S0-AFD-396

**The men—and women—
who built and ruled an empire:**

Bolivar Chandler: stern, God-fearing, born to poverty, he comes to dominate the cotton industry in the South.

Heath Chandler: heir to a fortune, he defies his father and marries Pearl, a scrawny illiterate who develops into a cultured beauty. Together they flee the tyranny of the family and the mills.

Andrew Ford: low-born, ambitious, he marries a Chandler and rises from mill worker to head of a vast textile empire.

"The novel is a big one in length, strength, and narrative."   —*Columbus Dispatch*

"...a roomy history, rich in melodramatic conflict, crises of conscience, and distinctive tarheel flavor."   —*The New York Times Book Review*

THE CHANDLER HERITAGE
was originally published by Simon and Schuster.

THE
CHANDLER
HERITAGE

Ben Haas

PUBLISHED BY POCKET 📖 BOOKS NEW YORK

THE CHANDLER HERITAGE

Simon and Schuster edition published January, 1972

POCKET BOOK edition published January, 1973

This POCKET BOOK edition includes every word
contained in the original, higher-priced edition. It is printed
from brand-new plates made from completely reset, clear, easy-to-read
type. POCKET BOOK editions are published by POCKET BOOKS, a division
of Simon & Schuster, Inc., 630 Fifth Avenue, New York, N.Y. 10020.
Trademarks registered in the United States and other countries.

L

Standard Book Number: 671-78256-8.
Library of Congress Catalog Card Number: 74-156148.
Copyright, ©, 1971, by Ben Haas. All rights reserved.
This POCKET BOOK edition is published by arrangement with
Simon & Schuster, Inc.

Printed in the U.S.A.   Cover art by Alan Magee.

This book is for Agnes and Joe Taylor, with love and gratitude, and for the Hendersons, Belle, Douglas, and Virginia, with the same.

Contents

PROLOGUE — 1

BOOK ONE

    PART ONE — 21

    PART TWO — 194

BOOK TWO

    PART ONE — 265

    PART TWO — 339

    PART THREE — 418

THE
CHANDLER
HERITAGE

Prologue

1   ALL THAT SUMMER the boy watched the road.

A narrow band of deep, powdery dust when dry, a rutted swamp of blood-colored mud when wet, it spilled into the valley from the north, followed the river between wooded slopes barely scratched with feeble cultivation, and, ten miles on, at the valley's mouth, joined another, larger track. Because it was a shortcut from Virginia, it carried that summer a vast traffic of men and animals: the defeated soldiers going home.

The healthy, the strong, and those with mounts came first, a trickling vanguard swelling to a stream of hungry, bearded men, barefooted, most of them, and nearly all in rags, plodding and hobbling like a mindless migration of ants, in curious silence, as if still too stunned by disaster to feel exuberance at survival and being homeward bound. Or perhaps the poverty and desolation of the valley evoked that silence. In the absence of able-bodied men, its raw clay, long since ruined by crop after crop of cotton, sliced with red, ghastly wounds of deepening gullies, had been beyond the power of women and children to plant and till; now it had become a dreary wilderness of scrub oak and pine, broom sedge and briars. Only here and there along the road were occasional little clearings, around cabins long unrepaired and mostly near collapse. It was in such a clearing, on the porch of such a cabin, that the boy kept station, staring with a curious, breathless gravity at every face that passed.

1

He was not large; at twelve he had the physique of a child four years younger. Only his head had grown to maturity, round and massive, top-heavy, seeming to over-balance his gaunt, shrunken frame. And his thick, unkempt shag of tow-colored hair, giving it the appearance of a mushroom, made it seem even larger.

His eyes were pale blue, like painted china, his cheeks sunken, his mouth small, with thin lips. He wore a ragged homespun shirt, pants of the same material belted around his waist with rope; on the pipestem lengths of naked shins below, countless scratches and cuts that his body lacked nutriment to heal had turned to sores. Hungry as they were, the soldiers never bothered to beg food at the door of the place; the child, grave and motionless on the porch, was like a lettered sign proclaiming the uselessness of that.

And yet he had surprising strength and energy. When the full flood of soldiers dwindled with the passing months and he scraped in the corn patch with his hoe or cut firewood with the ax, he worked hard; and when some random group of latecomers appeared against the merciless August sky on the hill's crest five hundred yards away (they were the feebler ones now, and slower—the wounded, and the released prisoners) he ran with surprising speed to inspect them as they scrabbled past. But he never saw the face for whch he looked; always, when they had gone on, the thin body seemed weaker and more listless. Then it would be a long while before he got up momentum again.

By early September it was nearly over. Now entire days passed without a stranger on the road.

Then one hot afternoon, the month three-quarters gone, a solitary figure inched down the hill with the gait of a crippled insect. The boy, making a rabbit trap from a piece of hollow log, did not see it until it came opposite the cabin's dooryard. Then he sprang to his feet, staring, seeking to penetrate the mask of dust and beard. For a moment, tensely, he looked; then he let out breath and his shoulders slumped. No. It was not this one either.

The man's body was warped into a question mark by

rheumatism, arthritis, or bowel complaint. Hardly taller than the boy in that posture, he seemed swallowed by the filthy rags of what had been a uniform. As he helped himself into the yard with a dogwood staff, the boy gave way before him, mounted to the porch.

The soldier followed, wordlessly. His black eyes, perhaps because their pupils were the only part of him not dust-coated, seemed to glitter ferociously. He came to the porch's edge; then, with a sigh, sank down upon it, leaning back against an awry post. The voice from the beard was a rasping croak. "Boy, I gotta have a drinka water."

"Yes, sir." The boy backed into the house, brought out a brimming gourd dipper. The hands extended for it were filthy, trembling talons with yellow nails like horn.

The soldier drank with head thrown back, gripping the gourd with both hands, with a rhythmic series of gulps, a froglike sound, the Adam's apple in the scrawny neck convulsing. Then he lowered the vessel, knocked off his slouch hat against the post, and poured the remaining water over his great, filthy shag of hair. It rolled off, dripped from his ears, ran down his cheeks like tears.

"Lord," the man said. "Lord God, but that feels good." He handed back the empty gourd. For a moment he only sat there, head tilted against the post, eyes closed, big yellow teeth showing in the slash of his mouth, panting with exhaustion. Watching him, the boy felt no fear of physical harm; he had learned to judge which soldiers were likely to become violent at the refusal of food. This man was too far gone to worry about. But, inexplicably, he felt another sort of dread. Perhaps he sensed even now that this one was the last.

Presently, as if the cold spring water had given him new strength, the man peeled back his grainy lids and hitched himself erect. "Boy, I ain't et since last night. And that warn't nothin but musky-dines. I'm so hongry I cain't stand hit. Whut you got to eat here?"

"Nothin," the boy said. "Mister, we ain't got nothin."

"Ahhh . . ." The man shook his head. "You bound to have sump'n. Where's your mama at?"

"She ain't here. She down at the creek, fishin, she an' my baby sister."

"Well, what about your daddy? Where at is he?"

The boy licked his lips. "He ain't here neither. They . . . they say he got killed. Up north. At a place called Gettysburg or somethin."

"Gettysburg." He contracted the word into a sharp, explosive sound, like a rifle shot. His face twisted.

The boy went on, desperately, words tumbling out. "But it ain't true. I know it ain't. His name was Lloyd Chandler. Maybe you knowed him. Maybe—"

"Chandler. Lloyd Chandler." The man rubbed his face. "Yeah," he said. "I knowed him."

The boy fell silent. In that instant the whole world seemed to fall silent. "It ain't true," he said desperately after a moment.

"*I* don't know," the man said. "All I know is that we was in Pickett's Brigade. There was a hill we went up, I never even learnt its name. But, boy—" His voice trembled; the glitter in his eyes seemed to become incandescent. "Boy, nobody ever seen nothin like that before nor since. I looked back and there was dead men ever'whur. Jest heaps and piles of dead men. Like somebody had done been cuttin hay with a scythe an' raked it up. It . . . Chandler," he finished. "Yeah. But I never seed nor heerd of him again."

"No!"

The man looked at him and shook his head. "Boy, he warn't the only one."

"No!" said the boy again.

The man stared at him, and his voice rose, trembled. "But whut difference does it make, boy? Dead er alive, what difference?" He flung out his hand in a wide gesture. "Fer God's sake, look at this country. There ain't nothin left of it. I done walked all the way from Virginny, and hit's all like this. Jest empty and dead." He laughed, and it was a sound unlike anything the boy had ever heard before. "A dead country fer dead people."

The boy did not answer. He felt as if something huge, swollen, were in his stomach, forcing its way up his windpipe, strangling him. He felt his eyes burn and felt wetness on his cheeks.

The man saw the tears. "Aw, now," he said and rubbed his face. "There ain't no call fer you to take on like that." His voice dropped, to a confidential whisper. "Because, I'll tell you whut. He's one of th' lucky ones, you know? Your daddy. You ought not to grieve fer him." The shining eyes seemed to expand; the boy could not wrench his own away from them. "The dead is the lucky ones. You want to grieve, you grieve fer th' livin."

And then he scrambled to his feet. "Because, what we gonna do, huh? What are all us pore bastards that didn't get killed gonna do? You look at me, you look at Tom Capps, from Mecklenburg County. I got a wife at home and four young-uns, and what am I gonna do when I git there, how am I gonna live? Me, Tom Capps!"

He panted loudly, yellow teeth huge and horsy in his muddy beard. "Before the war I rented me a piece of land. I scratched some kinda livin outa it, I don't know how. Hit took all the strength I had, and I had strength in them days. But look at me now. You look. When I git home, if I ever do, what I gonna be fit for? How'm I gonna live?" Again that sweeping gesture. "I know what's happened. I already seed it ever'whur I been. My land's gone, growed up. The brush has done took it back. I got no money, not a dime, I got no credit with nobody, maybe I ain't even got the land no more. All I got is a wife and kids lookin to me to feed 'em, and I don't know how." His voice rose to a shriek. "You understand? I don't know how!"

Then it again became a whisper, like wind in pines. "Oh, the rich folks, they'll make out! The rich folks always do! The niggers—they'll make out too! The Yankees'll see to that. But what about folks like me and you? Where we gonna go, how we gonna live, who's gonna see to *us*?"

He shook his head. "Yet we gotta live. I don't know how, but we got to. That's why I say, don't you grieve fer your daddy. He's through with livin. It ain't his bother no more. He's the lucky one—Lloyd Chandler.

Hit's people like me, like pore Tom Capps, the ones they call white trash, call us that and send us to fight their Goddamned war that—"

The words exploded from the boy. "You better not take the Lord's name in vain."

"What?" The soldier stared at him. Then he gave a ghastly chuckle. "Oh. Oh, you got religion, huh?"

"Yes, sir," the boy said.

"So you pray?" Suddenly the man was serious—deadly, intently so.

"Yes, sir. We pray ever' mornin, ever' night."

"That's good. . . . Your name? What you say your name was?"

The boy moistened dry lips with his tongue. "Bolivar. Bolivar Chandler."

"Bolivar Chandler, that's good. You can still pray, you're lucky." The face of Tom Capps twisted spastically. "I useta be able to pray too. I've tried it since, but it don't work no more, you understand? I've tried—"

He moved toward the porch again; the boy, frightened, flattened himself against the log wall.

"It don't work. It don't work nohow." And now there were tears on Tom Capps' cheeks. "It jest rips you apart inside when you try, after you seen all I have." He broke off; then his eyes flared again. "That's what I need," he rasped. "Somebody to pray fer me!"

Bolivar's lips moved soundlessly.

"You'll do it?" Tom Capps climbed the porch, moved up close. Bolivar's nostrils filled with the sourness of decay, despair, as that terrible face came close to his. "You pray fer me? Fer ole Tom Capps?"

He looked into those mad, staring eyes, that were like nothing he had ever seen before. "Yes," he heard himself whisper.

The nails of horn dug suddenly into his shoulder. "Promise!" Capps snarled. "You promise! I cain't do it fer myself!"

"I promise!" Bolivar yelled in panic. *"I promise!"*

Then the hand slipped away. "Well, good," Capps wheezed and, slowly, painfully, he backed off the porch.

In the dooryard he continued to stare at Bolivar. "Don't you ever fergit that," he said quietly. "Don't you ever, long as you live, fergit that. Your daddy, he don't need your prayers. But Tom Capps does. Tom Capps and ever' other pore son of a bitch that lived through this war. You pray fer us. Not the dead, but fer the livin."

"Yes," Bolivar whispered.

Capps backed farther away. He seemed for an instant to swell, expand, glow, as if his body were on fire. It could have been a trick of light, but in that instant he was human, more than human, less than human, an image the terrified, grief-stricken child would never forget. Then, quite suddenly, he shrank into mortal flesh again, weak, ravaged, crippled, and his voice was sane but shaky as he asked, "Whur's the next place? Whur at might somebody have somethin to spare a man to eat?"

"Kessler's store," Bolivar heard himself say.

"Kessler's store. Whur at is that?"

"Two miles on, the crossroads. Only, Kessler don't give no credit."

Capps' mouth twisted. "Naw," he said, and spat into the dust. "Naw. None of 'em does." Then, without further speech, he turned; hunched over the staff, he shuffled away into the road.

Bolivar, still flat against the wall, watched him go, watched that bent and ravaged figure climb step by step, foot by foot, through the red dust up the hill toward the place where the road made a bend. When the crippled figure had reached that turn, it halted, pivoted awkwardly. On the height of the ridge it was dark against the flat, beautiful, impersonal blue of the notch of sky between the woods. It stood there, poised, shaking, and lifted the staff and pointed it. The voice from that distance was thin, high, like the mew of a hawk.

"Don't you fergit, Bolivar! Tom Capps! You pray fer Tom Capps! You pray fer us all! You pray for the whole damned, Godforsaken South!"

It waved the staff for a moment, then, strength exhausted, let it drop, used it to twist itself around, scrabbled past the bend, and then was gone.

Bolivar Chandler stayed flattened against the wall until the man was out of sight. Then he came erect. His chest rose and fell with heavy breathing. Suddenly he leaped off the porch and began to run.

He ran through the little patch of dried cornstalks, then up a hill, through vines and briars, into pines. He ran through the pines too, fast as his legs could pump, as if something dark and terrible pursued him. He leaped over logs, crashed through brush. He ran until his strength gave out. Then, in a stifling grove, he fell flat on the slick, dry pine straw. He lay there for a long time, heart pounding against the earth, legs bleeding from a dozen cuts and scratches. Something huge, swollen, agonizing within him expanded enormously, until it felt as if it would explode him. He dug his fingers into earth.

Then, suddenly, it broke. It broke, and he began to cry. He cried explosively for a long time, until there were no more tears in him, until he only lay there wide-eyed, unseeing, gasping, purged. Presently, after breath returned, he got to his knees. He saw the stump of a pine tree his father had cut years before, remembered the long, springy trunk and bouncing branches crashing to earth, the man standing there huge and triumphant with his ax.

Bolivar scrabbled on his knees to the stump. He folded his hands on its grainy, irregular surface, marked with the waxy rings of time. Then he put his tow-colored, shag-haired head down on his hands and began to pray.

2   IT WAS two weeks before Bolivar Chandler told his mother what he had learned.

She was not a tall woman, but hunger and hard work had shrunk the flesh on her bones until her arms and legs looked longer than they were. To Bolivar she seemed large, however, immensely wise, infallible, the cement that held the family's life together. It was she who told him how to get through the day—working in the corn, fishing, setting rabbit traps. And whether his efforts yielded success or failed, there was, nevertheless, always something for his sister and himself to eat, produced magically in ways beyond his comprehension, conjured up by the mystical power of an adult. When he awakened she would already be hard at work; and she kept on long after he crawled exhausted into bed by the fire at night. When he or Mary Lou, his five-year-old sister, fell sick, she was always there with touch of hand and tuck of blanket; yet she never seemed to tire and was never sick herself. Perhaps it was from her that he acquired the idea that weakness, even illness, was somehow unmanly and immoral.

They had prayers twice a day. She could read a little, and every night opened the only book in the cabin, the Bible, laboriously spelling out the hopeful or the threatening parts. From this, and from thundering sermons at the log meeting-house, Bolivar formed his vision of God—a huge old man, white-bearded, clad in robes of white, on a throne somewhere above the transparent canopy of the sky, glaring down unwinkingly at Earth, cold, watchful eye following Bolivar Chandler day and night. His reward for keeping His commandments was not to unleash on you His terrible, vindictive anger, not to consign you in that harsh, unflinching way of His to eternal torture. In that hard life His love seemed unfelt and abstract, but His punishment was very real, and they lived always too near disaster to dare incur even His slightest wrath.

Since his mother was the intermediary through whom Bolivar received these teachings, he assumed that her acquaintance with God was intimate, her knowledge of Him gained firsthand; she was only slightly less all-knowing, all-wise, than God himself. Only after Tom Capps had come and gone did he begin to question this.

Because she still believed. Bolivar's memories of his father were vague after four years. A tall man cutting down a tree. A bony lap, a hard chest against which he laid his head; smell of tobacco and sweat; the brush of lips beneath a downy beard; deep laughter. But just as somehow she brought God into the cabin as a living presence, so, too, did she conjure up the absent man with stories, memories—and hope. "Your daddy always used to say. . . . Do you remember the time Daddy . . . Your daddy . . . your daddy . . ."

And always, every day, the glittering jewel amidst the mud of their existence, the promise of surcease: "When your daddy comes home—" She filled the cabin daylong with God and Lloyd Chandler, and it was those two unseen, real presences that comforted all of them.

Now everything had changed. Bolivar could not say how or why—all he knew was that he accepted, that suddenly one of those presences had vanished. He was terrified by that knowledge, and even more so because he possessed it and she did not. And somehow he was going to have to tell her.

For two weeks, though, he kept it to himself, something making him balk at the thought of mentioning it. But finally it was more than he could bear. Early in October it burst from him.

Mary Lou had already been put to bed. The lean, hemp-haired woman in the dirty homespun dress sat before a fire built up high with wood that he had chopped against unseasonable chill. While he lay on the hearth she worked at the loom on which she wove their cloth, a gaunt silhouette in the flickering light.

He heard, outside the cabin, the constant cry of whippoorwill. He watched her deft hands and treadling foot. He felt it growing within him, huge, uncontainable; something shifted and slipped in his vision. He saw his mother for the first time not as deity, but as person, and had to share with her unbearable knowledge he possessed.

The loom made a rhythmic, whispering sound. She sighed. "I'll be so glad when your daddy—"

Bolivar cut in. "Mama," he said.

She turned to look at him, arrested by some adult quality in his voice, the unfamiliar sound of masculine authority.

"Mama," he said, words rushing out, "he ain't coming back. He's never coming back. He's dead. He really is dead. They killed him at Gettysburg."

She looked at him with a face like a blade. Then she said, quaveringly, "You hush that foolishness. You hear me, sir? You hush it. I won't stand to hear you talk like that. That's the worst way I ever heard anybody talk."

Bolivar sat up. "But it's true," he said fiercely. "It's true. A man told me, by the name of Tom Capps. Daddy's dead—"

"No!" she cried. "No!" Her face turned toward him, began, in the firelight, to quiver like the faces of the rabbits he took from his traps; when he hauled them out by their ears and they knew their doom was upon them, nose and lips wobbled like that and they made the same keening sound. "No, I will not hear talk like that from you, sir. It ain't been a year yet since they declared the peace! You understand?"

"But, Mama—"

"Not a year." She shot out her hand in signal of authority. "You go to bed, sir! You hear me! You go to bed right now!"

Obediently he did that. He eased himself into the blankets before the hearth in the one-room cabin. He heard, later, as he was sinking into sleep, her sigh as she dropped into the narrow, rope-slung bed that she shared with his sister. In the middle of the night a strange, gasping, animal sound awakened him, but he was so groggy he took it for part of a dream and sank back immediately into sleep. Of course, though, she was crying.

In the morning he crawled stiffly from the pallet by the hearth, expecting to find his mother up before him, the fire unbanked and blazing, her presence vital in the room. But for the first time in Bolivar's memory the fire was still inert beneath cold ashes, and she had not arisen from the bed.

His sister was up, though, clawing at him in her nightshirt. "Bol," she whimpered. "Bol. I'm hungry."

Bolivar went to the bed. "Mama? Mama?"

She lay motionless, hands folded over her breast. Between pale, parted lips, her teeth were visible, and he heard the slow, soft sound of her breathing. "Mama, are you sick?" The pale blue eyes, wide open, staring at the rafters, did not move; she paid him no attention at all.

"Mama, we—" He shook her. She was warm, the touch of her flesh familiar, and he waited, but still she would not respond; he might have been shaking a sack of cotton. "Mama—" It was some time before he gave up, apprehension changing to fear, and fear to panic, while the little girl whined around his legs.

There was, of course, no way for Bolivar to understand what had happened, how important believing had been to her, that it had been the one vital spark that kept her going day after hopeless day, that the necessity to keep him believing had been part of her own belief. And now that he could no longer be deceived, it had become impossible for her to fool herself, and she had, at last, simply given way. There was no strength left in her, not even enough to meet his eyes.

He could not understand all that, but, in fear and bafflement and confusion, he realized that if there were to be anything in the house to eat today—maybe ever— he would have to provide it. He found a scrap of leftover cornbread, gave it to the little girl to quiet her whimpering, and, abstractedly, gently stroked the silkiness of her hair as she gobbled it. He was very hungry himself, yet, at the same time, had no appetite. He would have to do something, but he had no idea what. He must have help, but had no idea where to turn for it.

Of course there was prayer. After he had tried and failed again to make his mother speak, he dropped to his knees, pillowed his head on a chair. He prayed for a miracle, and when he was through he half expected to see her arising from the bed and the table miraculously laid with a banquet. But there was no miracle, and he would have to think of something else.

At least the act of praying had calmed and reassured him; he no longer felt alone. Pacing the cabin, he tried to think. But there was nobody; there was nobody to summon and no one to turn to; they were totally and completely alone. There was only Kessler. Only Kessler at the crossroads store had food; and Bolivar was terribly afraid of the big meanspirited, tightfisted German. He had been with her the only time she had ever begged credit of the man and had not been too young to understand the brutality of his refusal and the shame and despair it had engendered in his mother. He dared not go to Kessler.

Anyway, it would do no good. There was not a penny of money in the house and not a thing that could be traded.

And yet, inexorably, the knowledge bore in on him that there was nowhere else to go. He would have to try it, anyhow.

Bolivar told his sister, "You stay right here with her. You hear? You stay right here beside her in case she wants a drink of water. I'll be back directly."

It was a fine, clear, bright morning, tangy with fall. The woods and briared fields stood out in almost hallucinatory clarity as Bolivar went down the road. Even though he shuffled slowly, reluctantly, his heart was pounding as if he had been running and he had trouble breathing. Fear built in him, wound him up like a spring, and suddenly, involuntarily, he broke into a run. Hard and wiry, he ran swiftly, pushing to his limit, seeking release in action, driven anyhow by the need for haste. The way was mostly downhill, and he made good time, and in less than twenty minutes he saw it, where the valley opened out—the big frame building by the bridge, where two roads and the river met. Its unpainted flanks weathered to a cast-iron gray, its high windows barred with steel, it was a fortress he would have to storm, unarmed and singlehanded. By the time he reached its porch, before which one saddle horse was tethered, his hands were sweating, his stomach queasy. Then his nerve failed completely and he halted. He could not. He could not go up those steps. He could not face the towering, contemptuous Kessler. Most especially, he could not bring himself to beg. That was something no Chandler had ever done but once—enough for him to know how terrible it was to do that.

And yet there was no help for it. He forced his mind away from himself, thought resolutely only of the woman staring at the rafters and not moving, and of his crying sister. He took a long, deep breath, rubbed his hands against his pants. Then he climbed the steps and went, hesitantly and with thudding heart, into the store.

Its interior was a vast, dim cavern, piled—it seemed to Bolivar—with unimaginable riches. People said Kessler had relatives in the North who arranged for him to be supplied with so much that was still scarce or nonexistent elsewhere. Bolivar was only vaguely aware of that; all he knew was that the tang of fresh-ground coffee, spices, crisp new cloth, leather, rope and iron combined to make this place smell like paradise. Just inside the doorway he stood blinking and inhaling deeply.

Kessler was at the counter and—Bolivar's heart sank— another man was with him, one tall and wide-shouldered, in black coat, slouch hat, and riding boots. He had prepared himself to beg of Kessler, but not to do it before someone else. He balked. Almost, he turned and fled.

But not quite. Later it seemed to him that a huge, unseen hand had shoved him forward roughly and against his will. At the time all he knew was that he was suddenly at the counter, Kessler staring down at him in surprise and then displeasure, eyes like black currants set in heavy, uncooked dough. And Bolivar was talking suddenly, unable to stop himself, more words pouring from him in that quick, incontinent flood than he had ever spoken in a single burst in his whole, short life.

He was aware of the other man, tanned, clean-shaven, looking down at him with gray eyes; aware, too, of the growing opacity of Kessler's stare, the impatience, disgust, in the small, pursy mouth. Then Kessler said contemptuously, "Nahh. Nahh, nahh." He waved a beefy hand, turned away, gross belly spilling over his belt. "Go on, boy. Git. Git out of here."

Bolivar stood there, words pinched off, shame clogging

his throat, disappointment stinging in his eyes. "But Mister Kessler—"

"Nahh! I said git out!"

"Wait." The voice was soft, but it had authority. "Hold on, Kessler." The other man tilted back his hat, dropped into a squat so that his eyes met Bolivar's. "Now," he said. "What's all this again?"

Bolivar began to talk once more. The gray-eyed man nodded. "And won't get out of bed?" And, "Gettysburg, you say? Yeah, I was there. No, never met him—I was in the cavalry." He hoisted himself erect once more, turned. "Kessler—"

The storekeeper stared at him, face reddening. "Now, Major. I tell you, you don't know these people. Trash! Just plain trash."

"I know this boy's daddy got killed fighting for your fat arse."

"It wasn't my war! I didn't—" Kessler chopped the air with a hand.

"You'd be wise not to talk like that around here," the man said in the coldest voice Bolivar had ever heard. "Maybe you already forgot what we were just discussing? I told you that we intend to look after our own."

"I gave you my contribution! Right off, when you asked! I don't see—"

"Well, maybe you had better increase it a little bit. What-say three dollars?"

"Three dollars? Major—"

"Not a gift. Credit. This boy looks strong; he can work it out for you. If he don't, we'll guarantee it."

For a moment he and Kessler looked at one another. "But I don't need nobody! I don't—" Under the major's gaze Kessler's voice dwindled. The fat lips pouted; he turned away. "All right," he grunted. "But throw it away. Might as well throw it away, out there in the high road for the wind to blow." Furiously, he began to bustle around the store, slamming item after item down on the counter, goaded by an occasional word from the major.

Bolivar blinked. He had no idea what was happening; all he knew was that it was some sort of miracle. Side-meat; beans; meal; molasses; these accumulated on the counter.

"If his mama's down like he says she is, she'll need some coffee too," the major observed.

Kessler's face contorted. "It's already three dollars! And now coffee? Coffee's like gold!"

"A pound, anyhow," the major said; and he stepped behind the counter, scooped out the beans himself, and ground them. Kessler watched with fury he could barely contain. Finally, though, he sighed, threw up his hands. "All right. That's three and a half. He can work it out at five cents a day."

"Kessler," said the major, smiling faintly, "you'd skin a flea for its hide and tallow. Ten cents." His voice was very soft, but the smile was gone as he looked at the storekeeper. "We've been away a long time," he went on, "but we're home now, and you've got a lot of goodwill to buy back—you are not a popular man at this moment. You would be well advised to stretch a little bit. Yankee soldiers here or no, now that we're home, we're going to run this country again. Do you understand what I'm trying to say?"

"I understand." Kessler looked at the floor.

Again the man squatted before Bolivar. "Now, son. Can you carry all this stuff?"

Bolivar stared at the flour sack full of unbelievable wealth and nodded dazedly.

"All right. I hope your mama gets better. If she don't, you tell Mr. Kessler, and Mr. Kessler will let me know—won't you?"

"Yeah. Yeah, I'll let you know," Kessler muttered.

"Good. Well, I've got a long way to ride, a lot of other people to see." The man stood up, put his hand briefly on Bolivar's head. "Thanks, Kessler, for everything. We won't forget your generosity." Then he strode out. They heard his boots on the porch floor, the squeak of saddle leather, the sound of hoofbeats.

Kessler towered over Bolivar, face the color of liver, eyes lambent behind the rolls of flesh. He stood there for a long moment, looking at the child as if at some sort of vermin. Then he seized the flour sack, thrust it at Bolivar. "Here, damn it," he growled. "Take it and git outa here. You understand me? Go!"

Wordlessly, Bolivar did. The sack was very heavy; he had to struggle to get it over his shoulder. He found a faint, frightened whisper of thanks. It affected Kessler not one jot. Still glowering, he watched as Bolivar went quickly to the door with his burden. Then Kessler's rage burst from him in a roar. "You be here six o'clock tomorrow mornin' you hear? Six o'clock! If you ain't, by God, I come and git you by the ear!"

"Yes, sir!" Bolivar exclaimed. Still dazed, he hurried out, lurched home under all that weight through a world that had changed completely in the last half hour. He had prayed and he'd had his miracle. With wonder, he realized that it had all been true, all of it. So long as he feared God, as he had always been taught, and lived a righteous life, anything was possible.

BOOK ONE

Part One

1 As ALWAYS, he was up before the first whistle blew, charged with energy and ready for the day. Cautiously, not wanting to wake his wife, he sat on the edge of the bed—a short, muscular old man in a cotton nightshirt, his head, crested with thinning, silvery hair, far too large for his body. Rubbing pale blue eyes, he presently arose and, as was his custom, padded straight to the high window of the bedroom, where he pulled back the curtains and looked out as if to reassure himself that all he had built in fifty years had not been taken from him while he slept.

It was still there. Sunrise came early at this time of year, and though it was not yet five, the sky was growing light. The big house had been deliberately sited on a high knoll so that Bolivar could always keep his empire under surveillance, and now it all lay before him: the broad valley of the Achoa River, the mills beside the stream, and the town that surrounded and served them. Towering over all of it was the huge riveted steel water tank on spraddled legs, its silver-painted flanks inscribed in huge black letters: CHANDLERVILLE.

And he owned it, all of it, totally—the great three-story building of dung-colored brick, their walls inset with rows of high windows painted blue to keep the fatal sunlight off the cotton. Crammed with machinery, they were capable, those huge structures of masonry and oak, of spewing out endless miles of yarn, vast acreages of good, honest, unfinished cotton cloth—and, now that

21

America was in the war, an amazing amount of profit. And he held title to them, and to the town that had grown up around them, and to a considerable acreage beyond. Every building and every street down there was his property; and of the fifteen hundred people, there was not one but who lived here at Bolivar Chandler's pleasure and on his sufferance, drawing nourishment from Chandler Mills.

That thought stirred something secret, illicit, in his loins, a satisfaction almost sexual. He stood unmoving for a moment longer. At any given time he knew almost to the penny his own net worth, and on this summer morning in 1917 it was a shade over two million dollars. He knew that pride was sinful, but he could not help feeling it. Presently, almost as if in shame, he let the curtains drop and turned away.

Elizabeth, ten years younger than himself, still slept. He looked down at her with affection, and then some of his well-being dwindled. He hoped for her sake that a letter would finally come from Heath today. It was so much worse for her, because he was too busy to feel the fear except at odd times like this; but he knew it haunted her all day long. Besides, a father's fears were diluted a little by pride in a son who was a soldier; but women— she at least—found no solace in the glory of defending one's country, saw only the danger. And then it was worse for both of them, too, because of Heath flying those infernal airplanes, which could kill a man whether he met the enemy or not. Well, Bolivar thought grimly, there was nothing for it but to resign themselves to the fact that, whatever happened, it was the will of God.

All this was, of course. Bolivar Chandler never for a moment deluded himself that he had done all this alone. By now he could see the pattern clear and whole and never ceased to marvel at how intricate it was, or how deft the Hand that had used him as instrument, shuttle, with which to weave it. And all, of course, stemmed from Tom Capps, who, he perceived now, had been an instrument too. As had the major, Kessler, all the rest . . .

Looking backward, it was easy now to see how it all

fitted together, but at the time it had been a matter of doing what he had to, from day to day. Working so hard for the German that Kessler kept him on, eventually even teaching him to read and write—not out of charity, but because by then he perceived in Bolivar a windfall to be exploited. As times got better he had even grudgingly raised the boy's pay, and by his fifteenth birthday Bolivar was in full charge of the store, while Kessler lolled and ate and drank and grew to enormous size.

Others might have wasted their substance on fine clothes or courting or a fast horse, but Bolivar Chandler had learned his lesson: there was no substitute for money when you needed it, and the only way to have it was to save it. When he was twenty Kessler paid the wages of sin, of gluttony—a stroke laid him low. That was when Bolivar had dug up his savings from behind the cabin, gone to Kessler's wife, and made a down payment on the store.

He had no capital, but he had credit with Kessler's suppliers, who had learned long since that his word was his bond. In that devastated region, laid waste more by Reconstruction than by war, credit was as good as capital. He became a supply merchant, advancing seed and tools and food to live on to the desperate farmers, taking mortgages in return on their crops, their land, their houses, their very beds and chamber pots. Inevitably many failed, and when Bolivar, not without reluctance, foreclosed, he promptly converted into cash what he took, even at a discount. He was not a farmer, but a merchant; by now he knew storekeeping was his calling, the one thing in the world at which he was superb. Certainly he knew nothing about cotton mills and had never dreamed of owning one.

Then, in 1880, they had come to him—the newspaper editor, the minister, and the president of the short-line railroad that served the county seat of Macedonia. The latter was a tall man, clean-shaven, with gray eyes; and he was thicker and heavier than when Bolivar had first seen him on that crucial day in Kessler's store. Everyone still called him "Major."

He listened without comment as they explained their enterprise. The poor whites, landless, unable to compete with Negro labor—their numbers had multiplied, their misery grown, until they were a vast, idle mass threatening to drag down the county of Macedon in particular and the whole South in general under their dead weight. Something had to be done about them, they had to be put to work. And these men were sure they'd found the answer. Cotton, waterpower, labor—it was all at hand in abundance. If enough money could be raised by subscription, they would build a mill on the Achoa, equip it with secondhand machinery bought in New England, and generate a payroll by the spinning of cotton yarn.

Bolivar recognized the need, but he recognized, too, the light of idealism, almost fanaticism, in their eyes, and a warning bell rang at once in his cool mind. "I tell you," said the major earnestly, "this will be the greatest thing ever done for these people. The finest act of Christian charity we could perform."

"Maybe," Bolivar said. And he did not tell them what he really thought, which was that the idea of their enterprise might be sound enough, but their conception of it was all wrong. A business was a business, and a charity was something else altogether, and that was where they were making their mistake. There could be no mixing of the two if the business were to survive. In the end, he agreed to invest a thousand dollars—one tenth of what they asked—and, in his own mind, wrote it off immediately.

Still, somehow, they raised the money, a nickel here, a dime there, a thousand elsewhere, and, with their hearts where their heads should have been, they built their mill. Siting it in the wilderness on the swift-running river, they moved sixty families into company housing, began operations after an elaborate dedication—and in two years were on the edge of bankruptcy.

Then the major came to him again, alone this time. His desperation showed in his eyes and in the trembling of his hands, and it was obvious that he had been drinking heavily lately. "Don't you see?" His voice was a husky, shaky whisper. "It's not your money that we need. It's your name, your reputation—and that brain of yours. With a man like you as president of the company, we could reorganize and refinance. You could keep us going."

"I'm sorry," Bolivar said, "but the interests I've already got take all my time. Besides, I don't know the first thing about cotton mills."

"You could learn. And—we'd give you a free hand. Anything you want, any terms."

"No," Bolivar said again. "It's impossible."

The major was silent for a moment. Then he said, voice trembling with emotion, "Mr. Chandler, in all these years I've never mentioned a certain day here in this store a long time ago. But now I'm going to have to—not for myself, but for those people out there, the millhands. Men, women, children, waiting for a miracle; and if it doesn't happen, they are doomed and finished. You owe me a certain debt. I'm asking you now to go out there with me and see what we have and how things stand before you give a final answer. A day of your time, no more. Give me that, and we are quits."

His gray eyes met Bolivar's, and there was more confidence in them now, for he knew that Bolivar Chandler always paid his debts and could not refuse him this. Bolivar knew it, too; and he came out from behind the counter, somehow already feeling trapped as he put on his hat and coat.

He had never been inside a cotton mill before. He was impressed by the structure's size and its ranks of elaborate machinery. Because the mill was shut down and none of this was running, the inside of the place was vacant and silent as a great tomb. Their footsteps echoed hollowly as they went from room to room and the major explained how the cotton bales were brought in, broken open, the fiber cleaned and loosened by the great carding machines, then converted into a series of strands of ever-diminishing size which were at last spun into yarn to be sold on the New York market. In spite of himself, Bolivar was intrigued. He knew nothing of machinery, but this much he understood at once: here was a great investment teetering on the edge of destruction, and he was a man who hated waste. He felt saddened when they emerged into bleak winter sunlight, but he was still convinced that there was nothing he could do.

But then he saw the people. They sat on the porches of the little houses clustered around the mill, gaunt men and women and spindly-legged children in ragged clothes; and as he and the major drove through the village in the major's buggy, he felt their eyes upon him. They looked at the vehicle and the men in it with a kind of breathless gravity, a desperate hoping, that he remembered only too well and that made him strangely queasy. Then they were out of the village and turning homeward. "A miracle, you see," the major said. "They're waiting for a miracle. . . ."

Bolivar did not answer, indeed hardly heard. Suddenly he was seeing something else, hearing another voice. It was eerie how clear the image was—the tattered, half-mad soldier, the gleaming, despairing eyes, the horny nails digging into the young boy's flesh. *Don't you grieve for your daddy. . . . He's the lucky one. . . . Hit's people like me, like pore Tom Capps, the ones they call white trash. . . .* And, the voice thickening to an urgent snarl, *You promise! I cain't do it fer myself!* And his own voice, frightened, yelling. *I promise! I promise!*

And then the figure limned against the sky, on the height of road between the woods, waving its dogwood staff. *Don't you fergit, Bolivar! You pray fer Tom Capps! You pray fer us all . . . for the whole damned, Godforsaken South—!*

The buggy rattled on. When Bolivar heard the major again, the man was saying, "Maybe, after all, you're right. Maybe the best thing is just to liquidate and have the agony over."

Bolivar said, "Where are the books?"

The major sat up straight. "What?"

"The books of account," said Bolivar. "Where are they kept?"

The major stared. "In the mill office."

Bolivar drew in a deep breath. "Turn the buggy around," he said. "If you don't mind, I'd like to have a look at them."

In the bath adjoining his bedroom, Bolivar turned on the hot-water tap and stropped his razor. He could see now how, once He had chosen you, there was no escape. For two nights he had agonized over the accounts; things were worse, even, than represented. And yet, he knew somehow that there was no help for it; not only did he remember Tom Capps, but he was haunted by the image of Kessler dying, reduced by self-love and greed to a great mindless, rubbery mass. Somehow he knew that he was being tested, knew that if he refused this challenge, he would end spiritually as Kessler had done physically. His bluff was being called; prayer was not enough, deeds were demanded, deeds and sacrifice. In the end, he put the books under his arm, harnessed his horse to his buggy, and went to see the major.

It was a hard bargain that he drove, but they had no choice other than to agree. After that, on a part-time basis, he worked ferociously to set things straight and undo the damage they had wrought. He had been right; charity was what had brought them low. In this case salvation hung not on generosity and on vague spiritual optimism, but on ruthlessness and a harsh, hardheaded objectivity. Those qualities he could muster, and bit by bit, almost single-handed, he brought the mill back out of the depths and to the break-even point. But by then it was a full-time job and one he could not abandon. He was forced to sell the store and give up his other interests. At that juncture, though, he knew that it would work, that he could make it work; and he used a good part of his fortune to buy full control and later, just before the enterprise showed its first profit, total ownership. From then on, his life had moved in a straight line, wholly tied to the fortunes of the textile industry, dedicated to profit and expansion.

Meanwhile, the Achoa mill was only one eruption of

the fever that had swept the South. All across the high Piedmont plateau, from Virginia down to Georgia, other mills sprang up. Year by year, decade by decade, that stretch of red-clay highlands was transformed from cotton-growing to cotton-spinning and weaving country, a vein of industry running through a region otherwise wholly agricultural.

Competition was ferocious; what had begun as a vast welfare movement settled down to dog-eat-dog, hardheaded business as the idealists were weeded out. Even so, the textile men had more in common with each other than with the rest of the South, and they had the cash, the payrolls, which bought them finally almost total political power in their states. Now the mill country was a state within a state, with its own potentates and its own rules and unwritten laws.

Once again, shaving, Bolivar felt that surge of virility in his loins. He had survived, and not only survived but risen to the top. That, he knew, was because he had done his Christian duty. *Blessed,* he thought, *be the name of the Lord. . . .*

Then dread hit him again. So many miracles already . . . dared he hope, beg, for one more? Heath. Would the Lord send his son back to him alive?

Suddenly, hand trembling, he put down his razor, went back to the bedroom. He knelt before a chair, pillowed his head on his fists. "Maybe," he whispered, "it's not Your plan to keep him alive. Maybe it's too much to ask. But at least his eternal spirit . . . please, don't let him lose that over yonder in that place, with all those foreigners and Catholics to tempt him into sin. . . . Please, at least not that. . . ." Then he finished his prayers in the usual way, not failing to ask for blessing on a man he had not seen since an afternoon in August more than fifty years before, keeping an ancient promise.

But when he arose, he still felt fear, wondering why Heath had not written. Even now, he thought, his son might be in danger beyond his ability to imagine—not of his life only, but maybe even of his soul. . . .

* * *

All that Saturday Olin Clutterbuck had roamed Paris.
A tall, stoop-shouldered man of twenty-two, redheaded,
freckled, with a great jutting chin and big hands, he
wore the uniform of the British Royal Air Force. He had
been shot down over the front four weeks before and had
barely missed death. Now he was on his first leave from
the hospital, making his first real contact with the city,
and he had never seen anything like it—not Boston or
New York or London. Even with windows boarded
against air and Big Bertha attacks, it had a richness, a
texture, on which his artist's eye and sensibilities became
almost drunk. The quality of the summer sunlight, the
brilliance of flowers in gardens and window boxes, the
grace and grandeur with which everything had been conceived, the nervous, volatile, yet fatalistic vitality of its
people—hobbling along with his cane, each new discovery
increasing his appetite for surprises, he crossed the Seine,
left the Boulevard St. Germain, and penetrated deeply
into colorful little neighborhoods studded throughout the
area like luscious fruits in an overrich cake.

Presently he entered a narrow, cobbled street lined on
either side with rows of shabby flats, their plaster flanks
streaked with soot washed down from chimney pots and
tiled roofs. Jammed side by side, the flats were separated
by only occasional narrow alleys offering access to small
courtyards in the rear. With no shops, cafés, or bars here,
and almost no traffic on the narrow street or rudimentary
sidewalk, it was less interesting than he had hoped; and
all at once his weariness struck him. He was about to
turn, go back, when he heard the voices—hard, angry,
American.

"All right, damn it! You want me, come and get me!"

"Don't think we ain't gonna, buddy! That monkey suit
you got on won't help you here!"

The first voice had been defiant, yet mocking, strangely
drawling. The second was crasser—Brooklyn, or the
Bronx. Clutterbuck hobbled forward, looked down one
of those narrow alleys. At its end a man crouched against
a locked gate, and he wore a uniform like Olin's own.
Capless, jacket open, a lock of brown hair spilling across

the forehead of a massive head lowered challengingly, like a bull's, he had obviously been drinking but he looked as if he knew how to use his upraised fists.

Confronting him, backs to Clutterbuck, were two American infantrymen—one a sergeant, a hulking giant, the other a corporal, small and foxy. They had the man trapped against the gate, and now they raised their fists and began moving in. Instinctively Clutterbuck struck the cobbles with his cane. "Look here, you men! We'll have none of that!"

The two doughboys whirled, startled. The sergeant stared at Olin with beady eyes, fish's mouth twisting in a pale face. "Two of you, huh? Suits me. Rollins, you—"

"No," the smaller one said quickly. "Wait a minute, Kelly—"

"That's right," Clutterbuck said coolly, and he clubbed the cane. "You'd better think it over, Kelly. Unless you want a court-martial and a broken head both."

"Ahh," the sergeant rasped, "you bastards don't—" He swayed a little, as drunk as or drunker than the officer against the fence. The corporal seized his arm. "Kelly, come on! The little French slut ain't worth it!" He looked at Clutterbuck imploringly. "Sir, Kelly's got too much cognac in him. We come to see his girl and caught this lieutenant with her. He's all right when he's sober, only . . . Dammit, Kelly, *come on!*"

Slowly, warily, Clutterbuck backed out and gave them room. "All right. You're free to go, both of you. But I'd advise you to be quick about it." He jerked his head, trying to be commanding, though his hand was sweating on the cane.

For a moment it could have gone either way. Rollins tugged frantically at Kelly's arm. Then the big sergeant let out a rasping breath, seeming visibly to shrink with the decision he had made. "You're right, Rolly, she ain't worth it. Hell, let 'im have her, there's plenty more where she came from." He moved forward unsteadily, rubbing his face. Clutterbuck stepped back to let them pass. Then, like a mahout handling a balky elephant, Rollins shoved Kelly down the street. Clutterbuck watched until they vanished around a corner.

"Well, I reckon I owe you a drink, or four or five." A voice at his elbow made him turn. "All they needed was feathers to make me feel like Custer at the Little Big Horn. My name's Chandler, Heath Chandler, Eighty-eighth Squadron. I ought to know you, but I don't."

"Olin Clutterbuck, Eighty-fourth Squadron." Olin thrust out his hand.

"You'd better give that to me again. My eardrums are paralyzed with Calvados."

Clutterbuck, used to the problem of his name, repeated it. Chandler grinned. "Clutterbuck. Got it now. Sounds like somebody shaking a sack full of rocks."

He was not quite as tall as Olin, although—wide-shouldered and slim of hip—not a small man either. His eyes were brown, deep-set, sparkling with amusement, as if what had happened had been a kind of joke. His features, Olin thought, were straight out of a Charles Dana Gibson drawing, handsome, almost beautiful, save for the three-inch scar puckering his right cheek near his mouth. His nose was straight, his mouth almost like a girl's, but when he grinned his teeth were curiously defective— white, but crooked and irregular—and Clutterbuck had a fleeting impression of almost carnivorous sharpness. Chandler's hand was firm, his grip strong and vigorous; there was a warmth and frankness in his manner that captured Olin immediately. And now, as Chandler pulled his cap from his belt and clamped it on his head at anything but a regulation angle, something clicked in Olin's mind. "Yeah," he said, "wait a minute. I've heard about you. You're the one they used to call back in London the Commander of the Flying Four-posters."

Chandler's laugh was deep, rich. "Yep, that's me. A bunch of us rented this house in Berkeley Square—didn't you ever come there? Everybody else did, all the brass hats and the girls, God, the girls—" He tapped Olin on the arm. "Makes me thirsty just to think about it. Come on, let's find a rail to prop our feet on while we talk. It's on me, anything you want." He moved off, limping a little, and Clutterbuck followed, not entirely sure he wanted a drink, but curiously interested in Chandler, who, after all, was something of a legend. He fell in beside the other man.

"Clutterbuck. Where does a man with a name like that come from?" Chandler asked.

"Boston. You?"

"Place you never heard of. Chandlerville, North Carolina. Cotton-mill town."

"Named after your family?"

"After my father. He owns it, lock, stock and barrel. A company town." He said it simply, with no pride, even with distaste. "If you could call something like that a town. It's more like a scab. Here, this ought to do."

The little bar was rank with the smoke of bad tobacco, spilled wine, and its primitive *pissoir*, jammed with old men and younger ones minus arm, leg or eye. At the counter Chandler ordered two cognacs in fairly good French, and when they came paid with francs from a roll as thick as his wrist. Clutterbuck drank slowly, shuddering a little at the sour burn, but Chandler tossed his off at a gulp, then ordered two more. He drank the second as swiftly as the first and, since Olin lagged, ordered a third for himself alone. But as if a deep, initial craving had been satisfied, Heath drank the third more slowly.

"You really saved my bacon back yonder. I was bluffing like a puffin adder. With my game leg, that big mick would have masticated and expectorated me if you hadn't come along in the nick of time."

"What was it all about?"

Chandler grinned. "Poontang, what else? I bumped into this little Fifi in a bar across the river, went home with her. Had barely got my hat off when those two doughboys charged in and I learned that I was fishing in somebody else's pond. I tried to calm 'em down and leave quietly, but the big one wouldn't let me. He was even drunker than me, which is a hell of a thing to say about anybody. You in hospital too?"

"Yes."

"Where'd you get yours?"

"Armentières," Clutterbuck said. He felt cold sweat breaking out on him and didn't want to talk about it. Chandler sensed that, with a delicacy Olin had not expected, and changed the subject to himself. "Mine over Wipers. Went down on three Hun two-seaters at once; must have been out of my head. Or maybe it was the hangover I had—they always make me vicious. Well, I got one of 'em, but the other two diced me like a carrot. Took a bullet in my leg, lost my engine, went down like a rock. Damnedest thing, fully conscious the whole time, you know? Jesus, I'll never forget that last second before I hit; it must have lasted two centuries. Then I woke up draped over the cockpit with two Tommies shoving my teeth back into my mouth, another bandaging my leg, and a fourth waving a bottle of cognac, which I badly needed, under my nose. There was a lot of other stuff broken too; they had to put me back together like a jigsaw puzzle. But they say I'll stay glued." He finished his drink. "Hey, I know where there ought to be a party. Plenty of booze and lots of girls. Not mademoiselles either, or whatever you call distaff Frenchmen. British nurses. Would you by any chance be game?"

Olin frowned, very tired, yet strangely reluctant to part from Chandler. A kind of aura seemed to emanate from Heath, as if there were so much vitality in him that it forced itself out through his very pores. He roused a curious excitement in Clutterbuck, and almost against his will, Olin said, "Why not?"

Outside, the afternoon was waning, the sunlight changed from the color of white wine to that of good peach cordial; there was a barely perceptible vibration of air that they recognized as the shock of an enormous barrage very far away. "Somebody," Heath murmured, "on one side or the other is catching hell, poor bastards." Then he said, "You look tired. Wait here, I'll run down a cab." Before Olin could answer, he limped off and, almost immediately, returned walking beside a clattering, one-cylinder taxi. They piled in, and Chandler gave the driver instructions in French.

As it carried them back toward the Seine, Chandler

looked out at the city, his face grave. "Lord God," he said, "but this is a beautiful place. You can almost smell the life in it. I would like to live here forever." He paused, head turned away from Olin. "The only thing that really scares me about this war is the chance that I might live through it and have to go back home again."

There had been more than two hundred of them—volunteers in the Aviation Section of the U.S. Signal Corps—and, with no available planes or training facilities in the States, they had been sent to England to be trained by the Royal Flying Corps. Divided into several sections, they had been stationed all over England, and many of them had been killed or become mentally unfit for flying long before they had been sent to France.

Among them Heath Chandler had been a legend. He had been made an acting sergeant on the boat, and from the beginning had been a commanding presence, not at all averse to pushing his ambiguous authority to the limit, ambitious, hungry for accomplishment and prestige, and yet somehow managing to retain the regard of the majority. Olin, in a different section, had heard of him from the outset and knew that he had been both hated and admired, had heard it said that Heath took himself too seriously and not seriously enough.

Rumor also had it that he was possessed of great personal wealth; certainly he spent money lavishly. With a coterie of friends, he managed, while stationed near London, to rent a house in Mayfair for use at night, on weekends, and furloughs. There his skill at organizing parties and finding hard-to-come-by whiskey had drawn to his soirees not only certain daring ladies of the aristocracy but even officers of high rank, who, so to speak, checked their insignia at the door.

Anyhow, Olin had heard that while yet a cadet Chandler had established connections in high places, and, armed with these friendships, a suspected capacity for blackmail if it came to that, and his own charm, he had soon organized his own flying corps within the Flying Corps. A chance remark by an awed colonel—"*If those boys can fly aeroplanes the way they fly four-posters, God help the Huns!*"—had given his coterie its nickname. Of all this, Clutterbuck had been vaguely aware; he himself cared little for that kind of life and had never made any effort to force his way into that circle of wenchers and carousers. Now, though, he felt an inexplicable pleasure at being in Heath's company. This had been such a remarkable day that it seemed only right to climax it by falling in with such a man.

In the cab Chandler smoked incessantly, one strong Fatima after another; his fingers were stained yellow, his nails bitten close, and, Olin saw, his hands were not too steady. "There's this apartment up in Montmartre," he explained. "Belongs to our squadron's Number Two. He's had it since before the war and lets us use it and there's something going on every weekend. God only knows who'll be there, but the place ought to be crawling with females." Silent for a moment, he looked out the window. "Funny what the war does to women. Damned near pathetic how glad they are to get a chance to take off their corsets and be human. . . . But, what the hell, it does a lot of things to a lot of people. Maybe, if Jerry doesn't get me, one of these days I'll write a play about it—the way it really is—and shock everybody back home down to his toenails."

"A play?"

"Yeah." Heath laughed with a touch of self-consciousness. "I went to Harvard. My old man never went to school, but he figured his son ought to have the best. Anyhow, I took Baker's course in playwriting, and I think I've seen enough now to have something to write about." He flipped the cigarette butt out the window, shook out another Fatima. "The hell I will," he said suddenly, harshly, bitterly. "If I don't get killed I'll have to go home and wind up ass-deep in lint, like my father!"

"You don't like the textile business?"

Heath jerked around, stared at him. "Good God, man, you're from Massachusetts, you ought to know what it's like. Besides, after all this—" The hand with the cigarette made a jerky gesture. "Cloth? Yarn? The thought doesn't exactly bring me to climax." He tapped his jacket. "It's all here, though, in the last letter I got from him. He's got it all laid out for me. When I get home I start at the bottom, work my way up through every job in the mill. Maybe five years, more or less, then I'll be allowed to enter the holy sanctum, the office. And eventually, if everything goes well and I mind my manners and don't put my foot in any bucket, someday I inherit Chandler Mills and . . . that'll be the end of it. The end of a lot of things. Then I'll turn into another Bolivar Chandler, I guess, and—Oh, shit. You don't want to hear my sad story. Anyhow, Jerry will probably take care of all my problems in his own ineffable way. How many kills you got?"

Clutterbuck told him.

"Not bad. Me, only three confirmed and five I know of that I couldn't confirm. In my squadron, if you don't bring his scrotum home to tack on the wall of the mess, it don't count. But I'll get more." He laughed, a cold sound, and stared into his cigarette's curling smoke. "Before I'm through I'll get so many they'll have to build a monument to me—posthumously. That would make him happy—a nice, pure, white shaft of marble; that ought to meet the old bastard's standards. That's what he wants for a son anyhow." Clutterbuck was shocked at the profound despair in Heath's voice; but as quickly as it had materialized, it vanished. They were on a narrow, nearly vertical street in Montmartre now; behind the rooftops Clutterbuck could see the dome of Sacré-Coeur. Heath stopped the cab, paid the driver, took Olin's arm, and led him through the entrance of a nearby three-story house. With some effort, since both had bad legs, they climbed two flights of narrow, dingy stairs smelling of generations of humanity's ingestions and excretions. At the second landing there was a door, and from behind it came loud voices, laughter, music. Without knocking, Chandler pushed it open and they entered.

2 THE FRONT ROOM of the flat was large and thronged with people—men in Royal Air Force khaki or French horizon blue, pretty women in colorful dresses. The place reeked of smoke, alcohol, perfume, and wool, and above a babel of many languages a gramophone in one corner scratched out shrill, nervous ragtime music. Heath slammed the door deliberately, and those closest to it turned and stared. Then a kind of cheer went up. "By Jove," someone cried, "here he is at last." Men and women alike surged toward him, and Olin saw a transformation come over him, all signs of bitterness and fatigue vanishing. He seemed to glow and somehow looked younger as, with Clutterbuck behind him, he allowed himself to be swallowed by the crowd. As if he were the guest of honor or a celebrity, people of both sexes reached out to touch him, seeming hungry for physical contact with him.

Then a woman in the uniform of the British Nursing Corps broke through. She was tall, with chestnut hair piled high, and must have been at least five years older than Chandler, perhaps as much as ten. Her face lit with delight and relief. "Heath!" She threw her arms about him, kissed him hungrily on the mouth, then wrenched away, dark brows drawing down over huge dark eyes lustrous with exasperation. "You beast! You promised you'd come early! I've been nearly frantic. Where have you been?"

Chandler grinned, patting her casually on the rump. "You wouldn't believe me if I told you. But the fact of the matter is, I was attacked in a dark alley by fifteen Apaches who tried to cram me down a sewer. Only the intervention of my friend here saved me from an unspeakable fate. Lieutenant Olin Clutterbuck, meet Lieutenant Agatha Chisholm."

"How do you do?" She took his hand, frown vanishing. "Another American. I might have known. Thank you for

37

rescuing Heath. I understand the Apaches are very bad this time of year. Or was it cocottes?"

"Aggie, you've got a dirty mind." Chandler grinned. "Actually, Olin and I got to drinking and talking and lost track of time. Reggie come with you?"

"Yes, she's here somewhere."

"Well, round her up. I want Olin to meet her. Anybody made the punch yet?"

"No one would dare. We were waiting for you."

"*C'est bon!* All the ingredients at hand?"

"I managed to steal the grape juice from the commissary. No luck on the Scotch though."

"That's all right. Tommie Warner ought to be around here somewhere. He owes me a quart. Come on, Olin, watch a master hand at work. No party's complete without Chandler's Carolina Cat Sweat." He led Clutterbuck to a table laden with whiskey, gin, wine, cognac, and cans of fruit juice, all ranged around an enormous punch bowl. "No ice, of course," Heath said, "but after one drink your circulation stops and you don't need it anyway. Slosh something sustaining in a couple of glasses to hold us while I'm concocting, will you?" Then he turned, nudged an officer standing nearby, glass in hand. "Hello, Ralph, was Tommie able to come down this weekend? He owes me a bottle of Scotch I need for the punch."

The man, a captain with a cavalry mustache, was very drunk; he blinked once, focused his eyes carefully. "Tommie, did you say?"

"Yes, dammit. Tommie Warner, from the Hundred and Twenty-fourth."

"Oh, that Tommie." Pulling his mustache, the captain swayed precariously from side to side. "Why, I thought you'd heard. Didn't you hear?" He took a long drink of straight whiskey. "Thought everyone had heard."

"Heard what?" Heath asked tensely.

"Why, Tommie bought it last week. They got his bomber over Zeebrugge, and it burned up before it hit the ground. Sorry about the Scotch." Turning, he lurched away into the crowd.

For perhaps ten seconds Heath did not move. Then he

let out a long breath, shrugged, turned back to the punch bowl. "Well," he said tonelessly, "scratch one bottle of Scotch. That ruins the punch. Damn it, Clutt, I said pour us something!" He slammed down an opener into a can of grape juice.

Olin half filled two glasses with cognac. As he set down the bottle a woman's voice said, "Here they are." Agatha was there, and with her was another girl, also a lieutenant. She was shorter, younger, blonde, with milk-white skin and a snub nose and round, smooth, babyish cheeks. The breasts beneath her blouse were very large. "Heath, darling," Agatha said, "will you do the honors?"

"Olin Clutterbuck, Lieutenant Regina Wilson," Chandler said tersely. He shoved the can aside. "I'll get back to the punch later. Come on, Aggie, let's dance." He seized her roughly, pulled her close, and they shoved through the crowd.

Regina Wilson put out her hand. "How do you do, Lieutenant . . . forgive me, what is it?"

"Clutterbuck. Olin Clutterbuck."

"I'm sorry. There's so much noise in here." She pointed at Heath's untouched glass. "Please, may I have that?"

"Of course." Clutterbuck gave it to her. For a moment, even in the midst of the racket, there was an awkward silence between them. She bridged it gracefully, smiling warmly and lifting her glass. "Cheers." When they had drunk, she took his hand. "The sofa seems to be vacant for the moment. Let's sit and get our bearings."

Beside her on the sofa, Clutterbuck realized all at once how tired he was. He looked for Heath, saw him dancing with Agatha on the far side of the room, their bodies plastered together, hips moving in a way that had nothing to do with the rhythm of the music. "So you're an American," Reggie said. "In hospital, of course. I suppose you're an old friend of Heath's?"

"No. No, we came over on the same ship, but I only really met him this afternoon."

"Isn't he fabulous? They say he's a marvelous flyer, and no party is any fun without him. Poor Aggie, she's madly in love with him, and I'm afraid it's utterly hope-

less. I don't think he really cares for anything or anybody, and I don't know that I blame him, the way things
are. Have you a cigarette?"

Clutterbuck lit one for her, and as she drew on it like
a man he found himself looking at her with his artist's
eye, translating the essence of her into paint on canvas.
At first he would have said that, pretty as she was, she
offered small challenge to his talent. Then he realized
that beneath the smooth, round, babyish surface there
was something else, perhaps beyond his ability to capture, a paradoxical weariness and tensity, as if she were
really a haggard old woman encased in fresh, young
flesh; something in her eyes gave that impression, and
in the set of her rosebud mouth, the way her hands, not
at all chubby, but hard and competent, moved quickly,
almost spastically. He remembered what Heath had said
about the effect of war on women.

And he had made her uncomfortable. "You're looking
at me so strangely."

"I was just wondering whether or not I could paint
you."

"What color?" She laughed, then was serious. "Are you
an artist?"

"Not now. But I will be, I hope, if I live."

"*If you live.*" Lines appeared at the corners of her
mouth. "Why does everyone say that? Why should it be
necessary for all of you to qualify everything you say that
way? In the name of God . . . How old are you?"

"Twenty-two."

"Yes, of course," she said wearily. "A child. And I'm
six years past that."

"That's not old either."

"Yes it is. When you've seen what I've seen, it's old,
old, terribly old; I'm the oldest living woman." She drank
and shifted her body; and his hand, dangling across the
top of the sofa, came in contact with the soft cushion of
her breast. He started to move it and then decided not
to. "Yes," she said. "The things I have seen. I was a surgi-
cal nurse in a private hospital in London, and I thought
that I was hardened to anything I could be confronted

with over here. But that was before I was assigned to a field hospital. And then . . . what they brought back from the lines. My God, there have been times when I've thought that touching one more chunk of bloody flesh that used to be a human being—That's what this war is, of course. Bloody. Bloody, bloody, in every sense of the word." She turned, pressed her face against Clutterbuck's sleeve, and now the front of her breast was fully against his hand. Clutterbuck looked down at the bent, blonde head and took his hand away and used it to stroke her back, comfortingly, almost as if she were a child. He looked up, saw that Heath had left Agatha, and now, at the table, was surrounded by fascinated onlookers while, with bravura flourishes, he mixed the punch. Then Reggie sat up. "Enough of my doleful history," she said crisply. "Now, yours. Only, I hope, not so doleful. Where in the United States are you from?" She moved against him, so that now he was embracing her, and leaned her head on his shoulder.

He told her about Boston, and about his father, an underwriter of bonds and securities, and of his two younger brothers, one at an Episcopal seminary, the other in infantry training at Camp Jackson, South Carolina. As the oldest son, he was expected to join the firm after the war, but he did not want to. He could not imagine himself as a financier; the need to paint amounted to a compulsion, an obsession. He was full of confidence in his own talent and certain that it would make him great and famous. He had never told so much to anyone before and, realizing that he must be drunk, was relieved that she took him seriously and did not laugh at him. That and the cognac helped to vanquish the doubts that, secretly, always gnawed at him, and he felt very grateful and loving toward her for taking him seriously. Then Heath loomed above them with a glass of purple liquid in each hand.

"I hate to interrupt," he said thickly, "but it's time for your medicine, children. Dr. Chandler's Ancient Indian Compound, brewed from a formula given me by an old Tuscarora chief named Running Moose Nose, whose life I once saved from Broncho Billy Anderson, containing a mixture of health-giving roots, herbs, berries and other revivifying simples. Guaranteed good for man or beast, immediately cures heaves, hives, shingles, shakes, catarrh, split hoofs, and hernia in mules. Drink."

Clutterbuck did, and found it faintly sweet, marvelously refreshing; only after several swallows did he realize how shot through with alcohol it was. Reggie drained half her glass at a swallow and giggled. "Heath, darling, you have surpassed yourself."

"Careful," Heath said. "It'll put hair on your chest." Swaying, he made a gesture of benediction. "God bless you, my children. Clutterbuck, take care of my little girl." He turned, went to the gramophone and cut it off. Then he sat down at a cigarette-scarred upright piano in the other corner and, jacket open, hair tousled, struck some chords, moved into a rendition of what Clutterbuck vaguely recognized as a passage from the "Appassionata." It gathered strength and feeling, and Olin was arrested by the music and by the skill with which Heath played it, but it broke off suddenly into the cheap, ragtime rattle of what was then called a coon song, as if Chandler were making fun of his own mood. Hardly anyone paid attention to him anyway. The punch bowl was being raided. It seemed to Clutterbuck that the room itself and the people in it swam in a chiaroscuro of wine-colored light, and he was full of emotion—excitement and a sense of doom that sweetened it; and he wanted to kiss Reggie, and he did.

She was waiting for it, and her mouth was already parted when his came to it, and he felt immediately the tentative tip of her tongue. He had not kissed many women like that and was profoundly aroused and stirred, and he pulled her to him desperately and she clung, and for a long time after that they did as so many other couples were doing, wherever there was a chair in which a man could pull a girl down on his lap or a corner for them to be in, and took what they could in the time they had.

Much later the sound of furious voices made him raise his head.

Across the room a group of men stood by the window, Heath in its center, Agatha desperately circling outside it. The captain Heath had spoken to earlier was scarlet-faced, mustaches bristling. "By Jove, Chandler, that's the absolute last straw. What you want is a good lesson—"

"Please, Ralph, Heath, Willard, please—" Agatha's voice was frantic. They ignored her. "And who's gonna give it to me?" Heath's tone was sneering, mocking. "Bomber men? Why, hell, one good pursuit pilot could mop up a dozen of you tram conductors—"

"Oh, you bloody imp!" the captain roared, taunted beyond endurance. He lurched at Heath. "I'll show you!" He seized Heath, who only stood there laughing, wrestled him. "Come on, you fellows!" the captain yelled. "Help me! We'll show this insolent pup." Somebody whooped assent and others seized Heath. "*Wait!*" Agatha screamed. "If you want a test of bravery, we'll give you one!" the captain snarled. Heath kept on laughing. "Out the window with him!"

Clutterbuck stared, unbelieving. Someone threw up the sash, a surge of bodies engulfed Heath, lifted him off his feet. He was giggling helplessly and made on effort to resist. Then, as Agatha screamed again, they pushed him through the window.

"Good Lord," Olin whispered, suddenly remembering that they were two stories up. He shoved himself to his feet, scrabbled across the room without his cane. Agatha clawed in terror at the backs of the cursing, laughing men around the opening, and they disregarded her. Looking over their shoulders, Clutterbuck went cold. Heath hung dangling, head down, above the cobblestones thirty feet below, at the mercy of the captain and of a major, each of whom held a booted ankle.

"Now, damn you, Chandler, an apology or we'll drop you!" the captain snarled. In horror, Olin realized that, so drunk they could hardly stand, he and the other officer meant it. But Chandler did not answer. Dangling precariously, his body bouncing against the wall, his head sure to be smashed like a pumpkin on those stones if they let go, he was, inexplicably, still laughing, too convulsed with mirth to speak.

"Pull him in!" Clutterbuck yelled frantically. "Damn it, you fools, pull him in!" He stood helplessly, afraid to reach for Heath for fear of making them drop him. One boot had already begun to slip loose from Chandler's calf. "You'll murder him!"

"And good riddance!" Ralph snapped. Still, from below, the laughter boiled up in a manic gurgle. "He jokes about poor Tommie Warner, not yet cold in his grave, insults our squadron, he asked for it, and now, by George, he'll get it! I say, Chandler. Are you ready to apologize?"

"Go to hell!" Heath yelled back, finally finding voice. "I dare you to let me drop! You haven't got the guts!"

"Then—at the count of three! One . . . two . . ." He paused. "Your last chance, Chandler!"

Still laughing, Heath yelled up something obscene.

"Three!" the captain shouted. And it seemed to Clutterbuck that his own heart stopped. The captain released his grip. The major leaned out the window. Clutterbuck rammed through the crowd, caught one kicking foot; the major still gripped the other. Olin turned furiously on the officer. "Pull him up!" he snapped. "God damn you, help me pull him up, or—"

The major blinked at him owlishly. Then he seemed to come to his senses. Cold sweat stood out on his forehead. "Of course," he whispered. "We only meant to frighten him." He shook his head uncomprehendingly. "My God." He turned to the others. "You chaps bear a hand here." Then others caught Heath's legs and, inch by inch, he was hauled up and through the window. He slid into the room, face crimson, but he was on his feet in an instant, perfectly steady, and his grin was taunting. "I called your bluff, didn't I?"

"Why, you bastard—" the captain began, but Agatha was suddenly between him and Heath. "Be quiet," she rasped ferociously at Chandler. "You fool, be quiet. Ralph, he apologizes, he—Don't you, Heath?"

Mocking grin still lingering, Heath looked at her and then at Ralph. And suddenly his smile changed; now it was warm, frank, and even humble. "Of course I do," he said. "I'm sorry, Ralph, I was out of line. Thanks for not letting go, Willard. I owe you a drink." He clapped the captain on the shoulder, then shoved past him, put a record on the gramophone. At once it bleated ragtime. Then he seized the trembling Agatha, performed a spectacular and dirty maneuver with her in the middle of the silent, staring circle around them. The tension broke; all at once the room thundered with laughter. Ralph laughed hardest of all. "By Jove, Chandler, I'll see to having you transferred. With a little seasoning, you just might make a bomber man!" And he caught up a dark-haired French girl and, still laughing, swept her out on the floor to dance.

Clutterbuck turned away, quite sober now and with no amusement left in him. For a moment, while Heath had dangled above the cobblestones, there had been something dark, rank, animal, in the room that had frightened him and that now left him depressed with the realization of how little value any of them placed on life anymore. Watching Heath dancing lasciviously with the nurse, he thought that Chandler himself was somehow the author of that darkness, had deliberately roused, encouraged it. A shudder went over Clutterbuck, as if he had witnessed some awful perversion; and then it occurred to him that maybe he had. All at once he understood that it had not made the slightest difference to Heath Chandler whether they let him drop or not.

3   THE PARTY seethed for hours, and Clutterbuck fought the black mood the incident had created in him by drinking more of the punch. Outside, now, it was dark; within, the apartment filled with hysterical noise, like the amplified shrilling of insects on a summer night. He and Reggie, back on the sofa, pawed and kissed each other wetly and determinedly, while other couples mounted a considerable traffic through the bedroom door. Then —he heard vaguely that a newcomer had brought word

of another party elsewhere—the crowd began to thin. Presently, like wrack cast up by a storm, Olin Clutterbuck, Heath Chandler, and their women were left alone amidst the debris.

Heath seemed to strike a certain level of intoxication and hold it. As the others left he sat at the piano and played and sang bawdy music-hall ballads in superb imitation of the entertainers Clutterbuck had seen in tawdry places in London. Then the music changed to something inexpressibly sad, which Olin at last identified as Negro spirituals. That broke off, and then Heath and Agatha passed through the bedroom door and closed it. Sprawled across Reggie on the sofa, Olin got his hand under her dress, but when he tried to pull down her drawers, she fended that maneuver. He was insisting drunkenly when the bedroom door opened much later (though it had seemed only a moment or two) and, with perfect insouciance, Heath and Agatha emerged. The girl had let down her chestnut hair, and it fell almost to her waist.

Immediately Heath complained of being hungry and disappeared, evidently to find food. Reggie, wriggled from Clutterbuck's grasp. "Excuse me, please." She smiled, touched his cheek, and went to Agatha. The two of them whispered together, and Reggie said, "We won't be a minute, but we do need some repairs." They vanished into the bedroom, closing the door gently but firmly and leaving Clutterbuck alone.

He sat there, queasy with alcohol and aching with desire, and confusedly rubbed his face. He felt stunned by the events of the afternoon; impressions were blurred in his mind as if he had had a long ride on a runaway horse. And all this from a chance encounter with Heath Chandler. . . . He arose, began to walk, aimlessly about, went to a bookcase containing a mixture of philosophical works, poetry, Russian novels, and a stock of yellowbacked, paperbound, explicitly illustrated pornography in French, on which guests had evidently already made heavy inroads. He took out a volume, thumbed through it, too tired to try to read the French and too brimful of desire already to be stirred further by the incredible but elegantly executed illustrations. Then Chandler came in, and Olin hastily, guiltily, returned the volume to the shelf. "Well, that's done," Heath said. "I finally sweet-talked the concierge into rustling up some Frog slumgullion for us. What, pray tell, have you done with the women?"

"In there." Olin pointed to the bedroom.

"Oh. Deciding your fate." Heath dropped with utter weariness to the sofa, took out cigarettes.

"What?"

"Christ, man, don't you know anything about females? They're in deep conference. Reggie's telling Agatha all the reasons why she, Reggie, shouldn't, and Agatha is knocking them all down, just as Reggie wants her to." He lit a Fatima and made a face. "Gahh. My mouth tastes like a condor rookery."

"Wait a minute," Clutterbuck said, staring at the door. "Do you think—? Really, would she?"

Heath lay back. "Why not? They both like you and you've already got Reggie worked up. Besides, there's a war going on." He closed his eyes. *"The fire moths can never be too hot or bright, the flame too fierce; they come from the four corners of the night, bright wings outspread, avid for the burning kiss . . ."* "Who wrote that?" Clutterbuck asked. "I just did," said Chandler. "I frequently think in poetry when I'm drunk." He closed his eyes and softly began to snore; then the bedroom door opened and the two women were coming out.

In the milieu in which Olin Clutterbuck had grown to manhood it was nearly impossible for a young man, unless he were very daring, aggressive and lucky, to consort sexually with any women but prostitutes. There had been six of those in the last few years, including two in London, but afterward he always thought of that as the night on which he really lost his virginity. A single lamp burned on the bedside table. The bed on which he sat, watching Regina take down her hair at the dressing table, had been spread with fresh linen by the two women. The light

glinted on Reggie's bare shoulders and on her gold-
colored hair as she probed it with her fingers; then she
bent her head and the mass came loose in an astonishing,
shimmering cascade over her face, with a rain of pins on
the marble tabletop. With one hand and a jerk of her
head she tossed it back; it fell down over her naked
shoulders and the top of whatever it was, corset or cami-
sole or vest—Clutterbuck knew nothing about the taxon-
omy of the female undergarment—magnificently. The
nervousness and fear left him and the artist in him roused
as she unhooked herself at the edge of lamp glow; it was
as if he were seeing a naked woman for the first time
without the smudged glass of either prudery or cheap
vulgarity blurring the sight. "No," he said as she came
toward him a little shyly. "No, just stand there and let me
look at you for a minute." And unwittingly he had said
exactly the right thing in the right tone of voice. She
moved her half-shielding arms away from large breasts
that fell down a little of their own weight and allowed
him to stare at them and at the gentle swell of her belly,
the lyre-shaped curve of hips, the milky smoothness of the
thick female thighs of her rather short legs, and he was
aware that he was smiling gently and with pleasure at
her. "You're very beautiful," he said with absolute sin-
cerity, and although there had been a faint overlay of
nervousness on her own features, that vanished now, and
she returned his smile in a way that illuminated her. Then
she came to sit beside him on the bed. Only then did he
become aware that he himself was fully dressed. She
helped him take off the clothes, and, curiously, there was
no urgency, no fumbling. They were comfortable together.
Then they got into the bed, pulling the sheet up over
themselves, and lay together; and he kissed her and began
to model and repeat the curves and swellings of her body
with his hands, at first curiously and wanting to get the
aesthetic feel of them and then with a growing urgency;
and his touch changed; suddenly they were kissing each
other very hard and she was jerking and gasping with
excitement and after that they made love. Nearly an hour
later, when they came out of the room, he felt a great

tenderness toward her, and it seemed to him that he himself was a totally different man from the one who had earlier entered the room. Heath lay on the sofa, head on Agatha's lap, and on the table, cleared now of bottles, there was a huge ragout emitting savory steam, a great loaf of crusty bread with real butter, and a bottle of excellent wine. Presently the four of them ate in a warm, unique atmosphere of intimacy, as if they were survivors of a catastrophe that had, for the moment, passed by them. Heath presided, witty, relaxed, even jolly; and Clutterbuck, cherishing a new kind of euphoria, reluctant to let the moment go, felt overwhelming love and admiration for the man across the table and hoped that neither Heath nor himself got killed in this war so that their friendship might continue forever.

Then it was time to leave, and at once Heath's mood changed. While the girls got ready to return to the hospital Clutterbuck straightened himself up. He came back from the *pissoir* to find Chandler standing at the window in the darkened room, staring out into the night.

Clutterbuck searched in dimness for his cap. Heath paid him no attention. Clutterbuck put it on; the girls came out, were ready. Olin said, "Heath?"

Chandler turned, almost startled at the sound of his name. There was just enough light for Clutterbuck to see the look of agony his face had worn, quickly erased as he came back to himself. "What were you thinking about so hard?" Olin asked.

"Nothing," Heath said. "Nothing of any consequence." He grinned bitterly. "Just wondering how, after all this, I can ever go home again."

4   IT WAS SUMMER, the land gripped by searing drought, the air breezeless and devoid of moisture. Inside the mill it was worse; the steam of boiling water, poured over the oaken floors to raise the humidity to the proper level for working cotton fibers, combined with

August heat to create a stifling hell in which only by an act of will could men maintain the unending, rhythmic exertion of tending machinery. Lint flew everywhere in the dead, dank air, drawn into the mouths and nostrils of the gasping mill hands; meanwhile, the unceasing thunder of the machines beat deafeningly on the eardrums, shook floor and walls and even the very air. In the card-room the reddish-brown dust of the trash and rubbish, worked out of the cotton by the cleaning action of the steel monster Heath Chandler tended, added to his misery as the card gulped the blanketlike soft laps of fiber and spewed out white, ropelike silver coiling endlessly into metal cans, as it had been doing since six o'clock that morning. In khaki shirt and bib overalls, bathed in sweat, Heath went about his work mechanically, too exhausted and dazed by noise for thought, yearning only for the whistle to signal the shift's end.

Then it came, a loud, bellowing hoot like that of some giant, wounded beast. His relief was there, and smoothly and without shutdown, the transition was made. Heath turned away groggily, blowing and picking at lint-clogged nostrils, raking white tufts from eyebrows. He hurried to the stairwell that led into open air, where he could breathe again.

It was clogged with weary mill hands—men, women, children—all, like himself, bathed in sweat, dusty white with lint, and completely drained after their ten-hour ordeal. As Chandler Mills was presently scheduled, they would put in five and a half such days a week; and this, Heath thought despairingly, was only Tuesday. He eased into the crowd, let it carry him down the stairs.

When it emerged from the mill into daylight, that shambling stream of dazed humanity, the outdoor silence was stunning; in it their raised voices were preternaturally loud. Moving to one side, Heath greedily lit a cigarette, drew in smoke, and tried to appear casual as he watched the hands file by.

They could all have been kin—brothers and sisters, or at least cousins. Many, in fact, were. Beginning almost forty years before and continuing through the war-born expansion of Chandler Mills, whole families had moved in off the land from which they could no longer wring a living and, desperate, had as a last resort relinquished the freedom they and their kind had always prized to go to work for wages, indoors, at machinery and under the tyranny of clocks and supervisors. In 1917, when labor was short, the demands on Chandler Mills heavy, and the market for its products unlimited, Bolivar Chandler had brought more of them down from the dark coves and hollows of the westward mountains. Pure Anglo-Saxon stock, all of them, descendants of pioneers and frontiersmen, the men still had a gaunt backwoods lankiness, shared by those women who had not run to gross fat on starchy rations. Coming slowly back to life now, they made their jokes with a nasal twang and dry understatement and salted their speech with traces of their ancestors' Elizabethan turns of phrase. The woman for whom Heath waited was one of them.

And she was late. He finished the cigarette, ground it out, lit another, wishing she would hurry up. He felt conspicuous standing here like this, but he had to know about tonight. After all, he must get the whiskey; and time was short.

Then he saw her. The other women moved on sociable coveys, groups and cliques, but she always walked alone. It was not her fault; it was only that she gave off, without being able to help it, a kind of sexual radiation as palpable as musk, which brought men into rut even as it frightened, angered and disturbed the women. So she came toward him apart from the crowd, barefooted, with a slow, indolent gait that caused broad hips to shift and heavy thighs to rub together in lazy invitation beneath the clinging, sweat-moist gingham that culminated higher in a rhythmic bobbing of big, soft, unhaltered breasts. Heath stared at her in helpless fascination, feeling instant stirring in his loins: a heavy woman, bovine even, belonging, he thought, in a painting by Rubens, with broad, rosy ass planted on greensward and the folds of flesh at her belly dealt with as another artist might deal with draperies. Then she had seen him and raised her head.

He looked into large, brown eyes, almost cowlike, yet with a strange sultriness and not totally stupid or insensitive. As she passed she nodded slightly, the ripe, pink lips forming a single word: *Yes.* Heath felt exultation mixed with fear and shame. Then she was gone, trailing in her wake like dust settling behind her a diminishing stream of sexuality, a sort of electricity with which her passage charged the air, lessening in intensity with distance.

When she was through the gate Heath hurried after her and crossed the road into the parking lot, while she turned to the right, ambling homeward toward the mill village on the hillside. As a few Model T's bought with war-fattened wages, sputtered into life, he started his own big, yellow Marmon, maneuvered it out of the lot, and eased it into the street and through the crowd of people going home on foot. There was a knot of apprehension in his belly. He did not have much time before supper to pick up the whiskey.

As he worked the car westward through the town Heath thought of Olin Clutterbuck, whom he had last seen six months before in Greenwich Village, with envy and with longing.

After their encounter in Paris he and Olin had done the town together as often as they could until both were discharged from the hospital and sent back to their units. Then fate had thrown them together again, when the Americans had been withdrawn from British units and formed into wings of their own. He and Olin had, through the luck of the draw, wound up not only in the same squadron but in the same flight. Flying wing to wing, they had played dice together with the enemy for their lives, and, as the war dwindled, Heath, in a final burst of recklessness, engaged and shot down so many Germans that he had soared high in the ranking of American aces. Then, to his despair, the war ended suddenly, and he was still alive.

He'd put off coming home as long as possible, wandering over Europe, seeking every excuse to postpone the inevitable. Finally, though, he had had to come back to Chandlerville.

In New York again he delayed, astonished and fascinated by what had happened in his absence. The girls had flung away their corsets, picked up cigarettes, learned to savor gin, and the city had become one vast party. He had been astonished not only by the dawning of this new era but by finding Clutterbuck in the heart of it in a grimy downtown loft full of unfinished paintings, with a girl who served both as model and as mistress. Heath had moved in with them, and the next week had been a blur. There were so many people he knew, survivors, all stunned, dislocated, still keyed up, like himself, who, startled and finding themselves still alive and accustomed to the pace of war, had created a kind of ferment that changed the city. While they drank, made love, danced and partied they sought some new style of life that would fit the people into whom they had been transformed by war, groped for something to replace the intensity and glory they had known, which would never come again.

And he himself knew at once that this was the place he had been seeking, not only through that postwar year of roaming but all his life. Drinking with Olin in the big, dirty studio, he had cried out, "Clutt. What am I to do?"

"Go home," Clutterbuck said, "and then come back."

"I can't. You don't understand. It's not that easy. *He* won't let me."

"Look," Olin said, "he's only a man. I know how you would have to get drunk before you could even bear to read his letters overseas, but— Hell, he's your father. Talk to him, tell him you don't want to stay."

"Oh, sure, just like that." Heath drank. "Listen, let me tell you about Bolivar Chandler. The Old Man, they call him down there, and the name fits him. He's been an old man since the day he was born. Never roamed a big, strange city, hungering to see what was around the next bend, never flown through clouds or risked his life or made love to somebody he would never see again or read a book or looked at a painting or heard a symphony or seen a play. He's old inside, and the only thing that ever stirred him, aside from a rip-roaring hell's-fire-and-damnation sermon, has been his bank balance or a rise in the yarn market."

"He's a businessman," said Olin. "So's my dad. I know it's hard for them to understand, but—"

"Hard? Impossible!" Heath laughed bitterly. "Clutt, do you know what working in a cotton mill is like? I can't even begin to describe the noise—like a barrage that goes on and on—but just the . . . act itself. Ten hours a day of it, the same thing over and over, because it's what you've got to do to keep the machines fed and running, what the machine demands of you, the same actions, repeated second after second, minute after minute, day in, day out, week after week. Not thinking, just hurrying to keep up, not to miss a beat, because you've got to be a machine yourself to match the machine you're working on. That's what he's asking of me, five years of it, five years of wasted life, the best part of my life. And he can't even see why I should balk at handing him those years on a silver platter just because he tells me to."

He paused. "I guess I've got too much of my Charleston kin in me. My mother was a Hampton, and the Charleston Hamptons were a wild bunch, whiskey drinkers, poker players, hell raisers. I often wondered why she ever married him—maybe he was a change after all that swashbuckling, I don't know. Anyhow, I'm full of Hampton blood, and he can't stand that, he's determined to rub it out of me. He has never understood what I wanted, the things that were important to me. His real offspring is Chandler Mills. He took them when they were busted and built them up, and they're all he really gives a damn about, everything else and everybody exists only to serve them, only for their benefit. That's all I exist for where he's concerned."

"Oh, don't be—"

"I'm not." Heath was grave. "It took me a long time to understand that, Clutt. He doesn't want me, he wants a replacement part for Bolivar Chandler. When I was a kid I was always in Dutch with him, just for being myself. I used to assume it was some flaw in me, some failing, that I was damned and doomed because I couldn't be perfect like him. And I guess he felt the same way, because he never quit trying to straighten me out, make me into another Bolivar Chandler. Funny, he never spanked me. But, God, when I used to get his lectures on what a disgrace and disappointment I was, how, if I kept on the way I was, what would I do when I had to step into his shoes—I used to wish, then, that he'd beat the hell out of me instead." He was ashamed of the way his voice broke. "I don't know how to tell the way I used to feel then. I would just shrivel up inside, just want to die, literally. There was never any doubt in my mind that I'd be better off dead and that he'd be happier to see me that way than in disgrace. And it'll be the same thing now when I go home. Because there's no way I can be myself and not disgrace him. Not according to his lights."

"Then don't go home at all. You've got the money your grandmother left you. Stay here and try to write the plays you keep talking about."

"I can't. I've got to go home." Heath shook his head. "And once I'm there I'm trapped. I'll never get away again."

"I don't see why not."

Heath had been silent for a moment, trying to find exactly the right words. Then, in utter honesty, they tumbled out of him. "Because I love him, Clutt. And, God help me, all I've ever really wanted is for him to love me too. And maybe I'm crazy, but right now that's all that seems to matter."

The speed felt good. It was not like flying, but it was better than nothing. Well, that was one promise he'd not broken, anyhow—even after he'd discovered a man in Macedonia with a hangar full of surplus Jennies. It had taken all his willpower to resist renting one, taking it up, shaking it out—but he would no sooner have landed than Bolivar would have known about it. His spy system was almost flawless; the mills and town alike were riddled with informers, ready to run to him with tales of any transgression of his stern code by any of his subjects, and the risk was not-worth it. Besides, he had promised. But, he thought wryly, he had not made any promise about corn whiskey and women. If Bolivar had taken his abstention from those for granted, that was just too bad.

He was out of Chandlerville now, racing through a countryside of scrubby woods and rain-starved pastures and a few fields of nearly withered cotton. It seemed to Heath that even the land had turned ugly, as if nature itself conspired with Bolivar to make his existence as brutally depressing as possible. Now, he thought, he could understand why a man sentenced to life imprisonment might choose to hang himself, unable to endure the awful frustration of living death while, outside, a world of richness, adventure, love and action from which he was forever closed off went on without him. Wrenching the last notch of speed from the car, he remembered England, France, New York, all he had seen and done and felt and would never see or do or feel again, and it was almost more than he could bear. Not even the prospect of the woman eased a pain almost physical or brought him any joy; she was a necessity, no more. He needed the sexual relief, but more than that he needed the risk, the excitement, after a long day's boredom. That was all he could get from her and all he really wanted.

But, God! Compare her with Celia! Even the thought of her, the only woman he had ever really loved, increased the pain. He gripped the wheel tightly. Remember how she had looked that first night when she had appeared at the Berkeley Square flat with the Guards colonel—cool, lovely, poised, just past thirty, with pale blonde hair, huge gray eyes, and that small, compact, trim and thoroughbred body that had catapulted him into a new, unimagined world. The moment they were introduced, something amazing, almost shattering, had arced between them; and the colonel had left the house alone that night and it had been himself who'd taken her home to her own place near Grosvenor Square.

Her husband had a title and a brigade in France and had been away for so long, was so obviously doomed, that he had not even counted; all that mattered was what they felt about each other, which was something that made everything right and perfect from the beginning—though his cheeks still burned as he imagined how ignorant and naïve she must have found him that first night, with no more refinement than a young bull. But maybe a young bull had been what she wanted then; anyhow, she was a good teacher and he a fast learner; and beyond that there was their love for one another. When he'd flown across the Channel he'd worn one of her stockings, black silk, beneath his helmet like a skullcap, a lady's favor to her knight. He wondered if she'd kept the impassioned letters he'd written her; he still had hers to him. They had come promptly at first, tapered off later, and, still later, without explanation, had ceased entirely. That had cost him agony, but he had learned something from it, and the pain was a cheap price to pay for the grandeur of the experience. . . . *And now,* he thought savagely, *tonight, that damned fat slob!* He had come to that, disgusting, humiliating, and yet needful. He hated himself for sinking so low and hated Bolivar for making it necessary that he do so.

Then he slowed a little. He was nearing the road to Fox's now, and a little of the blackness seeped out of him. Thank God for Fox Ramsey! When he reached Fox's place he'd have a drink or two, talk to Fox and listen to him, and take a while to let his overstrained nerves unwind. At Fox's he could regain some, if not all, of his good humor and become human again for a little while at least.

Then he saw the turn ahead, almost invisible in the woods that flanked the road, and wrenched the wheel.

Originally a wagon track, the way to Fox Ramsey's house was now rutted by the narrow wheels of many Model T's; a considerable traffic passed back and forth along it. Still, it was only wide enough for a single car, winding intricately through a dense forest of second-growth oaks and hickories, and it took all Heath's skill to hold the Marmon in the ruts and dodge tree trunks and stumps.

For two miles he wound deeper into the woods. Then the road descended steeply and the forest thinned a little, and presently, in a basin-shaped hollow not more than a couple of hundred yards across, he saw in the deepening twilight Fox Ramsey's house.

Not house so much as shanty, a two-room structure of unpainted boards with rickety porches fore and aft. Behind it wet wash hung lankly on a line; a couple of pigs grunted in a stinking pen, and a few scrawny chickens scratched in the thick leaf duff or amidst the pile of junk and garbage—old cans, broken bottles, discarded shoes—on the clearing's edge. Despite the shabbiness and clutter of the place, Heath felt as if he had reached a kind of refuge when he stopped the car before the cabin. As he mounted steps that trembled beneath his weight an ancient, drowsing hound beside them stirred enough to raise his head, blast a single bugle note; then, recognizing a familiar scent, flopped again.

The door of rough boards was closed. Heath knocked and waited. In a moment he heard bare feet shuffling over the floor within. Then it squeaked open and he looked down at the girl standing in the doorway and smiled and said, "Hello, Pearl."

She was seventeen, tall, skinny, almost breastless in the patched gingham dress that hung down around her like a tube. Dingy, straw-colored hair was pulled back tightly from her temples, piled in a bun behind her head. Her face was sallow, wide at cheekbones that were almost blades, narrowing to a sharp, pointed chin; her nose was straight, her mouth colorless and unremarkable. Only her eyes were of any interest: huge, they were a strange, arresting green, slanting toward her nose and giving her, in conjunction with the other features, a curious resemblance to something shy and wild—perhaps a vixen. "Howdy," she said in a nasal, expressionless voice.

"Your daddy home?"

"He's down at the crick. Be back directly."

"Can I come in?"

She nodded wordlessly, pulled the door wider. He entered a small room furnished with an oilcloth-covered

table, a few rickety chairs, an iron cot neatly spread with
a quilt of the kind handmade in the mountains, an old
food safe, its tin doors perforated in a floral pattern, and
a shotgun on pegs above a blackened fireplace of stones
chinked with mud. Only a crayon portrait of a pretty
young woman in turn-of-the-century dress, and Fox's discharge from the Army after the Spanish-American War,
framed above the bed, brightened the unpainted walls.

Again with that sense of sanctuary, Heath let out a long
breath as Pearl closed the door. "What about pouring me
a drink?" he asked. "A big one."

She looked startled, frightened. "You know Daddy don't
allow *me* to serve no whiskey," she whined.

"Okay, I'll do it, then. I know where he keeps it." He
went to the food safe. Pearl raised thin hands, work-
reddened. "You ought not to—" Then she let her arms fall
helplessly; as if frightened by his audacity, she hurried
through another door into the other room. Heath looked
after her with a mixture of pity and distaste. Fox kept her
shut up here like a prisoner, guarding her from all outside contacts with fanatic paternal zealousness. Despite
all the time he had spent in this house, Heath hardly
knew her and still could not decide whether she was
stupid or merely shy and ignorant. Anyhow, he thought,
the least she could do is wash her hair.

The safe contained a dozen cloudy glasses, five quart
fruit jars of corn whiskey. He took two glasses and a jar
that had already been opened and brought them to the
table, poured a big drink, held his breath, and tossed it
off greedily. The liquor was smooth, palatable, product
of a master craftsman, but still rackingly strong. While he
waited for it to take hold he lit a cigarette.

He had discovered Fox Ramsey within a week of drinking up all the Scotch he'd brought home from New York.
Not only Chandler but every millowner in Macedon
County strove to keep the area bone-dry. Drinking meant
hangovers, lost working time, fighting, gambling. Except
for Fox, they had succeeded in stamping out every source
of liquor.

But Ramsey had defied them all and somehow got

away with it. Originally a mountain man, he'd come down from the hills to work in the mills. But the routine, taking orders, the indoor work, had been too much for the frontiersman in him; his mountaineer's pride could not bear that abridgment of his freedom. So he had quit, found this lonesome hollow, and turned for his living to an art learned from his father and his grandfather—distilling corn and selling his moonshine by drink or jug.

And it had been almost like the thing with Celia, Heath thought. From the moment he and Fox had met, there had been something between them stronger than the relationship of buyer to seller. There was no explaining it; he was a Harvard graduate and Ramsey was an almost illiterate man twenty years his senior, and yet each had found something in the other that he needed, admired. Maybe it was a mutual contempt for petty rules, maybe the fact that they both despised cotton mills and everything that went with them, maybe the fact that, in the eyes of Bolivar Chandler, they were both, in their natural state, outlaws. Anyhow, Fox was a man in every sense of the word, tolerating no infringement on his masculinity, and there was something at the core of him to which Heath responded. Over the past few months their relationship had become something even more complex than friendship; it was, Heath thought now, the kind of thing that sons who were very lucky, as he was not, might have with their fathers.

Outside, the old hound gave his single, pro-forma bay of greeting. A voice said, "Hush," and the house trembled slightly with footsteps on the porch, the door scraped open, and Fox Ramsey came in, pausing just inside the threshold.

He was short, slight of build, with faded overalls and sweaty workshirt hanging on him baggily. Beneath his tipped-back and stained Fedora tendrils of thin, ginger-colored hair curled above a face that was a lined, tanned, older and masculine version of his daughter's: the nose longer, sharper, the chin more pointed, the slanted green eyes more vulpine. His cheeks were covered with two days' beard the color of his hair, but dulled with a peppering of gray. He looked at Heath and at the fruit jar. "Hallo, young feller," he said tonelessly. "You couldn't wait, huh?"

"Fox, I felt a snake bite comin on. I knew you wouldn't want me to have a spasm."

"Uh-huh." Ramsey crossed the room, trailing a rich, fruity odor of fermentation, and put the .30-30 Winchester rifle he carried on pegs beneath the shotgun. Then he turned. "Okay. You kin get away with it this time. But not again, you hear? Nobody pours whiskey in this house but me."

"I'm sorry," Heath said, meaning it. Fox ran this place by rules and did not take their breaking lightly. Small and easygoing as he seemed, there was something violent within him that was not lightly to be tampered with. "Come on and have a drink," Heath added, trying to mollify him. "I'll buy."

"Fair enough. I reckon it's time." Fox drank only once a day—two shots before he had his supper. He watched as Heath poured, held up one hand. "Whoa." He took the glass, sniffed its contents, then sipped lightly. When Heath gulped down his own drink in a single swallow, something moved in Fox's eyes.

"You drink that like it's gonna run away from you," he said.

"I need it."

"Bad day?"

"They're all bad," Heath said bitterly. "That mill's no place for a human being." He reached for the jar again, but before he touched it Fox moved it away.

Heath sat up straight, stared. Something in Fox's manner was strange. At the same time, the second drink exploded in him, and the craving for a third was strong, imperious. "I want one more, Fox."

"Maybe in a minute. First I want to talk to you."

Heath felt apprehension, reached instinctively for a cigarette. "What about?"

Fox Ramsey sat down, took out a corncob pipe, tamped it neatly and methodically with tobacco from a pouch. "You been swillin a powerful lot of that stuff lately."

"That's what you make it for, ain't it?" Heath laughed a bit lamely.

"Maybe," Fox said. "I don't mind you drinkin it. But I don't aim for you to use it to kill yourself with."

Again, nervously, Heath gave that tinny laugh. "Oh, hell, Fox. I can hold my booze. You should have seen me overseas."

"Umm." Fox lit the pipe. Then he scraped back his chair, went to the door, and, with his back to Heath, stood looking out at the chickens scratching in the leaf mould. After a moment that seemed interminable he turned, and the green eyes were serious, the thin face grave.

"Look," he said, "I was in a war one time myself. I know what it's like to go off to furren places, git all keyed up to fight, then come back home whur ever'thing is different. Kind of dead. Flat. Because when I come home from Cuba back to the Toe River valley, I recollect how ever'thing had changed while I was away. Seemed littler, slower, quieter. And how . . . there wasn't nobody I could talk to about what I had done and seen and no way I could explain how I had changed. I reckon a war is kinda like a whorehouse, no man ever comes outa one feelin the same way he did when he went in."

He paused, sipped from the glass. "From the time you first come here I made allowance for that. Knowed that after bein in all them far places and flyin them airplanes and shootin down all them Germans you had to have time to kind of unwind, git your feet on the ground again. On top of that, I know the mill." His mouth curled. "I served my time in the mill. I met my wife there, married her. And it was the mill that give her the TB that took her off—what they call the Kiss of Death from drawin in the warp yarn with her teeth, passed on from ever'body that uses his mouth on that damn heddle—"

He broke off. "Well, that ain't here nor there. All I'm sayin is that I know how you feel, maybe made more allowance for it than I ought to have. But . . . well, I kinda admired you, for all you done and ever'thing. Only—" He sat down again. "Anyhow, I been waitin. I been waitin all this time for you to do somethin, go one way or the other. Either to settle down, make up your mind to do what your daddy wants you to, or else to tell him to go to hell and take off on your own, do whatever it is you got to do that you think will make you happy. Only you ain't done neither one. You won't do nothin except drown your sorrows in all the likker you can lay your hands on and drive around the country in that yaller car of yourn like the devil was on your shirttail."

Heath's face felt frozen, his cheeks burned. "Fox, for God's sake. Don't you get on me too." Involuntarily he reached for the jar again; this time, as if from compassion, Fox let him have it.

Heath had sense enough to make the drink a small one. He held on tightly to the glass, as if it represented his salvation. "Fox," he whispered, ashamed of the trembling of his voice, "what brought all this on?"

"I'll tell you what brought it on," Fox said, and looked back at him coldly. "Sonny Ford was in here last night, drunk before he come, drunker when he left. And he knows all about you and his wife."

Heath stared at Fox Ramsey, totally unable to speak. Not fear of the wronged husband, but shame had literally knocked the wind out of him, clenched his stomach and his throat. He felt himself shrinking under Fox's gaze, as if the man had caught him in some perversion. "Fox—" Finally he managed that much.

"Don't Fox me!" And now the small man's voice was angry. "Damn it, don't tell me you couldn't have plenty of other women! A man like you, all them nice gals, them society gals in Macedonia . . . Why don't you go to them, your own kind, git what you want from them?" He shook his head. "Why *her?* Why a woman that's had ever'thing around here but the ax handle stuck in her already, and, on top of that, is married to the absolutely meanest snake in all this dadburned county?"

"Fox, I can't explain . . . I mean . . ."

"I know." Ramsey's voice was weary, disgusted. "I've seed her myself. Like a heifer that never goes outa heat. And I was young once too, recollect what it was like to need somethin, *anything*, to ram that in or else you'd go crazy! But none of that's no excuse—not with a married woman. And specially not with Sonny Ford's!" Fox paused. "He swears he aims to kill you," he finished flatly.

Heath sat there wordlessly for a second, still paralyzed by shame. Then, with hollow bravado, he said defiantly, "Shit."

"You keep your voice down! Pearl's back yonder!"

"I'm sorry. But I ain't afraid of Sonny Ford."

"Then you ain't got bat sense."

"Listen, Fox. She don't love him. He beats her. She's shown me the bruises, he beats hell out of her—"

"And you think she don't ask for it? Lord God, boy, that's why she's put the horns on him with ever' man in this end of the state and likely rubbed his nose in it! Listen, I know about both them Fords—They're both crazy! He's served time on the chain gang for a killin already, and that's why they run him out of the Butler mill over at Brackettville before he come here! If he says he's gonna kill you, he'll shore God try it! Anybody else, you bein the Old Man's son, might back off—but not him!"

Heath relaxed a little. "I don't need my name to protect me." Now his defiance was genuine, the whiskey biting home. "If it comes down to that, I've killed more men than he has."

Fox sighed. "Now you're talking foolishness. You think if he comes after you, you're gonna have a airplane to fly away in or a machine gun to shoot at him with? He'll git you when you're not lookin for him—and, damn it, I can't say that I blame him. Well . . ." Suddenly his whole manner changed. All at once passion left him; now he was wholly matter-of-fact and distant. "Well, it's your affair, not mine. Now, finish your drink. It's the last drop you'll ever git from me." He arose, took the jar to the food safe and put it in. Closing the door with finality, he turned. "And then git out. I don't ever want you in my house again."

Heath was unable to speak for a moment, disbelief and pain balking his words. Then he whispered, "Fox. Fox, you can't mean that. You don't understand. I need this place. I need you—"

"No," Fox said.

"But we're friends, you're the only friend I've got, there's nowhere else I can come—" He fought to master the emotions that clogged his throat. "You don't understand," he said again.

"I understand that I got a daughter to look after. I got a business to run. And I'm not gonna give Bolivar Chandler any excuse to ruin me."

Heath sank back in his chair. "So that's it," he said bitterly. "All the time I thought you were the one man he couldn't scare. But you're just like the rest, scared shitless of him just like all the others."

Something flared in Fox's eyes, then died. "You're welcome to think what you please. A damned fool always does. But I ain't no damned fool, and neither is your daddy. You think he don't know I'm here? How do you reckon I've managed to stay in business all this time when ever'body else has been run off or sent to jail? Bolivar Chandler hates whiskey, but he's smart enough to know people are gonna git it somewhere, and that what I sell won't poison 'em or drive 'em crazy. And he knows I got rules, that I'm careful about who I sell to. And so he ignores me, figurin better me than somebody else—as long as I don't force his hand."

"You mean there's been a deal." Heath sank back. "The two of you have—I knew *he* was a hypocrite, but—"

"There's been no word ever passed between us!" Fox's voice was sharp. "We understand each other well enough without that. I took a long risk the first time I ever sold you a drink—I started not to, but I seed you needed it, and I liked you. But I figured in time you'd straighten out, taper off, not start guzzlin the stuff. Now it looks like you ain't gonna stop this side of gittin yourself killed, or maybe worse, and I got no intention of lettin you drag me and Pearl along with you. The time comes that Sonny Ford cuts you open, there won't be no whiskey of mine in your belly! You can go to hell in your own way, but

I won't he'p you do it no more, and you ain't gonna take me and my daughter with you!"

He broke off; the room was silent. Heath could not meet his eyes. Everything Fox said, he knew, was truth, and again he felt shame, at having driven Fox to this extremity.

Then, more softly, Ramsey went on. "You're a young feller who already has more than any one man has got a right to. Good looks, strong as a horse, college education, famous, traveled over half the world. Your grandma's money, more than I'll earn in the next five years, maybe ten. I don't know what else you need, could want. But, boy, you got to find out soon."

"I know," Heath said miserably.

"Whatever it is, it ain't in the bottom of a jug or between the legs of some linthead slut."

"I know that too." Heath shook his head in agony. "Fox, it's just . . . I don't know. I've just got to get away from *him*."

"You're powerful hard on him," Fox said after a pause.

"He's hard on me."

"Maybe he figures he needs to be."

"That's not it. It's . . ." The words ripped from Heath— "Fox, it's the mills. That's what it is, the Goddamned mills."

He sucked in a long, shuddering breath. "That's what's torn us apart ever since I can remember. All I ever wanted was for him to care for me more than he did for them. Just see me as *me,* a person with his own . . . own *necessities.* But he couldn't, never has. All he could see is another Bolivar Chandler, a future president of Chandler Mills. That's all I've ever meant to him, I'm not a son, I'm a machine, and all he cares about is gettin me in perfect workin order by the time he needs me . . ."

His words choked off. Fox looked at him strangely, frowning. Then he did something he had never done before—touched Heath. He came to him, put a hand on his shoulder. "All right. Now steady yourself. You just steady yourself."

"I'm steady," Heath said, eyes burning. "I think."

Fox took his hand away. Again he went to the door, looked out; it was nearly dark now. "I know what you mean," he said after a while. "But you got to see his side of it too. There ain't nobody less alike than me and him, but I'll give him his due. Forty years ago he give up his own business, his store, they say, and took over these mills when they'd gone broke, and that was somethin he didn't have to do. You're too young to remember what it was like then, and I wasn't here, but I've heerd 'em talk, the old 'uns that was in the first bunch that hired out. Since the war they hadn't knowed which way to go or where to turn. Then the mill opened, and they thought finally they'd seed the light. And then it went broke, and . . . they thought they was finished. Would have been if it hadn't of been for him."

Fox turned around. "Even today," he said, "there ain't nothin here but cotton mills. Anywhere around here, if a pore white man can't make it farmin, there's the only place he's got to turn to keep hisself alive. Maybe it ain't the best work in the world—myself, I couldn't abide it. But it's better than hearin your baby squallin with an empty belly." His voice was low, intense. "Don't you ever underrate what your old man did fer this part of the country—"

"And got rich at it."

"Sho. Because he was smart and took his chances and beat the odds. Anyhow, you're wrong, you can't see past your nose. He don't think of you like that. Maybe he's carryin a big load, maybe he's a mite too anxious to git rid of some of it, shove it off on you, but—I've heerd 'em talk, the Chandler hands, about all the other folks they've worked for, and they'll all agree on this: maybe his ideas of what's good for 'em don't suit 'em, but he's the onliest one they know of that they ever felt did give a damn about them. And if he feels that way about them, how do you reckon he feels about you?"

"I don't know. All I know is that he's got a hell of a way of showing it."

"People show things in different ways," Fox said.

"Maybe you're right," Heath said tiredly. "But the fact

remains—the mills are there, and I'm fed up with 'em, don't want any part of 'em. And where does that leave me? Fox, Fox. What am I going to do?"

"Why," Fox said, "you're a grown man. And your feet ain't nailed to any floor."

"I can't leave. I wish I could, but I don't have the nerve. Fox, I'm a coward."

"Or love him too much," Fox said.

"Maybe. Anyhow, I don't know. I'm so mixed up, I don't know anything—except that if you send me away, I'm . . . finished."

"Don't put it off on me," Fox said. "All you got to do is stay away from that woman. I mean, *away!* But that's up to you, nobody else."

Heath sat there in silence. He could now see himself through Fox's eyes, a great, cowardly, whining baby. That thought sickened him. If he hated anything, it was cowardice. He could not bear being diminished like that in the eyes of someone he loved. He drew in a long breath. Fox was right. The choice was his, and he had to be man enough to make it.

"Fox," he heard himself say, "thanks. You're right, of course. I've been behaving like a brat. Either I leave or I stay and take my medicine, shut my mouth and mind my manners. But I've been trying to have it both ways, and I can't do that."

"Nobody ever did."

Heath stared at his hands on the table before him. "Suppose I made you a promise."

"What sort of promise?"

"That I was through with Evelyn Ford from now on. That I wouldn't go near her again. Would that . . . change anything?"

"It might," Fox said cautiously after a moment.

"If it comes down to you or her, I choose you," Heath said. "I mean it, Fox." He paused. "I'm sick, anyway," he said. "Sick of the way I've been. Just in some kind of . . . spiral, going down and down—tailspin, we used to call it." He shook his head. "You're right, I've got to pull out of it." He could see it all clearly now, understand

and believe every word he spoke. There was no other way. "Get a grip on myself, make up my mind what's best to do and just do it." He raised his head, looked at the other. "Anyhow, I'm through with her. I mean it."

Fox stared at him long and hard, and now Heath could meet his eyes. Then Fox's face relaxed, suddenly it was warm with relief and pleasure. "In that case," he said, "you kin have one more drink while I take my last one."

5   In 1880, when they had built the mill, no town of any kind had existed in this steep valley, to which the swift flow of boundless water had drawn the promoters. They had provided a cluster of houses around the plant for the workers, and a company store; not until Bolivar had driven his hard bargain and assumed full control of the bankrupt mill had there been more than that. Chandlerville was his creation, connected with the county seat of Macedonia by a short-line railroad and an unpaved highway; but it was still isolated, a world in itself. Now, as Heath re-entered the town at a much slower speed, the great ranks of blue windows in the mill, lighted from within, were a surprisingly beautiful touch of color in otherwise total drabness; and a twilight hush, broken only by the cold sound of water pouring over the dam, had settled on the place. Men off shift sat on the steps or in the porch swings of the monotonous little company houses and talked with weary softness; the main street was deserted, all business closed. Only the mill was alive; Heath could hear the muted rumble of its machinery as he passed it: the pumping heart that kept the company town alive.

He followed the road up the valley wall. There, on a knoll's crest, Chandler House gleamed white in dying sunlight. An enormous Greek Revival structure, almost a parody of the great southern plantations of antebellum days, it had been built by Bolivar in 1915 in an inexplicable burst of extravagance. The columns on its veranda were oversized and fluted; a hundred windows winked with sunset, and, on either side, lawns and formal gardens spilled down the slope. It was, Heath had thought from his first sight of it upon coming home, like a banner planted on the heights, proclaiming to the South Carolina Hamptons and the world at large: *BOLIVAR CHANDLER HAS ARRIVED.*

Tucking the jar of liquor under the seat, he parked in the garage, entered through the side door beneath a porte cochere. No one was around, and he went quickly up the long winding stair to his own room on the second floor.

While he was away it had been moved to the mansion intact from the smaller, more conventional, two-story house they had lived in downtown, closer to the mills. His childhood books were there: Ernest Thompson Seton, Stevenson, the more innocuous of Mark Twain, Tom Swifts, plus a great deal of Henty and Alger, and even more leaden, pious, and inspirational juvenile horrors that had accompanied every adventure novel his mother had ordered from Charlotte, forty miles away, there being no place closer where one could buy a book. His shotgun—unused so far; he seemed to have lost his taste for hunting since he'd been back—his fishing tackle, and the phonograph he'd bought in New York, with the stack of jazz and ragtime records, were all in place, as were the books he'd acquired in college; and some fairly spectacular pornography that he'd smuggled in from Europe was well hidden in his closet.

It was a kind of sanctuary, and when he'd locked the door behind himself, he felt curiously safe as he stripped off stinking, sweat-wet clothes. Naked, he went to the closet, fumbled behind the boxes containing his baseball gear (he had always loved the game—one interest he and Bolivar shared) and brought out another fruit jar. This one held only a single drink. He drained it at a gulp and sat down on the bed after he had hidden the empty jar.

Yes, he thought, Fox was right, absolutely right. If he kept on this way he was hell-bent for disaster. Somehow he had to get himself in check, get straightened out.

Maybe Fox was right, maybe he should find some nice girl in Macedonia or in Charlotte, but, Christ—! Celia. Celia had spoiled him for girls like that, and so had Aggie. To listen to their banal mouthings, endure their vapid, virginal flirtations, to know that the penalty for seduction of one of them was marriage . . .

But somehow, somewhere, he had to find an answer. He could not go on like this, he absolutely could not.

He arose, went to the bath and ran the shower he'd installed with his own money. When he came out some of the fatigue was gone, and he was mildly, pleasantly drunk. But a sickness lingered in him; Fox knew. He had come within an inch of losing Fox's respect. And that would have been the worst disaster of all; nothing was worth that.

He brushed his teeth, staring at his face in the mirror. It was still a good face, thanks to his mother's beauty, but after six months in Chandlerville it was changing. The lines on it had altered, those that had used to turn up now turned down; it was becoming a sour countenance, and he hated that.

By then, it was time for supper. He brushed his hair, then hesitated. He had to come to some decision.

Really, there was no decision to come to. He had made Fox a promise. He would have to keep it. He could live without her. Maybe it would do him good to try clean living for a while. Maybe it would be good to face his father again without secret guilt and fear of what rumor might have brought to Bolivar. Maybe there was virtue in chastity and hard work. He would explore that, anyhow, and find out.

Full of resolve, knowing now that she would have to wait in vain for him tonight, he went downstairs. In the dining room his parents were already at the table, Elizabeth in a print dress, Bolivar in the black suit he wore summer or winter. It was the first time he had seen either of them that day.

"Hi, Mamma, Papa." He made his greeting cordial, breezy.

"You're late," Bolivar said.

Heath sat down heavily. "I'm sorry," he answered carefully. *I will not get wrought up with him tonight,* he thought. "I had to take a shower. It was hot in the cardroom."

"Hot everywhere," Bolivar grunted. The food was already on the big oval table. "You want to say the blessing?"

Since he had been able to speak they had taken turn about, he and Bolivar, the two males. "Yes, sir." He bowed his head and said, not thinking about the ritual words lest that cause him to forget them, "Good Lord, bless these gifts which Thou hast given us for the nourishment of our bodies so that we may accomplish Your will. In the name of Jesus Christ, our Lord and Savior, we ask this. Amen."

Bolivar gave a gusty sigh of satisfaction. "Amen," he echoed.

Heath looked across the table at the stocky man with the big head and the seamed face and cold, china-blue eyes. Carefully he fought down the automatic irritation that just the sight of Bolivar had come to arouse in him these last few months. Then he turned to his mother, feeling compassion. She was the one caught in between, this handsome, sweet-faced woman in her fifties. He still could not understand how someone like her could live with his father for so long and not go mad. He knew her intelligence and her quick mind, her vivacity, and he could not comprehend how she managed for so long to turn herself into a mere looking glass, reflecting her husband's attitudes and wishes with total faithfulness. But he understood this: if it came to a showdown of any sort, the two of them were united, and she would have to stand with Bolivar.

Well, he vowed, there would be no showdown. They could not change, so it was up to him. He would exert every ounce of will and strength he possessed to be like them, and maybe if he tried hard enough, it would work; maybe he could kill whatever it was within him that made him different, and then he would be all right and happy.

Now, as Bolivar served, he tried to remember how good it had been to come home, how surprisingly good. He had not expected the emotion the southern countryside evoked in him; after the lovely delicate greens of England, the more vivid hues of that part of France undevastated, the magnificence of the Alps, he had not expected to be stirred by this uncouth land. Here there was chaos: raw, tangled, uncombed frontier; even the red earth of the Piedmont was like flayed flesh. So much of this lovely country remained unsubdued, dramatic. In Europe the earth had long since been conquered and turned effeminate; here it fought back with masculine savagery, as if, encouraged by the sun, it waged a final battle for supremacy over man, its weapons wild, tumultuous growth, vine, briar, weed and scrub, ready to move in, usurp, at any letdown of humanity's guard.

But man was winning on the high Piedmont plateau, refusing to do battle on the sun's terms. Here they had fenced out the underbrush, shut out the sun with the blue-painted windows of the cotton mills. He had been astonished at how much of the textile industry had spilled south from New England since he had left: new plants and towns all along the railroad track, from Danville through Greensboro, Thomasville, Salisbury, China Grove, Kannapolis and Charlotte, on to Gastonia, Macedonia, and Chandlerville. South Carolina was full of mills now too: York, Lancaster, Spartanburg, Greenville; everybody seemed to have given up growing cotton and gone to spinning it.

Anyhow, at first it had been good to be back; maybe the coal miners in the hideous fields of Wales and Cornwall had felt the same emotion on their return—nothing to do with the quality of the land, only that they had been born upon it. But Bolivar had quickly killed that.

He had determined to accept his fate, do everything in his power to make his parents happy. They were, after all, entitled to something after his long absence. That resolve had still been in him when, on the first day, he and his father sat together in the privacy of the Old Man's office in the big house. But he saw at once that, no matter what compromises he was prepared to make, Bolivar would make none at all.

He waited for a word of praise. He was, after all, America's sixth-ranking ace, holder of the Distinguished Service Cross, the Croix de Guerre, and other decorations. His name and picture had been in all the papers; he was the most famous Chandler who had ever lived. Facing Bolivar, desperately yearning for the impossible drink, Heath took out a cigarette and lit it. Bolivar's first words had been, "Those things will ruin your heart and lungs, you know. I want you to quit that rotten habit."

"I'll try." He tossed the butt into the fireplace; there were no ashtrays.

"All it takes is a little willpower." Then Bolivar said, "Why didn't you come home sooner? All that running around over there, wasting that good money your grandmother left you. And you never signed the power of attorney I sent you so I could invest it for you. Put in Chandler Mills stock, it would have doubled by now. We've made a lot of money since the war started."

Heath closed his eyes. *Fuck your money,* he thought desperately. *Just, for God's sake, say you're glad I'm home. Just that, I ask no more.*

"I had the bank give me a statement of your account," Bolivar went on. "I don't know how you could waste so much."

Heath sat up straight. "The bank gave you a statement . . . *my* account?" Then he slumped back; of course— Bolivar was a director of the Bank of Macedonia. "I don't know," he mumbled. "I just spent it."

"Well, that's past. You've got what—twenty thousand left?"

"About." Heath's voice suddenly crackled. "But I'm not putting it in Chandler Mills. I'm leaving it where it is."

Bolivar's pale eyes had met his. "What for?"

"Well, I . . . I might need something. Clothes, a car."

"I've got a car. You want to use it, all you've got to do is ask."

"I know, but I might want one of my own."

Bolivar had been silent a moment. Then: "All right. If you want to throw your money away, I can't stop you. But your mother and I ask you for one promise."

"What's that?"

"This airplane business. It's worried your mother sick. I hope you've got that foolishness out of your system by now. Anyhow, we want you to promise not to go up in one of those things again."

Heath did not meet his eyes. "Papa, I can't promise that."

"Why not?" Bolivar rasped.

"Because—" He made an uncertain gesture. "Because I love it."

"It's dangerous. You'll get yourself killed. You're not to fly anymore, and that's that. If you won't think of your mother and me, think of everybody else who'd suffer if something happened to you. After all, the day's not far off when you'll have to take responsibility for all those people—" His short, jerky gesture encompassed the mill, the town, even, somehow, the two other mills acquired during the war in distant towns. "They're depending on you. It's not fair to them. There is, in case you don't know it, a lot more than your having fun. Now, this is something I won't take no for an answer about. I'll have your promise."

Heath set his mouth, tensed his body. His father's eyes were like cold mountain lakes in the rugged, seamed topography of that old face. Beneath their gaze, balanced between displeasure and approval, his defiance could not gain headway. He seemed to feel himself shrinking, growing smaller, younger, helpless; was aware, bitterly, of his own inadequacy before the old man across from him. Suddenly it was more important than anything to see those eyes change, embrace, approve him. "All right, sir," he managed. "I promise."

Then he had his reward. Bolivar relaxed; the frosty face regained its warmth. "Good," he said in a deep, relieved and loving voice, "that's a great load off everybody's mind." And then, to Heath's surprise, he added,

"Thank you." Then it was worth it, all of it—for the moment, anyhow.

Now Heath sat tensely at the supper table, eating without appetite. Meanwhile, to Elizabeth Chandler fell conducting what table talk there was. By now, of course, she sensed the tension between son and husband, and the brightness of her expression, the chirp in her voice, had begun to be spurious and apprehensive. Her only duties outside the household were to represent the Chandler family in the women's activities of the Baptist Church and to serve as liaison between the mills and the pathetic little women's groups of the other churches —Presbyterian, Pentecostal, even the holy-rolling Blood of the Lamb True Gospel Church.

Tonight she milked for all it was worth a petition for more games at the YMCA Community Hall, but when Bolivar approved the request with a gruff syllable, she lapsed into helpless silence. Bolivar had no topics save business and religion; the first he never discussed at home, and now he was too busy eating to consider the latter. Heath, pitying his mother, searched his mind for something to add that would lighten the atmosphere, but without success. Since he had begun work in the plant, every day had been like every other, and shut up inside the cardroom, he was as cut off from any outside stimuli as a prisoner in solitary. The only excitement his life contained, after hours, he dared not speak of. And so the silence hung beneath the crystal chandelier, around the oval table, broken only by the mushy, animal sound of Bolivar's chewing, the quick rhythmic clink of his fork on plate. And Heath began to feel as if a spring within him were coiling tighter and tighter.

Then the Old Man swallowed audibly, mopped his mouth with a napkin. "McDowell's agreed to come," he said.

"Sir?"

"The Reverend Carl McDowell. He's a great revivalist, a good, solid old-time preacher. Knows how to tell the True Word. Two weeks from now, Saturday afternoon and all day Sunday. He'll pitch his tent down on the baseball field. Gonna bring his own band and singers." He took a drink of water. "I'm anxious to hear him preach. We need him here."

There was silence.

Bolivar looked at Heath. "I want you there. It'll do you good to go. You'll get a lot out of it."

Heath's hand clenched beneath the table. Then he remembered his resolve. Do it, he thought. Do it; maybe it will start the killing process inside you. "Yes, sir," he said. "I'll try to attend. I mean, I will attend."

The graven lines in Bolivar's face softened a bit. "Good," he said. Then he served himself to more potatoes and began to eat again.

There was a clock in the nearby living room. Heath heard its solid, monotonous ticking. He looked at his mother and she looked down at her plate. The spring within him was winding tighter. He had promised Fox . . . But he could not stay here tonight. He absolutely could not stay here tonight.

He cleared his throat. Bolivar raised his head. "After supper," Heath said, and his voice squeaked and he started over. "After supper I think I'll drive over to Macedonia and see the picture show."

"I think that would be nice—" Elizabeth began. But Bolivar's mouth thinned. "On a week night?"

"Why not? There's nothing else to do." Then he couldn't resist adding, "If you'd let them start one here, I wouldn't have to drive so far."

"I see no reason," Bolivar answered crisply, "to expose young people to more temptation than they've already got, much less encourage them to waste nights when they ought to be restin. If you ask me, you're settin a bad example for the hands. They know you're seein all these picture shows, they'll start goin too, and what can I say to 'em then? Besides, you've been out three nights in the past week, ten days, already—missed evenin prayers every time."

It was strange how he could feel skin tightening over

his face. "I'm sorry. The show's not out until late, but I'll get back soon as I can."

"No. I think you'd better stay in tonight."

Heath raised his head, cheeks burning, and now there seemed to be pressures inside his skull, pushing at his temples. He fought down the impulse, necessity almost, to smash the table with his fist. *You've got to learn . . .* But he heard himself say, "I don't want to stay in tonight." He met Bolivar's eyes, and then suddenly he was terrified. *God, does he know? Those spies of his . . .* Then he relaxed a little. *No. If he had any idea, all hell would already have broken loose.*

Then Elizabeth spoke faintly in the silence following. "Couldn't we have prayers right after supper, Papa? Then I don't see where it would do Heath any harm to go."

Bolivar didn't even look at her, seemed not to hear. His mouth was pursed. "All right," he said at last, grudgingly. "But you be in early, you hear? Come home right after the picture show is over."

"Yes, Papa," Heath said, and even to himself he sounded like a sullen child.

"Because you need your rest," said Bolivar.

6 FOR A LONG TIME Pearl Ramsey lay wakeful in the darkness.

In the front room Fox snored softly, a rhythmic sound like the muted growl of an animal in its den. Beyond the hollow, in the deep woods near the branch, whippoorwills called with mindless regularity. In this weather the hogpen's stench was overpowering; she had closed the window, shut the door, and the heat in the kitchen, which was also her bedroom, was terrible.

When she arose, groped for the lamp, her nightgown, made from sacks that had once held sugar Fox used at the still, clung dankly to her thin body. She struck a match, touched it to the wick, blinked owlishly in the flickering light. Then she sat down on the rumpled bed and rubbed her face.

Not even the dreams had helped. Not real dreams, sleeping dreams, but the ones she made, told to herself like stories in a magazine, when she lay down to sleep. They were something she looked forward to, those fantasies she put together when each long day was over—only then did life seem real and full of promise. One year from now, two, maybe three, and they would all come true. How it would happen she did not know, but it would happen somehow. She would lose her shyness, quit freezing up before him, and suddenly, like girls in *The Saturday Evening Post,* she would know exactly the right thing to say, laughing in thrilling fashion, as they always did. And when that miracle happened he would look at her—for the first time he would really see her. And his face would change, his eyes . . . Stunned with the sudden realization, he would come to her. And then it would be different, it would all be different. He would take her from the cabin to a house of their own, not large, but pretty, in a pretty yard, with grass and garden and a yellow kitchen with running water, and she'd buy curtains for the windows and—

She broke off the thought, breathing hard, suddenly aware, as she always was at such a time, of her breasts; instinctively her hands went to them, pressed them. The sensation was, physically, delicious; she closed her eyes, pressed harder. Then she jerked her hands away, despairing. They were so *small!* So little, not the swelling bosom of the story girls! They were awful!

The last wisp of fantasy fled. All at once she saw it clearly—the ugly little room of boards with its rusty iron stove, the warped shelf with the dishpan, the scrap bucket for the pigs and chickens, the few cracked plates and worn utensils. And saw herself as well: a scrawny, sharp-faced girl in sweaty nightgown made of sewn-together sugar sacks; and her mouth twisted and she felt the hot burn of tears. *Foot!* she thought savagely, venting her strongest curse. *Oh, Foot!* A hatred of this place and of her father and most strongly of herself racked her. Sure she was going crazy, she rubbed her temples. What was wrong with her, anyhow? Why did she have to be so different? Why couldn't she be the way she was supposed to, the way her father wanted her?

The heat was too much to bear; pig smell or no, she went to the door, soundlessly pulled it wide. Cool air rushed in to displace the heat, touched the sweaty gown, moved over and around the body beneath it like a caress, and she spread her legs to let it go between her thighs and dared to draw in a long, grateful breath, and found that the wind had changed. Instead of pigs, it bore the warm, stirring night scent of woods: of growing plants, rocks, water, the sweet decay of leaves and the poignant, overriding perfume of the honeysuckle that grew heaped and crawling over piles of junk and garbage from all the years that they had lived here. That scent went through her nostrils down into her lungs and then, it seemed, into every other vital organ and into her very blood; and she caught her breath quickly, as if strangling. Her legs spread wider, she raised her arms, let the cool, perfumed air make a kind of love to her as it blew in the door. Her breasts seemed to come back to life and, even better, there was a wild, sinful, delicious stirring, a helpless wetness, between her thighs, that the wind touched and cooled and emphasized; and for a long moment she abandoned herself to the night and sin.

Then bedsprings squeaked as Fox rolled over; she jumped in guilt, held her breath until his snoring resumed. That broke the mood; she came back to reality.

And yet the excitement the wind had stirred would not abate. Fox was sound asleep again, and she once more in wicked privacy and freedom. She could not resist; with cold hands she shrugged off the nightgown. Knowing the sick fascination of the criminal, she let the night wind have her unhampered for a moment, and this time, while it stroked her, naked, unshielded flesh responded more strongly. Squeezing her breasts, she felt the nipples rise; then she ran her hand down her stomach, marveling at how smooth it really was, so soft and unlike the exposed parts of her body she was accustomed to touch. She even pressed one hand between her thighs, excited at how her hips pushed forward to meet it; then, blood burning in her cheeks, jerked it guiltily away, suddenly closed the door. Anyhow, the pig smell had come back again, drowning out the honeysuckle.

She cocked her head, heard Fox still snoring. A new temptation grew in her. She had to see herself. Not with her eyes, but with his. If *he* were here now, if *he* were looking at her, what would he see? For better or worse, she had to know.

But it was too difficult to accomplish. Her only mirror was too small, its glass dim and wavy, and worse by lamplight. She had to set it on the shelf, all the way across the room, contort herself to get even a three-quarter view. Even then, all she could really make out, it seemed, was eyes and nipples, as if only they were real enough to reflect. She shook her head in frustration, then again donned the clammy nightgown.

A corner of the room had been curtained off with muslin to make a closet. Pearl went to this, groped in its depths, and brought out two copies of *The Saturday Evening Post* and one of the *Delineator*. These at least Fox did not grudge her, for he was proud of how well she read.

She had, after all, finished the fifth grade in Chandlerville before her mother had become too sick to work and Fox, raging against the mill, had left the town and brought his wife and child here to this lonesome hollow, where he could make whiskey for a living in stealth. That had been the only real good time of her life, she thought: when she had been with other people in the town all the time and Mama was alive and . . . She had been good in school too, had made the highest marks in her class, and the teacher had even come to talk with Mama about how smart she was, how she ought to go on with her schooling. . . . Well, anyhow, Fox let her have the magazines. He would not always let her go with him on his Saturday trip to town, but he never failed to bring back the new *Post* and sometimes even *Woman's Home Companion*, *McCall's*, or the *Ladies' Home Journal*. Without them, she thought, she could not have kept on living; they were the raw material for her dreams. She saved every copy, nearly memorized the articles and stories, but most of all she loved the illustrations and the advertisements. She had learned how, by an effort of will and imagination, to project herself into them, actually enter the lovely rooms they depicted, and, most important of all, could somehow make herself into each beautiful girl held tightly by each handsome man. Now she clung desperately to the magazines in her hands as she sat down again on the sagging iron cot. But she did not open them. Instead, she thought of Heath.

Suddenly she laid the magazines aside, arose, and turned back the lumpy cotton mattress. From beneath it she brought out a copy of Street & Smith's *Love Stories* she had once dared to buy and smuggle home. She opened it, and her hand shook a little as she took out the newspaper clipping and the postcard hidden between its pulpy pages.

The clipping first, months old and ready to fall apart. From the front page of the Macedonia *Herald* a headline proclaimed FLYING ACE RETURNS. Beneath a jaunty cap the handsome, ink-blurred features of Heath Chandler smiled at her.

Though she knew it by heart, she read it again, excited by the triumphs it recounted. Then she laid it aside, picked up the postcard, which bore a gaudy view of the Battery in Charleston, South Carolina: green park, blue sea, a lot of big old cannons. She turned it over. *Mr. Fox Ramsey, c/o Post Office, Chandlerville, N.C.* The message, in a bold, flaring hand, was only two sentences. *Hot as you know where and twice as dry. Love to Pearl. H.C.*

Love to Pearl . . . Her lips moved soundlessly as, for the thousandth time, she tried to interpret the real meaning of those words. How had she come to be in his mind, what had he been thinking of when he had put them down? What did she dare believe they meant?

She sat there, card in hand, staring at nothing. Until *he* had come she had not really minded the way Fox kept her shut up here, would never let her go to town alone, had exploded in fury when, once, she'd timidly suggested that she could take a job in the mill. She knew he needed her, could not bear to lose her, that she was all he had.

But Heath was too much like the men in the magazines, could have stepped out of the *Post* or *Journal*. In fact, there was one drawing by James Montgomery Flagg —she knew the names and styles of all the illustrators— for which he might have modeled. At first sight of him, something had come to life within her, new and glorious and agonizing. And yet there was no way to tell him, make him know. When he was before her in the flesh, looked at her and spoke to her, she froze, went dumb and tongue-tied, the way she had tonight. Why, when he'd asked her to pour that drink, hadn't she had the courage to take that much risk to show him that she loved him? She might even have dared to sit and talk to him while he drank it. Instead, she'd stood there like a knot on a log, then run off and hid.

But, of course, had listened at the door, as always, while he and Fox had talked. And then it had seemed her world had fallen in, as Fox had banished him. That awful Evelyn Ford, that terrible married woman, leading him on—she had almost ruined everything! Pearl's whole body seemed to fill and clog with hatred for the woman she had never seen, and who threatened to take the man she loved away from her forever.

But it was all right now; her father had made him see the light, got that promise from him. She'd begun to breathe again as the atmosphere in the front room seemed to change and, finally, Heath had even laughed, and so had Fox. And then Heath had asked, "Well, am I still cut off?"

Pearl had stood tensely, hating that he drank so much, but knowing that that was what brought him here, and if Fox would not sell to him, she would never see him again. Fox had been silent for an interminable half-minute. Then he said, "It depends on who you drink it with."

"Not her. I gave you my word. My solemn promise. I'm through with her. Fox, I'll swear that."

Again silence.

And Heath's voice, low, persuasive. "But all the same, Fox, I've got to have some booze. It's the only thing that keeps me from going crazy. All day long in the mill, and then back to Chandler House and *him*—My God, you can't expect me to get along without it completely. You wouldn't expect any other millhand to do it. *You* couldn't do it, not if you had to live with *him*."

"Jest the same," Fox said.

"Well," Heath sighed, "I can't say that I blame you. I won't argue; everything you've said about me's true. All I can say is this: I might mess up myself, but I'd die before I'd do something to mess you up." When Fox did not answer, he said, "All right. I understand. I reckon I can find some somewhere in Macedonia."

"And poison your fool self," Fox said. His chair scraped back. "One quart," he said. "I'll gamble that on your promise. But I warn you—"

"I know," Heath said. "And I told you, I'll keep my promise."

"Yeah." She heard him getting it, heard Heath say warmly, "Thanks, Fox. I'll guarantee you won't be sorry." Then he had gone; she'd run to the kitchen window for just a glimpse of him in the yellow Marmon as it vanished in the dusk. After that she'd served Fox supper, then had gone to bed, read awhile, dropped off to sleep while, as he often did, Fox sat on the porch and smoked his pipe.

Once she'd awakened in the night to hear him still moving around the front room, but she was too drowsy to worry about it. Anyhow, he had these bad nights sometimes since Mama died. Now it was her turn to be restless while he slept like a log.

Suddenly she was stricken with a loneliness she could not contain; tears welled in her eyes, hot and stinging. Through them she stared at the cheap clock beside the stove. Shoot, it was after four o'clock! He'd be up at daybreak and want his breakfast! Somehow she had to make herself sleep again!

She stood up, remade the bed, hid *Love Stories,* clipping and postcard beneath the mattress again, blew out the lamp. Outside, the whippoorwills kept on calling, managing somehow to express exactly what she felt, loss and sorrow and loneliness unbearable. In desperation she reached for the ancient doll that always lay beside her pillow, one that had belonged to her mother. Its small body was of cloth, its head and limbs of china, its eyes wide, blue, with big, painted lashes. Its name was Pearlie's Baby. She clasped it tightly to her breast, and it helped.

For a long time she lay in darkness, one arm around the doll, while she built a fantasy, made herself a drowsy dream. *Love to Pearl . . .* She clung to the words until she slept.

7 WHEN HEATH had left the house that night he should have felt relief at escaping with such comparative ease; instead, closing the door of Chandler House behind him, striding to the garage, he was as close to tears of rage and humiliation as a man his age could come, his fury directed not so much at Bolivar, who, obviously, could not change, as at himself for his lack of courage, for allowing himself to be treated like a child. What he should have done, he told himself, settling into the Marmon, was to have it out, assert himself as a man in his own right. Defy Bolivar to his face, demand the respect due him, and, since he was turning over a new leaf anyhow, establish a whole new relationship between them, one he could live with and which Bolivar, like it or not, must accept.

But he could not. Something in the Old Man's eyes, some set of that stern mouth, dissolved all bravery, all self-assertion. It was uncanny; confronting Bolivar, he *was* a child. It was as if his father had enchanted him, cast

a spell over him that he could not break. He could not
defy him to his face; he lacked the guts to withstand
even the slightest expression of disapproval on that countenance; that still terrified him, just as it had done ever
since he could remember.

Slumped behind the wheel, he gasped for breath, as if
he had run a long way. He beat the wheel with his
hands, cursed almost soundlessly, a long string of mindless oaths, like a boiler venting steam through a pinhole.
He would drive very swiftly to Macedonia tonight, he
thought, fast as this damned car would go. And if he
wrecked it, killed himself, what the hell! He didn't care,
he just didn't care! He put his head down on the wheel
for a moment, hearing the rapid beating of his heart,
knowing that in this mood he was truly dangerous, especially to himself. Then he remembered the bottle under
the seat.

He had to ease off, gear down. He groped instinctively
for it. A drink, two—they would dull the cutting edge of
his shame and fury, bring him back to rationality, help
him regain control. In the darkness and privacy of the
garage he gulped the whiskey, sat with eyes closed,
waited for it to catch. Presently he sighed and drank
again, as, physically he relaxed. But, emotionally, it did
not help him; instead, it seemed to wind him tighter. He
put the jug away, slammed the car backward out the
door, whirled it around, crammed down on the accelerator, roared down the hill. He raced through the town—
there was almost no traffic now—and out the Macedonia
road. Once clear of Chandlerville, he pulled over to the
side, looked around, drank again, and sat there with the
headlights on, the engine idling.

She would be getting ready now. He imagined her, in
the three-room house in the mill village—naked, probably: those great breasts, buttocks, thighs. She would be
excited, looking forward to the night. Well, she would
have to find some other relief; let her wait; he had
promised Fox. And Fox was right. Trouble with Sonny
Ford . . . not that he was afraid of Ford; he was afraid
of no one, save Bolivar. But that would tear it, the Old

Man would find out right away and— Besides, what difference did it make if he stood her up? She was just a linthead girl who cheated on her husband, only an instrument he had used to ease his tensions, and that was all he was to her too, an instrument. They used each other in a kind of masturbation; it was not a question of love or feelings, not like with Celia. Grief welled up in him. *Oh, Celia, Celia, where are you now? And Agatha and all the rest—*

He drank again, thinking of everything of which he was being cheated, of all the irreparable waste. One thing the war had taught him: time was short. For a man like him there was no future; the minute was everything and all, and there was so much yet undone to crowd into each one. But he was letting them go by unused, spilling them like money through his hands, at drudgery, here in this backwater far from everything he valued. And now he had let go of even the one poor straw at which he had grasped, denied himself the only interval of danger and sensation that served to remind him that he was even alive.

And to which, he thought savagely, he was entitled.

That was it: neither Fox nor Bolivar could understand. They had no idea of the sacrifices he had already made, the misery already endured. They could not see that he had earned that much anyhow, a few hours a few nights a month, or envision what would happen to him if he were denied them. They were old men, with desire long dead within them, and they did not understand.

He thought of her again, of the wet mouth and heavy tongue, and his body stirred even as he felt a kind of shame. And yet . . . and yet, she was all he had. Without her and the defiance she represented he was not a man at all; he was nothing.

And anyhow, he thought, it was lousy to let her wait, wondering, not knowing. Even if he saw her, he did not have to make love to her. He could take her somewhere, they could talk, he could tell her that it had ended. She was entitled to that much consideration. There was nothing wrong with that. It was the right and honest thing to do.

Part of him, drunk and wrought up, believed that; another part, standing aside with cool objectivity, mocked. Still, he drank again and put the car in gear and turned around in the middle of the road with a strange, almost unreal feeling of uncaring fatality and a desire for vengeance on someone—on whom, he was not quite sure.

He had to circle Chandlerville, come up on its north edge. There all the dreary rows of company houses lay below him, lamps shining through a thousand windows. The road led past a grove of locust trees in which honeysuckle heaped itself above the ruins of the house of a farmer driven off the land—and this was where she should be waiting.

He approached with head lamps off, but there was more than half a moon silvering the valley. When the car stopped, a shadow detached itself from deeper darkness, moved into light; and until he saw that thick, full-breasted, round-butted body, moving with its slow, lumbering gait, he had not realized how afraid he'd been that Sonny Ford might have kept her home, locked her in. But Sonny worked the night shift and would have been gone by the time she got home.

If he was tumescent, she seemed more so, her whole body swollen within a dress that fitted her like sausage skin. He opened the door, and she slid in beside him, moving against him at once, hand reaching for his thigh, face turned toward his with open mouth. He kissed her, and her heavy tongue sought his. When they pulled apart, she breathed, "Sugar, you late. I was gittin worried."

"Had some trouble gettin whiskey."

"You got some, though?" Her voice twanged with the mill village accent. "Where at is it?"

He found the bottle, gave it to her. She uncapped it, drank greedily, like a man, sighed, drank again, then put the top on. "Less go, baby." As he started the car she threw herself against him, breast and thigh. "Oh, sugar pie, we goan have a good time tonight."

"Yeah." The road blurred before him and he squinted as he pressed the accelerator. "What about Sonny? He went to work, didn't he?"

"Shore he did."

"Good." He found the bottle, drank again and let her have it. He came down off the hill and struck the valley road, going north.

As he drove, her hand played over him boldly until he was in a fever of excitement. Likely, she had not bathed—the mill houses included no running water—but she had doused herself in cheap perfume, and, mingled with the musk of her body and the clean night air, it jangled his senses. They groped at each other frantically, not talking, for neither had anything to say to the other, the communication between them was not verbal. He had read Havelock Ellis and some Freud already and knew what she was; there was no need to talk. Once he almost ran the car off the road, and she squealed. "Honey, slow down a little bit. You done been at that whiskey too much!"

He slowed, for they were nearing the place to turn anyhow, and it took all his concentration to find it. "Right thur, baby," she said. "You near went past." He swung the wheel, the car lurched through the notch in the brush and bounced downhill toward the river.

After a hundred yards he pulled it off the trace into a patch of cane and briars. Not far below, the river poured coldly over stones, its bank shadowed by huge red birch and sycamores. "Don't ferget the jug," she said and giggled, and he took that and the lap robe and, arm in arm, they staggered down the hill, stopping once to kiss messily. Then they were in darkness beneath the trees, beside the cold-running river. He spread the robe, heard her giggle and heard the whisper of hard breathing as she undressed. He took off his own clothes, and the air was cool on his hard-muscled nakedness. Then she caught him, pulled him down. They groped for the fruit jar, drank, then wallowed against each other. Her breasts were great spongy cushions; her mouth drooled against his face and neck, kissing, licking. His hands explored all that heavy flesh, slid between spread thighs, and his fingers were engulfed. Then neither could wait longer; she moaned as he mounted and entered her, slamming brutally from the beginning; it was what she wanted, measured manhood by, size and force, and she jerked convulsively and made crazy animal sounds of pleasure, gasping and crying out like some night creature in the darkness, and he was lost to everything but flesh, the sharpness of his own desire, head swimming with whiskey and with lust . . .

The hands grabbed him by the shoulders, pulled him up and out and threw him backward on the sand. He sprawled, and a hard-shod foot slammed into his ribs. "Honey?" Evelyn Ford moaned mindlessly, cheated, and then she sucked in breath, opened her eyes. "Oh, sweet Jesus!" she cried. Heath tried to rise; the brogan-shod foot kicked him down again brutally. He shook his head, his vision cleared; then he saw the carbide lantern of the kind used by coon hunters as a white dazzle over him, and, in its light, the pistol pointed at his head. Behind it the eyes of a tall, slat-thin man gleamed like tiny flames. "What the hell is this?" Heath blurted, blinded.

"Watch 'im, Odie," a voice grated. The light shifted, focused on the woman lying on the robe, eyes wide and blank with fear, huge breasts saggings, heavy thighs spread wide, the mound between them a dark shag of hair. "You bitch!" Sonny Ford rasped and bent and hit her with his fist. She fell back on the robe.

"Don't you move, damn you," the husband said ferociously. She sprawled obscenely, whimpering. Then Ford turned, shining the light on Heath again. "Odie?"

The man crouched over Heath with another gun was short, stocky, and Heath recognized him: he worked the night shift in the weave room. "Don't worry, Sonny. He's covered. He ain't goin nowhur."

In the back glow of the carbide lantern Evelyn's husband towered over Heath, pale blue eyes shining beneath lank, tow-colored hair. His cheeks were narrow, his mouth small, red, wet. He wore a white shirt, collarless, sleeves rolled up to show tattoos on long, thin, vein-roped arms. "Well, now, Chandler, ain't you a purty sight," he said, and a hand went into the pocket of his khaki pants. It brought out a huge clasp knife and deftly flicked open a serrated blade designed for scaling fish. Heath stared at that six-inch length of steel glittering in the lantern light and felt cold all over. At the same time he knew a curious sense of unreality, as if it were not himself lying here naked, as if he only stood to one side and watched.

"Maybe you think that jest because you're the Old Man's son you got a right to light on another man's nest." Bad yellow teeth shone in the lantern glow. "Well, buddy, you got another think a-comin. You see this feesh knife? You know what I goan do with it?" He squatted, thrusting the blade toward Heath's loins. "I'm goan fix you so you never fuck another man's wife—"

Somebody, Heath supposed himself, said coolly, "Ford, don't be a fool. You'd better let me up, or—"

"Er you'll yell fer Daddy. Only Daddy ain't here. You yell all you want to. You won't yell when we throw you in that-air river. Odie, you got that tow chain?"

"Got it."

"Wrop it around this sonbitch, wrop it good. Then I'll go to work on him."

"Shore." The squat man jerked Heath to a sitting position. His pistol barrel was centered on Heath's forehead. "Lemme git this thang around ye." For the first time Heath realized that it was he, himself, they had captured and would hurt beyond endurance and then kill. Still, he felt strangely indifferent. I can bear that too, he thought. Maybe it's what I deserve, have been looking for —Then the cold chain touched his flesh and his indifference vanished. "No!" he cried. "No!" He tried to struggle, but he was wrapped in it now, arms pinned. "Now, Sonny, wait a minute." He despised himself for begging and could not help it. "Now, just wait—I'm sorry. For God's sake—"

"He's tight, Sonny," Odie said, latching the chain.

"Good. Here's his jug. Less have a drink, then I'll go to cuttin.'" Ford turned back to the robe, where Evelyn lay, still sprawled, open, wide-eyed. He grinned at her, picked up the jar, drank and passed it to Odie. Without taking the pistol off Heath, Odie drank long and deeply. Then he passed the jar back to Ford, who drank again, wiped his mouth with the back of the hand that held the knife, and squatted before Heath again.

"Now," he said. "Pull his legs apart, Odie."

Hands seized Heath's ankles, pried and spread his thighs. Ford placed the lantern to beam on his loins. In the glow his face was ghastly, dark eye sockets, white cheekbones, red mouth grinning. "Well, lookathere. That thang done gone plumb down, ain't hit? Knows whut goan happen." Then he rasped, "Awright, Chandler, now" —and he pushed the knife blade forward, and Heath tensed his buttocks and closed his eyes.

And then Fox Ramsey's voice said, "Don't you tech him with that knife, Sonny. This here's a thutty-thutty rifle pointed at you, and you lay that blade on him, I'll blow you plumb to hell."

There was a moment when the only sound was the cold, constant ripple of the river, ten or fifteen yards away. Heath opened his eyes, stared at Ford, frozen motionless, like some obscene, carved, squatting idol, knife still outstretched. Then he turned his head and saw, beyond the lantern light, a small, tense silhouette.

Fox said harshly, "Lay it down, Sonny."

Ford said, "Fox, this ain't your put-in. My wife—"

"I know that." Leaves crunched, then Fox was in full lamp glow, the muzzle of the rifle swiveling. "All the same, you lay down that fish knife."

Heath tried to sit up. "Fox." His very viscera seemed to dissolve with relief. "Fox, they got pistols—"

"Shut up," Ramsey said. "Sonny, I done tole you—"

"Fox, don't make us come after you too."

"You do, you'll be damn sorry. Throw the knife away."

Fox and Sonny Ford looked at each other for an endless space of seconds. Then Ford's mouth curled. "Sheet," he said, and tossed the knife aside.

"Good. Now, both of you. Stand up, back away."

They did it. Fox said, "Drop that pistol, Odie." When it landed on the sand, he moved forward, scooped it up without taking eyes off them. After that he relaxed a little, looking at Evelyn Ford on the blanket, one hand over her mouth.

"Fox, we caught him in the act," Ford whispered.

"Sho. I can see that."

"And I got a right to—"

"I didn't say you ain't. But for God's sake, man, you want to go to the electric chair? You cut him, kill him, where you think Bolivar's gonna send you?"

"I don't give a shit for Bolivar Chandler!"

"Well, you'd better. I do."

"Whut you want, then? Let him go? Let him fuck my wife and git away with it?"

"No," Fox said. "I didn't say that." He jerked his head. "Odie. Up yonder in my Model T. There's an extra inner tube on the front seat. You go fetch it. And no tricks, or Sonny'll suffer."

"A inner tube?" Then Ford comprehended. "Sheet, that ain't enough."

"You kin make it enough. So long as you stop this side of cripplin him fer good."

For a moment Ford and Ramsey stared at one another. Then Ford grinned slowly. "All right," he said. "Go an fetch the inner tube, Odie." His eyes flickered to the woman on the robe. "And she gits her dose too."

"She's your woman," Fox said flatly.

"Oh, Jesus." And Evelyn Ford began to whimper.

With an effort Heath sat up. "Fox—"

Fox turned on him savagely. "Don't 'Fox' me!" he snapped, and in the lantern light his green eyes blazed, his mouth twisted with fury and disgust. "And don't you try to git away! You lyin sonofabitch! Give me your word, sweet-talk me into sellin you whiskey, then fast as I turn my back you break your promise, do edzactly what you swore you wouldn't! By God, if it warn't fer th' fact that I'm in this too, thanks to you, I'd let him go ahead and cut your balls off! That's what you really deserve!" He spat. "God knows what this foolishness is gonna cost us all!"

"Fox, I'm sorry."

"Sorry." Fox looked at him with the greatest contempt Heath had ever seen on any human face and turned away. Then Odie reappeared, the inner tube trailing from his hand.

Fox jerked his head at Heath. "Take that chain offn him. He ain't goin nowhere."

"Yeah." Ford did that. "On your feet, Chandler."

Numbly Heath obeyed. The terror he had felt was gone. Replacing it now was a kind of sickness, a hatred of himself so deep and racking that it made him tremble. He looked at Fox, who stonily avoided his gaze, tried hard to think of something he could say and found nothing. Then Odie pushed him forward. "Let's git 'em out in the moonlight where we kin see."

"Right." Ford went to Evelyn, jerked her to her feet, hammerlocked her arm behind her. "Down on the riverbank—" She made a blubbering sound. "Oh, Sonny, no, no, darlin, no—" He shoved her forward roughly, paying no attention, as Odie hustled Heath along behind. Fox followed, carrying the rifle at the ready.

They reached the river's rim, brush and catbrier raking Heath's naked flesh. Sonny's eyes searched the bank, then he laughed shortly. "There. Down there. Made to order." He pointed. Below, a great sandbar shelved out into the current, silvered with moonglow. From the bank itself a thick willow tree grew out horizontally above it, then, after five feet, curved up. Ford pushed the woman down the slope; she landed sprawling on the sand. He slid down after her, caught her as she scrambled to her feet, shoved her forward. Odie pushed Heath; he, too, went tumbling down the bank, and Fox and Odie came behind.

"Fox," Ford said, "you'll watch him, won't you?"

"I'll watch him," Fox said.

"Then, come here, Odie, and gimme a hand."

Odie moved past Heath, carrying the tube, eyes gleaming, a grin of anticipation on his face. Evelyn was moaning now. "Oh, please, Sonny, I promise, honest to God, I promise I'll never—"

"Shut up." He slapped her, and the words pinched off into a mewing whine. Then he pushed her facedown across the willow trunk, her buttocks, huge and globular, gleaming in the moonlight. "Hold her shoulders, Odie." Odie stepped across the trunk, pinned them. Heath saw that, in the process, he managed to touch her dangling breasts. Then Ford let out a kind of sigh, stepped back, the inner tube dangling from his hand. "Now, you whore, you're gonna git your medicine."

"Watch the valve," Fox said.

Unanswering, Ford raised the tube, slung it high, slammed it down. It made a solid, meaty, slapping sound. Evelyn howled, exactly like a dog. Ford laughed; Heath saw the growing bulge in the front of his overalls. Then, mercilessly, he really beat her.

It went on and on, across her buttocks, up her back, down her thighs. She howled and howled, the sound echoing up the cold, swift-running river like the baying of a pack of hounds, and then the howling stopped, became a whimper, drowned out by the repeated crash of rubber against her flesh. And now Heath's bemusement broke; suddenly all this was real, and he no longer felt shame or fear, only anger. He took a step forward. Fox's cold voice said, "You stand fast."

"Damn it, Fox, that's enough."

"Sonny'll decide what's enough. She's his wife, not yourn or mine." But Fox's face seemed pale beneath the beard. A moment more and he rasped harshly: "Ford. All right."

Sonny half raised the inner tube.

"Damn it, I said all right!"

Ford stood there a moment, then nodded and let it drop. Evelyn, twitching, moaning, lay limply. Her husband seized her shoulder, threw her off the trunk. She fell like a bag of grain, curled in fetal position, knees against her breasts, tangled hair across her tear-swollen face. Ford turned, looked at Heath. "Now you," he said.

"No," Heath said.

Fox made a sound. "Boy, go on."

"No," said Heath ferociously. "You'll have to kill me first."

"I said, go on. Take your medicine."

"No." He half turned, as if to run. Fox tripped him. He sprawled on the sandbar, face grinding into rock and gravel. "I guess I'll hafta help you," Fox said bitterly above him. "Come on, the two of you." Before Heath could rise they had him, Fox's grip like iron on his biceps, Odie's arm locked around his neck. They jerked him to his feet, Ford caught his ankles. He was propelled across the sandbar; the abrasive willow bark ground into his naked stomach. Fox's spring-steel hands pinned his shoulders, Odie took his feet. He was aware of Ford stepping back. He sucked in a deep breath, then let himself go limp.

He had learned how to endure pain; the half-dozen crashes had taught him that much anyhow. He did not even close his eyes; throughout he kept them open, staring down at the sand—every grain, every rock, every pebble standing out in astounding clarity. Ford began to beat him. At first it did not seem to hurt very much; he thought he could bear it in silence. But it went on and on, and the effect was cumulative, and presently, through a kind of mist, he heard an ugly hurt-animal sound and realized that it came from himself. Then he was on fire everywhere, all over. Still it did not stop.

And when it did, much later, he kept on making that ugly, degrading, involuntary sound. Next he was off the tree trunk and lying on the cold sand, feet shuffling around him. He heard Ford's voice, the words incomprehensible through his own whimpering and the blaze of pain. Presently he knew that some of them were gone. Then Fox's voice said above him, "Roll over. Roll over in that cold water. It'll help to stop the hurtin." But he had neither strength nor will to obey. Fox's hands were on him; he groaned as Fox rolled him like a log. Then he was lying on his back in the icy, shallow flow at the sandbar's edge, the water swirling over him. Fox, panting with exertion, said from above, "There. Your clothes are where you left 'em. It's up to you to git home. And you listen to me, God damn you. Don't you ever come around me again. Don't you ever come anywhere near me." Then he was gone.

Heath lay in the water for a long time. It numbed his flesh. Presently, experimentally, he moved. It cost him agony. Somehow he managed to get to his feet. He was alone beside the river. The moonlight fell on the swirling current; above, the woods loomed darkly. He scrabbled up the bank, and by the time he made the top, his wet body, plastered with mud, was one vast throbbing ache. Somehow, in the darkness, he found his clothes, and tears of pain flowed down his cheeks as he got into them. He turned to attempt the almost impossible climb back to the car; as he did so, his foot kicked something: the capped whiskey jar. It gurgled. He managed to bend, pick it up, uncap it, take a long, long drink. That made it possible to reach the Marmon. He nearly screamed at the effort of getting behind the wheel, dared not let his back touch the seat. Somehow he got the car started, out of the brush, on the road.

He drove slowly to Chandlerville. When he ascended the hill he saw that all the lights were off in the house except the ones to light his entry. He parked the car in the garage, crept to the side door, opened it, made his way across the big drawing room to the stairs. By the time he had climbed them, the fear of encountering his parents was worse than the hurt. But they were asleep; he made it to his own room all right. There he managed to strip off the muddy clothes and stow them. It was well after midnight. What he was going to do about tomorrow was something he lacked strength to think about. He crawled painfully into his pajamas. Then he threw himself facedown upon the bed. Shame, rage, humiliation and agony racked him. He lay there crying into his pillow like a child for more than an hour. Precisely when he finally went to sleep he could not say. But his sleep was fitful, a nightmare sleep, haunted by a sense of doom.

8 AT FIRST they had breakfasted together every morning. Then Heath got his car and, to Bolivar's dismay, had begun to sleep too late. That came from going out at night so often, missing his proper rest. Now he slept every morning until the last minute; Bolivar would already have eaten and gone before he came sprinting down the stairs, gulped a cup or two of coffee, refusing breakfast, and drove in his reckless fashion to the mill in his own Marmon. Today, when Bolivar had prayed and washed and shaved and dressed, he left the master bedroom, went down the corridor, and, as always, hesitated before Heath's door. He had lain awake long last night himself and had not heard his son come in before he drifted off to sleep. It must have been very late when the boy got to bed; it would be well to see that he did not oversleep.

Bolivar turned the knob and discovered that the door was locked. His lips compressed; he did not like to be shut out of any room in his own house. He hammered on the door. "Heath? Son—" his voice was harsh. "Wake up in there! The second whistle's blown." He knocked again, paused.

An interval of perhaps a minute; no sound. Then an audible stirring, something like a groan. Bolivar hammered once more. "Wake up, Heath!"

"All right." Heath's voice was sullen. "All right. I'm awake."

Bolivar stood there thirty seconds longer, face engraved with a frown. "You're running late," he snapped. "You'd better hurry." Angrily he wheeled and went down the stairs.

He felt baffled, confused, as his hand slid down the satiny rail. What more could the boy want than he had? Look at the house he lived in—huge, spacious—the security he had, never missing a meal or having to worry about where food was coming from. It enraged the Old

Man that Heath could not appreciate that. He had to put a stop to this, he thought. The boy was ruining his health with those late hours. Dangerous for him to be driving around in the dark everywhere too. He would have to have another talk with him.

In the breakfast room the cook had his meal waiting: fried ham, three eggs, grits and biscuits. Bolivar ate rapidly, ferociously, face almost in his plate, arm shielding his food as if afraid it would be snatched from him.

Still, he had to admit, the reports from the mill were fine. He'd made it plain to all the supervisors that, good or bad, he wanted the hard truth about Heath's performance; and there was no doubt about it, the boy was a worker. Nor, so far as he could learn, had Heath transgressed in his time off. No drinking, no bad women; his spies had reported nothing of the sort.

That, he thought, wiping his mouth with the napkin tucked in his collar, was what had really worried him. There were two lives a man could lose, mortal and immortal. He could have borne it if Heath had lost the first, but the second . . . He had seen so many young men destroyed by the war in which his father had died, had seen them come home seemingly alive and yet dead inside, unable to settle down or turn their hands to anything productive. *I can't pray,* Tom Capps had mourned, and to lose that ability . . . Oh, he had watched them throwing away hope of heaven on whiskey, bad women, cards, finally drifting west, bottle in one saddlebag, pistol in the other, to disappear forever. The living dead—that was what he had feared for Heath.

But the boy was coming along. Fractious, yes, but gradually pulling at the harness, dragging his own weight. And that was another miracle, Bolivar thought, another answered prayer. He quenched his anger, realizing how fortunate he had been. And this morning even lingered a moment longer at table, hoping Heath would come down before he left. But though he heard stirrings overhead, the young man did not appear. And finally it was time for Bolivar to leave.

Walking through the labyrinth of the great house, he

felt once more the sense of potency that came with wealth. Elizabeth had wanted this, designed it, and he had scoffed and dragged his feet, but all along he had known that he wanted it too, and had been secretly grateful to her for giving him chance and excuse to build it. Then he went out to the huge black limousine awaiting him. He opened the door himself—he always opened his doors—and got in and let the chauffeur drive him down the hill.

After the wake-up whistle, the ready whistle had given its mournful hoot, and now, streaming out onto the main thoroughfare from all the little dusty feeder streets, mill-hands went to work. Some drove in Fords, but most of them walked, in a long winding stream on either side of the road; and Bolivar looked at them and felt kinship with them. He was, after all, sprung from the same origins. But for the grace of God he could have been one of those lank men shambling down the road. He knew and understood them and even loved them and was proud of what he had done for them, of how he had more than kept and fulfilled his promise to Tom Capps.

Well, the proof of the rightness of his decision was how he had prospered. That was the reward for following, at whatever danger, God's will. Now, as the limousine wound down the hill, the lines of millhands smiled and waved at it, and he returned their greetings. He knew them all by name, their wives, their children. There was no other way to manage them. You had to be one of them, no better and no worse, only a little luckier. They would accept the fact that you were set above them if you were pious, would take it as God's verdict that you had been better than they, religiously speaking. Still, they were fiercely independent, and, clinging to that independence, they would work only for a man whom they admired and felt kinship with, one who had the common touch. He never deceived himself: he was not their boss, he was the leader of their clan. They were his responsibility, a weight bearing down on him. But one he was glad to carry. He thought about a cabin by a red clay road, thought about the man limned against the sky's scalding, terrible blue. *Pray for the South—*

The limousine drew up before the entrance to the general office of the mills. Bolivar got out, dismissed the black driver with a wave of hand. The man would sit there, before the main gateway, until Bolivar needed him.

Inside, Bolivar greeted Miss Jane Gurganis, his receptionist for nineteen years. Then he went through double doors into the main office of Chandler Mills. Men seated at rows of desks nodded to him, and he nodded back. Next, down a corridor, between lines of cubicles divided by frosted-glass partitions. In each, one of his executives was at his desk; he made sure by poking in his head, reaping a "Good morning, Mr. Bolivar" from every one. At the lane's end a door bore on its opaque glass the legend: PRESIDENT. He entered it, spoke to his secretary (of whom he stood in secret awe, because she knew how to run the typewriting machine he still considered an innovation). Then his own sanctum, a large Spartan room with file cabinets and tables overspread with drawings and plugs of cotton samples. There was an old rolltop desk in the corner of the room, and he seated himself there and waited. Presently it was time; he arose and went into the spinning room, where banks of machines were lined up for hundreds of yards, cat's-cradled with the thicker lines of roving that would be reduced to yarn. There he led everyone in prayer. Then he went back to his office and thought of Heath again. By now his son would be hard at work in the cardroom. But it was almost time to move him up, make him a supervisor.

However, there was not time now to think of that. His desk was piled with reports from his three mills, and soon he would have to deal with matters of the town; this belonged to a separate corporation wholly owned by Chandler Mills, of which Bolivar was also president. At ten, in an austere conference room, he met with the managers of his water works and burgeoning electric system, his fire chief, the supervisor of town property and construction, the ministers of the various churches, and the principal of the grammar school.

There was nothing unusual about his ownership of Chandlerville. Since, in the beginning, most mills had been built in remote places, such towns had had to be constructed, and nearly every company owned at least one and sometimes more. It was a wholly efficient arrangement, for, mostly illiterate and inexperienced at managing the simplest personal affairs, the people who had come in from the farms and down from the mountains needed a lot of taking care of. Like children, they always wanted things not good for either them or the business on which their welfare depended. It was his responsibility to deny them things injurious and to see that the lives they led were frugal and upright. Thus, before the conference was over, he knew everything that had happened in his domain for the past week. Nothing escaped his notice: if a supervisor reported inefficiency or undue absenteeism, every aspect of the delinquent's personal life would be investigated. There was no room in Chandlerville for drinkers, gamblers, backsliders from the church, adulterers or wife beaters, nor for the lazy or the thriftless. When all the evidence was in from his network of informers, Bolivar reached his verdicts swiftly, and they were beyond appeal.

Nevertheless it was a taxing business. He recognized in himself a tendency to err, an undue tolerance and willingness to be merciful that was, in the last analysis, no favor to the defendant and harmful to the rest of the people of the mills and town. He had to guard against and compensate for it always; and the summary decisions he had to make affecting not only men but their wives and children were often privately exhausting. There seemed a lot of them today, and he dealt with them as always, with his mind, not with his heart; and when the session was over he was tired. Maybe, he thought, this was the logical next step for Heath. Let the boy assume some responsibility for the town. It would give him another view of life and its seriousness, a vision of the importance of the mission that lay ahead of him. And it would take some weight off his own shoulders, which would please Elizabeth. He made that decision quickly, like all the rest, was pleased with it, then leaned back in his chair, eyes sweeping the packed board table. "Anything else?" He looked at Buck Higgins, the chief of the force of special deputies whose salaries he paid and who comprised the town's police force. Higgins had seemed strangely quiet, almost distracted, throughout the session. "Buck, anything you want to report?"

The beefy man jerked erect. "Sir? Oh, no, sir."

"Then, meetin's adjourned."

Bolivar went to his office while they filed out. The more he thought about it, the better the idea seemed. Heath was resentful at having to work in the mill, but he had done his job, learned more quickly than Bolivar had expected. Maybe that was the advantage of an education. He had sent Heath to St. Paul's and Harvard because that was where the sons of the people in New York and New England with whom he dealt went, and he had always felt a certain sense of inferiority dealing with them in view of his own limited education. He had not wanted Heath to be hampered by that. And even though he had not liked the idea of exposing the boy to all sorts of strange, Yankeefied, and maybe harmful ideas, apparently it had paid off. He reached for the telephone to call Elizabeth and tell her of his decision. But his hand had just touched the phone when the door from the conference room swung open, and Buck Higgins was there.

Bolivar drew back his hand. "Well," he rasped, "what did you forget?"

"Nothin, Mr. Bolivar. Only—" The Chief's voice shook. "Only I got to talk to you alone a minute. It's . . . somethin important."

The pain was bad. But what was worse was that they already knew.

He'd seen it in their eyes at once—the curious, shifting stares, people drifting through the cardroom to look him over, as if his wounds would show through his work clothes. They knew, all right; the grapevine had been at work, the news flying through the plant like lint.

But he was determined to stick it out. There was, after

all, nothing else to do. He did not even want to think of what lay ahead of him, much less remember last night —Fox's blazing, contemptuous eyes and his own efforts to get back to his car. Even the mildest, simplest of movements cost him agony, which combined with dread to scrape his nerves so raw he felt like screaming. In a daze he went about his work, full of a sense of doom, each minute as interminable as that for a prisoner awaiting the headsman's ax.

It fell just before noon. The foreman was there, tapping him on the shoulder, a kind of awe, a certain pity, in his eyes. Even with his words almost lost in the thunder of machinery, Heath read their meaning well enough from his lips: "Your daddy wants to see you. In his office. Right away."

"Yes," Heath said. He left the man to do his work, went out the fire door and down the stairs, every jarring step of the descent sending waves of agony through a body nearly one solid, purple bruise. He held the rail, closed his eyes, groped his way down.

Limping along the corridor, he wondered how the Old Man would look, what he would say. How many times had he seen displeasure, disappointment, rage, on that face, the blue eyes too terrible to look at, the mouth thin, ferocious? How many times had he felt the need to vanish, to cease to exist, before that presence? Almost his earliest memories: the feel of warm, wet wool scratching his thighs: *A boy your age doing such a childish thing!* Or *It's not that you can't learn; it's that you don't apply yourself. A report like this . . .* Each sin, each reprimand, of increasing intensity, and now, like a discordant symphony building to a crescendo, this, the ultimate. Although there was nearly nothing in his stomach, he retched, tasted hot bile and swallowed it. And then he was at the door of the outer office. He paused there, willing time to stop, wishing himself to explode into a mist of atoms and end, finally, once for all, before he had to turn that knob. But there was no help for it; he entered.

The secretary's smile was motherly, and so, of course,

it had not yet spread from the plant's grapevine to the office. "Mr. Bolivar's expecting you. Go right in."

"Thanks." Heath moved across the room, opened the door.

There he sat, behind his desk, amidst the clutter of files and papers and plans and broken gears and cotton plugs. His white hair, caught in a slant of sunlight through the dusty window, made a nimbus around his head. But the expression he wore was not the one Heath had expected. His face seemed inexpressibly old, pale, drawn, stricken. "Come in, please," he said in a soft, trembling voice, "and shut the door behind you."

Heath did so and moved to stand silently before the desk. His head pounded with hangover and tension; his body was a total entity of pain; his stomach churned. He was exhausted, neither physical nor spiritual strength remaining in him. Vaguely he managed to think that this was what Judgment Day was like: to stand stripped of all sophistry and bravado before a merciless accountant who, never having sinned, could feel no compassion. For a dazed instant it seemed that he faced not his father but his father's God.

Still in that muted, shaky voice, the Old Man said, "I reckon you know what I have heard. About you and last night. Now I am waiting for you to tell me that they have got it all wrong. I want you to tell me what really happened. I want to hear what you have got to say for yourself, sir."

Heath had never heard him sound like that before. The voice was almost a whisper, drained of vigor.

He shook his head, searching for words. He found none, and the silence in the room, absolute, profound, not even affected by the clearly audible rumbling of machinery, lasted forever.

And during that eternity Bolivar Chandler's face began to change. Slowly life seeped back into the blue eyes that Heath could barely meet, manifested itself in a glitter, light seen through a shield of ice. Then color seeped back into the pale flesh. Still the silence stretched between them. The eyes glittered with more intensity, yet cold as stars; the face took on a normal hue, then altered, as blood surged into it. Redder and redder it became, a remarkable phenomenon, Heath thought with strange detachment; it was scarlet now, like a turkey's wattle, and the eyes were becoming wild. All at once he recognized what he saw as fury, an insanity of fury. His father, sitting there before him, was going quite mad with rage.

Then Bolivar scraped back his chair, stood up. "So it's true," he said, the words seeming to come from deep in his barrel chest. "It's true, then."

Heath's head moved in a faint nod of assent, the only motion of which, in that moment, he was capable.

"My own son." Bolivar's whispered words seemed strangely ventriloquial, his lips nearly motionless. "My own son—you—guilty of all that. After all we've tried to teach you. After all the prayers . . . Drinking yourself mindless on rotten whiskey, wallowing in it like a swine . . . an adulterer, in Godless intercourse with a *married* woman . . ." He broke off, lips moving soundlessly. "And being beaten for it like a dog. Being stretched out naked, whipped . . ."

Suddenly Heath feared for the man's life. All that blood in Bolivar's face, that strange trembling. Desperate words came to him, anything to mitigate that terrible pressure in his father. "Dad, I'm sorry . . . I . . . repent . . ." His voice was a croak.

"Sorry. Repent." His father repeated the two words blankly. "Yes, we'll all repent. We sinned too. We were too lax with you. We'll all repent. *The wages of sin are death!* We've let you go to your death! Through our kindness, our love for you, we— But there'll be no more of that. No more automobile for you to drive around in. No more being out at nights. If you're to have any salvation, it can only come through work and prayer! From now on, you will go directly to your work in the morning and come directly home from your work in the evening, and you will not leave that house at night except to go to church and we will pray with you . . . we will all pray with you, your mother and me and you, and maybe—" He broke off, face engorged, stocky body shaking as he leaned forward across his desk, supported on his two clenched fists. "I don't know," he said. "I've already prayed. I've already prayed as hard as I know how, but maybe if—" Suddenly he came around the desk. The blood color of his face deepened, his eyes were flares. "Yes, that's it, we'll pray together. Now." Suddenly he roared the words. *"Down on your knees!"*

Heath stood dazedly, stunned by the sight of his father like this. His moment of hesitation was too long. His father's big hand flashed out, seized his wrist, twisted, forced him downward. *"I said,"* roared Bolivar Chandler, *"down on your knees!"* With iron strength, he jerked.

Heath's bruised, stiff legs would not comply, they would not bend; he staggered, fell, and Bolivar, standing over him, forced and twisted with a right arm like an oaken beam, and Heath sprawled on the floor and his body turned to fire; he squealed with the sudden, unbearable pain. In the flash of it, he wrenched loose and struck out, and his clenched fist was like a hammer against Bolivar's chest. The old man let go, reeled back, came up short against his desk. Then, retching with pain, Heath scrambled to his feet.

The blood was gone from Bolivar's face now, the twisted countenance swam before him pale as paper, a hallucination in the mist of agony and sudden, mindless, explosive rage.

"You hit me," Bolivar said wildly. "Why, you hit me—"

"Yes, by God, I hit you!" Heath shrieked. He no longer felt the pain. The act, the blow, had ruptured something in him strained beyond its ability to contain his feelings; now it all poured out, a gushing pus of frustration, hatred, despair. "What the hell did I do, anyhow?" he howled. "Get drunk, lay up with a woman— You think it was the first time for me, you think it's gonna be the last? You think I'm going to live like you the rest of my life, down on my knees in front of God and a cotton mill? Dead, the way you're dead? You talk about sin!" He flung the words, fiercely, contemptuously. "You don't know what sin is, you never had the chance to learn. You don't know what joy is either, or love. All you know is money, fear, and ugliness. From the day I was born you never gave a shit about me, all you cared about was making sure I grew up to be the right tool, the best instrument you could use to run your mills with! All you ever wanted was to chain me to these mills the way you've spent your whole life chained, not living, feeling any joy or any love or any greatness. That's sin for you, Bolivar Chandler. My God, you talk about mortal sin— To be alive and waste it, to be able to feel and not let yourself feel anything, to be afraid of feeling—" He broke off, his own panting loud in his ears. "If I go to hell," he said thinly, "for drinking whiskey and loving women and trying to feel alive, then I'll go a lot more gladly than I'd go to heaven for wasting my life the way you have done and never even being able to love my own son—"

He stopped. The room swam. He had reached the end of his tether; could feel himself swaying. Bolivar stared at him, eyes two blue dots in chalk-white face, a wraith. Then Bolivar drew himself up.

It was, Heath realized, even in the midst of delirium, the most astonishing feat of self-control he had ever seen. He gaped in amazement as Bolivar stood erect, like a granite statue unaffected by age, time, fury. "Young man," he said, "you're overwrought. You get yourself in hand." He reached for Heath. "We'll pray together."

Heath stared. "You don't understand," he whispered. "Do you? You just can't understand."

"Get down on your knees," Bolivar rasped.

"No," Heath whispered.

"I said, get down on your knees!"

They looked at each other. There was a moment then when Heath wanted to do nothing in the world so much as to obey. But it was beyond his power; in a flash of clarity he perceived that if he did, he was truly lost.

"I can't," he said. "I'm going."

"No!" Bolivar muttered.

"Yes. Yes, I'm going now. I'm—" His throat was clogged, his eyes were full of tears. "I'm just going, that's all," he said and turned away.

His hand touched the door.

"Heath!" Bolivar's voice was imperious.

He halted.

Bolivar said, words freighted with cold warning, "Don't you go out that door."

Heath sucked in his breath. "Goodbye," he said. Then he went out and closed the door behind him.

9 SHE STILL could not believe it, comprehend it. One moment life floated along as always, a slow, steady river. The next, they were there—the sheriff and his men. And suddenly it all changed, and she did not know why or how, or what to do. All she knew was that everything had stopped. Fox was gone, and she was here alone.

Beside the stove the clock ticked loudly. She looked at it. Three o'clock. They would be coming back now, any time, to take her into Macedonia. Fox had said they would. So had the sheriff. She had best get some clothes together.

Pearl got off the bed, where she had sat for more than a half hour, just staring at the wall, trying to make sense of it all. Going to the closet, feeling strangely as if she were not inside the body that performed these acts, she pulled back the muslin curtain. The old leather suitcase that her father had bought for his and Mama's wedding trip was there, scarred and battered. She took it out, laid it on the bed, and opened it. Then she began to pack: her underwear, much of it made from sugar sacks; her three everyday dresses from the store in Chandlerville, her extra pair of shoes. Meanwhile she let it all run back through her mind again, trying to make sense of it.

Fox had been at the table in the living room eating dinner—side meat, cornbread, black-eyed peas. He had been strangely quiet all day, and once, when she had occasion to go to the food safe, she had found it empty; when she asked if he had sold all the whiskey last night, he only grunted. Then they had heard the cars.

Because there was more than one. That was unusual—
two at a time, and in the middle of the day. Fox sat up
straight, his nose twitched, his eyes turned hard. She
said, "Wonder who that is?"

"The Law," Fox said.

Pearl froze where she stood, a glass of buttermilk in
her hand. "The Law." It was as if he had announced that
God was coming down into the clearing—or the devil.
She knew nothing about The Law, except that it was a
constant threat, one so terrible that even her father
feared it. They lived in the shadow of The Law; and yet
it had never bothered them, and so she had almost
ceased to believe in it. Now she stared at Fox.

He looked back, face pale beneath his beard. When
he spoke, the words came rapidly, distinctly: instructions.
"I'm likely to have some trouble with The Law. Maybe
it won't amount to nothin, maybe it will. I done hid all
the whiskey, and you don't know nothin about it, you
understand? *You don't know nothin about it.*"

Now the cars were in the hollow, engines roaring. Fox
stood up. "No matter what happens," he said, "you don't
say nothin. Absolutely nothin. And no matter where
they take me or what they say, don't you worry. I'll be
all right and so will you. I'll see to that."

Pearl only opened and closed her mouth. Then she
said, "Yes, Daddy."

"All right." He came to her, patted her shoulder. "Now,
don't you worry," he said again, smiled faintly, and kissed
her on the cheek. Then he put on his hat, went out on
the porch. Pearl moved closer to the door.

The old hound bayed as the engine sound died. Fox
said, "Hush. You hush." Through the doorway she saw
the men swarm out of the cars, eight of them, four from
each vehicle. Some carried shotguns.

A lean, rangy man in a dark-blue suit, a holstered pistol
on his hip, came forward a few paces, saw Fox and
stopped. "Howdy, Fox."

"Sheriff. Howdy."

Pearl saw how the other men aimed their weapons

at her father. "Fox," the sheriff said, "we got to talk a little bit."

"Sho," said Fox. "Y'all come on in. You want some cold buttermilk?"

"No," the sheriff said. "We'll talk out here. Fox, I got a warrant for your arrest."

"Is that a fact? What I done wrong?"

The sheriff's lips moved beneath his mustache. "That's for the court to say. But you're charged with a federal warrant the United States Commissioner has done sworn out against you. Violation of the Volstead Act."

"You mean sellin whiskey?"

"I mean makin it *and* sellin it. We're gonna have to search your premises, Fox."

"Sho," Fox said. "You won't find nothin, but go ahead."

"It don't matter whether we find anything. I've got two men along with the treasury agent down at your still right now."

"My still? I don't know what you're talkin about."

"Down by the branch. On your land."

Fox smiled. "Sheriff, I don't never go down there. If somebody has snuck in and put a still on my property, it's a surprise to me."

"Yeah," the sheriff said, "I reckon it is. Well, we have to make a search."

"Do," Fox said.

"You won't oppose us?" The sheriff looked relieved. "Come ahead."

They did. They went through everything. Pearl had blushed and felt petrified when they raised her mattress; luckily Fox did not see the *Love Stories* magazine. She still understood nothing, had no idea what was going to happen. Finally Fox said, "You see?"

"It don't make no difference. You've got to come along. You won't make us put irons on you."

Fox looked at him with a different expression. "No, Holding," he said, "you don't want to try that." He sighed. "I'll come along peaceable. One thing. You gonna let me make bond?"

"That's up to the commissioner." But Pearl saw how

their eyes met, and the sheriff shook his head. "It ain't likely, Fox, I'm afraid."

Fox nodded. "That means I'll be in the jailhouse for a while. What about my girl? She can't stay out here by herself."

"I'll see to her. If you want her brought on into town, I'll send a deputy back after her—there ain't room in the cars right now. I'll make sure she's got a decent place to stay."

Fox nodded. "I'll hold you to that, Bert." He turned to Pearl. "You hear, sugar? I got to go off with these folks. You pack up and git ready. They'll send somebody out here to pick you up and bring you to me directly." He patted her shoulder, kissed her again, and said, "Now, don't you worry. Everything's gonna be all right."

Pearl sought words and found none.

"There's some other things," Fox said, turning away. "I got a dog, two hawgs to be looked after, and there's my car."

"Fox, you leave all that to me," the sheriff said. "We'll bring your car in, and I'll store it in my own garage. I'll take care of that redbone too. Does he hunt?"

"He used to, but he's gettin old. He's still a good strike dog on coon, but he drops out before they tree."

"I'll run him with mine ever' now and again; I need a good strike dog. I reckon Willis Gaddy will come out and git your pigs and put 'em in with his—go halvers on 'em with you if you ain't around at killin time."

"All right," said Fox. "I'm much obliged to you, Bert. I'll depend on you to see to everything."

"You know I will," the sheriff said. "I swear, Fox, I hate this—"

"Don't let it worry you," Fox said. "You folks ready to go?"

"Any time you are."

"Then we might as well." He turned to Pearl. "I'll go with these people now. Don't fret, I'll see you later on today." He turned to the sheriff. "One thing more, what about keepin my guns for me? I don't worry much about the pistol, but the rifle's worth money and the shotgun was my daddy's."

"I'll hold 'em," the sheriff said. "Let's go, Fox."

"Sho," he said; and they went out.

That was it: The Law. The Law had her father and it was coming for her, and the world had fallen in. She knew this much about The Law, anyhow; when poor folks got mixed up with it, they were doomed. All her life she had heard that. And they were poor folks.

With a misery of fear throbbing within her like a tooth just beginning to twinge, she numbly put things in the suitcase—the clock, Pearlie's Baby—and then she remembered. Taking the magazine from beneath the mattress, she dropped it in. After that she stripped off all her clothes, put on fresh underwear, donned her one good dress, bought from Sears, Roebuck two years before, almost outgrown, far too tight and short now. Then she carefully arranged the hat she had inherited from her mother and that she almost never wore.

She went into the front room. Fox's plate was still on the table. She took it to the kitchen, washed it, stacked it with the others. Then, again to the front: she took her mother's portrait and Fox's army discharge from the wall, packed them. With a heightened perception that was new and strange, she looked around the place again, and it seemed to her that she could see the grain in every board; each thread of yarn hanging from the frayed quilt on Fox's bed stood out. This was awful, terrible; and yet, struck through with guilt, she felt excitement: she was leaving here, going to Macedonia; everything was changing. She could not help a surge of anticipation. As bad as things were, things were also different.

When she had fed the last scraps to the chickens, rinsed out the bucket, everything she could do had been done. Pearl went out on the porch to wait.

Here again, the world seemed to have, this afternoon, unnatural clarity. It was as if every leaf stood out on every heat-stricken tree, each feather on every scrawny chicken. She saw details her eye had never caught; only once or twice had she known this sensation before, when sick, in fever. Then the eye saw things this way. She felt as if she were sick now; her entrails seemed choked and clogged.

The Law. If only she knew more about it. She clasped her hands, paced back and forth on the porch, wished that her dress were newer, fitted better. And what would they do, how would they live? Was The Law going to put her father in the jail? For how long? A week? Forever?

Then she heard the car.

It came whining down through the woods, traveling fast. The deputy, of course. She turned to look, and then her heart seemed to stop. Through the livid greenery she caught a flash of yellow.

Oh, no, she thought with a rush of blood to her cheeks. Oh, no, not now, not him—what will I tell him?

But then it was there: the Marmon. It halted before the porch; she saw the familiar, handsome head, its very shape stirring something wild within her. Then, moving strangely, Heath got out.

And stopped short. He had never seen her in anything but the usual gingham dress or with a hat on. He frowned; and in that interval she sensed somehow that he was changed too. His eyes were deeply circled, discolored, every muscle in his face seemed taut. He said, "Pearl. Hello, where's Fox? I've got to see him."

"He ain't here."

"Down at the still? I'll go down—"

"No. He ain't there either." It burst from her. "The Law done come. The Law done come and took him off to Macedonia."

Heath stood rigidly. "The Law," he said. "The sheriff?"

"Yeah." She got out the one word; then her throat closed up.

Heath said in a croaking voice: "So. God damn him. God damn him to hell."

"Who?"

"Never mind," he said. "Not Fox." Then he sat down

on the running board and put his head in his hands. "Oh, Christ."

She only stood there, while he sat like that for what seemed a very long time. She wanted to go to him, lay her hand on his head, comfort him somehow in whatever grief he felt. But she could not move.

Then Heath raised his head. "You're dressed for traveling."

"A deputy was comin for me. To take me to Macedonia. I thought you was him."

Heath got up as if each inch of movement cost him agony. "I've got to see Fox. I've got to." He knuckled at his eyes. "All right, I'll go into Macedonia."

The words burst from her without volition. "Take me with you!"

He dropped his hands. "Huh?"

"I'm tired of waitin on that deputy. I want to see my daddy. I'm all packed to go—take me with you."

Heath blinked, then nodded. "Sure. Why not?" He started forward, halted. "You'll have to bring whatever you've got yourself. I'm . . . not in shape to carry anything."

"I'll git my suitcase." Pearl whirled, ran inside. To ride in a car with *him!* She pressed her hands to her breasts. She had to hurry before the deputy came and she was forced to ride with *him.* Snatching up the valise, she ran out of the house, went rapidly down the steps, then stopped. The old hound raised his head, looked at her with rheum-veiled eyes.

"Oh, Lord, Trail," Pearl said, with something huge and awful in her. She bent, caressed the crop-furred skull as if in farewell; if she could have, if Heath had not been watching, she would have hugged the dog. Then, in a gesture of finality, she took her hand away, strode forward. "I'm ready," she said.

Her voice grated on his nerves, but he had to find out all that had happened. So as they sped toward Macedonia he drew her out, and in that whining, nasal drawl she told him what she knew. "They said he couldn't make no bonds."

"No, of course not." He said it harshly.

"What does that mean?"

"It means he'll have to stay in jail until they try him."

"You mean take him up in court?"

"Yes," he said. They were entering Macedonia. Its main street paralleled the railroad tracks. The town had grown, its population now nearly fifteen thousand, maybe more, the nucleus of a cell composed of dozens of cotton mills. Heath reached the square, turned right on Butler Street. The big, Greek Revival courthouse in its grove of oaks looked curiously like Chandler House.

He tried to fight his mind away from that, blank out the span of hours that encompassed his confrontation with his father, and then with his mother. He had surged in on her in hot blood, still in that mindless hysteria that had possessed him in Bolivar's office. At first he had imagined that she was his enemy too; that was how he gathered courage to face her, to blurt, "I got something to tell you."

"All right," she said. The eyes, so much like his own, scanned his face. Then she said, "I think I already know what it is. Come and have a cup of coffee and talk to me."

"No, you don't understand; it's terrible."

She took his hand. "Come and tell me."

The cook was in the kitchen, but Elizabeth dismissed her, made the coffee herself, went through all sorts of drawn-out female rituals before she served it. He sat seething, ready to explode with words. Then she turned, disarmed him, putting down the cups. "If you want to leave," she said, "go ahead."

He gaped. "How did you know?"

What both of them said after that ran together in a blur. They talked as they had never talked before. He told her everything, couching it in the most careful terms he could, so as not to shock her. What baffled him was that, once, she smiled.

Then she stood up, went to the icebox, got more cream. "Hampton blood," she said.

"What?" Heath blurted.

"Don't you think I know what it is? I remember when my father told my mother that he had lost his last piece of what used to be the homeplace in a poker game. He was roaring drunk; it was the only way he could face her. Son," she said, "don't you think I know? My heavens, I raised you. Watched it in you."

"The Hampton blood?" He stared at her.

"Some. The Chandler blood too." She shook her head. "And both of them mixed in you."

Still he could not comprehend. "But what I've done—"

She set down the cream. Then she turned and looked out the kitchen window. "The thing about it is," she said, "that you've got to remember that your father had to work all his life."

He looked at her, this small woman, and a kind of wonder welled up in him. Her back toward him, silhouetted against the window, in her unfashionable chocolate-colored dress, she conjured up in his mind the image of a piece of spring steel. He had never thought of her that way before.

"He is a fine man, an admirable man, and if I had not thought so, I would never have married him or lived with him this long. But he has his limitations; we all have them, even you." She turned; her brows had drawn together, her lips quivered slightly. "There are some things he doesn't understand because he's never had the chance to learn them. But he's a great man all the same."

She dropped into her chair. "What you did . . . is beyond excuse. But maybe you wouldn't have done it if . . . if a lot of things. In Charleston it would have been a scandal and all my brothers would have bought you a drink afterward. I don't know. Just . . . I've thought about it a lot. You go. You need to go. I'll tend to him."

Dazedly, Heath said, "You really mean that?"

"He hasn't called me yet, or come home. When he does, I'll have to . . . change and stand with him. Hurry. Pack whatever you can and get out. I'll send you the rest later."

"Oh," he said. "Oh, Mother—" He looked at her. "You must have had an awful time here."

"I've had a fine time here. I'll never regret it. Hurry."

"All right," he said, got to his feet, limped upstairs. He did not waste much time packing. He came down with one small bag. She clung to him for a moment, then broke away, her cheeks wet. "You're too damned much like him," she said, and it was the first oath he had ever heard her utter. "Go on, now—" She took his hand. "Please write," she said.

He limped out to the Marmon. She stood on the porch and waved to him. He waved back. Why, he wondered, had she waited so long to let him know that he was not alone? He raced the car.

Chandler House fell away behind him. He tried not to think, he had no idea what his next move would be. All he knew was that he had to face Fox Ramsey before he went.

The sheriff's office was in the courthouse, its wooden moldings and wainscots of dark wood, its walls an ugly tan. Holding looked at Heath narrowly, trying to assess, Heath supposed, whether this could mean trouble for him. Finally he nodded. "Sure, you can see him, if he wants to see you. Come on." He led Heath and Pearl up a dark, narrow stair that smelled of generations of unwashed humanity; a kind of hopelessness seemed to freight the hot, lifeless air. Then into the jail itself with its iron bars, its mingled stench of people, excrement, and disinfectant; beside Heath, Pearl caught her breath. They walked down the cell block, past curious faces peering from cages, and halted at the last cell; the jailer handed Holding the keys, and the sheriff said, "Fox."

He got up off his cot, then saw Heath and stopped. The nostrils of that sharp nose flared; he showed his discolored teeth like an angered animal. "What you doin here with her?"

"Fox, I had to come. I . . . had a falling out with *him*. I'm going away, and I had to see you first. When I went by your place the deputy hadn't come to bring her in, so she rode with me." As if he were the prisoner, Heath wrapped his hands around the bars. "Fox, what can I say, how can I make it up to you?"

"Just leave me alone," Fox said heavily.

"Look, have you got a lawyer yet? And what about Pearl? I've got some money. Nearly twenty thousand. You can have it all."

"I don't want your money. I wouldn't touch your rotten money," Fox said with hatred. "Just git outa here and leave me with my girl." He looked at the sheriff. "Holding—"

The officer took Heath's arm. "Come on, Mr. Chandler."

"But, Fox—" Heath would not let go the bars.

"Git him out, Holding!" Fox yelled.

The sheriff pulled. "I think you'd better come along," he said firmly.

Leaving Pearl behind, they went back down the stairs to Holding's office. Heath paced the floor, his shirt wet with cold, unwholesome sweat. "I'll pay anything, do anything to see that he's got a fair trial."

"Didn't you hear him? He wouldn't take your money. Besides, it wouldn't do no good."

"He's got no chance of getting off?"

"No. And you know why. He'll have to pull some time, boy, and there's no way out of it. Three years, that's what they'll hand him, eligible for parole in eighteen months—but there again, that'll be up to—you know. But if he minds himself, he'll be out in two, anyhow—good behavior. Fox will get along. Federal prison ain't so bad. Nothing like the chain gang."

"But what about the girl? How will she live all that time?"

"I don't know, I got to talk to Fox about that. He ought to have some money saved up she can use. Anyhow, there's a constable named Bailey lives over on Jordan Street, his wife runs a boardinghouse. I've arranged for her to stay there for the time bein. She'll be all right; Mrs. Bailey is a good Christian woman. After things settle down, the trial's over she won't have no trouble gettin a job in a mill. Anyhow, don't worry about her. Fox and

I are old friends. I already promised him I'll keep my eye on her."

"All the same—" Heath began. Then Pearl came in, her face pale, tear marks on her cheeks. She sniffled, found her voice. "I reckon I might as well go on to where I'm to stay."

Heath looked at this lanky, awkward, breastless girl in the old, ill-fitting dress. A child, he thought, a vulnerable child, stranded, frightened, helpless—and all his fault. He turned to Holding. "Give me the address. I'll take her there."

"I reckon not. Come along, missy." The sheriff arose, reached for her arm. She moved away.

"Why can't he take me?"

Holding pursed his lips. "Because," he said flatly, "he ain't the kind of man you ought to associate with."

"That's foolish." Her voice was suddenly so strong that both looked at her in surprise. Standing very straight, hands locked in front of her, fingers twisting nervously, she went on quickly. "My suitcase is already in his car. I want him to take me. Besides, I got somethin to talk to him about."

"Now, you know Fox wouldn't—" Holding began.

"He's up there in jail. This man is the reason why he's there. He says he's leavin this part of the country, but he ain't goin until I git things straight with him. Now, what's the address?"

The sheriff stared at her a moment. Then he looked coldly at Heath. "Boy—" he began.

"All I'm gonna do," Heath said wearily, "is take her to the boardinghouse. What—what do you think I am, anyhow?"

Holding was silent for a moment. Then he made a gesture of resignation, took a pen from its holder, dipped it in ink, scribbled and blotted the address. He gave it to Pearl. "I'll call in a spell to make sure you're settled all right. You can come back to see your daddy tonight after supper if you want to."

"Yes, sir. I . . . appreciate everything, Sheriff."

"Glad to do it," Holding said. He looked at Heath

sourly. "I'm jest sorry the necessity arose. You be careful drivin over there, young man."

"Don't worry," Heath said thinly. "I don't have any intention of causing any more trouble."

"I just wish you'd taken that attitude yesterday," the sheriff said, and turned away.

10 "PEARL, I . . . DON'T KNOW what I can say." Heath's voice was low as they went down the courthouse steps very slowly, for his body was still one vast, painful bruise. "I only wish it was me up there in that cell instead of him. I wish he'd just stayed clear and let 'em kill me—"

"Don't talk foolishness!" Again that unexpected sharpness, that strength in her voice. "Don't say nothin like that."

"Well, it's true." They walked to the car. "But—Anyhow, you're going to need money. I've got plenty. I'll go to the bank after I get you settled, and then I'll come back by the boardinghouse and—"

"I don't want your money." She got into the car without waiting for him to open the door. When he slid gingerly behind the wheel, he saw that she sat very straight, looking forward. Curiously, she seemed older, more confident, as if the removal of the pressure of Fox's presence allowed something within her to work its way out.

He started the engine. "I thought you said—"

"That was because the sheriff wouldn't have let me come with you no other way. But I already seen that he's scared he'll have to loan me some of his own money. He won't, nobody will, Daddy told me where it's at and he's got plenty. More than I ever dreamed." As the car pulled away she turned to him. "But I still had to talk to you. I—" For the first time her voice broke. "I couldn't let you go off thinkin I hated you."

"If you don't, you should. God knows, I hate myself."

"Well, there jest ain't no call to," she said fiercely.

"Daddy's been worried about The Law ever since I can remember; they was bound to take him up sooner or later."

"Maybe a lot later, if he'd stayed away from me. I still haven't figured out how he showed up when he did."

"He told me that. He was settin out on the porch last night, Sonny Ford and that other man drove up, wanted to buy some whiskey. He wouldn't sell it to 'em. They bragged they was out to git you last night. When they drove off, he followed 'em."

"Oh, hell," Heath groaned.

She put a hand on his wrist. "He knowed what he was doin."

"That's why he shouldn't have done it." The car bounced across railroad tracks; she took her hand away. "Well, anyhow," she said, "I didn't want you to go off worryin about me."

"I'll worry about you for the rest of my life. Fox too."

"No. You done had your punishment. He says they beat you real bad."

They were in a section of town now sooted by railroad smoke. A switch engine huffed and plumed in a coal yard. Ahead, on a sharply rising street, big houses with wide porches were set close together, dormered and gingerbreaded, paint peeling, front yards almost nonexistent, sterile and grassless. Beyond hulked the ugly, smudged flank of a mill, its blue windows closed and lightless; the Butlers had laid off their hands in this ancient plant to work down their inventories. Even in the febrile, breezeless sunlight there was an invincible ugliness about this place, a miasma of defeat and poverty. And it was Jordan Street. "Good Lord," Heath said, "I hope your boardinghouse isn't along here."

"I reckon the sheriff thought I'd best stay somewhere cheap." But some of the bravado had vanished from her voice. "It can't be no worse than our own place." She pointed. "There," she said faintly. "Two-ten. I guess that's it."

Heath stopped the car and they both stared, appalled. Once, when this end of town had been more fashionable, it must have been an expensive house. But for at least twenty years, along with the rest of the neighborhood, it had been sinking into squalor; and now it was about to be swallowed by it. Once painted a dark brown, now it had turned a sooty, neutral color, from its high roof of warped shingles down to its rotting porch. A cardboard sign on a decayed pillar said: *Room and Board*. Half of the gingerbread scrollwork dangled loosely from the porch eaves. Behind the scabby, formerly ornate railing three men sat in rocking chairs, looking curiously at the Marmon and its occupants. One, in faded overalls, was very old, a bristle of white beard on a blasted face, eyes blank with senility. Another was younger, Heath's age, broad in the shoulders, dark of mustache, eyes glittering as they ranged over Pearl, booted feet propped on the banister. He showed white teeth in a grin, leaned over, whispered something to the old man, who cackled. The third arose from his chair. He was short, paunchy, well past fifty, face swollen and puffy, cheeks purplish with webbed veins, his eyes, like plums in uncooked dough, bloodshot. He wore a threadbare business suit, and a silver shield showed on his vest. As Heath and Pearl got out he came down the high, decaying steps with a curious, spraddle-legged, duckfooted walk, as if his paunch made it impossible for him to bring his knees together. On the sidewalk, he reached out and took Pearl's hand firmly between both of his and leaned close. "Well, young lady, I bet you the new boarder Sher'f Holdin sent over. We been waitin for you. Come right in." He managed to hold her hand for a full ten seconds more before she realized he was not going to let it go and withdrew it. "I'm Eddie Bailey, Constable, you jest call me Mister Eddie." A breath of home brew and the musty smell of wool long uncleaned mingled in Heath's nostrils as the constable turned to him. "Jest bring her traps right on in, young feller." He took Pearl's arm in his hand, squeezing. "You come right up, ma'am. Look out for them steps. They need fixin."

Behind them Heath halted, suitcase in his hand. He watched them climb the steps, the fat man holding determinedly to Pearl's arm. "Oh, hell," he whispered. Then, suddenly, he threw the bag back into the car. He ran up the steps after them.

On the porch, Bailey halted, but he did not let go of Pearl. "This here's my son Ned," he said. The young man rolled his eyes at Pearl and bobbed his head, letting the wooden match he chewed move slowly across his mouth. "And this here's Mr. Wilson, he's another one of our boarders. Now, you jest come right in and meet my wife, she'll git you settled down good."

"Please t'meetcha," Mr. Wilson said and cackled. With complete lack of self-consciousness, he scratched his groin.

"Fellers, this here's Miss Rumsey," Bailey told them. He opened a door with a tattered screen. "Now, you come on in, Miss Rumsey." Close behind, Heath followed them into a dark hall, a bulky, mirrored coatrack on one side, closed doors with chipped paint all along its length. A dim electric bulb dangling from the ceiling far back gave just enough light to reveal figured paper the color of tobacco juice, billowing and sagging overhead, stripped and marred along the walls. The place smelled close, of cooking greens and pork—not today's. It was as if no new air had been let into it this week.

Bailey halted, resisting Pearl's effort to pull her arm away. "Hey, suuuugggaaarrr," he called. "New boarder's here."

There were footsteps on the stairs. A slat-thin woman in greasy long dress and even greasier apron appeared, pushing at frowsy, silver-brown hair. She halted halfway down, staring at Pearl with hostile eyes. When she spoke, Heath saw that most of her teeth had rotted away to stumps, accounting for the puckering of pale lips above the almost nonexistent chin. "Howdy," she said tersely.

"Shug, this Miss Rumsey."

"Ramsey," Pearl said, voice reedy, trembling. "Pearl Ramsey."

"I thought the sher'f said Rumsey. Well, don't matter. You got her room ready, shug?"

"It ain't ready yet, it'll be ready directly." The Bailey

woman snapped the words, turned away, labored up the stairs, panting audibly.

"Well, shore, you come on out, sit on the po'ch with us," Bailey said. "We'll git acquainted. You'll like Ned. It's always good to have young folks around." He turned, still grasping her, saw Heath. His eyes narrowed. "Where at's her bag?"

"I . . . forgot to bring it in," Heath said.

"Fergot? Well, go git it. You can set it in the hall, then be on your way."

"Yes, sir," Heath said. He drew in a long breath, turned, plunged out of the house, down the steps. *No*, he thought. *No, Goddammit!* He ran to the car, opened the door, fumbled inside. Then he turned. "Hey, Pearl—Come here a minute."

"Jest git her bag, young feller," Bailey called irritably.

"I can't tell which one's hers."

"Wait!" Pearl's voice rang out. "I'll show you." She pulled away, came running down the steps. "Get in," he said fiercely in a low voice.

"Yes," she answered quickly. As he, disregarding pain, slid across the seat she leaped in beside him, slammed the door. "Hey, wait a minute!" Bailey squawked from the porch as the engine ground to life. Heath jammed down the gas pedal, the car roared off. "Wait!" he heard Bailey yell. "I'll call the sher'f—"

The car leaped forward. "Jesus," Heath grated. "Jesus Christ." He whipped it around a corner, climbed a hilly street lined with more of those once proud houses bought so low. "You can't stay there."

"No," she was gasping as if she had run hard. "No, not that place, I don't care how cheap. Somewhere else."

"Yes," Heath said. The car sped down a hill; now they were back at the railroad. He pulled over beside a vacant lot and stopped, letting the engine idle. "But where, dammit?"

"I don't know. Back to the sheriff." She was twisting her hands in her lap.

Heath shook his head. "He'd only talk you into it— Or another place just like it. Come on, a decent hotel—I'll pay." He turned to her angrily. "But I owe Fox that much. You'll not stay in a place like that."

"I can't take your money," Pearl said. She sat up very straight, staring directly ahead. Her hands knotted. "I ain't goin to."

"Goddammit, woman, don't you understand? You're my responsibility!"

"I ain't neither."

He seized her arm, squeezed it savagely. His back was afire, his head throbbing, he'd had all he could take. "Don't say that! I've got to see to you."

She pulled away. She made a strange sound in her throat, and he saw the almost imperceptible breasts rise beneath the silly dress. "Where're you goin when you leave here?"

"Huh?"

"I said, where you goin when you leave here?"

"I don't know. Somewhere. New York."

Pearl said, "Take me with you."

"Take you—?" Heath stared at her, unbelieving.

Then suddenly she turned on him, those green eyes enormous. "If I'm your responsibility, take me with you! New York! Anywhere outa here! Don't you see, I ain't got no chance but this!"

"But Fox," he whispered.

"I can't help that!" Her voice was strangled. "He'll be put away. You think I want to spend two years in this place waitin, workin in the mill or scrubbin floors somewhere? And then, when he comes out, what? Back to that shack out yonder? I'm all packed, ready, I won't be no trouble, not ask you for no money. Just take me outa here. Take me," she almost screamed, "outa here *while I still got the chance to go!*"

Heath looked at her. "Your father . . ."

"I got to be free!" she cried.

He turned away. His head hurt, his body ached, he was wearier than he had ever been in his life. He could not think, nothing made sense. The stench of boarding-house and jail still seemed to clog his nostrils. He looked at the vacant lot, lush and rampant with high weeds. The carcass of a dead dog half sprawled out of the greenery, ants crawling in and out of the open, white-fanged mouth. He wanted to vomit.

The world seemed to swirl in upon him, kaleidoscopically, a jumble of colors. It was as if he were in a spinning plane, the earth leaping up at him, and it was all over, all finished, nothing mattered. He laughed hoarsely, raised his hands high, brought them down hard on the wheel. He had no idea of what he was doing or of the consequences; it was all a joke, a monstrous joke. "Hang on!" he shouted and put the car in gear.

11

"I GOT TO BE FREE!" Pearl had cried.

And the agony of that plea had triggered something in him. It was as if he suddenly were prescient, able to see with utter clarity what lay before her unless she was rescued. Bailey, the musty boardinghouse, the stallion of a boy with glittering eyes, the old man scratching his crotch—he saw all that with *her* vision and understood the depths of fear and longing. And suddenly, in one flash of maniacal clarity, it came to him. All at once he knew what he could do to put everything right, shrive himself, expiate it all. The decision came with the bright, stunning force of lightning; a bolt from nowhere, it struck, exploded, irrevocably altering what it hit. He laughed, brought his hands down hard, decisively, on the wheel. "Hang on!" he yelled and put the car in gear.

It roared northward, slammed across the railroad tracks. "Wait!" Pearl screamed. "Wait, wait!"

Suddenly Heath turned it, ran between two wooden warehouses, stopped. She was staring at him in terror. Her chin trembled. "Wait— You mean . . . You don't mean . . . you'd really do it?"

"Yes," he said. "I owe it to you. Do you want to go?"

Her eyes did not leave his. She was, unconsciously, clasping her breasts with her hands. Then she whispered, "I said I did."

His voice was rough. "Make up your mind, Pearl. Bailey's already called the sheriff, you can bet. Holding will be looking for us right now. I can either take you back to his office or I've got to drive like hell to get out of Macedonia and across the county line. It's your choice, but there's no time to dally over it. Tell me where you want to go."

She shook her head unbelievingly; then she did a strange thing. She laughed; and at the same time she was crying. "With you," she said. "I won't be no bother. With you."

"All right," he said. "It's settled You've got from now until we hit the county line to change your mind." He put the car in motion with a lurch, then drove madly through back street after back street, one ear tuned for any protest. But she only clung tightly to the door, and no word passed her lips.

And then they were clear of town, ripping through outlying hamlets, the mill villages that ringed Macedonia like a bracelet. Still Pearl was silent, and Heath himself was careful not to think, only watched his driving, and now the last town was far behind and they were roaring northward through open country, and then, ahead, Heath saw the bridge across the creek that marked the county line. He slowed, his mirror revealing nothing on the road behind him. God help Holding, caught between Fox and Bolivar, he thought wryly, and once more he looked at Pearl. "It's not really your last chance," he said more rationally. "If you change your mind, I'll put you on the train and send you home."

Pearl stared at the wooden sign on the bridge rail. "I ain't got no home," she said in the most desolate voice that he had ever heard issue from a human being. "Let's go on."

They crossed the bridge.

And then, suddenly, it hit Heath; it all caught up with him; the reaction set in. He pulled over to the side of the road, shaking uncontrollably. "Oh, God," he said.

"Whut's wrong?" she asked him fearfully.

"Nothing." He closed his eyes; his head swam; bright

lights seemed to flare, explode, behind his lids. This was wrong too. No matter what he did, it was wrong. He sucked in air; his hands shook as they searched for a cigarette. He could not light it for the trembling. "Here," she said, "let me do it," and she took the match and held it. The smoke steadied him. He raised his head, looked at her, and said, "It's only that I'm tired. But we can't stop now. We've got to get across the state line as soon as we can. Bolivar Chandler's got long arms and so has Holding."

"But you look like— You look awful. You're too tired to drive."

"I'm all right."

"Maybe . . . maybe what you need is . . . a drink of likker."

He turned forward again, stared at the road ahead. "I don't know what I need," he said dully. "Maybe that would help."

"Why don't you stop in the next town and see can you find a little?" She suggested it as matter-of-factly as if recommending aspirin. But then, why not? Whiskey had been a part of her life for years, the sovereign remedy that her father sold. Because Fox made it, sold it, there could be in her thinking nothing wrong with it. He smiled wryly at such innocence; but all at once he knew she was right. He could not go on without it; and he had to go on.

He started the car again. "I think I'll do that," he said.

Nor, once out of Macedon County, was it difficult. This was back country; stills flourished in its hills and creek bottoms. A country store, a guarded inquiry, a keen, appraising glance that satisfied the vendor he was no undercover man . . . He came back to the car with the quart in a paper bag, drove swiftly to the next side road, turned there and parked the vehicle. His hands still shook so that he had to get her to untwist the cap. He raised the jar, drank long and greedily, and felt new strength and reassurance flow into him at once. Suddenly everything was all right; suddenly he was ready

for adventure, without regret. He lowered the jar, and
saw Pearl watching him intently. All at once he felt great
compassion and admiration for her, despite her frowzy,
watery-eyed appearance. By God, beneath that unpalat-
able exterior she had a streak of Fox inside her; he did
not see how she had borne up under all that had fallen
on her today. And she was entitled to the same surcease
she had allowed him. "Maybe," he said, "you'd like a
drink yourself."

Her eyes widened. "Oh, I've never tasted the stuff in
my life. Daddy would—" She broke off. "Whut's it like?"

"You'll have to try it for yourself," he answered. But
she'd already taken the jar.

"I always wondered what people seen in it." She drank
too, gagged and coughed and spat. "Oh, gosh, ugh. That's
turrble."

"Not like Papa used to make." But before he could take
it back she held her breath and tried again; this time
she got down a large swallow. Wheezing, eyes watering,
she passed the container back.

He drank again, capped the jar, put it on the seat between them. He was all right now, steady. He felt fine.
And he drove on.

They wound north through the hills across one more
county, then turned east, struck a main road that followed
the railroad track; and then they were back in mill
country once again. The towns reeled past as twilight
fell: Concord, Kannapolis, China Grove, Salisbury, Lex-
ington, High Point, Greensboro, Burlington. The huge
buildings that ranked the road in all those places thundered with the whirl of many spindles, the clash of loom
shuttles; their lights blazed behind the blue that made
the dusk colorful. Heath drank several times again; Pearl
tried it once more. But it was not the whiskey that made
her eyes wide, that brought from her more than once
a high, excited laugh or a gurgle like a child's chuckle
of wonder. She had never been so far from home before,
nor seen such sights. His mind loose, unfocused, he smiled
wryly. There were a lot of things she had never done,
and now, because of him, her life had changed. His, too,

he thought, but the whiskey protected him from fear or apprehension; now it was a joke. A great, monstrous, practical joke, the first he'd played since coming home. On himself, on her, on Bolivar and Fox and Holding—on everyone with whom his life had come in contact today; he was playing the hugest, most satisfying joke of his career on all of them. He drank, and they pressed north, for Danville, Virginia. Where, he promised himself, the rest would take final fruit.

Six hours after the start of their hegira they reached it. Pearl stared in awe at the huge old houses along its main street; beyond, in the valley by the river, the Dan River Mill was on its night shift, blue windows gleaming. In the little business section Heath pulled the car over and stopped. It seemed to him he floated as he got out.

"Where you going?" Pearl asked, suddenly fearful.

He pointed to a drugstore still open. "To get some cigarettes."

He bought the Camels, got the directions he needed. Two blocks down the street, two blocks right; the character of the neighborhood changed; modest bungalows. Then he saw the sign, stopped the car. He reached down and opened the jar and drank. Without offering it to Pearl, he capped it, put it back and got out. He had exactly the same feeling he had experienced just before a crash; a sense of doom and a curious uncaring happiness. Very drunk, he went around, opened the door. "Come on," he said.

"Where?"

"In here." He pointed to the house. "There's . . ." His voice was thick, blurred; he would have to do better than that. "There's somebody in there I want you to meet."

She looked puzzled and worried, but there was trust in the way she took his hand. He tried to imagine what had been in her mind all afternoon and found it beyond him. But she came easily and meekly, maybe a little giddy from the drinks she'd had as he led her up the walk.

He turned the bell knob on the door decisively. In a moment shuffling footsteps sounded; the door opened; a woman with a kind, rawboned face stood there, "Can I help you?"

"Yes, ma'am, if your husband's in," Heath said, pronouncing every word distinctly, still holding Pearl's hand. "We'd like to have him marry us."

Beside him, Pearl made a stifled sound; in the porch light her face swam in his vision, mouth wide, green eyes staring. She stood there like that, speechless, for a full half minute. Heath tried to stand without swaying, smiling down at her.

"Well," the woman said, "come in." She stepped aside.

Still Pearl did not move. Heath touched her gently, but with pressure. "Go ahead," he said.

Her mouth closed. Numbly, mechanically, she crossed the threshold. They were in a lamplit, shabby living room, with threadbare carpet on the floor, an ornate pedal organ in one corner. "He was just fixin to go to bed," the woman said. "Excuse me. I'll go and git him." She vanished into a hall.

Pearl shook her head. "I can't," she whispered. "I mean . . . You're not yourself."

"I'll not have Fox say I didn't make an honest woman of you," Heath muttered, trying to suppress the idiotic laughter welling in him. He thought of Bolivar; suddenly he giggled, then bit it off.

"But I can't," Pearl said again, her voice now choked with tears. "This is mean. You ought not to—"

"Why not? Didn't you want to get away?" His whisper was suddenly furious, persuasive. "Don't you understand? Once this is done, they can't take you back. You'll never have to go back again. Besides, if I don't, Fox will kill us both when he gets out. Besides, I want to."

She shook her head slowly, her face screwed up, twisted, ugly with emotion. "You . . . want to?"

Down the hall the woman said, "Daddy, there's some young folks here."

"Yes," Heath said. Words. It did not matter what he said. He had lied to everyone and broken all his promises. Words had no meaning any longer. "I want to marry you."

She just stood there, stunned. The joke was getting better all the time; it was perfect, absolutely perfect. After what Bolivar had done to Fox, what finer, more symmetrical, poetic justice? And he himself did not matter any longer; the plane would crash any minute now. Then the old man was there, shorter than the woman, coatless, but in vest, and blinking sleepily; he looked like Santa Claus. The woman held his coat for him, an artificial carnation in its lapel. "Good evening," he said. "You folks have come to me to be joined in wedlock? How nice." But his eyes were suspicious as they played over Heath and Pearl.

"That's what we've come for," Heath said carefully. "Ain't we, honey?" And he put his hand in the small of her back.

She did not answer; she was crying silently.

"Only," Heath said, "I ain't got any ring."

"That's all right," the magistrate said. "I get a lot of folks like you, and I keep a nice assortment on hand. You'll find something there to suit the little lady at a price you can afford. Now, if you'll just come this way . . ."

"Yes," Heath said, and once again pressed Pearl. At his touch she moved forward wordlessly, compliantly, like a sleepwalker.

12 MUTE AND MOTIONLESS, she stood beside him in the lamplit room while the old man droned. She was afraid—not of what was happening, but that it might not happen, that some random unlucky word or motion might break the spell that held them; each second was a breathlesss agony as she waited for him to make a joke of this, halt it, pinch it off. She had no idea how this had come about: a million questions moiled in her mind, but none of them counted now. For, as the old man's words inched toward finality with awful slowness, she had comprehended. And she thought of the postcard, realized in an astounded flash that the phrase must have meant exactly what it said. The questions could be dealt with later. For the moment it was enough that she was at last in a story, and that it was ending perfectly, as all such stories ended, and that finally something wonderful was happening to her, if only nothing spoiled it.

Then, incredibly, it was over, Heath slipping the cheap ring on her finger, the magistrate proclaiming with tinny exultation, "Husband, salute your bride!" She turned to Heath, but he only looked at her blankly, face glistening with sweat, not understanding. "Kiss your bride, fella," the justice of the peace said impatiently. Heath blinked; then, like a mechanical toy just wound up, he bent and touched her lips with his very briefly. But that was enough, more than enough, for now. The woman, who had served as witness and played the organ, handed her the marriage booklet, at that time the only certificate needed. Marveling, she took it, responding to the beauty of pink roses, doves and cupids emblazoned on the two cardboard pages signed by the old man and tied with bright red cord. Heath passed money to the man. "God bless you," the woman said tonelessly, and took Pearl's hands in her own rough, cold ones. Then Heath said dazedly, "Let's go," and shoved Pearl toward the door. In the car he slumped behind the wheel, motionless, breathing hard. As she climbed in, he reached for the fruit jar, took a drink, and set it down. Still he did not move.

"H-honey." Pearl formed the word with trepidation, even though she had the right to say it now. She could not think of anything else to call him as she took his hand. "Honey, what's the matter? Are you all right?"

Pulling away, he let out a gusty breath that was almost a groan. "Yeah. Yeah, I'm fine. Well, we did it, didn't we?" He straightened up, put both hands on the wheel.

"Where we goin now?" She imagined the two of them riding on through the night. That was what she wanted, to ride on with him beside her, her husband now.

"We got to stay some place. He told me about a hotel." Starting the engine, he drove off, leaning over the wheel, squinting as if there were rain or fog, though the night was dry and utterly clear.

As he circled confusedly through the town, trying to find his way to the place the man had told him of, his silence made it hard to suppress the questions and the fears. Fox. For the first time she allowed herself to think of him, of his dreadful hurt and terrifying rage when he found out. She had totally betrayed him. Oddly, she was not shaken by that thought; a cold-blooded selfishness she had never suspected herself of possessing made it curiously easy to set aside the thought of Fox, made her even glad that he was penned up where he could not have blocked or spoiled this. Tonight was her night, her own night, her dream come true, and she was entitled to it. Questions or none, whatever the reasons, Heath had made her his wife, and she was forever beyond Fox's reach now, anyhow. What frightened her more was her own ignorance, a terror that he would find her stupid and silly for not knowing what came next.

But she didn't know. She had never read a story that would guide her past this point, and now she was in a situation utterly beyond predicting. When they reached the hotel, what happened then? She understood the mechanics of it only vaguely, for no one had ever told her, and she had never seen a man totally naked, not even Fox, especially not Fox. She looked at the dark form beside her. She could smell the sweat and whiskey odor of him, and, since she was very close, even feel the heat of his body. Well, he loved her and he would teach her. He would know all about it. And she would learn as quickly as she could. Then she thought of Evelyn Ford, not in jealousy, but in triumph and contempt. *Hi!* she thought, *now you like this, you old Evelyn Ford?*

The hotel was near the railroad tracks. She had never been in one before. He parked the car; a Negro man came shuffling out to take the bags, his eyes seeming to add them like a column of figures, then mock them both; and she did not like him. But her dislike vanished when he followed Heath into the lobby. She had never seen anything like this: all marble, soft rugs, pretty red plush furniture. She was lost in wonder until she heard Heath mutter, "I want a room for me and my wife, a double room. With a bath, if you got it."

For me and my wife. Then they rode an elevator. She gasped as it went up. Then the room, a splendor she had never imagined. The bathroom, too, was a miracle. She had never bathed in anything but a galvanized tin tub in all her life, and she stared at the ornate and massive vessel of gleaming white on its lion-paw feet, the spotless tile; and then she saw herself in the full-length mirror on the door and caught her breath.

It was her first really clear look at herself in all her life, and it was ghastly.

The wind had ripped her hair until it fell in frowsy tatters all around her face. Her dress was rumpled, dirty, with ugly sweat stains beneath the arms. Her hands and feet so big, her face so sharp and ugly— Suddenly her heart sank. Oh, Lord, how could he love someone who looked like that? She moved numbly back into the main room, from which the bellboy was just taking leave. The door closed behind him with finality, and they were alone, and Pearl was sick with apprehension and knowledge of her own unloveliness. This was wrong; the girls in the stories were all so thrilling.

She did not feel thrilling. She felt sad and confused and absolutely bone weary. But she must not show that to him; she must not disappoint him.

He turned from the door. Seeing him in good light, her heart dipped further. His eyes were sunken in his head, darkly circled. His white shirt was filthy, as soaked with sweat as her dress; his brown hair was windblown and tangled. He was, in that moment, almost ugly and certainly frightening. Sitting on the bed, she waited for him to say something.

He did. He said, "Christ, I'm tired and I hurt all over." Then he went to the dresser. He had brought up the whiskey jug in its brown paper wrapper. There was not much left in it. He drank and dragged deeply on a cigarette and then turned and passed the jug to her. The smell of it made her sick and she handed it back wordlessly. He capped it and put it on the dresser. "Pearl," he said. He was beginning something, and she was afraid of what.

Quickly, for the protection of both of them, she said, "You look turrble tired. You ought to git some rest."

He blinked. "Rest?" Then he laughed, a sound that deepened her apprehension, and rubbed his face. "Yes. Jesus, that's what I need. Rest. Excuse me." He simply threw himself across the bed, face down, beside her, and groaned softly. She was afraid he'd burn himself with the cigarette and took it from his hand. He made no protest, and she got up to put it out. Just before she stubbed it in the ashtray, curiosity overcame her. She sucked a long drag from the end wet with his saliva, found its taste bitter, and extinguished it. When she turned around he was snoring.

And Pearl sighed with relief.

For the moment the fact of marriage was enough. It was all she could cope with, all she needed now. Her head was bursting with new experience, unabsorbed. They were alone together. That was enough wedding night for her.

Then it occurred to her that she should undress him. She had the right, and he should be put in bed properly and made comfortable. Besides, it would give her some idea of what to expect; if she could see him naked while he slept, she would betray no surprise or shock when whatever it was that had to happen happened.

He still wore the heavy work shoes of the mill. She unlooped their laces from the metal hooks, removed them from his pungent feet, and stripped away damp socks. He did not stir.

"Heath, honey," she said, "lemme help you git them clothes off," but his snoring rasped on. He was heavy, but she rolled him over, and he did not even flicker an eye. She tugged until he lay properly on the bed. Once he said, "Look out. There's another one up yonder." Otherwise he was inert as a sack of flour.

Unbuttoning his shirt, she worked it off. Beneath it, B.V.D.s, sweat-plastered, clung to his body. She hesitated, then unbuckled his belt and tugged pants down the long

length of thighs and calves. He helped her there, uncon
sciously arching his body. Then he was stripped, but fo
the suit of one-piece underwear. She hesitated, looking a
the long, hairy columns of his legs, the outflung arms
strong and muscular even in repose. She was a little awec
by the difference of his body from hers, the hardness o
it and the latent, hairy, brutal power. Then she decidec
to remove the underwear as well.

Of course she knew how it worked; Fox wore the sam
kind and she had washed it often enough. She went abou
it carefully, peeling it from him slowly, staring curiousl
at each inch of the body that now belonged to her an
had become her responsibility. When she got it dow
past the thighs, she froze. She stared at what was there
with no response at first but curiosity. So that was wha
a man was like. Yes. Now, this went into her. She knev
that much. And even as she tried to imagine how i
would work and feel, she was a little repelled by it
ugliness and at the same time excited by the sense of sin
an illicit thrill. She touched it, finding it soft, damp
flaccid. He did not stir.

For a moment, then, with a sense of luxury that ha
nothing really to do with sex, she examined him, satisfie
herself as to how he was made and what he felt like
Heath snored raspingly. But as her hand touched an
moved him, a curious thing began to happen. She let g
in surprise, then touched again and watched. Now sh
understood. Now she thoroughly understood. Only . .
was she supposed to receive *that*? Could she? Suddenl
she dared not pursue this any longer. She stripped th
underwear off. As it cleared his feet, he made a sound i
his throat, rolled over, and Pearl sucked in her breath i
a sob of pity and of outrage.

His body was a hideous reddish-purple mass, from
shoulder blades down across the compact buttocks t
the bend of knees. Good Lord in heaven! she though
He done all that today when he was in that sort o
shape? No wonder that he drank so much whiskey, n
wonder he was tired! She stood up straight, grimly. No
only Sonny Ford, she thought, but her own daddy! Sh

had heard enough today to know what happened. Her own daddy had stood there and let them do that to him. Suddenly, teeth grinding hard, she hated Fox. That he could stand by and let them beat Heath like that—

But, curiously, she was glad, too, that he was hurt. Because it gave her a chance to take care of him. She would find some medicine tomorrow and rub his back, make him well. She would be so tender and loving with him— He would love her even more for taking care of him, and at the same time she had a chance to prove her love for him. She pulled the covers from beneath him, then drew them over him.

He slept. She was, really, alone in the room. She went into the bathroom, closed the door. Taking off her clothes, in the light of her new knowledge she appraised her body. Whatever it felt like, good or bad, she would endure it, she decided. Because they loved each other.

She experimented with the tub, and enjoyed for the first time a bath that she had not had to carry or heat and that she would not have to empty by hand afterward. There was soap, and it was not like her own homemade stuff, but smelled like flowers. She laved herself all over with it and felt different at once as its perfume filled her nostrils; she submerged, boneless, disembodied, savoring the perfume, dreaming fantastic dreams. A long time afterward, having washed her hair with the same sweet-smelling soap, she dried herself on the fluffiest, most luxurious towel she had ever felt against her flesh, vowing she'd never use a sugar sack again.

Naked, wet hair plastered down around her shoulders, she crept out into the room, timidly, but he was still unconscious. She opened the suitcase. Every nightgown in it was made of sugar sacking. She felt a stinging in her eyes; she could not wear such a thing to bed and have him find her in it when he awakened. She tried to think of what to do and found no answer. Then she made up her mind with a boldness that startled even her. Better to wear nothing than such ugly sleeping clothes. Nothing at all. Her heart pounded; her breasts were taut, her nipples hard. She pulled back the sheet and counterpane and saw his poor, purple abused back again. She got down in beside him, turned off the lamp on the table. She moved against him. For the first time her naked flesh touched that of a man. It was warm, exciting. She rolled over, gingerly touched her breasts to his back, pushed her body against the hard round curves of his buttocks, put her arm about him. Suddenly she wanted to push her breasts hard against him, but she knew that would hurt him. She savored the warmth that emanated from his body. Almost before she knew it, then, she slept.

It happened in the middle of the night.

Only half awake, she felt it, hard and probing, against her legs. She had, at first, no idea what it was. Then she put her hand down and touched something like warm, moist iron, and even in her daze of sleep she understood, and at the touch of that hand something happened, he moved and shoved hard. Slowly her head cleared, she began to pant with excitement and with fear. "Heath," she whispered. "Honey . . ." He did not answer.

But, imperiously, that hard thing moved against her. She bit her lip. His body was plastered tightly against her, she felt his breath on her neck. Something strange was happening to her too, a loosening and a sudden wetness. Her own hips moved in response. Behind her breasts her heart was like a hammer. Then a heavy thigh was thrown across her, that gouging motion harder, more insistent. It jabbed blindly at her thighs and belly, and she put down her hand again and guided it. Then, with sudden decisiveness, she twisted, impaled herself. Immediately she felt the pain, sharp, ugly, and more wetness. It was most unpleasant, but it quickly faded, and there was new sensation. . . .

In the darkness, then, he mounted her, his body crushing hers. "Heath," she said again, hoarsely, but he did not answer, his face buried in her neck. Instinctively, she began to kiss him, the side of his head, his ear, the sweat-wet hair.

She was fully awake throughout, intent on the fading pain, the growing pleasure, the novelty of it all, learning,

learning. Her body had its own will, moving rhythmically beneath him; large as that instrument was, she found no real difficulty in accepting it. Her legs came up, as she suddenly had a need to feel it more deeply within her; she clasped him to her with them, quite unthinkingly, only trying in a strange, pleasurable haze, to get more of him in her. At that instant something happened. He went tense, she felt him jerking spasmodically, outside and within her. She thought there was greater wetness now. Then he groaned, oddly, and his body ceased its ramming, seemed to die upon her, its great weight crushing down on her thin and fragile form. She held him tightly, strangely disappointed that it was over, yet thrilled with her new knowledge. So that was it, that . . . Not bad at all, good, in fact, and well within her capability. Relief flooded through her, and a sense of well-being, not at all tainted by the uncomfortable burning. His breathing became regular again; she felt him diminish within her. Then he pulled away. "Honey," she said. "Oh, honey." But he was lying on his back, and now his snoring deepened.

Pearl lay there for a while. Maybe it was just as well he hadn't awakened, but how could a man do such a thing in his sleep? He hadn't even kissed her. Then she thought, with a burst of revelation like a sunrise, *Now I can have his baby!*

Through with the present, her mind raced ahead, formed more pictures. They hazed through her consciousness in colorful, ecstatic blurs. But at last the body intruded, she had to get up and go to the bathroom. There she looked appalled at the blood on her thighs, but it had stopped flowing, and would never come again; the seal she knew was there had at last been broken. Suddenly she felt older, stronger, capable of facing anything. Coolly she ran water in the tub and bathed again. When she got out, the burning was gone and once more she smelled like flowers. Her hair, dry now, was mussed and frizzy, but certainly it was cleaner and lighter than she had ever seen it. In the lighted bathroom she combed her hair before the long mirror, brought it to a glisten

and a sheen, and stared at the thin body that only a
little while ago had been a child's and now belonged to
an experienced woman, and smiled at herself in the glass
with a confidence she had never known before.

13   HEATH HAD only vague recollection of de-
flowering her in sleep; the act had been an explosion
of tension, as instinctive and impersonal as the mating of
frogs, on his part totally selfish and even brutal. In fact,
until he saw the blood on the sheets next morning he was
not entirely sure he had not dreamed it.

He awakened with throbbing head and burned-out,
sticky mouth; then, as he rolled over, it all came back
like a blow between the eyes. She was there—straw-
colored hair fanned across the pillow, sharp face in profile, lips peeled back from teeth, one of which was
crooked, as she breathed between them. "Oh, Christ," he
whispered, as the full import of it all sank in.

Shaking violently, he eased from bed. The sheet was
half thrown back, the little breasts, the ribby flanks,
exposed and naked. That was when he saw the tiny spots
of dried blood. He clenched his teeth, ran to the bathroom.

That interval alone in there, facing his beardy, stinking self, rank with whiskey, sweat, and the aftertaint of
sex, was the most terrible and racking of his life. He
vomited dryly into the toilet bowl, raising nothing but
greenish bile. Then he turned on the faucets of the tub.

*Well, you've really fixed it, ain't you, you stupid bas-
tard? You've fixed everybody—Fox, Mother, the Old Man,
Pearl—hell, even the Fords. Not to mention yourself. You
God damned idiot.* Scrubbing frantically, as if to wash
away his sins, over and over, he recited the dreadful inventory. *Why didn't you just kill yourself and save everybody a lot of trouble? You drunken, stupid asshole!*

Then, reaction. All right, he'd bitched everything for
everybody. There was no punishment dire enough—except to live with what he had done. Somehow he had to

force himself to do that, to face the music, to stop re-
treating into drunkenness, flight, and the search for death.
Death was too good for him; life, with all its complications, was what he had earned. "You made your bed," he
rasped at his image in the mirror as he shaved. "Now,
God damn you, you're gonna lie in it whether you want
to or not." A towel wrapped around his loins, he returned hesitantly to the bedroom.

She still slept; quickly he dressed in clean clothes and
felt less helpless. As he buttoned his shirt Pearl stirred,
awakened. She turned her head, looked at him with a
glow in those green eyes that was unmistakable. God help
them both, the fool girl loved him! No wonder she had
let him do it—she had a silly crush on him!

"Good mornin, honey." He tried not to flinch at that
nasal whine. "Good morning," he answered tonelessly.
This is your bride. . . . She lay motionless, looking at him
with that absurd expression; she expected him to come
to her, had that right, but he could not bring himself to
do it. There was an awkward silence. Then Pearl sat up,
holding the sheet about her. Her voice was timid. "I
reckon I had better git up and dressed."

"Yes," Heath said. "I need some cigarettes. I'll go
downstairs and buy 'em." Before she could answer he
went out and closed the door.

On his way he thought: We have got to talk. The only
thing to do is to give it to her straight. It's cruel to let
her think . . . It would be kinder to her to let her know
exactly where she stands without deception. I'm through
with deception—I've had enough of that. While he bought
the unneeded cigarettes, paced a lobby coming to life
with traveling salesmen preparing for their rounds, giving her plenty of time, he made that resolve. As soon
as he went upstairs they'd have it out, talk over every
aspect of the situation, calmly and with common sense.
After all, it was not, come to think of it, totally his fault.
If Holding had not sent her to such a sleazy place, if she
had not begged him to take her with him, if Fox had kept
out of that incident at the river . . . They all bore blame,
including Bolivar. And so they would all have to help

him straighten out this mess. His mind was sure, made up, when he went back to the room.

He went in without knocking, to find that he had not given her time enough after all. He surprised her in a tattered slip, pawing desperately through the pile of clothes thrown onto the bed. "What's the matter?" he asked.

"I ain't got nothing— I mean, I'm wondering what to wear." Her cheeks turned pink, her eyes slid away from his.

"Let's see."

"No, wait—" But he was already sorting through the things, saw the underclothing and the nightgowns made of sugar sacks, their faded labels still visible, the old and formless dress or two. Appalled, he felt a thrust of pity. Nevertheless his face was hard, his voice almost brutal as he said, "Put on this and this. Then I'll cash a check and you can buy some clothes and we'll eat." He turned away. "Holding said Fox had money. Didn't he ever give you any to spend?"

Her voice was faint, apologetic. "I never needed much out there."

"Well, you're not going to New York in those things. Hurry up."

And now, somehow, his resolve had vanished. What he felt instead was a smoldering fury at the cheapness and narrowness of them all: the ignorant moonshiner who had kept his daughter prisoner and in rags, the sheriff who had sent her to a place like Bailey's to save a dollar . . . By God, beside them both he was a monument of decency, a knight in shining armor. His pity for the girl made his brutal decision impossible to carry out. Later, he thought. Later, when I have given her at least something to justify it, to lessen the sting. The opportunity for charity, for doing favor, restored a little of his self-esteem.

Also a mill town, Danville was about the size of Macedonia, but with a certain saving grace of antiquity and tradition. Even so, its best shop was nothing special. Within it Pearl was awed and helpless; it was obvious that she knew nothing about what to wear or how to buy it. Heath placed her in the hands of a saleswoman, warning the latter with his eyes against sarcasm or condescension. Then he went to cash a check.

There was no trouble; the name of Chandler was well known here, and his own especially, because of his war exploits. When he returned to the store the woman had laid out a great deal of stuff, and Pearl was standing in the midst of it, baffled and near panic. Heath took over; consulting with the clerk, he ignored Pearl, choosing what seemed to him the best. In addition to dresses and undergarments, silk stockings, shoes and a hat had to be purchased. When it had all been taken care of, he sent Pearl with the woman to change. Waiting for her, he rambled aimlessly through the store.

This, he knew, was stalling. This and breakfast—temporary reprieves; then they had to face the bitter part of it. Somehow the news must be broken to the Chandlers and to Fox. The thought of that sickened him with fear. It should be done, of course, by long-distance telephone; but even if they could get through, he thought he lacked the nerve. Letters were the safest way; in letters he could explain himself more fully. But perhaps he'd have to find the nerve.

Then Pearl came out in sand-colored, tailored suit, lowered straw hat, walking awkwardly in shoes with heels higher than she was used to. Her face a study in mingled delight and apprehension, she halted while he looked her over. "I feel kinda funny in this git-up."

"It's all right," he said. "You look good." In a sense it was true; as much had been done with her as was possible. At least he could walk the street or enter a restaurant beside her without embarrassment—so long, he thought, as she kept her mouth shut. He was rewarded for the compliment by a light of pleasure that, wholly spontaneous, sprang suddenly from within her, illuminating thin features, sallow skin, and huge green eyes in an almost startling way.

The hotel dining room was large, with gilt scrollwork on its walnut columns. They sat at a large table with linen

cloth and napkins, sturdy silverware, attended by a so
licitous Negro in white uniform, and while Heath or
dered enormous breakfasts for both, Pearl looked aroun
covertly, her wonder plain.

Watching her, it came to him how many millions lik
her, especially in the South, lived lives of utter, primi
tive drabness, squalor. She was not unique in never hav
ing been more than thirty miles from home, or, unti
now, never having slept in a hotel, used a modern bath
room or eaten in a decent restaurant; there were horde
of people condemned forever to the darkness of ignor
ance, grinding labor, and utter poverty, from which sh
now marveled to find herself delivered. The differenc
was that most of the others would have recoiled in frigh
from the opportunity to escape, would have lacked th
nerve to seize it. Not her. That one, flickering, outsid
chance, and she had taken it bravely, boldly, withou
hesitation. His eyes narrowed as he looked her ove
Where had she found the courage? *I got to be free!* sh
had cried. There was, perhaps, more to her than met th
eye, something in her he did not understand. Then sh
looked at him, and he dropped his eyes to his coffee.

They both ate hungrily, and at last, with food in hir
coffee, his body no longer a throbbing torment, hea
clearer now, he had to come to grips with reality. Pear
he realized suddenly, was necessary to him after al
Maybe that was what he had been about subconsciousl
last night—using her to lock up, guarantee, the impossi
bility of his ever going back. Maybe, in a way, she was a
necessary to his freedom as he to hers. At any rate, sh
was not the only one whose life had changed last nigh
clearly, completely, forever. Sitting here, she was proo
that his break with Bolivar was final; and, strangely, h
began to feel lifting from his shoulders a huge, invisibl
weight that had borne him down for months. The di
was cast.

And so, calmer, possessed now of justification, he coul
face what he had to do. "The next thing is," he saic
laying down his fork, "we've got to tell them. My parent
And Fox."

She paled. "Yes. Oh, Lord. Daddy. I . . . I don't think I kin do it."

"You won't have to. It's up to me. But we're not leaving Danville until I can get through long-distance calls to Chandler House and the Macedonia jail."

Two hours later he had done it, and then, once more, he went to the jar on the dresser and drained it, sick and shaken.

His mother had been incredulous, then wept, tried to brave it out, and wept again.

Fox Ramsey, brought down to Holding's office from his cell, had listened quietly. Then, in the coldest, most dangerous voice Heath had ever heard, he said: "You got jest as long as it takes them to turn me loose. Then, if you ain't looked after her the best you can, I'll find you wherever you are and kill you dead." He hung up before Heath could protest or speak or make any of the promises that bubbled to his lips.

Next he talked to Bolivar, who was at his office. He had half expected the Old Man to refuse the call. However, Chandler took it. "Hello," he said.

"Dad, it's Heath. I—"

"I know," said Chandler. "Your mother told me. The doctor's with her now."

"Oh, Lord, Papa, I—"

"That's enough," said Bolivar. "I don't ever want to see or hear of you again." His voice was steady, businesslike. "From this day forward your sins are on your own head. I have no son."

"Papa—"

"Goodbye," said Bolivar tersely, and something clicked.

Heath said, hoarsely, into the mouthpiece, "Dad. Dad, I—Papa?"

The operator said, in a motherly voice, "I'm sorry. The gentleman has hung up."

"Yes," said Heath. "Yes, I know he has. Thank you." And he put the receiver in its hook and went upstairs to tell Pearl, who had not dared be with him when he placed the calls.

She listened in silence, drawn face paper-white, hands

twisting nervously. Her voice was small when she asked, "Whut do we do now?"

Heath threw the empty jar into a wastebasket. "Just what I said," he told her grimly. "We go on to New York."

14   THEY BURST IN on the party unannounced. By then, while she had goggled at the unimaginable city, trying to restrain the impulse to laugh and cry and shout with excitement to vent the emotions the soaring buildings and heavy traffic stirred in her, Heath had already found a speakeasy and acquired two bottles of gin as a gift for his friend with the funny name, Olin Clutterbuck.

Then Greenwich Village and up a dirty stair that smelled bad, and when Heath flung the door open, the noise, laughter and frantic music all leaped out at Pearl, frightening and exhilarating her. A tall, redhaired man in shirtsleeves and paint-smeared pants, glass in hand, stared blankly at Heath on the threshold. Then he whooped and launched himself. She stood back shyly as the two yelled and hugged and pounded one another. Then Heath said something that made the redhead's face change, go blank. Heath's lips moved again; she read the words somehow: *A long story.* Then Clutterbuck—it must be he —recovered. He strode to her, embraced her, swept her into the turmoil of the loft. "Well, Pearl, you've accomplished the impossible! Congratulations!" Swaying a little, he kissed her on the mouth.

Everybody seemed to know Heath. Pearl saw faces light up with pleasure at his presence—and the women! She did not know what to do when girl after girl embraced Heath, kissed him. Then he began to try to introduce her, but in the uproar she caught no names. They understood though that she was Heath Chandler's wife, and she saw more than once the same blank look of astonishment that Clutterbuck's face had worn. All at once she realized that Heath was gone; he had been swept off to be the center of a knot of people who were laughing, shouting; she saw women put their hands on him. She tried to get through to stand beside him, but there were too many bodies; they shut her out.

Unutterably lonely, she withdrew, found a vacant corner. It had taken two more days of traveling to reach the city, and during all that time he had never said what she had been waiting for, the one phrase that would complete the pattern of the story. Not even when, last night in Baltimore, *it* had happened for the second time. First he had shown her the city, fed her supper in a good restaurant; she had never before eaten anything that had come from the ocean, had been hesitant, overcome her qualms, and found the shellfish delicious. But they could not stay out all night; at last they had to be alone in the hotel room. *It* had happened almost as if it were easier for him to do that than talk to her. To her dismay she had not really enjoyed it; she had been too tense, and he had been a little drunk and had hurt her, although not very much, and afterward had rolled over and gone to sleep almost at once. She had lain awake for a long time. Of course she knew that the way old Bolivar Chandler had taken the news had almost driven him crazy; he tried to hide it, but he had drawn into himself, been quiet, snappish, touchy. Curiously, she hardly thought of Fox or what he must feel; she had written him a short letter but had not been able to get out of her mind the fact that somebody else would have to read it to him, and that had kept her from saying very much. Finally she had arisen, switched on a little lamp on the dresser, opened her purse, and taken out the two stiff little pieces of cardboard bound with the red ribbon. They *existed*, in all their rose-emblazoned reality. She was his wife. Nothing could change that. For the rest, she had to be patient, let everything work itself out. He had already done so much for her. . . .

But today, as they drew closer to New York, he had begun to brighten. When they reached the city he was different, a person she had never seen before. The gloom was gone, he smiled, whistled, and once, in their room at the Algonquin Hotel, even put his arm about her and embraced her briefly, as if he could not contain himself. Then he had dressed for the first time in suit and tie, and she had caught her breath in pride that such a handsome man belonged to her.

Now, though, she understood the reason for his gaiety. It had nothing to do with her; it was just that he was back where he belonged. Encircled by the crowd, his laugh—deep, rich with pleasure—sounded often, and he was talking a streak, as if a dam within him had burst, releasing a torrent of pent-up words. There was no sign that he even remembered she existed.

She decided to make the best of it. If these were the kind of people he liked, she wanted to know, understand, and learn to be like them. They were all young, of course, and for the most part unlike anything she had ever seen before, even in magazines. Some of the men were wildly dressed, and a surprising number of them wore their hair almost as long as women; in fact, a few bore themselves eerily like females. Conversely, she was startled by how short the girls had cut their hair; moreover, most had painted faces, skirts halfway to their knees, and smoked and drank without shame, just like men! Two of them, with very short hair indeed, she glimpsed in a dim corner across the room, holding hands and nuzzling each other in a most curious way. Then she became aware of a presence over her—Clutterbuck.

"Gosh, woman," he said, "you don't even have a drink. Here." He thrust a glass of something yellow in her hand. "Try an orange blossom."

She looked up at the gaunt, kind face beneath the tousled red hair. She liked him at once, hoped he would stay and talk. "You need a sponsor," he said. "I don't blame you for being wary of this crowd." Turning, he called, "Hey, Jeannie! One moment." He leaned out, caught the wrist of a lush, striking girl in a red dress and loops and loops of clicking black beads. "This is Heath's wife, Pearl. Pearl, this is Jeannie Vann. The two of you'll see a lot of each other; you might as well get acquainted. Show her around and introduce her, will you, Jeannie?" Then he drifted off.

Jeannie had short, chestnut hair, a face round and almost childish, enormous eyes smeared with some sort of black paint, a tiny, full, red-painted mouth. Her breasts were large white slopes showing beneath the beads that covered the lowcut neckline of the dress. She had a glass of gin in one hand, a cigarette in the other. "So you're the one," she said.

"The one what?"

"Who finally caught *him*." Jeannie jerked her head. "Don't you just know every woman in this room just hates you?"

"Hates me? Why?"

"For God's sake, honey!" Then Jeannie sobered, really looked at Pearl for the first time. "That the way they wear their hair down south?"

Instinctively Pearl touched the pinned-up mass. "What's wrong with it?"

"Nothing, I guess. Only, it's not New York—you understand? I'll take you to my hairdresser, you can get it shingled. Olin's right, I guess we'll see a lot of each other."

"Are you his girl friend?"

She had a raucous laugh. "Yeah. And his model. See?" She gestured, and for the first time Pearl saw the half-finished painting propped against the wall by a washstand. She stared. It was undeniably Jeannie, and Jeannie was undeniably naked. "Okay, you're shocked. Well, I was, too, when I first hit this town. It's a long way from Zanesville, Ohio. It takes some getting used to. But don't panic. We'll make a New Yorker out of you in no time. You and Heath *are* going to stay here, aren't you?"

"I . . . I don't know." It occurred to her that he had said nothing about the future.

"Oh, you will. This is his kind of town." She gripped Pearl's arm, leaned close. "Only, if you can, just keep him out of those damned airplanes—you understand? That's all you got to worry about, those damned airplanes. He and Olin, they're worse about those than liquor and women. Olin's got all these friends that he was in the

Army with, and they fly, and he goes up with them sometimes, and my heart just stops . . ."

"You're in love with him."

"Mad about him. He's lucky I am too. If he didn't have
me to look after him he'd starve to death or run around
naked. You should have seen how he lived before I moved
in—"

"You live here with him?"

Jeannie looked astonished. "Sure. How do you think
he gets along? He couldn't even afford a model if it
weren't for me, and what I make posing for other people
buys the groceries. Come on now, I'll show you around.
The men'll really fall for that cute little old southern
accent of yours. You're going to have to teach me how to
put it on."

The rest of the evening was a blur. Pearl drank the
orange blossom and then another and one more after that.
Jeannie gave her a cigarette, and she felt awkward with
it, but all the other girls—the ones Heath seemed to enjoy
so much—were smoking. It made her cough at first, but
after two more she could draw smoke into her lungs and
blow it out like any of them. The music! The phonograph
played all the time, sometimes slowly, sweetly, and sometimes with a wild, jarring rhythm that, she found, stirred
her blood. People were dancing in the most shocking
way. Once one girl did a solo while everyone watched.
It was as if somebody invisible were making love to her.
She shook her breasts, thrust with her hips. Pearl felt hot
blood mount to her cheeks.

A man asked her to dance. He was tall, muscular,
bearded. She did not know what to say—she had never
danced in her life. Before she could find an excuse he
had her in his arms. She tried to imitate the movements
she had seen. The giddiness she felt, the slamming beat
of music, helped. She caught its rhythm, but she was
knotted up inside the whole time. When the music
stopped she tried to escape, but he held her, and then
they danced again. Midway through that dance she felt
a hard, gouging bulge against her that she would not
even have recognized a few days before, but which she

now understood thoroughly, and she was frightened. Not so much by its pressure as by the fact that it excited her—and he was a stranger! When that record ended, confused and flustered, she broke away, at last found her way through the crowd to Heath.

He glanced at her briefly, then went on talking. She could not really understand a word he said: "Immelman . . . Archie . . . SE-5 . . . Squadron . . . Spad . . . Fokker." The bearded man seized her again. Helplessly, she danced with him once more. In a corner he tried to kiss her, but she evaded that. He put a hand on her breasts, and she pushed it away. He grunted something and left her alone. She could feel the pressure of his palm, it seemed, for a long time afterward.

Now Heath was talking with the only older man at the party. They were in one corner, engaged in earnest conversation. The man was blocky, in his forties, well dressed, with an aggressive, bullish look. He kept waving the hand that held his drink. She tried to engage Heath's attention, but he was rapt. "Listen, Colonel," she heard him say, "if it sold for the right price—" She gave up, drifted off. Moved up to two young men who kept waving their hands and clutching each other as they talked. When she heard one of them call the other "My dear," she was no longer even surprised; anything could happen here. "There is still room for elegance," one of them was saying; the other kept shaking his head and shrilling, "No, no, no, no . . ." A mannish-looking woman engaged her in conversation next, her eyes seeming to go right through the dress, so that Pearl felt naked and uncomfortable. She was glad when Jeannie claimed her again. She had to go to the bathroom. It was down the hall, and there were roaches in it. When she came back, there was a flow of movement toward the door. Then she, Heath, Clutterbuck and Jeannie were finally alone. They all sat on the floor, with a bottle of gin and another of orange juice in the middle. But at least she could be near him, although she and Jeannie were still ignored. Heath, with drunken intensity, wagged his finger at Clutterbuck. "Baldwin. God, he was magnificent. Remember

how he stole the six Spads from the depot in Paris? I'll
bet the Goddamned Frogs are still trying to figure out
who lifted all their airplanes."

"All the same," Clutterbuck said, "all the same, that's
a lot of money."

"I'm no fool, I'll check it first. But I trust Baldwin.
And, my God, Clutt, if this comes off, think of the
market!"

"Just the same—" said Clutterbuck.

"You'll look adorable with short hair," Jeannie said.
"It'll feel funny at first, but you've got just the face for
it. Look, if you ever need to, I can get you some
modeling . . ."

Then, somehow, through a city glittering with lights
even at such an hour, the magnificent buildings towering
high above, they were back at the hotel. The lobby was
thronged with men in evening dress, women in revealing
gowns. Pearl stared as they crossed it to the elevator. In
their own room, Heath uncorked a bottle, poured another
drink. He pulled down his tie, unbuttoned his collar.
Without removing coat and vest he sank into a chair,
propped his feet on the bed. "Well," he said, face flushed,
eyes glittering, looking at her. "Well, how did you like
it—your first taste of New York night life and *la vie
bohème?*"

"I don't know," she said. "It was different." Suddenly
she felt a need to show him what she'd learned. She
took a cigarette from his pack, lit it, inhaled. He looked
at her with surprise, then wry amusement. "You learn
fast," he said.

"All the girls were smokin 'em." She blew smoke. "Tomorrow, if you don't mind, Jeannie's gonna take me to
git my hair cut."

"Good," he said. "I'll shell out some money. You need
some more clothes, good ones, the kind you couldn't
get in Danville. Try some makeup too."

"I aimed to," she said.

"Well," he said, "you're way ahead of me, ain't you?"
Then he laughed. "You and Jeannie go your way. I've

got business to attend to. I struck it lucky tonight. If everything works out, I've already got a job."

"What? What kind?"

"Baldwin. Colonel Alec Baldwin. I got to know him when Clutt and I were transferred to the AEF. He was in charge of aircraft procurement. Everybody wanted Spads, they were the only things that could really out-fight the D-7s. But the French tried to keep them all for themselves. God knows how many of 'em Baldwin stole for us, but he was a man who got things done, a real go-getter."

She only vaguely understood, but already she felt cold. "Airplanes?"

"Yeah. He's got a company out on Long Island now. The Army bought a lot of Jennies and DH-4s and now they've got no use for 'em. Congress has just passed a law that they've all got to be broken up and sold for scrap. Baldwin's made arrangements to buy 'em. A little greasing of the palms, and they won't be broken up too badly. He's got a shop that will cannibalize them, make new airplanes out of old ones. He can buy them as junk, resell them as first-class flying machines. On top of that, he's designed a plane of his own, a marvelous thing, the way he describes it. Sort of based on the old Fokker monoplane that came out just before the end of the war. Calls it the Tiercel—that's a male hawk, the female's a falcon. It'll be a plane for businessmen. Flying's the thing of the future, you know—there's nothing like it for getting from one place to the other, and sooner or later the American businessman, whatever he is, will get the idea. When he does, Baldwin aims to be in on the ground floor. He wants me to come in with him, invest a little money, be his test pilot." He drained his glass. "Oh, God. Oh, God, it's so good to be back in civilization. You don't know how good it is."

"Airplanes," she said again, and remembering what Jeannie had told her, it seemed to her that her heart faltered.

"Yeah. The automobile made the horse obsolete, now the airplane's going to make the automobile obsolete. It'll carry the mail, fly passengers— Why not? There's no limit to what an airplane can do. If I go in with Baldwin, there's no limit to how much money I can make either, when it catches on. I'll help him with his design, with sales, and in between-times I'll take each new plane up and shake it out. Right down my alley."

Her hand was on her breast. "But it's dangerous . . . isn't it?"

He laughed. "It's fun," he said. "That's the main thing. Gosh, it feels good to be where it's not illegal to be alive." He finished his drink, seemingly very sober. "Of course I'll examine the proposition, I'll examine it very closely, but if it works out the way I think it will—" As if he could not sit still, he bounced to his feet, began to pace the room, radiating so much strength, vitality, force that it was almost frightening. She felt a need to shield herself from it, found one of her new nightgowns, went into the bathroom. There she washed, cleaned her mouth with the first toothbrush she had ever owned. She could hear him pacing out there, the clink of bottle and glass; and she was still afraid and could not imagine why. But he was even more of a stranger now than he had been before; just as she had become accustomed to one person, he had become another.

When she came back into the bedroom in the nightgown, which was frilly but modest, he was sitting on the bed, glass cradled between his palms. He was staring down into it as if he saw pictures there. Then he lifted his head, looked at her for a moment with a kind of cold objectivity, as if she were a purchase he had made without thinking, and now that he was home with it was trying to decide what he had got for his money. After a moment he said in a perfectly sober voice, "You know, this is a hell of a complicated situation we're in."

"I reckon," Pearl said faintly.

"I mean—" He gestured. "I promised Fox I'd look after you. So don't you worry. I'm going to do it. I'm going to keep that promise."

She found nothing to answer him with except a small

"Thank you," which sounded silly even to her. But he had arisen, was pacing again.

"Only, there are some things we have to get straight, now that we've finally made it, now that things are shaping up. I mean, we've got to be honest with each other. There's no point in trying to pretend about anything—" He stopped, seemed to be searching for words as he went on pacing, not looking at her now. "I mean, everything was happening so quickly, it was all so Goddamned confused, and there had to be decisions made, and—"

And all at once she knew what he was trying to tell her. She had known it all along, but she'd refused to admit it to herself. He stood there with his back toward her. "But don't worry. You're going to have everything you're entitled to. Good clothes, and an allowance to spend and—"

"Only what you're trying to say," Pearl cut in, summoning every bit of courage she possessed to get the truth spoken and get it spoken quickly, "is that you didn't really mean to marry me."

"Yeah, I did too." He turned quickly. "But I should have talked to you first about why. It wasn't fair to either of us not to have done that first. It was—"

She began to move. Not willing herself to, but as if someone else were pushing her, jerking her arms and legs and body as if she were a puppet on a string. Her eyes burned with tears, but what she felt was, for the first time, total rage directed at another human, fury that left no room for grief, shame, or humility. With a jerk that tore the lace, she stripped off the nightgown, threw it on the bed. Unmindful of her nudity, she seized the clothes she had just removed, began to dress. Heath stared blankly. "What the hell?"

She sat on the bed in her chemise, pulled on her stockings, did not answer. Suddenly he was on her, seized her arm, yanked her to her feet. "What do you think you're doing?" he grated.

She tore loose with a strength she had not dreamed she possessed. Without answering, she reached for the dress. It slid over her head; she looked around for her shoes.

"Now, listen!" Heath rasped. "I don't know what—"

Pearl stopped. She was racked by rage—all at once it exploded from her. "No, *you* listen!" Her voice was thin, cold, ugly, cutting—a stranger's voice, old, hard, bereft of tears. "All I asked you to do was bring me up here. I didn't ask you to buy me clothes or marry me or nothin else! I jest asked you for the ride."

"I know, but—"

"Shut up!" she screamed. "You shut up and let me talk! I know you did it while you were drunk, you didn't know what you were doin! I know I ain't the kind of woman you want, the kind I saw crawlin all over you tonight! Well, don't worry, Heath Chandler, I ain't goin to git between you and them. It wasn't my idea to stop off in Danville like that, I tried to talk you outa it. You talk about lookin after me!" Her lips curled, she nearly spat. "I've looked after you all the way up here. I don't need you to see to me!"

His face went red, then white. "Pearl, wait a minute—"

"No, dammit!" she yelled, and stamped her foot. "I think you've looked after us enough! You already put my daddy in jail and done with me the same thing you done with Ev'lyn Ford and are now lookin around for somebody else to do it with! I think that's more than enough lookin after! Well, you don't have to worry about me, you kin ease your mind. I don't know why you think I need *you* to see to *me*. I don't want your money and I don't want you feelin sorry for me and I don't want anything else you got! I'm Fox Ramsey's daughter, and, thank you kindly, I can see to myself well enough!"

She drew in a long sobbing breath and, feeling as if her body were of chilled iron and had a cutting edge, strode to the closet, yanked out the suitcase. She threw it on the bed. "Go guzzle your gin and sleep with your short-haired women and have a good time and don't worry about me. I'll find somethin to do and send you the money you've done spent on me as quick as I can!" Then she thought of something, went to her handbag on the dresser. She snapped it open, fished out those two cardboard pages with their red cord binder. Coldly, she threw them squarely in his face. "If you don't want that, neither do I." They struck him right in the mouth, fluttered to the floor. She jerked open a drawer, blindly seized a double handful of new garments. Throwing them into the suitcase, she said hoarsely: "Thanks for the ride, Mr. Chandler. Thank you very much." Then they threatened to break loose—tears. Not of grief, still only of fury. But he would mistake them; she gulped them back, stayed cold.

She was aware of Heath behind her, silent, but breathing hard and audibly. She went on with her packing, motions furious and choppy. "I don't know who you think the Ramseys are," she managed hoarsely, "but they're good as the Chandlers any day. Any time the Ramseys need help from the Chandlers, they'll let you know." There were more clothes in the dresser and the closet, but she did not want them. All she wanted now was to be out of there. She closed the suitcase, did not bother with the straps, but left them dangling. She snatched it up, turned.

He stood there, between her and the door. His face was absolutely white, and that made his working mouth dark red. His eyes stared at her with a fury that matched her own.

"We don't beg from nobody," she said. "And we don't let nobody look down on us." Her voice shook. "Git outa my way." She hated him in that instant and loved him too, and the combined emotions made her feel as if she were made out of flame, cold and blue. If she had had a gun, she would have killed him first, then wept over his body. "Move," she said.

But he only shook his head.

"I said, move!" She bared her teeth, stepped forward, raised the suitcase like a mace. She was someone she had never been before, proud, immeasurably strong. He caught her wrist in a grip that hurt, squeezed until bones grated; she dropped the suitcase. Then he had her pinned, powerless, with the other hand, his face so close to hers that she smelled the liquor and tobacco on his breath. Something happened in his eyes; they changed, stirred. She saw a look of wonder on his face, felt a surge of triumph that at least he saw her now as someone human. Then he said, "No!" He pushed her backward, shoved, and she fell sprawling on the bed.

She looked up at him without fear, only rage, as he towered over her. Again his face had changed, and what she saw in it now startled and froze her for an instant: suddenly, she realized, he wanted her. Whatever she had done, it had made him, for the first time, want her. All at once it felt as if wings were beating in her. He could not want her like that, she somehow sensed, without seeing her. Not just an object, not just a woman, not just Fox Ramsey's daughter, but her, herself, Pearl! The surge of triumph mounted in her; no matter what happened from now on, she was someone new, with a power over men, power over him. She sensed at once how she had won it, and she was not about to quit now. She came up off the bed quickly, but he caught her, bore her down again. Now he was sprawled over her, pinning her, and she fought furiously, viciously, with all her strength, but counting on the fact that he was so much stronger.

Of course he was; he pinned her and she was helpless, except for the ferocity she could put in her face, her eyes. She lay there with him holding both wrists, his weight keeping her immobile, her lips peeled back in savagery, a wild excitement and delight hidden in her body. "Let me go," she managed.

"No." He threw a thigh across her; she felt a hard bulge against her. Her skirt had ridden high, one stocking had come down. She clamped her legs together. "No," he rasped. "Not until we get a lot of things straight. I'll admit—"

She bucked. "I don't care what you admit." She snarled the words. "Jest let me up. I ain't no Evelyn Ford—"

"I know you ain't."

"I'm Pearl Ramsey and I won't—"

"No," he said harshly. "You're Pearl Chandler. You'd better get that through your head."

"I won't. I didn't ask you—"

"I don't care what you asked me. I asked you."

"Stop it, you hear? You've got lots of other girls—go to 'em! Let me up, I want to leave."

He said only, "No." Then he said coldly, distinctly, "If I want another girl, I'll find one. It'll be up to you to make sure I don't."

"Go to hell," she said. "I ain't gonna do it with you. Jest because you feel sorry for me."

"I don't. I did, but not now. You tried to kill me with that damned suitcase."

"I wisht I had." But, crying now, somehow she laughed through the tears.

"You'll get another chance, you'll get lots of chances. If you'll just stay."

"You don't want me to."

"I didn't. But now I do. I really do."

She began to cough, sob. "No," she said. "Jest because Fox Ramsey is my daddy—"

"I don't give a damn who your daddy is."

"Heath, please—" She rolled her head aside. "Jest let me up and let me go."

"You don't want to go and I don't want you to go. I said, I don't give a damn who your daddy is. Not now. I don't give a damn about the other women either. Just—" His hand was tugging at her underwear. "Pearl," he said, "I want you to stay."

"Oh, Jesus, sweet Jesus." She closed her eyes.

"We've got so damned much to work out. I don't know who you are, I don't even know who I am. But we'll never find out unless you stay. Unless you give us both a chance. . . . Will you stay?"

She kept her eyes tightly closed. Then suddenly her body went lax, no more strength left. "For a while, anyway," she heard herself say.

"That's all I ask," he murmured, and she felt his lips on her ear. She knew she was a fool, but she knew that she was, also, being terribly wise. She lay quietly as he fumbled with the dress. She felt his mouth on her breasts, on the flesh between them, on her stomach. Her body moved involuntarily. "The only reason I married you," she heard herself say, "was so that we could both be . . . happy. . . . Don't, now; don't please." But he would not quit. His mouth came down on hers; she wanted him and knew now that if she took him it would not be as a beggar. While she still felt strength enough in her to resist, she made her decision. She did not have all she hungered for, but she had more than she had guessed she would get, and now she felt so much older, wiser, and experienced that at least what she wanted was not impossible. She gloried in the power she had over him, even as she was appalled by the power he had over her. He could not master the underwear; she helped him, almost numbly. Then she was naked, except for the frock crammed up around her neck. She felt him enter her, and it was different this time; she had moved up on the mountain to stand beside him as an equal; they were both out of the valley. She sighed as his mouth came down on hers. Later she always remembered that as really being her wedding night.

15   OLIN CLUTTERBUCK, seated across from Heath at the table in his studio, watched his friend pour another glass of gin. He felt not only pleasure in Heath's company again but a sense of reassurance. Lately he had begun to lose confidence in himself. The almost instant success as an artist he had half expected, even while telling himself that such expectation was foolish, had not come. He had attained no recognition at all; and he was learning now what poverty and insecurity really were. His father would have helped him, but his pride would not allow that, and lately he had felt strangely adrift and, even waking, in a dream of falling.

Now that sensation was gone. In Heath he had a partisan, someone to turn to, and, he admitted to himself, someone with money, which was even better. There was still much he did not understand about what had happened; even two days had not been time enough to get the straight of it. He had, however, already decided that he would like to paint Heath's wife. She was no beauty, true, but there was something about that gaunt, concave, foxy, curiously innocent face that had captured him.

Then he bent his mind to what Heath, who had just returned from a conference with Baldwin on Long Island, was saying. "Instead of the Army smashing those surplus planes, he's swung a deal—you know his connections. They'll just make a few token cuts with a saw. Then we bid 'em in as junk, repair 'em, sell 'em!"

"Who to?"

Heath laughed. "Maybe back to the government, if this airmail thing works out. But we see another market too. They can be fixed so one man could fly a plane to Canada and bring back ten cases of Scotch in one trip. Clutt, do you know what the average profit on a case of real Scotch is? Eighty dollars! And the Prohibition agents don't have planes! Baldwin's already been approached by certain people—"

"And this other plane he's designed—?"

"The Tiercel? That's going to be a real beauty. Cheap, fast as a scalded cat, simple to handle—you wait and see how many businessmen we can palm those off on! When they find out how much faster they can travel by plane instead of car or train . . ."

"And what about the plays you were going to write?"

"They can wait! Right now I want some action; I've been penned up too long. When Baldwin and I get this thing going, then I'll think about those, but right now—" As if it were a subject he did not want to pursue, he broke off, looked at his wristwatch. "Where're the girls? They ought to be back by this time."

Clutterbuck laughed. "With all that money you gave 'em? Jeannie hasn't seen that much cash in one hunk in her whole life, much less had it to buy things with. She and Pearl'll squeeze every drop of ecstasy out of it."

"I hope she does," Heath said. "She's entitled to a little

ecstasy." He was serious now, grave, thoughtful. "This started out as the damnedest mess—"

"I know. You told me."

"Now I've got to unwind all the damn tangle I made." He was silent for a moment. "Of course, I was drunk, but I had no idea it was gonna be this complicated. I mean, the whole time—well, I guess I was just thinking of her as some sort of . . . object. The ignorant little country girl, and me, the great Heath Chandler, conferring on her the royal favor, and not about to have his style cramped by it any more than any baron or duke. Hell, all I ever dreamed about in Chandlerville was the girls up here, how I was gonna cut a real swath. And then—" He stared at his clenched fists. "It's not working out that way. She's not going to give me the chance to work it out that way. There is . . . more to her than I counted on. Knowing her father, I should have realized that."

Clutterbuck waited. "Anyhow," Heath went on, "she's not going to let me get away with my act. She's perfectly willing to spit in my eye and tell me to go peddle my papers." He laughed shortly. "There's an old story about the balky mule, just stood there, and nothing the farmer could do would make it move. Finally a stranger volunteers; he picks up a huge wooden club, walks up to the mule, slams it across the head as hard as he can. Then he tells the mule to giddap, and it giddaps. 'That's how you make a mule go,' the stranger tells the farmer. 'First *you got to git his attention!*'" Wryly, he grinned. "Anyhow, she sure as hell got my attention the other night."

"So . . ."

"So I've got to back up and start over again. I've got to do the best I can by her, at least put on some sort of decent act."

"But you don't love her."

"Come on, Clutt. You've seen her and heard her talk. But . . . Her old man's pulling three years in the pen because of me, and I don't know how I'll ever make that up to either of 'em. Still, I've got to try. It's gonna be rough, with all these other dames right under my nose, real live ones. But I guess that's part of my punishment. Anyhow, if I can't do anything else, I can at least prepare her to look after herself. No matter what happens, I couldn't let her walk out or turn her loose the way she is now; she wouldn't last any longer than a snowball in hell in a place like this. Whether it works or not, I've got to take responsibility for her while she grows up a little, and try not to hurt her any more than necessary."

"It's a hell of an act you're talking about putting on."

"I know. I don't know whether I can sustain it or not. The trouble"—he laughed bitterly—"is that my good intentions are like a soldier's will: writ in sand. But I'll—" He broke off at the sound of footsteps on the landing. "Here they are now," he said in a lowered, guilty voice.

Then the door opened and the two women came in, and both men stared as they halted just inside the threshold.

"We didn't go to my regular place," Jeannie said. "We went to another one, uptown, on Fifth Avenue. That's where she got her hair fixed."

Pearl stood there with hands twisting anxiously on her new pocketbook. Her new white suit accentuated the huge, green eyes. Her hair had been washed thoroughly, and now, gleaming almost like sunlight, it curled around her face, framing wide, sharp cheekbones. Mascara, lipstick, powder—she wore them all. What stood there apprehensively, undergoing their inspection, was a striking, vivid girl, possessed of a beauty still partly incipient, totally unconventional, but absolutely real.

"Judas Priest," said Heath.

Pearl laughed, an embarrassed giggle. "You like it?"

"Monsieur Henri went nuts over the way her face is made," said Jeannie. She took Pearl's hand. "There are a lot of packages out there. You two bring them in. Then —we've got another surprise."

"No, wait. Let me look." Heath, his face grave, stood before the girl, his eyes ranging over her, while her face reddened under his scrutiny. Then, as if inspecting a statue, he circled her. Pearl stood without moving while he did that.

"It's all right," he said at last, voice faintly touched with awe. "It's fine. It's just fine."

"Thank goodness," Pearl said, and her shoulders slumped. She dropped into a chair. "I've had fun," she said, "but whut a day!"

"Me too," said Jeannie fervently. "Honey, I'll make us both a big, stiff drink." She poured gin from the bottle, added orange juice. Meanwhile the two men lugged in the enormous pile of boxes and packages. When the last had been retrieved, Heath stared down at the great mound of them. "You spent it all, I take it?"

"You bet your boots we did. Oh, we had so much fun! But that isn't the half of it!" Jeannie cried. "Wait until you see what comes next."

"No," Pearl said quickly. "That was just talk. We don't need to— Maybe he wouldn't like it."

"Oh, no, it's got to happen. We bought the book, didn't we?" Jeannie opened her handbag, took out a volume bound in yellow paper, threw it on the table. Clutterbuck read the black legend. *What Shall We Name Baby?* Heath blinked. "What the devil—!"

"Really, it was Monsieur Henri's idea," laughed Jeannie. "After he'd done with her, he sized her up. Then he said he didn't like the name—it didn't go with the hairdo. He's a crazy little man. Anyhow, we talked about it in the cab. After all, she's got a new hairdo and a new last name —why shouldn't she have a new first one too? That's the thing about it, you see? When you come to a place like this, all you've got to do is decide who and what you want to be and be it! Now, we've got to find a substitute for Pearl. That sounds so countrified and backwoodsy." She riffled through the book.

Heath was looking narrowly at the girl. "You don't like your name?"

Her eyes shuttled away. "I don't know. I mean—" She shook her head. "I just don't . . . don't feel like Pearl . . ."

"Well, I'll be damned," said Heath softly. "Well, I'll just be damned." Suddenly he laughed. "A fresh start. Clean slate. Well, you're entitled to that." As if the idea had caught fire within him, he whipped out a fountain pen. "Here, use this. Just close your eyes and choose."

"Oh, no," Jeannie protested. "We'll have to consider—"

Heath thrust the uncapped pen into Pearl's hand. "Give me that." He took the book, riffled through it, then said, "Close your eyes."

Pearl did so. She raised the pen. Heath laid the book before her. "Now," he said. "Choose."

The room was very silent. Pearl waved the pen, her face pink beneath the makeup. Then, slowly, she brought it down. "There," she whispered.

Jeannie leaned forward. "Cl— Claudia. The Patrician. Oh, I like that. Claudia . . . Claudia Chandler! Say, that sounds good!"

Pearl opened her eyes. "Claudia." Her lips moved as she savored the word. She looked at Heath. "Do you like it?"

"That's not for me to say."

She nodded. "Yes. Yes, it is."

He was silent for a moment. "I like it," he said at last.

Her face lit suddenly with relief, pleasure and excitement. "Then I'm really somebody new!"

Heath laughed with her. "Yep," he said, "you are indeed!"

To Clutterbuck that day seemed symbolic. It was a time when New York was exploding with a million fresh starts, which somehow seemed to generate a tidal wave of change. As if the past were an old, drab garment of which they all had wearied, they cast it off and wove a new one from the threads of hope, youth and sheer exuberance. Everyone was beginning again, and Pearl was not alone. They were all caught up in it, all swept along in that great freshet of innovation, the last remnants of the old and ugly flushed away to reveal a new and shining world made only for pleasure. The four of them, he, Jeannie, Heath and Claudia, explored all its strange dimensions together.

The Chandlers rented, furnished, a small apartment on East Eighth Street, to be near the Village, the center, nexus, of all that ferment. Heath invested ten thousand dollars with Baldwin, threw himself into the business of the company with an energy and determination that astonished Clutterbuck, a kind of drive he had never before displayed—except in search of pleasure. He left early in the morning, returned late, but was never too tired for a party—nor, for that matter, never too hung over the next day to be about his business.

As to what went on between the man and woman in their apartment, Clutterbuck had only vaguest knowledge. What adjustment Heath made, how they got on at home, he could not learn. He did know this: in public Heath acted carefully the role of fond, indulgent husband. There were a dozen women who would have been overjoyed to break up the marriage, or take him for a lover even if it held, but he gave none of them, so far as Clutterbuck could tell, a chance. And yet, it must have been a terrible temptation, for, despite new clothes, new hairdo, and new name, Claudia stood out among those wise, experienced, brittle, hungry girls like a sore thumb. Her naïveté, her total ignorance of form and custom, much less of the special jargon and ritual of the arty, jazzy, sophisticated society in which they moved, made her a monument of gaucherie, and more than once a laughingstock. She must have suffered tortures if she had any pride or ego whatsoever; and Clutterbuck well knew how much pride and ego Chandler was possessed of. She must have shamed him many times, made him want to wince and cringe at this ridiculous faux pas or that; Olin himself sometimes had the same reaction—and she was not even his woman. And yet, instead of withdrawing, the both of them seemed to go out of their way to court such embarrassments. It was a full three months before it dawned on Olin what they were about and he perceived the subtle change in Claudia.

Then he realized that it was her doing: the girl cherished within her some secret image of herself. It could only be fulfilled by learning and experience, and there was only one way to learn—the hard way. So she had leaped into deep water at the beginning. At first she almost sank; then she began at least to dog-paddle. For, very slowly, but surely, she continued to change.

To begin with, she gained nearly fifteen pounds. It was the first time in her life she had a chance to eat a balanced diet or even cultivate an appetite. As she told Jeannie once, "Daddy would never have nothin but pork and grits and biscuits and greens. I got so tired of fixin the same thing over and over I didn't even want no food." Now she explored menus the way Stanley covered Africa, with courage, curiosity and delight, and the added weight —which soon was stabilized—wrought changes. Her breasts were larger, her hips and rump more rounded, her face lost its starved, pinched look, and the sallowness left her skin. Watching her with artist's eye, Clutterbuck saw blooming there a beauty that had been caught just in time, before malnutrition and neglect snuffed it out forever. A dentist repaired her one bad tooth and cleaned the rest; her hands began to soften, lose their work-roughened graininess; she learned how to groom herself, and had the time to do it right. Meanwhile Clutterbuck discovered that she had a knack for picking brains. She dug every bit of knowledge out of the delighted Jeannie that she could probe, absorbed and made it all her own, including many misconceptions. Then she began on Olin. She inveigled from him as much of Heath's history as he dared tell her, and everything he knew of Heath's likes and dislikes as well. She made him explain the theory of colors, and he soon discovered that her sense for them was delicate, perceptive, and accurate. She got him started on a series of informal seminars in art, borrowed books from him, and, he noticed, actually digested them. Meanwhile he could mark the stations of her progress by his own reactions. At first he tolerated her, then was amused. Then one day it occurred to him that if she had not belonged to Heath, he would have enjoyed making love to her. That was a revelation not so much about himself as about how far she had come in so short a time. He began to watch her more closely and with curiosity, and he saw what she was doing.

She exposed herself to every possible experience and

learned what she could from each—from mistakes as well as triumphs. He heard the subtle alterations in her speech, first full of echoes of Jeannie, himself, Heath, and others whom he recognized. She did a great deal of reading too; the apartment overflowed with books, ranging from an enormous Emily Post to the galvanic *This Side of Paradise*, which had become all the rage. Once, dropping in unexpectedly, he and Jeannie caught her with the dining table set beautifully for six, although they were scheduled to eat spaghetti at Clutterbuck's studio that night. She was only practicing, she explained, blushing, while Caruso sang "Vesti la Giubba" on the phonograph. She made Heath take her to the opera and to the better speakeasies; but still her appetite for improvement remained unsatiated. She was worried about her accent—that nasal whine negated every attempt at impressing anybody verbally; and her movements, although she had almost grown up to the large hands and feet, were still awkward and undeniably rangy. Then Heath, over drinks, told Clutterbuck with a mixture of amusement and awe about the speech classes. "This threadbare Englishwoman," he said. "She dug her up somewhere, and now two afternoons a week . . ." A month later he reported something else. "Dancing . . . ballet, for God's sake." He laughed perplexedly, indulgently. "Where will it all end?"

"You should feel flattered," Olin said. By now he was her staunch partisan. He had not forgotten Heath's remarks about how it might fall apart in the end. He found himself now half-hoping it would. "It's all for your benefit."

"I guess so. But I'm gonna have to call a halt somewhere. She spends money as if she were to the manor born. The stockpile's running a little thin."

Nevertheless, even though the enterprise with Baldwin was apparently not going as well as he had hoped—the competition was terrific; dozens of ex-flyers had gone into the business of building airplanes—he let her continue. Slowly, subtly, the effects became noticeable. Her voice dropped in register, left her nose, became deeper, her tones more rounded, and even the ghost of an English accent appeared—strange at first, for her grammar still left much to be desired; but as that too improved, it all seemed to fit together. She had become, Clutterbuck learned by dancing with her as often as he could arrange it, an excellent dancer. She was shedding her old personality like an outgrown skin, assembling a new one out of whole cloth. Presently no one laughed at her anymore. She was not yet what she was obviously trying to be. But she had come a long way from what she had been.

That was when Clutterbuck began to notice the change in Heath. At first it seemed inexplicable. But it took place in direct proportion to the change in Claudia. With all she was doing to please him, to make him take pride in her, a curious counterprocess began in him. Where once he had been meticulous in his public show of devotion to her, he began to look at other women. *A soldier's will: writ in sand.* But there was more to it than that. The old Heath Chandler began to re-emerge, and now at parties he laid himself open to the approaches of other girls. They flocked to him, and he did not turn away as he had before. It puzzled Clutterbuck, and it took him a long time to figure out what was happening.

Heath was discharging his obligation to her. The more she fitted into this milieu, the more capable she became of taking care of herself, the less responsibility he felt toward her. He still had not come to love her, despite all she had done, become. He was still paying a debt; a year had passed, and it was well on its way to being discharged. In his mind there was some point at which that obligation would be canceled. The faster she became a New York woman, as hard and self-reliant as any other, and with no disadvantages in open competition, the faster that point approached. As if she were not his wife at all, but a child he had undertaken to raise until she was old enough and wise enough to stand alone; and when that moment came . . .

Olin could not understand it. He thought she was becoming something magnificent. He knew now that he himself wanted her; more and more, guiltily, he found himself longing for the two graph lines, Heath's conception of full payment and her conception of herself, to intersect. When that time came, he felt, there would be some sort of explosion. And then— In a way he loved Jeannie. But Claudia was fascinating. He could not understand why Heath could not feel that fascination. To live with her, to watch her bloom and change like this, every night to come home to a woman subtly altered, different, new and unpredictable . . .

But, of course, he thought, she was the past. No matter how much she changed, she remained a symbol of a time and place Heath hated, yearned to expunge completely from his mind. No matter what she did, she could not overcome that handicap; each time he looked at her he must have thought of Chandlerville, her father and his, and old griefs, regrets, must have been awakened.

For he had cut himself off from that life completely. Or, more accurately, thought Olin, his father had cut him off. Disinherited him, flatly and finally. There was no doubt of that; Heath had told him that in this entire year there had been no word from either Bolivar or Elizabeth Chandler. *I have no son.* Heath did not seem to mind, only seemed to be relieved. If it were not for Claudia— Pearl-Claudia—that world would no longer have existed for him at all. It was her misfortune that, no matter how hard she tried, Claudia could not escape the fact that she was the last remnant of it he had to deal with.

Meanwhile Heath flew. He flew every day, and sometimes Clutterbuck flew with him. They would take up each new plane put together out of the wounded, surplus Jennies and de Havillands and test it, high over the Island and the Sound. Mock dogfights, conjuring old memories; they dived and rolled and turned and zoomed, with that old, familiar sound of wasps enraged. Then Clutterbuck gave it up. One day it simply occurred to him that this was too dangerous. It was as if he had simply outgrown the need for useless risk; making his living as an artist seemed risk enough.

Besides, the Tiercel frightened him. Day by day the first one took shape in the huge tar-paper shed near the water, and to Olin's eyes it began to have the appearance of some sleek, predatory beast. Built like a bullet, with stubby, swept-back wings, a tremendous engine, there was something malign about it, and at last he decided what it was: too much power. But when he tried to explain that to Heath, Chandler only laughed.

"Listen, it's all been tested. Every element, rib and strut. We've racked models through everything we can think up, used engineering and aerodynamic theories nobody's even thought of before. I'll admit that our conception of it's changed a little—this first one isn't the plane we'll eventually produce. We're making this one to race. We need the prize money and we need the publicity. If I can win enough races to make the Tiercel famous, then we can modify it and sell 'em like hotcakes. I'm not afraid of that plane. I've had my finger in it every inch of the way. Hell, I can't wait to take it up."

Arguing with him was hopeless. But as it neared completion, Olin did not even want to look at it; he stayed away from the place where it grew. Perhaps it was not Heath he feared for so much as himself. His emotions were becoming tangled. He had come to depend on Heath, not only as a source of encouragement when his own self-confidence dwindled but in a practical way— for little favors, small loans, meals when he and Jeannie were broke; it was as if the four of them constituted a tribe and Heath were its chieftain, with responsibility for them all. And yet, mixed with that, and with love and friendship, was something else. He began to build sick, guilty fantasies, which disturbed him profoundly, but which he could not help. Claudia was beyond him now, but if something happened to Heath, if the Tiercel got him—

16 HEATH TRIED HARD to hold to all his good resolutions. He had the work with Baldwin to siphon off the flood of pent-up energy and creativity accumulated in Chandlerville. Baldwin was a superb engineer, an ingenious designer, and an awful businessman. Before Heath realized it, most of the administration of the little company had been dumped on him simply because Baldwin went to any lengths to avoid it. Knowing almost nothing of profit and loss, sales and financing, he still had to, willy-nilly, straighten out the mess Baldwin had allowed to pile up and make sure no more accumulated. To his own surprise, he managed this with a certain flair, even took a creative pleasure in bringing order out of chaos; but, of course, the flying was the best part of his job.

He had plenty of that. For a while they sold their reconstituted aircraft, assembled from junked Army planes, in fair volume. Their standards were meticulous, and no plane left their shop without a thorough testing in the air. Heath gloried in the task; he had not realized until now how totally frustrated being earthbound had made him. The kind of hysteria that had gripped him for so long oozed away; he felt whole once more, capable of joy, exaltation. In the sky his soul expanded, seemed to purify itself, shed the pettiness and sordidness of the flesh. The danger, too, was good; just enough to give intensity to living, make each heartbeat sweeter.

On the ground, of course, he had to deal with Claudia. There was no question of ever feeling for her the wild, transforming passion he had known with Celia, but he had to find and strike some sort of attitude. At first he settled on kindliness and the tolerance of teacher toward pupil. Indeed, it was impossible not to feel admiration and a certain affection as, day after day, she surprised him or sent him into hilarity or dumbfoundedness with some new accomplishment—or effort, anyhow. She was brave and proud and gentle, and if he did not simulate the intensity of a newly married man, he gave a fair approximation of an affectionate husband. She had had so little that even that seemed more than enough for her; sharing various adventures together, they achieved a balance that made it possible for her to love him—something she did not conceal—without his being embarrassed or hurting her. And the lustiness with which he initiated her into sex was real; he needed a woman, and needed one often, and she was new to him and ever-changing, and for a time it was fascinating to be her instructor, even as Celia had once been his. He was tempted, agonizingly, by other women—they still swarmed around him, marriage or no. But for the moment there was enough other excitement, accomplishment and stimulation in his life to make up for that part of freedom he had sacrificed.

Besides, he still had a vast debt to pay. That was rammed home to him when they returned to Macedonia for the trial, six weeks after their flight. Fox was dumbfounded by the transformation in his daughter, but not necessarily pleased. He held his peace with her, though, for her pride and pleasure in herself and in her marriage disarmed even him. But he spoke to Heath privately in his cell, and his eyes were hard. "I'm gonna be in that pen for a long time, young feller," he rasped thinly. "But don't you forget what I told you. If she ain't been tooken care of right when I come out, if you've done one thing to hurt her, hell won't be hot enough to hold you when I git through with you. You hear me?"

Heath could not meet his gaze. "I hear you."

"Then we'll leave it at that," said Fox.

Neither of them had the courage to tell him that she'd changed her name. Fox got three years, as Holding had prophesied, accepting the sentence stony-faced, consoling Pearl when she broke into tears before he was taken away. He held her tightly against him, his face still threatening as he looked across her shoulder at Heath; their eyes met, and Fox's reinforced his warning. Then he was gone.

Only then, when the trial was over, did Heath Chandler call his mother. Her voice trembled on the phone. "Oh, Heath . . ."

"He's not there?"

"No, he's at the office."

"Then we can come over, see you."

There was silence. Then she said forlornly, "I don't think you'd better."

"Why not?"

"He will find out you've been here in this house. And then he'll be furious."

"At you?"

"Yes." There was a world of misery in the single word.

Heath was racked by anger. "There's no reason for him to take it out on you."

"He can't help it. It was all too quick. There hasn't been enough time. He . . . is very deeply hurt."

"I know. I guess you are too." His voice was weary.

"Yes, but I love you, you know that. But I love him too. I couldn't see you without telling him, I couldn't hold it in. And then that would hurt him again. It's just all too soon, darling. Oh, Heath, it's . . ." Her voice began to fade, dissolve in sobs.

He drew in a rasping breath. "Okay, Mom, I won't put you on the spot. I understand. I still intend to write you, though, whether you read the letters or not. And if he ever comes to his senses . . ."

"He will, he has to, someday." She struggled for control. "It's just a matter of time." Then she said, "Heath, There's something else you ought to know."

"What?"

"He has—" She broke off, could not say it. Intuitively he finished the sentence.

"Disinherited me?"

"Yes."

So the rage had been that great, the wound that deep. It was not that he cared about the mills or money—to hell with all of it! To hell with him too, the old fart! To take out his venom on Elizabeth, vent his spite and anger on that gentle woman . . . And yet in the long run it was not Bolivar's fault, it was his own. Something else he had to expiate. "All right, Mom, I'll stay in touch as best I can. Don't worry about it, don't worry about anything."

"Oh . . ." That was a moan of impossibility. Then "Son."

"Yes, ma'am?"

"You're not . . . flying, are you? Please don't fly."

Heath was silent for a moment. "No," he lied, "I'm not flying."

"Thank heavens," she gasped. "That was what really worried me. Yes, write. Please write, and I'll write you. I love you, child."

"I love you too," he said and hung up, pale-faced and sweating. He turned away from the phone and looked at Claudia, who watched him with wide eyes. She was his only instrument, the only way he could justify it all. In a sense she was his salvation; he had to use her well to restore his self-respect.

And so he had taken good care of her for a long time and made her happy, and it was almost enough, with all the other things. In fact, it gave him an additional outlet for his creativity; he vowed coldly to use every bit of skill and ingenuity and tenderness and money too, for that matter, that he could muster, to fulfill the promise that she showed, to make her into a woman, finally, who would justify it all. Maybe even one with whom at last he could fall in love.

He made it through a solid year like that, as, with amazing speed she transformed herself. It was a delicate adjustment, almost an eerie one, but somehow it worked. Then bit by bit things began to come loose, to fall apart.

It began with the business. The supply of surplus planes ran low; meanwhile the partners started to feel the bite of competition. All over the country, veterans like themselves were making, selling aircraft. At the same time the rumrunners, who had been a primary market, organized into large, efficient gangs. With power to corrupt, suborn, and threaten, they could haul whiskey by the truckload now, even by the convoy. The few cases that could be carried in an airplane were chicken feed, and that trade dwindled, almost vanished. Before long it was obvious that they had one hope and one hope only of survival: Baldwin's Tiercel.

But Baldwin's dream was almost too large, the technological leap he attempted nearly beyond achievement. Snag after snag developed in the prototype, problems demanding solutions for which there were no precedent. For every step forward, it seemed they slid two backward, and while that was happening, their money was running out.

For the first time in his life Heath Chandler felt the pinch of real financial hardship. He and Claudia—and Clutterbuck and Jeannie, for that matter—had denied themselves nothing in the vast, never-ending party of New York. He had the new experience of watching bills pile up unpaid and—at the office—dealing with urgent, pushing creditors. It became necessary to find new capital; Baldwin scraped up some from God knows where; Heath found matching it one of the knottiest problems of his life. Suddenly he realized that he owned nothing, had no net worth, except his share in a tar-paper and pine-board aircraft factory with a payroll that could be reduced no farther and its entire future pinned on a refractory aircraft that would not let itself be put in working order. Finally he borrowed from friends.

And yet, if they could only succeed, if they could make the Tiercel do what they demanded, both he and Baldwin were convinced that it would all come out right in the end. The plane as conceived was so far ahead of any other aircraft flying that it would sell itself, if only they could get it in production. Now they began to work desperately, around the clock, flogging themselves into wakefulness with cigarettes and coffee, and at last, exhausted, unable to ease off, using gin to let them down. Heath lost weight, felt haunted, tense, desperate; his sense of well-being evanesced. The bills piled up at home, and yet it seemed as if they were on a merry-go-round they could not climb off; both had become so accustomed to extravagance that they could not break the habit. He was worse than Claudia; it seemed absurd to deny themselves things they wanted; when the Tiercel flew, soon, there would be more money, plenty of it.

Meanwhile he began to lie awake at night, adding sums in his mind, dreading the answers his calculations yielded. He learned how to placate creditors with cool half-truths or outright falsehoods, which demeaned and humiliated him, gnawed at his image of himself. He become short-tempered, senselessly ferocious, and now something else crowded in on him, a need to escape from reality, find surcease from the strains that racked him. And Claudia could offer him none.

At this moment in their lives she was in a kind of limbo of the personality, it seemed to Heath—neither one thing nor the other; and he found that irritated him. Besides, she was part of the very reality he felt the need to hide from. No matter how tender she might be with him, how much she tried to understand, he could get nothing from her that he needed—she could not offer him the release, the forgetfulness, that suddenly he had begun to crave.

He was in that mood when he met the most beautiful woman he had ever seen; in fact, one certified by acclamation to be the loveliest in New York.

He and Baldwin had worked late that night. Nearly hysterical with coffee and cigarettes, neither could go home yet; instead, they sought a speakeasy on West Fifty-fifth Street. Its proprietor, Joe Capriano, had bought two planes from them to bring liquor across the border. Something about the slender, dark-haired man, always jovial, smiling, yet with a core of case-hardened steel, had struck a chord in Heath—the wild, outlaw streak that he himself possessed. He and Capriano were good friends, and though the place was full and Joe was busy at this hour—nearly two—the neat, almost dainty Italian joined them at their table.

"How's that airplane with the funny name going? Think you'll ever get it off the ground?"

"One of these days," Heath said. Instinctively, as he had learned to do at any expression of interest, he went on, "You wanta get in on the ground floor? We've got some stock to sell. Make you rich."

"You lemme see it fly, then I'll talk to you. If it looks good, I might make a small investment. But right now—" He broke off as, slowly, like a breeze bending down a wheat field, silence spread across the room. The door had opened, closed; and, instinctively, Heath and Baldwin turned to look.

That was when for the first time he saw her in the flesh, although her pictures had adorned every tabloid on sale in town. After the opening of this year's Ziegfeld Follies, in which she danced and sang almost nude and invariably stopped the show, she had become a celebrity. But the pictures had not done her justice: in blue satin dress, she was a heart-stopping confection of blond and creamy splendor, on the arm of a powerful-looking, gray-haired man in evening clothes. Well aware of the sensation her entrance caused, she halted for a moment, savoring it; and Capriano sprang up and ran forward to greet them.

"That's Betty Hammond," Baldwin murmured. "Damn, what a baby doll!"

"Yeah," Heath said. His eyes took in the lush breasts and moving, rounded buttocks beneath the clinging satin; and suddenly he thought of Evelyn Ford. Since her he had never seen a woman who radiated such unalloyed sex appeal . . . and knew it.

It was a long time before Capriano drifted back. Betty Hammond and her escort had the best table in the house; and a kind of miasma of lust and envy filled the room for a long time as she endured with aplomb riveting stares from two hundred curious eyes, taking all that tribute matter-of-factly as her due. Heath was no better than the rest; immediately he ached with longing for her.

"Somethin, eh?" Capriano rolled his eyes.

"Prime," murmured Baldwin. "Totally, absolutely prime."

"The cat's pajamas. She comes in here every night after the show. Best business-builder I got."

Heath still had his eyes on her. "Who's the joker with her?"

"Everybody's gotta have a sugar daddy. Let's just say this one's in banking; she don't come cheap." He looked at Heath with a glint of amusement. "You like that, hah?"

"I like that." Heath returned the look. "What about an introduction?"

Capriano smiled faintly. "I thought you were a married man."

"Let's just say I ain't that married," Heath murmured after a moment.

"Very few are." Capriano chuckled. "Well, with all them planes you shot down, you're a kind of celebrity yourself. Wait till the guy with her's had a few. He'll be a little more receptive then."

Baldwin sighed. He looked at Heath strangely, then stood up. "This is all too rich for my blood. I think I'll go on home. See you in the morning." Then he went out.

Heath stayed; Claudia would assume he was working, but it made no difference anyhow. After what he had been through, he was entitled to some relaxation.

Actually, when her escort learned Heath's identity, he began to fawn, but, of course, by then he was very drunk. He had, he swore, exhausted every effort to join up, but they all insisted he was too valuable on the home front. But nobody outstripped him in his admiration for those heroic boys who had won the war, and especially for the flyers. God, yes, he'd read all about Heath in the *Times* and *Sun;* this was a very real pleasure. The drinks were on him. Heath sat down; he felt Betty Hammond's deep gentian eyes on him like rays of heat. He had not been there more than five minutes when her knee touched his beneath the table. Later, when the man named R. T. something went to the bathroom, she leaned over, touched the scar on his cheek. "I like that," she said in a husky, silken voice. "It makes you look wicked." The lush, red lips curved. "There's something fascinating about wicked-looking men."

That was the beginning of it—an addiction like morphine, cocaine or alcohol. Whatever she saw in him, for Heath it was like entering a hothouse or a tropical jungle, a place where everything rank and livid could grow without restraint. She gave off an emanation of steamy, decadent fecundity, which was fully justified when he bedded her for the first time. Here was no woman whom he had to teach or be taught by; although she already had another lover, that rank, ripe flesh could, like fertile

soil, support an infinite number of them. She had no mind
to speak of, but a mind was not what he sought; what
he wanted was a warm bath of sex into which he could
sink, submerge himself, find forgetfulness. She gave him
that, usually in the middle of the day, and she was everything he had come to New York to find. And because of
her he began to look at Claudia with different eyes. Now
he found himself judging her degree of self-sufficiency

In the long run, wasn't that all he owed her? When
she no longer needed him to tend to her and bolster her,
could stand on her own two feet as an urbane, knowl-
edgeable woman of New York, hadn't his obligation
ended? His debt to Fox, was large, but after all, a debt
by definition could be paid. He had already given her
more than she had any right to expect, had sacrificed
enough. Not that he loved Betty Hammond or thought
of marrying her; he would tire of her too, eventually, but
. . . now the precedent was set. There were other Betty
Hammonds, lesser and greater, and he could have as
many of them as he wanted, and something in him craved
them all.

And so he walked a tightrope of stealth and furtiveness,
making thrice-weekly visits to Betty's Fifth Avenue apartment, a huge, lush sprawl of gilt and satin and even
ormolu, mindless and humid and erotic as herself. At
home—he could not help it—he was distant, withdrawn,
partly from fatigue, partly from guilt, and partly because
he had a greater vision now. When the Tiercel flew, when
it made him money, so that he could afford a generous
settlement with Claudia . . .

Tortuously, bit by bit, the airplane was fought toward
completion. At last, very late one night, Heath and Baldwin stood, hollow-eyed, trembling with fatigue, in the
cavernous, feverishly lit expanse of shop, reeking with the
smells of paint and glue and steel and oil and resin oozing
from the pine boards of the sidewalls. Squat and shark-
like, gleaming with layers of sanded paint, the Tiercel
crouched on three wheels, lacking now only its propeller.
The compact, powerful, lightweight engine of Baldwin's

design, custom-made, had been installed, its preliminary tests passed at last, after many failures and revisions. Both men looked at the airplane with a dazed incredulity, and Heath rubbed a dirty, greasy face. "There must be something else," he muttered. "You're sure there ain't anything else?"

"No." Baldwin shook his head. His voice was vibrant. "That's all there is. Tomorrow we install the prop, and then she's finished."

"My God," Heath said in awe. "Then we've finally done it."

"I hope so."

Chandler laughed. "Just like the U.S. Cavalry in the movies. Right in the nick of time. Alec, I can hardly wait to get that bitch up. Can you have her ready tomorrow afternoon?"

"Hell, no," said Baldwin. "We've got to check her on the ground first. Slow and easy. Three days, anyhow."

"Too long."

"No. Maybe not long enough."

"Look," Heath snapped, "you don't know the situation; I ain't bothered you with it. But we've got lawyers on our ass like snapping turtles. We're just before being sued, backward, forward and sideways. We've got to buy some time, and every day counts."

Baldwin frowned. "I didn't know it was that bad."

"If we could get all these people we owe out here for the test, let 'em see that this thing really works . . . And the Air Corps and air mail people. When they see the old Tiercel there go into orgasm, really do her stuff, they're bound to get excited. Then we re-establish confidence; they'll back off and give us time. Most of 'em didn't think the thing would ever work, but if we can get 'em out here to watch it with their own eyes . . ."

"All the same," said Baldwin, "we can't push it."

"Goddammit, man, we've *got* to push it!" Heath's shredded self-control ripped again. "Otherwise we'll be so tied up in judgments we'll never get into production. Even Joe Capriano, he'd put money in the company if he saw her fly—you heard him say that. Maybe even Betty would!"

"I don't want Betty in it," Baldwin said thinly.

"All right. Anyhow, we've got to fly her."

Baldwin let out a heavy sigh. "Only when I'm ready. Three days. You get 'em all together, I'll rake up the money for whiskey and a spread, we'll make a party out of it. Get reporters too—you know a lot of 'em. But after all I've put in it, I'll not skimp. There's a lot at stake here, you know. More than just the company."

"What do you mean?"

Baldwin turned to look at him. "If that thing doesn't stay up there," he said quietly, "you."

"All right," Heath said after a moment. "I just wish it could be sooner."

"Don't wish your life away," said Baldwin wearily. He ran a hand through his thinning hair. "Let's go home."

That was what Heath did, tired, yet full of elation. It was the uncertainty that twisted a man's guts; soon all that would end. All he wanted now was to prove the airplane, get it into production—he knew it would sell, nothing else could equal it—and recoup his finances. If he could only make some money to buy his freedom . . . His mind, nearly hallucinating with fatigue, built wild fantasies. He had waited so long, taken such a devious path to freedom . . .

He fumbled with the key, let himself into the living room of the apartment. Then he stopped. Contrary to her custom, Claudia was still up, sitting with legs tucked beneath her on the sofa, a copy of *Smart Set* on her lap. Her hair was a wheat-straw gleam about her face; she wore a champagne-colored nightgown, a frilly peignoir of the same color over it. Heath closed the door behind him. "You're still awake?"

She smiled, a glint in those slanted, brilliant eyes. "Uh-huh."

"Why?"

"Waiting for you." She laid the magazine aside. "You look absolutely frazzled." There was no trace of backwoods whine in her voice now. "Would you like a drink?"

"God, yes." He had intended to have several, but in solitude, nourishing his triumph and his plans alone, unshared. But he was too tired now even for resentment at her intrusion on his fantasies. He dropped into a chair, pushed his shoes off without untying them, unbuttoned his shirt, raised his arms to let the air reach beneath them. Claudia disappeared into the kitchen, returned with a cocktail shaker and two glasses. "Martinis. I made them from the book." She poured and handed one to him, then came and sat on the arm of his chair, her own glass in her hand. Heath stiffened slightly, sensing something offbeat and out-of-phase about all this.

"How did it go?" she asked.

"Believe it or not, it's finished. Tomorrow we install the prop, then check the damned thing. Three days from now I take her up."

"Oh," she said with a slight, sharp intake of breath. She had watched him fly, was very good about that. Nevertheless he caught the sudden fear in that implosive sound and laughed a little harshly.

"Don't worry. It'll be perfectly safe. I wanted to shake her out tomorrow, but Baldwin wouldn't go along. He's going over her with a fine-tooth comb before I take her off the ground."

"That's good," she said. "I won't worry so much, then."

Heath—it seemed to take great effort—twisted his head wearily to look up at her. "Since when do you worry about me flying?"

"Well, the other planes, I guess they're different. You've been flying them for a long time. But the Tiercel . . . That's so *new*."

"It's not new by now," he grumbled. "It's Goddamned old." Again he had that sense of something strange, maybe wrong. He pulled away from the hand that rested on his head, stood up, confronted her. Even though he had only sipped his drink, she was blurred in his vision; he was that tired. "What the hell's going on here?" he snapped. "What are you doing up and martinis already made?"

She met his eyes, then looked away, as if what she saw dismayed her. "I . . . had some news."

Immediately something cold clutched at Heath's heart. "Fox? What about him?"

"No, not Fox." Suddenly words burst from her in a stream. "Heath, I went to Doctor Vincent last week, I had to go, Jeannie went with me, and he did some things, made some tests. He phoned me today, it was so exciting—"

His mind leaped ahead. Even before he spoke he saw with despair all of it tumbling about him: the bright structure he had built in imagination—freedom at last. "You're not pregnant?" His voice was stunned.

"That's what he said." She smiled expectantly.

But he only stood there, desperately trying to decide how he must react. There was fury in him, at her, himself, and most of all at fate. He had already perceived what this meant: new bondage, new obligation, just when, at last, he had seen light at the end of a long, dark tunnel.

His silence baffled, dismayed her. "I'm sorry. I should have waited until tomorrow morning when you weren't so absolutely tired."

"No," he heard himself say. He wanted to be brutal, he wanted to smash something, anything, from frustration and disappointment; but not even he could be that much of a swine. She's right, he told himself. I'm too tired. This is something I've got to think about later. And he lied again, for his sake as much as hers, unable to summon strength right now for any complications. "No, it's all right, it's fine." He pulled her to him, kissed her briefly, then let her go. "Only—" Rubbing his face, he said, "Only, you're right, I'm absolutely bushed. And a baby, right now—"

"I know. I was half-afraid to tell you. But when you said the Tiercel was ready . . . Everything will be all right once it's in operation, you said." She laughed, took his hand. "Drink your martini, you look like you need it. Maybe it will be a boy. I hope it is, don't you? I've already written Daddy and . . . and I wrote your mother too. You don't mind? I thought she ought to know."

He gulped the martini. "No, I don't mind," he said and dropped wearily into the chair again. He held out his glass. "Another drink." He had that one and another, not hearing anything Claudia said, and at last he made it to the bed, his mind locked and frozen, not thinking about anything, and promptly fell into a deathlike sleep. When he awakened in the morning he did not remember it at first; then it hit him fully with all its implications. But there was nothing he could do about it, nothing at all, except put on the best face possible and cage his real feelings within him like gnawing rats.

17 IN ANY EVENT, there was no time to brood. Their creditors made clear that even the three-day extension was a major concession, and there was no question about the deadline they had to meet. That yielded barely time enough to give the Tiercel the meticulous ground tests on which Baldwin resolutely insisted, much less prepare for what was turning into a major party on their airstrip. The guest list grew—the roll of people whom they owed was lengthy—encompassing, too, delegations from the Army and Navy, plus a swarm of reporters alerted by Heath. The importance of their guests protected them from Prohibition authorities, and liquor must be procured, a bar set up, catering arranged. All that cost money, nearly the last they had; but the successful flight would open up new lines of credit to tide them over until the inevitable orders came in.

Nevertheless what should have been for Heath a triumphal occasion was spoiled by Claudia's news. Suddenly the success of the Tiercel lost much of its significance for him; it would restore his finances, but it would not, after all, give him freedom. Well, he thought grimly, free or not, he would not relinquish Betty or whoever her inevitable successors might be. Bolivar and Claudia: the two of them had managed to ruin too many years already. Now he was going to take something for himself, no matter how he had to get it.

With effort, though, he kept up a front; if anything, he became more affectionate, acting well the part of the pleased, dazed father. It was smoke screen, a kind of smoke screen he would have to maintain if he were to have his double life, keep Claudia off guard. Meanwhile he invited Betty Hammond to the test: good publicity, he told Baldwin, who only grunted sourly.

They ran the ground check, broke the engine in, pushed it to capacity, checked and readjusted it. Brakes locked, the Tiercel quivered with eagerness, wanting to take flight; taxiing, it seemed to fight the bit, try to slip the reins, surge free. Its stubby wings almost flapped with lust for being airborne; in its cockpit Heath felt a sense of power and of rightness—this airplane was perfect. Years of experience had given him a sixth sense; like a fine horse and knowing rider, he and the Tiercel were one from the beginning. It was a superb and honest machine; and it would advance aviation a full decade in an afternoon. Nothing, he was certain, ever built could match it for sped, range, and maneuverability.

Still, Baldwin was not satisfied. He tinkered, checked, tightened and reworked, and Heath tested and retested, and performance improved each time. At last, glowing with delight, Heath told his partner: "Leave it alone. We've got a gold mine here! Don't mess with it any more!"

Clutterbuck brought Claudia to the airstrip, along with Jeannie. Fully a hundred people roiled in and out of the hangar, around the plane itself, cordoned off by the few remaining employees against the depredations of curiosity seekers. It was a fine, hot afternoon, sea and sky melding into an intense, almost incandescent blue. It was a color that reminded Heath of something; then he had it: exactly the same hue as the windows in a mill. He grinned wryly. There was a difference: one was the color of slavery, the other of freedom.

In flying garb, helmet and goggles, he cut a figure and he knew it, wanted to. Let the reporters and photographers have their field day. He savored, as well, the admiring gazes of women. He searched the crowd, but Betty had not yet arrived; she was late, but she was always late. Standing with Claudia, Olin, and Jeannie for a few moments—he could barely spare the time; the creditors and prospective buyers, especially the colonels and commanders took first priority—he felt a certain disappointment.

Claudia herself was splendid in white summer suit trimmed with gold. They had been photographed embracing. Now she took Heath's hand, and her own was soft and cool and damp with apprehension. Only once had she watched him in a test flight; after that she had refused to see another. Now, though, she squeezed tightly, and Heath returned the pressure automatically, feeling admiration mixed with pity for her. He pitied, for that matter, all of them who had any stake in this; the waiting and watching was the excruciating part—his was the easy job, embodying the release of action and control. Baldwin looked phlegmatic, but Heath had known him long enough to realize how tightly wound the man was. Then his attention was diverted by a kind of tidal wave in the crowd as a long, low Deusenberg limousine pulled up, stopped; and he caught a glimpse of golden hair and creamy flesh and clinging fabric. Betty had finally made her entrance.

For a while she was smothered by reporters and admirers. "Isn't that the Follies girl?" Claudia asked, frowning slightly. "You know, Betty whatshername?"

"I think it is."

"What's she doing here?"

Heath avoided Clutterbuck's eyes. "We thought it'd be good publicity to invite her."

"Oh," said Claudia. "I didn't think you knew her."

Olin said thinly, "Heath knows everybody."

Then two photographers seized him, pulled him away before he knew what was happening. In a moment he found himself in a circle in the crowd, with Betty kissing

him on the cheek while cameras clicked. "Good luck,
darling," she whispered in his ear. By request, she had
to do it three more times before all the photographers
were satisfied. Once she took his hand, squeezed it just
as Claudia had, but only briefly; later it would appear
preserved in halftone on a tabloid's front page.

As soon as it was over, Claudia, Olin and Jeannie closed
in on Heath once more. A lull, a curious silence, fell
around them. They were all acutely aware of the time—
two-fifty; takeoff was at three o'clock. Olin took the initiative, thrusting out his hand. "Good hunting. But don't
get carried away up there. Don't get too gay with your
new toy."

Heath grinned. "You're envious, that's all."

Clutterbuck's handshake was hard, firm. "Maybe."

"I want a kiss before you fly," said Jeannie. "Everybody
else has had one."

Heath grinned. "Sure." He bussed her soundly. Beneath his lips her mouth opened slightly. Inwardly he
was amused; so she was available too. Hell, they all were.
Then he let her go. Now Claudia stood before him. Her
green eyes were huge, swirling with emotion. They
looked at one another for a moment. Somehow in that
instant it seemed to Heath that she was lovelier than
Betty—but of course that was absurd. Then Claudia took
both his hands, her eyes still locked on his. She smiled
faintly. "Make them all sit up and take notice," she whispered. Then she kissed him on the mouth lightly. "We'll
get out of your way now. Olin—" That was all she said
as they turned away.

Then it was time. Flanked by Baldwin and some Army
officers, Heath went to the Tiercel. "Good luck," was all
Baldwin said as he climbed into the cockpit. "Thanks,"
Heath answered; and he was photographed shaking
hands in turn with all of them. The reporters and camera-
men were like jackals, scavengers, he thought, as he went
through the routine for them. They were the only ones
here who hoped he crashed; it would be even bigger
news than a successful test. Then he turned, forgot them,
forgot everything but the Tiercel, buckling safety belt

and going through preflight routine as the crowd drew back.

Baldwin himself spun the propeller; the engine caught, fired with a steady, guttural roar of power. Deliberately, to impress those present, Heath throttled it up to maximum RPM's; it made a kind of thunder that hushed the crowd. Totally confident, he savored that powerful engine sound. Nobody but himself and Betty knew what was beneath his flying helmet; one of her stockings, worn as favor to a knight, just as he had worn Celia's when he crossed the Channel. That had been a conceit of his. Then he released the brakes, throttled down, taxied to the runway's end, and turned, neatly, smoothly, aware of how much impression even that easy maneuver must make on the experienced airmen in the crowd. *Now,* he thought, made one last check, gave full throttle, released the brakes, gripped the stick, and kicked the airplane off. It hurtled down the runway, airborne in a time incredibly short, and something cried out inside Heath, a silent shout of jubilation.

Then, blessedly, he was alone with the magnificent airplane. It was like making love as its quivering frame responded to his every demand. Climbing, soaring, reaching for the peak of ecstasy, it flung itself against the poised sun in the glittering blue. Inside it Heath was in two places at once, in the cockpit and down below; he knew what a shimmering speck he was in the high reaches of the cloudless sky. He pushed it higher, still higher, knowing what it could do and straining for the utmost, just as in the act of sex; and then it reached apogee, trembled in a way that told him it had found fulfillment, could climb no more, and he leveled off.

Below, Long Island and the mainland were laid out in bright relief. The hangar was a tiny dot, the sprawled crowd around the runway but a smudge. He and the Tiercel were alone up here and making love to one another. He would have preferred to stay at this ultimate ecstasy indefinitely, but there were people down there he must impress. He told his darling what he wanted and she responded, hurtling down obediently on her stubby wings, willing to risk self-destruction at his command.

The ground rushed up, the smudge became a crowd again; the Sound, bright blue like mill windows, but capped with little white foaming ridges, edged the Island. The Tiercel whined and shivered and roared with excitement, and he pulled her up and rolled her, and she shook all over with delight and peeled, belly to the sun, back to the sky. He whipped her out, rolled over and over and again, weight straining against the belt, mind blurred with an ecstasy of blue sea and sky, dived her down and brought her up once more and sent her soaring. He wanted to climb, had to, until he and the airplane both became a single star, lost forever. The engine growled and purred with pleasure at the demands he made; then the stubby wings lost their lift in the high, thin air, and he kicked it into a spectacular left spin and came straight down, whining and turning, plunging toward a sea as limitless as the air, laughing between his teeth as the revolutions of the Tiercel spun his vision on an axis, seemed to whip the water into a seething vortex around that given point. He knew that, on the shore, breaths were held, men were cursing, women even screaming, and the jackals all licking chops. Then, at the last minute, he and the plane both were racked as he brought it out; it shuddered with the ferocity of his requirements, but obeyed, leveled, went hurtling toward the Island like a bullet, rich prop pitch biting in the thick air of low altitude. It roared over the antlike, excited crowd and out across the water, and he kicked it around and brought it back again, even lower. In a moment he would climb once more, engage an imaginary opponent in a dogfight for the benefit of the military, but for now—

Then the engine quit.

Not a stall, a sudden failure. Something in there had seized and locked. The silence was tremendous. The Tiercel hurtled on, borne by momentum. In a curious suspension of time, beyond fear or even haste, Heath worked calmly with the controls. But nothing happened, the engine would not catch; now in place of its growl and purr there was a banshee wail, a high-pitched demoniacal keening of rushing air, as, caught by gravity, the Tiercel sped like a flying bomb straight toward the crowd on the runway. Now there was no time left for restarting. His mind computed airspeed, lost altitude, trajectory . . . For the first time panic seized him. The runway hurtled up, metallic, shining; he saw all those upturned faces, white, like daisies in a field, the bright pattern of women's dresses, all those bodies frozen with terror and amazement, flesh and blood to be scythed down by wood and steel— In the pair of seconds he had left he pulled back desperately on the stick; obedient in that, anyhow, the plane responded, nose lifting slightly, enough so the wheels just cleared that blotch of white, fearful, staring faces. Then the end of the runway was coming up as the Tiercel mushed, dropped again; and now he was over sand and scrub, and then ahead there was the grove of pines and stunted oaks; and, he thought, with an astounding clarity, utter coolness, he was going to smash into all those trunks head-on in just one second, and that was going to be the end of it. He pitied them all, condemned to watch this: Baldwin and Claudia especially, their whole lives about to crash with him, and then there was nothing in the windshield but greenery, no sky that he could see; and he just had time to be shocked and astonished by how titanic such an impact was, the blow of a huge, vindictive hand. Flung against the belt, he felt things crush within him, and the smashing, crunching, shattering of wood and metal filled his ears just before the darkness came, blanking out the world as quickly as the closing of an eye.

Part Two

1 THE VILLA perched on a steep hill overlooking the Danube, and the morning after Clutterbuck's
arrival they had breakfast on the terrace. Below, the
woods along the river—which Clutterbuck had been as-
sured by Heath and Claudia, was indeed blue when the
wind came from a certain quarter—were a vast palette
of delicate springtime greens. Just down the hill from the
big, yellow, three-story house a cherry orchard had exploded in riotous blossom, and the staked vines in the
nearby vineyards put out new leaf. Behind the house a
lush, green meadow, blazing with thousands of huge,
yellow dandelions, sloped upward to the shadowy edge of
the Vienna Woods. The sky was cloudless, the air so
transparent that every detail of the village in the valley,
the little towns across the river, the great castle on a
peak four miles away, and the city of Vienna itself, beyond the brooding hulk of two dark almost-mountains,
stood out with amazing clarity. Clutterbuck felt some of
the tensions of these last failure-ridden years ooze away.
Everywhere else the world was crumbling, but here
Heath, Claudia and the two children seemed to have
found a hiding place from the cancer gnawing at western
civilization in the wake of last year's stock-market collapse. It was as if, he thought, the Chandlers had somehow earned the special favor of the gods.

"More coffee?" Claudia took his cup, poured from a
silver pot, added hot cream from a smaller one. Her hair,
still the color of clean wheat straw, was worn short, curl-

ng around her face, emphasizing the remarkable struc-
ure of her cheekbones, the magnificence of green, slanted
yes. At twenty-seven there was nothing matronly about
er, even after two children. The figure beneath the dress
f white, light wool was superb, breasts small, but well-
efined and sharp, legs long and excellent. Clutterbuck,
ppraising her both as man and artist, thought that she
as at the very peak of her development and wished
ery much that he could both paint her nude and make
ve to her. He felt a twinge of envy; Heath had more
an one man deserved.

Now she turned to her husband with the pot, but he
ook his head. "No, thanks, I'm bubbling over now.
Vhat's your agenda for today?"

"Unless you've got plans that include me, I think I'll
ke the children to Vienna for their spring outfits. Frau
layer can go along and take them to the Prater while
have lunch with Karen von Nordhof and her White
ussian princess at the Sacher. Care to join us?"

"No, thanks. I had enough faded nobility at that party
e other night in Grinzing. While you're in town, though,
hone the bank, will you? My agent was supposed to
ansfer the next payment from *The Last Squadron*
rect, and I left instructions to have it converted into
old. See if it's come, will you?"

"Surely. All right, we'll leave you and Olin to your
wn devices. Excuse me." Both men watched as she
rode gracefully across the terrace. Her departure
emed to reduce the quality of the morning. For a mo-
ent they were silent; then Clutterbuck became aware
at Heath was watching him sardonically.

"I'm sorry," Chandler said. "There was a time when
d have been willing to give her to you if you'd have
ken her off my hands. But you missed your chance."

"It's fantastic. Absolutely fantastic."

"No, it ain't. It's just proof of the unshakable American
elief that if you work hard enough, you can be any-
dy you want to be. God knows, she's worked hard
ough."

"But she doesn't have to work now."

"No. She's not trying to become, she *has* become; sh
is." Heath lit a cigarette. "Look, if you *want* to go in
Vienna—for that matter, if you want to paint—"

"Uh-uh," said Olin. "I've had all the cities I need fo
a while. Painting too. What the hell's the use of paintin
any more when I've got stacks of stuff nobody'll buy o
even hang?"

Heath said soberly, "It's a rough way to make it, isn
it?"

"No worse than yours, I guess."

"No, that's not true. I try to make my plays as good a
possible, I *aim* for art, but I'm not fooling myself. I wa
just lucky, that's all. I had something the public wante
and I'm still writing it. War and more war. Hell, th
way they flock to the box office, you'd think they can
wait until another one. But the first two used up every
thing I had to say, now I'm just using the old tricks ove
and over, and the suckers still keep plunking down the
cash—" He broke off as the back door of the vill
slammed. "Aha. What have we here?"

The twins ran across the garden, boy and girl in matcl
ing sailor clothes, bubbling with the natural energy o
seven-year-olds. They leaped into Heath's lap like pup
pies, their round, smooth faces lit with delight as he pu
his arms around them; and Olin thought of a baroqu
chapel fresco, full of cherubim with soft blond hair an
shining eyes and small, delicate rosebud mouths.

He watched as Heath pawed and kissed them like a
animal with its frisky young, off guard in that insta
and beaming with parental pleasure, all irony and cyn
cism vanished from his face. When, gently, he put the
down, Olin saw him, with faint surprise, really vulnerabl
for the first time. "All right, you two," Heath ordere
smiling a little foolishly. "Say *Grüss Gott* to your Unc.
Olin."

Running to Clutterbuck, the boy scrambled up to perc
on his knee. "*Grüss Gott,* Uncle Olin." Of his own a
cord he gave the stranger a quick damp kiss. Clutte
buck caught the clean babyish perfume of the hair, th
brush of soft velvet cheek. "Hello, fat boy," he sai

punched him gently in the stomach and set him down.

"My name's not 'fat boy.' My name's Hampton Olin Chandler and Mama says I must thank you for the toy soldiers." It came in a forceful burst, devoid of shyness.

"And you're welcome, Hampton Olin Chandler, even if you did steal my name." He looked at the girl.

She clung to her father, staring at him gravely from green slanted eyes beneath straw-colored, pigtailed hair. Heath tapped her gently. "Say hello, Ramsey."

But she only looked at Clutterbuck with those enormous eyes. He had always thought twins, even fraternal ones, were similar in personality and response, but these were, he guessed, vastly different, maybe because of the fact of gender. Hamp was the quintessential male, already adventurous and bold; she was something else, more passive, and yet, somehow, he sensed, more complicated—but then females always were. Finally, as Heath nudged her again, she said quietly, "*Grüss Gott,* Uncle Olin."

Before he could answer, Hamp was clawing up his father's knees, reaching across the table, "We're going to the Tiergarten! Want some sugar for the el'phants."

"Knock over that coffee pot and Frau Mayer'll feed you to the lions." Heath crammed a handful of wrapped cubes into his son's pockets. "Here, divide with your sister. And one each for y'all to eat and rot your teeth with. On your way now!" He whacked both of them on their bottoms, and they ran together toward the house. Again there was that feeling of diminished vitality on the terrace, and when Heath turned to Olin, his face still shone with a kind of afterglow.

"You're simpering," Clutterbuck said wryly.

"Likely. I'll admit I seem to have discovered an untapped vein of paternal instinct in myself." He watched the children vanish through the door. "They're good kids, Clutt—and, yes, I'm a pure fool about both of 'em." Then he sobered. "Of course, maybe I'm just compensating. Anyhow, by God, I'm going to see that the sins of the fathers aren't visited on *them.*"

Olin caught the bitterness in his voice. "Still haven't heard from *him?*"

"Not a peep." Heath lit a cigarette. "My mother writes fairly often; I answer faithfully, send her pictures. But . . . he won't even read the letters, look at the pictures. Where he's concerned, I don't exist, neither does Claudia or the children." He laughed harshly. "Anyhow, nobody can accuse him of inconsistency." Then his face softened. "Clutt, I was sorry to hear about *your* old man."

Olin, having come to terms with that, shrugged. "He built his life around money. When the money went last year, the life went too."

"But at least y'all were still talking."

"Yeah." Clutterbuck toyed with his cup. "Maybe I should have listened to him too. Maybe he knew all along that I was third-rate."

"Crap. Don't—"

"Oh, yeah. I've proved that to my own satisfaction now. It's just too bad it took me ten years to find it out. But a man can only live off his own ego, like the yolk in a hatching egg, for so long. Sooner or later he has to face the truth. But, yes— It's a little rough, when you're thirty-three years old and there's a worldwide depression to face the fact that there's not a damned thing you can do to earn your living. There's not much market now for SE-5 pilots and even less for hack painters. . . . The trick is," he said, "to distinguish between a knack and a talent. The way to tell the difference is that you'll do anything to cherish your talent. But when Jeannie had to go out whoring so we could eat and I could paint . . . I couldn't bear that. For her own good I had to blast her loose. When I'd finally made myself so revolting to her that not even she could stand me, she got the message. She met some rich American kid whose father had sold out just before the crash, and it worked out fine for her. And I spent the winter shoveling snow, on the payroll of the *arrondissement*. But the snow ran out. If you hadn't written me—" He shrugged. "I wouldn't have had any problems if I could have just arranged for it to snow in Paris all year round."

"Listen," Heath said, "I know this shit of feeling sorry for yourself—I've been through it. Knock it off. You don't need anything but a rest and a chance to pull up your socks."

"All the same, I can't—"

"The hell you can't. We've got more room than we can possibly use. And as for money, every time the Austrian currency drops, my dollars go up. If I don't earn another nickel in my whole life, we can still get by. So you stay with us as long as you take a notion to. I need you, anyhow. I've got to have somebody to bounce my novel off of, and aside from Claudia, you're the only one I know who'll give it to me straight. You're staying with us, and no argument."

Clutterbuck had known all along that Heath would offer and that he would protest, then yield. "Well, I'll hang around a while. Maybe you'd like a portrait of Claudia, if that would be some compensation . . ."

"Love it. But with her clothes on—let's have that understood, you horny bastard." Heath arose. "Come on. Let's take a walk and I'll show you the Vienna Woods and fill you up on the wine of the country."

The three of them had sat up talking and drinking for a long time, and when Heath and Claudia had gone to bed, they were still excited and had made love. Now, in darkness, his arm around his sleeping wife, Heath Chandler, keyed up yet, lay awake.

Claudia's steady breathing was a sound that comforted him, the warmth of her body deeply, primitively satisfying and reassuring. It had become a necessary communion, to roll over and find the other there; he supposed it was part of love.

The windows were wide open, the moist, warm air of spring flowing into the bedroom like a caress, perfumed with the smell of night and growth. Presently Heath swung out of bed, acutely aware of a body satiated with exercise and sex, a strong, responsive vehicle for his brain and spirit. After the crash it had taken a long time to repair his body, and the struggle to regain its total use had given him an appreciation of the luxury of strength and health. At thirty-three, he thought, padding

barefoot through the darkened villa, he was at the peak
of all his powers; perhaps he would never feel so strong
again. As always, sensuously, he savored every aspect of
the moment.

The children's bedroom was next to theirs, a night-
light burning in one corner. He entered it, stood for a
moment staring down at them with love and wonder. It
seemed incredible that such marvelous, complicated,
lovely organisms had come into being through the agency
of his and Claudia's embrace, the rightful fruit of love.
Small heads and rounded cheeks, pink, delicate lips
pursed with breathing, hands formed exquisitely—Hamp
had one thumb thrust comfortingly in his mouth—little,
almost animal feet, like a possum's or a coon's, thrust
from beneath the covers . . . He could not resist the
temptation to touch his son. In awe and pleasure his
hand capped the silky hair. Hamp stirred slightly, making a piggish noise with the thumb; when Heath withdrew it gently, his lips worked in deprivation like a
goldfish's, then quirked in a small, dreamy smile. Heath
wondered what he could possibly give them in recom-
pense for what they had given him—at least a partial re-
capturing of a kind of innocence that he supposed he
himself must once have possessed but had willfully
warped and soiled and ruined and squandered. They had,
in some measure, restored it to him, had made it impossible for him to believe in life again and want it. In
return he could help them grow, reach for that same
prize. For this much, at least, he was grateful to Bolivar:
the Old Man had taught him all the pitfalls, all the mistakes he must avoid with Hamp.

And with Ramsey too, of course. He looked down at
her briefly. He loved her as deeply as he loved her
brother, but his commitment to her was of a different
kind. Shared masculinity made Hamp his specific responsibility, but Ramsey was Claudia's. Another man
would someday take over his responsibility to his daughter, but his obligation to his son was lifelong. On his
skill, strength and love as a father depended the boy's
whole growth and survival as a man. There were things

he had to give Ramsey too, before she sheered off into the world of womanhood, where he could not follow; but his life and Hamp's would run together until the day he died. He pulled a blanket over Ramsey's foot. Hamp's thumb had found his mouth again; this time Heath did not remove it.

He left the bedroom, went down the stairs, then out onto the terrace. The moon was high and full, the lawn silvered, the nearby orchards and vineyards patterns of light and shadow. The Gothic spire of the little village church thrust against the sky. If this were North Carolina, a mockingbird would have sung deliriously, but there seemed to be no night birds here. Instead, as he sat down, savoring the touch of breeze through the thin fabric of his pajamas, something small moved across the terrace, waddled into light. Heath smiled. The hedgehog, not much bigger than a kitten, ignored him as it sought the saucer of milk Frau Mayer and the children put out for it every night. Finding it in the usual place, it thrust in its snout and drank, prickly spines across its back laid down, unalarmed. When it had had its fill, it shuffled on to wherever it lived here in the garden.

Heath leaned back in the chair. For this moment at least he never wanted to leave this place. And yet, he thought wryly, what a circuitous course of triumphs and disasters had led him to it. He had staggered into happiness like a drunken man slamming into doors and lampposts before he finally found his bed.

Later they told him that once, on the first night after the crash, he had no pulse at all, was actually given up for dead. Somehow that correlated with the one impression from that long interval of nonbeing he carried with him into recovery. There was a time when he stood alone in a deep bluish darkness of a special quality, enormous as space itself. Then, ahead, appeared two high, white pillars, pristine, fluted and free-standing, set apart to form a kind of gate. It was as if someone had built a temple on a midnight plain and then removed it, leaving only this pair of lovely columns, deserted, perfect,

glimmering. He stood before them, wanting to pass between, full of curiosity and a strange yearning to learn
what lay behind them. But it was a decision he himself
had to make, and he understood how momentous and
irrevocable it was; once he took another step, he could
not come back outside. Desperately he wanted to go
ahead, but the finality of doing that checked him, made
him quail. He hesitated there for a long time, fighting
with all his logic, will and fear the almost overpowering
desire to enter. Somehow he was conscious of too much
unfinished business to make that move; easy as it was,
as great as was his yearning, it was indulgence he could
not afford. By a deliberate act of will, at last he turned
away; the columns disappeared behind him in the boundless darkness as he retreated with a sense of loss and yet
of fear at how nearly he had passed between them; then
he was swallowed up again in that blackness that robbed
him of all consciousness of self until, much later, he
began to feel the pain.

He had hurt in his time, but never like this. The
penalty he paid for choosing life was exquisite agony. A
thousand long, dull skewers seemed to pierce him, turned
brutally and constantly within his flesh. No man fully
conscious could have borne that; drugs, he supposed, and
delirium turned it into a sort of dream. He and the pain
engaged in single combat, the worst battle he had ever
fought, requiring of him every scrap and scratch of
courage and endurance he could muster. Nor was it only
pain that he was fighting; something real, tangible, some
presence brutally impersonal, almost overpoweringly
strong and terribly efficient, wrestled with him, to drag
him back to that threshold he had refused to cross. He
could not relax his guard or slacken his resistance to this
grim, yet unmalign, adversary for one instant; he had
to fight beyond endurance and keep on fighting, his survival depending on nothing but a force of will that must
be like steel. He had never known how much courage
he actually possessed until that battle; for there was no
ally anywhere, no help, he had to do it all alone, in terrible and frightening solitude, beyond the reach of any-

one. He had never known either what loneliness was until then, nor how grievous it could be. Yet there was no help for it, no way any other human could enter that shadowy place in which he fought; it was the time when every man must stand alone, unarmed but for his own strength, a Jacob wrestling through the night with a powerful, unseen enemy.

Then, somehow, he knew he had won. Presently (ten days after the crash, he found out later) he opened his eyes, his vision cleared briefly, and he was no longer alone. Claudia was there, her face above him, her hand on his, and he had never known a sensation like the vanishing of that awful loneliness, the joy of touching, making connection with someone else. He would have wept, if he could, with returning to the world again. It was a miracle, and she was part of it, all he had, his only bulwark against that dark terror. He had won this battle, but there would be another one to fight someday, and he would not win that one. Knowing what he must face again, he understood how short time was, and how crucial it was not to be alone in the time remaining to him; and he found strength to close his hand and cling to hers as if it were a lifeline, a man with new knowledge he could not yet assess, but understanding the importance of the only shield anyone ever had against that ultimate time of solitary and inevitable defeat: love.

For weeks that was enough, strengthening him for the rearguard action he had yet to fight. The force with which he had been thrown against the seat belt had done hideous things to him internally; the broken ribs, compound fracture of the leg, cracked skull and lacerations had been the least of it. The battle against pain, the struggle for every new returning ounce of strength, was brutal, but at least, now, it did not have to be fought alone. He had to concentrate all his physical and emotional resources on it, and she was there, constantly, throughout his lengthening periods of rationality, whether they came by day or night. Not only did her presence reassure him; she was someone for whom he had to put together the shattered pieces of himself, become a personality again.

Like a frightened actor, he found courage in an audience, refusing to betray to her any fear or discouragement and thus conquering those things within himself. The two of them gave strength to each other, and in the process, as if he absorbed her in the healing, she became part of him in a way that no one else ever had, his very flesh; it was something beyond the definition of love that he had used until now. It was only part of the miracle of returning life, but the most important, the greatest discovery of this experience that had changed him, he could sense, in ways that he could not even yet begin to guess. "I love you," he said to her instinctively in those flashes of full consciousness, and found satisfaction in the saying; she only smiled and held his hand.

At last the pain diminished, enough strength returned for him to take an interest in the world beyond it; he began to ask questions, get answers that first were guarded, then more honest. Slowly he pieced together what had happened and understood affairs as they now existed. Fortunately he was too weak, passive, and drugged to be immediately concerned by their disastrous state.

The Tiercel's engine failure remained inexplicable. Baldwin, Claudia said, could only conjecture that he had designed into it more power than the alloys from which it was machined—and they were the strongest then existing—could tolerate. He took full responsibility for that; Heath himself, it seemed, had been acclaimed, lionized by the press for his skill and daring in maneuvering over the crowd, avoiding ghastly and seemingly inevitable slaughter. He was still something of a popular hero, with occasional bulletins on his condition appearing in the papers.

Then brief visits were allowed, and Baldwin came himself, told Heath the rest of it. The company was in receivership, beyond revival. Reluctantly, as Heath began to probe, he made the dimensions of the disaster clear. There were judgments against both of them and no hope of starting over. But his courage was not one whit less than Heath's; he was cheerful, optimistic. Despite its failure, the aircraft's design had engaged the interest of other companies; there was a chance of selling or licensing certain patents that the company held for individual components, enough to recoup partially. But that would be a long process; meanwhile Baldwin was selling bonds for a brokerage house.

They were alone in the hospital room at the time. And curiously, not until then did Heath remember Betty Hammond. She, like everything before the crash, seemed something from another world; he asked Baldwin about her with an odd indifference. The man only shrugged—nothing had been heard from her. He understood that shortly after the crash she had gone to California to make moving pictures. "I don't think she even called the hospital. I'm sorry."

"I'm not," said Heath, vaguely relieved. "It doesn't make a bit of difference." He was glad Claudia had not had her to cope with along with all the rest.

Which brought up a host of questions. One of them was answered when his mother appeared. Reduced to infantile helplessness in the bed, he was almost overwhelmed by the impact of her presence. But it turned out that she had been there, off and on, all along. Of course Claudia had called her as soon as it had happened; she had caught the train and had come at once. She looked old and tired and drawn, and Heath hated to ask the question, but he could not help it. At first she tried to put him off. "He's so busy. Things aren't going at all well with the mills." Bit by bit, though, he drew from her the facts; but when he understood, he quit, knowing how it must torment her.

Bolivar would not come. Bolivar would not even ask her how he was. Bolivar Chandler had no son, and thus was not affected one iota by what had happened. Heath fought back hatred of his father. Not for his indifference to his son, but for his brutality toward the mother of his son. For the first time his triumph over death seemed to diminish. Suddenly he had the childish thought that it would have served Bolivar right if he had not lived.

Other facts began to fit together in a bleak mosaic.

Six weeks had passed since the crash. He had months more in hospital, though the doctors were optimistic that he would regain almost total fitness eventually. Meanwhile, he realized suddenly, he was a pauper—worse than that, over his head in debt. And helpless, unable to earn a penny. How had Claudia lived so far, how would she live? Of course, there was Chandler money—but Bolivar controlled all that and Bolivar had no son. For that matter, Heath, in the mood in which his mother's visits left him, would have died before seeking a single penny from his father, even if it was available, even if Bolivar had not arranged things so that Elizabeth was a virtual pauper too, except for what he chose to give her.

Finally, he learned, she had borrowed money from her own family, the Charleston Hamptons. They were closely knit by blood. Even though their fortunes failed now in the postwar slump that had hit the cotton market, they had scraped up some cash. So had Fox Ramsey, still in prison in Atlanta. He had made what he had left—not much—available to Claudia. Neither sum would come close to amortizing all the debts. And, on top of that, Claudia's pregnancy became more noticeable every day. At first he had almost forgotten that, it was part of the blur of his precrash life; and, curiously, Claudia did not remind him. But he saw and remembered and understood with a kind of horror that long before he could do any gainful work he would be a father, with an obligation to another human, and one he could not fulfill.

Amidst a growing frustration and despair he perceived then something he had never known before, though it must have been instinctively and grimly bred into the bone of the lowest, most ignorant mill hand he had ever met. Life never gave you rest. Like a relentless employer, devoid of sympathy, it demanded its due, fairly or unfairly, caring not one whit how you contrived to give it. Neither better nor worse than death, but only different, it played no favorites, not even him.

That was the hardest knowledge. Until now he had thought it worked another way. He had conceived that, because he was himself, Heath Chandler, its rules were

uspended for him, that he could awe it into yielding a
:ey to the magic door, beyond which lay fulfillment, un-
nding happiness, perfection. Now he understood that,
eally, life cared not a damn about him. There was no
nagic door. No rules would be suspended for him;
ruelly and impartially it would continue its demands,
nd not even winning that battle in the darkness with the
ingel would earn him one second's time off.

He would have sunk then into despair, despite Clau-
lia's unflagging courage, if it had not been for the miracle
hat Olin Clutterbuck wrought.

As soon as he could call for anyone besides Claudia,
.e had asked for Olin, and Clutterbuck had been there,
upplying a different kind of strength. Olin—like Bald-
rin—had some inkling of what he had been through, the
esperation of that solitary battle. Both men understood
eath in a way that Claudia could not possibly have
:arned to; and both were just contemptuous enough of
to keep Heath from sliding into either self-pity or self-
lorification because of his victory over it. Because they
new how serious that battle was, they could joke about
; and that was what he then most desperately needed:
iat cool, hard, masculine restoration of perspective. It
ould have been easy to wallow in Claudia's concern and
is own childish helplessness, but it would have de-
ieaned him before the men; and the two of them
elped restore his masculinity, his sensation of having
ender during the long and sexless phase of helplessness
irough which he passed. But Clutterbuck did more than
iat. He was the one person to whom Heath could talk,
infess misgivings; and when he understood what was
appening in Heath's mind, he took action.

When Heath was able to sit up, use arms and hands
id mind, and when the hours stretched longer and
inger every day, despite Claudia's presence, Clutterbuck
ppeared with a thick notebook, a box of sharpened pen-
ils, and a stranger. Actually, what he bore was hope.

"Heath, this is Phil Montague. Phil, Heath Chandler."

Montague was in his thirties, small, dapper, with a
ark mustache and quick, gray, intelligent eyes. "Mr.

Chandler, it's a pleasure. You don't know how happy
am to see you on the road to recovery. Now I'll get to th
point. Olin tells me that you've got a play in you—I under
stand you've had Baker's course at Harvard—and"—h
smiled faintly—"it looks like you've got time to write it.

"A play," Heath said dully, not quite comprehending.

"Surely you've seen or heard of my productions, *Th
Hearthfire* and *The Deaths of Kings*. Both hits, I'm prou
to say, critically and at the box office." Something flare
in Heath's mind, a quick, vaulting interest, as the ma
went on. "Now I'm looking for a new one. What I reall
want is a play about the war. Olin tells me you've ha
one in mind ever since you fought in France. The wa
he describes it, it's to be something new, absolutely au
thentic, the way it really was. I don't think there's bee
such a play yet, and I think that now the time is ripe fc
one. The romantic glamour has faded; people know no
that it wasn't all beer and skittles. I believe they'd lik
a real look behind the scenes. I think they're ready fc
the straight, unvarnished thing."

Already Heath felt excitement beating in him. "But
he said, "I've never written a play before—not really."

Montague's mouth curled in a smile. "I know that. An
I'm making no promises. But you've got the insid
knowledge, you've had the training, and you've got th
time. And I'm a gambler. Everybody in the theater is
but you ask anybody, they'll tell you Phil Montague's
little crazy and makes it pay off. Well, I've got a gan
bler's hunch. Can you write? Are you equal to th
sustained effort?"

"I don't know," Heath said. "I can try."

"Then, fair enough. This is the time for me to strik
while you're undistracted. If you'd undertake a pl
about the air war, the *real* air war . . . Of course, the
are limitations; it all has to take place on the ground, yc
know, except that I think I could put a real Spad on th
stage, think what a sensation that would create, when i
engine started— Well, we'll talk about that. Anyhow, I
like to have you try it and I'd like to work along wi
you on it. You're going to make false starts and have tro

ble, no two ways about it, but I can save you some mistakes. Would you undertake such a thing for two thousand dollars' advance against a standard playwright's contract?"

"Two thousand dollars." Once it had seemed a paltry sum, but he was acutely aware now of what a fortune it really was. Then, because it was so magnificent, he had misgivings. "I don't know—"

"No one does until opening night." Montague's smile stayed fixed. "On the other hand, Mr. Chandler—may I call you Heath?—you have a certain advantage. You're not an unknown. You've been twice a hero in the papers—during the war and . . . recently. Your name alone would insure a certain interest. Enough so I'd risk the two thousand now on your signature and, say, another three as we progress and finish satisfactorily, against royalties, unrefundable if the play's not a success. That's the Phil Montague way; I'll gamble if you want to gamble too."

Heath was silent, unbelieving, for a moment. Five thousand dollars. And, what was more, he could do it; he felt in his bones that he could do it. In that instant the world shifted, changed again, and he came back totally to life. He looked at Olin with gratitude for this miracle, at Montague as if afraid the man would vanish. He drew in a long breath.

"Mr. Montague," he said, "I'll do my damnedest."

Montague's smile widened. "Call me Phil," he said and put out his hand.

Eight months later, after a nightmare of hard work, *Squadrons High* opened in a theater on West Forty-second Street, shocked the public with its grim realism and brutal, obscene soldier talk, became a smash hit and created a new genre in legitimate drama. Heath Chandler, using two canes, was present at the premiere. So was Claudia, who, a month before, had given birth to twins.

The wind had turned a little cool in the garden of the villa. Heath arose, went inside. Claudia breathed with sibilant regularity and instinctively moved against him as he slid gratefully beneath the cover to share the

warmth created by her body, rolled over, cupped her
right breast in his hand, and clung to her as if she were
life itself.

The next day he got the cablegram.

2   THE RAIN had poured for two days now
and showed no sign of slackening. Late April, and it was
chilly as February. Fox threw more coal into the mouth
of the potbellied stove that heated the little store and
spread his hands to warm them, while, overhead, the tin
roof vibrated with a constant rhythm, like a muted snare-
drum. Then, restless, he went behind the counter, got a
new pack of cigarettes, and, opening it, strode to the door
pulled it open, and looked out.

The road from Chandlerville to Macedonia had been
paved now; otherwise it would have been a sea of mud
like the drowned fields across the way. Through the gray
curtain and the white, constant sheet of spill from the
porch's gutterless eaves, the grove of pines on the hill
beyond looked dark, forlorn. Fox shook his head at all
that bleakness and shivered beneath the heavy sweater
A bad spring, he thought, I've never seen a worser one

He sighed, closed the door, and turned to survey the
small room. The stock on the shelves was scanty, only
bare necessities, but no one had money to buy anything
else, anyhow. What little he did sell, on top of that, was
on credit. Or no, not on credit, even—just on hope
Credit was a business thing, with a kind of logic, certain
rules; it presupposed the buyer could pay eventually
When that assurance vanished, then the whole nature of
his trade had altered into something inexplicable, nearly
every transaction now motivated not by hope of profit, or
even of payment, but by necessity, buyer and seller alike
stripped of those identities, reduced to two humans in
time of crisis, one with goods, the other in need, and the
emergency so great that nothing else really counted. Be

ath his salt-and-ginger beard Fox's mouth twisted.
pression. The papers—he had learned to read in prison
vere full of it. But they did not even know what De-
ssion was, those Yankees who were howling loudest.
them it was something new. But here it had been a
t of life for nearly a decade now, like sunrise and sun-
and the rain and heat.

3y the time he had been released, in 1922, the bottom
1 already dropped out—in Macedon County, in North
rolina, in the whole South. He came home to a land
m with poverty after the brief flare of wartime pros-
ity. Cotton had once again betrayed them all. Not
y had the boll weevil made its appearance, rapacious
hail, but there was no market for the crop that survived
silent gnawing. The world was full of cotton, glutted
h it, and yet it was the only thing these people knew
v to grow; even when each crop was foredoomed to
aster, they went on planting it, whether as an act of
h or simply of insanity, madness, Fox could not tell.
t there was no place to sell it, neither abroad nor at
ne—especially not at home.

Rayon, they said, that was part of it. The new fiber
de of wood that felt almost like silk. Women were go-
crazy over rayon. It seemed ridiculous, Fox thought,
urning to the stove and soaking up its warmth, that
whims of women, a change in what they took a notion
wear, could plunge a whole section of the country
o poverty, that the bellies of men, women, and children
ld be dependent for their food on women's fashions.
1 yet it must be so; everybody said it was. But it
med to him that it was more than that. People had
nted on the war lasting a lot longer; down here, new
ton mills and additions to the old ones had exploded,
operators grabbing for the dollar while it was there.
n the Armistice had blasted all their dreams. The
rtime demand had tapered off, then vanished. Mean-
ile new workers had been lured down from the
untains and off their farms and made dependent on
h wages. Barely had they become used to living off
checks when the paychecks first were sharply cut,

and then, for many, stopped entirely. For almost t
years now the jaws of the hard-times vise had clos
notch by notch, a little tighter every year; and now,
last, their clamp was brutal. This was it, this was the en
something had to happen.

Something was, in fact, already happening. The unio
and the Communists were moving in. Look at Gastor
last year, what had happened at the Loray Mill, in t
town that prided itself on operating more spindles th
any other city in the world, even Macedonia. The Yank
management there had tried the stretch-out, increasing
the limits of human endurance the number of machin
each worker had to tend. Promptly the National Text
Workers Union had moved in and organized seve
hundred of the nearly two thousand workers. Twen
were fired, and the union called a strike.

Its demands had frightened and outraged mill own
all across the South: a twenty-dollar weekly minimu
wage—for women and children as well as men; aboliti
of piecework; a five-day week and eight-hour day; bett
working conditions; improvement of mill housing and re
reduction; and, most terrible of all, union recognition.
federal mediator had been called in, advised the own
to have no dealings with the union. Then the strikebrea
ers came, the scabs, and with them five companies
militia sent to protect them. Immediately war broke o
The whole power of the state was thrown behind the eff
to stamp out something that, if allowed to grow, wou
menace the entire foundation of the cloth and ya
industry, indeed, of every business: the right of a
owner to use his property as he saw fit and to hire and f
at his own discretion. If the strike succeeded, it cou
bring tumbling down the whole southern, indeed, Ame
can, structure of life.

Charges, countercharges. Violence, counterviolen
State Guard and special deputies. Union headquart
raided, its commissary looted, kerosene poured on foo
Then the gun battle, when the chief of police and f
deputies raided the tent colony built for strikers evict
from the village. Men were wounded, Chief Aderh

illed. The explosion was total—the town, the state, the
ills, against the strikers, their spearhead a "Committee
f One Hundred," a private army. Almost a hundred
trikers were charged with murder, assault with intent to
ill, conspiracy to murder, or felonious assault. Organiz-
rs were kidnapped, beaten; a woman on her way to a
nion meeting was shot and killed. The attention of the
whole country was drawn to the final trial of the union
rganizers in September: the northerners, four of them,
rew the stiffest sentences—seventeen to twenty years
or second-degree murder; two southerners got twelve
o fifteen, and one five to seven. Of course some were
admitted Communists.

The whole thing had bothered Fox, nearly turned his
tomach. Partly it was his own prison experience. Two
ears in a federal pen had been bad enough; with his
bred love of freedom, the thought of twenty in a state
rison, where the men would be singled out for special
reatment—damned hard treatment—was appalling; he
ondered if he wouldn't kill himself before enduring it.
esides, his loyalties were divided. A victim himself of
he high-handedness of one of the most powerful textile
agnates in the state, he knew how, caught up in the
ils of The Law, they must have felt: powerless, help-
ss; indeed, they were. And yet . . . and yet his mountain
eritage cried out against their rebellion.

If they didn't like their jobs, they were free to go, find
hers, if they could. A man's property was his property:
st so, no question about it. You worked for him, you
d his bidding; if he made you do something against
e grain, you spat in his eye and walked off; that was all.
was a matter of pride; and when you came down to
a man had little else. He would not have struck; he
ould only have left, or, if the grievance were severe
ough, maybe have got some dynamite and thrown it
gainst the mill before he went. He couldn't make head
tail of it at all, but he knew this: things were changing
own here; some kind of seed had been planted. If things
t worse instead of better, no telling what bitter shoot
sour fruit it would send up.

He saw no prospect of their getting better. Mills a
over the state had closed down or ran on short tim
while they strove to sell their inventories. No mill han
knew from one day to the next how many hours or hov
many days he would work or get paid for. Except—h
amended the thought—Chandler's people.

It was astonishing. The Old Man refused to yield. Har
times or no, he somehow kept all three plants running
paid his help on time. He had cut wages, yes, cut ther
to the bone. But still the Chandler people drew the
weekly cash; and, God knows, he made them earn i
which was only just and fair. Nobody knew how he mar
aged when all his competitors had ground to a disma
halt. Only the driblet of hard money from the Chandle
payroll kept Fox himself alive. He could have made
fortune in moonshine whiskey in these times; the wors
things were, the more people drank. But he'd had enoug
of prison, would not risk it again. What money he ha
left when he came out he'd put into this little store, hal
way between Macedonia and Chandlerville. Now tha
there was only himself, so far he had managed to surviv

But for how much longer? There had not been a cus
tomer all morning. Of course, with the way things wer
that might be a blessing.

Then, above the drum and splash of rain, he heard th
car. It stopped outside. There was an interval, whil
instinctively, he went behind the counter. Then, foo
steps on the porch, the door opened, and Bolivar Chandle
came in.

Fox Ramsey stared incredulously.

A few times in the past eight years he had passed th
Old Man on the streets of Chandlerville, maybe twic
maybe three times. And not in nearly a year. They ke
away from each other, well away. Chandler knew he wa
here, of course, but never until now had he set foot i
Fox's store.

He paused, just inside the door, clad in a black wint
suit and an overcoat drenched by the cascade from th
porch's roof. Water dripped from the brim of his sodde
gray hat. Before he even looked at Fox he shuttled blu

eyes around the room, coolly, professionally, and that gave
Fox time to assess what the years, the months just past,
had done to him. He must be nearly eighty now, Fox
thought—and, Lord, he looks it!

For Chandler had become an enormous head and a
big paunch on withered pipestems of legs, a caricature
of the bull-like little man that Fox remembered. His face
seemed to have collapsed, as if, made of wax, it had been
left too close to heat and had begun to melt. When he
finally turned that huge dome slowly and focused those
cold blue eyes on Fox, then came toward the counter, he
walked slowly, delicately, as if not entirely sure his legs
would carry him. His brows were dead white, so were
the shaggy strands escaping beneath the hat. His lips
were colorless, and the seams around them were deep;
his chin, seeming to recede, supported wattles of loose
flesh.

"Howdy," Fox said tonelessly.

"Howdy," Chandler said. He dug into his pocket,
brought out a small suede purse. His blue-veined, mottled
hands shook as he pried it open, dug in it. "Have you
got any Juicy Fruit chewing gum?"

"Sure," said Fox. He took a pack from a box, laid it on
the counter.

Slowly, with begrudgement and calculation, Bolivar
disbursed the nickel. His nails clawed at the counter as
he picked up the pack of gum; arthritis, Fox thought
then. Suddenly a shiver racked the old man. Fox said,
"You better go stand over by the stove a minute and warm
yourself. It's mighty cold outside today."

"Yes," said Chandler. To Fox's surprise, he did that,
backing up to the heater, rubbing the withered, crippled
hands together. He did not look at Fox.

A moment passed, in which the rain sound seemed even
louder. Chandler did not open the gum, but put it in
his pocket. Fox came around the counter. "I'll throw in
some more coal, it's gittin low." He did so, as Chandler
moved aside. The fire roared, gulping the fresh fuel.

More silence. Then Fox understood. He could not say
how he knew, but he did, as surely as he knew he lived

and breathed and stood here. The silence stretched, as he waited for the Old Man to speak. But Bolivar did not. At last he dropped his coattail and turned to go. As he shambled toward the door Fox drew in a deep breath.

"I had a letter from 'em last week. There was some pictures in it. You want to see 'em?"

Chandler halted.

"They are mighty likely-looking young-uns," said Fox, feeling deep pity all at once.

"I'm sure," said Chandler. He coughed then, deeply, and it racked him. The coughing went on for nearly a minute. During that time Fox went back to the counter, took out the cigar box in which he kept the letters. "Here. If you want to look."

"I ain't got the time." Bolivar pulled out a handkerchief, blew his nose, snuffled ropily. But otherwise he did not move.

Fox waited. Bolivar sniffled some more. Then he said, "I might need two packs of gum. You got another one?"

"Yeah."

"Let me have it." Bolivar came stiffly back to the counter. The envelope lay there. While he got out his purse again, Fox opened its unsealed flap, shoved the photographs out across the counter top, arranged them. "I reckon you at least know their names," he said. "One's named Hampton—the boy; the other one, the girl's, named Ramsey. They are all healthy and doing well."

"Let me have my chewing gum, please," said Bolivar.

Fox turned to the shelf behind him. He kept his back to Chandler long enough to give him time to look. "They seem happy over yonder. Them plays of his keep runnin and runnin and they got a lot of money. The kids speak German good as they do English."

Bolivar made a thick, hawking sound. He was full of phlegm.

"Heath's totally recovered. You'd never know he was so banged up." Fox turned with the pack of gum in his hand; then he stopped. Bolivar was not even aware of his presence. He was staring hungrily at the pictures: Heath and Pearl and the young ones all in a group before some kind of statue. Another one of Hamp and Ramsey feeding an elephant in a zoo.

"They're likely-lookin kids," Fox said. "Here's your gum."

"Thank you," said Chandler, and he laid down another nickel.

"I've got lots more pictures. You can take them with you if you want 'em."

"No," Chandler said. He was shivering again beneath the overcoat.

"You better go on home," Fox said. "You're catchin cold."

"I'm all right," Chandler said. He looked around the store again. "You got a good stock. Not too much, not too little."

"Keepin store is a hard thing," Fox said.

Chandler, coughing, nodded. "It sure is," he said. "There's an art to it." He turned away.

"They sent the same pictures to your wife," Fox said.

Chandler did not answer. He opened the door, went out. Fox caught a glimpse of the big, black LaSalle parked outside, the chauffeur behind its wheel. He saw the old man hunker through the downpour off the eaves, open the door for himself, work himself painfully within. Fox went to the door, stood there as the car drove off. He watched it move along the road toward Chandlerville in the rain.

"Hell," Fox said as he closed the door and went back to the stove. "Two packs of gum. Shit." He spat on the stove's top and watched the spittle hiss, sizzle away.

3   CLAUDIA TRIED to sit immobile while Olin sketched a preliminary study for the portrait. Outside, on the terrace, Frau Mayer supervised the children's play; in the room overhead, Heath's footsteps were audible as he arose from his work table and stretched his legs. The day was warm for April, and a drowsy,

sunlit silence trembled unbroken in the air. It was pleasant to sit here in the place allocated to Olin for a studio and have the excuse to be as still and quiet as a resting cat.

She felt like a cat today, one full of cream—smug, self-satisfied. Her mind could drift, without even minor concern; she was so content that she had no more fantasies to weave. It was, she thought, almost frightening to have achieved such a Nirvana, no longer to need or want anything but for this voluptuous stasis to continue always. . . .

Of course it could not. Someday there would be another change; in what direction, she could not imagine. Maybe she would be ready for it then; maybe this very contentment would bore and cloy her. But until it did . . . Instinctively she crossed her fingers.

Meanwhile there had been changes enough; she had lived through enough incarnations: Pearl, the bootlegger's daughter; Claudia, the would-be flapper, sure that the right lipstick, the perfect hat or the latest book would somehow magically unlock her husband's love.

That Pearl, that Claudia, were dream figures now, children at whom she could smile with amusement and compassion. Not until the crash had she found out what it meant to be a woman.

There she could take some credit to herself. Any woman faced with such an ordeal—husband suspended between life and death, herself pregnant for the first time, flat broke and in what was still a strange city, a hostile, foreign environment—well, either she would come apart or she would develop strength enough to see her through the rest of life. And she had not—say that for herself—come apart, though the margin of survival had sometimes been precarious, her despair almost more than she could bear.

But that was over now, mercifully almost erased from memory. And she had gained from it, more than she'd had any right to hope. Heath's survival would have been enough; that some sea change had taken place within him while he drifted in unconsciousness, transmuting tolerance to love, was greater miracle. Perhaps she would never understand it, but she did not care about that; it was fact, proved and proved again. She was content to accept it.

And then the other miracle—she looked at Olin fondly as he stared back, not seeing anything but planes and lines, as if she were a cone or cube—the one he'd wrought, the play—and all the money and success. Add to that Hamp and Ramsey—her eyes shuttled to the window—it was eerie. So much good luck. She was the most fortunate of women.

And yet neither Heath's love nor his triumph had meant the end of struggle, not for her. Quite the contrary; there were new challenges. They had moved uptown, into a different world, when *Squadrons High* had clicked, one as foreign to her as the Village had been after Chandlerville.

It was a world of grace and privilege, inhabited by the elegant aristocracy of success and wealth as well as birth. In the Village, propriety was despised; here it was everything. Tradition, rules, and style counted and were valued, and understatement was a way of life. This world had its codes and its demanding rituals, and she had to learn them all, for its inhabitants had standards and required that they be met. There were boors, fools, and drunkards among them, of course, but even when they broke the rules, the rules were valued all the same. Heath, purged of the agony and confusion that had hagridden him ever since she had known him, now seemingly certain of his own identity and strength, drifted to them naturally—many of them had been his Harvard classmates or fellow officers. Seeming to have outgrown Clutterbuck and his raucous circle, they were, apparently, what he needed; he felt at home with them.

Not so Claudia. At first she was staggered and dismayed at how much she had to learn, simply not to disgrace him in this company. But, curiously, she was accepted more readily here than even in the Village. Finally she realized that the basic teachings she'd absorbed from Fox and her dimly remembered mother met their basic

standards. She had that foundation. Moreover, she also,
it dawned on her, knew who she was now; she, too, had
her own identity. She made mistakes, but as long as they
were honest, without pompousness or pretension, no one
minded. Suddenly it seemed to her that this was a very
good world indeed and one she had a talent for. It contained things she wanted, and she set about getting them,
watching, learning, accepting, rejecting. In two years she
was as much at home in it as Heath; and if there had
ever been a time when she was not, she and everyone
else seemed to have forgotten it.

Except Fox, of course. Released from prison, he had
come to visit them. He was quieter, too, muted, seemingly
purged of any need for outlawry. They tried to be as
natural with one another as they could, but he was uncomfortable in this world, and she could no longer revert
to his with ease. Sometimes she caught him looking at
her with a kind of awe. But his reconciliation with them
both, with her and Heath, was total; his grandchildren
ensured that. He was almost ludicrously doting with
them, and they adored him, and he could feel at ease
with them. Still, after he had gone home and bought the
store with the money she had borrowed from him and
which Heath had repaid with interest, he visited them
only infrequently, though his appetite for letters and
photographs was insatiable.

"Turn your head," said Clutterbuck. "Just a little, to
the right."

"Like this?"

"There. Fine."

But they never went to visit Fox. Not once did either
of them propose it, and neither did he; and, of course,
that was because of Bolivar Chandler.

Unwittingly, Claudia shifted on the chaise longe, and
Clutterbuck said, "Watch it."

"Sorry." She resumed the posture. She wished she had
not thought of Bolivar; it tore the pleasant fabric of the
day. But if there was one person in the world for whom
she felt genuine hatred, that was the Old Man, as Heath
still called him.

But how could you help hating a man like that? One whose son lay dying and who never even asked after him, much less offered help. One whose wife was a nervous wreck, torn between son and husband, and still, not even for her sake would he unbend that iron neck. A man who would never acknowledge the existence of his two grandchildren, who had never sent congratulations to his son, the most successful playwright of the decade. No wonder just the mention, the very thought, of Bolivar was enough to menace Heath's balance even now. His mother's letters always ended, *Your father is well.* Delicately, carefully, never any other word of him, but still Heath drank heavily every time a letter came. Sometimes she thought he did not read them at all.

"Ready for a break?" asked Olin.

"No, I'm not a bit tired. Go on if you like."

"Okay, I'll strike while the iron's hot."

She could not understand the workings of a mind like that, had quit trying. Still, she hated him because he remained a threat, the only one, to Heath's well-being. She was pretty sure it was because of him that Heath had grown restless once again, insisted on this move to Europe. As if he had wanted to put as much distance between the two of them as possible, as if not even nearly seven hundred miles was quite enough to keep Bolivar out of mind as well as out of sight.

Of course, there were other reasons. Everyone was going; even Clutterbuck, by that time having failed in New York, had left for Paris. Besides, New York—or was it America in general?—had seemed to cloy Heath. With his second play's success, it became harder for him to find time to work. Beyond that, he had a love for Europe that had baffled her until she had come here herself; then she understood it. Whatever kind of people they had become, it was a place for people like them.

Because of wartime connections, he was known, received, everywhere. She spent weekends in chilly English country houses, drank cocktails in brightly lit Mayfair flats; they made love in their Ritz Hotel suite; she ate *escargots* in Maxim's, drank cognac on the Left Bank, acquired a tan at Juan-les-Pins, and marveled at each new world that opened to her, seized whatever she could find within it that pleased her, in the way she had learned, and made it hers, subtly altering with every experience. Then that part of it, the initial blast, was over. It was time for Heath to go back to work, for her to digest what she had learned. They sought a place, found the villa outside of Vienna and fell in love with it at once. They were now in their second year here, and it seemed to her that she had lived here always. Chandlerville was a dream, New York not much more than that. The reality was the countryside, the marvelous, baroque, and various city itself, with its charming, careless people, and the fact that they loved each other and were enough for one another. Of course it would change, it had to change, and yet . . .

Her leg cramped. "I've got to move," she said.

"Sure. No professional would have held a pose nearly as long." Clutterbuck laid down the charcoal, and they both arose and stretched. "Want to take a look?"

"No, it might dismay me if I look before you finish."

"You're smart. It's pretty dismaying." He took out cigarettes and lit one. His hands were steadier, she noted, than when he had first arrived. She hoped he would stay a long time. He was good for Heath, and she thought both of them would be good for him. He needed reassurance, maybe a little mothering. She would have to find a girl for him, with just the right combination of intelligence, beauty, and sensuality. There were plenty like that in Vienna, and she had friends she could inquire of frankly. Inwardly she smiled. A man would call it pimping, she supposed, but women called it matchmaking.

Then she heard Heath's tread in the corridor. Dressed in white shirt, flannel trousers, canvas shoes, he halted just inside the door. "I see you haven't got down to the part yet where she has to take her clothes off, Clutt."

"That comes later, when you're away," said Olin.

Heath came up behind him, peered at the easel. "Strange, I never noticed before that she had three eyes and a nose like a piece of chewing gum parked on some-body's bedpost."

"You go to hell," Clutterbuck and Claudia said simultaneously.

"Not without a drink to keep me cool. The sun's over the yardarm."

"I'm ready." Claudia came toward them. "Have a good, productive day?"

"I've got writer's cramp and a numb butt. Occupational hazards. I should have gone into this line of work"—he gestured at the easel—"with nothing to do but sit and look at naked women all day."

"I'm not naked."

"Yes you are. Clutt's been undressing you with his eyes." He seized her. "Come here," he said, kissing her briefly but with force. "Get back a little of my own. Who wants Scotch and who wants wine?"

"Scotch," said Clutterbuck.

"Me too," Claudia told him.

"Okay, let's go out on the—" He broke off as the bell at the front gate rang. "Oh, hell, somebody soliciting for the Old Soldiers' Home again, I reckon."

"Frau Mayer'll see to it." Claudia slipped her arm through his. "Which one of you gentlemen will offer me a cigarette?"

"Those things'll ruin your heart and lungs," Heath said. He took out a pack. Then a door slammed in the back of the house, they heard Frau Mayer's footsteps in the corridor, and Claudia could tell immediately that she was agitated. Her hand froze with the cigarette halfway to her mouth, and for some reason her heart kicked strangely. Then the woman knocked, bustled in, plump, apologetic. "Entschuldigen, bitte. Aber . . . für d' Herr." She held out a folded square of white paper.

"Cablegram?" Heath took it, frowning. "Must be from Montague. About the script revisions— Danke schön, Frau Mayer."

Full of curiosity, the governess reluctantly left the room. Claudia was aware of apprehension rising in herself like the faint malaise of incipient sickness as Heath, a little clumsily, opened the sealed paper. She watched his face as he unfolded it, began to read. Of course, he often got cables from producer, publisher, or bank. Nevertheless . . .

He gulped the phrase with his eyes as always; the swiftness with which he read was incredible. For a couple of seconds his face revealed nothing. Then it went hard and his lips peeled back in a kind of snarl. "Shit," he said.

She had not felt this way since the sheriff had come for Fox. Her hand trembled as she reached for the message. In German script, the words, copied painstakingly by the postmistress, leaped up at her: BOLIVAR CHANDLER VERY SICK PNEUMONIA DOCTORS FEAR WORST MAYBE YOU SHOULD COME NO TIME TO LOSE REGARDS FOX.

With a kind of numbness Claudia gave the paper to Olin.

Heath's face was an unwholesome pasty white. Jerkily he took out a cigarette, thrust it into his mouth. Around it he said harshly, "I'm not going. The hell with him."

Claudia felt a vast relief flood over her. In that instant she had felt a black menace that had been terrifying. And yet . . . It was not of her own volition that she said it. "You have to."

Heath turned on her swiftly, furiously. "No, I don't! Why should I? He doesn't have a son! Don't that mean I don't have a father?"

"I don't know." Her knees felt weak; she sank into Olin's chair behind the easel. Why had she said that? What had wrenched it from her when the last thing she wanted was to go back there? Why was she so afraid, feeling confronted by two evils from which they must choose the lesser?

"I don't know," she said again. Then she thought of Elizabeth, the aged woman, thin, nervous, terrified, who had braved her husband's wrath so many times—to let Heath escape; then to come to him when he lay almost dying. She was a mother too; maybe it was that instinctive kinship, allegiance . . . No, she realized suddenly, more than that. Some wisdom she had not known she possessed steadied her voice, for now she knew she spoke elemental truth. "If you don't go, later you'll wish you had. All right, he didn't forgive you. But you've got to forgive him, don't you see? Now. He'll be dead, whatever hatred he felt will be ended. But you're alive. When his is gone, why should you carry yours around with you forever?" She stood up then. "Go home," she said fiercely. "Go on home, bad as it'll be, and clean it out, end it all now. Get it out of you, and—Don't be like him. Finish this business now, once for all."

Heath stood there looking at her. "No. No, I don't want to. You don't understand."

"I understand this. That if you don't go home right away, you'll carry around a wound the rest of your life that'll never heal." She made a gesture. "*He* doesn't matter; your mother does. She's had enough, why hurt her more?" Then Claudia gripped his wrist. "Look," she said, "it's only for a little while. You go, we'll wait here."

Heath pulled his hand away.

Claudia stood up. "He's little," she said fiercely. "You're big. But if you don't go now, you'll be little too, from now on."

Heath turned away from both of them, stared at the easel with its charcoaled board. "You make it sound so easy." His voice was hoarse. "It ain't that easy."

"He can't hurt you. He's dying."

"Claudia," Olin said then. "Maybe you don't know—"

"Hush, Olin. I know." She was silent for a moment, looking at her husband's back. "All right," she said. "We'll go with you. All of us. The children. Maybe even Olin. We'll leave Frau Mayer in charge, and if you'll go into Vienna tomorrow and make the ship arrangements, we'll be ready in a day's time."

Still he did not speak.

"Heath," she said. Then she looked at Olin. "Will you come too? We need you."

Olin gestured helplessly. "Yes, I guess—" His face changed then, became more decisive. "Claudia's right, Heath. I've been through this, I know."

"So have I. I was dying and he didn't come to me."

"Strangely enough," Olin said, and he put a hand on

Heath's shoulder, "you'll find out that makes no difference now. You don't have to live with him any longer. But you've got to live with yourself. It'll be easier if you go."

Again that silence. Then Heath said in a muffled voice, "All right. If you'll go too. If you'll all go."

"We will," said Claudia. She felt neither triumph nor relief; if anything, that sense of being menaced intensified. But she had to live with herself as well, and this was a price to pay that could not be avoided. But she was fortunate. For her there was much to do; Heath could only wait and seethe.

4   THEY WERE, in the event, too late.

The Old Man hung on doggedly; each day while they were at sea the cabled message was the same: FATHER'S CONDITION UNCHANGED ALL MY LOVE MOTHER. But his lungs were full of fluid, he was drowning from the inside out. The night before they landed in New York, as they sat in the ship's bar, the steward brought Heath another message. Even before he opened it, all three knew what it contained.

He had been drinking steadily, but he was not drunk, nor had he been at any time. All the way he had been under control, as if this were any ordinary, pleasant crossing; and he had taken great delight in showing the children around the ship. Now, as he read the slip of paper, his face was expressionless. He passed it to Claudia. "Well," he said quietly, "that's the end of it."

MR. L. HEATH CHANDLER CARE S.S. AQUITANIA. FATHER PASSED PEACEFULLY TODAY STOP FUNERAL PENDING YOUR ARRIVAL STOP CALL FROM NEW YORK ALL MY LOVE MOTHER.

Claudia gave it to Clutterbuck. "I'm sorry," she said. It was inane, but there was nothing else to say.

Heath smiled faintly, shrugged. But his hands were nervous, drummed the table, and he smoked incessantly as they sat in silence. Presently he arose. "Excuse me for a while," he said and went out. When he had not returned in fifteen minutes, Claudia and Olin went looking for him. From the first-class promenade they saw him at the stern, alone, a wind-whipped silhouette, watching the swirl and foam of the wake in the glare of the after running lights. They left him there.

Claudia was already asleep when he returned to the stateroom. She was only vaguely aware of the weight of his body in the bed beside her. He kept the light on for a while, reading, then turned it off, rolled over, put his arm around her, held her very tightly, and went to sleep.

Fox Ramsey met them at the Macedonia station.

It had been a long time since they had seen him, and Heath was startled at how old he'd become, how small he looked, especially in the unaccustomed shabby suit and tie. He had developed a pot belly, round as a watermelon, though the rest of him was almost scrawny. Presently the children's excitement at the reunion had ebbed and he had a chance to talk to Heath. As the chauffeur loaded the baggage in Bolivar's big LaSalle he said, "Your mama's takin it kind of hard."

"That's to be expected," Heath said.

"Yes." Fox met his eyes. "I hope you ain't going to—"

"No," Heath said. "You know me better than that. I'm not going to make it any worse for her."

"Besides," Fox said, "I think he was changin a little there at the end."

"You two go on, get in the car," Heath said. He gave the children a push. Clutterbuck hustled them into the sedan. Heath looked at Fox. He had been very careful to feel nothing at all so far, had allowed himself neither grief nor hatred, had maintained, by a delicate adjustment, a total numbness of emotion. Now Fox's words threatened that. "What do you mean?"

"You know, since I been back from down yonder"—he meant the prison—"I never swapped a single word with him. Until week before last. Jest before he come down with it. Then he come by the store. It was pourin cold rain and he already had a hackin cough, but he had to have two packs of chewin gum. A devil of a long way to go to buy two packs of gum."

Fox took off his hat, ran his hand through thinning hair. "I knowed blame well he never come for no chewing gum. He piddled around there, but he couldn't git up nerve enough to ask. So I made it easy for him. Put out the letters and the pictures. Then I had other business. If it means anything, he looked at 'em."

Heath was silent for a moment. *If it means anything* . . . No. No, it had no meaning. "You're wrong, Fox. He didn't have to come to you. Mother had all that stuff."

"And you think, with his pride, he'd ask her to let him see it? I don't know," Fox said. "I only know he was sick already. Gittin wet as a drowned rat to buy two packs of gum didn't help him; the next day, I understand, he went to bed. Maybe he knowed something already—I couldn't say." He turned toward the car. "Anyhow, that's what happened."

Carefully Heath put what Fox had said out of his mind. Instead, as they drove toward Chandlerville, he looked out at the countryside. Stubbornly, determinedly, men with mules worked the blood-red land. "It's been powerful hard times here," Fox said. "About the hardest I can recollect. Bottom's dropped outa cotton, the mills are closin everywhere, the whole country jest seems to be dryin up. I'll say this for him. He kept his runnin as long as he could."

Heath jerked around. "The mills are closed? Chandler Mills?"

"For the first time. When the Old Man got down, days ago, and when they seen he couldn't git up, couldn't talk, tell 'em what to do, they come to your mama, his office people. They told her they couldn't keep on goin. They told her there warn't nothin to do but shut down, lay ever'body off." Fox leaned out the window, spat, settled back. "From whut they said, he'd been livin off his fat, and the fat was all gone, and now he was to the lean, and not long before to the bone. Warehouses full of cloth he couldn't sell, everything goin out, nothin comin in." He was silent. "Maybe he had jest come to the end of the line. Maybe that was it. Maybe he jest died before he'd face it. It mighta seemed to him that there was no other way out."

Heath looked away. "If you're trying to make me feel sorry for him—" His voice was harsh. It was going to be hard enough anyhow, without Fox's yammering. "Besides, it's none of my concern. I'm not his son, remember? He didn't have a son. My mother will inherit the mills, not me. If she asks, I'll advise her to put them up for sale."

"You won't git nothin for them," Fox said. "Not nowadays."

"She'll get enough to keep her the rest of her days. That's all I give a damn about. I'm all right, I can take care of myself and family. Take care of her too, if it comes to that. We can give the damned things away to get 'em off our neck, and that'll be all right by me."

"Sho," Fox said, and he was silent. All he said after that was, "I reckon it'll be one of the biggest funerals this end of the state has ever seen. I know for a fact the governor is comin. The Old Man, he drawed a lot of water."

They came to Chandlerville. By this time Heath was aware of a curious tension within himself; it had nothing to do with any sense of homecoming. It was fear, a sense of danger. Nevertheless when he saw, ahead, the huge dark flank of the mills, inset with blue windows through which, for the first time in his memory, no light gleamed on a weekday, he drew in a long, sharp breath, and still it did not seem to provide his lungs with oxygen.

The children were excited, curious. "What's that big place, Daddy?" Hamp fidgeted, staring.

"That's a cotton mill," Heath said. "Chandler Mills."

"That's where Grandfather worked. Grandfather Chandler."

"That's right."

"But he's dead now."

"Yes," Claudia said.

"May we see him? May we see him dead?"

"Hush," said Claudia.

"I've never seen Grandfather Chandler. I want to see him."

"You'll see him," Heath said.

"And I said, be quiet," Claudia added with severity. Ramsey only looked and was silent.

They swept past the towering, silent hulk of the plant; ahead, like some big-bellied monster on incredible steel legs, the silver-painted water tower gleamed against the pale brightness of the sky, fading into sunlight, only the huge black letters—CHANDLER—immediately visible, like an inscription written up there by a giant celestial finger. The gates of the mill were closed; it seemed strange not to hear the roar and throb of machinery within as they passed.

Then they were on the main street of what Heath saw with surprise was no longer just a hamlet. The street was longer, there were more buildings, signs, stores, offices. "Well, I'll be—" he began.

"I know," said Fox. "I felt the same way when I come back. And that warn't a patch to what it is now. It's half again as big, maybe more, than it was when you took off. I reckon people that couldn't make a livin farmin drifted in. And somehow he found somethin for them all to do. There's two car agencies here now, and even a moom-picture show—he give in that much, finally."

There were paved sidewalks, and Bolivar Street itself bore a coat of macadam. It seemed to Heath the place swarmed with people; then he realized that was because the mills were closed. They stood in idleness in doorways and on corners, gaunt men, soaking up the sunlight in groups and clusters, or they sat on benches, whittling, spitting. When they saw the big black car, they ceased whatever they were doing and fastened their eyes upon it and swung their heads and watched it until it passed.

"They been waitin," Fox said. "Wonderin when you would come."

Heath saw familiar faces, was surprised at how many he could connect with names.

"They don't know where they stand," Fox said. "Every-thin has jest quit, like a clock with its mainspring busted. They are wonderin when somebody is goin to fix it up and git it runnin again."

"I'm afraid they've got a long wait," Heath said.

"Sho," said Fox. "I guess there ain't no help for that."

They swung to the right, crossed the railroad, climbed up through the mill village. In the sunlight the little houses in their neat rows looked scabby, in need of paint. So it was that bad, Heath thought; only dire necessity would force Bolivar Chandler to leave property unmaintained. Children played in the dusty streets; women sat and gossiped on the porches, men lounged on the steps. They, too, looked at the car as it went past. There were many more houses than there had been. Hamp and Ramsey watched with noses pressed against the glass. "Who lives here, Daddy?"

"The folks that worked in your granddaddy's mill," Fox answered for Heath.

Clutterbuck, too, was watching with interest. "It's different from New England." He turned, stared at Heath. "This *all* belongs to you?" There was wonder in his voice. Although he had heard descriptions of Chandlerville for years, apparently the dimensions of Bolivar's empire had never been real to him till now.

"To the estate, I guess," Heath said tersely.

"Incredible," Clutterbuck said. "Just incred—" Then, ahead, he saw Chandler House, enormous, gleaming whitely through the bright spring foliage of its shielding trees. "Well, I'll be da—"

Heath laughed shortly. "Quite a monstrosity, eh? That's the only self-indulgence he ever allowed himself, not counting my conception."

Clutterbuck just shook his head. "What are you going to do with it all? What can you possibly do with all this?"

"Let the lawyers play with it," Heath said. Then they were at the house, the limousine halting in the drive. Elizabeth had been watching for them, because she was there, on the high, columned veranda, even before it stopped.

• • •

A ghost, thought Heath, holding her tightly in his arms; a frail, thin, ancient wraith, the body her spirit had actually inhabited cold in its coffin somewhere inside the house. For the first time he felt emotion as the little old woman, ravaged by years and grief, began to cry, rackingly, painfully, as if she had been waiting for his arrival before allowing herself this release.

And yet she did not cry long. Pride and courtesy overrode her mourning, and she pulled away self-consciously, marshaling her resources, embraced Claudia, then beamed with real joy as the impatient children, outgoing, loving, hugged her, even though they really knew her only from her photographs. She was introduced to Clutterbuck and, with her face still tear-stained, greeted him warmly with that Charlestonian, instinctive hospitality, as if his arrival were really what this reunion was all about. "You'll have to forgive me for letting myself go like that."

"Forgive?" said Clutterbuck incredulously.

"Yes, please. Now, all of you must be very tired. Please come inside. Isaiah will bring your bags." They entered the dark, cool foyer of the enormous house. The almost sickeningly sweet smell of many flowers hit Heath like a blow across the face; he stopped, swallowing hard.

Elizabeth halted too. Her voice was reedy as she pointed to the drawing room to the left. "He's . . . in there. If you'd like . . . but maybe the children shouldn't—"

Heath only stood helplessly. Claudia said quietly, "I think they ought to see their grandfather." She looked at Heath with what he read as a touch of defiance.

He did not care; he felt spiritless and enervated. He nodded, and they filed into the big room, Fox Ramsey trailing behind with Heath and Olin.

The coffin looked so large for so small a man, almost hidden by great banks of wreaths and arrangements, colorful in the muted light. Claudia took the children by their hands, led them to the massive metal casket. "That's your Grandfather Chandler," she said quietly.

They stood on tiptoe to look in. Ramsey glanced briefly, then settled back, but Hamp stared with aggressive curiosity. "Gee, he was *old*."

"Yes," said Claudia. "Very old." She looked down, then raised her head. "Come," she said. "Come, now." She led them away. Elizabeth looked inquiringly at Heath.

He did not want to do it. He did not want to see what was in there. He stood motionless; then somebody touched his back, maybe Fox or Clutterbuck. It moved him; he approached the coffin.

Bolivar lay on rich velvet beneath the glass, hands folded, eyes closed, scalp's flesh sallow beneath the thinning strands of silver. Heath stared down at his father, and suddenly he felt vast relief. All at once he realized that he had been afraid of discovering in Bolivar's face in death something that would menace his adjustment, make a claim on his emotions, some hint of pain or fear or love or grief or even happiness, something to make Bolivar human to him again. But the waxen countenance, beneath cosmetics, was dour, deeply graven lines of disapproval about the thin, pursed, angry mouth; it was the same face lodged in Heath's memory—forbidding, disapproving. He was safe. Grateful that he still felt nothing, he turned away, seeking some word for his mother, who stared at him tensely, hands clasped together.

All he could find was, banally, "He looks like he's asleep."

But it was all she needed; visibly she relaxed. "Yes," she answered shakily. "I've seen him sleeping so many times. That's just . . . how he's always looked."

He supposed there must be a great deal of business to be seen to, but he had no heart for it; caught in a strange lassitude, all he wanted was to get this over and be gone, selfish as that might seem. Even in death his father seemed to menace him, hold some threat over him, from which he must escape as soon as possible—in this case, he thought, the endless complications of the estate.

"Well, he did me one favor, anyway," he told Olin. They sat together in Clutterbuck's room while Fox watched the children play on the vast, landscaped lawn and Claudia and Elizabeth were closeted in the kitchen with the cook, preparing for the huge influx of Charleston kin expected that night. "Cutting me out of the will. That makes it simple."

Clutterbuck still looked awe-stricken by the actuality of Chandler's holdings. "Somebody's got to do something with all this."

"But not me. I'm in the clear." He arose, paced restlessly. "All I want is to get this over with and get away from here. If Mother wants to come along, fine. But I'm not going to stick around one minute longer than necessary. If that makes me a monster, I can't help it."

That afternoon the Charleston people filled the house to overflowing. He remembered almost none of them, but they all knew him, and he received more gushing commiseration than he could stand from countless aunts and cousins, while the men made quick trips to the clandestine bar, stocked by whiskey Fox had got from somewhere. The horde ploughed through mountains of food, and presently it was less an occasion for mourning than a jovial, raucous family reunion—but that was the way of that breed of southerners. It went on far into the night, that in-gathering, and the next morning, day of the funeral, he awakened with a hangover, not from whiskey, but from strain.

Like most men, he abhorred funerals and weddings as pagan ceremonials designed only to satisfy some need rooted deep in the souls of women. It was with a kind of weary dread that he faced the crowd that early began to gather, but before long that dread turned to awe, amazement.

This was not the Bolivar Chandler he had known who was today being buried, not the sour, joyless, narrow-minded little man whose corpse lay imprisoned in the heavy casket. This was a giant, a leviathan, the toppled pillar of a temple, a fallen hero. They came in waves, contingents, not just from across the state but from across the South, the country. Two senators and a clutch of congressmen down from Washington; the governor and his entourage; bankers, judges, cotton kings, laymen and ministers, and even, from New York, Gorman, the senior partner of the commission firm that had sold the Chandler output—or failed to sell it—for so long. And of course the Springs, the Cannons, the Butlers, the Stowes, the Cramers, all the satrapy of the textile industry, its emperors and archdukes, counts and barons; they filled all the house and its verandas, overflowed into drives and yards. Reporters scribbled, photographers made white, startling lightning flashes; and not so much the corpse itself as Heath became the center of all this. With astonishment he realized that he was being courted. Bolivar had held wealth and power. It had now to flow to someone; they all assumed to him.

With the high and mighty came the lowly; and he saw the same assumption on their faces, in their bearing: the mill hands, the card hands and fixers and roving haulers and spinners and doffers and weavers and creelers and slasher hands; the sweepers and the laborers—and the office workers, the clerks and secretaries. They came, briefly, shyly, some greeting him as old friends, the grief most genuine, their commiseration real and heartfelt. Somehow that touched him, as did the confusion and woebegoneness of the small handful of elderly executives who had helped Bolivar run his kingdom, most of whom Heath had known from childhood. By the time they left for the Baptist church he was dazed and, like it or not, swirling with emotion himself, but what emotion he could not say.

The church—How often had he seethed impotently through prayer and sermon here, hating all its narrow senselessness!—could not come close to holding everyone. Of course the men of power filled it; outside, the hands, in their shabby suits and Sunday dresses, clustered in a huge throng, to catch as much of the service as they could through the wide-open doors and windows. Beside Heath on the front pew his mother sat rigidly, staring at the casket almost hidden beneath the mass of flowers; Hamp and Ramsey fidgeted between Claudia and Fox; Clutterbuck's presence was comforting, a prop. The organ —three-quarters of its cost donated by Bolivar, the rest raised by the congregation—murmured a melancholy threnody. Then it began, endless eulogies and prayers, in which every minister in town and representatives from the State Baptist Convention must have their say. Whatever Heath had been about to feel withered under all those droning, meaningless words; he sat there unhearing, mind blank, holding his mother's hand. He was taken by surprise by what followed.

For it was over now, except for a final hymn—and suddenly the organ blared as they all arose, and then the choir began to sing, and so did the people who filled the church, and the hymn was caught up by the crowd outside, the mill hands, and nearly a thousand voices swelled in an old song that they all knew, that had been Bolivar Chandler's favorite. And as the church seemed to shake with that great chorus, Heath found himself singing too, and all at once the short hair prickled on the back of his neck, and he felt clogged and distended from within by emotion, and there was a burning in his eyes. Almost he could see the Old Man beside him on a Sunday morning, cawing those words loudly in an offkey voice:

> Amazing Grace, how sweet the sound
> That saved a wretch like me . . .
> I once was lost, but now am found,
> Was blind, but now can see . . .

Almost he expected Bolivar to rise from his coffin and join in. Tears were wet on his cheeks. Then it was over, and he was leading the procession from the church. His mother leaned on him and his own knees felt weak. Then they were in the bright sunlight of the cemetery beside the church, where not even massed flowers could disguise the red gape of grave. But suddenly, as the talk began again, he was all right. What he had felt at the sound of music evanesced; he came back to himself, in tight control. Well, he had paid tribute; all right. He felt nothing of any consequence through that part of the service except relief that soon it would all be over and, of course, great pity for his mother.

Then it was finished: and, at last, Bolivar Chandler was gone. It seemed incredible, and yet it was true; earth would shortly swallow and contain all that packaged energy and ferocity, and no man would feel its impact again. Heath held his mother tightly as they went back to the limousine, thinking that, as religious as her husband, perhaps she felt no such sense of finality, perhaps she was certain of being reunited. He hoped so; it was all she had to sustain her.

The rest of the day was a blur. Somehow, though, they got through it, as the crowd melted like wet snow, so that once again in Chandler House there was room to turn around. Heath had thought the place was cleared when a tall, handsome man of about his own age, beautifully dressed in tailored suit, appeared thrusting out a soft, damp hand. "Heath, you know you have all our sympathies."

Dazed, he had to search his mind for identification. Then it clicked. "Thanks, St. John. Good of you."

St. John Butler, now, after the death of his own father a year before, president of the vast complex of Butler Mills sprawling across Macedon County and lapping over into two beyond, withdrew his hand. "I know this great loss leaves you with an awful lot of problems. I know, too, you've been away from the mills for a long time. If I can be of any help in advising you . . ."

Heath looked at him; something on the man's face engaged his interest. "I appreciate it, St. John. But I don't expect to have any problems. I'll leave those to the lawyers."

"Oh? I know this isn't the time or the place, but . . . you're not going to, ah, well, take over?"

"Not if I can help it," Heath said, watching Butler closely.

Butler smiled, nodded. "You're wise. After all, I understand you're well established in your own career. Besides, the textile business right now is nothing for sane men to deliberately get mixed up in. So . . . your family may consider disposing of the mills?"

"I said, it's up to the lawyers—and my mother."

"Well . . ." Butler seemed undecided whether to go or stay. "You will be here for a few days, though?"

"I guess so. But not very long."

"I wonder if it would be . . . out of line if I . . . well, could we get together some afternoon, at your convenience, before you leave? Frankly, Heath, if it turns out you do want to dispose of Chandler Mills, well, I'd like to talk to you about it."

"The lawyers," Heath said. "Talk to them. You know Wade, Ross and Flythe."

"Yes, of course. All the same . . ."

Heath smiled faintly. "All right, St. John. Come around day after tomorrow, if that suits you. We'll have a drink together."

Butler looked shocked, as if expecting lightning to flash down and strike them both, but he masked it quickly. "Sure. Thanks, Heath. I'll call you first. Well . . . God bless you. They never made another like Mr. Bolivar. We'll certainly miss him." He took his leave.

Heath watched him pass through the door, thinking. He's got a scent in his nostrils. Instinctively he rubbed the hand Butler had shaken against his trouser leg. If unctuousness sold for a penny a quart, he thought, that man would be worth a hundred thousand dollars. All the same, he may be an answer to the problem.

He turned away. Then he halted. "Hello, Mr. Wade."

The lawyer had appeared from the drawing room, where the rest of the family was clustered around Elizabeth. Short, paunchy, gray-haired, with keen brown eyes, he looked toward the door just closing. "Didn't I see St. John Butler talking to you?"

"You sure did."

Wade hesitated. "Do you feel up to some more talk? I know you're tired, but—"

"But there's a lot of stuff hanging fire and the sooner we get it out of the way, the better. That suits me exactly. Let's go in the Old Man—in Dad's office."

"Excellent."

There Heath went to a file cabinet, took out a bottle and two glasses. "I don't know about you, Mr. Wade, but

I need a drink." He smiled. "I took the precaution of putting some toddy where I could get to it on the sly. Will you join me?"

The lawyer glanced around uneasily, as if Bolivar might be watching. Then he nodded. "It's been a strain on me too. You've lost your father. I have lost one of my most valued friends."

Pouring the liquor, Heath said, "You thought a lot of my father."

"He was a great man, a very great man. I don't say that lightly." He looked uncomfortable. "I know you two had your difficulties. I—"

"That's a matter we'll let drop."

"He never spoke of them to me, anyway." Wade sipped the whiskey carefully. "We haven't had a formal reading of the will, but I suppose your mother has discussed it with you. I've given her the gist of it."

"As a matter of fact," said Heath, "no. I haven't even mentioned it to her and she hasn't brought up the subject. There's been too much going on. As long as she's provided for, that's all that counts. I assume I'm right in that she gets most of the estate?"

A strange expression crossed Wade's face. "No, as a matter of fact, you aren't."

Heath's hand halted with the glass in midair. "For God's sake, he didn't go crazy and leave it all to the Baptist Church?"

"No," Wade said with a touch of anger. "I thought your mother would have told you. He left most of it to you."

Heath dropped the glass. It fell on Bolivar's desk, sloshing its contents unheeded across the mahogany, to dribble onto the carpet. He stared at Wade, and in that shocked instant he was certain he had misunderstood. Even so, though, he felt a sick kind of terror. "That's absurd," he whispered. "He disinherited me long ago."

The attorney sighed strangely. "True. You had been disinherited. But some days ago your father came to my office. I was concerned about him even then. The weather was bad, he already had a cold, and he'd got himself soaking wet somewhere along the line—"

"When he bought the chewing gum from Fox."

"What?"

"Never mind." Suddenly Heath's voice was sharp. What difference did it make? What difference could it possibly make? "Go on."

"For nearly ten years the will had stood as he had written it. I had been after him recently to make some adjustments in it; there were cash bequests that I knew the financial position of the company and of his personal holdings could no longer reasonably honor. But he had refused. Very old people are like that; after a certain age they often avoid the subject of wills altogether, as if they feel they're signing their own death warrants. At any rate—" He drank. "Mr. Chandler appeared unexpectedly. We changed the will that afternoon while he was in the office; he signed the revised one before he left. Under the new terms your mother gets the house and the proceeds of a trust that will keep her in comfort. A small percentage of the stock is distributed among his executive staff, a fairly substantial bloc does go to the church. But by far the greater portion—in all the interlocking corporations, certainly an easily controlling interest—comes direct to you."

"The hell it does," Heath said numbly. He arose, went to the window, pulled back the curtain. It was nearly twilight, but out on the lawn Fox led a pony back and forth, Hamp and Ramsey, laughing, on it together, bareback. Heath wondered where Fox had got the animal. Then he whirled. "Did he say why?"

Wade blinked. "Mr. Chandler never gave reasons and I never asked him. But it seemed natural—"

"Natural?" Heath's laugh was raucous, bitter. "Yeah, of course it was for *him!*"

"I'm afraid I don't understand."

Heath gestured with a clenched fist. "Good God, man, it's plain as the nose on your face! He couldn't let go, wouldn't, not even from the grave. Even from there he had to reach out and try to grab me, make one last effort to control my life, screw it up—"

"Young man." Wade stood up. "I'm afraid it was a mistake to discuss this right now. You're overwrought—"

"I'm overwrought, all right"—and Heath gave that ghastly laugh again. "He didn't say he was changing his will because he had any regrets, was sorry, or that maybe even"—he caught the tremor in his voice, ironed it out—"maybe even just because he loved me?"

"He said nothing."

"That's what I mean." Heath let out a long, shuddering breath. Then he dropped into the chair behind the desk and poured another drink with a hand that shook, the bottle neck chattering against the glass. He tossed it off in a gulp. "I'm sorry, Mr. Wade. It's not your fault. But—" He stared down at his hands, clenched on the desk before him. "He made it plain that I was no longer his son. Once I nearly died, after an airplane crash in New York. There was no word from him then, not a single expression of concern. He had two grandchildren. He made no gesture to even acknowledge they were alive. For ten years none of us existed. Now . . ." His mouth twisted. "This."

"All right." Wade spoke quietly. "I'd be a liar if I pretended that I didn't know the situation. It distressed me and everyone who knew about it. After all, I have children of my own. I can understand your feelings. But he was a proud, exceptional man, maybe even a genius; and people like that operate in their own way. The fact remains that he *did* change his will, he *did* make you his heir—"

"Yeah, but not on my account." Heath's voice was cold. "Not because he loved *me*. But because he loved Chandler Mills. And because he couldn't accept defeat, not ever. All my life he tried to turn me into a carbon copy of himself. I wouldn't let him, I insisted on being a person in my own right. That made me the only one who ever defied him, whom he couldn't bend or break. Then he saw the chance to kill two birds with one stone. Find somebody to run his mills when he was gone—and teach me that I couldn't escape him, not ever, not even when he was dead. He didn't say that he loved me, not to you. Not to my mother either, or that would have been the first thing she would have told me. Not even on his death-bed would he say that. Nor did he tell *me*. Any time . . . any time within ten years he could have sat down at this desk, right here,"—and Heath slammed it with his fist—"and written a half-dozen lines. That's all it would have taken, just a lousy half-dozen lines." Now his voice broke. "I went into his office that day prepared to eat dirt. To try to be what he wanted me to be. All I . . . cared about was to make it right with him again. If he would just have met me halfway, acknowledged that I was a human being too, not . . . not just another tool or machine that belonged to Chandler Mills. If he had just loved me enough to do that . . . But it wasn't me he loved, it was all these Goddamned big buildings with their blue windows. I had betrayed them, and alongside them I counted for . . . for *nothing!*" He raised his head, looked at Wade without trying to mask his grief and rage. "And still don't," he said. "That's why he did this. Not because he loved me, not even because *he* needed me. But because he knew the mills would. Like he would buy a machine—"

Wade said, "I'm sorry. I know nothing of all that. I'll say this. I'm old enough to know that nobody can look into anyone else's soul and see what goes on there. Just remember that."

"I remember a lot of things!" Then Heath, with great effort, pulled himself together. "It doesn't matter. I defied him once; I can do it again. If I own the mills, I can sell them."

Wade was silent for a moment. "Yes, of course. If you can find a buyer."

"I can find one. You saw St. John Butler. Like a buzzard circling a dead horse. He'll make an offer."

"Uh-huh. Butler. He'd already made offers. Twice. Your father turned him down both times." Now Wade helped himself to the bottle; he looked drawn and grief-stricken, and Heath realized he was exhausted. "Mr. Wade," he said, "we can talk about this later."

"No. Several thousand people are hanging between heaven and hell this minute, waiting for things to be settled." Heath was surprised by the lawyer's asperity. "Everybody in Chandlerville. All the personnel of the other two mills, and the towns that depend on their payrolls. A damned good hunk of the economy of this end of the state. Bolivar Chandler's been holding it up singlehanded for a long time."

Now it was Wade's turn to begin pacing. "Okay," he said. "The Butlers—St. John and his brothers. They'll buy you out, all right, at a fraction of the real value of the estate. But you're correct; they want Chandler Mills and they've got cash."

"Then that's all I care about. I'll leave it up to you—I don't care if you sell for a nickel on the dollar. I've got money of my own and a career of my own and— I just want to unload."

"The reason they've got the cash," Wade went on, as if he hadn't heard, "is because of the way they operate. Have always operated. Or don't you know about that?"

"I know they're a bunch of cold-blooded businessmen. But so was Bolivar Chandler."

"Was he?" Wade halted, looked at Heath. "You, of all people, should know better than that." When Heath didn't answer, he went on. "The Butlers have money, yes. They got it by . . . all right, reinstituting slavery. Only this time with white people."

"There's not a Goddamned cotton mill in the South that doesn't practice slavery."

"Maybe. But not like the Butlers. There's a difference between slavery and paternalism. My Lord, I've lived and worked here all my life; I know every mill owner in the Carolinas! They're a hard lot, right. They've got to be. We haven't come out from under Reconstruction yet, and a dollar means even more here than anywhere else in this country, has to do twice the work. But damned few of the other operators can stomach the way the Butlers run their mills."

He paused. "There are still not enough jobs and too many people in this region. Especially since the war—

I mean the one you fought in, when everybody expanded and got caught short when Germany surrendered. Then everything else changed too. Rayon, and more than that"—he made a gesture—"moving pictures, automobiles, now the radio . . . It used to be that a mill could specialize in one product and know it would sell so much of that every year. Now . . . fashion. Some harlot shows up on a movie screen in a certain garment and all the women won't have anything but that. That's made it worse—everything's all up in the air. Nobody knows in this business from one day to the next what the market wants. Now for every job there are ten people fighting to fill it. The Butlers know that and use it for all it's worth. They're the kind of people who would own a horse for twenty years and then shoot it or let it starve. They feel the same way about their people. And that's why they've got cash when everybody else is broke. But if you want to sell to them, I can't stop you."

Heath said, "I've got myself to think about."

"So did your father. But he kept his mills running. Right up to the time he lay down on his deathbed. It'll take an audit to show what that cost him. But— Did you ever hear of a man named Tom Capps?"

Heath laughed. "At family prayers, twice a day."

"You know the story, then?"

"He had a lot of ways of justifying what he did. That was only one of them."

"Yes, maybe. In good times. But it wasn't that easy a justification in the bad ones. Still, it was what he used."

"You said he never gave you reasons."

"Sometimes he had to. I had to handle a lot of his financial affairs. When they got worse and worse, I had to make him justify himself; it was my duty to a client. He needed to shut down, work off his inventory. He needed to decide whether to accept or reject the Butlers' offers. After all, even at a discount, he could have lived well for the rest of his life off what the mills would bring—not to mention his holdings in the town. I got him in a corner one day; he told me that story, finally, reluctantly. He thought of himself as a man to whom God gave a mission; Capps was the symbol of that. Every man he ever put on the payroll was Tom Capps to him."

Heath sighed, stood up. "Bluntly, Mr. Wade, I don't give a fuck about Tom Capps. I'm a writer, not a mill man. And I have no mission. If you can find another buyer besides the Butlers, fine. But if they're the only ones, take their offer."

Wade only looked at him. Heath saw the disapproval in his face. "You won't even *try?*" he asked.

Heath shook his head. "Even now that he's dead," he said, "I wouldn't give him that satisfaction."

Wade stood there a moment longer. Then he shrugged. "It's your decision. I'll get right on it." He did not offer to shake hands as he left the room.

5 AFTER THE HUBBUB of the funeral the enormous house seemed almost tomblike. Alone now in Bolivar's office, Heath stripped off coat and tie with hands that trembled and threw them on the sofa. Then he sat down heavily in the Old Man's chair, its leather permanently cupped and dented by the weight of those solid buttocks. Chandler's desk bore a picture of Elizabeth at the age of forty, a pen, inkwell, calendar, and nothing else. He spread his hands on it, afflicted now with sudden memory, a picture from his childhood, flashed on the screen of consciousness like a slide in a darkened theater: Boliver seated here (no, not in this room—that was before Chandler House was built—but at the same desk in the big house in town). It was late, his father was in shirt sleeves, writing by the light of a lamp with a bell-shaped shade of stained glass on the cabinet behind him. The man Heath saw was not the silver-haired, pursed-faced thing in the casket of this afternoon, but a small, solid shape (which nevertheless had seemed very large to him then) radiating limitless strength and durability, the hair of the massive head not yet gray, still mostly the color of straw. Heath, perhaps eight, stood

in the doorway, watching, wondering at the secret ritual
his father practiced here every night. It was something
important—Business. Business was something like religion, a stern master and yet the source of all good, a
mysterious kind of magic. He had stood there for several
minutes, looking at Bolivar, watching him do Business,
wanting to go in and ask about it, but afraid to. When
Bolivar was at Business he hated interruptions. He
would only tell Heath briefly to go straight to bed. Then
Heath decided that it was worth it; on the pretext of
giving Bolivar the customary goodnight kiss, he had
entered, hoping Bolivar would interrupt himself, take him
on his knee, as he occasionally did, maybe even explain
what went on at the desk. Heath already had the questions in mind; if he asked enough, Bolivar might hold
him a while and talk to him, a luxury and pleasure for
the boy almost exquisite. Instead, interrupted, the Old
Man had turned briefly, abstractedly, looking at him
without quite seeing him. "Good night, son," he said
tonelessly, ritually, "sweet dreams." He accepted the kiss
on the hard, bristly cheek (he smelled of sweat and
witch hazel), pecked Heath lightly in return, and then
swung the chair around in dismissal. Heath had gone out,
but somehow he had never forgotten those moments of
looking on Bolivar unaware, seeing his father whole and
in every dimension, instead of only as face, hands, voice,
presence.

Now he drank from the glass he had poured while
Wade had talked to him. He was exhausted, every
muscle aching from the day's strain. Yet it seemed to
him that even attempting to relax would cause him to
fly apart. Wound up, engine racing, he wanted either
the artificial oblivion of liquor or the release of action;
what he did not want to do was to have to think about
what Wade had told him.

Because it meant nothing, anyway. Except that even
in the last extremity, his father's scheming brain had
gone on working—on behalf of Chandler Mills. Like a
football player, a quarterback, rushed, about to go under,
desperate to pitch the ball, needing a receiver, any

receiver. And mixed with that, probably a kind of spite, stemming from his determination never to be thwarted, to have his own way in the end, regardless of the cost to others—especially of the cost to Heath. That was all it meant, all it could mean and— Now Heath was racked by hatred, grief, and disappointment. It hit him then, the revelation that for years, beneath his bitterness and hatred, he had been waiting for the gesture. Until now he had not even known that. But, God damn it! he thought bitterly, all that time he had been waiting, just as he had waited in the doorway that night and then at his father's side, like a kid wanting to be picked up and held. And coming home— He stared at the wall opposite without seeing it. He had been hoping then too; almost breathless with the hope, burying it beneath indifference. Like a puppy—his mouth twisted in self-contempt—abjectly craving any word, yearning for a pat . . .

Shit, he said soundlessly and jumped to his feet. Again that picture of the Old Man at this desk . . . Why couldn't he? he thought. Damn it, why couldn't he? It would have made it all so different. Fox could do it; if it were Hamp, I would do it; why couldn't he do it too—forgive?

But no! Without realizing it, he was at the door; brutally he struck his clenched fist against the jamb. Pain flared in his hand, yet he hit the jamb again, harder. He did not know what he wanted to smash; he must smash something. Then the pain brought reason back, and he got control again.

Suddenly he had to talk to his mother. Why hadn't she told him? Well, this had to be got straight, and got straight right now. He left the office, ran up the stairs. No unfinished business, tell her now. It wouldn't work. If she thought it would work, she might as well know right away. He topped the stairs, then halted. Claudia was emerging from Elizabeth's room.

She stared at him as, quietly, she shut the door. He knew what he must look like to her; she could read his every expression. That accounted for the quick concern that crossed her face. But she raised a finger to her lips.

Heath jerked his head toward the door. "I've got to see her."

"Not now. She's worn out. I just got her to sleep."

He went to her, took her arm. "Then, our room. I've got to talk to you."

"What's wrong?" There was apprehension in her voice.

He didn't answer until they were behind their own door. Then he whirled on her. "Do you know what he's done? Do you know what that old fart did? He changed his will." His arm went out in a wild gesture. "He left this all to me!"

For a moment she only looked at him, stunned, unable to assess the meaning of that news. Then she sat down heavily on the bed, forming unspoken questions, her mind charting the possible impact of this on their lives.

"Don't worry," he rasped. "I've got no intention of taking it. I mean I'll take it, but then I'll sell it! I'm not going to let him get away with it! It won't change anything at all!"

Relief, deep, instant, touched her face. Even so, she shook her head. "I don't understand."

Tersely, he repeated his conversation with Wade. "If nobody else will buy us out, the Butlers will. I don't give a damn what they offer. Hell, I'd pay them to take it over and get us out from under."

"But why?" She blinked. "Why did he do it?"

"Why do you think? He thought if he presented me with a *fait accompli* he'd have his way at last. By God, he was going to have his way even when he was six feet under!" He whirled, began to pace the room. "With not much as a by-your-leave, not giving a damn about what it meant to anyone else—to me, you, the kids—nobody but his fucking mills!" He stopped, flung out his arm toward his mother's room. "*She!* She knew about it, but she didn't tell me. Did she tell you?"

"Of course not," Claudia said. "She was under too much strain to think about anything like that."

"But anything else? Did she say anything else?" He lowered his voice. "Did the Old Man even discuss it with her?" He swallowed hard. "Was there any other reason why?"

"What do you mean?"

"You know what I mean." Then Heath let out a long, shuddering breath. "Of course not. He never even mentioned me to her, did he?"

And now she read his face again, and the hurt beneath the anger was as surprising to her as it had been to him. She took a moment to assess its depth, then she stood up, came to him. "Darling," she said, "I'm sorry. But don't. Don't let him keep on hurting you."

"If it'd been me, Hamp, don't you think I would have—?"

"All right." She pulled him down beside her on the bed, held his head against her breast for a moment, ran her hand through his hair as if he were a child. "I know." Then she said, "But he did, you know, anyhow. He did go to Daddy's store, he must have wanted to—"

Heath pulled away, but he felt better. She had divined his true need, not to have his anger fed with her own agreeable, sympathetic outrage, but to have the hurt lessened. "All the same," he said. "That was a great concession, after ten years, to sneak a look at pictures of his grandchildren, wasn't it? If he had asked Mother for them instead, it would have been different, but—" He was choking up, whether with renewed anger or disappointment or grief, he could not tell. "Anyhow, you're right. I'm not going to let it hurt me. I'm not going to let that or anything else ever sour me the way he soured. We have our life, and we're going to live it as we please, and— I'll just turn everything over to the lawyers and it won't take long. I don't know what we'll do with Mother. Maybe she'll come back to Vienna with us."

"Maybe."

"You won't mind?"

"You know better than that."

He looked down at her, full of love and admiration for her, wonder at his own instinctive wisdom—or blind luck—in having married her. Then she stood up. "Why don't you and Olin have a drink together? Have a lot of drinks. Poor Olin, he's at loose ends."

"I know, I'm sorry." He stood there, rubbing clenched fists against his thighs. "I don't want another drink. I've been cooped up too long—the ship, the trains, now here. I'll see if Olin wants to take a walk. I'll show him the town and the mills." Then he saw the flicker in her eyes. He took her hand. "Don't be afraid. He won't get away with it. And . . . I don't know what the whole thing's worth, but surely we'll get at least a million out of it. Enough to do anything we want to, live any way we choose."

"I just want to go on the way we were," she said, so deeply, vibrantly that he was almost startled. "I don't care about the money; I don't want anything but that."

"Neither do I." He said it softly. "Well, I'll go find Olin."

Clutterbuck's position had been almost unbearably awkward, and he was obviously glad to have attention paid to him. They left Chandler House and walked down the drive, then halted. Below them the boxy houses of the mill village lined dusty streets. Then the railroad tracks; beyond, the business district; northwest of that the pleasant area of big old houses, lawns shaded by oak and elm, where Bolivar's hierarchy dwelled; southwest, nearer the mill, a lesser enclave of bungalows, which, though of varying design, were all modest, where lived the foremen, the clerks, the small artisans and tradesmen of the town. Beyond, the great idle sprawl of the mills— multifaceted blue eyes dulled as if with sleep; another clot of mill houses; then the shimmering surface of the river, blood-red in the slanting evening light, bridged here and there to make room for more development (this with the last ten years), where the growing middle class had found another toehold. Thus the town was checker-boarded into sections by rank and function.

Heath watched Clutterbuck's face. A kind of awe moved into it. "And so, whether you want it or not," Olin said, "you become the Duke of Chandlerville. Hell, there are European principalities not this big." He shook his head. "And that little old man did it all? Single-handed?"

"Yes," Heath said. For a moment, then, a curious thing happened. Looking at Chandlerville through Olin's eyes, he felt the same awe. Viewed objectively, it was indeed amazing. For an instant, then, he knew a quick, strong pride. It had, at least, taken a real man to do this; whatever the bitterness between them, he had to give Bolivar his due. There were not many like him, maybe none. It was something to have such a man's blood in your veins, regardless of all the rest. In that respect, anyhow, he had been fortunate. He might hate his father, but he need never be ashamed of him. If only— He began the thought, then cut it off. "Yeah," he said. "I guess I'm royalty, if inheriting a royal pain in the ass means anything."

They moved on down the hill, entered the mill village that lay below. Almost at once Heath knew this was a mistake. As usual when the mill was idle, people were out in swarms, on the porches and the steps. And, of course, they all knew him and he knew many of them. And he tensed, for fear they would approach and ask questions he was not yet ready to answer.

But they did not; they only followed the pair of them with their eyes, nodding courteously as he and Clutterbuck strode along, dodging shirtless, barefooted boys, and girls in short gingham dresses, who played in the street. Slowly Heath relaxed; it was as if they had decided not to press the issue for fear of learning more than they wanted to know.

Clutterbuck looked around with curiosity; maybe it was his presence that inhibited them and shielded Heath. "Like some kind of enormous dog kennel," he murmured from the corner of his mouth. "But it's better than the same thing up north or in England. I saw the mills there —did you?"

"Yes," Heath said, thinking of narrow, dark, sooty streets and ugly warrens. "I guess it is. At least they've got fresh air and a little room to move around in. The houses are cheap, but they rent cheap too—about a dollar a room a month, and that includes light and water. They make up a big hunk of the total cost of doing business."

"It's funny," Clutterbuck said. "You notice it? Most of these people look so much alike. They could be brothers and sisters or cousins."

"A lot of them are. The poor white, run flat out to seed, who couldn't look after himself, had to commit himself to the care of somebody else. That was a kind of degradation, the end of the line for a southern white man—like a woman having to go on the streets. It cost 'em something in self-respect, and the rest of society has always looked down their noses at 'em. In a way they're sort of like Jews in a ghetto or Negroes in a shanty town. They've got their own customs and morals, and naturally they tend to inbreed with each other, and, really, I guess an anthropologist would classify 'em as a sort of subspecies by now. They're a hard bunch to explain to anybody who doesn't know 'em—totally dependent, and yet they've got a kind of pride, too, in being what they are, in being different, maybe a kind of defiant pride, a compensation. It's not enough to pay 'em, you've got to have their allegiance too; it's something they're very touchy about. They won't even take an order unless it's phrased right. God help the supervisor who doesn't start every order with 'If you don't mind,' or 'What about doing me a favor and—'"

He laughed, then sobered. "They're mostly illiterate and not worried about that at all; sometimes kind of proud of it. If you understand their psychology, know how to handle 'em, you can manipulate 'em like so much putty. But you've got to do it just right. That's one of the reasons the unions haven't got much of a toehold down here—just a quirk of psychology. Once they join a union, they're not on a man-to-man basis with the bossman any longer. They don't want to make that admission, not even to themselves."

"And you don't work any Negroes in the mill at all?"

"Good lord, no! Except outside, at the lowest jobs. The three things these people hate worse than poison are niggers, Yankees and the Pope, not necessarily in that order." He broke off. "Let's get out of here. All those eyes are bothering me."

They swung back to the main road into town. "The Old Man ruled 'em with an iron hand," Heath went on. "But he could get away with it, because he knew what made them tick. In a sense he was one of 'em himself—as narrow, as bigoted, just as proud of being what he was, and the hell with anybody who tried to change him."

"It sounds like you understand 'em pretty well too."

Heath's laugh was hollow. "I've worked with 'em, grew up with 'em. They're the ones who almost set a limit on my life." He looked back at the village. "That was what he was trying to do—define *me* by what *they* are. Make sure that I was more like them than like myself."

"So you despise them."

"No. No, I don't despise them. I have friends among 'em, good friends. It's just that I flatly refuse to live my life by standards set for me by them. Royalty, you said. Well, royalty is always the prisoner of its subjects."

They walked on down the hill, reached the town. "Here's another expression of his personality—and theirs. Not a dollar spent for anything but utility and durability. The hallmark of the company town." Heath gestured at the drab and sooty buildings of the business section, the sidewalks splattered with the stains of decades of tobacco spitting. "Everything comes from the ledger sheet; you can't write any aesthetic values into the profit column. And since *he* owned everything, no incentive for anybody else to attempt to improve it. He set the tone; this town is what he was and felt."

"He built that big house, all those landscaped grounds—"

"At my mother's urging."

"It's ugly as hell, all right," Olin said, looking around. "I'm surprised she didn't suggest—"

"He would have balked if she had. Goddammit, he was just suspicious, frightened, of anything beautiful. Or maybe there was another reason—I just thought of it."

"What's that?"

"Maybe it would have menaced his control. Maybe this deliberate ugliness was a sort of discipline. The more you remind people that they have human responses, the more likely they are to insist on their own humanity. The closer you can keep them to living like animals, the easier it is to handle them like animals."

"There's another possibility," said Olin.

"What?"

"Maybe all this"—Olin swept out his hand—"maybe all this, from scratch, was work of art enough for him. Maybe he felt it didn't need any more adornment."

Heath halted, looked at him. Then he shrugged. "Who knows? You want to see the mills?"

"Why not?"

He knew the watchman on duty at the front gate, an elderly man in overalls. "Hello, Uncle Frank."

"Heath." The old man put out a hand. "Son, it's good to see you back. You know how we all feel about your daddy—"

"Yes, sir. Olin, this is Uncle Frank Watkins. He's been with Chandler Mills—how long, Uncle Frank?"

"Lord, goin on thirty year now. Started out when there warn't but this one buildin here."

"This is Mr. Clutterbuck."

"Pleased to meetcha, Mr. Clutterbuck." Uncle Frank put out his hand, shook Olin's limply, briefly. Then he looked at Heath with that same question in his eyes. Heath avoided his gaze. Instead, he got the keys from the old man, led Olin into the office. "You notice how he looked at me," he said, closing the door behind him. "Goddammit, they all think I've got nothing to do with my life except see to them—" He led Clutterbuck through the outer offices. Then he halted. Ahead was the frosted door with its black legend, PRESIDENT. "No," he said. "We won't bother with that. Come on, I'll take you through the plant."

In the huge, machinery-cluttered rooms the light from the blue windows had an eerie cast; it was like being in a deserted cathedral. Their footsteps seemed loud, echoing, on the oaken floors. Heath led Olin from area to area in the proper sequence, explaining to him the steps of making yarn. They went from the opening room, where the bales were broken and the fiber loosened, through the cardroom, through the other areas, where the ropelike slivers from the cards were combined into roving and then twisted into strands from which the final spinning was done. He showed Olin the ranks of spinning frames and the spoolers, where the bobbins were combined to make cones of yarn; the slasher room, where the warp threads were sized before weaving, and the weave room itself with its vast rows of looms. Everywhere there was lint, and the machines were still webbed with white, the looms turned off with half-finished cloth still stretched on them.

"Like Sleeping Beauty's castle," Heath said thinly. "Only it will take one hell of a lot more than a kiss to get all this back into operation." Hands on hips, he surveyed the weave room. "Hell, he was still making the same yarn and the same constructions of cloth they were turning out when I left. And on the same machinery." He shook his head. "No wonder . . . no wonder . . ."

They left the manufacturing areas. Heath began to prowl the warehouses, with Olin close behind. It was nearly sunset now. The cotton inventory was low, startlingly so; Heath remembered when these warehouses had been crammed with bales. In other warehouses, though, he goggled at the huge piles of gray goods, unfinished cloth, mountainous inventories of it, crammed wherever there was space. Even when it couldn't be sold, the Old Man, he realized, had just gone on and on making it, stubbornly, determinedly, idiotically, as if he were obsessed. Struck by something, Heath chuckled grimly. "You know what? If only once he had gone to a moving picture."

"Huh?" Olin looked at him blankly.

"He wouldn't go to movies; they were the devil's invention. Or nightclubs, or parties, or any place where women might have been seen wearing the latest clothes. Great Scot, Olin, the Old Man was living in a vacuum. Gingham and duck, gingham and duck; he didn't know women don't wear that stuff any more. Look at this crap! Out of touch, just out of touch!" He turned away. "Thank God, it's not my problem. I hope St. John Butler knows where to sell it." He led Clutterbuck out, slammed the huge sliding door, relocked it with a key from the ring Uncle Frank had given him. They walked down the splintered loading dock, entered another door, which led them back to the office. All at once Heath felt very tired, and he went to the small, deserted switchboard in the entry; it had not been modernized either, and he still knew how to operate it. "That's a long climb back to the house. I'll call for a car to retrieve us."

The fatigue persisted; it was good to be, much later, in bed with Claudia, her head cradled on his arm, her body in its accustomed place by his, while he smoked a final cigarette. "I was right," he said.

"Right, how?"

"About my getting out this afternoon. Only it wasn't the walk that made me feel much better."

"Oh?"

"It was seeing the mill." He inhaled, blew a plume of smoke. "That lifted a kind of burden from me I didn't know I was carrying."

"What do you mean?"

"They've all been looking at me. Eyes following me everywhere I went. Asking me, *What can you do? What are you going to do for us? What sort of magic are you going to perform to make everything all right?* Waiting for me to say, *Okay, fellows, I'm here, let's get to work.*" He ground out the cigarette. "What he was hoping I'd say, of course. But that trip through the mill today . . . that made it clear that there's nothing I *can* do but sell."

He paused. "It's hard to believe, but it turned out that he was fallible. In business. It's like finding out that Jesse James robbed the poor or that Michelangelo was color-blind, but it's the truth. He'd lost his grip. I don't know when it started, how far back, but it must have been months ago, maybe years. Anyhow, that's a mess down there—just an absolute, utter, profound mess."

"In what way?"

"In every way. I know just enough about the business to recognize that. The machinery's worn out and obsolete, the warehouses are jammed with unsalable goods. But he was like a snapping turtle; they say if one bites down, you can cut its head off and it still won't let go until it thunders. Well, he had bitten down, and he wouldn't let go— And nobody can accuse me of cowardice or bad faith because I can't undo the damage. Even if that were the only aim I had in life, even if there was nothing more I wanted than to pick up the old family torch and hold it high, I couldn't. He's made such a wreck out of Chandler Mills that it's going to take a genius to put the company back together—and not only a genius but one who knows this business backward and forward. That lets me out. Now I can turn loose with a clear conscience."

Claudia rolled over, put an arm around him. "I'm glad," she said. "I . . . I didn't know what to feel. When you told me about the will this afternoon, for a minute the bottom just seemed to drop out of everything. I didn't know what to say. No matter what I said, it would have been wrong. All I could do was hope that . . . this wouldn't tear everything to shreds."

Heath laughed softly. "And what would have happened if his gambit had worked? Suppose I had decided it was my duty to stay here, be the new Old Man of Chandler Mills?"

"I don't even want to think about that." She laughed ironically. "I suppose I've got above my raising. But there's nothing here for me. There never was, really. Any more than there was for you. We're like . . . like the first two creatures ever to crawl out of the ocean and live on land. We . . . in a sense we invented ourselves. I feel sorry for Daddy; there's nothing he'd like better, secretly, than to see us come back. I feel sorry for your mother too. But we have our own lives, and the children have theirs and— After all the trouble we both went to to get out of the ocean, learn to live higher up . . ." She was beginning to sound drowsy now. "I've always thought that, in a sense, we were creating a work of art in the way we lived. It took us so long, so many false starts, to get it right, but once we did, the two of us . . ."

"I know," he said. His arm tightened about her. "I know."

"I'm glad . . ." He could smell the perfume of her hair. "I'm glad you feel better about it." Then she said nothing else. Presently he knew that fatigue had claimed her.

He was equally as tired. Every muscle, every nerve, had been stretched so taut that now, in relaxation, they ached. He waited for sleep to take him too; but, perversely, it would not come. He was too tired to sleep. He lay awake for a long time with Claudia curled around him; then he disengaged himself and rolled over. That did not help either. He was, within himself, still tautly wound, his engine racing. He could not gear down.

After what seemed hours, he could bear it no longer. Lying here in darkness, too many memories came back, too many regrets, too many foul-breathed monsters of guilt were stalking him in the night. Gently, needing to move around, he got out of bed.

He went downstairs, vaguely thinking that a glass of milk might help. Or a drink. Yes. That was what he needed. A good, stiff drink. Maybe two, maybe three. Maybe a whole bottle—he didn't know. All he knew was that he had to turn himself off, no matter what it took. Damn the Old Man. Damn the old snapping turtle who would not let go.

The bottle was in Chandler's office. In its doorway, having flicked on the light, he paused. The house was huge and silent around him; the short hair on the back of his neck prickled. Almost, in that instant, he had expected to find Bolivar seated there, turning slow, cold, disapproving eyes toward him. He would not have been surprised if he were.

But the chair behind the desk was empty. Heath went to it, dropped into it, feeling his own buttocks fit into that hollow worn into leather by the solid rump of Chandler over the years. The bottle was still on the table where it had been left after Olin, Fox and Claudia had taken nightcaps before retiring. In the ice bucket there was still cool water. He poured it into a glass, drained the last of the Scotch in on top, shook it up, leaned back in the chair.

All he had wanted that night was for his father to pick him up and hold him for a moment. He often held Hamp that way; and it was possible to feel currents of strength and love flowing between them, nourishing them both. But, of course, Bolivar had not needed nourishment. Bolivar was strong enough. And so it had never occurred to Bolivar that he might need it, that there were others not as strong. "Shit," he said aloud, and he drank.

The whiskey tasted sour.

All right, Heath thought, I'll take my share of guilt. But I am a father, too, now, and I think I understand a few things. . . . He was great on the Bible. How did he miss the parable of the Prodigal Son? What is it like to live so locked up in your own self-righteousness that you can never get out? "Hell," he said, and he drank again.

The whiskey was helping, all right. It was getting to him promptly. This one drink and there'd be no need of another. Rolling the glass between his hands, he looked at the desk top, with the picture of Elizabeth, the pen and inkwell. That was typical. A place for everything and everything in its place.

There was a center drawer, long and shallow, and two larger drawers on either side. "What," he said aloud, "was he working on when he died, I wonder?" He opened the center drawer. It held nothing but an array of pencils, paper clips, erasers, and the like—all orderly in a tray. He closed it again, went to the side drawers.

They were empty too. Of course, he thought. The lawyers. They must have searched for documents and petty cash, cleared everything. He felt cheated. It was as if his father had never worked at this desk. He drank again, wheeled the chair back on its rollers, opened the center drawer once more. It was deep, had to be pulled a long way before it was fully open. As it happened, it came out, dropped in his lap. Then, in a neat stack in one corner, he saw the envelopes.

He recognized them at once for what they were and recognized, too, the crabbed, yet fully legible handwriting on them. Meticulously, Bolivar Chandler kept his household expenses separate from those of the company. How many times had Heath seen him writing checks to pay them here at this desk? These envelopes were neatly addressed, stamped, enclosing payments, ironically enough, to companies that he owned himself. The first one, for coal; another to the drugstore— Even as he felt a sense of triumph in finding something the lawyers, the vultures, had overlooked, Heath was surprised at the impact of that familiar handwriting. How many letters had he received in it, carping, admonitory, at college or overseas? He was, he thought, like one of Pavlov's dogs; automatically he felt foreboding when he saw it.

He laid the stack of envelopes on the desk. Bolivar had written checks, addressed, sealed, stamped all this, and then . . . He must already have had the cold. Maybe the chill, the fever, a scratchy throat and nose . . . He had to be very sick to go to bed and stay there. Heath could remember only one other time—an attack of pleurisy. And then people had trooped to his bedside with decisions to be made. . . . He had intended to mail these the next morning when he got up.

And didn't get up, thought Heath.

He drank again, remembering what it had felt like to almost die. That loneliness, that utter, terrible loneliness, in which no one could reach you. And that was what Bolivar had lain down to, sank into, once he had got beneath the cover. That must have been what he had felt at last. What a shock it must have been then to realize that he was severed from his beloved mills, drifting away, could never get back . . . And from Elizabeth, from everyone . . . Heath shuddered. With a sudden vicious gesture, he struck the stack of envelopes, sent them fanning across the desk. And that was when he saw it.

Mr. Heath Chandler
Schumann Gasse 14 . . .

"Well, I'll be damned," he said aloud blankly.

He just sat and stared at the address, and it did not change; he was seeing it correctly.

It was a long time before he reached out and picked up the envelope.

There were no stamps on it. Bolivar had run out by then—another sign of fallibility.

It was sealed, though. Heath held it without attempting to open it. He did not want to read it. The last thing in the world he wanted to do was to open this letter and read it. He hated to open letters from the Old Man, he had always had to get drunk to do it overseas.

"No," he said. He crumpled it in his hand. But he did not throw it away.

Instead, he sat there with it in a wad inside his sweating palm for a long time. During that interval he drained the glass, smoked a cigarette.

Presently he could bear it no longer. He found a paper clip, straightened it out with hands that shook, used it to penetrate the side of the flap, open the envelope with careful, very precise delicacy. Then he took out the single folded sheet of paper it contained. He unfolded it and began to read:

My dear son

I know you will be surprised to get this letter [Word scratched out.] I only hope you will read it. I [Here a whole line completely obliterated with ink-splattering pressure on the pen's nib.]

[Then suddenly plunging ahead:] I beg your forgiveness. I love you more than you've got any idea.

I am very happy about your success and proud of you and your wife and the two fine children. They look just like your mother.

I miss you. I wish you would come home for a

while. I have a cold now but I'll write more when I feel better.

I am sorry about everything. I love you.

Your loving father.

Bolivar Chandler.

"No," Heath Chandler said. "No, no, no." He read the letter again. "No. No, no, no."

And read it once more. Then he made a strange, anguished sound, stood up from the chair, dropped into it again, read the letter a final time, and put his head in his hands. "Your loving father," he said. "Christ."

He sat there for a long time.

Then, still holding the letter, he got up, went through the house, out the French windows to the terrace. He walked in the moonlight, through a night as warm as breath, the grass soft and dew-wet under his bare feet. He walked back and forth repeatedly, one hand over his face, while his shoulders shook as he began to cry. He had no idea how long he was out there like that, alone in the night. Much later he went back into the house. He did not see how, now, he could possibly sleep.

He went upstairs, awakened Claudia.

She was groggy at first; her eyes cleared as she read the letter. She looked at him with a mixture of grief and fear.

"We've got to talk about this," Heath said. "Because it changes everything. Don't you see? It changes everything."

BOOK TWO

BOOK TWO

Part One

1 WHEN OLIN CLUTTERBUCK came down for breakfast he realized immediately that something momentous had happened in this house while he slept. At the table Claudia was pale, silent, and her hand shook slightly when she raised her cup. Heath seemed grave, withdrawn, almost sullen; and Olin had the feeling that he had stepped into the aftermath of a terrific family battle. At any rate, this was more than the normal hang-over from the strain of yesterday.

It was an uncomfortable, nearly wordless meal. Then Heath looked at Olin strangely, as if hesitant, embar-rassed. Suddenly he whipped a folded sheet of paper from his shirt pocket, thrust it at Clutterbuck. "Here, read that. Tell me what you make of it."

He felt the eyes of both of them on him, as if he were being summoned to referee their dispute. Unfolding the letter, he read it once and did not quite comprehend. The second time, he felt the shock of it and knew at once what its impact must have been on Heath. But he did not know what to say and passed it back with only his eyes asking questions.

"Last night I found it in his desk," Heath said, voice a bit unsteady, charged with emotion. "He . . . must have written it the day he got really sick, not knowing that when he went to bed that night, he'd never get up to mail it. And naturally he couldn't ask *her* to do it for him, not even tell her he'd written it." Heath swallowed. "And then I guess it was too late, he was too sick even

265

to remember it. But . . . it was there. Had been ever since the day he went to Fox's store and looked at the pictures, the day he changed his will."

Groping, Olin finally managed, "I know this makes things easier."

"No," Heath said. "No, it only makes them harder. Because I can't do it now, Olin, don't you see? I can't sell Chandler Mills. Now I've got to stay here and run them."

For a second Clutterbuck sat blank, unmoving, with surprise. Then his eyes went to Claudia, and when she did not meet them, he knew there had been argument all right. Still, he could not believe Heath meant it. Although surely that letter must have gone straight to his core, Olin had seen him too often intoxicated with his own emotions. Today, in shock, regret, grief, and maybe a kind of joy, he was on a jag. But later, when that wore off . . .

"I don't want to," Heath went on quickly. "But I have to, you understand? There's no way I can get out of it." He gestured with the letter. "Not after this."

Claudia raised her head, green eyes lambent, mouth set thinly. "Yesterday you told me it was impossible, such a mess nobody could set it straight." She was still fighting, Olin saw, the very structure of her life, everything she had made of herself, the future of her children, menaced by this unexpected message from the grave.

Heath was carefully reasonable. "I know—it is a mess. Maybe I can't. But . . . Christ, I thought about it all last night." He looked at Olin, eyes pleading for understanding and support. "Because I can see now. All that time he was hurting worse than I was. I couldn't understand it at first, but I should have known it now that I'm a father myself. After Hamp was born I should have realized. But I didn't. I was too damned stupid!" He struck the table suddenly with clenched fist, and china jingled. "I could have written this letter, should have! Ever since Hamp, seven years ago— But I didn't. It was left to him." He let out a gusty breath. "And so he died. Without knowing that I gave a damn at all."

"Just the same," Claudia said fiercely, "that doesn't mean—"

Heath's voice was thick, almost strangled. "It means that I've got to make it up somehow. And I only know one way to do it."

Claudia stared at him with a face almost hawklike. Then her expression softened; Olin saw that she was changing tactics. She laid her hand on Heath's. "Darling, we know how you feel, you know that. But—"

He pulled his hand away. "I didn't want to come home," he said defensively. "You're the one who made me do it. Remember? What you said about carrying around a wound that'd never heal? Well, you were right. That's something I can't afford to do—and don't intend to." He paused. "It would be different if the mills were in good shape and running. Then there wouldn't be anything I could do, or had to, except see to Mother. But they aren't, and he would expect me to—"

"Heath," Claudia said, and she was close to tears now, "that's absurd. You couldn't do it even if you wanted to. And why should we just . . . pull our lives down around our heads and wreck them to . . . I've worked so hard to get out of Chandlerville, we both have, and now you say—" She shook her head. "This isn't where either of us wants to live, and it's not where we want our children to grow up."

"I know," Heath said bleakly. "But I can't help that either. Wade said it yesterday—there are thousands of people out there hanging between heaven and hell, waiting for a Chandler to bail 'em out, put 'em back to work and feed 'em. And I happen to be the only Chandler left."

"All the same, it's not—"

He turned on her. "Yes, it is, damn it! They're expecting me to do it, and they're right, I have to, because"—his voice rose and his eyes flared—"the fact remains, *I am his son!*"

He and Claudia looked at each other then for a soundless moment, and her face worked, and in that instant Clutterbuck knew that she had lost. This was no quick emotional jag; those words, wrenched from deep inside

the man, rang with agony and triumph alike, and now
Olin knew that Heath had found something he had been
seeking all his life and would not easily give it up.
Maybe Claudia could have won if she had exerted all
her power over him, but it would have been a Pyrrhic
victory, costing more than losing.

He felt pity for her, robbed in that moment of a life
that she had built block by block, like a mason con-
structing a cathedral single-handed, waited for the flash
of final rage and bitterness. But it did not come. The silence continued a few seconds more. Then she nodded
slowly. "Yes," she said softly. "You're right, of course."

Incredulity spread over Heath Chandler's face; then it
twisted in a kind of grimace that combined relief, gratitude and love. "Oh, hell," he whispered, and reached for
her hand.

"You're right," she said again. "You do have the obligation. I guess there's no way out of it."

"Not and live with myself," he whispered.

"That's what I mean. So—" Her body trembled slightly;
she was gathering all her will and sensibility to compose
herself. Then, amazingly, she smiled. "So we'll do it,"
she said in a totally different voice, light and devoid of
grudge or bitterness. If she were not suddenly wholly
reconciled, she was a marvelous actress. "Maybe it's time
we came back anyhow, for Hamp and Ramsey's sake, if
nothing else. And Fox's. Oh, he'll be ecstatic when he
hears." She drew in a long breath. "There, it's settled."
Her laugh was only a little shaky. "Hometown boy and
girl return."

Both men looked at her with a kind of awe. Then
Heath said, "Thanks. Christ, I love you."

Claudia laughed again. "Then we're victims of the
same affliction." Then she was serious. "But can you do
it? As bad as things are, do you really have a chance?"

Heath sat up straight, purged of sentiment, full of
vitality and purpose. "I'm pretty sure I have. Hell, the
mills are there, they *exist*. Somebody's going to open them
up again, it might as well be me. I've got some ideas already, and I think they'll work. But—" He hesitated.

"There's one thing. I'll have to sink some of our money in them. Maybe most of it."

Only the briefest flicker came and went in Claudia's eyes. "That's up to you. But what difference does it make? Three mills, the town—you said last night they were worth a million, even at rock-bottom. That's more than we've got now. So how can we lose?"

"We won't lose," said Heath quietly. "No, I promise you that." Once again they looked at each other and Claudia's smile widened. She was once again wholly her husband's partisan, and Olin, excluded from that intimacy, felt an outsider's thrust of envy, jealousy, sadness, and even fear. Now it ended; now he lost them both, Heath and Claudia, and that was worse even than the prospect of leaving their bounty to return to poverty and the frustration of the failed artist. In that instant he hated Bolivar worse than Claudia ever had.

Then Chandler turned to him, something kindling in his face, grin wide, eyes dancing, showing that mercurial enthusiasm of his which, while it lasted, acknowledged no obstacles. "And you, Clutt, are you in it too?"

"Me?" Olin blinked.

"Damn, man, you don't think I can do something like this without your help? I can't go it alone! I need you!"

"But I— I don't know anything about textiles! About any business!"

"So what?" Heath was like a locomotive with steam up and brakes suddenly off, pent-up power translated all at once into speed and action. And, Olin understood now, he had been bored. Happy, but unchallenged; and challenge was the fundamental force that drove him. "Who cares what you know? I don't know either. But all those grand viziers of Bolivar's ought to—they've been here long enough! What they need is somebody to get them off their duffs and make them use their knowledge. Then you and I, we can get by on brass. Come on, Olin. The two of us, we can get this thing rollin again and have ourselves a real high time in the process!"

"I don't—"

"Listen, chum." Heath was pleading with him now.

"This is the dreariest, most monotonous racket in the world. I won't be able to stand it without somebody to help me liven it up." And then his grin broadened. "And, boy, do I aim to liven it up!" He bounced to his feet. "I've already been thinking, made some plans. Do you know what's behind this whole business? *What women want to put on their bodies!* Things have reached a point where whole companies rise and fall on what some dumb blonde wears in a hit movie! Fashion—and you know what fashion is: sex! That's where the Old Man tripped up—he didn't know a thing about either one. Hell, I told you, he'd never even seen a moving picture." He laughed. "And if you've never made love to any female who wasn't wearing a flannel nightgown, how can you help being out of touch?"

He wagged a finger. "So that's the answer, see? Fashion, sex, using a little imagination to stay ahead of the game. Ever since it started, this industry's mostly been run by people like the Old Man, and that's what's wrong with it now. It needs some people who've been around, wastrels like us who've misspent our lives partying and traveling and living it up. And that may be our edge, the way we can get things on their feet again!"

Quickly he lit a cigarette, rushed on, the locomotive gathering speed. "I thought about it all this morning when I couldn't sleep, and I don't see why it wouldn't work. What we've got to do is get there fustest with the mostest. Bolivar had to depend on what his selling agents in New York told him about what would sell, but what I aim to do is find out myself before anybody else does, beat out the competition. Look, the three of us know, or can get to, everybody in New York, in London, and in Paris who counts—not the people who follow fashion but the ones who make it. The thing to do is use those connections and squeeze 'em dry."

Olin and Claudia both stared at him as he rushed on.

"We may not know the nuts and bolts of this business, but we know giving parties, socializing. And you can learn more over a martini than you can from a hundred calls and interviews. What I want to do is this: rent a suite in some good New York hotel and get back in the swing of things. Throw some of the damnedest parties the town's ever seen, and get everybody who's anybody there, especially in the garment trades and fashion—not only the buyers, but the executives, the designers, the creative people. And the movie stars and all the rest who set the styles and make things go." He turned to Claudia. "And Paris! You can attend the showings there, report right back on what's coming into style. While everybody else in this game sits home and waits for the phone to ring and somebody to tell 'em what to make next, we'll already be way ahead of 'em! Do you see? There's not one of our competitors who doesn't know a million times more about making yarn and cloth than we do, but we're the only ones with the special talents and connections that we've got! So why not use 'em for all they're worth, and have some fun at the same time?"

Again Olin blinked. Heath's enthusiasm infected him, but it was frightening too. It did not sound like business as he had always thought of it. Dreams, air castles—

Claudia voiced his doubts. "How can you do that? Party in New York and run things here?"

He shrugged. "Simple. I'll buy an airplane."

"Oh, no." Her voice caught, face paled. "Now, wait—" Olin saw again, as she must have, the Tiercel hurtling toward the trees.

"Now, don't panic." Heath's voice was reassuring, almost amused. "Not some hot race job. Something practical and safe and conservative—likely a Tin Goose, a Ford Trimotor. They're just as safe as any railroad train."

"I don't care! I don't want you flying again!"

"Look. To make this thing work, I've got to have a plane. It's one more edge nobody else will have. With a Ford I can get from here to New York and back the same day if I have to. Be on top of things when they're breaking, hit customers before anybody else can get to 'em, build good will by taking them for rides, hauling 'em where they want to go. It's important to the whole deal —I can't make things work without it!"

Claudia only shook her head swiftly, mutely.

Heath went to her, put his hands on her arms. "I promise. No wild flying, no crazy tricks. Business, business only, and safely, responsibly. I give you my word of honor."

She turned her head away. He was asking too much, too quickly, Olin thought; how could he expect any woman to have that much capacity for giving? But she knew that it was useless to deny him. Presently she said, dully, "All right. But I'll hold you to that promise."

"Ahh." With a sound of delight Heath embraced her. "Damn, Olin, did you ever see another like her?" He held her tightly, and once more Olin felt that bitter thrust of envy, exclusion, and looked down at his plate.

"Well, Clutt? What do you say?" Heath released Claudia. "The old girl's in. Will you buy chips?"

"I'm not a businessman, I'm an artist." There was a sullenness in Olin's voice he had not meant to betray.

"That's the point! I'm not going to run a business—I'm going to create a work of art!" Heath swept out his arm. "There's one out there now, waiting for an artist to bring it back to life and shape it up, make it perfection! Clutt, come on, please. I can't promise you a mammoth salary, but you'll have some stock that may or may not be worth the ink it's printed with, and I'll give you my *droit du seigneur* over all the nubile female mill hands. And we'll have fun, I'll swear to that." Now he was serious, pleading. "I can't do it without you, no way at all. Please, Clutt, will you?"

Olin shook his head. This was not what he wanted, no part of it appealed to him; he did not like Chandlerville or what he had seen of the mills. But, on the other hand, how could he sustain himself without the Chandlers? He was through with painting, burned out, they were all that had kept him from ultimate despair and maybe even self-destruction . . .

"Olin," Claudia said softly, looking at him with enormous eyes. "Will you, please? We both need you." And he saw that, for her at least, that was absolutely true, and it turned the balance.

Knowing then that he had to be near her, he nodded slowly. "Okay," he said. "Why not?"

Her eyes met his, and the gratitude he saw there was real and reward enough as she said quietly, meaning it, "Thank you, Olin, thank you." And thus he was committed.

The formal reading of the will was held immediately in the drawing room at Chandler House. According to a preliminary inventory the estate amounted to something like five million dollars—but that was property, buildings, machinery and inventory, with pathetically little cash on hand. What money there was had been set aside by Bolivar in trust for Elizabeth, along with a substantial block of stock. Smaller blocks went to the churches of the town, to the senior executives, and one was, startlingly, bequeathed to Fox Ramsey, as if in atonement and compensation. There were trusts for Hamp and Ramsey, and all the remainder went directly to Heath—70 percent of outstanding shares, complete control.

When that was over, Wade addressed the group that had gathered for the reading. "Ladies and gentlemen, this must be probated, and it will be some time before actual distribution of bequests can be made. Meanwhile, as executor, I intend to ask the court to certify Heath Chandler as president and board chairman of Chandler Mills and all its affiliated corporations. Do I hear any objections from those stockholders present?"

There was only silence. "Then we're all in agreement." Wade sat down and Heath, an imposing figure in gray suit and dark tie, arose, his handsome face serious.

"Gentlemen, I don't have much to say. I know you've got a million questions, but I can only answer one right now. Let me make this announcement." His eyes swept the group. "It is my intention to put Chandler Mills back in operation at the soonest possible moment and to run the company at a profit. In order to accomplish that, I'll need the help, support, and advice of everyone here. And I'll take this opportunity to ask for that."

He paused; the room was very silent.

"One thing more. I owe my father a fitting memorial. I intend to give him one, and not of granite or of marble. Once the doors of Chandler Mills are open, as long as I am president they will never close again, except on Sundays and legal holidays. Once the mills are running, they will never be shut down again for anything or anybody. That is a resolve I have made. Thank you. Now, there is no time to waste. I'd like to see every member of the staff in the president's, my, office at nine tomorrow morning for a planning session."

The old men who had served Bolivar for so long looked at one another, and life and hope seeped back into their gray old faces. There was a spattering of applause. When they had arisen, shaken his hand, and filed out, Heath smiled faintly. "Poor old codgers. I'm afraid they're in for a shock when they see what happens next."

As the last one left, the phone rang. The maid answered and called Heath to it; when he returned to the drawing room his face registered a mixture of distaste and wry amusement. "St. John Butler. We had an appointment for tomorrow, but he must have got wind that the will was being read today, and the vulture couldn't wait. 'Just happened to be passing through and wondered if I can drop in.' So I told him to come on."

"Would you prefer that I deal with him?" asked Wade.

"No. I'll reserve that pleasure to myself and Olin; I want him to see what the competition's like."

"In that case I'll be going."

Heath nodded to Olin, and they walked with Wade to the door. When he had departed Chandler said: "I'll fill you in on the Butlers. In a way, St. John and I are sort of in the same boat. Old Sam Butler came out of the War Between the States with a lot of money. He was a cotton factor and a man who knew how to set his sail to catch the wind, got in with the carpetbagger government and made a fortune in Confederate cotton that was condemned as contraband. Later he started buying up bankrupt cotton mills. Butler Mills is a big outfit now, and St. John and his brothers are their father's sons. Nothing means more to them than a nickel, unless it's a dollar, and they're notorious for the way they treat their people. Next to them Bolivar was a liberal spendthrift and a real humanitarian. You'll see what I mean when he gets here."

Nevertheless Clutterbuck found the slender, handsome, soft-spoken man impressive at first. "I just thought, Heath, I'd stop by and see if there's any way I can be of help to you. Any burdens I can lift from your shoulders."

"That's nice of you, St. John." Olin caught the streak of irony in Heath's tone. "But everything's under control."

In the deep leather chair in Bolivar's study Butler looked a little startled. "Oh, well, that's good. Of course . . . there is that matter we discussed the other day."

"What matter? Oh, the offer you were going to make for the mills." Heath was casual. "Well, how much?"

"I— Well, frankly I wasn't prepared right now. I only wanted to—"

"Come off it, St. John. We'll both save time if we don't beat around the bush. What's your best offer?"

Butler recovered, but could not quite mask the pleasure in his eyes that they had come directly to business. "Well, we don't really *need* any additional plant capacity right now. In fact, we've shut down half of what we already have. But maybe someday, in the distant future, things will get better and we'll be looking toward expansion again. And our thinking—very tentative, of course— was that it might be more advantageous to buy your mills and hold them until that time than to have to build new capacity from scratch when it comes."

"That sounds smart. You still haven't mentioned price."

"Well, naturally, it would be a matter for negotiation. We'd have to audit and appraise—"

"St. John," Heath said. "You know already what these mills are worth as well as I do, maybe better. And you know exactly what you aim to pay."

Butler smiled faintly, shrugged. "Well, this day and time the truth is, we couldn't possibly go over a million."

"Oh?" Heath's brows went up; he looked impressed. "A whole million dollars?"

"Yes." Butler leaned forward eagerly.

"And then how much more for the town and all its assets?"

"What?" Butler's face went blank. "Why, I meant for the mills and town both, for all the holdings of your company."

Heath sat up straight in the chair behind Bolivar's desk. "I see. Don't you think that's rather low for three mills and a whole town?"

"In this day and time a million dollars is a lot of money."

"Sure. Come to think of it, it is." Heath took out cigarettes, lit one with slow, elaborate gestures. Then said, "But not for properties worth five million at the very least."

Butler bit his lip, then laughed softly. "Oh, now, Heath, be sensible. Maybe your books show some figure like that, but it doesn't mean a thing. Not with the mills closed and no way to reopen them. Maybe if they were running profitably they might be worth that, but right now they're just so many big buildings—liabilities, not assets."

Leaning back, Heath propped his feet on Bolivar's desk. Butler looked shocked. "Sure enough," Heath said, "that's right. I've thought about that a lot. If I can get them back in production and in the black. I'll make four million, just like that."

St. John Butler's jaw dropped. "You—?"

Heath nodded. "That would be good business, wouldn't it, St. John? Make a going concern out of my inheritance, instead of selling it for a song on a distress market?"

"Why . . . why . . ." Butler groped for words. "You can't be serious."

Heath took down his feet. "But I am. I'm sorry if I misled you the other day, St. John. But certain things have changed. I don't see how I can give away four million dollars; I know I don't have that kind of money just to donate to you."

Slowly Butler nodded; and Olin saw that he had a quick mind, and in that second or two of hesitation it was scurrying ahead through the implications of Heath's speech. His poise was completely recovered when he said, "Let me be sure I understand you? It's your intention to take over Chandler Mills and run them yourself."

"It is at present."

"Well, I hope you won't take it amiss if I speak frankly to you as your friend. I really don't believe you know what you're letting yourself in for. After all, you've been away a long time. Heath, today the textile industry, especially cottons, is in the worst shape it's been in since the War Between the States. Demand and prices both are at rock-bottom, and even the strongest mills, run by the most experienced people, are struggling to survive. Do you have any idea of the amount of capital you'll need just to start up again? And even if you get it, frankly, there's no substitute for experience. I know you're Mr. Bolivar's son and that some years ago you had a certain amount of training and exposure to the business. But that was in a different market and a different world. To be honest, I just don't see how you can do it. I don't believe you know what you're biting off, and as your friend, I can only warn you that I'm afraid, if you attempt this, you'll be very sorry indeed."

"That's entirely likely," Heath said. "But a chance I've got to take."

Again Butler paused thoughtfully. "I'll tell you," he said at last. "This is without authority from my board, and I'm opening myself to criticism. But I could probably squeeze out another two hundred and fifty thousand dollars. And believe me, the interest you could earn on that extra quarter-million alone is more than you'll earn in profits for a long, long time, even if you are successful in reopening. I don't ask you to take my word. You look around, check with banks, check with Mr. Bolivar's commission agent, check with everybody. Then I'm sure you'll realize that you'll be better off taking a reasonable offer and leaving the headaches and heartbreaks to people who are used to them."

"I don't doubt that either," Heath said. "But as long as I can feed my family and keep the rain off 'em, I'm not going to concern myself too much about the profits. If I can put my hands back to work and break even, that'll keep me happy for a while."

Butler blinked, then smiled almost pityingly.

"You think I'm being naïve," Heath said.

"I think you're being sentimental. And I think it won't take long for you to see that sentiment's a luxury a businessman can't afford—not nowadays."

"Maybe you're right," Heath said easily. "Tell you what, St. John. I'll accept your offer if you'll guarantee me that you'll find a job for every hand who had one with Chandler Mills before my father died." He leaned forward. "I'll take a million and a quarter and your undertaking to see that everyone who wants to work can."

"Oh, for—" Butler shook his head.

"Well, that's my aim," Heath said. "It's a kind of . . . remembrance I can give my father."

"A decision made in grief. You'll feel different later. Look, Heath, the only way anybody can survive right now is cut expenses and useless overhead to the bone. We're all struggling to do that—all the members of the Textile Manufacturers Association of this state—and to do our best to keep the market up. Right now it's flooded with goods, and inventories are our biggest problem. We're laying off people, shutting down mills, and all of us are operating on a quota system until the glut in gray goods has subsided and things pick up again. Even if you went back in business, your quota wouldn't be big enough to allow you to work all your hands."

"I see. Then it wouldn't be smart for me to join the association and let you inflict a quota on me, would it?"

Butler's face went hard. "Surely you don't intend to operate outside the association? In times like these everybody's got to pull together. The quota system's the only way to do it. And it won't work unless everybody sticks to it. If only one man breaks it, there'll be chaos."

"Maybe. But it sounds kind of hard on the hired help."

"The hired help be damned!" Butler flared. "A company's first responsibility is to its stockholders! Right now the surest way to go into bankruptcy's to coddle your labor! If you don't believe that, look at the situation Mr. Bolivar worked himself into! Heath, I'll tell you bluntly: it's a mistake for you to try to reopen Chandler Mills yourself. But it'll be a bigger one for you to try to go it alone, without the cooperation of the rest of the industry."

"Is that a threat, St. John?"

"Of course not, only fact. In times like these there's no room for a maverick. We've struggled to build a system to keep ourselves alive. Much as we like you personally, we couldn't, any of us, tolerate anybody else—you or anybody—who, out of ignorance, threatened to tear it down."

"And what would you do to me if I did?"

"I . . ." Butler was openly perturbed now. "I don't want to get mixed up in any sort of discussion like that, especially at this time."

"But all the rest of you, working against me, could make it hard on me."

"I think that's obvious," Butler said thinly.

"Well . . ." Heath shrugged. "I guess it's just something else I'll have to face." Then he sat up straight, and his face was hard, completely devoid of humor. "Because here's how I stand, St. John. I intend to do my damnedest to get Chandler Mills back in production. Maybe I will, maybe I won't, but if I do, I'll be in business to make and sell every yard of cloth and inch of yarn I can, and nobody's going to set any limits on me at all or tell me how to run my company, you or your association or anybody. Once I get these mills open, they're never gonna close again, and if the rest of you can't keep up with me, then it's devil take the hindmost."

"That's big talk, Heath," said Butler harshly.

"I know it. Maybe I can't back it up. But I'm going to try."

Butler was silent for a moment more, then he relaxed. "Let's not quarrel. I understand your feelings at this time and admire them. But when you actually come to grips with things, you'll see what I'm driving at. I'm afraid you're in for a rude awakening."

Heath laughed. "It won't be my first."

Butler stood up, took his hat. "Well, you're sure there's nothing I can do, I mean of a personal nature, for you and your family?"

"Not right now, thanks, St. John."

"Please let me know if there is. Feel free to call on me for anything you need. Good afternoon, Heath, Mr. Clutterbuck. You both come to see us, hear?" They shook hands, and Heath ushered him out. When he returned to the study his face was grim. "That sanctimonious son of a bitch," he rasped. Then he smiled wryly. "Come on, Clutt, let's have a drink. What the hell, it's not every day a man gets to turn down a million dollars!"

Once committed, Claudia moved as swiftly and decisively as Heath. Olin wondered whether she was really a wholehearted partisan of the enterprise or, with feminine deviousness, had set out to cut off Heath's retreat and by doing so force him to think twice.

When she broke the news to the children, Hamp, surprisingly, was not dismayed that they would not return to Austria. Indeed, he was delighted. If Chandlerville had not captured him, Fox Ramsey had, with promises of guns, hunting, fishing, a whole spectrum of masculine adventure. Ramsey took it less well; for her it was a painful uprooting, but whatever Hamp wanted, she would, in adoration of her brother, accept. If they had not been twins, Olin thought, her attachment to him would have been almost unwholesome.

Claudia would not hear of keeping the villa, despite Heath's insistence. With their money invested in the mills, they could not afford it. Heath was obviously reluctant to part with it, but she was firm, merciless, leaving him no escape route, no tie with the past. So within a few days Olin and Chandler saw her and the twins aboard the *Carinthia,* returning to Vienna to terminate the lease and handle the shipment of their belongings. As the call for visitors to go ashore rang out, the children embraced their father and he clung to them almost desperately. Then Claudia moved into his arms, and Clutterbuck again felt that sense of exclusion, loneliness.

Reluctantly Heath released her. "If there's any trouble, cable me."

"I don't expect any. Besides, you'll have problems of your own." She turned to Clutterbuck. "Olin, watch over him."

"I'll do my best. Don't forget the portrait. I want to finish it." Then he kissed her briefly, and it was good to hold her at all, even like that.

Standing on the dock, as the vessel was tugged out to sea, Heath's face was grave. He raised his hand once, dropped it. The ship was too far out now for the passengers at its rail to be more than dots. Then he turned to Olin. "All right, Clutt," he said, "let's go to work."

2   WORTH STREET, on Manhattan's lower West Side, was the center of the wholesale textile trade, an unprepossessing street lined with storefronts full of cloth offered by brokers and dealers, reeking with a sordid taint of cutthroat competition and desperate hustle. But the Arkwright Club, at 40 Worth, where Heath and Olin lunched with Norris Gorman, president of the sales agency that serviced Chandler Mills, was insulated from all that, and in its dining room Clutterbuck smelled money in vast amounts.

"Of course I'm delighted with your decision," Gorman said. He was a curious mixture of cultivated New Yorker and dour New England Yankee. "After all, Chandler Mills was one of our prime accounts."

By now Clutterbuck had learned enough about the business to comprehend the symbiotic relationship between Chandler Mills and the commission house. From the beginning the southern manufacturers had lacked either financing or knowledge to set up sales forces of their own and had turned to agents in New York, already well established as salesmen for the New England industry. For a commission Gorman had sold Chandler's output, and the Old Man had been dependent on him both for sales and for market information on which to base his planning. Since big commission houses like Gorman's represented many different mills, some in competition with each other, their clients, totally in their hands, had to rely on their energy and integrity for their survival. It seemed to Olin a ramshackle, inefficient arrangement, providing too many opportunities for skulduggery by an unscrupulous agency, but it was the way things had always been done, and it kept down the overhead.

"I'm glad you approve," Heath said. "I'm going to need all the help I can get." He took an envelope from his pocket, handed it to Gorman. "There's our current inventory; and it's a brute. We've got an awful lot of duck and gingham in our warehouse for a prime account."

"Yes." Gorman put it in his pocket without opening it. "Well, toward the end, I'm afraid, Mr. Bolivar was a difficult man to deal with. We tried to advise him, but it was hard to get him to listen. He went on making the same constructions he always had, no matter what the market wanted. Of course he lacked the modern machinery necessary for the quick changeovers you've got to make nowadays, when flexibility is all."

"Sure. Anyhow, I'm stuck with a lot of cloth."

"Eventually we'll find a market for it. But it'll take time. Right now, things are . . . chaotic."

"That's what I hear. All the same, I need operating capital."

Gorman smiled. "I think we can help you there, inventory or no. It's been our policy to make selective advances to good clients who're in a short cash position. Not to everybody, but for Chandler Mills we would certainly—"

"Mr. Gorman," Heath said crisply, "I don't want an advance. I've seen that deal work before. An agent advances money to a mill, the mill defaults, and then the agent takes over to protect his investment. I don't mean that you'd do it, but there are plenty who've worked that angle just to get control of mills and milk them dry for their own profit, no matter how much damage it does the mill itself. I don't want to get caught up in that, I just want you to sell my inventory."

Gorman's eyes went opaque, his mouth thinned. "Mr. Chandler. We've been your father's sales outlet for forty years. If you doubt our ability and good faith—"

"I didn't say that." Suddenly Heath smiled, summoning total charm. Even Gorman's flinty face relaxed under that warmth. "I have complete faith in you. That's why I'm being frank about my problems. All the same, understand my position. I'm sinking my personal resources into Chandler Mills, but they aren't nearly enough. I've got to unload that inventory and do it fast and get some cash out of it. I thought surely you could handle that for me in the best way."

"Oh, we could give it away, yes. But dumping all that on the market would ruin the price structure—for you, for everybody."

"Do you know, Mr. Gorman, I don't really give a damn about the price structure right now, or about anybody else, for that matter. Chandler Mills is all I can concern myself with. If you were to move into the market quick with that inventory, slash hell out of prices for a quick sale—anything to get it out of my warehouse and get me even a few pennies on the dollar for it. Speed, that's what I need, speed and action."

Gorman leaned back. "Young man, I don't think you understand—"

"Oh, yes, I do. I understand that I've got thousands of people down in North Carolina starving while they wait for me to get my mills open and put 'em back to work. And that they can't hang on much longer." His smile vanished. "Mr. Gorman, I want that inventory sold, and I want it sold fast. Now, if you tell me you can't do it, I'll take a whirl at it myself. I don't mind pounding the pavement up and down Worth Street and Seventh Avenue."

Something, perhaps alarm, flickered in Gorman's eyes. "That's absurd. You couldn't possibly make as good a

deal yourself as we could make for you. And if you di●
you'd put us in the position of having to . . . relinquis●
your account."

"My account," Heath said crassly, "won't be worth ●
fart in a hurricane unless I get my mills in operation●
Now his voice was full of iron. "Mr. Gorman, I'm gonn●
do that. Somehow, whether you help me or not. And whe●
I do, we'll make cloth—one pluperfect hell of a lot ●
cloth. And not to rot in warehouses either, but to se●
Before I'm through, somebody's going to get rich o●
Chandler Mills' commissions. I hope it's you. But if wor●
comes to worst, I'm prepared to set up a sales force ●
my own here in New York and dispense with commissio●
agents altogether."

It was bluff, sheer bluff, and Olin knew it. But th●
utter assurance in Heath's voice had its effect. Gorma●
bit his lip. "I shouldn't think that was necessary. O●
course, if you're absolutely determined to unload no●
and take a loss—"

"I am. I'm a little ignorant at present, but I learn fas●
I'll expect you to set just the right price to make th●
inventory move and give me maximum return. Maybe ●
won't know how well you've done that for months b●
in a year or two I'll be able to judge—and I have a lon●
memory."

Gorman bridled. "You are a most impertinent youn●
man. Not like Mr. Bolivar at all."

Heath smiled. "You've just learned the two most im●
portant things about me, then." His smile came bac●
"Mr. Gorman, I have every confidence in your outfi●
You'll just have to overlook my impatience, it's the wa●
I'm built. Maybe when I'm older, I'll settle down. Mea●
while I'll be in touch every day or so on the long-distan●
phone."

"There's no need to go to that expense. I'll write—"

"I'll risk the phone calls. Maybe I'll learn somethin●
from them."

"Very well," Gorman said. "At any rate, you've cha●
lenged us, and it's up to us to meet the challenge. I a●
sure you, Mr. Chandler, we will."

"I never doubted that. And, please—it would be a favor if you would call me Heath."

"God damn it," Heath said, "if your business is like mine, I don't see how you survive. Nobody wants to do anything but sit and moan. They won't spend a dime to make a dollar on telegrams or phone calls even, much less airplanes. I don't see how you stay alive, Alec."

Baldwin, in the hotel room, was a little drunk in the fervor of reunion. "Oh, it ain't as bad as you think. Back in the twenties you and I had the right idea; it was the car that put a crimp in us. When Ford came along with a cheap automobile, everybody forgot about airplanes. But the novelty's worn off of putting along at forty miles an hour—and then Lindbergh, God bless old Slim . . . People are beginning to look at airplanes again." He leaned forward, belly spilling over belt, wagged a finger. "Believe me, another ten years and you'll be able to fly anywhere you want to go on an airplane."

"Can't wait. I need a Tin Goose. You're a broker. Can you get me a good one cheap?"

Baldwin blinked. "Ford Trimotor? Hell, Heath, you want something hotter than that!"

"Later. Right now I have to break Claudia in easy to my flying again at all. Besides, I need a big, safe, reliable plane that'll haul a lot of passengers, so I can fly customers around and butter 'em up."

Baldwin shrugged. "Okay. A Ford, then. How much you want to spend?"

"The least I can get by with. Find me something cheap, put it in shape in a reliable shop, double-check it, add your profit, and break the bad news."

Baldwin shook his head. "There won't be any profit add-on."

"The hell there won't."

"Listen, you helped bail me out of that Tiercel mess with your play royalties until I could shop my patents. If it hadn't been for that—"

"If I could have kept the damned thing aloft where it belonged, there wouldn't have been any mess."

"Shit," Baldwin said. "Anyhow, my patents are payin, off now. I don't need your lousy money. You'll take prime Ford at cost and keep your fucking mouth shu' Selah."

Heath grinned. "Okay. You want to screw yoursel' have fun. Just get me a good airplane."

"You'll have it." Baldwin was silent as he took anothe drink. Then he said, "Have you seen that new shov *North Wind?*"

"No, why?"

"Because," Baldwin said, "Betty Hammond's the star.

Olin watched Heath. Chandler only rolled his glas between his palms. "So what?" His voice was toneless

"Nothing. Just thought you might be interested. Sh got good reviews, it's a hit."

Heath said nothing.

Baldwin laughed thickly. "Probably wouldn't make an difference. They say now she goes mainly for girls."

Clutterbuck saw Heath's brows draw down. Then h said casually, "Well, that's what Hollywood will do fo you. Alec, what about another drink?"

If Heath had shaken up Gorman, he created pani among the executives of Chandler Mills. These men wer old in every sense, gutted of drive and initiative by year of Bolivar's one-man rule. In his reign he had reserve the final decision on every matter, regardless of hov inconsequential, to himself. When Heath tried to outlin his new approach to a staff not one of whom had eve flown, or even taken a mixed drink, much less attende a cocktail party, he might as well have spoken Sanskri His plan to dump the inventory met with stiff oppositior The cloth had cost money to manufacture. No matte how figures were juggled, there was a level below whic it would be disastrous to sell; as long as it was in ware house, artificially valued, the books balanced.

Heath listened with a patience Olin had not expecter and when he spoke, it was at first with humility. "Yo gentlemen may be right. But the whole point is, we'n starting fresh. As if . . . well, as if we're foreigners who'v bought out Chandler Mills and know nothing about the past, have to find our own way through the future. And don't know what's possible or impossible until we try it."

"All the same, your father never would have—"

"I know," Heath said. "That's what I'm driving at. We buried my father three weeks ago."

In the shocked silence that followed he added flatly, "We'll try things my way and see how they work."

Then he began to pick their brains while he and Olin pored over books, ledgers, past correspondence and billings. In the beginning Clutterbuck found most of it incomprehensible, but Heath's grasp of the mill's affairs was lightning-swift. Patiently he tried to explain things to Olin, but the more he comprehended, the more Clutterbuck was appalled by the seeming illogic and confusion of the whole enterprise.

"We're in the middle," Heath told him. "Raw cotton accounts for half our costs, and we buy it on a market that goes up and down from minute to minute. And sell what we make on another one that does the same thing. All we can do is ride the roller coaster between them and try to keep our balance. If we fall off, we're finished."

He went on, phrasing it in elementary terms. "First of all, we spin yarn. Out of that yarn we weave cloth. What we don't use in our own weaving we sell to other manufacturers. The cloth we make is unfinished, called gray goods. That we sell to finishers and converters, who dye and print it and sell it in turn to wholesalers or the cutting trades, the garment makers. By the time it gets on the customer's back it's been through more hands than a mademoiselle on Saturday night in 1917—and there's not a single son of a bitch we deal with who wouldn't steal your eyeteeth to make a nickel and come back for your gums to sell for a penny.

"The upshot of the whole thing is that we have to watch ourselves every minute. We can get screwed by making a mistake in the cotton market, screwed again in the cloth and yarn market, and screwed even by our selling agent, who, after all, handles our competitors too and won't hesitate to play both ends against the middle if he can make a buck. When you come down to it, it's like walking a barbed-wire fence barefooted with a bobcat under each arm."

They had been working that night in the conference room. Now they got up, went into the adjoining office, which had once been Bolivar's and now was Heath's. Chandler halted, staring at a picture on the wall. It had been made in the early days of the mill: sixty lank workers ranked in rows, and, standing in their forefront, small and proud, the little man with the big head, hand thrust Napoleonically inside his frock coat. Then Heath went to his desk, and a curious sound drew Clutterbuck's attention.

Heath stood there, spinning the wooden swivel chair that had once been Bolivar's, a strange expression on his face.

"You know," he said, "when I was a kid I used to sneak in here and sit in this and whirl until I got dizzy. Thought it made a fine merry-go-round. I guess it still will." He looked at Olin with a smile that was curiously shy. "I didn't come near filling it. It seemed to me like the biggest chair in the whole world."

He gave it another spin. "And I guess it is," he murmured.

3   WHEN HEATH AWAKENED, the room was still dark.

He lay motionless beside Claudia for a while, drawing comfort from the warmth and presence of her after a month, while she was in Europe, in which the bed had seemed huge and barren. Then, with acceleration of heart and pulse, he knew what day this was and could lie still no longer. Easing from beneath the covers, he walked across the room, pulled back the curtains, and looked out at Chandlerville and the mills down in the valley.

It was half past four. Only a few lights winked in the

darkness below. He searched for the outline of the mills, thought he saw chimneys thrusting against the sky, but dawn was still too far away to be sure. Then he went to the table by the bed, picked up a handbill. In the bathroom he switched on the light and read it again, although he himself had written it.

Attention, Employees of Chandler Mills!
At 6:00 Monday morning, July 2, work will start again in all plants. In the beginning we will run only one shift. Within a few weeks we hope to add a second one. Meanwhile we will try to arrange things so at least one member of every family will have work and draw pay. Apply to Personnel Manager for job assignment.

Notice! If you are not at your machine exactly at the shift starting time, your job will go to somebody else!

With your help we will run as many shifts as we can and hope never to close down again. The cooperation of every worker will be needed if this is to be.

HEATH CHANDLER
President, Chandler Mills

The handbills, put out in every store and church, actually were superfluous. The grapevine in the mills had long since spread the information; the bills only made it official.

When Heath came back into the bedroom, dressed, the sky was lightening a little. He looked down at Claudia, at the wheat-colored hair, the clean, sharp features, the faintly parted lips, the crease of breasts almost wholly revealed above the nightgown's neckline. And his mind went back to that other night, when he had handed her Bolivar's letter.

It had been the most bitter battle of their marriage. At first she refused to believe what she must already have understood from his face. Then she tried to reason with him, cajole and woo him from what she must have taken for only an aberration of the moment. That failed; and then she had really begun to fight. Playing for the highest stakes, she met him head-on with ferocity. "I won't let you! I won't let you throw everything away because of that—that old bastard!" She hurled the letter at him; it fluttered to the carpet like a leaf. "Words! Words are cheap! What did they cost him to write?" For the first time he saw clearly the depth and virulence of her hatred for his father. "Why didn't he write them after the Tiercel crash? When I was pregnant with his grandchildren and we were broke and your mother and I both going through hell, why didn't that vile, selfish, stupid man come to us then? That was when we needed this—" She slashed a hand toward the fallen letter. "But, no! And now—" She almost spat. "Words—cheap, lousy words! Sucker bait!"

She went on like that, her fury, because so uncommon, shaking him profoundly. But the stakes he played for were even higher than hers. He had already sensed that for him this was a matter of self-preservation. Until now he had been a man drifting, floating, without an anchorage in the past. And no man, he had realized, could deny his father and create himself and still be whole, complete. Nor could that man's children. If he denied the past to himself, he denied it to Hamp and Ramsey, condemned the three of them to go through life rootless, and somehow unfinished. He had endured ten years without that vital anchorage, and only he could know how much damage that had done him. Now, if he seized this chance, he could heal the wound, repair the damage, restore, he felt, some part of himself vital and missing too long from the rest. Find, with linkage to both past and future—Bolivar the past, the twins the future— a completeness in the present that he could not exist without.

He did not blame Claudia for being unable to understand. Fox was still alive and had always loved her, so she had never lost her father. But he had, and he was entitled to regain him, not only for himself but for Hamp and Ramsey. They were due continuity, assurance of the part of their identity that the Old Man was, and without it they, too, would be damaged, crippled; and it seemed to him that he fought as much for their welfare as she thought she did.

Anyhow, she had thrown herself against his resolve like a battering ram, had sought, failing to break it down, to undermine or go around or over it; and, in all that, had failed as well. Near dawn she had recognized defeat. No—he amended that thought—achieved understanding. He had seen comprehension come at last into her reddened eyes. And then he knew it was going to be all right again. As, right now, his identity and self-respect was bound up in Bolivar, so hers was bound up in him, in being Heath Chandler's wife; and if this was what he absolutely had to have, it was her duty to help him get it. But not before she had tested in every possible way its necessity and become convinced.

Then, after the final challenge at breakfast, she had yielded, the need to meet the obligations imposed on her by love greater than her hatred of Bolivar or even her own desires. Since she could not beat him, she had joined him, with the grace that made her unique among all the women he had known. What lingering bitterness and disappointment she must have felt, she had swallowed and kept carefully concealed.

He put out a hand and touched her cheek, and even as his fingers played over soft skin, it came: the hoarse, agonized bawl of the whistle from the mill, like a gigantic, primeval creature in pain or lust. It howled and rang across the valley, and Heath shook Claudia's shoulder. "Wake up," he said. "Wake up, sweetheart—it's time."

The five of them breakfasted together, and, save for himself and Hamp, they were silent and groggy with the earliness of the hour. He himself was wide awake, juices flowing, exuberance and triumph swelling within him, making food superfluous; he ate little, but savored his coffee. And Hamp, beside him, bounced on his chair and gobbled eggs and bacon and chattered continuously.

Hamp. From the very beginning he had been capti-
vated, fascinated, by the mill. They had roamed its depths
together so many times, exploring the long, echoing
rooms with their forests of untended, frozen machines,
and Hamp's interest never flagged. Amazingly, he
grasped effortlessly the processes through which raw
cotton was spun out into yarn and yarn woven into
cloth. Instinctively, he understood machinery and how
it worked to make things. Neither Ramsey nor Claudia
had that knack, and it came hard to Fox and Olin. But
there was a breed of people—he had known such mechanics overseas—for whom machinery lived and had
heart and soul and to whom it gave up its complicated
secrets willingly; and Hamp was one of those, more so
even than his father. Watching him as they made their
rounds, Heath felt a kind of awe of his son. He saw in
Hamp evidence of a talent, a calling even, that reinforced
his certainty of having made the right decision. He himself was only a stopgap, a caretaker. The mills, by right,
belonged to Bolivar and Hamp, and by reviving them, he
served them both: past, future. And that was what
counted, made it all worthwhile, worth all the effort,
strain, and heartbreak.

Which had been more than even he had expected.
His confrontation with Gorman had borne fruit: the
inventory was dumped quickly, almost revengefully, at
a price savagely low. Even so, the cash it yielded to sup-
plement his own fortune—loaned to the company at no
interest—was not enough. He needed more money, lots
of it, in a hurry, and there was only one place to get it.
So he took what capital he had accumulated and plunged
into the cotton-futures market.

All mill owners gambled in such a way, simply to
survive, but it was no place for an amateur. The risks
were long: a few mistakes, some bad luck, and that
volatile exchange could bleed him of his slender backlog, abort all his plans. But it was gambling that could
be done on margin, requiring scant cash and offering
high returns almost overnight. Still, he would not have
risked it without the help of Neal McLendon, the com-

pany treasurer. Under Bolivar's supervision he had been dealing in futures for the mill's account for decades. He knew the ins and outs, lacked only the gambling instinct, which Bolivar had once supplied and which Heath now provided. Together they made a team, and they had been lucky, realizing a quick and startling profit. Not enough for the modern machinery the mills required, of course. But enough to get back into production and run for a while at least. And that would give Heath a chance to convince the dubious bankers and manufacturers, who were still all too aware of his reputation as the rebellious, party-loving playboy. Charm was not enough for them; only deeds, success, could win them over.

So, in a sense, the miracle he'd wrought was fragile, his achievement tenuous. For three months, maybe four, Chandler Mills could exist on what he had accumulated. If in that time they could not be made to pay their way, then they would close again—and if they ever reopened, it would not be with a Chandler in command.

Heath looked at Hamp. "Calm down, kid. You'll shake your breakfast out again."

"Can I stay all day, Daddy? Can I stay all day and watch?" Hamp's green eyes were huge, shining.

Heath grinned, rubbed gently the silky hair. "We'll see. Maybe you'll get tired."

"I won't get tired, I promise."

Heath laughed softly. "Maybe you won't." He took his hand away. Damn it, he thought, it *had* to work. Not for him, for Hamp!

They went down in Bolivar's old limousine, Heath driving, Olin beside him, Claudia and the children in the rear. Dawn, fresh and bright, washed the ugly little town, the whole valley. As they neared the mill village the crisp silence exploded with the sharp bark of lesser automobiles coming to life, backfiring: sporadic at first, soon it was as if a gun battle reached crescendo among the little houses on the hillside. Then from the unpaved streets the cars poured out onto the main road; and so did the walking men in faded overalls. There were not many women among them, for preference had been given to heads of families. As the big, black car rolled by they turned, raised their hands in greeting, and their faces were lit by the rising sun. Heath felt a powerful stirring in his loins. "They're coming," he whispered. "Look at them come."

He returned their greetings as the car threaded through their ranks. Now, ahead, the plant itself took shape, multiple smokestacks phallic against the sky above dark, bulking buildings; and the blue windows were touched by dawn. Again Heath felt that surge of potency. Though their output depended on female whim, there was something about the mills wholly, brutally masculine; and he responded to it.

Then they were beneath the towering walls, and Heath parked the car. As they got out he took Hamp's hand, and Fox came toward them across the parking lot, having driven over from the store. He set Ramsey on his shoulder, and with Claudia walking beside Olin, they crossed the street, entered the office.

"Good morning, Mr. Heath," said the desiccated woman behind the switchboard, with awe and excitement in her voice.

"Morning, Miss Anne." In the common area every clerical desk was occupied. Over and over came the greeting, *Morning, Mr. Heath.* Going down the corridor, Chandler peered into every executive's cubicle. Gray heads lifted; there was respect and surprising vitality, even excitement, in the old voices: *Morning, Mr. Heath.* They entered the president's office, where yellowed plugs of cotton still lay scattered on the tables amidst faded shop drawings undisturbed since Bolivar's hand had last unrolled them. Before Heath could seat himself, Hamp ran for the swivel chair behind the desk, leaped into it, face bright with laughter, and whirled himself around and around. Through the open window came the voices of the mill hands streaming through the gate and chattering with the hysterical animation of survivors just comprehending that they were no longer doomed.

Then, save for the sound of the whirling chair, the

room was silent. Heath glanced at his watch. *Thirty seconds.* He moved instinctively to Claudia, and she put her arm about his waist. Olin Clutterbuck cleared his throat. Ramsey began, "Granddaddy?" but Fox said, "Hush a minute." Two more hands ran desperately across the yard, through the door. Then the steam whistle blew.

For a full sixty seconds its crass, hoarse howl filled the office, drowning them in the cry of triumph that echoed up and down the valley. Hamp stopped the chair; Ramsey stood motionless, even frightened, hand thrust in Fox's. Claudia's fingers dug into Heath's flank; Olin Clutterbuck puffed jerkily at a cigarette. The wild, conquering moan went on and on, then ebbed, died, leaving behind it a silence of an intensity almost equal to the sound.

Then the plant awakened. Throughout its corpus, dormant organisms came to life. Switches clicked, valves turned. Flywheels fought inertia, then pulled themselves over and around with increasing speed. Along the ceilings the huge drive shafts revolved, reluctantly at first, then with eagerness. Leather belting, under tension, slapped and roared. Like a giant arising from a sickbed, Chandler Mills went into action.

At first the vibration was slow, gentle. Then it grew as the machinery gathered speed, in seconds became a solid, rhythmic pounding, exactly like the beating of an enormous, noisy heart. That mounted as each work area added its own thunder to the roar, and then it reached crescendo, shaking floors, walls, ceilings, the very air itself, before it leveled off into a steady, driving stampede of enormous energy released in service of moving card teeth and whirling spindles and flying strings of fiber and yarn, of slamming loom shuttles and all the other myriad mechanisms driven, pulled, geared, picking, biting, twisting, and, with luck, transforming fiber into money. Still Heath did not stir; he stood there, head cocked, listening as if searching for any telltale falter, any disrhythm, that might be a symptom of less than total health and strength. There was none, and suddenly he whooped, exactly like an Indian, startling them all.

"Oh, by God," he yelled, "we did it! I don't know how, but damned if we haven't done it!" On the wall the picture of the little man with hand thrust inside his coat shook so much the image blurred. "You hear?" he shouted at it, half laughing, half crying. "You hear? We're back in business!" He seized Claudia and squeezed her crushingly. Hamp ran to him. "Daddy! Daddy, can I stay, please?"

Heath gathered the boy against his thigh with his free hand. "Sure," he said thickly. "Sure, you can stay."

"Hot dog!" Hamp yelled, and pulled away, ran back to the swivel chair, freeing Heath to take Clutterbuck's outstretched hand.

4   THE PARTY had begun at three, and by four, this Saturday afternoon, the suite at the Waldorf-Astoria was crowded, tainted with odors of whiskey, gin, hair oil, and expensive perfume, shrill with conversation and high-pitched laughter. Heath drew a little apart for the moment, ran amused eyes over the cluster at the bar, the confusion around the buffet, and the ring of men encircling Claudia, who was breathtaking in an afternoon dress of gold on white, every stitch of it—designed in Paris on her commission—made of cotton. That dress represented a terrific investment, but it had already repaid its cost. The competition from synthetic fabrics, rayon and its imitators, was brutal, and Heath had risked the money to show the designers and buyers who flocked to these biweekly parties what could be done with natural fiber. Already buyers for two big department stores were interested, and a chain of cause and effect was set in motion that would redound to the interest of Chandler Mills. There would be orders, and, by careful manipulation, Heath would insure that his company would furnish the fabric. It was only one facet, a minor one, of the campaign, plotted with the precision of a military expedition, that had revived Chandler Mills.

Even before the plants were back in operation he and Claudia had worked out their strategy. Baldwin's superb Tin Goose made commuting to Manhattan easy, and they had rebuilt old connections and cultivated new ones, capitalizing ruthlessly on Heath's still-viable prestige as playwright, easing back into the slot in society that they had abandoned years before. Soon invitations to their parties—or Claudia's salons—were coveted by everyone who counted. Then, using such guests as bait, they had mixed in the most important people in the cloth and garment trade, who made up in money what they lacked in social cachet. Thus, subtly, they mingled two vastly different classes: those who set the styles and those who made their livings from the styles. It was a feat comparable to mixing oil and water, but the Chandlers brought it off, catering to the democracy of pleasure that was beginning to be called café society. And they quickly reaped rewards. Like horse racing or the stock market, this was a business in which a scrap of inside information could be worth a small fortune. Heath worked hard to make sure he missed nothing that alcohol-loosened tongues could tell him, and presently he was putting together deals in the hotel that Gorman could not equal in the open market.

And that martini-induced advance intelligence was what had saved Chandler Mills. Across the South the Depression deepened; mill after mill faltered, fell into the hands of loan-shark agents, or went bankrupt outright. Those that survived did so by locking out their workers when their inventories became unwieldy, slashing wages to the starvation point, or resorting to the stretch-out, doubling the number of machines one operator must tend, wringing the last ounce of strength and productivity from people desperate enough to endure anything to feed their families.

But Chandler Mills ran steadily, closing only on Sundays and legal holidays, and not only ran but added a second shift; all this without resorting to borrowed money or more than a small degree of stretch-out, though Heath was merciless in demanding the utmost from every hand

on the payroll and at paring unnecessary expenditures.
He had learned to be cold and hard when that was
what it took in order to survive; and he drove no one
more ruthlessly than himself. Seven days a week, twelve
or fifteen hours at a stretch, he labored, in the office or
prowling the whole country in his airplane, seeking any
tatter of business to keep his schedule full.

His remorseless energy finally convinced the bankers
and suppliers who had been wary of Heath Chandler,
flying ace and hard-drinking playboy. They saw him now
as superb businessman and risked the needed financing
for equipment with which to modernize and skim the
cream from new market trends before his competitors
learned of their existence or could set up to meet them.
Flexibility, Gorman had said; he was achieving that,
now—

A hand touched his arm. "Heath, you've been avoiding
me."

He looked down into a swarthy face capped by black,
curly hair, made vivid with paint and barbaric earrings.
Nita Pappas was buyer for an enormous mail-order house;
five years his senior, striking if not beautiful, he knew
she would welcome an affair with him. He smiled inwardly. There had been a time when she might have
tempted him, but now he felt no desire. There was no
room left in his life for anything but Claudia, the children, and the mills. In fact, he needed nothing else; with
these he had everything he wanted, was totally alive,
constantly challenged. Still, Nita was important, could
be used, and he would use her, within self-imposed
limits, quite ruthlessly.

"You're the last person I'd avoid. But if I did—slap
my wrist."

She laughed. "You might hit back. Honestly, though, I
wish we could get together for lunch someday." She
added bait. "I've got some problems I need your advice
about."

"Personal or professional?"

"Both."

"The professional ones I can help with right away. What's the trouble?"

She looked disappointed, then shrugged. "Okay, if that's the best I can do. Listen, we're going to need several thousand gross of cotton pajamas, junior size, for next spring's catalogue, and I'm having trouble getting price and delivery commitments. I think they're trying to use this labor trouble down south to jack up prices. Will there really be a general strike? Can the unions really shut down all the mills?"

"Some, maybe. Nobody's going to shut down Chandler Mills. You can count on that. Who're you dealing with? I'll cut the ground out from under him. Give him a firm price on any quantity and construction he needs and guarantee delivery."

"You sound awfully confident."

"I am." As he went on, she listened closely, business taking precedence even over sex. "The unions have been trying to organize the southern mills for years, but they're barking up the wrong tree. You saw what happened to 'em in Gastonia in 1929—the big strike there, the shootings and the trials. They used everything they had and never got to first base."

"But aren't things different now?"

"No. Oh, they've got a sympathetic administration in Washington now, they're stronger, and, yes, they have organized and struck some mills. But the only ones they've had luck with were those that were closed anyhow. Now they say they're going to branch out, close every mill below the Mason-Dixon line until the owners come to terms. Well, they won't close mine, I'll guarantee you that."

"Why not?"

"It's too long a story to tell you. It's one thing to strike a mill that runs only half the time, anyhow; it's another to shut down one that's run full time for the past four years. It's a matter of how much people have to lose, and I've seen to it that my people have too much to lose to listen to the unions."

"But what about the flying squadrons—isn't that what

they call them? Armies of strikers roaming up and down
the country trying to close mills by force . . ."

"They haven't hit me yet, and I don't think they'll
dare to. Yeah, that's their brag, that if the hands won't
walk out they'll break into the mill and occupy it and
shut it down anyhow until the workers join the union
and management comes to terms. And it might work
in some places. A lot of my competitors treat their people like pigs and leave themselves wide open for that
sort of stuff. But I've played it straight with my hands,
and if anybody comes in and tries to close my mills
they'll fight. Not for the union, for me."

"You're sure?"

Heath grinned. "Listen, let the flying squadrons use
all the force they can put together. They can't use half
as much as I can. When I reopened Chandler Mills I
swore that they would never close, not for anybody, and
that includes the unions. My hands know how many
sacrifices I've made for 'em and they'll stick with me.
Don't worry, Nita. My plant'll stay open, and I'll undertake to furnish anything your suppliers needs, even with
a penalty clause if necessary."

"Then you'd better talk to Hauptman and Sons. Don't
let them know I've tipped you off, but when you've made
an offer, give me a call. Then I'll know exactly how to
deal with them."

"Delicately, of course. I do a lot of business with
Hauptman—"

"Very delicately." Nita smiled. "Now that we've disposed of that, it only leaves my personal problems, and—"
Then she broke off. The chatter in the room had suddenly
faded, died, as if something had withered it. Instinctively
she turned, but Heath had already seen, over her shoulder, Phil Montague come into the suite—and Betty
Hammond was on his arm.

She had changed. The years had replaced the milky
freshness of youth with full-blown maturity, an almost
obscene lushness. The spurious innocence combined with
sexuality—he knew better than anybody what an illusion
that innocence was—had become an unabashed, ever

flaunted decadence, a weary, jaded sensuality, as if the core of her finally showed through nakedly, unmasked. And yet that change somehow enhanced the impact of a body still carefully maintained, not quite overflowing its sheathing of bias-cut sea-green crepe, which hugged breasts and hips like a second skin. As always, every man in the room stared at her with lust and admiration, and every woman who was not a Lesbian with envy and resentment.

Heath frowned. He had not invited her, or, for that matter, Montague, who he had heard was in Europe evading creditors and past-due taxes. Instinctively he shot a glance toward Claudia.

Not once had she mentioned Betty Hammond, and to this day he was still not sure how much she knew or guessed about that involvement. Now, glass poised, she stared like all the rest, face unreadable, eyes, after the first flare of surprise, without expression. Then she murmured something to the men around her, and the ring they made parted. "Phil!" she cried, went to the producer and embraced him. Heath's paralysis broke too. "Excuse me," he told Nita, and he strode across the room.

When he came up, the two women had touched hands briefly, looking guardedly at one another. He heard Claudia say, "Yes, of course. It's perfectly all right. I'm so glad you came."

"Thank you." Betty's gaze curiously tabulated the changes in her since the Tiercel incident; then she became aware of Chandler. She jerked around. "Heath!" she cried, and threw herself into his arms, presenting her open mouth for his kiss.

He touched his lips briefly to her cheek. "Hello, Betty."

Her hand closed on his. Her eyes, enormous, blue, and eloquent, met his. "You look marvelous. Very handsome."

"Thanks, you're not bad yourself." Then, quite deliberately, he pulled his hand away and turned to Montague. "Phil, this is fine!"

They shook hands with genuine delight, Claudia flanking them on one side, Betty Hammond on the other.

Heath was acutely, uncomfortably, aware of those two presences, could smell the sensuous fragrance of Betty's perfume; from only the brief kiss, it seemed caught in his nostrils. He talked rapidly. "Where've you been, Phil, you old bastard? This calls for a drink." He pulled Montague toward the bar. Betty started to follow, but Claudia engaged her in conversation.

Montague, a drink in hand, said, "Well, I finally got my taxes straightened out and got up nerve to come home. Everybody talks about your parties, and Betty asked me to bring her this afternoon. I didn't think you'd mind. Hell, nobody who doesn't show up at a Chandler party is anybody, and I'm tired of being nobody." The words rattled from him with a kind of desperation; his face was pinched, his suit, though expensive, rather shabby. "Besides, I want to talk a little business with you."

The two women were coming toward the bar now. "Then let's talk it," Heath said, and drew the man aside.

"I'm sorry," Montague said when they had found a corner. "I mean about her. I know some of the story—it wasn't the smartest thing to do, was it? But she's a star, and a producer needs stars, and when one asks a favor, he doesn't turn her down. Claudia. Maybe it's okay. She's changed. She looks like she can hold her own with Betty now. Or is that the right thing to say?"

"Claudia can hold her own with anybody. But right now we'll drop the subject."

"Okay," said Montague. "What's this crap I hear about you running cotton mills?"

"It's not crap." Briefly Heath told him what had happened.

"And you like it?" Montague asked incredulously.

"I eat it up," Heath laughed. "I know, I'm as surprised as you. But that's the truth. I like it more than anything else in the world except flying and maybe sex."

"I can't understand that. You're a writer, an artist, not a manufacturer or a peddler."

"Don't kid yourself." Heath sipped his drink. "Those plays of mine, after the first, they were two-finger exercises, piddling substitutes for reality. This, by God, is reality itself. Like the war." His face flushed with his intensity. "Plays— Nobody will remember them after I'm dead. But Chandler Mills— Long after I'm gone the mills will still be there. When my son's an old man he'll be able to look at them and say, *By God, my grandfather and my father built all this!*"

Montague stared down at his shoes. "You're totally engaged in this?"

"Totally."

"That's too bad." He raised his head. "Heath, I've had nothing but turkeys since your last play. I need another script from you. Christ, I do. Not about the war—that's finished, played out. What's hot now is the labor movement, the proletariat. And this big cotton-mill strike in Gastonia a few years ago—that's a natural! The workers killed, the sheriff shot from ambush, the National Guard with bayonets. The whole power of a state brought to bear on the workers to crush 'em. There's a hell of a play there, Heath, and you're the only man can write it!"

Heath looked at him with a kind of sadness. He owed Phil Montague so much. "No, Phil. I can't write it."

"Why not?"

"First of all, no time. I'm going day and night, week in, week out, right now, trying to keep my company alive."

"You could find the time. Everybody needs a change of pace."

"Not me. Every day's a change of pace, new problems, new decisions. One day I'm buying, the next I'm selling, then I'm dealing with machinery or talking to bankers or . . . everything. I've never done anything like this before."

"Still—"

"Listen, I haven't forgot how much I owe you. If you need money, backing, I can scrape up a few dollars to invest—a couple of thousand now if that would help. But I can't write a play for you—and especially not a play about that Gastonia strike. That would be like cutting my own throat."

"I don't get you."

"Maybe you haven't read the papers. The unions are back in North Carolina, threatening to close down all the mills—"

"That's the point, the timeliness—"

"No. The point is, you want an outraged play about the treatment of the workers and the unions in Gastonia. The death of Ella Wiggins, the kangaroo courts, the beatings and . . . well, all that from the mill hand's viewpoint. And I can't do it. Maybe the workers got a raw deal in Gastonia, maybe the unions did too. Maybe the organizers they slapped in jail were really railroaded; I wouldn't doubt it a bit. But, God damn it, I'm a mill-owner myself now, and if I wrote a play like that, it would be issuing a standing invitation for the union to come in and organize my mills!"

"What's wrong with that?"

"Oh, for God's sake. All right, let me make it simple. I took over bankrupt mills and put them back in action again, and the only way I did it was because I had complete freedom to do anything I took a notion to. Right or wrong, nobody could tell me what to do. A business ain't like a play, it's not a collaboration, it's a one-man thing, and it's got to have a boss. One boss, at the top; not two, not a committee of them. Well, I'm the boss of Chandler Mills. But if the union came in, it would try to be boss along with me. And I won't have that. I can't survive that way. And neither can my people."

Montague looked puzzled. "That's funny. I remember—"

"You heard me talk, yes. About working in the mills under my father. But I didn't understand the facts of life then. Now, since I've sat in his chair, I do. I understand a lot of things I couldn't even comprehend before."

Heath paused. "There are a lot of bastards in our business, sure. We've got a nasty reputation for exploiting the poor, and we've earned it. But my father wasn't a bastard, he was a man doing the best he could the best he knew how, giving more of himself than any hand. If I wrote the kind of play you're talking about, I'd be repudiating him, and I won't do that, certainly not just to pick up a

quick buck. No, Phil. I've got more now than I can say
grace over. It's a bigger thing to run a company and run
it right than to write a play."

"Listen," Montague said. "I just came from Germany.
Only a year of Hitler and it's got me scared already.
This business of one man knowing what's best for
everybody—"

"I know what's best for Chandler Mills."

"Maybe." Montague looked at him keenly. "All the
same . . . you go away and then you come back. And
what do you see? Chaos, revolution—you can smell it in
the air. Something's wrong, the system's broken down.
And what's the answer, Communists? Fascists? Nazis?
Labor, or the industrialists? I don't know. But I know
this. We'd better find an answer and we'd better find it
quick, or things are going to fall apart." He looked small,
weary, despondent. "Maybe you're right, Heath. Maybe
the answer is a man, or a bunch of men, who know what's
best for everybody. But I keep thinking about Lord
Acton's aphorism. And the more I think about it, the
more frightened I get. Especially of men who confuse
themselves with God."

Heath laughed. "Which reminds me, I've got some
stone tablets to deliver. Hell, Phil, perk up and have
another drink. Who knows, it might change your whole
philosophy."

In the next half-hour he committed himself to lending
Montague six thousand dollars at no interest, and was
glad to do it, relieved to buy himself clear of obligation.
Still, watching Betty Hammond and Claudia from the
corner of his eye, he clung to the man as long as possible.

Each woman now was the center of a group of men,
well separated and he was relieved by that. "Betty," he
asked Montague. "Are you laying her?"

Phil laughed, a little drunk now and giddy with the
relief of Heath's promise, which had lifted obviously
crushing pressure from him. "Me? Thanks for the
compliment."

"Maybe it's not one. She's like another girl I used to

know. Somebody said she'd had everything but the ax handle stuck in her."

"Send her one. She would hate to miss anything."

"I understand she goes for girls now."

Montague laughed again. "For anything that walks or crawls and can climb up on a bed. But she still likes money, success. There's not enough of that tainting me right now to attract her. You're not—" Montague looked at him quizzically.

"Hell, no."

"Then, good. She's poison. Nobody with a woman like Claudia should need a broad like her."

"I don't."

"That's a sign you're growing up." He shuffled uneasily. "Hey, there's Laird Thornton over there. I've heard some talk he might angel a production—"

"Go ahead. This is a business party anyhow."

When Montague left, Heath moved instinctively toward Claudia, but Betty Hammond, magically detached from all those men, blocked his way. "Heath."

He looked down at her. Some women, he thought, remembering Evelyn Ford, were nothing but flesh, desire —not people, succubi. Even with what the years had done to her, he could not be insensible to her presence; too much raw sexuality emanated from her for that. He raked his eyes over bare flesh that seemed to have a quality the flesh of ordinary women lacked, and, quite helplessly, was aware of a stirring in his loins, a dryness in his mouth—and fear.

"Would you give me a minute? I have some things to explain to you. There was so much I wanted to say to you, do for you, after that accident, and I never got the chance."

"Yeah, I know. You left for the Coast."

"Things broke for me. I had to make a choice."

"You made the right one."

Her eyes shadowed. Her lips always seemed slightly parted, soliciting. Suddenly he thought of a toilet seat, a public facility, open, indiscriminate. And her attraction no longer reached him, he felt immune and somewhat revolted, even as she said, "I'm not so sure of that."

"I am, though." Brusquely he turned away. "Excuse me, I need to talk to Claudia." And he moved on, leaving her standing there.

Shouldering through the group encircling Claudia, he put his arm around her. "You predators," he said. "Take off."

"Now, wait a minute, Chandler," someone protested.

"I want to speak to her alone. Go have some gin."

They withdrew. Claudia looked at him questioningly.

"I love you," he said, and kissed her on the lips. "That's all."

"Well, how nice." She looked toward Betty, and was not puzzled.

"I've got a tip on a big order with Hauptman, and you've probably done all right too. Let's cut this thing short if we can, or at least not let it run overtime."

"Seven." She moved against him, understanding. "Everybody clears out by seven, even if I have to use force."

"Good," he said.

Claudia looked again at Betty Hammond. "Even her."

Heath's arm tightened about her. "Especially her," he said.

5   THE SEPTEMBER HEAT was humid, sullen. Bad enough in the offices, it was almost unbearable in the plant. There was not yet enough money in the company treasury even to consider investing in the still-unperfected air-conditioning systems, which would have required complete remodeling of the ancient buildings. So in all areas of the factory, behind blue windows cracked only faintly to admit some breeze without fading the fibers, the mill hands pitted flesh against steel. The flesh felt the heat and suffered; the steel, impervious to it, ran remorselessly. It was up to flesh to keep pace.

In his office, cooled by an electric fan's blast, Heath Chandler stared sourly at the pile of forms on his desk, each with a note of inquiry from a department head. The damned government, he thought. It was worse even than the unions.

He had fought a running battle with it since the passage of the National Recovery Act, the "Blue Eagle"—or the Violet Vulture, as he sardonically referred to it. He had refused to join the Textile Manufacturers Association and accept its quota system; had sold what he could where and when he could, and had made a lot of enemies doing so. Now the United States was trying to force him to do what his competitors could not: cut back production. The act's textile provisions had been written by associations of the manufacturers themselves, and they had tailored it to suit them and been given responsibility for policing it. In effect, it was aimed at bringing people like Heath Chandler into line, and now, since what had been an informal agreement had become law, he was facing head-on conflict with Washington.

Clutterbuck, sitting across the desk from him, said: "Well, do we give them the information they demand or don't we?"

"We tell 'em to jam it up their ass," Heath growled. "Why should I spill all my secrets, all my production data, into the public record so that every two-bit competitor can use them? Why should I cut back on the hours my machines can run when I've got work to keep 'em busy? And why the hell should I pay people good money to fill out this crap?" He thrust the papers back at Clutterbuck. "Perforate 'em and put 'em in the warehouse for all I care."

Hesitantly Clutterbuck took them. "You're risking trouble."

"I'm not risking anything. That stuff's not constitutional on the face of it, and the Supreme Court's bound to rule against it. All we've got to do is stall until the whole mess is moot."

"I hope you're right. Otherwise we're in hot water up to our nostrils."

"I'm right." Heath looked out the window toward the west. "Besides, we've got other things to worry about."

The room was silent for a moment. Then Olin said, "You think they'll come?"

"Yes," Heath said. "They'll come, all right. Sooner or later." He meant the flying squadron. By now the union effort to bring about a general strike had reached its apogee. All during that molten summer the high, red-clay plateau had seethed with picket lines; and convoys of shouting men—no longer docile laborers, but revolutionists now, as their forefathers had been at Kings Mountain, Manassas, and in a hundred other battles—rushed up and down the paved arc of Highway 29, through the heart of textile country, flinging themselves in fury against the mills. Although they had still not hit any Chandler plant, they were established now at Butler's Plant Number One in Brackettville, twenty-five miles away. Closed for nearly two months, its hands locked out without warning, it had been easy pickings for the organizers. And, wageless, starving, the desperate men would not be satisfied for long with carrying signs and marching up and down; sooner or later they would strike out at another target, and the nearest one was Chandlerville. The union was still determined to close every southern mill, hoping that when no spindle turned or shuttle moved in the whole land, the owners would be forced to bargain. That meant violence, of course, but violence was a welcome outlet to men with hunger-pinched and crying children, men with no other chance, and born and bred in violence anyhow. "They won't pass us up," Heath went on. "They know if they close us, they can close anybody. When that time comes I want everything ready."

"Everything is ready."

"Let's keep it that way—everything we discussed, on a moment's notice."

Clutterbuck nodded and arose. Heath followed him with his eyes as he went out.

His judgment had been right. Without Olin he could not have accomplished anything. It had not been just friendship or sympathy for a discouraged, penniless man that had moved him to ask Clutterbuck to stay. The qualities that had marked the man as a combat pilot—courage, imagination, utter reliability—these were what he had had to have to back him up. Olin now was indispensable, sharing responsibility both in New York and Chandlerville, a second-in-command, with full authority to act in Heath's stead.

He knew, too, that Clutterbuck had not stayed with him entirely out of friendship or financial self-interest. Claudia—poor Olin was in love with her, and it was she more than anything else that held him here.

And that was all right too. He knew both of them too well to feel the least suspicion, much less jealousy. In fact, this was a welcome added insurance. If anything happened to him, Olin would take care of Claudia—and the mills. If the king died—and the king knew himself well enough to know that he was not through with risk and jeopardy yet—a regent was at hand.

It was Fox's pleasure and custom to pick up the children at the Chandlerville school every afternoon, deliver Ramsey to Chandler House, and bring Heath's son to the mill. There Hamp gloried in acting as his father's "office boy." Swollen with importance, he scurried here and there on minor errands, hovered in the background as Heath made decisions, and went with his father on the necessary daily rounds when, as chieftain of the clan, Heath visited as many departments of the mill as he had time for, stopping to chat with workers, sealing their fealty with personal contact.

Hamp was growing swiftly, and even at the age of eleven he was, Heath thought, an impressive person. Melded in him were Bolivar's cool, objective mind and Heath's imagination, daring, the Charleston wit and grace. Still, of course, completely a child, even babyish at times, especially when sick or tired, a man of great power and intelligence was, Heath thought, foreshadowed in him, and there were times when, looking at him the father felt, mingled with an almost uncontainable pride, a strange, cold dread. Handsome, well-coordinated, Hamp seemed to embody almost too much perfection; and in a world where mediocrity was the rule, perfection was a challenge to the fates. In France it had been the brilliant and aggressive who put themselves in jeopardy again and again and consequently died, while the dull and timid held back cautiously and lived; and while he loved his son, he feared for him.

He loved both his children, of course, but what he felt for Hamp was different from his love for Ramsey. A man invested so much of himself in his son, and with every year that investment increased, the commitment grew. Each year of growth demanded more of the father's hard-accumulated store of knowledge, patience, strength; a son was the dearest thing a man could purchase in the most painfully earned coin. And now Heath could understand the hell that Bolivar must have endured while he had swooped and fought and lived from one second to another over France. The very thought of Hamp's having to do such a thing chilled him, and, putting himself in Bolivar's place, with his son far away—waiting, dreading, hoping, praying—he was by no means sure that he would have the Old Man's strength. Bolivar, after all, had leaned on God; Heath lacked that prop. Sometimes he wished he had it; he could see the value of it now.

This afternoon in early September the day was nearly over, and Hamp was flagging—shirttail out, socks fallen around his ankles, wheat-colored hair mussed, and the brassy smell of boy-sweat pungent on him. As they returned to the office after a circuit through the spinning room Heath felt the need to touch the boy and hold him. He put his arm around Hamp's shoulder, and when he dropped into his chair, pulled the boy to him, hoisted him on his lap. Hamp leaned back tiredly, contentedly, against the hard torso while Heath nuzzled the damp neck, ran his face through the silken hair. Then he thought of something that would give Hamp pleasure. "Hey, I just remembered, there's a circus in Charlotte next weekend. Sells-Floto, with Tom Mix in the Wild West Show. You and Ramsey want to go?"

The boy's weariness vanished at once. "Tom Mix? And *Tony?*"

"You know ole Tom wouldn't come without his horse. Matter of fact, I can probably arrange for you to meet him when the show's over. Maybe he'd even let you sit on Tony."

Hamp stared. "*You know Tom Mix?*"

"Met him a couple of times. He might not remember me, but we'll find out. Maybe, if he'll be there overnight, he might have supper with us. I'll—" The phone rang. "Reach that for me, will you?"

"Yes, sir!" Hamp squirmed, took the receiver from its cradle, passed it over. He leaned back against his father while Heath spoke into the phone. "Chandler here."

"Cap'n Chandler? This is Josh Temple, dep'ty shurf in Brackettville. I thought you better know. The flyin squadron jest took off from here, a mighty lot of people in cars and trucks. They're bound for Chandlerville, aimin to shut down your plant."

Heath pushed Hamp off his lap. "When did they leave?"

"Not five minutes past. I was out of town deliverin a writ, and they formed up in secret. Was jest pullin out when I got in, so I called you right away."

"All right," Heath said. "Thanks." He slammed down the receiver. "Hamp, go get your Uncle Olin. Tell him I want to see him right away."

The boy looked at him curiously, catching the harshness in his voice. "Yes, sir, but—"

"Move!" Heath roared. Hamp ran out. Heath waited until he was gone, picked up the phone again. "Get me Chandler House."

Claudia herself answered. "Hello?"

"Listen, the flying squadron's coming."

"Oh," she breathed.

"No need to get worked up. But it just left Brackett-ville. Where's Ramsey?"

"Out on her pony."

"Find her, get her in. We've got an hour, more or less. Do you know where Fox is?"

"Drinking coffee with me here." Her voice was cool, steady now.

"I'll send Hamp home right away. Put Fox on."

Then Fox was there. "So they finally got up nerve enough, huh?"

"Looks like it; a big crew from Butler's plant. Listen, I'm sending ten men up to Chandler House, Hamp along with 'em. They'll all be armed, and you're in charge. Put 'em upstairs, where they've got good fields of fire. Claudia'll give you the key to my gun rack, take any weapon you want, there's plenty of ammo. I figure we've got an hour, maybe more if I can slow 'em down. They'll make the plant their main target, but they'll send people up there, too, to raise hell. I don't care how much they whoop and holler, how many windows they break with rocks; long as it's no worse than that, nobody's to fire a shot; I'll skin the man alive who does. But if they try to get in a door or use guns of their own, then you do whatever's necessary and don't worry about it—I'll back you up."

"Nobody's comin in this house," Fox said. "Don't let that worry you."

"Right. I probably won't be home tonight. It'll be late before the troops get here." He hung up.

Olin came in, Hamp jittering beside him. "Flying squadron?"

"Yeah, on their way." He told Clutterbuck what the deputy had said. "Let's get moving. I want ten men with guns at Chandler House right away. Send Hamp with 'em."

"No!" the boy exploded. "I wanta stay!"

"You will in a pig's eye. You've got a job of your own. I want you to look after Ramsey. Your granddaddy's in charge at Chandler House, and the two of you do exactly what he tells you or I'll have your hide. Understand?"

"Yes, sir. Do I get to use my twenty-two?"

"You do not." Heath hugged him briefly, then slapped his rump. "On your way." Thank God, he thought, for Fox. He would die before he let danger come to Hamp or Ramsey.

The boy ran out. Heath turned to Olin. "Send all the women home to stay until further notice. Tell the men to go home, get their guns, and come back here. And get those trucks out and rolling."

"Right. The police are to guard the power plant. And what about the machinery—shut it down?"

"Hell, no. Bring in men from the other shift to replace the women. I want every machine in this mill running when they come, and I want 'em to keep on running."

"Sure," Olin said, but he was not immune to excitement either, and his eyes glinted. As he went out Heath reached for the phone again.

By political arrangement the governorship of North Carolina was held alternately by representatives of east and west, the tobacco and textile interests controlling the office in turn. The man Heath now talked to was a member of what was called the Macedon Ring, backed by the mills. With that sponsorship and half his own fortune tied up in mill stock, he had, so far, moved quickly and determinedly against the strikers. When Heath said tersely, "The flying squadron's on the way to Chandlerville. I want troops," the governor answered without question or debate, "How many?"

"Two companies. And I need 'em damned fast. They're bound here from Brackettville, and that ain't far. I've sent out trucks to dump bales of cotton on all the bridges block 'em, but that won't slow 'em long. They'll still be here by nightfall."

"Well, we're in a pinch, most of the soldiers are already out at other mills; these'll have to come from over east Can you hold out for two hours, maybe three?"

"I can hold out for as long as I have to. I've held mass meeting in every plant this summer, told my folk this was coming. I gave 'em a choice: if they wanted th union, they could have it, and I'd shut down my mills an sell 'em off and go back to Europe. But if they wanted t keep on working, I'd bust a gut to see they had th chance. They were with me a hundred percent, and I'v sent 'em all home to arm themselves now. I won't let an of 'em shoot unless this bunch actually tries to force entry to the mills or to my house, but if they do, I aim to hurt 'em."

"You'll be fully protected long as you're defending your property against the mob."

"Right. But I'd still rather the troops did it. Get 'em in here fast, and— Bob. Send a couple of machine guns."

On the other end of the line the governor sucked in his breath. "You think it'll be that bad?"

"No. But I want 'em here for effect. I don't want anybody in that flying squadron to be under the least misapprehension about what'll happen if they get violent. The sight of a couple of machine guns may save some lives."

"All right, you'll have those too. Heath, remember, the whole state's on your side. Don't let these Reds take over, no matter what you have to do! By heaven, I'm not going to let the Communists—"

"Spare me the campaign oratory and just get the fucking troops moving, will you? Thanks. Keep me posted." Heath hung up. Then Olin was back. "The trucks are out?"

"Gone. The women and children cleared, the men gone for their weapons. The fire trucks are being brought into the yard to stand by. Hamp's been sent home with the detail. Anything else?"

"Nothing but to wait. Bob says he'll have troops here sometime tonight. Meanwhile we're on our own."

He arose, went to the window, looked out. People were streaming from the mill, chattering with excitement. Heath sighed. "Well, now we reap what others have sown." The anger he felt trembled in his voice. "All the lousy, greedy, penny-wise and pound-foolish bastards like St. John Butler. The ones who don't give a damn for anything but a dollar, the ones who treat their people like animals, like shit." His voice rose. "I don't blame those hands in the flying squadron; hell, if I was in their place I'd be doing the same thing. But I sure as hell hate the sons of bitches who've brought us to this pass and tarred me with their pitch."

"Don't worry." Olin's voice was wry. "They hate you too."

"Good. I can take satisfaction in that at least. I'd be damned ashamed of myself if any of 'em liked me." He paused. "This country's on the edge of revolution, and all because there are so many bastards who want everything they can lay their hands on and begrudge an honest nickel to anybody else. Sometimes, just to spite them, I think I'd like to let the union in. Embrace it with open arms. But, of course, I can't. Not if I'm gonna keep my promise. But . . . hell"—and his voice was full of disgust. Then the phone rang. He moved to his desk in a single stride and scooped it up.

His secretary said, "Captain Heath. A man named Jess Hook is out here from Macedonia and says he's got to see you right away."

Heath frowned. "Jess Hook?" Then he remembered. "All right, send him in." He hung up and turned to Olin. "Well, now my bucket of snakes runneth over.. We're about to have a visit from the Exalted Cyclops of the Macedonia Ku Klux Klan."

6 OF MEDIUM HEIGHT, with the heavy chest and muscled shoulders of a workingman, Jess Hook had a square redburned face and eyes like small brown marbles. In his mid-thirties, he wore white shirt and khaki pants, and the hand he put out for Heath to shake was hard and rough as a block of cedar. "Cap'n Chandler. I heerd from my people in Brackettville that the flyin squadron was on its way here, so I drove over from Macedonia fast as I could." He took the chair Heath indicated. "I've come to offer the services of the Ku Klux Klan. You say the word, I can have a hundred men with guns here inside an hour to protect your mill from those Communists. And we'll find those Yankee organizers and teach 'em a lesson they won't forgit very durn soon."

Heath's smile was faint and cold. "That's mighty generous of you, Mr. Hook. Thanks—but no thanks."

The hard brown eyes pressed at him. "Whut do you mean by that?"

"I've got plenty of men and plenty of guns of my own. We can handle our own problems."

Hook bit his lower lip. "Listen, Cap'n Chandler—"

"No, you listen; my time's limited. When I came back to Chandlerville one of the first things I did was to break up the den, or klavern, or whatever you call it, of the Klan I found set up here. I disbanded it and laid down the rule that any Chandler employee who belonged to the Klan was automatically fired."

"You think I don't remember that? That's one of the reasons I come; I want to prove to you that you need the Klan."

Heath's mouth twisted. "I need the Klan like I need a third ball. I don't like the way the Ku Klux Klan operates, Mr. Hook. When a man joins it he's got to swear that his first loyalty's to the Klan. Anybody that works for me, after his church and his family, his first loyalty had better be to Chandler Mills. Be that as it may, there's not gonna be any organization in any of my towns that I don't ramrod myself. That's why I chased the Klan out, and that's why I don't want it back, and that's why I'm telling you now I appreciate your concern, but don't you bring any of your Ku Kluxers into Chandlerville or any other of my towns, flying squadron or no." He got abruptly to his feet. "Thanks for coming over, Mr. Hook."

Hook got up slowly. His eyes met Heath's. "We'll be on hand anyhow, Cap'n Chandler. You might need us worse than you think."

"Mr. Hook." Heath's voice was cold, thin. "Let's get one thing straight right now. I own Chandlerville, lock, stock, barrel; you can't even stand on the main street of the town without trespassing on my property. You bring your people in here and I'll have 'em dealt with the same way I'll deal with the strikers—and worse if they're armed. Nobody is going to tote guns and take on the responsibility of using them to protect Chandler Mills except my own

people and the State Militia. Anybody who brings a weapon into Chandlerville, striker or Klansman either, is
gonna find himself put in the jailhouse, and he'll be a
long time getting out. That goes for you too. If I see you
back in Chandlerville while this trouble's on, you'll be arrested so fast it'll make your head swim."

Hook's eyes glittered. "You're talkin pretty big, Cap'n
Chandler. You better be careful you don't say somethin
you'll regret."

"I've said everything I aim to say, Mr. Hook. Now, I've
got one hell of a lot of things to do. Good day." He turned
away.

Hook stood there a moment longer, face brick red. He
let out a long breath. "So be it, then. We'll remember this,
Cap'n Chandler."

"Good. So will I. Yonder's the door." After another second Hook went out.

They gave him time to get beyond earshot. Then Olin
Clutterbuck, who had sat wordless, said, "You were rough
with him."

"I meant to be. Goddammit, everybody wants to tell me
how to run my own affairs. That son of a bitch, he thought
he could ingratiate himself with me and I'd let him reopen
in my towns. Well, the last thing I need is a bunch of
strikebreakers in bedsheets." He went to the window.
Across the yard men were filing back into the plant with
guns. He turned to Olin. "As soon as everybody's here, be
ready to barricade those gates."

Then the waiting. That was the hard part as the afternoon stretched on, sunlight slanting. Heath passed part
of the time in the plant with his men.

This was a land in which every white man owned a gun,
and he had long since provided each of them with ammu-
nition. They circled around him, the mill hands, as he reinforced his orders: no shot to be fired without the express
permission of himself or Olin Clutterbuck. They looked
disappointed; their lives were woven of such dreadful
boredom that the prospect of a fight exhilarated them.
They all had this in common: the belief that, in the end, a

man's honor and salvation depended on himself alone, not on courts, laws, society or organizations. And, by comparison, they were "haves"; they had jobs, they could feed their families. The men who were coming aimed to take that away from them; and they would not let that happen. They felt no bond, no solidarity, between themselves and the jobless of Brackettville; if a man needed work, let him go and find it for himself. They were glad to have excitement and they were glad to have an enemy.

Though this was to Heath's benefit, he felt a kind of sad disgust as he returned to his office. It seemed to take no more than that to manipulate people in the mass: give them an enemy, especially one threatening their pocketbooks and property. That was something Hitler understood, and Mussolini, and the labor organizers, and even Jess Hook, the Klansman. Huey Long understood it too, and probably Franklin Roosevelt. How, Heath wondered, could anyone lead people and not become a total cynic?

Well, he had his own responsibilities, and they spread wider and were more complex than anyone but himself could know. He looked at Bolivar on the wall, hand thrust forward, eyes challenging.

He would use anybody, do whatever it took, stand any cost, to pay his debt to the figure in the picture.

They came an hour later in a blare of honking horns, a howl of raucous voices, pouring out of the high westward hills in a long stream of Fords and Chevvies and Plymouths and rickety stakebodied trucks, every vehicle crammed with people. The blocked bridges had delayed them for a while, but the tons of baled cotton were nothing against determination and collective muscle experienced at handling cotton bales; and they flooded into Chandlerville an hour before sunset, long before any sign of soldiers. And when Heath saw them, whatever lingering doubts he had about opposing them evanesced like smoke.

Outside the plant the street filled quickly with cars, each disgorging its load of men and women already bellowing senseless noise, two hundred at least and maybe more, in khaki, denim, calico and rayon. Mostly they were young; Heath saw a lot of pretty girls among them. One big truck full of shouting strikers rolled on past, and Heath knew it was bound for Chandler House.

Then before the main gate, the mob coalesced and picket signs arose and waved: THE STRIKE IS ON! . . . THE UNION NEEDS YOU! . . . TO HELL WITH BOSSES . . . FEED OUR CHILDREN! And beneath them a sea of contorted faces, angry eyes, twisted mouths —and Heath was startled at the wave of hatred roiling from that gobbling, yowling throng. This was his first real confrontation with an angry mob, and the reality of it dwarfed what he had imagined; it was as if he'd awaited a swarm of alley cats and faced instead a gigantic, deadly tiger. He'd thought of a mob as a crowd of humans, with grievances, and reason to discuss them; there was nothing human about this surging, furious beast, bent not on re- dress, but on destruction, vengeance. It could not be dealt with; could only be fought. The organizers, he thought —he had them spotted now, a half-dozen of them hurrying through the crowd, yelling orders, forming ranks—knew their business: they had made sure the mob knew its enemy.

He whirled toward the phone, snatched it up. "Get me Chandler House. Hurry!"

The second or two he had to wait seemed interminable. Then Fox snapped: "Hello?"

"They're on their way."

"Hell, I can see 'em comin!" Fox hung up. At the same instant there was a crash of breaking glass. Rocks hurtled through the office windows. Olin Clutterbuck grabbed Heath, jerked him sideways as a hail of stones bounced off his desk. More flew, aimed higher; the windows of the plant smashed and tinkled, blue shards raining down. *"The strike is here, the strike is here, come out and join, come out and join!"* The yelling of the mob rose and fell in waves.

"The sons of bitches!" Heath snarled, furious.

"Don't be a scab, come out and join! One for all and all for one!" A surge of bodies slammed against the main

gate; the whole fence line rippled, shook but heavy woven wire and cotton-bale barricades held. The rocks still flew, arching high above the lawn. *"End the stretch-out! Stand up like men! To hell with bosses!"* And with those slogans, curses, obscenities, jeers and hoots. They crashed the fence again. The three-inch pipe posts set deep in concrete, braced and diaphragmed with heavy woven wire, topped with outward-tilting strands of barbs, shook but held. But the hatred roiled through the mesh and toward the mill like the hot, rank, tainted breath of a huge carnivorous animal. It seemed to fill the office with its muggy foulness; and there was something dirty, polluted, about it. Heath felt a kind of sickness. What in God's name, he thought, had happened to this country, to his South and to his America that all across it wounds had been inflicted and allowed to fester until this noxious pus burst out of all those economic abscesses? Whose guilt, for Christ's sake, and how could passions such as these ever be stilled, such wounds healed? Suddenly he felt a sense of doom; it had not worked, America had not worked, and if it would not, what could? All at once he almost wished he had not called the troops. They would only deepen the wounds, infect them further, and he would then bear a kind of guilt himself, of which, until now, he had felt smugly free. But they were on their way, and when they came he would use them. "God, this is a rotten business," he growled at Clutterbuck. "Get out there in the plant, make sure nobody shoots. I wish to hell those bastards yonder would calm down so I could go talk to 'em!"

Olin stared at him with startled eyes. "Don't be a fool!" he rasped. "You hear me? Don't be a fool!" Then he hurried out. At that instant a furious animal roar went up outside. Hands pointed, eyes turned upward, gaunt faces gawked. Heath could not see what had caused that outburst, but he could guess—gun barrels poking through the broken windows.

And now there were no more chanted slogans. The sight of weapons sent the flying squadron into an insanity of outrage and hatred. The air clanged with obscenities and ugly screaming; like shapeless birds, a new barrage of hurtling rocks filled the sky. Again the crowd threw itself against the fence; the whole line shuddered, but it still stood. Then the organizers, howling to make their orders heard, indistinguishable from any striker save for their recognizable authority, struggled in the mob to force it back. The guns had frightened them. They knew they would be used if it came to that, mass slaughter might occur. They needed time to appraise that possibility, decide whether, if it happened, it would be useful or detrimental. One martyr, Heath thought cynically, might be acceptable, very useful—maybe even two. But they had to weigh the risk of getting them.

And so, gradually, they fought the crowd back across the road and quieted it a little; but they could not quiet the women and the girls. These surged to the forefront, gesturing and screaming defiantly, insultingly, at the catcalling men in the windows of the mill above them. Olin reappeared, looking shaken. "Jesus, that was close! If they hadn't pulled back, somebody would have shot into 'em, sure as fate! What are they up to now?"

"I don't know. This might be the first mill they ever hit that was defended by its own hands. Having a council of war, I reckon—whether to go all out and risk some killing or fall back on a waiting game." Outside, floodlights came to life on the mill roof, dissolving the dusk in yellow glare. Suddenly he made a decision. "Those guns took some of the starch out of their brass hats. I think now's the time to go out and talk to 'em."

Olin stared. "For God's sake, you idiot! They'd stone you to death!"

"Maybe a few minutes ago. Not now, I don't think."

"All the same, it's stupid! You've got nothing to negotiate about! The Guard will be here soon and—"

"I know. But I think I'll try it. Maybe it'll save some trouble in the long run."

Olin's mouth thinned as he looked at Heath. "You don't think that at all," he snapped. "It's just that you can't stand it, can you? The risk's there for the taking, so of course you've got to take it—"

Heath laughed softly. "Maybe that's part of it too. But

there are other reasons. Anyhow, I'm gonna try it." And before Clutterbuck could stop him he left his office.

All the women had been sent home from the outer offices, and the men looked at him with wondering eyes as he walked through to the front door. "All right, boys," he told the armed guards there. "Let me out."

"Cap'n Heath—" one protested, flabbergasted.

"I said, let me out." He pushed between them, unlocked the door with his own key. "Leave this open. I may have to come back in a hurry." He passed through, and then he was in the yard, bathed in floodlight glare.

He halted just outside the door, stood motionless for a full minute, giving them a chance to see him, identify him, and wonder; giving himself time as well to assess their reaction and retreat immediately if necessary. Behind him the guards muttered, and Heath grinned faintly. The legend was building already. Olin did not understand, even after all these years, how important legends, heroes, were to southerners. Even if he won this battle, sooner or later the union would come back, maybe next time with stronger cards. A gesture of this kind right now would inflame the imaginations of his hands, buy their loyalty in a way that money never could. After all, no general had ever kept his troops' esteem by hiding. When you walked the firing line and shared their risks, they loved you—and you awed the enemy. Anyhow, reason aside, it was something he had to do. He could not bear to let the union men out there brag that their courage was greater than his, let them use the smear of cowardice against him.

And now they saw him. A murmur rippled through the crowd, and a surge of movement that quickly checked itself, from curiosity, not discipline. Heath stood motionless a few seconds longer, and there were a few scattered yells, shouted curses, but these trailed off. The organizers called and motioned the crowd to silence. Heath judged it would hold; he might have to dodge a rock or two. Curiously calm, dispassionate, he began to walk down the concrete path from the front door to the main gate.

Three men in work clothes detached themselves from the mob and came to meet him. A single stone sailed over the fence, fell just short. One of the men whirled, barked something, and no more rocks came.

Heath walked around the barricade of cotton bales at the gate, went to the fence. The three organizers met him there.

"I'm Heath Chandler," he said. "I guess you people wanted to see me." He made his voice loud enough to carry, though his tone was wryly understated. The mob across the road laughed, bitterly, but with admiration.

"I guess we did, Mr. Chandler." The leader of the three was a man of thirty, in a dirty white shirt and rumpled pants. He was of medium height, gaunt, with tired, sad eyes in a wary face. His voice had a northern tang. "I'm Howard Freeman, Textile Workers Union, AFL." He ran hand through lank, dark hair.

"I can't say I'm overjoyed to meet you. Now, tell me— are all these people here just from a desire to raise general hell, or have you got some specific demands?"

Freeman blinked. "You know our demands. Either let your people join the union or we'll shut your mill."

"My people don't want to join the union."

"That's what you say."

"That's what those guns up yonder say. Look, Mr. Freeman, Chandler Mills takes care of its own. When it needs help from the union, we'll let you know. That's not just me talking, it's every hand that works for me. Now, I won't argue with you that there are a lot of places where you might do some good, maybe are even wanted, needed. But not here. So I'm asking you to disperse this crowd, let my people go about their business."

Freeman shook his head. "Either this mill is organized or it don't run; that's final. Chandler, you got the reputation of being kind of reasonable, anyhow. We don't want to have to use force . . ."

"Is that a threat?" Heath's voice was knife-edged.

"I'm saying that this time the general strike's gonna succeed!" Freeman's voice rose, tinged with the hysteria of desperation and fatigue. "Nothing's gonna stand in the way of that, not you, not nobody! We've tried for fifteen years to organize this industry, and this time we'll do it. And we'll blast you or anybody else gets in our way!"

"Blast?" Heath looked into tired, muddy, floodlit eyes. "What do you mean, blast?"

"I mean, you can't stand against us! Nobody can this time." Freeman shook his head wildly, crazily. Heath thought he smelled, emanating from the man, something of the suppuration of insane hatred that the mob had given off. Suddenly he realized that Freeman was hopeless: this man had run headfirst into too many stone walls, tried too hard too long against odds too great, and he was no longer balanced, reasoning. He had been that way himself in France when the fatigue of too much fighting had warped reason, judgment, almost driven him mad, knew what it felt like, felt a strange, sudden kinship with the man. For the first time he knew fear. He knew what a man in the grip of that emotion was like, the mad nihilism that sought not goals but its own destruction in destruction. It was like talking to a mirror image of himself in his younger, wilder days. Freeman, under constant strain, had written himself off, and no one was more dangerous than a man who thought of himself as already dead.

For a moment he felt a strange, pitying, paternal sympathy, wished he could put a hand through the fence, touch the young man and calm him. But he could not, of course. Nothing now would ever calm Howard Freeman, not even success. All he sought was to immolate himself for a cause, and no force could turn him from his eventual aim of glorious self-destruction.

At the same instant, in that realization, Heath felt a justification of his own. Freeman might be a stronger, deadlier enemy than he had counted on, but it would be wrong to deliver his people into the keeping of a madman, a zealot.

The organizer's fingers slid through the woven wire, curled around its shining strands like sallow worms, the forefinger of the right hand stained with nicotine. Guts and cigarettes, Heath thought, the fighter's diet.

"Freeman," he said quietly, "look, I'll make you a deal." A compassion for the man that he could not shake was in his voice. "Listen to me: I've sent for troops, the State Guard is coming. You don't have a chance against them. I've sent for machine guns, and I'll use them if I have to. But if you'll take these people back where they belong, to Brackettville, and then come and see me, I'll talk to you and try to explain the situation here. Believe me, it's different from what you've run up against before. We can't talk out here like this. Take your people back, then come to my office. I'll guarantee your safety."

Freeman only looked at him, eyes shining in the floodlight's glare. Then he said, coldly, distinctly, with an awful hatred distilled in his voice, "If you won't talk to me now, you never will. Fuck you, Captain Chandler."

Heath stiffened, and in that moment felt his first real fear for Claudia, Hamp, Ramsey, even for Fox and the men on guard. Words bounced off this fanatic like stones off the hard brick wall of the mills; Freeman was past reason, caught up in violence. "Fuck you," he said again, "you God damned *boss*," and he put in that last word a lifetime of loathing, hatred, oppression endured. Things for a moment shifted; Heath had the eerie impression that he himself stood across the wire, facing Bolivar on this side. Then the world snapped back into focus.

This man frightened him even as he saddened him, and fear purged him instantly of compassion. "Suit yourself," he said thinly. "All right. I had the guts to come out here and talk to you. You got the guts to let me go back inside without getting crowned by a rock?"

"You go," Freeman whispered. "You go on back, you'll be all right. But you can't beat us. You hear? We're too many for you. Hundreds, thousands— You go back. Don't worry. You'll be all right—until we really come and get you." He stared at Heath a moment more, eyes huge in the direct glare of floodlights. Then he said tiredly, "Come on fellows; I've had enough of this," and turned away.

Heath stood there a few seconds longer, then also turned around. He felt exposed, vulnerable, his back to the crowd as he walked toward the plant. It took all his will power not to shield his head and run. Then he stiffened. Far away, in the distance, he heard the shrill vibration of approaching sirens. Only an intimation at first, nearing, it became distinct and comprehensible. Suddenly he began to run, knowing that the strikers would interpret it too. He made it inside the door of the mill just ahead of a fresh barrage of rocks.

The army trucks rolled into town in a tight-packed convoy. Even before they fully halted, soldiers spilled over their sides, floodlights shining on dishpan helmets and the long, sharp blades of fixed bayonets. A kind of squall went up from the mob outside the gates. Then, from the command car in the lead, a man bearing major's oakleaves on his collar leaped out, flanked on either side by lieutenants with drawn automatics.

The crowd surged across the street to meet the soldiers. The young, frightened Guardsmen formed ranks to meet it, rifles out, thrusting with their bayonets. The major strutted forward, his pistol-pointing guards brushing shoulders with him. "Give way there!" he roared. Short, stocky, with a black mustache and pot belly, he rested one hand on the flap of his pistol holster. "Give way, I warn you! By order of the Governor of the State of North Carolina, I command you to disperse!"

Through the shattered office windows Heath and Olin saw the women again surge to the front of the mob. Young girls, mostly; and they came with breasts outthrust, protuberant, faces contorted with mockery and hatred. As if, Heath thought, their breasts were armor, shields; they did not know the state. Not even the breasts of women could stand against the God of Property; the situation now beyond his control, he almost turned away, still feeling afraid and dirty, and, psychologically now, more with the strikers than the Guard.

But he had to watch. With savagery and withering contempt, the girls threw their breasts at the bayonets, dared the young soldiers to pierce those objects of desire and nourishment. Screaming like banshees, they waved clenched fists and shouted taunts that only women would have dared, against the masculinity of the young soldiers. The major's face was passionless; he snapped orders; the lieutenants relayed them in bellowing shouts; the phalanx of bayonets arose, bristling, and the abatis of teats drew back before their points touched them, soft flesh yielding, as always, to sharpened steel. Then Freeman shouted something, and the crowd began to flow in a different direction. A few rocks sailed out, one bounced off a helmet; then the strikers had retreated and were huddling in the parking lot. The soldiers occupied the space before the fence, shaking with surprise and emotion. This was something they had never counted on: being hated for wearing this uniform—by pretty girls. They could not understand it. The major rattled the gate; Heath, with a detail of armed men, went to open it. It took some time before the bales of cotton were shoved aside so the officer could enter.

"Captain Chandler? Coy Lawrence." The major's mouth flickered in a nervous smile beneath his mustache. Money and power could awe him in a way the crowd had not; he was proud, too, of his own potency in rescuing what Chandler represented. His palm was soft, moist, as Heath shook it.

"Damned glad to see you, Major. Just in time, like in the movies."

"Got here as quick as we could. The machine guns are in the truck."

"Good. I want them removed from the truck with the maximum amount of display. Be sure everybody sees them. Then put them on the mill roof."

The major squinted. "Yes, a good field of fire."

"Right. But, Major." Heath looked the man straight in the eye. "If one of those guns fires without my personal order, I'll have your ass. Every last scrap of it."

The major blinked. "Now, Captain Chandler—"

"You heard me."

Lawrence bit his lip. "Very well. My orders are to follow your orders. But . . . you'll be here all through the night?"

All through the night. Sleep my love and peace attend thee . . . "I'll be here," Heath said.

"Very well." The major turned away, brisk with competence and self-importance.

The machine guns then were taken from the truck. At the sight of them a hoarse, eerie cry arose from the crowd. The mob trembled, shuddered, then was motionless as the guns were brought in through the gate; and its silence was more ominous than its outburst. At first they could not believe it. Those weapons, designed for use against a foreign enemy, were here to be turned on them—Americans! Heath himself felt the same disbelief, the same refusal to admit that it had come to this. Could he even give such a command if it were necessary? He did not know. But he knew that, if he did, the major would carry it out promptly and dispassionately.

Almost then, like the crowd's, his resolve faltered at the sight of those impersonal, trim machines for mass slaughter, the use of which he himself knew only too well. Then he relaxed a little, his judgment vindicated. The sight of them had its effect. Because they were here, perhaps the rifles or the bayonets would not have to come into play. The crowd, awed, intimidated, drew back, began to fragment as the guns were mounted on the roof.

And then only Freeman remained, alone in the center of the street. In the floodlight glare, hands clenched, he looked up at the muzzles of the Brownings. His upturned face was defiant, yet somehow pleading, his chest swollen, as if he presented himself for slaughter, defying, yet soliciting, martyrdom. For a long time he stood like that, tensely, in the yellow light. When minutes passed and nothing happened he lowered his head, pale face bitter, turned, and rejoined the crowd in the parking lot. Watching him go, Heath felt no sense of triumph, only a cold foreboding.

Neither Chandler nor Clutterbuck left the plant for sixty hours. That was how long the flying squadron remained, held at bay by rifles, Brownings, bayonets. Meanwhile details of soldiers escorted shifts of workers back and forth, and the machines kept running, their thunder constant in the night, what was left of the shattered windows colorful in darkness, lit from within. The men and women of the flying squadron, over and over again, surged against the cordons of Guardsmen escorting the workers, screaming, shaking fists; but even they knew it was over, finished, and that they were beaten. Toward the end Heath saw Freeman again, in the middle of the street, alone, looking at the mill, his face a mask, eyes sunken, features almost skull-like. Then he turned away, and, not long after, the people whom he could not feed or house climbed wearily into the cars and trucks; and, much more slowly than it had come, the flying squadron left.

Heath waited another hour, until he was sure it had gone for good. Then, bearded, rank with grime and sweat, groggy with sleeplessness, too much coffee, too many cigarettes, he went to Chandler House. There the lower windows had been broken by strikers, no other damage done. Claudia ran to him, embraced him, and he held her tightly. Without bathing or shaving, he dropped, dead beat, into bed. But it was a long time before he got to sleep, keyed up as he was, and all he could see when he closed his eyes was Freeman's enigmatic, skull-like face.

7   A NIGHTMARE that she could not remember awakened Ramsey, whose heart was pounding, body rigid, flesh cold. Terrified, sick with fear, she lay there for a second staring at a ceiling dimly lighted by the night-lamp across the room. She could not stay here alone; she had to have somebody; she needed Hamp. Breaking the paralysis that held her, she swung out of bed, ran through the darkened house, with chilled spine and goose-pimpled skin, for the sanctuary of his room.

It was cold upstairs, the furnace fire banked. Her teeth chattered as she pushed through Hamp's door. He disdained a night-light, and his room was wholly dark. She groped through it to the bed. Quickly she slid under sheet, under quilts and blankets, nightgown riding up about her lean thighs, and found the warmth and reassurance she sought and pressed her breastless body against it, and then everything was all right. Her teeth stopped chattering; the chill left her flesh; the fear subsided.

She still could not understand why they had been separated, why, since they had come to Chandler House, they had to sleep in different rooms. The explanations given her by Mother had seemed foolish. Of course he was a boy and she a girl, but what difference did that make? They were brother and sister and loved one another. She put her arm around Hamp, shoved belly and loins tightly against his back and buttocks. He was so warm . . . Then he stirred groggily, turned beneath the arch of her arm, and she felt his breath on her face. Something else pushed against her stomach, small and hard. "Huh?" he murmured fuzzily. "What is it?"

"I had a bad dream," she whispered.

"Oh. Okay." He put his arm about her, held her to him tightly, as he had always done, and she felt comforted, safe again. He went back to sleep. She did not. Instead, she savored the change in herself, the end of fear, the comfort and warmth of safety.

She liked to be held by people who loved her. It was the best feeling in the world. There were four of them: Hamp first, then Father. After that Grandfather, and then Mother. But only with Hamp did she feel truly all right, truly safe. She hated not being in the same room with him any more, and she hated, too, that he did not really seem to mind that they had been forced apart like that and that, whenever she felt the need, she could not simply slide from her bed to his and snuggle up against him.

The hard thing still poked at her, and while he slept she touched it. It was what made the difference. That was why he spent so much time with Father and she with Mother. She knew what it was; it was what a boy put inside a girl, a man put inside a woman, and then a baby was the result. Someday she would marry and a man would put that inside her and she would have a baby too. She began to drift a little in warmth and sleep. Why couldn't it be Hamp? She touched it again and it seemed to grow under her fingers. Why couldn't she and Hamp just stay together and then he could— And it would be his baby, and—

But that was wrong and sinful, and she took her hand away and moved a little apart, feeling guilty. All the same, she did not really want to get married. Not to some strange man. To go off, leave them all: her father, mother, and most especially Hamp. Maybe if she got married, Hamp could come to live with them. She did not want to be away from him. She could not bear the thought of being away from him.

That was why they had been put in separate rooms, of course. But Hamp felt so good against her, she had to have him against her, have him touch her. She—

He awakened, because she held him tightly when he tried to turn over. "Sis?" He seemed surprised to find her there.

"I had a bad dream," she said again.

"Oh." He lay still, sharing warmth with her, not moving his arm. "It's all right now, ain't it?"

"Oh, it's all right now. Yes."

He came wider awake. "What time is it?"

"How would I know?"

Hamp sat up, switched on the light. He looked at the wristwatch he had got for his birthday. "Four o'clock. My God."

"You're not supposed to take the Lord's name in vain." She giggled. She liked to hear him do it; she didn't have the nerve herself. It sent a kind of thrill through her to hear Hamp use bad words. He had learned a lot of them down at the plant.

He rubbed his eyes; then he was fully awake. "Hey, you know what? I'll bet they've put some more presents under the tree."

Only then did she remember that tomorrow was Christmas Eve. She thought of the huge, glittering tree that they had helped to decorate, the great tree shining with glass balls from Europe and dripping with silvery tinsel, a marvel, a wonder, the most beautiful thing in the world. She thought of all the heaped boxes and packages beneath it, which she and Hamp had shaken, rattled, agonized over, wondering what their contents were. "You think so?"

"Hell, I know so." He swung out of bed. "Let's go down and see."

The prospect was irresistible, though she hated to leave the warmth beneath the covers. "Sure." She jumped out too, shivering immediately, teeth chattering. "You'd better put on my bathrobe," he said.

"You mean your bathroom." That was what he had called it when he was very little, and her parents still made a joke out of that.

He did not answer, but got it from the foot of the bed, held it for her while she slipped into it. It was heavy, warm, and smelled like him, and she nuzzled her face into its shoulder. Then he took her hand. "Come on."

"My feet are cold."

"Here, take my slippers."

Once they had been exactly the same size; now he was larger. The shoes, fleece-lined, were too big for her, but they kept her feet off the icy floor. Without a robe, barefooted—he did not seem to mind the cold—he led the way stealthily through the hall, down the stairs.

On the first floor they wound through labyrinths of corridors and rooms until they reached the spacious living room never used except when there was company or on holiday occasion. There the magnificent cedar with sweeping branches was only a blackness in the gloom until Hamp plugged in the lights with which it was festooned. Ramsey gasped. He had been right. The pile of packages beneath the tree had doubled in size since they had gone to bed. Huge, enticing, brilliantly wrapped boxes; and they sought out those with their names and passed them to one another and shook and pinched them in an agony of greed and anticipation.

"I can't wait," Hamp whispered. "Gosh, I don't see how I can wait."

"Me either. Golly—" They sat there, contemplating the mysterious riches until even Hamp shivered. Then he stood up. "I'm cold. Let's go back to bed."

"All right. We can snuggle up."

"No. No. I'm going down to the office with Pop. You know what they say about— You'd better go back to your own bed."

"I had a bad dream."

"That was a long time ago. He'll be in to wake me up in another . . . half hour."

"I don't want to go back to sleep. I might have another dream. I'll go with you."

Hamp hesitated, looking disappointed. She knew that look. He hated to have her, a girl, intruding on his time with Father. But then, with a burst of generosity, he said, "Okay. You can be *my* office boy."

"Girl." She giggled.

"Office girl. Let's go." He ran upstairs, and she padded soundlessly behind.

"Go on to bed now." It was an order. He sounded like Father. "It's not but a half hour."

She took off his robe, kicked off his slippers. "All right." She turned, ran into her own room, jumped beneath the covers, lay there huddled, shivering. She made a fantasy in her mind. No matter what they said, she would never get married. Neither would Hamp. They would go off together. Somewhere. He would look after her and she would look after him. When it was cold they could sleep together, and no one would stop them. They could snuggle up as much as they wanted. It was a delicious dream. In slow-growing, delicious warmth she sank into a drowse and knew nothing else until her father's hand awakened her.

"You don't look very bright-eyed and bushy-tailed," he said. "You sure you want to go down to the plant? You look like you ought to crawl back in your *Schlafwinkel* and get some more shut-eye. It might not be a bad idea for you to stockpile some sleep. I expect tomorrow night's going to be kind of restless."

They were eating breakfast in the kitchen. Her mother was not there; Father always let her sleep. No sense, he said, in rousting her out at five o'clock just to look across the table at him like a poleaxed heifer—whatever that was.

Ramsey hesitated. Now that she had slept and awakened again, she really did not want to go. She could not see what Father and Hamp saw in the place, why they were always so eager to get to the plant. But then something rebelled inside her. They kept trying to separate her from Hamp; even he himself tried to escape her nowadays every chance he got. Well, she wasn't going to let them do that to her. It was time she had a turn with Father, anyhow. He never spent any time with her, it was always Hamp— To spite them both, and not to lose them, she said, "I'm sure I want to go."

"Okay." Just then someone knocked at the back door. "Get that, will you, Darla? It's probably Ike."

The Negro cook went to the door, opened it.

"Howdy, Miz Fisher," said the old colored man who stood there in a neatly pressed chauffeur's uniform. Then, past her, "Good mawnin, Cap'n Heath. Mawnin, young cap'n, mawnin, young lady."

"Good morning, Isaiah." She could not tell whether her father was angry or amused. Maybe a little of each. "Well, I can't turn him away," he had told Mother last night. "After all, he did drive the Old Man around for twenty years. It's not his fault I'd sooner drive myself. And he needs money for Christmas over and above his regular pension, just like anybody else. And to remind us he exists when it's time to yell 'Christmas gift!' It's only a few days every year at this season, so what the hell. He can run us down there and piddle away the day as he sees fit until we're ready to come home." Now he turned in his chair. "Cold out there, ain't it?"

"Yes, sir. Powerful nippy."

"You'd better come in and have a cup of coffee. Give him some coffee, Darla. You want some breakfast, Ike?"

"Naw, suh. I done eat. But . . . if they's a little left over . . ."

"I expect Darla can rake up some ham and biscuits."

The two Negroes moved down the large kitchen to a smaller table in one corner. Ramsey finished her eggs. The yellows were runny and her mouth felt sticky. She licked her lips with her tongue, as her father scraped back his chair, lit a cigarette. Then he stood up and called, "Ike. You about ready to go?"

"Yassuh, Cap'n Heath. Any time."

"Well, go start the car and bring it around. Be sure to let it warm up good. Get your jackets on, kids."

Hamp had long since finished eating, and now he sprang to his feet impatiently. He scooped his jacket from the back of his chair, shrugged it on as the old man limped toward the back door. "Come on, Ramsey."

Not wanting to be left behind, she got into her own coat. Hamp and Isaiah were already at the back door. "Wait a minute, I'm coming." She knew why Hamp was in such a hurry. Isaiah would let him turn the key and step on the starter, bring the car to life. She started after them, but her father caught her shoulder. "Hold on, young lady. You've got egg all over your mouth."

"No, I haven't."

"Oh, yes, you have. Come here." He picked up a napkin, led her to the kitchen sink. His right hand cupped the back of her head gently, and his left, rougher, scraped at her mouth with the wet cloth. She looked up at him, and all at once she felt good about having decided to go this morning. The light in his eyes, the curve of his lips, told her how much he loved her, and, in that moment, having his hands on her was just as good, maybe better, than snuggling Hamp. Then he laid the napkin aside. "*In ordnung,*" he said. He salted his speech with German phrases to help them remember what they had learned in Austria. "Let's go." He took her hand, and together they walked to the door.

The icy cold of the outdoors slapped her across the face as they left the warm kitchen. Outside it was still totally dark; the garage, a hundred feet behind the house, was a black bulk, only barely discernible. From within it she heard car doors slam, Ike's voice trailing off and Hamp laughing. The screen door eased itself shut behind them. Her father was whistling softly "God Rest Ye Merry, Gentlemen." His big, leather-gloved hand was tight around her small, mittened one. Then she heard the ratchet of the starter button. Next, across the paved drive, there was a great red-orange puff of flame, larger than a house. Ramsey thought, How beautiful. Like a flower, I must be dreaming.

Something flew by her head, slammed into the house. At the same instant her father shrieked, "Down!" She was on the asphalt and he was over her. It seemed much later that she heard the sound, like a clap of thunder, only much louder, louder than any thunder she had ever heard. Then metal, clanging on the pavement like a strange rain. Suddenly there was no more weight on her. "God, oh God," she heard her father sob as he sprang up. "Oh, God, God, God. *Hamp!*"

She sat up, dazed, ears ringing. Then she sprang to her feet, ran after him. He stood before the garage, staring at crumpled iron and tattered cloth with some red substance all over it. There was no sign of the car. Ramsey blinked. Then she heard the cry, "*Daddy. Daddy. Daddy. Ramsey.*"

It had to be Hamp, but calling in a voice she had never heard before. She and Chandler turned. It lay to one side of the splintered garage. She stared at it. It was black all over and it lacked arms and legs. It just kept calling.

"Get back! Turn away!" Her father's voice was a roar. But it was too late. She had already seen it, heard it. She stood there frozen as he rushed to it. "Hamp," he cried. "Oh, God, son—" He reached for the thing, picked it up, cradled it in his arms.

"Hamp—"

As he lifted it, it screamed.

She had never heard anything like that before. Not even in her nightmare. It was a short, high, thin scream, and it quickly stopped. Her father was a huddled knot in the darkness; she could not see him plainly. That was Hamp, she realized. That was— Everything suddenly turned blurry, foggy. She tried to run toward it, but she could not move. She only stood there. Then suddenly she was sitting down, the pavement icy under her thighs. Everything was going around and around, and—

She heard the screen door open: She saw the rectangle of light, recognized her mother's silhouette framed in the kitchen door. "Heath!" her mother yelled. "Heath! What—?"

Her father straightened up. The ray of light fell across his face and across the thing shielded and cradled in his arms. His face was twisted, ugly, wet. He turned to hide with his body what he held. His voice was high, almost like a woman's, furious, desperate. "Don't come out here!" he screamed. "Get back, you understand? *Don't come out here! Don't look!*"

Ramsey sat there on the cold pavement. Then, exactly like a movie, the whole scene faded out into total blackness.

Part Two

1 ANDREW HAD NOT PLANNED to stop in Chandlerville; it was the car that caused it.

It was a 1940 Chevrolet, and as soon as he had left the separation center at Fort Bragg he had bought it from a rapacious dealer in Fayetteville for the equivalent of what he had earned in his last two years in the Army. Then, still dressed in issue khakis, the "Ruptured Duck" discharge pin on his shirt, he had driven across the state to Brackettville. Not that he really wanted to go back. But for years, in the Pacific, he had listened to others talk longingly of home, and it seemed somehow shameful not to return, like everyone else; besides, he had nowhere else to go.

So he drove west across the sandhills until the land shelved upward, changing to thick red clay; and presently he was almost in the shadow of the mountains. He passed through Macedonia and its circling outskirts of mills and villages into a countryside wild and resolutely rural. Along the way he gorged himself on cold beer and milk and hamburgers and all the other things he had missed for so long. Presently, in a steep-sided river valley, almost a ravine, he came to Brackettville.

Outwardly nothing there had changed. The ancient mill, with its blue windows in dirty brick walls, squatted by the river, and the village was strung out along the hill, no more, no less than the seventy houses that had been there when he left. The same two short blocks of cracked concrete sidewalk with the dry-goods store, the barber shop, the drugstore, and the grocery. Although a railroad spur ran through the valley behind the town, there was no station. The loading platforms at the mill warehouse served that purpose.

When he saw the place again, he wondered why he had come. He knew that Will Doggett and his family had long since left, gone north to war work, swallowed up in Chicago or Detroit. Instead of nostalgia, he felt a kind of revulsion, the same suffocation that had afflicted him until the Army had taken him out of here. But he drove up into the village anyhow and stopped before the house where he had once lived and which now was occupied by strangers. On the porch next door a short, dumpy woman with legs like bolsters swept vigorously. At the sight of her something stirred in Andrew, and for the first time he had a sense of homecoming. He got out of the car. "Mrs. Royce."

She stared, squinting. "Law— An*drew!* Andrew Ford?" She threw her arms wide as he ran up the steps, hugged him to thick, maternal softness. She smelled of fried pork fat. Suddenly it was a good, a comforting smell. She had been more mother to him than the woman who raised him, and she had always smelled of cooking, ever since he could remember. Then she sat down in the porch swing, and he on a chair, and she fired questions at him and he gave her the answers and asked questions of his own and quickly learned that there was nothing or no one else to hold him here. "Vic's done come home and gone off again," she told him. "Said he warn't goin back into no mill. Got his heart set on becomin a lawyer, and he went off to Northwestern University up in Illinois now. He asked about you in his last letter, but we didn't know nothin to tell 'im." And Paul McCloskey's family had moved back to Massachusetts, whence they'd originally come.

So that severed the last tie with Brackettville. Vic Royce, Paul McCloskey, Andrew Ford: they had grown up together in the same row of mill houses, had been inseparable from the first grade of grammar school until they reached an age at which the war had parted them.

Andrew got Vic's address, but doubted that he would ever write. He was not much at writing letters; that was how he had lost track of the Doggetts. But then, they had been even less than he when it came to that; they were the ones who had given up the correspondence first. He doubted now that they even thought of him. It was just as well. Brackettville was the old world, prehistoric, with no relation to him now. Ahead lay a new, unknown one, freshly minted, glittering. Suddenly he was eager to get away. Collards simmered on the stove and Mrs. Royce invited him to stay and eat, but he declined. As he went down the rickety steps she called, "They're runnin three shifts down yonder if ye want a job." He only grinned and shook his head, waved and got in the car.

Leaving Brackettville, he took a shortcut east, through the hills, presently struck another paved road north of Macedonia. Meanwhile the car was heating up again. It had been doing that all across the state. Twice he'd flushed the radiator, had replaced one bad hose. Still the trouble persisted—worse in the hills. By the time he entered another valley, a broader one, where Chandlerville lay shimmering in the summer afternoon, its silver water tank a giant dazzle in the air, the heat indicator was all the way over, the stench of rusty iron and dirty steam rank in his nostrils.

He cursed and nursed the car onward, through scattered outskirts—pleasant little houses, not the mill-village kind; these had well-grassed lawns and shrubbery and some even had fences; a few stores; but no service station. Then, ahead, he saw a wide, graveled parking area before a shabby little building with a plate-glass window bearing the inscription BEER. He let the car coast in and stopped.

He was already sweating, and when he got out the heat struck him like a hammer. Opening the hood he carefully removed the cap, then jumped back from jetting steam. He watched it spout until only waves of heat arose from its single nostril. Then he went into the tavern.

As always upon entering such a place, he stopped just inside the door and looked around for women; but there were none, except for Rita Hayworth in a black lace nightgown on a calendar behind the bar. Beneath it his own reflection looked back at him from a dirty mirror: a man of twenty-five, a little taller than average, wide in the shoulders and thick in the chest, his close-cropped hair dark brown, his eyes an even darker shade. He had vanity, and he appraised himself for a split second, and was not displeased with what he saw. No movie star, but girls had told him often that he was good-looking.

A half-dozen men in khakis or overalls drank beer and played the pinball machines, and from behind the counter, a beefy man in a dirty apron said, "Come in the house." Andrew gasped with gratitude at the play of an electric fan on his wet shirt, sat down, ordered a cold beer and drank it quickly. When the second was before him he asked about a place to get the radiator boiled out. That brought everybody into the conversation, and the damnation of all car dealers was unanimous for the next ten minutes. There was a garage farther in, near the mills that could take care of the trouble; and by then they felt free to ask questions about the war, in which all had been too old to serve. He told them what he could, but that was not much. There was not really any way you could tell somebody who had not been there what it was like. Presently the conversation tapered off.

"Well, I'll tell you," the counterman said. "I'm glad it's over, but I bet I ain't half as glad as you are. You lookin for work, incident'ly, the mills are hirin here, and the Old Man gives veter'ns first crack."

"I don't think I'll go back in any damned cotton mill. I had enough of that in Brackettville before the war."

"Well, I sure as hell don't blame you. I put in my time too, till I got smart and bought this place. To my mind anythin beats workin in a mill. All the same, it's a lot different here than what I heard it's like in one of them Butler mills." He scrubbed the counter with a rag. "The Old Man's just about doubled the plant here since the war, and the new part's somethin else—air-conditioned, them floo-o-rescent lights, real fancy—not a bad place to work. Of course, that old part's still a damn sweatbox but they say he's aimin to fix that up too. There's a lot worse places to work than Chandler Mills." He put another beer in front of Andrew. "This 'un's on me. Least I can do for a feller that's been off fightin. What do you aim to do, now that you're home?"

"I don't know," Andrew said. He looked at his reflection in the mirror. "Something. I don't know what. Something. I think maybe I'll go to college."

"Now you're talkin!" A stubble-bearded old man at one end of the bar spoke up. "That's th' thing to do—git the eddication. A feller cain't amount to nothin without the eddication. Lord God, I worked in them mills for near thirty year, and that's whut held me back. If I'd been able to read and write real good I coulda been a second hand at least. A man cain't git nowhere in this world without he's got some schoolin!"

"I know," said Andrew. Instinctively he touched his wallet, which held the clipping and the letter Willie Morgan had written. "Actually, I—" He broke off. Outside, wheels crunched on gravel. The counterman was staring over his shoulder. "Wheew. Look at that, will you? She finally got delivery on it."

With the others, Andrew turned. A red Cadillac roadster, obviously factory-new, had pulled into the drive. "She said they had it on order," the counterman murmured. "I reckon the Old Man give General Motors such fits they had to ship it in self-deefense."

Andrew stared, not at the car but at the girl who slid from beneath the wheel, revealing briefly a long stretch of suntanned thigh under a short yellow summer dress. Then she walked across the drive. She was tall and slender, her breasts small, yet definite, pointed beneath the cloth, a bright scarf bound around her hair, so that Andrew could not tell its color. The dress was what he had heard girls call a sunback, and it showed a lot of flesh and all of it was darkly tanned like her leg. She came into the tavern and went to the counter, rope sandals barely whispering on the floor. She looked neither to the right nor left. "Hello, Billie Ray," she said, her voice soft, with a husky undertone.

"Howdy, Ramsey. See your new car done come."

"Finally. Look, I want four cold Schlitzes to go." Under all those covert male eyes she opened her handbag, took out cigarettes and a lighter. She thrust a cigarette between lips painted dark red in the fashion of the time, snapped the lighter into flame, bent her head. Andrew's gaze was not covert. He had never seen a face like that before. The cheekbones were high and prominent, tapering to a narrow chin, the nose straight and perfect, the mouth wide. But it was her eyes that held him. They were enormous, long-lashed and smoky green, slanted curiously, giving that V-shaped face a cast that was almost foxy, a look at once unique, arresting.

She was beautiful, he thought, but with a different kind of beauty, one wholly individual, strange. This close he saw how darkly burned her arm was and how it was overlaid with a faint down of sunburned hair. The flesh looked soft, yet solid. Then she snapped shut the lighter, raised her head, and by accident her gaze met Andrew's. For perhaps two seconds he looked full into those curious, slanted eyes; and that was long enough for something sudden, unexpected, to stir within him. Then she turned away as Billie Ray handed her the bag of beer. A strange sadness gripped Andrew, an unease, as if he felt the first intimation of a sickness coming on.

"Put it on the ticket, please," the girl said. Then clutching the bulky parcel with its chill contents against her breasts, she went out. No one stirred or made a sound as all eyes watched her slide gracefully into the Cadillac. Then, like a startled animal, the car plunged backward, dug gravel as it spun around, sprayed more as it roared out of the drive, and vanished from their frame of vision, leaving behind a kind of sad, longing silence strangely devoid of lust, that was not broken until its engine sound had faded.

Then someone said with a lewdness almost forced, "Headed fer th' river."

"Yeah." The words dissipated the strange chastity of the hush. A fat man in a dirty tee shirt and faded blue jeans said, "You ever had any of that, Billie Ray?"

"No," said the counterman. "And I don't want it neither. I got troubles enough as it is."

Andrew Ford frowned, trying to make sense of this. "Who *was* that?"

The counterman was still looking at the driveway. "Ramsey Chandler."

"Who? Wait a minute." He made the connection then. "You mean—?"

"The Old Man's daughter. Yeah."

"Her?" He twisted on the stool, but of course she had long since disappeared. "In *here?*"

"She comes in occasion'ly. The town's dry, but this is outside the limits, the first place you hit. She buys beer from me once in a while."

"When she runs outa liquor," the fat man said.

"If I had her money," somebody put in, "I'd never run out."

Billie Ray snorted. "Didn't you hear her put it on the credit?" he asked shortly. "She ain't got no money. Not except what *he* allows her to have. Otherwise she's broke as you and me. Been like that ever since she married that Mexican feller and it took a fortune to get her loose from him."

The fat man's eyes were wet, glittering. "Whut you reckon she's gonna do—drink all four them beers herself?"

"Why not?" Billie Ray snapped. "Hell, you can swill four in no time flat."

"Awright, don't git your back up. Jest that I heerd so many stories about her. How she'll pick up somebody from over in Macedonia someplace, anybody, it don't make no difference, take 'im out to that River House, even furnish the whiskey . . . They do say she likes that old thang stuck in her."

"I don't know," Billie Ray rasped. "All I know is you better keep any damn stories like that to your own big self. What she does is her own damn business. But if word gits back to Heath Chandler that you're badmouthin his girl, he'll jerk a knot in you four men and a boy cain't untie! That'll be enough of that in here!"

The fat man stuck out his lower lip. "You sound like you're sweet on her."

"I'm sweet on my beer license and stayin in business. This may be outside the town, but Heath Chandler still owns this property. I don't want no shit like that gittin back to him from here!"

"Awright, awright." The fat man subsided. Somebody began to play the pinball machine. Andrew sat there with his beer bottle cradled between his palms. He looked at his image in the mirror, this time objectively, trying to see himself as he had appeared to her. That strange feeling was still within him, that sad queasiness, that curious sense of loss and regret that had descended upon him as she had driven off. And those eyes— What he felt was upsetting, yet somehow delicious, and he withdrew into himself, neither speaking nor listening.

Not that this had not happened before. At twenty-five, he walked a perpetual tightrope between raw lust for woman-flesh and a deep, fundamental yearning for something more. To satisfy the first was comparatively simple; it was the other that was so hard. He had within him the conviction that somewhere he would find a woman magnificent and unique, one special woman set apart for him, waiting for him to love her and to love him in return. And he had never found her.

He had come close occasionally, but it had never quite happened with any of the girls he'd known. Something always spoiled it before it could happen; either too much intimacy or not enough. And yet he persisted in the quest. How many times in how many strange towns on how many frantic weekends, with the knowledge of the shortness of life, the running out of time, at his heels like a pursuing hound, had he felt this same sense of significant encounter—on the street, in a crowded railroad station or bus terminal. For only seconds you met the eyes of a girl whom you had never seen before, and in that brief interval something passed between you; both knew that, if only time and place allowed, each had something to give that the other desperately sought. But the moment passed always; the high heels clicked on; the train pulled out the bus was called. And you never saw them again; but those eyes, those faces, were vivid long after the features of the women to whom you'd made real love were forgotten. He turned again, looked out at the driveway.

"You want another'n?" asked Billie Ray.

That broke the spell. He laughed softly, derisively, at himself. "No," he said. "Not now. I got to have that car fixed."

"Well, good luck," said Billie Ray. "And you come back."

"I'll do that," Andrew said, and went out into the terrible heat.

2   THE BUILDING that housed the general offices of Chandler Mills had been completed just before Pearl Harbor, and every brick and furnishing of it proclaimed not only Heath Chandler's antic imagination but his respect for quality. Three stories high, separated from the plant itself by a rolling, landscaped lawn, it had seemed much larger than necessary at the time it was built. Now, following five years of wartime prosperity, it was far too small, and when materials became available, an addition was scheduled. Only the tower would not be enlarged.

That soared an additional three stories above the roof of the main building, like the keep of a castle, or the upthrust of a lighthouse, perfectly round, even its huge windows curved, housing on its lower floor certain executive offices, on its second the board and private dining rooms, and, at the very top, the offices of Heath Chandler and Olin Clutterbuck. On its roof was a small, pleasant garden, where, in clement weather, the hierarchy of Chandler Mills held informal lunches and meetings.

Olin Clutterbuck's suite, like Heath's, was finished in rich, rubbed cherry, and the interior of the room was curved, following the arc of the wall. Heath had not bothered to justify this whim except to say, "Let's make it round so nobody can corner us. Besides, nobody else has got a tower. It makes us stand out. And if I can't be the biggest in the industry, I at least want to be the damnedest." Well, Olin thought, he had succeeded thoroughly at that, anyhow.

Shoving back his chair, he arose wearily from his desk. With Heath in New York, the entire burden of Chandler Mills and all its ramified subsidiaries fell on his shoulders, and though by now he knew every aspect of the business, he could not and never would be able to handle things the way Heath did. Sometimes he felt like an apprentice juggler bound to a master of the art; Heath not only kept an incredible number of projects going simultaneously but did it flawlessly, deftly, by instinct. For him it was play, the exercise of a natural talent, exhilarating and enjoyable; for Olin, even after all these years, management and administration took effort and concentration.

But, then, there was only one Heath Chandler—and by now everybody knew that.

Dress in the Chandler offices was informal in the summer, and in his private bathroom Clutterbuck stripped off his sport shirt, washed his face, then combed his hair. He backed off a little, looking at himself in the mirror. At forty-nine, his hair was thinning, his body thickening; that, he thought, was the penalty for being a capitalist. With his holdings in Chandler stock, his own investments of his lavish salary and yearly bonus, he was, he realized with a kind of awe, very close to being a millionaire. North Carolina was a long way from Paris, but being executive vice-president of Chandler Mills was better than starving in a garret. He put his shirt back on, went through his own office to the outer one. His secretary was young and very pretty; Heath had scoured the South for girls who combined efficiency, intelligence and beauty. "I'll be damned," he'd growled, "if I'll have a building that cost this much uglied up by a bunch of old maids. Besides, a little touch of lechery adds tone." Clutterbuck told the girl that he was leaving for the day; if anything came up during the last hour of business he would be at Chandler House.

In the private elevator he rode down to a large, ex-

tremely modern lobby, where a quartet of telephone operators and receptionists occupied a round glass booth. Like
most of the furniture in the building, the sofas, chairs
and tables here had been designed by Heath and himself
and made in the company's own shops—of discarded textile machinery and equipment, transformed by imagination and the lavish use of rare woods into works of art.
Old looms and loom beams, slubber cones and calendar
rolls, even broomsticks had been pressed into service; the
very flowerpots and ashtrays had once been part of the
antiquated equipment Heath had inherited and long
since replaced. In the long run all this had cost more
than conventional furnishing by half, despite Heath's
claim of saving money, but it helped achieve the effect
he sought. No one who had ever been in the general offices of Chandler Mills would forget the visit—or the
company itself.

Olin's big Lincoln in the parking lot was prewar, but
the engine started smoothly and purred as he drove out,
turned left, and passed the plant. A vast, sprawling complex of buildings now—many of them single-storied, win-
dowless, climate-controlled and modern, though the blue
windows still made rows of color in the older areas—it
had tripled in size since that day, so long ago, when
Heath had first led him through it. Then it had seemed
to him a mystery; now the never-ending processes within
it were as familiar as a human body to a general surgeon;
he knew its organs, arteries, nerves, in every detail. And
not only this one but the other five too, sprawled across
three counties, each specialized, with its particular, calcu-
lated place and function in Heath's meticulous scheme of
things. The whole process, he thought, had been like
creating the original of a superb piece of sculpture in
clay or plasticine, a delicate business of adding here, sub-
tracting there, until an organic whole emerged with grace
and balance. Heath had been right—business could be an
art; and they had prospered by using art in business.
They had applied the creative, free-ranging imagination
of the writer and the painter; and that had made the difference between Chandler Mills and companies run by

men whose minds had been bounded all their lives by the rules and shibboleths of commerce. It was curious, he thought, that the legend had arisen that artists were poor businessmen. Actually, every word that went on paper, every stroke that went on canvas, was the product of analysis, decision, foresight, the ability to grasp entire a complicated vision. Business demanded no more. And if the same intensity, concentration, and vast energy were devoted to a company as to a work of art, it could indeed become one.

There was no reason why the town should not be one too, he thought, swinging through its center. It had grown, expanded—its population now was over twenty thousand—but it still offended him profoundly with its harsh, industrial ugliness, overlaid with a trashy glitter of prosperity and commercialism. He yearned to attack it with money and materials, reshape it from end to end make of it something new and remarkable in the way of a city. In theory, it was possible: Heath had here an opportunity possessed by no more than two or three other men in the country. He still owned this place almost outright. It was his personal property, to do with as he chose, and no one in it could put restrictions on him or say him nay. The town remained unincorporated, and despite various artifices to give the illusion of popular government, under one-man rule. But, realistically, it was not feasible. Besides the huge cost of such an undertaking, beautifying Chandlerville would have upset and baffled its citizens.

"You don't *understand*," Heath had insisted. "They think it's beautiful now. Look, when I was a kid I used to know a man who trapped raccoons for their fur."

"What's that got to do with it?"

"You know what the best bait for a coon is? Something shiny and bright, fastened to the trap. Anything that glitters—a piece of tin, a hunk of mirror glass . . . they just can't stay away from it. Well, these people here are just like coons. The more something shines and glistens, the prettier they think it is. For God's sake, look at the grill and bumpers on the new cars—or take a jukebox, with

all that bubbling neon and colored lights—that's their ide
of beauty. You want to make Chandlerville into a garden.
They'd hate the idea. But if you proposed to make it into
one great big jukebox, they'd fall all over you and love
you for it. So why waste the money on something they'd
hate? Forget it, Clutt."

Heath was, as usual, right; and Olin tried not to look
at the place as he passed through. Turning toward Chandler House, he forgot all that, anyhow; his mind went instead to the strange undertone in Claudia's voice. She
had not asked him to dinner because she was lonely and
wanted company; there had been a purpose. Something
was wrong, and he supposed it had to do with Ramsey.

Well, regardless, he was glad of the excuse to spend an
evening with her. He was reconciled now to the role he
played in her life—and she in his; but he still loved her.

And whatever she asked of him he would give, even if
it meant coming into conflict with Heath.

Waiting for Olin, Claudia thought, Someday it has all
got to be finished. Even the biggest rock thrown into the
water can't send out its ripples forever. Someday . . .

Not until after Elizabeth Chandler had died quietly,
prematurely, in the spring of 1933, seemingly from no
cause save a determination to be parted from Bolivar no
longer, had Claudia begun to imprint her own personality
on the house. A slow, tentative process at first, it had
become in time almost an obsession: therapy. Now, wandering restlessly from room to room, she remembered
how, alone with Ramsey in Vienna and Zurich, she had
haunted the great auction houses of Central Europe for
furnishings and art, in an era when the entire contents of
a chateau, *Schloss,* or even palace could be bought for
almost nothing—the heirlooms and possessions of gentry
and nobility brought low by defeat, depression, and democracy. She had, she thought, spent money like a drunk-
en sailor; but it had been a time when she and Heath,
equally shattered, had sought refuge, surcease, in manias
of their own.

She had been in despair then; it seemed the whole

world had fallen in upon her. The clinics, the doctors, their endless talk and explanations; and, through it all, Ramsey unmoved and unhelped, withdrawn, never smiling, never speaking except when spoken to, shocked into some secret, safe world of her own, from which, it seemed, she would never emerge to confront a reality that could do to humans what it had done to Hamp. And Heath himself, thrown into a crazy spin, the agony of which she could only imagine, all the forces of self-destruction, so long suppressed, released within him again, only this time more viciously, more savagely than ever. And yet she could not blame him any more than she could blame Ramsey. She had not seen what they had seen, not had imprinted on her brain the images they sought to erase.

She remembered, though, Heath's high-pitched scream as she stood there unmoving on that winter morning in the doorway, shocked and baffled. Remembered how he had forced her back, had stalked into the kitchen, coat covered with soot and blood, face unbearable to look upon, Ramsey unconscious in his arms. How he had laid her on the table, and the utter flatness of his voice: "Don't go out there. Don't you dare to go out there." He made a gasping sound. "Hamp's dead. The union put dynamite in the car." And then she had cried out herself and tried to run past him, and he had knocked her back, hard enough to send her reeling and cut her lip. "I said, don't go out there." Tears were streaming down his cheeks. "Call Olin, for God's sake, call Clutt." Then, to the cook: "Darla. Find me a sheet. I've got to go and cover him up."

So he had spared her. Her last memory of Hamp was when, the night before, he had kissed her before he went to bed. And that was tolerable; her sanity could deal with grief no worse than that. But she could only imagine what Heath and Ramsey had had to deal with, and she could condemn neither of them, only decide which of them needed her more.

That was, of course, the child. When Ramsey had regained consciousness she had been disoriented and withdrawn—wholly, deadly calm. Grave, contained, in a way that had stricken Claudia all through with chill. She would not cry or rage; she simply refused to acknowledge a world in which Hamp was gone. And so, at a time when Heath's need of his wife was greatest, she had had to go away, leave him with Olin as his only brace, support. American doctors all said the same—psychiatry. Maybe in Vienna, in Zurich—

She tried the ones in New York first; there were not many, and they all failed. And then there was nothing left but to take the girl to Europe. Heath would not go with her. The company—

She had raged about that at first, Claudia remembered. He needed her, but she needed him too; and so did Ramsey. But the company seemed to come first, the mills. She could not understand; only later did she realize that some deep, instinctive need turned him to them. He could not withdraw like Ramsey, but he could seek his own oblivion in work, massive doses of it—long, draining hours that, Olin told her, left him staggering with fatigue. And when even that could not erase whatever it was he must wipe from his brain, there was whiskey; and when that did not work either, there were women—or one woman, Betty Hammond. Maybe it would have been different if she could have stayed; but the imperative of Ramsey's need had not allowed that.

Claudia went into the kitchen, gave instructions to the cook. Then she walked through the house out onto the terrace. Below, Chandlerville spread out like an ever-widening inkblot on soft paper; every day its circumference grew. She hated it. Even to this day she hated it. She turned away from the prospect of it, lit a cigarette, sat down at a wrought-iron table. Olin should be here any moment now.

The damned clinics, she thought, the jargon; all the bearded men who worked with the maturing, yet still-silent child, and gave elaborate excuses for their failures. Their diagnoses were all the same: the girl had simply lost a part of herself; she and Hamp had been one, a single organism. Dr. Hochmann in Vienna had made it clearer than all the rest: "The relationship between twins, even fraternal ones, the fact that they were of opposite sexes—one can compare it only to that all too uncommon phenomenon, the truly happy marriage, when two people join together wholly, each capable of perceiving the world through the mind and senses of the other, each incomplete without the other. . . . In a sense, Mrs. Chandler, your daughter has just been widowed. And for her there is nothing that psychotherapy can do. Here we fall back on proverbs: Time heals all wounds. Eventually the subconscious will cope with the raw, physical fact of violence; in time it will bury the factual incidents of that tragedy, as scar tissue encysts an object that cannot be removed by surgery. Then the child will emerge from her withdrawal; and not before. The matter, however, of incompletion— That is a different case. It will depend on the men she encounters in her life. Just as the widow of a happy marriage seeks the nearest duplicate of her late husband that she can find—" He gestured, smiled faintly. "One can almost forecast the type of male to whom, in future years, your daughter will be drawn."

"That's all well and good, but for now—"

"For now, waiting. Patience, attention, and parental love." He had drawn deeply on his pipe. "In such cases, and in this one in particular, the father can be of vast therapeutic benefit. I think you should return home."

Claudia had stiffened. "Why?"

"Your daughter needs a substitute for the male personality that was part of her and of which she was suddenly deprived. The father can be an effective surrogate. He can provide the support, the sustaining masculinity, can stand in for the missing brother as a crutch substitutes for a missing limb. But, naturally, there is risk."

Claudia was silent for a moment. "I think I see what you mean."

"Of course you do. You are an intelligent woman, and as you say, have consulted authorities far more eminent than myself. The psychosexual relationships between sister and brother and daughter and father are very complex, but basically they are not too different. If your husband is willing to make the effort, he can, in some measure, substitute for the dead brother and make good the loss. Do you see my meaning?"

"I see it," Claudia said.

"I think you waste your time here without the only other male who, at the moment, can fill the void existing in her psyche. Therapy cannot do it. She needs only a substitute for the brother who, at the moment, will help her to accept a better substitute when he comes along. If this can be managed, there is an excellent prospect that in future years she can make a reasonably normal adjustment to the world." He smiled faintly. "Not wholly, perhaps; but then none of us ever wholly does."

"I understand," Claudia had said; and for the first time she truly did. She arose. "Thank you, Doctor. Please send your bill to me at the Hotel Sacher."

"Of course." As she left he said, "Mrs. Chandler."

"Yes?"

"May I congratulate you on your knowledge of German? Many people speak it well, but when it comes to the terminology of psychiatry—"

Claudia smiled without any humor. "Thank you, Dr. Hochmann. I've spoken a great deal of German to a lot of psychiatrists in the past year." Then she went out and got into the hired car.

It took her from Schwarzenberg Platz along the Ringstrasse to the Hotel Sacher, behind the great, gray, colonnaded pile of the opera. She was glad to enter the slightly ratty lobby of red velour, red satin and marble, to be out of the chill blast of the November wind, which sliced even through her mink. She went upstairs to the suite, where Frau Mayer was looking after Ramsey. The woman, who had forsaken better employment to come back to her, was not in sight; only one person was in the living room when she entered, and Claudia halted, staring at him. Then she let out a real squeal of pleasure, her first in years, and ran into his arms. "Olin!"

He held her tightly, the pressure of his embrace easing all the loneliness, helplessness and fear. "Oh, Olin . . ." She was crying. Then she pulled away, looked at him. "What are you doing here?" The habit of expecting the worst had fastened on her, and as her eyes raked over the tall, lean, redheaded man in the gray suit she felt a sudden thrust of fear. "Heath—?"

"He's all right. For the next three weeks, anyhow, he'll be in Chandlerville, working like hell. I'm on vacation. He wanted me to defer it, but I put my foot down. I was homesick for Europe." His eyes met hers directly. "Among other things."

She felt an inward kick of a different kind of fear. She had known for so long how Olin felt. For so many years now the three of them had been melded in such intimacy, a kind of incomplete *ménage à trois*, certainly a mutual dependency. It was a relationship that Heath had dominated, but now— The fear she felt was of herself, of her own loneliness and despair. And the knowledge that Olin would not have come to her if Heath had still wanted her.

His very presence here told her something she could not force her mind to dwell on. He had come, and Heath had not. She knew how Olin felt, all right. What she did not know was how she felt.

They had gone, she remembered, up the river to a *Heuriger* at Klosterneuburg, one of those uniquely Austrian public houses run by vintners who sold to the public new wine made by themselves from their own grapes. She had been afraid of drinking, alone and with Ramsey as her responsibility; now there was someone to take responsibility for her, and she relaxed, taking in two *Viertels* of the potent new wine quickly, with smoked wild boar, black bread, and cheese to ballast it. The food had little effect, Olin's presence and the wine a great deal. What she could not forget, though, was that it was Clutterbuck who had come, and not Heath.

For a long time they talked around that. Then Claudia had another glass of wine, and when it was half finished, she said: "And how will Heath manage with you gone? He'll have to stay in Chandlerville, won't he? He won't be able to get to New York. But maybe, then, he'll have her brought down."

Olin sat up straight, the freckles on his skin standing

out against paleness. He looked as if he had been struck, unexpectedly and hard.

Claudia laughed shortly. "You think I don't know about her? I've got friends in New York too. Some of them are only too eager to let you know when—" Then she took pity on him. "You don't have to make excuses for him, Olin. You don't have to say anything in his behalf at all."

He relaxed a little. "All right. I won't make any excuses. Except this: I don't think he would have gone near her if only he could have found out who did it. If he could have just laid his hands on the man . . . Maybe it's better this than murder; if he could have got his hands on Freeman, he would have killed him. Personally. Outright. But Freeman's vanished—"

"It wasn't Freeman who killed Hamp," said Claudia.

"It wasn't—? You mean that theory about the Klan. Because he ran them out of town. He turned the Klan inside out—"

"It wasn't the Klan either." Claudia's voice trembled. "It was Bolivar."

He only looked at her.

"Don't you see?" she went on. "He did it! He reached out from the grave to do it. It all goes back to him." She turned her head in a quick gesture of agony, hatred, face twisting. "If he hadn't written that letter, determined to save his God damned mills— And he's the one I can't fight, never will be able to. Not Betty Hammond, not any other woman—I could fight the other women! But . . . but not that damned old dead man."

She regained control. "I tried," she said softly. "God knows, that first night, when he handed me that letter, I tried. Right from the start something inside me went cold. But—" She moved her hands in futility. "Chandler," she said harshly. "Sometimes I wish I'd never heard the name."

Olin did not answer.

"It's like a curse, being a Chandler. Sometimes, at night, I think how different it could have been . . . if I had never heard the name, never met him— Oh, I wouldn't be here in Vienna in a plush hotel; there's a lot

I never would have done or learned. But— I might not have lost a son either." She drew in a long breath. "Sometimes I wish he had never come near me. Had left me to grow up what I was—a barefooted, ignorant bootlegger's girl, maybe working in the mills now, maybe happy with that, maybe never missing what I never had—"

"You don't mean that," said Olin.

She was more than a little drunk, and knew it, did not care. "I'd have a husband and a swarm of children. And if something happened to one, he could give me a new one to ease the hurt."

She was aware of the narrowing of Olin's eyes. "But Heath can't do that," she went on recklessly. "He's sterile, did you know? Not impotent, just sterile. The Tiercel crash—that was one of its aftereffects. That's why my children were so precious, Olin. They were all there would ever be. And now . . . one dead. The other . . . in that hotel suite back there, just sitting, half-dead herself; and it tears my heart out every time I look at her. That's what it's come to, Olin, that's my wedding gift, somewhat belated, from Bolivar Chandler!" In a nervous gesture she knocked her glass skittering, spilling wine; it crashed on the floor and everyone turned, then looked away politely. "I'm sorry," she said as the owner hurried over with a fresh glass, cleaned up, reassuring her it amounted to nothing.

When he had gone, Clutterbuck said, "I didn't know that. I guessed. But I didn't know."

"I thought he told you everything."

"Not that," Olin said. "Christ, that makes it worse for him too—" He looked down at his glass.

"I know. I shouldn't condemn him. I know, but—I'm tired, Olin. I'm just plain tired. Let's go back."

"Yes," he said. He arose. Gently he took her arm. "Let's go back."

In the corridor before the door she opened her handbag, took out her key. She stood there with it in her hand, looking up at Olin. There was silence between them as their eyes met. Claudia drew in a deep breath.

Then Clutterbuck said gently: "Good night, Claudia,"

and kissed her lightly on the lips. "I'll see you in the morning." He took her key, opened the door for her, let her in. When she had crossed the threshold they looked at each other again briefly. "Get a good night's sleep," he said.

Wordlessly, she nodded, and then, as he turned away, she closed the door.

That night she lay awake for a long time. She knew why he had come and what his coming meant; and now she had to decide what she was going to do. She was grateful to Olin for not forcing a decision on her that night, or even part of a decision, the first step toward one. But it was as momentous a move for him as for her, and . . .

Because he would not be here if he had not long since decided that his coming to her was not a betrayal of Heath. What his presence meant was that it no longer mattered to Heath what became of either of them. Whatever world he had moved into, it was one in which they, and Ramsey too, had no place. And Olin had decided that Heath was never coming back from it, and that was why, at last, he had taken the initiative. Olin had made up his mind and was telling her as gently as he could that something had ended forever for both of them, and that it was time to make a fresh start.

And maybe he was right.

Something in her broke, snapped. She rolled over and cried rackingly until at last she went to sleep, hands clenched tightly in the pillow.

Then Claudia heard Olin coming through the house and arose from the chair on the terrace and went to meet him.

3   THE ARMY AIR FORCE, in which Baldwin had served as a major general, had been good for him, Heath thought, not without a pang of envy. The war

seemed to have taken years off his age, pounds off his belly. He had eaten sparingly at dinner, and now, in the hotel room, he drank sparingly too. "And of course, I'm checked out on jets," he was saying. "But, God, flying one of those things is a young man's job. They're so damned hot you wouldn't believe it—" Then he must have read the expression on Heath's face. He broke off. "I'm sorry," he said. "Hell, don't let it worry you. In the long run you probably had more to do with winning the war than I did. Major generals are a dime a dozen; people who can make as much cloth as you are damned few and far between. Anyhow, you know I did everything I could, pulled every string—"

Heath shrugged. "Sure. You know I appreciate it."

"They say your application for a commission got all the way up to Roosevelt himself."

"It did." Heath made a wry face. "He called me personally to explain why he had turned it down—and Clutt's along with it. You know him, he could have charmed a knot off a tree, and he used it all on me, but you could feel the iron underneath. Well, I guess I was essential and so was Clutt, but that didn't make it any easier. I'd have defied him, enlisted as a private, but I couldn't pass the physical. Not with as many things broken up and busted inside me as there were—" He shrugged. "Well, it's over, the hell with it. If there's ever another one, though, I'll guarantee you I won't miss it. Not if I have to recruit my own private air force and pay for it myself."

Baldwin grinned. "You could probably afford it."

"Probably. War's good for business. Even with the prices cut to the bare minimum, we got well. The whole industry got well, for the first time in twenty years. It's a hell of a way to make money, but I must admit, it feels good to have some capital for a change."

Baldwin nodded. "What about these kids I recommended to you? Any work out?"

"Harry Frankel, that major. I took him on as sales manager. He's impressive as the devil, and he learned the business inside out before the war."

"Harry's aggressive, a real go-getter. He'll be a good man. What about the others?"

"A little wet behind the ears yet. I may gamble on Whitworth and Schuman. I've got three others I rounded up myself."

Baldwin ground out his cigar. "This is quite a gamble you're taking, isn't it?"

"Maybe. But ever since I took over the mills I've planned to have my own sales office. I'm tired of being at the mercy of commission agents. I'm going to integrate my company into one complete operation. Why let everybody else skim the gravy? I'll make the cloth, finish, dye, print it, eventually maybe even sew it. Meanwhile this is a first step. There are a lot of people who say it won't work, but they've been yelling that at me for years."

"You'll make it work." Baldwin arose. "Well, I've got to get to bed. My plane for Washington leaves early." He was liaison man with the Pentagon for an enormous aircraft manufacturer. "Heath, it's been good . . ." He stuck out his hand.

When Baldwin had gone, the room, deprived of the vitality of his presence, seemed empty, lonely. Heath restlessly mixed another drink he did not want, went to the window, stared down at the midnight traffic on Forty-fourth Street. More and more, as he grew older, he missed Claudia and Ramsey when he was away from them. He thought about what might have happened; how close he had come to losing both of them. He sipped his drink, shook his head as if he had water in his ear. That interval now had the quality of a nightmare.

Actually, he could remember very little of those first months after that winter morning. He supposed that outwardly he had seemed to function. He had walked, talked, carried on rational conversations, made decisions, even laughed at times. But that was only part of him, a façade; inwardly he had been quite unbalanced. What he had seen that morning had been, for a while, more than he could bear, more than he could live with.

While Claudia and Ramsey were in Chandlerville he had managed. They had needed his strength, and in giving it to them he had gained strength of his own. But when there was no hope for the girl but to take her to Europe, the props beneath him had been pulled out; Heath Chandler had funked, collapsed.

In his own agony he had lashed out at anything and everything. The Ku Klux Klan—he had broken it in Macedon County, but without finding any trace of guilt it bore for the bombing. That it had been capable of such an act, there was no doubt; but he'd proved to his own satisfaction that it had not done it. No. Freeman. He saw again the lonely figure standing in the floodlights of the street, deep in secret thought, possessed by some dream, some hatred in defeat, that racked it. The fanatic, temporarily defeated, but not through with vengeance yet.

And he had sought Freeman and had not found him. Some said the man had gone to Russia; anyhow, his trail had vanished. The union itself had to bear the brunt of his hatred; but it, too, had pulled back, the general strike broken, its efforts come to nothing. There was no way he could hit at it. And so he had taken out his need for vengeance on poor Olin and on himself.

Betty Hammond . . . His mouth twisted in revulsion. And yet at the time he had welcomed what she offered— a way to blank out all reality. Reality could not enter, reach, that dark labyrinth of corruption in which, like a female Minotaur, she lurked, waiting for victims of either sex. In there it was possible to forget everything except flesh, sensation; and he had plunged into the labyrinth desperately. For a while that had been everything and all, forgetfulness, however gained. He had not even had to worry about the mills. Olin saw to those efficiently.

Now he could not even remember how long he had been down in that darkness with her. Weeks? Months? All he could remember was coming out into light again And perhaps he never would have if it had not been for Olin's wire: URGENT YOU RETURN CHANDLERVILLE IMMEDIATELY. CLUTTERBUCK.

It had come directly to her Fifth Avenue apartment He had not even known that Olin knew; his stomach clenched with the shame of discovery. Suddenly he realized that everybody knew.

It was ten in the morning. The apartment was a shambles; the maid would not be in till twelve. He tipped the messenger and turned away. His head ached, his body felt smeared and grimy. In the bathroom he vomited dryly. When he returned to the bedroom she was awake, hair tousled, lines showing in her face, eyes redveined.

"What's that?" She squinted at the paper in his hand. Her breasts, bruised and pendulous now, were obscene globes, dangling as she sat up.

He showed it to her. Suddenly he did not want to look at her. Olin knew. Of course Olin knew.

When she had read it she rubbed her mouth with the back of her hand. "It can't be anything important. He'd have phoned you."

"I don't know. I'll call him and see." He went to the telephone. The place smelled of stale smoke, spilled whiskey, the lingering reek of various perfumes. He called Chandler Mills. Olin was out, the switchboard said. He talked to Neal McLendon, the treasurer. "I had this wire from Olin Clutterbuck. What's happening there?"

"I don't know. Why don't you talk to Olin?"

"They said he wasn't in."

"Why—" McLendon's voice was baffled. "Wait a minute."

Time passed. Heath lit a cigarette, crushed it out after the first drag. He could hear Betty moving around the room. He heard her take a drink of straight whiskey; she did that now first thing upon arising, every morning. In the bathroom she began to cough and gag, cursing between spasms in ferocious, mindless gutter language, like a cheated whore. McLendon came back, a strange quality in his voice. "I was wrong. Olin is out. Shall I have him call you?"

Heath hesitated, looking around the room. "No. I'll call back."

He began to dress. Betty came to the bathroom door,

leaned against the jamb, staring at him with blurred eyes. "Where you going?"

"Back to the hotel."

"You'll be back tonight . . . You know what we've got planned—"

"I'll try to be." He buttoned his clothes swiftly. Suddenly he had to be out of there. Suddenly he needed air. "That new little girl," she went on, "the one with the big—"

"I'll try," he said again. He started for the door, then halted. "I've got a business to see to, you know." Before she could answer he went out.

The fresh air helped, but not much. Back at the hotel he showered in nearly scalding water, scrubbing himself fiercely, trying not to remember last night. Then, somewhat revived, he called Chandlerville again.

He tried three times that day. Olin would not take his call. In the Tin Goose then he flew home and reached Chandlerville at dusk.

Olin's house was across the town, on the opposite side of the valley, a small, neat place, wholly unpretentious. Heath parked the car in the drive, lights gleamed through the windows. He strode up the steps, full of apprehension and defensive anger, slammed open the door, entered without knocking. Olin had heard the car, stood there in the center of the living room. His face bore no expression.

Heath did not even take time to shake hands. "What the hell does this mean?" he snapped, waving the telegram.

"Just what it says," Olin told him.

"I called you all morning long. They said you were out! Where the hell were you?"

"Out—to you." Olin turned away. "I'm going to have a drink. Want one?"

"I want to know what the hell—"

Then Clutterbuck whirled. "All right," he said evenly. "The wire was the only way to get you back. If I'd talked to you on the phone, you'd have put me off." He threw up his hands. "It's all yours," he said.

"What?" Heath blinked.

"The company!" Olin yelled. "Chandler Mills! That's your name on it, not mine! Goddammit, if you want it, you crawl out of bed and run it! I'm taking off!"

Heath froze. "You're what?" he asked incredulously.

"Taking off," Olin said, now quietly.

"You don't mean for good."

"I don't know what I mean." Again Olin turned his back on him, went to a table, began to pour. Heath saw that his hand shook with suppressed tension, emotion of some kind. "Anyhow, I've had no vacation this year. I've got that coming to me. I skipped it when you decided, it seems, to take up permanent residence in Betty Hammond's bedroom." He thrust a drink at Heath, held one himself. "But I'm going to take it now, with or without your leave—at least a month." He drank. "Maybe more. I haven't decided yet. Maybe I'll make it permanent. I'll think about that later. Meanwhile, if you haven't forgotten how to find your office, it's still there."

There was a disgusted finality in his voice Heath had never heard before. They looked at each other; Heath's eyes dropped first under the impact of Olin's.

"I can find it," he said, voice shaking a little. "Where are you going?"

Olin hesitated. "I think Vienna," he said, and he was still looking hard at Heath.

Chandler tensed. "Clutt—"

Olin tossed off the drink. Then Heath saw the coat across the back of the sofa, the two packed suitcases by it. Olin threw the glass into the fireplace; it smashed. He slid into the coat, picked up the suitcases. "I was only waiting until you got back," he said thinly. "I guess the coast is clear now. McLendon can catch you up on anything you need to know, and I left you a long memo too. Lock the door behind you when you go out, will you?" And, carrying the luggage, he stalked past Heath out into the twilight. Chandler stood motionless, staring after him. Outside, he heard a car door slam; then its engine coughed into life, roared. The sound dwindled as Olin drove down the hill. Presently it was gone entirely.

There were no servants now at Chandler House; it was enormous, empty. When Heath closed the front door behind him its sound seemed to echo. He halted in the foyer, switching on lights.

The housekeeper who came in to dust had stacked the mail on a table in the hall. He sorted through the letters, all addressed in Claudia's hand, bearing Austrian stamps. An accumulation of more than three weeks; and he did not open any of them. He could not; he was afraid to. Just, he thought, as he had been afraid to open those from Bolivar when he was overseas. He laid them aside, found some whiskey, went to the kitchen, made a drink. He had that one, and another, and another after that, careful not to think about anything at all. Presently, upstairs, he fell asleep fully clothed. The next morning he found where his cigarette had burned itself out on the carpet; only a miracle had saved him from being burned alive. He was hung over again, and sick. He ate a little breakfast, washed, shaved, had another drink. Then he got in his car and drove to Macedonia.

The manager of the airport would have let no one but Heath Chandler take up the old Jenny, though the ancient biplane was still in superb condition. It was Saturday, a fine, clear, bright November day, Indian summer warm. The plane climbed as if glad to be unleashed; when he rolled and looped it, it seemed to frolic. He straightened out, the world now remote and far away, flew through heaped clouds, and once again he was in utter loneliness, high cleanliness, all connection with the earth severed. Here, at last, he told himself, he could think.

Presently he sideslipped downward. The land below resolved into detail as he left the cloudbank: the winding coil of the Achoa River, blood red in the sun, not far away the sprawl of Chandlerville, the shining silver dazzle of its water tower. He pushed forward on the stick. The plane lost altitude, its wires singing as it rushed downward.

The red water of the river came swiftly up to meet him. At the last minute he came out, kicked the rudder bar, sent the Jenny skidding upstream at full throttle, wheels just above the surface. He held the stick tightly, laughing, but not with humor. Five, ten feet—a little forward pressure would be all it took . . . Then he saw the bridge.

It loomed ahead, a lacy arch of riveted metal braced on massive concrete piers, around which the current swirled with turbulence. It seemed to hurtle toward him; the airplane's top wing was far below the roadway's level. In five seconds more—three, two—he had to pull up— Then the time was past, and he had not touched the controls. The bridge kept coming; he sat quietly, waiting to see what he would do. At the last second he kicked the rudder bar again. Then, with a roar magnified by its enclosure, he rushed between those great concrete piers, beneath the bridge, with inches to spare on either wingtip. For that moment he was in shadow, chill; then he emerged in sunlight, still alive. Something stirred within him. The plane almost grazed a boat of gawking, startled fishermen; roughly he pulled it up. He sent it climbing, climbing, then looped spectacularly into a hurtling dive. He watched the water rush up again, waited until the last minute to move the stick. The Jenny shuddered, racked with pressure, then bit the air and leveled out. He gave more throttle and again slammed along the surface toward the bridge, aiming the airplane like a rifle. Shadow and the engine's roar swallowed him once more; then the sunlight came again. He pulled up, climbed, leveled off, flew back to Macedonia, landed, turned in the plane and paid the rental. Back at Chandler House, he opened the letters, read them. Then he called Neal McLendon. After that he phoned ahead for a ship ticket and caught the midnight train to New York.

He turned away from the hotel window. Well, he had tried to make it up to them, to all of them—to her, to Olin, and to Ramsey. In some measure, certainly he had succeeded; surely by now those obligations were paid off. Life had texture for them all again, and meaning, and he should have been content. Except . . . except that he had no son, no successor. And, without one, he could not pay his final obligation, complete the pattern.

And yet, he thought, beginning to undress, it was not hopeless. There was still a chance. He would not give up yet. He had long since put depression and despair and grief behind him. Ramsey was almost well now, and someday she would marry . . .

He had enjoyed the evening with Baldwin. He slipped into bed, read a new novel for a while, turned off the light, and soon slept soundly.

One more miracle, he thought, as he drifted off. That was all he asked.

4 CLAUDIA WAS WAITING for him on the terrace, and when he closed the French windows behind him, she smiled, green eyes lighting. "Hello, Olin. You're right on time. But then, you always are."

At forty-three, she had not entirely escaped the ravages of middle age; faint fans of lines at the corners of her eyes, a slackening of the skin beneath her chin. Still, she had made good use of the great preservatives of a woman's looks: leisure, money and self-discipline. As always, Clutterbuck felt the impact of her beauty; to him the marks of aging were only accents that emphasized rather than detracted from her loveliness.

He kissed her on the lips briefly. "Well, I sensed matters of great import in your voice. Besides, I wanted to get out of that madhouse. The New Orleans market went crazy and I've been juggling futures all day. That's Heath's meat, but not mine; it always makes my hands sweat and my stomach burn. I guess I'm just not a natural-born gambler."

"Thank God for that. It's a mark of sanity. We can use all the sanity around here we can get. What would you like to drink? I'll do the honors."

He dropped into a wrought-iron chair. "Anything. Gin and tonic?"

"Right." She went to another table set up as a bar. He lit a cigarette, watched her admiringly as she deftly mixed the drinks. In that interval his mind slipped back in time again, to that November in Vienna . . .

He supposed, he thought, he should have known what her answer would be. He remembered the two of them, on his third night there, in the living room of the suite; it was late, Ramsey long since in bed. They had been to the opera, then a late dinner and *Sekt* in the Sacher bar; and she had been almost more than he could bear to look at. After all those grim months, abandoning herself again to irresponsibility, she laughed readily, her wit flashed, years peeled away; her beauty made something clinch within him, physically ache.

And then they had gone upstairs, and there had been more champagne, and—

It had happened naturally; they had simply come together at the same time, and her kiss was greedy, hungry, and she clung to him fiercely, and exultancy flared within him. He had been right; she, too, had abandoned all hope of Heath; she wanted him, needed him. He kissed her again, bore her backward on the sofa; instinctively his hand went to her breasts. She sighed, relaxed in his arms as his mouth played hungrily over the curve of the white throat. He felt her body move beneath him . . . and then she had gone rigid. "Olin," she said.

He hardly heard her.

"Olin," she said with more urgency. He raised his head. Then, suddenly and with surprising strength, she had pulled away, slipped from beneath him. Trembling, face pale, she stood up.

He sat up, dazedly. "Claudia— Damn it, I love you."

"I know," she said. "Olin, I'm sorry. What a rotten damned way to treat you— But, I can't. Not yet. Not right now."

"Claudia, he's lost and gone." His voice was hoarse. "You know I wouldn't have come here otherwise. Wind it up, forget it, forget him. I love you, I have for so long— And we've both got to start all over again. We're not leaving him, he's already left us."

She nodded wordlessly, came to sit by him again, took his hand. She licked her lips, seemed groping for words. "Maybe you're right. You probably are. But—"

He should have known, he thought. Any other woman, maybe, but not her. Oh, she wanted him, at least for this one night; he knew that, and he could sense it now in the pressure of her hands. And he could push it a little further, have her, at least for the next few hours. More times than one he had thought even a few hours would be worth anything. But now he was playing for bigger stakes, and he had to be careful not to spoil anything.

"Olin," she said, "I want to be honest with you. Right now everything in me just cries out to . . . finish what we started. I didn't mean to tease you, it was what I wanted, needed. You probably won't believe this, but in all these months I've been here by myself I haven't . . . there hasn't been any other man."

"Oh, I believe it."

"And not because I'm some little tin goddess. But sooner or later I've got to face him, there has to be some settlement, some resolution. I can't just throw up my hands, turn my back on all these years, all we've got bound up in each other, invested. I can't start something, commit myself to something new until I am sure the old is ended." She pulled her hands away, got up, moved across the room, stood there with her back to him. He wanted to go to her, but he did not.

"It's all too complicated. I'm a lousy liar, and I'd make a rotten cheat, and it wouldn't be any good for either of us. You're probably right, maybe he has just gone away and left us both; and if he has, it will be you I turn to. But before then I still have to go back to him, even for Ramsey's sake if for no other—the doctors say she needs him—and when I do that I don't want anything . . . any new obligation . . . haunting me. Do you understand what I'm driving at?"

"I think so," Olin said heavily.

She turned. "Oh, damn it," she cried angrily, "I wish I were different. It's silly, isn't it? What difference could a night make? Olin—" She stood there poised, and then he knew that all he had to do was speak and move, and for a little while at least—

The last thing he felt then was nobility. The need to take her, and right now, pushed him, drove him. But he fought it back with reason. "It would make a lot of difference to you," he said, knowing that was the truth. The very importance she attached to things like this, to honesty, to the keeping of her bargains, was what made her different from any other woman he had ever met. He could have her now, but when it was over she would have changed, some irretrievable step would have been taken that might poison everything, cost him what he really wanted. Besides, he could afford to wait. He knew how Heath was now. She would have to find out for herself that there was not any way she could keep her bargain, salvage anything, that what she was talking about was hopeless.

He stood up. "All right," he went on. "There's plenty of time."

"Olin . . ." She could not look at him. "I feel so terrible, so foolish, so . . . so God damned prissy."

He laughed shortly; that broke a little of the tension. "Maybe a little prissiness is what this situation needs. God knows, nobody else has displayed any." He came to her, took her by the upper arms. "I didn't come here lightly, and I don't want to be taken lightly, and what you have to decide can't be decided lightly." He paused. "Will you be going back to Chandlerville?"

"If he doesn't come here."

"He won't. Well, we'll talk about it in the morning." He kissed her on the forehead. "Good night." Then, certain that in his own self-interest he was doing the right thing, making the right move, he stepped past her and out the door.

In his room he sat up for a long time before he undressed and went to bed. *It will be you I turn to.* For the moment that promise was enough. That it would come to that there was no doubt, and now he could plan. Exuberantly, his mind raced forward. Within two weeks, he thought, if she went home promptly, it would all be over between Heath and her. Cleanly finished. The divorce would take some time of course. Reno would be quickest. And then— He had money now, and, more important, he had experience and reputation as a businessman. He could get another job somewhere, far away from Chandlerville. And he would make her a better husband, give her more than Heath ever had—

Presently he went to sleep. The next morning he awakened with that eagerness still in him, washed and shaved and dressed very quickly. The world seemed wholly different, and he felt young and curiously light-headed, foolish. He hurried down the corridor to her suite. Then, with his hand raised to knock, he froze.

The sound came again from within, and, with incredulity and sudden fear, he recognized it. Ramsey had not spoken six syllables to him in all these days, but what he heard now was her laughter. It was a sound that turned him cold. He knocked.

Claudia herself opened the door. She looked up at him with a face full of pity and joy. And, staring across her shoulder, he saw, in the middle of the room, Heath Chandler, with his daughter held high in his arms.

And Heath saw him and met his eyes.

"Hello, Clutt," he said.

And only Heath could have done it, he thought, as Claudia crossed the terrace now with the drinks. Only Heath, with a curious mixture of unaccustomed humility and apology and that damned charm of his could have rewoven all that ripped, frayed fabric of their lives, wiped out the past, restored all those relationships to their former balance. But he had known, of course—and had used the knowledge—how great their need of him was, how incomplete their lives must have been without him. What passed between Claudia and him in privacy Clutterbuck never learned; what passed between himself and Heath was strange, elliptical—apology from Heath, no questions asked of Olin, and an assumption, infuriating and yet somehow reassuring, that everything would be as it had been before. No pressure, no urging, but the way was open, the choice clearly his, and Heath's need of him reiterated. And, helplessly, he had chosen in Chandler's favor. Because he could live without Heath if he had Claudia, but without either of them the future was only frightening emptiness.

Eleven years now, and good ones for all of them, Clutterbuck supposed, taking his gin and tonic from Claudia's hand. Heath as sane and balanced as he ever was, his joy in life, his outrageous sense of fun, wholly restored; Claudia's relief and happiness almost painfully unmistakable; and Ramsey— Heath had never been more attentive to Hamp than he was now to her; and the doctors had been right. Her father filled the void that had been for her unbearable, wooed her carefully back to reality with all the force of his magnetic masculinity. She was not, perhaps, wholly healed, nor ever would be. Olin knew that lately there had been trouble . . . But she was a person once again, a young woman almost frighteningly beautiful, who, when she chose to use it, was possessed of a charm inherited from both parents and almost dangerous in its intensity. Like Heath, of course, she was mercurial, swinging from one pole to the other, but she functioned. That was the main thing—she functioned now.

Claudia sat down opposite, raised her own drink. "Cheers."

"Cheers." He drank.

Then she stirred uncomfortably, took out a cigarette; he lit it for her. "Okay. What's on your mind?"

She sighed. "I need some help. I always seem to need some help, and I always seem to call on you. But Heath will listen to you sometimes when he won't to me."

"Not very often. What's the deal? I'll do what I can."

Claudia sighed. "Well, it's Ramsey. I had a letter today from Marta Hoyt. I don't think you know her, but she and I were close friends in New York before the war. She lives in Honolulu now, and she suggested that Ramsey come out and visit her and stay a while. Olin, she ought to go; there's no reason why she shouldn't. But she won't.

Not unless *he* tells her to. And you know how much chance there is of that."

"Maybe she just doesn't want to go to Honolulu."

"She doesn't want to go anywhere away from *him*." Claudia's voice rose. "It's not right. She's twenty-three years old, and there's nothing in this place for her. She ought to be back in Washington or New York or Los Angeles or somewhere. Anywhere she can be on her own . . . stand on her own two feet without him."

"She tried that once without notable success."

"It might have worked. But you know what happened. He made her choose. Between him and Emiliano."

"Emiliano was a fortune-hunting bastard."

"You're echoing Heath."

"He fed her a line about what immense holdings his family had in Mexico."

"They had holdings. Not as much as he claimed, but you've got to make allowances for a young man trying to impress a girl with a lot of money. Anyway, that's not the point. It might have worked if it hadn't been for Heath. He never gave it a chance to work."

She paused. "I thought when I'd persuaded him to let her go to Washington and into war work, I'd made some progress. And when she married Emiliano without getting *his* permission first—well, maybe I should have been distressed, but I wasn't. Even if it was a bad match—and I wasn't sure of that—the main thing was that she was acting on her own, doing something independent of Heath. But of course he wouldn't let her get away with it. He brought her back, had the marriage annulled; despite everything I can do, he's kept her here."

"Well, maybe she's better off."

"How could she be?" Claudia's voice was scathing. "In a place like Chandlerville?" She ground out her cigarette. "I could think so, maybe, if she had moved into a circle somewhere—Macedonia, Charlotte; if she had friends and knew people and lived a life she didn't want to give up. But she doesn't have any of that, won't bother to try. Why should she when he's enough for her?" She hesitated. "This is something the doctors warned me of long

go. When it was healing her, I didn't resent it. But now
the time has come to turn her loose, and he's got to be
persuaded to do it." Suddenly there was intensity in her
voice. "Olin, tell me what you think. I'm afraid that, con-
ciously or not, he's using her."

"For what?"

"You know for what," said Claudia. "Bait."

Olin did not answer. She looked into the distance, toward the upthrusting chimneys of the mill. "He's not free
himself either; you know that. All this expansion, this
building—he's still paying off the interest on that same
old debt."

"Bolivar?"

"Bolivar," she said tonelessly. "And if he lives to be a
thousand, he still can't pay it off. Nothing would pay it
off but to guarantee that old man immortality. He thought
he could through Hamp, and now Hamp's gone and Ramsey's all that's left and—I don't even know whether he's
doing this consciously, Olin. All I know is that he's not
thinking like a father, he's thinking like . . . like a stock-
breeder. He's going to hold Ramsey until he finds the
right man—not for her, but for the mills. And use her to
tie that man down and hold him, use her to find himself
another Hamp."

"You make it sound pretty cold-blooded and dreadful."

"When people use love that way, it always is. Oh, I'm
not *blaming* him, he was used too. And I'm sure he
doesn't see it the way I do; he thinks that what he's doing
is for the best. When I try to explain to him what he's
really doing, he can't seem to understand it. Of course,
with Heath it's hard to tell when he's being devious. He'll
swear she's free to do anything within reason—and then
he'll turn on so much charm, become so damned affec-
ionate toward her, that she's just helpless, beyond exer-
ing her own will at all. Then, when he's gone—as he is
right now—the reaction sets in. She's at loose ends, she
just seems to *haunt* the house. And she wanders off, and
when she comes home I know she's been drinking. Hard.
Harder than a girl that age should—and in the middle
of the day. And . . . I don't know what else she might be

doing. I've heard rumors. For the moment I've put them out of my mind. But she needs to get away, Olin. She's strong enough to do it now, if he'll only let her. And, in time, she can be completely well."

Clutterbuck nodded. He could tell by the intensity of Claudia's face how deeply troubled she was; and there was nothing he would deny her. "When he comes back," he said, "I'll talk to him."

"Thank you," she said quietly and with affection. She looked toward the mill again. "If Ramsey only goes away, learns to stand on her own, builds a life for herself away from here, maybe that will end it. Maybe that will lay that damned old man's ghost once and for all." Then she brightened. "So much for that. Let's have one more drink and dinner."

"Fine. Will Ramsey . . . join us?"

"I don't know," said Claudia. "When Heath's gone, I never know what she will do."

5   IT WAS, HE KNEW, damned foolishness, but somehow he could not leave Chandlerville. Even after the car was ready he kept the boardinghouse room, in which he had meant to spend only one night. Every morning he slept late, then, near noon, drove to Billie Ray's. There he ate a hamburger, drank beer, and waited, not admitting even to himself for what. Sometimes, in a booth, apart from the other customers, he read the clipping again.

Yellowed now, creases reinforced with transparent tape, the newsprint worn thin and fuzzy, it was dated January 12, 1943, and bore the heading OVER THERE, BY WILLIE MORGAN. It had appeared in 108 daily newspapers in the United States, and he could recite it by heart, but it was better to read the words in print.

No grown man enjoys admitting he needs a nursemaid. But Guadalcanal is no place for an amateur, and when I secured permission to share this rifle company's fortunes in combat, Captain Eli Walker, of Alpine, Texas, decided that a fifty-year-old war correspondent needed a mother hen.

"Stick with Ford," said Captain Walker. "He knows the score."

Sergeant Andrew Ford does indeed know the score. Yesterday I accompanied the twenty-two-year-old former North Carolina textile worker on a routine patrol, if such a thing there be here. We made our way through a devastated coconut plantation into the jungle . . .

Andrew's eyes skipped lower.

At the first shot Ford hurled me flat, covering my body with his. Lead from a hidden machine gun mowed the leaves above us. The patrol was pinned down.

"Stay here, damn you." Ford and Platoon Sergeant Jerry W. Hammacher, of Milwaukee, Wis., crawled into the impenetrable foliage. An interminable ten minutes passed, during which at least one inexperienced member of the patrol cringed beneath the unending hail of lead. Then there was the dull explosion of grenades. Immediately the machine gun's chatter ceased. Then the rest of the patrol disposed of two snipers assigned to cover the gun from nearby treetops.

Ford reappeared, sweating profusely, but grinning with relief that his charge—myself—remained unharmed. He and Hammacher had crawled behind the gun, under sniper fire, and grenaded it. Dangerous as it had been, Ford tried to dismiss the incident. "Hell," he said, "I'm too ignorant to be scared."

I didn't believe him for a minute. Like many excellent combat soldiers, Andrew Ford has had his troubles with the Army; he has not always seen eye to eye with those who impose the regulations and restrictions in the rear areas, and he makes no secret of the fact that this is the third time he has worn sergeant's stripes, having been "busted" twice before for insubordination or the like. Rebellious he may be, but there is nothing ignorant about

Sergeant Ford. Indeed, his courage and native intelligence should take him far in civilian life. Meanwhile it
is comforting to have him as my nursemaid.

And, as he folded the clipping and returned it to his
wallet, Andrew would think of Willie then—the wry-
faced, gray-haired little man whom, in a few short weeks,
he had come to love more than anyone else he had ever
known—and he would feel a warmth tempered by grief
at Willie's death. Then, his own image clear in his mind
once more, he would order another beer.

After four days she came.
It was early, the tavern deserted save for Billie Ray and
an old, hunched man sitting at one end of the bar, droning on about the days under the first Chandler, when
each shift in the mill had begun with prayer. But
drowned in senility, beer, the buzz of the fan, his voice
trailed off. Each time the door opened, Andrew turned
and looked, but it was always a casual take-out customer
—until now.
"Hello, Ramsey," Billie Ray said. "How you doin?"
"Fine, thanks." The cool, husky voice, with its accent
neither southern nor Yankee, but—almost English? Remote, seemingly miles away.
"You want some to go?"
Andrew, twisting around, eyed her boldly as she stood
near him at the counter. She wore the same yellow dress
now, though, her hair was unbound. It fell, clean and
shimmering, to her shoulders. She hesitated, looked
around the room, at him and yet through him, as if he
were an object. She seemed gratified at the emptiness of
the place. "Not yet," she said. "I'll have one to drink here
first."
The counterman's brows went up slightly. His eyes
flickered to Andrew and away. "Sho." Ramsey sat down
while he delved in the cooler, leaving a vacant stool between herself and Andrew. Once she turned, looked over
her shoulder at the driveway, as if afraid someone might

be watching her. "How do, Miss Ramsey?" the old man said from the other end of the bar.

She had to look past Andrew. "Hello, Uncle Bud."

"How your daddy and mama?"

Go to hell, old man, Andrew thought. He tried to catch her eyes, but she would not let him. "Fine, thank you. How are all your people?"

"Doon right well, much obliged."

"That's nice." She turned forward, opened her handbag, took out a cigarette. Andrew tensed, hoping that this was a gambit, but she quickly lit it herself, returned pack and lighter to the bag, blew smoke. The counterman poured beer into a glass for her. She watched him intently, and Andrew looked at her, the curves and planes of her profile. He could not say why, but each feature seemed perfectly to match some pattern, some template, he had carried in his head for a long time. He was very tense, heart pounding, palms sweating. He had thought she might be older than he; now he decided she was a little younger. He racked his brain desperately for some way to get past that cool self-containment. For the first time since he could remember he felt apprehension at trying to pick up a girl.

Ramsey sipped her beer, staring fixedly at a sign over the mirror, *If You Don't Like It Here Get Your* (drawing of a donkey) *Out,* as if something important but difficult to decipher was written there. Long, polished nails tapped lightly, nervously, on the counter. Once again she looked over her shoulder outside. Andrew followed suit.

Then he turned around and heard himself say, "That's some car you got out there. Brand new?"

"Yes," she said. Something leaped in him; he had not really expected her to answer. "I've had it about ten days."

He sucked in an emboldened breath. "I don't reckon you know what it'll do yet, do you?"

Now she laughed slightly, as if the question was absurd. "A hundred and ten."

"You've opened it up? And it not broken in?"

She still looked at the donkey. "Oh, it's broken in; break 'em in fast."

"I'll bet you do." Andrew licked dry lips, striving to keep any mill-hand slur or twang from his speech. Somehow, quickly, he had to impress her, engage her interest. "Well, maybe that's what I'll buy when I get out of college. A Cadillac."

She turned slowly, and he could not tell whether it was interest or amusement flaring in those huge green eyes. But at least she was looking at him. "Oh, what school are you in?"

"None, yet, but I'm going." He rushed on. "To Chapel Hill, to study journalism. You know, newspapers. Willie Morgan—you've heard of him?"

She frowned slightly, then there was genuine interest. "The war correspondent?"

"Yeah, him. He was a good friend of mine," Andrew said quickly. "I've got a letter in my wallet from him to the Dean up there now. He wrote it before he was killed." He hesitated, then added: "You're Ramsey Chandler, aren't you?"

"Yes."

"My name's Andrew Ford."

"Oh." Then she said, "Have you ever been in Washington?"

"D.C.?"

"Yes."

"No."

"That's funny." She looked thoughtful. "I thought I'd seen you somewhere before."

"You did. I was in here when you came in the other day."

"Maybe that's where. Where did you know Willie Morgan?"

This was what he had been waiting for. Immediately Andrew whipped out the wallet, moved to the stool beside her, handed her the clipping. "Read this," he said eagerly. "I'll order a couple more beers and we can move over to a booth."

She glanced down at it, surprised, then looked warily

at the counterman, who was carefully busy stacking cases, the old man drowsing in the sun at the room's other end. Andrew held his breath. Then she nodded. "All right," she said, and got up and moved across the room.

Ramsey read so swiftly that at first Andrew could not believe she had taken it all in. But when she leaned back against the wall of the booth and raised her head, he saw to his delight that she was impressed. "Very good," she murmured. Then she added, "It says you used to be a textile worker. Who'd you work for?"

"Butler, in Brackettville," he answered reluctantly. "But I'm not going back, you can bet on that! I'm gonna go to school! I've got the G.I. Bill and I've got money, over three thousand dollars—"

"You must be awfully thrifty." Her voice was faintly mocking, as if that sum did not impress her.

"I won it playing poker. Where I was, there were always big games on payday when we weren't in the line. I'm a good poker player, if I do say so myself, and Willie helped me set up a bank account by mail in San Francisco. Then, boy, when I hit Stateside again, did I ever have myself a time! But I didn't spend *too* much; I've still got plenty stashed away. Willie and I spent a lot of time on Guadal, and he made me see that nobody's gonna get anywhere without a college education. . . . I guess you've already been to college."

"No, not really." Now she was looking at him openly and with genuine curiosity, as if really seeing him for the first time. "I was . . . sick when I was younger, and mostly I've been tutored at home." Suddenly, as if deciding to take him into her confidence, she leaned forward, lowered her voice a little. "Look, you've been in the Pacific, what do you know about Honolulu? My mother wants me to visit somebody out there, and I'm not sure I want to go. What's it like?"

His heart sank. After all this, would it be like with the others? Moving on, just when he had hoped— "I never saw it, except from a troopship. They wouldn't let us go ashore. What do you want to go out there for?"

"I told you, it's my mother that wants me to. I'm perfectly happy right here."

That startled him, though. "In Chandlerville?"

"What's wrong with Chandlerville?"

Then, disgusted with his own stupidity, he remembered that her father owned it. "Nothing," he said lamely. "Only, I thought— You know, you'd be happier in a big town, someplace where there's excitement—"

She smiled, almost laughed; and the way her green eyes lit, just the lift and curve of cheeks and lips, made him strangely and instantly happy. "You sound like my mother." Then she drank the rest of her beer. "Say, would you like to try out my car?"

Andrew blinked. "The Caddy?"

"Why not? You wondered what it would do. Besides"— she made a wild, restless gesture—"I feel like doing something, going somewhere. Just not to Honolulu, that's all. Why don't we go to Charlotte, find someplace there and have another beer?" She looked around. "This is a little public, if you see what I mean."

Something soared with Andrew, and he could not quite believe it, for this was more than he had dared dream of, hope for. "You really mean it?"

"Sure I do."

"Then, hell, yes!" He got up quickly. She stood up briskly, seized her bag, all solemnity gone; she looked happy and excited herself, vivacious.

"Goodbye, Billie Ray!" she called from the door. "Uncle Bud."

Billie Ray looked up. "So long, Ramsey. Come back." The old man did not even hear. They went out, and as they crossed the drive Ramsey gave her keys to Andrew, waited until he opened the door for her, slid in and pulled down her skirt.

"Let's go," she said, smoothing back her hair, and Andrew, hands sweating, got behind the wheel.

He had never driven such a car in his life, all power and responsive smoothness. Racing down the steel-colored highway through the summer afternoon, as intensely aware of the girl beside him as if she were a bonfire, it was all he could do to keep from crying out with sheer exultancy, total excitement and sensation, the triumphant joy of being himself, Andrew Ford. He knew a sense of revelation, as if a door, swinging wide, had revealed possibilities, challenges, glorious beyond imagining and all designed especially for him.

"Don't worry about the cops!" yelled Ramsey above the rush of wind. Her face was vivid, green eyes brilliant with the thrill of speed and danger. "They know this car, they never stop it!"

So he drove faster, and at eighty turned to look at her. Leaning back, eyes closed, she basked in risk and speed as if in sun, throat a smooth, lovely curve, breasts sharp and definite beneath the wind-plastered fabric of the dress. Andrew ached to touch her, but did not yet quite dare, and sent the Cadillac hurtling on.

They roared across the river bridge, along a four-lane highway, into the outskirts of the city, the largest in the state. She directed him at a more sedate pace through wide avenues shaded by gigantic oaks and maples and lined with luxurious, huge, expensive houses, and presently they came to a drive-in restaurant and parked in shade in the lot behind, which was almost deserted at this time of day. A black carhop brought beer, and they drank it slowly while music trickled softly from the radio of the car.

"This is much better," Ramsey said lazily, well away from him on the end of the seat. "Nobody's likely to recognize me here and I can . . . relax a little. How did you like the car?"

"It's a dream."

"You're a good driver. You drive as well as I do, and that's saying a lot, because my father taught me." She seemed happy, at ease, as she stared off into space, glass cradled in her hands. Then he saw a strange thing happening. It was like watching a cloud shadow move across a sunlit meadow; her expression changed, smile mutating into something colder, almost sardonic. "Well, now you know it's all true."

"What?"

"What they say about me in Billie Ray's."

"I don't pay attention to what people say in places like that," he lied quickly, desperately, face burning as he remembered exactly how much attention he·had paid.

"Oh, don't you? Then why did you think you could pick me up?"

Suddenly feeling stranded, caught by this changing mood, Andrew's mind flailed, seeking words. "I didn't. I mean— Look. But I saw you before, the last time you came in there. And— This sounds crazy—"

"What?" She turned on the seat, tucking one leg beneath her, and her eyes, meeting his, almost paralyzed him. She was frowning slightly and her expression was serious, intent, somewhat puzzled. Words poured from him, and he felt foolish, because he was used to controlling the situation with any girl, and this one had him as flustered as a kid.

"I said I saw you, four days ago. And . . . damn it, I just couldn't get you out of my head! I was supposed to be rollin on, but I couldn't *leave!* It wasn't what they said in there, they didn't say much, and anyhow, that wasn't it. It was just that I couldn't *help* myself. For four days now I've gone back there, just waitin for you to come in again—"

"Four days?" She kept looking at him, not into his eyes but staring at his face as if there were something on it or something wrong with it, and he pawed at it. "You could have found a lot of other girls in that time."

"I didn't want another girl, I just— Hell, I said it was crazy."

Then her mood broke again, changed, and she turned away, laughed. "Well, you certainly get what you go after, don't you?"

He found no answer for that. They sat in silence for a moment, Ramsey staring at the fence before them that edged the parking lot. It was heaped with the green vine and white blossoms of honeysuckle. Beyond it a creek polluted to dead blackness by the dye houses of mills up stream, gurgled drowsily.

"All right," she said after a moment. She kept lookin

at the vines. "I'll tell you something. I was wondering if you *would* be there today when I came in."

"You mean that?" whispered Andrew incredulously.

"Yes, I do. I saw you that first day. You know when I asked you if you'd ever been to Washington? I thought sure I'd met you there, some place. It's funny. Today I didn't really plan to be so obvious, sit down so close, but . . . then I was sure again, and I wanted to find out. And you never worked at our mills?"

"No. Only at Butler. And I'm not going back there either."

"Good!" she said. And then another shift in mood, and suddenly she turned toward him again, and now the brightness had come back in her face, her smile was open, natural, happy. And something taut within Andrew seemed to ease and break, and quite unconsciously, baffled, he shook his head, and then he put out a hand to touch hers. She let him keep it there a pair of seconds, then drew away, laughed softly, and said, "This is kind of—eerie. Then, what about you? I mean, besides the clipping." Andrew hesitated. "I know you just got out of the Army," she prompted. "And according to the clipping, you must have been a good soldier—"

"I did all right."

She was almost teasing now. "But rebellious, it said. And demoted twice?"

"Yeah," he said grudgingly, "they busted me." Then suddenly he made up his mind. Tell her everything; it was important to do that. If she became disgusted with him, rejected him, let it happen now, not later, when he was in too deep. Because he knew he was on the edge of something very deep now, and— "Okay," he said defiantly. "Here it is the middle of 1946, the war's been over almost a year and—you wanta know why I'm so late comin home? Well, I was in the stockade for six months. I had what they call bad time to make up before I could get an honorable discharge."

"The stockade?"

"I mean a G.I. jail. I lost my stripes three times, all told, and the third time they stuck me in the pen. So I'll be honest with you, truthful. The first two times I got in trouble, it didn't amount to anything. Officers try to crap on you, you know, when you're an enlisted man, they wanta make damned sure you don't get any ideas about being human. And I'd had enough of that at Butler."

"So you insisted on being human?" Her insight, the way she phrased it, surprised him.

"Yeah," he said. "Yeah, that's the whole thing. But then I learned the ropes and got some sense and found out I could crap on them too, and— It would have been all right if I hadn't gotten framed."

"Framed?"

He swallowed beer, set down his glass. "I had a buddy, we went overseas together, a kind of kid in a way, I looked after him, we went through it all together. Then the war was over and— Well, he had married this girl he knew in high school. Damn, but he was crazy about her. I remember one night before we shipped out, he got drunk and told me about their wedding night. She was only seventeen and had never even . . . I mean, she didn't have any idea of what to do, he had to teach her. Anyhow, all he ever wanted was to get back to her. He'd write her letters all day long, and once he had me take some pictures of him naked, in the shower, and send 'em to her. And he made some money gambling, and then in the black market, sent it all home to her— Then the war was over. We were all waiting to go home, only there weren't enough ships. And he got this cablegram—"

"Oh," she said softly. "From his wife."

"No. From his mother. His wife didn't have the guts to write him." Andrew laughed harshly. "But she'd learned a lot from that weddin night, I reckon, and wasn't about to let it go to waste while he was overseas. Anyhow, she'd got knocked up by another man, took all his money out of the bank, and run off with the guy. Left him high and dry, ten thousand miles from home. He would have killed her if he could have got back Stateside then—"

"What did all this have to do with you?"

"I said he was my friend—and younger. Hell, he looked almost like a girl himself, not much beard, no hair on his chest . . . And we had a major in the outfit—" Andrew drew in a long breath. "The bastard was queer as a nine-dollar bill, and he had, well, this whole group of guys he had gathered around him. Like Browne, my buddy, you know, all young kids. And he wanted Browne too, and played up to him and— Well, when that cablegram came he finally got his chance, I guess."

He picked up his glass, drank. "It was enough to turn your stomach, a sickening thing to watch, the way he moved in. So slick, and Browne half crazy and hating women and— Well, I could see he was gonna screw the poor guy up for the rest of his life. And finally I had a bellyful of it; I just flat out told him to his face to leave the kid alone, to be satisfied with the fairies he already had and not make any new ones. And I warned him, if he didn't lay off of Browne, I'd blow the whistle on him."

He paused, breathing hard as he remembered. "Two days later they had a surprise shakedown inspection on his orders. Two Colt automatics they said had been stolen from battalion headquarters were found in my gear, where he'd had 'em hidden. I pulled a special court-martial, he saw to it that I was convicted, got the stockade . . ."

"I see," she murmured. "And your friend? What about him?"

"I don't know—I never saw him or the major again. They'd both gone home by the time I got out." He broke off. "But that's the way it is. They'll shove you around if you let 'em—"

"Who?"

"Anybody, if you let 'em. Anybody that's got the power to do it. Willie Morgan used to talk about that a lot, before he got killed, explained to me how this war started, all the power a few people had and how they used it, and — That's why he was always out in the field with the troops instead of hanging around the rear echelon lapping up the general's whiskey. He wanted to be able to see plain how people with power were usin it, the truth about what they did with it—" Then he spread his hands. "What the hell, it's over. Maybe it was even a lucky break for me. While I was in the stockade and then pullin my six months of time to make up for it, I made up my mind nobody was ever gonna catch me helpless again, not if I could do anything about it. I studied USAFI courses and got my high-school diploma, and I'll get the rest of my education, and—"

"You hadn't finished high school before you went in the Army?"

"Hell, how many people finish high school in Brackett-ville? They don't even have one there, you have to go fifteen miles. Anyhow, when you're sixteen you go to work, you don't loaf around in school. Besides, I wanted to get out of there so bad I enlisted as soon as I could. But Willie made me see what I had to do. I worked like hell, got a diploma any college will accept. I even passed enough Latin, for God's sake, to get into Carolina, because you got to have it there. And I'm gonna get me a degree too, and—"

"And then what?"

"I don't know. Maybe get me a job where I can be like Willie, on a newspaper or magazine or something, where I can blow the whistle on people like that Goddamn major—" He broke off. "Let's forget about all that. Let's have another beer." And he pushed the horn.

Ramsey was looking at him strangely. "All right," she said, and then said, "No, wait. Get several. Get some to go, and we'll take 'em with us."

Andrew stared at her. "Take 'em with us where?"

"Just someplace else. I'm tired of here."

"Well, sure," he said quietly, puzzled and yet beginning to wonder if— "I didn't mean to upset you," he said.

"You didn't upset me." Now she leaned over, fiddled with the radio, not looking at him. "I want to know the rest about you too."

Before he could answer, the carhop came. He ordered six bottles to go, then turned to her. "There isn't much rest," he said. "I've told you." He could not look at her now, because he could not bring himself to tell her the rest; that would surely revolt her, ruin everything. "I'm just an ex-mill hand, ex-soldier, future I-don't-know-what.

But something. Willie used to say that a war splits time in two. What the world was like before has nothing to do with what it's like afterward, maybe the only reason for a big war is to wipe the slate clean, tear down everything, give everybody who comes out alive a chance to start all over again. Like an amnesty, if you know what that is."

"I know what it is," she said.

"Then what difference does it make what I used to be? All that counts is that there aren't any limits on me now. I can do anything and be anybody I want to be."

She cut off the radio. "Yes," she said, "I believe you can."

Andrew felt a sudden rush of not only desire but strength, decision. "Damned right I can," he grated, and reached for her then, and pulled her around and to him. For a moment he thought she would resist, was prepared for that, but she didn't. Then, holding her tightly, he kissed her, feeling her lips part slightly, her breasts push against his chest. Almost always, kissing a woman, he kept his senses, savored his triumph with a conscious mind. This time it was different. His consciousness was swallowed up in something else, the touch, the feel, the fragrant smell of her, and he seemed to float, mindless, drifting. He did not know how long the kiss lasted; she was the one to break it after an interval of increasingly hungry response. She pulled away, and he came back to reality just as the poker-faced carhop thrust a bag of beer at him.

Ramsey slid away, patting quickly at her hair, shielding her face with one hand. Andrew gave the man two dollars, sat there, face flushed, holding the beer. It was cold through the paper sack. Then Ramsey turned to him, they looked at each other solemnly for a moment, then laughed in wry amusement at the interruption. She reached out. "Let me take that." He could see, he was sure, the outline of her nipples beneath the fabric of the dress.

"Yeah," he said. "Thanks." Suddenly his voice was hoarse. "Now. Where was it you wanted to go?"

With that rapidity to which he was becoming accustomed, her face went curiously grave again. "I thought maybe," she said a little uncertainly, "to the river house."

His heart leaped. "How do we get there?"

"Go ahead," she said. "Back the way we came, and then I'll show you."

6 THE CHANDLERS, Andrew thought, lying drowsily in sunlight on the dock with Ramsey cradled on his arm, scattered houses along behind them the way other people dropped gum wrappers. Rolling his head, he looked at the structure of white clapboard perched on the hill above the wide cove the river made here; save for its pilings, it could have been transplanted from some good residential section of a city. Add to this Chandler House in town, the apartment in New York, the house on Hilton Head, and another in Florida . . . First class, he thought. All the way. The only way to go.

Ramsey stirred against him, and he held her more tightly, feeling a kind of awe at the way his world had changed in less than two weeks. Looking at the river house again, he remembered how surprised he had been at first sight of it ten days before, expecting only a cabin or a lodge of some kind.

That day came vividly back to him. When they had left the parking lot behind the drive-in she had moved to the far end of the seat again, and she spoke only to give him directions. This time she did not lean back in enjoyment of the speed, but sat tensely, upright. He himself had not talked either. He had been afraid to risk a single word that might have popped the bubble. He drove swiftly back through Charlotte, out the highway, across the county line, swung north. Even at eighty miles an hour, it seemed to take forever before she directed him to take a narrow country road that wound through forests and old fields. Presently she had him halt before a narrow, graveled drive that turned off abruptly into thick pine woods, its entrance barred with a heavy chain suspended from concrete posts. He got out, unlocked it with a key from her ring, drove through, locked it behind them again, and they wound down a slope through the woods until, after nearly a mile, white clapboard and the shine of red, muddy river appeared through branches; then the drive widened into a big, graveled turnaround, and they were there.

Andrew shut off the engine. There was a vacuum of silence, no sound except the wind, like running water, in the treetops.

He and Ramsey looked at each other. Then he reached for her, but she eluded him, opened the door, slid out. "Let's go inside," she said. "Give me the keys." He did, and, heart pounding, took the beer. She unlocked the back door of the place and they went in.

Andrew looked around a living room dominated by a rough stone fireplace with a hewn, stained-oak mantel over it. There was carpet on the floor, sofa, easy chairs. The far wall was of sliding glass and, beyond, a spacious, glassed-in porch with other sliding panels was cantilevered out above the river bank. Below that was a floating dock, and then only the placid surface of the huge cove, with no other houses visible around its jungled edges.

He was impressed. As a soldier bound overseas in wartime, he had been invited into one or two upper-middle-class homes; otherwise, surroundings such as these had been accessible to him only in moving pictures. "Nice," he said.

"Yes, it's all right. Let me have the beer." Ramsey took the bag.

He followed her through an arch and down a step into a kitchen shining with appliances. Leaving out two bottles, she stored the beer in a refrigerator, then got two tall glasses from a cupboard. As she turned from the counter with them, he could not help it, the silent intimacy of their surroundings more than he could fight. He seized both her wrists, pulled her to him, kissed her again. He ground his mouth down on hers determinedly, brutally. He sensed a hesitation in her, then she was responding, kissing him with enthusiasm, if not with total passion. But when his right hand left her wrist and after pausing on her back moved hungrily down to stroke the curve of buttock, she broke away, stepped aside. Breathing hard, half smiling, she looked at him without reproach, with warmth. Then she said, "Why don't you open the beer, and we'll go out on the porch."

That was the last thing he wanted to do; he had already glimpsed a bedroom through an open door. But something in him warned against forcing the issue now. Let her set her own pace.

On the big porch overlooking the river he would have, despite his resolutions, reached for her again, but she sat quickly in a deep, basket-bottomed chair, put her feet beneath her, and her knees jutted out protectively. Reluctantly he took another chair just like it, not far away, but too far to reach out and touch her. Sourly now, he wondered how many men before him had sat in it, looking at her like this as she teased them. It was not a thought he liked. But it struck a chord in him: curiosity. Suddenly he was as hungry to know more about her as he was to hold her. Besides, it was plain that she was not ready yet, and, in an ambivalent way, even that made him feel better. Even as he had yearned for her to be easy for him, he had dreaded that she would be, and that it would devalue everything that had happened so far. "All right," he said, control regained. "Now, it's your turn."

"My turn for what?"

"To talk. You had me spoutin. Now you do it."

"Oh," she said, looking out across the water, "you know all about me. You must have heard at Billie Ray's."

"Damn it, I told you, I don't—" Then he broke off. She was looking pleased, and suddenly he realized that this was what she had wanted, teased him into—probing to see how much interest he had in her beyond taking her to bed. Well, that was all right, he did not begrudge her that. "Go ahead," he said. "I want to hear."

"What is there to tell?" Then, reciting like a child:

My name is Elizabeth Ramsey Chandler. I'm twenty-
three years old, height five feet six inches, weight one
hundred and eight, no identifying scars and birthmarks—
visible, anyhow. Unmarried and—"

"You were married once."

She made a wry face. "Oh, you did listen to the stories
after all." Then she was serious. "Yes, I was. But it only
lasted a week before my father had it annulled. That was
when I was in Washington, working as a file clerk, my
only useful occupational specialty, in the Office of Price
Administration." He listened in fascination, as much for
love of the sound of her voice with that clean, precise
pronunciation, that accent almost, not quite foreign, as to
learn what had happened. "His name was Emiliano
Vásquez-Rojas, and he was a colonel in the Mexican Army
and an attaché at their embassy. His family was supposed
to be very rich, but it wasn't. He wanted money, and I'm
afraid he got it. After that my father made me come
home, and I've been here ever since, more than a year
and a half now. What else do you want to know?"

There was one thing he wanted to know very badly
indeed, but he had no way of putting it, sat there in-
articulately. Then she understood.

"Oh," she said crisply. Now her mood had changed
again, her voice was ironic, detached, cool. "All those
other stories. Of course." Her mouth twisted. "Well, obviously they're true, aren't they? Otherwise you wouldn't
be here now, would you?"

"Ramsey, I didn't mean—"

"The thing about me is, Andrew, I'm not a very stable
person." Her voice, her whole attitude, frightened him
slightly now, inexplicably. It was as if she were discussing
someone else entirely, whom she did not like very much.
In fact, you'd be shocked at just how much time and
money has been spent in trying to make me stable, without much luck. When I was young I was . . . very sick."
She touched her temple briefly. "I guess I still am, a little
bit."

"Sick—how?"

"I don't want to talk about it," she said. "That's something I never talk about." She took a long, deep swallow of beer. "The truth," she went on mercilessly, "is that most afternoons I come out here dead alone and drink and swim all by myself, or kill time some other way. That's my chief occupation now, just killing time. But, yes, Andrew. Once in a while. Like today—you understand? Not a tenth as many as they say. But a few." There was almost pleasure in her chill voice now, but he could not tell whether it came from demeaning him or herself. "Maybe three, four, since I came back from Washington." She stopped, drank more beer.

The porch was very silent; he could hear the water lapping at the dock below. His throat seemed clogged with something he could not quite swallow, and there was a sickness lower down, in his belly. "Guys like me," he said. "That you just pick up?"

"You could say that, yes," she answered offhandedly.

"Why?" Even he was surprised at the agony in the single word, the outrage at being reduced, in that instant, to something faceless, shapeless.

His intensity startled her, and she stared at him; then her face changed again. Now it had softened, was even melancholy. "Andrew," she said swiftly, "I'm sorry, truly," and she arose and came to where he sat and knelt beside the chair and took his hand. "That was an ugly, lousy way to say it, but I'm so damned ugly, lousy, sometime that— No. Not the way I made it sound. How can I explain? I don't know how to explain. Partly because I'm only human, sometimes I want, have to have— Like anybody else, you understand? But even that I can control. But sometimes I see a person, like I saw you, and then it's different, it's like something pushing me, something I have to find out—"

"What?" he rasped.

"I don't know, I can't explain. Something I've been searching for, something—" She broke off. "Oh, I'm not making sense. And you've been sweet this afternoon, and this has been fine, and I've spoiled it. I'm sorry." She straightened up, and, reaching, with one hand pulled down his head. Then this time she kissed him, and with

out restraint, mouth open, tongue seeking his. He was
rigid for a second, and then he made a sound and pulled
her up and stood up himself and held her to him, and
she came easily and ground herself against him, and she
made no protest this time as his hand ran avidly over her
body, he himself amazed at how magical and wonderful
the sensation of touching her was, as if she were made of
something different from ordinary woman flesh. Against
the screen behind the open panel, wasps beat and buzzed,
as if there were something in the house they had to have,
and, across the cove, a kingfisher made a ratcheting
sound. Then they broke apart, stared at each other. Ramsey's eyes were huge, wondering, and her breasts rose
and fell as if she gasped for breath. "My God," she
whispered. "My God—"

Andrew moved toward her again. But then, all at
once, her face changed; she took a quick step backward,
head tilted strangely. "Wait," she breathed. "Wait. Be
quiet."

He halted, for she had half turned, was looking up-
river, had out a hand to fend him off. She stood motionless. The wasps bumped the screen; the kingfisher clattered again. Then, he, too, heard it in the distance, the
steady drone of the engine of a small airplane.

Suddenly Ramsey came to life. "Quick!" she snapped.
"We'd better go inside."

"What?"

"It's him," she said. "Off the porch, where he can't see
us. He'll be here in a minute."

"Who?" blurted Andrew.

"Father," she said impatiently. "He's been in New York;
he'll have landed at Charlotte, be flying his own plane
home from there. He'll pass right over and spot the car.
It's better if he doesn't see you with me."

"How can he, even out here?"

All at once she laughed, with an undertone of delight.
"You watch, you'll see. Come on, come on." She took his
wrist, pulled, and he followed her inside. There he
reached for her, but she moved away. "Watch this," she
whispered raptly, pulling back the curtains on a window

that faced the porch. "Come here and watch this." He stood beside her, and this time when he put his arm around her she made no objection; she was intent on the approaching plane.

It flew just too high to be seen itself, but the surrogate of its shadow moved out of the channel and made a traveling blot on the red, rippling surface of the cove. That shadow turned, pointed toward the cabin, skimmed over the water toward the shore. Now the engine roar seemed so close that Andrew thought he could, if he was outside, reach up and touch the plane. It growled overhead, then had passed, was gone.

Angry at the interruption, Andrew snarled, "You see? He couldn't near have—"

"Wait," she said. "He'll be back." And she gave that delighted laugh again, crouched at the window, almost jumping with excitement.

The fading sound, hardly louder than the buzzing of the wasps, changed pitch. Then it was returning. Its volume, intensity, swelled rapidly, back into a roar. It passed the house some distance upstream, then came back; he saw the shadow once again, and then sucked in breath as from below a masking line of trees along the cove the plane appeared, a Stinson hurtling just above the water, wheels nearly skimming. It shot out across the cove—clean, sleek, blue and white, its shadow racing it, wingtips below the level of the forest behind it. One wing dipped, almost touched the surface, as it turned spectacularly. Then, at the level of their eyes, it hurtled toward them. Andrew fought the desire to duck as the plane grew larger, enormous, blanked out his vision, seemed sure to smash headlong into the porch, and

—then, roaring, pulled suddenly upward, white belly flashing. It seemed almost to scrape the eaves; the house vibrated with sound and turbulence. As if its passage sucked her with it, Ramsey ran across the room to another window, looked up and out. Andrew caught a glimpse of blue and white vanishing beyond distant pines.

Then Ramsey turned, face so radiant that Andrew was startled, almost dazzled. "You see? That was his hello telling me he was back, to come on home—" She broke off then in self-awareness. Then she turned away. "Andrew," she said faintly, "I have to go."

"Not now, for Christ's sake," he blurted.

"I do, I really have to. He . . . he will be expecting me to hurry. If I'm late, he'll ask me questions, and besides . . . Please," she said. "I know it's rotten, but I really must."

Andrew only stood there, everything within him collapsed and heavy. For a moment he fought back the impulse to go ahead and take her by force, teach her a lesson—he could do that. But his disappointment and disgust bore down even anger. Then he said bitterly, "Go ahead. It's your car. What about a ride back to Billie Ray's? It's a little far to walk."

She looked at him with a kind of misery. "I really am so sorry, so truly sorry." Then, as if unable to face him, she went out on the porch to get her handbag. He followed her to the door.

"Ramsey?"

"Yes?" Her hands were shaking as she lit a cigarette. She did not look around.

"What about tomorrow? Meeting me here or at Billie Ray's?"

She snapped the lighter closed, turned, took the cigarette from her mouth. Her face was expressionless now. "Andrew, I don't know."

"I can wait at Billie Ray's."

"You don't understand. Things are different when he's home. I don't always have that much freedom."

"I can wait there," Andrew said doggedly.

Her expression softened. "All right, Andrew," she said. "Wait for me. But—"

"What?"

"If I don't come— Then maybe you'd better go on to Chapel Hill."

He was silent for a moment. Then he said, "Yeah. If you don't come, I'll do that."

They closed the house, and she drove at top speed back to the tavern and let him out. It was the rush hour;

there were many cars on the highway. He was surprised when, in public view, before he opened the car door, she leaned over, brushed her lips lightly against his.

"Thank you for the afternoon and everything," she said.

He got out. "I'll be here tomorrow."

She looked at him a moment, only nodded. Then she put the car in gear. Andrew stood motionless as she roared out onto the pavement, and watched her until she was gone.

That night was the longest he had ever spent. The next morning was interminable. There was no hope left in him as he drove to Billie Ray's at noon. He was a fool, and she was some sort of crazy woman, and out of his class anyhow, and—He drank no beer, only coffee, talked to no one and no one talked to him. An hour passed; two; his stomach knotted every time a car approached. At last he left his booth for the counter. "I've had all the coffee I can stand," he rasped. "Gimme a beer; then I'll be movin on."

"Sure," said Billie Ray. He took a bottle from the cooler, stuck its cap into the opener. Somebody put a nickel in the jukebox; Roy Acuff began to wail "The Streamlined Cannonball." The music drowned out the sound of wheels on gravel. Billie Ray shoved the bottle toward Andrew, and then, as the door opened, looked up and past him, smiling.

"Hello, Ramsey," he said.

At first he thought her gaiety of a different sort, the way she was full of life and eagerness, sparkling, was a fraud, an attempt to make up to him for yesterday's fiasco. By the time they reached the river house he understood that it was real, and no sooner were they inside than he understood something else too; she wanted him, and right away. As soon as the door closed behind them she was in his arms, and there was an almost frantic desire in the way she kissed him. When she pulled away, he himself could not wait to hammer into her. Together, Ramsey holding his hand tightly, they went quickly to a small, pleasant bedroom. He reached for her, and threw her down on the bed, and they rolled there for a long minute, hands everywhere on each other and mouths glued together, and then they broke apart and took off their clothes, watching each other as they undressed, and he saw how lovely she was naked, better than he had dared even hope, and her eyes were huge, glistening, and they lay down again this time, and her hair swirled around them as they made love. Lost in her, he again had that strange sensation that her flesh was different. Always before with a strange woman there had been the sense of touching unfamiliar, alien flesh; this was like touching himself. Melting together, he could not tell where he left off and she began.

When it was over, there was none of the usual awkwardness, none of the gulf between people who had no intimacy but that of coupling. They remained linked for a long time, not speaking, lips playing gently over one another until desire rekindled, and it went more slowly this time, was better for her, and she began to moan in a slow, eerie rhythm, and then cried out and clasped him with her thighs, arched her back, clung to him and trembled all over spastically; then that faded and she sank back, panting, making a sound almost like purring deep in her chest. He felt better now, knowing that he had given her satisfaction, dropped his body on hers for a while longer. Then both knew it was time for a cigarette. He lit two and passed her one, and they lay close together on their backs, an ashtray on her stomach, and smoked with a kind of sensuality that was almost sexual in itself, watching the twin gray threads rise and intermingle.

"Thank God you didn't leave," she whispered.

"I was just before doing it."

"I know. I wouldn't have blamed you. But I'm glad you didn't." Her hand moved over his chest and stomach. Then she said, "It was so strange last night. I'm always so glad to see him when he comes home. That whole house changes when he walks in; he just seems to light it up. And he had been away so long this time. But, funny. Even when I drove away from you at Billie Ray's I was feeling different. Going home, I suddenly realized that instead of being glad that he was there, I was sad that I was leaving you. I never had that happen before."

She paused, knocked ash from the cigarette. "And then I was home, and he was there, in all his glory, so to speak. A drink or two already and keyed up, on a high horse, at his most fascinating—and believe me, that's something. And then I saw something else."

She laughed softly. "I didn't realize it before, but when he's been gone a long time like that and just come back, Mother and I are downright silly. Why, suddenly I realized the two of us were competing for his attention like . . . like rivals, like two harem girls for a sultan. And not only that. He was enjoying it, amusing himself by playing us off against each other. Whether he knew he was doing that or not, I don't know—"

"He must be a real hell-roarer," Andrew said. "All I've heard about him, and the way he handled that plane yesterday—" He could afford to speak without bitterness now, even indulge his curiosity."

"He is a great man," Ramsey said simply, "and I love him very much." She closed her eyes, and when she went on, her voice was slurred and dreamy. He took the cigarette from her fingers and crushed it out in the ashtray as she spoke.

"That was really the reason, you see? Sometimes I don't feel *real*. Sometimes I don't even feel like a person, but like a . . . a *ghost*, and then I have to— That's when I drink too much and drive too fast and— That's why I don't want to go to Honolulu, to be away from him. I don't know, maybe that's really why I married Emiliano when I knew it would never work. To make him come and get me and bring me back. It's very funny, Andrew. There are times when I think I'm just . . . a genie in a bottle, only a cloud of smoke, shut up, formless, until *he* uncorks me, lets me out . . ."

"You're not making sense," Andrew said.

"No. I guess not. There's too much about me you don't know."

"Then tell me."

"No. No, it's something I won't talk about." Suddenly she moved away. "Can't talk about," she said, sat up, and all at once she was shivering as if a cold draft blew through the warm room and enveloped her; but there was none. "Not to anybody. Not the doctors, not even Mother, not even him. But I don't have to talk about it with him; he was there, he knows."

"Goddammit, Ramsey." Andrew was alarmed now. He, too, sat up, put his arm about her, pulled her to him. Held her, stroked her hair. "What is all this? Tell me."

"No, no," she muttered. "I don't dare even start to."

He held her a while longer, remembering what he had heard about her brother. That must be it, of course. The trembling stopped; he got up, went to the kitchen. She had brought a bottle with her; he poured two drinks, dropped in ice, a little water, came back to the bedroom. In the doorway he halted. She was getting dressed.

"Ramsey—"

She fastened the bra behind her, turned. "No," she said, looking at him gravely, her eyes big. "No, I'm not going. But . . . somehow it's easier to talk with clothes on. I don't know why. It just is." Then she dropped her hands, stood with them by her sides, naked save for bra and underpants, hair spilling down around tanned shoulders. Her face, with its wide cheekbones and almost pointed chin, looked pinched and was dominated wholly by her eyes. "Get dressed, Andrew," she said. "Let's go out on the porch. I think I do want to tell you, after all."

When she was through he sat there feeling chilled despite the summer afternoon's heat. She had told it carefully, completely, and without a trace of emotion, like a child reciting a hard but perfectly memorized lesson.

"Ramsey," he whispered, "for God's sake, listen. He couldn't have felt anything—not anything at all. I've seen that happen in the Army. Shock. They never feel anything. He didn't know—"

She raised her head, looked at him with a face so terrible, so contorted with grief and strain that it chilled him. The words came from her as if each had to be forced out by an effort of will. "He screamed," she said. "I heard him scream. And . . . he called our names." And then her control broke, she dropped her head, covered her face with her hands, and her whole body was racked as, dryly, convulsively, she began to cry. He stood over her, with no idea of how long the crying lasted, still feeling cold himself as he tried to calm her, quiet her with an occasional awkward touch, a stroking of her hair. He might as well not have been there; it went on until she was drained and empty, her face ghost-pale, almost phosphorescent in its whiteness, when she raised her head.

She swallowed hard. Wordlessly he handed her a drink. She sipped it for the wetness, not the alcohol. She sniffled, cleared her throat thickly. "I knew," she husked. "I knew I was going to have to. Yesterday I knew, just before he came in the plane, that I would have to tell you. And now I have." She said it wonderingly. "I did, didn't I? I told it to you, all of it."

"All of it," he said as she drank again, a long, deep swallow this time. Then she sat there silently, breathing hard, staring out across the cove, chest heaving as if she had just run a long way swiftly.

After a while she turned, mustered a weak smile, pushed at her hair. "I told you I was a little crazy; now you know why." And then she was suddenly serious, serious and terrified at once. "Andrew," she said urgently, "you won't leave me, will you? Not soon, please don't leave me soon."

He dropped to his knees beside her chair. "Hell, no," he said hoarsely. "I won't leave you. The last thing I intend to do is leave you."

They had made love this afternoon, as they had done every afternoon for the past nine days, and again, as had become their custom, had swum in the cove afterward, crawled out on the dock to lie together and dry off in the sun. They were used to lying together that way now, completely used to the rightness of it. Drowsily Ramsey turned, put her arm around his naked chest, kissed his shoulder. "Oh, good gracious," she whispered, "but I love you so much."

But he had been the first one to say it, holding her that afternoon when she had told him about Hamp. And when he had said it, a great weight had seemed to lift from him. And all she had said in reply was to answer simply, "I know. I love you too."

And they had said it to each other perhaps a thousand times over the rest of those days, and each time the change in her became more perceptible, the metamorphosis more astonishing. She had before seemed older than she was; now she seemed much younger. That tense, driven quality, the mercurial change of moods—mostly gone now; and she drank only about a third as much as before. She was happy, glowing with happiness, and that he could be the cause of such a change awed and flattered him. But, then, he had changed too.

He had not realized how much inner turmoil he himself had contained until she eased it. Had not perceived his own loneliness and incompleteness, or understood his own capacity for joy—and being hurt. One thing he had never done till now was to make himself vulnerable to any other human being, except, perhaps, for Vic and Paul, and, of course, Willie Morgan. But never to a girl, never before opening himself up, lying with his vitals exposed, so to speak, and giving her the power, if she chose, to rip them from him.

He had, after all, his own secret, his own memory, locked within him, that had always been almost more than he could bear. Paul and Vic and Willie knew it, but it had taken days before he could be sure enough of her, and of himself, for him to confide in Ramsey. Actually, insatiable for any scrap of knowledge about his life, his family, she had drawn it from him. And while he told her, he had been terrified that she would recoil.

It had made no difference—not to her. But there were people, he thought bitterly, to whom it would. Still, that could not be helped. He was what he was, and could not be blamed for what his mother had been. Ramsey, too, insisted on that. "You only deserve more credit," she said, "for growing up the way you have."

"Maybe," he said. "I guess the credit goes to my uncle. If he hadn't taken me in— I never liked him, but he was all right, I can see that now. Hell, with five kids of his own, and him hardly able to feed even them . . . You couldn't blame him for not bein overjoyed at bein presented with another mouth to feed. But I paid my way soon as I could, God knows. Maybe he didn't smother me with love, but he gave me a place to sleep, and was strict as hell with me, and— If I knew where he was now I'd thank him and try to pay him back."

Well, he thought, lying on the dock, it was temporarily out of his system, anyhow. But he was wise enough to know how hard it was going to make what lay ahead, what must lie ahead. He squeezed Ramsey almost desperately, and she let out a cry. "You're hurting me, wanta break my ribs?" Laughing, she pulled free, sat up, adjusting the halter of the two-piece bathing suit, throwing back her hair. She looked down at him, sobered, and stroked his lips with her fingers. "Andrew," she murmured, "please. Let's do it today. Now, this afternoon. We can go to South Carolina, only twenty, thirty miles. You don't have to wait there—"

"No," Andrew said firmly, sitting up.

"But it's the only way."

"No. It's the wrong way." He found a cigarette, lit it. "Damn it, don't you think I've thought about it backward, forward, sideways? And this has got to be right, absolutely right, every inch of the way. I may not know much, but I know this is the most important thing that ever happened to me, and I'm not going to let it be screwed up or spoiled by doing it some half-assed way."

"But once we're married, what can *he* do to us?"

Andrew looked at her. "Remember the Mexican?"

Ramsey's eyes dropped. "That was different."

"You and I know that. But, him— How's *he* gonna know it? We slip off behind his back, then show up married and drop it in his lap, just like that, he'll be mad as hell and come down on us like a ton of bricks, and I wouldn't blame him. No, not that way. I'm not gonna give *him* the least little thing he can use to break us up."

"What do you want to do, then?" Her voice was tinged with fear.

"What I told you. Go to him, tell him face to face."

"Andrew, you *can't!* It won't work, you don't know him, you don't know what he's *like!*"

"I know what I'm like," Andrew said. "Anyhow, if he turns us down, *then* we can go to South Carolina."

"Then we won't have the chance to. Look, he and Mother ran away, that was how they got married—"

Andrew shook his head. "I said no. Leave it to me. It's my responsibility."

She stared at him a moment, face pale. Then she made a helpless gesture. "All right. Maybe you can do it. Maybe you really can. But . . . give me a little while to pave the way. He'll listen to two people—Mother and Uncle Olin. Let me go to them first."

"There's no need for you to have to go through a lot of crap if you're afraid of him."

She sat up straight. "I'm not afraid of him. I'll . . . talk to Mother tonight and Uncle Olin in the morning."

"Okay," Andrew said. "But make it fast. I'm not good at waiting."

7 SHE HAD WARNED HIM she would not be able to meet him, and Andrew Ford spent the next day in a kind of limbo. All he could think about was the Old Man, the Captain, her father.

This was a legend he had decided to confront. Even in his childhood, admiring tall tales about Heath Chandler had been told in every mill town; here in Chandlerville he had been assaulted by them from every side. Out of bits and pieces, anecdotes and legends—and the memory of that airplane hurtling at the river house—he tried to put together some image of what he was up against.

Well, when he was young he tried t' drink up ever'-

thang that was wet and screw anythang that moved . . .
that was why him and his daddy had that fallin out.

They say one time he was barrelin down the road in
that Caddylac of hisn, eighty miles an ar, the way he allus
goes. This here State Trooper stops him, tells him he's
under arrest fer speedin. "Thet so?" the Ole Man sez.
"Whut's the fine?" Trooper sez it's fifteen dollar. Ole Man
hauls out his wallet, sez, "Here's thirty. I'll be comin back
the same way two ars from now and in a hurry."

Whut about that time them people from the govern-
ment come down here, back in thutty-seven, investigatin
lynchin in the South, they sez, like we hung a nigger ever
day around here. Ole Man knowed they was comin, met
'em hisself at the railroad station, was drivin 'em to his
office. Then they git downtown and, by God, if there ain't
a nigger hangin from ever other lamppost on Bolivar
Street. "Well, gentlemen," Ole Man says, plumb straight-
faced, "looks like you're in luck. Boys musta had a big
night last night." Them fellers like to shit until they
found out the Cap'n had done paid ten niggers outa the
boiler room twenty dollars each to let theyselves be
hoisted up there with a kinda harness around their shoul-
ders so the ropes around their necks wouldn't hurt 'em.

Maybe you think he's funny. You ask me, he's a son of
a bitch.

Well, he don't take no shit. You work for him, you
earn your pay, or man, you're gone! After the union killed
his boy, he was a dangerous man to be around.

That's all right. One night my little gal was down with
pneumonia, looked like she was about to die, he come by
the house and set with me for a whole two hours tryin to
cheer me up. And I never even knowed he knowed my
name.

He throwed my brother outa a company house, no
reason atall except he got drunk and said he wishta hell
the union would come in here. And that ole bastard hears
ever'thing, and next day th' cops come and moved him
out. . . . No notice atall!

Well, hell, he give me a loan to buy my house with,
and give my boy a scholarship to college.

He's makin money hand over fist, rollin in it, but you try to git a raise—

Why, you couldn't git me to work for nobody else but him!

And so the image grew in Andrew's mind, but he was not afraid, only eager to meet the challenge. He had survived a lot of things; he was not afraid of Chandler. Not as long as Ramsey loved him. Her love made him invulnerable, and nobody would balk him from possessing her completely, wholly, legally, not even Heath Chandler himself.

The first night, knowing he would not hear from her, he roamed the town, circling the huge mills with their rows of lighted windows, beautiful in the darkness. He was still able to interpret the thunder from behind them, separate the pound of spinning frames from the clash of looms. They were sounds he hated, and his mouth curled contemptuously.

He drove, too, through the mill villages, feeling pity for the tired people lounging on the porches, the dirty children playing Giant Steps and Red Light in the dusty streets. He knew their lives, how it felt to rise in a cold house at five, dress by the kitchen stove, gulp whatever was for breakfast, rush to be in place when the starting whistle blew, spend the day in a blur of monotonous effort, choking on lint, serving the merciless machines under the eyes of men with no regard for anything not made of iron . . .

The very thought of that clogged his gorge, made him sick. Let them waste themselves; he would not waste Andrew Ford. There was within him too much strength, power, magnificence, waiting to break free; he did not need the mills, all he needed was Ramsey and his abilities. In that moment, angry, exalted, full of himself, he could not wait to confront Heath Chandler. Presently he drove through the town and up the hill and followed the rising road to Chandler House.

He had seen it from below; like a monument, it was visible from every part of town. But now for the first time

he penetrated its grounds, with curiosity and defiance. H
was awed, despite himself, by the great, landscaped law
the huge columns, the many lighted windows—and th
fact that this was Ramsey's home. He tried to will himsel
inside, to see her in those unimaginable surrounding
which were to her so commonplace, and could not. In
burst of sudden, surprising panic he wheeled the ca
raced swiftly away before discovery.

The next day he stayed in his room because she wa
to call him. He hardly dared leave it for meals lest he mi
the summons. Then it came, her voice on the phor
downstairs, low, urgent, as if afraid of being overhear
"Well, I've done it. But I can't tell what they think. All
know is that they want to see you right away!"

He put on the new suit bought especially for this er
counter and drove to Chandler House more slowly tha
he had thought he would, trying to prepare himself f
anything. Despite his bravado, though, his hands we
sweating and his belly contained a leaden weight as I
mounted the steps, rang the bell. A Negro butler a
swered, appraised him with eyes that sorted and grade
him immediately and remorselessly, and, with chilly cc
rectness, let him in.

Inside the house Andrew found himself in an ali
world. Coming from an environment of boards and she
metal and barracks, tents, and foxholes, he was ove
whelmed, dazed, by high ceilings, ornate plasterwork,
sprial staircase, polished floors, great, glittering cut-gla
chandeliers, soft carpets, pier glasses, paintings, tapestri
He stared about with wonder and awe. Even the sm
was unlike anything he'd known—no taint of human u
as if all these expensive furnishings gave off an emanati
of their own, like that of a newly printed dollar. Th
he had adjusted; his mind clicked. A new environme
yes, neither welcoming nor hostile, but in the past fo
years he had confronted all sorts of new environmen
this was just another. Maybe a different kind of jung
His courage came back as the butler led him through
labyrinth to a small sitting room tucked away somewhe
in the depths. Ramsey emerged from it before they reac

ed it, lovely in summer white. Andrew halted. In this
setting, she looked different, a stranger. All at once he
was a little in awe of her. Then she said, "All right, Ned,"
and the butler nodded, vanished, and she took his hand.
His courage returned as she whispered desperately, "I
love you."

"I love you too. How is it?"

She bit her lip. "It could be worse. Come on." She led
him into the room.

Just inside the door they halted. On a sofa near a marble
fireplace sat a woman of breathtaking beauty, a froth
of chiffon veiling ivory shoulders above a bone-white
dress, her hair dull gold in the muted light, her face sculp-
tured, delicate, yet strong and spirited. Her eyes were
like Ramsey's in shape and color, and yet deeper, lit with
more than intelligence, with wisdom. She smiled slightly,
noncommittally, and all at once he felt a certain reassurance; he had not expected any smile at all, but hostility,
even weeping. He felt a thrill; this was Ramsey's mother
and what Ramsey should be, could be, twenty years
hence, and more of a prize worth fighting for than he had
even realized.

Then the man leaning against the mantel said, "Good
evening, Mr. Ford."

Andrew tensed. So this was his adversary.

Dressed in white sport coat, neat tie, and slacks, he
was not extremely large, and yet he gave the impression
of size, and the power within him could be felt at once.
His face was tanned and handsome and wore a certain
cool, cynical and yet quizzical expression that was not
what Andrew had expected either. Strangely, Andrew re-
axed a little as Chandler came forward; he had expected
hostility here too, and a man arrogant or at least dogmatic,
perhaps pompous. There was none of that in Chandler,
nothing wholly overpowering, just as there was nothing
weak or shy. Something about that controlled masculinity
struck a chord in Andrew. He sensed here a man enough
like himself to at least make possible communication in a
common language, terms they both understood. They
were not two totally different breeds, and it was possible

that Chandler was prepared to listen as well as talk. He took the hand, large and a little rough, like that of a workingman who had been for some years retired. In a voice that trembled with apprehension Ramsey said faintly, "Mother, Father, this is Andrew Ford."

"Captain Chandler." He knew enough to use the military title, which took precedence here over "Mister." He made his own handshake strong and vigorous, but not too much so, and then, as Chandler withdrew, turned to the woman. "Mrs. Chandler." She put out a cool, small hand. "How do you do, Mr. Ford? We are glad to meet you." It seemed to him that she offered reassurance.

Then Heath Chandler said, "What about a drink?"

Andrew hesitated; then, determined not to pretend or strive to make a false impression, he said, "Yes, sir."

"Tell Ned, please, Ramsey." She went out obediently. "Sit down, Mr. Ford."

"I'd rather stand, if you don't mind." Instinct told him not to lower himself below the man's eye level.

"Suit yourself." Chandler smiled a little, as if reading Andrew's mind. He went back to the mantel, leaned against it, and suddenly his eyes, like scalpels, seemed to peel away Andrew's skin, his flesh, opening Andrew so he could see inside. Quickly Andrew raised his guard again. Chandler's voice changed too, was harder, blunter. "Ramsey says she wants to marry you, and I assume you want to marry her. She's talked about you considerably, but I think you yourself ought to tell us who and what you are. She said something about a clipping from a newspaper. Maybe we ought to begin with that."

"Yes, sir." He whipped it out and passed it over, blessing Ramsey for giving him this chance to put best foot forward right away; she had done a real job. Chandler read it with incredible speed, handed it to his wife. She took it a bit more slowly, then gave it back to her husband, who returned it to Andrew, as if they followed definite chain of command.

"Not unimpressive," Chandler said crisply. "I knew Willie Morgan slightly. Apparently you were a good soldier, but I don't know that what my daughter needs is combat infantryman. Let's get on. She says you're from Brackettville, worked in Butler's plant before the Army."

"Yes, sir, I was a doffer."

"Uh-huh. And your people?"

This was what Andrew had dreaded, the cruelest ordeal. He realized that he had hoped Ramsey's telling them would be enough to satisfy them, but Chandler would not let him off so easily, was going with sure instinct to the point of vulnerability. Andrew sucked in a deep breath.

Defiantly he said, "All right. My mother was a whore."

The sitting room was hushed all at once. Chandler had not expected this. He stood up straight. "Now, boy, wait a minute."

"No," Andrew said, rushing on. "If Ramsey didn't tell you, she was supposed to. My daddy ran off and left her before I was born, no other way for her to make a livin. We lived in a shack on Bland Street in Charlotte. I remember the men comin in and out. When I was six years old I woke up one mornin and she was dead, somebody had beat her up. I never even heard it. The police came and took me. She had a brother named Doggett over in Brackettville, no other kin. Doggett took me in and raised me." He broke off. "That's what you wanted to make me say, ain't it? That I'm not anything, that I'm just dirt?"

"Andrew!" Ramsey gasped from the doorway. Chandler was looking at him narrowly, face very red, so that a scar on his cheek stood out whitely. Again that hush, and then the butler entered with the drinks.

Chandler gestured; the servant turned to Andrew. Andrew had never needed a drink more in his life; his knees felt weak, his heart was pounding. Still, he made himself deliberately casual as he took the glass. The silence held, stretched, until the others were served. Then the man went out, closed the door.

Heath Chandler said softly: "All right, Andrew. So much for where you came from. Where do you think you're going?"

"To college. To Carolina."

"To study what?"

"I'm not sure yet. Willie Morgan said I ought to wait at least a year, then pick a major. But something. Something I'll be good at."

Now Chandler's lip curled with faint amusement. "Naturally." He took a sip of his drink and looked at the two women on the sofa with silent command. Mrs. Chandler said something polite as she arose; she took Ramsey by the arm. The girl looked at Andrew almost wildly as she was led out, but at the last minute she smiled, conveying love and reassurance and heartening him. Then he and Heath Chandler were alone.

Somehow the atmosphere uncharged itself a little. Chandler took out cigarettes, offered them, and Andrew accepted gratefully. There was a further decompressive moment while they lit them. Then Chandler said quietly, "You haven't done badly so far. I'm not particularly worried about the past, but let's get to the future again. About your schooling: Have you considered the Textile School at State College in Raleigh? You've got a mill background; with a degree in textile engineering—"

"I'm not interested in textile engineering."

"Why not?"

"Because I'm not interested in anything that has to do with cotton mills. I got enough of that at Brackettville to last me a lifetime. I want to do something that's really important."

"I see." Again Chandler smiled a little, but it was not a pleasant smile. Then suddenly his face was hard and cruel. "So you don't want anything to do with cotton mills. All you want to do is marry my daughter. Has it occurred to you, Andrew Ford, that there is no way, no way on this earth, that anybody can marry Ramsey and not have anything to do with cotton mills?"

Andrew stepped back, opened his mouth, but before he could speak, Chandler went on, hammering at him now. "Has it occurred to you that she is my only child? And that I own all these mills myself"—he flung out an arm—"and have nobody to pass them down to except her and the man she marries?" He straightened up, almost contemptuous now. "When she marries, the mills go with her, and the man that marries her had better be prepared to do his share to keep 'em running, because there's no way he can get out from under them. No way, Andrew. It's as simple as that. And maybe that's something you'd better damned well understand before we go any further."

Andrew tensed. His instinctive reaction was to lash back at Chandler, but he squelched that. Nevertheless he raised himself subtly, stretching to emphasize his slight edge in height over Ramsey's father, forcing Chandler to look up to him. "And maybe there's something you'd better understand, Captain Chandler. I love Ramsey and I'm going to marry her, but I'm not going to marry your mills. I don't need your mills—and if you're afraid I'm after your money, forget it. I've been working for my living ever since I can remember, and I can keep on doing it, and I can look out for her too, some way! I'm not like that Mexican—"

"So she told you? All right. Then you know what a mess that was. I'll not have any repetition of it."

"Don't worry, you won't!"

"I know damned well I won't!" And Andrew despaired at the confidence that rang in his voice, the calm assurance of his own power. Chandler drank, set his glass aside. Then suddenly he was gentle, courteous, remote.

"Andrew, I appreciate your honesty, good faith, and, yes, courage, in coming to me like this. It makes you quite a man. All the same, it's necessary for her mother and myself to take a certain responsibility for Ramsey. I'm not sure you know certain matters—"

"I know everything," Andrew said. "About your boy—everything. She told me."

It was as if somebody had hit Heath Chandler. He whirled around, stared at Andrew. "She *told* you?"

"Exactly how it happened."

"I see." Chandler picked up his glass again, drained it. Then he had recovered. "In that case you know how delicate her balance is. Which means she cannot be entrusted—"

"She can be trusted to me. She loves me. She'll be all right when we're married."

Suddenly Chandler, who had half turned, whirled on him. "That's your contention; I'll not accept it!" Then he calmed. "Anyhow," he said crisply, "it makes no difference. You came in here from nowhere, you don't know where you're going, all you know is that you're young and full of piss and vinegar and everything seems simple to you. Well, it's not simple."

His voice rose. "Do you know what Chandler Mills, Incorporated, really is—do you have any *idea*? Six plants all going full blast! This town, growing like a weed, chunks of other property spread out across two states, the cottonseed-oil mill, the banks, the railroad interests . . Can you imagine, have you ever stopped to think what that all represents? How many millions? And the complexity—? Listen, Andrew, this isn't General Motors, no Du Pont or R. J. Reynolds, but it's no one-horse operation either. More than twelve thousand employees, Andrew, and more to come, and all their families and the trades people who live off what they earn, what Chandler Mills, what I, pump into all those towns— And it goes, Andrew. It goes like clockwork, because I made it go that way, put it together wheel by wheel and spring by spring.

"And what will happen if somebody gets hold of it who doesn't know how it works, smashes all that delicate machinery? Can you conceive the consequences to all those people?" His lip curled. "Of course not. You, a kid all randy, full of yourself because you've been to war with no idea of who you are or where you're going or what you want to do— You come in here cold and tell me you're going to marry Ramsey, selah, amen, over and out, march in, appoint yourself custodian of the one person on whom all that hangs, with no more idea of what you're doing than a baby playing with an automatic pistol, and think, because you and Ramsey have decided that you love each other, that's all that matters! Well, you'd better think again, Andrew Ford, and so had she!"

Suddenly he looked faintly abashed at having lost control. He changed his voice again, made it level but no less firm. "Look, boy, I don't give a damn about your background, what your mother was or where you came from,

But I sure as hell care about who you're going to be. I have to, don't you see? You say you're bound for school, to get an education. All right, that's admirable, a step in the right direction, but only a step. Bluntly, I'm not so damned sure you'll make it, considering handicaps I'll admit you can't help; the odds are against you all the way. But that's your problem. Anyhow, I'll give you this chance. You go on to Chapel Hill. Then, after your first year, you come back here, and we'll see how you've grown and where you stand. Then, if both of you are still interested, we'll talk some more."

"A year?" Andrew cawed. "With Ramsey and me apart?" Unconsciously he took a step toward Chandler.

"At least a year. And I'll tell you now you'd better not try to finesse me by talking her into running off—or I'll make you regret the day the Japs didn't get you!"

"Listen," Andrew raged, "don't try that stuff on me. I've been—"

"Scared by experts?" Chandler's grin was ugly. "I don't doubt it. But what makes you think I'm not an expert too?" Then he changed again. "Andrew, I don't have anything against you. But I've nothing for you either. So you'll have to wait at least a year; maybe, if that's not enough, another one."

"And meantime somebody else comes along you think is better and you push Ramsey—"

"It's a chance you'll have to take." His face closed. "Everything I've said is final. Good night, Mr. Ford."

"Captain Chandler, I won't—"

"Good night, sir."

Seething, Andrew hesitated. "It's not final," he said harshly. "I'll tell you now, it's not final." He wheeled, stalked out. In the hall the butler waited to show him to the door, and there was no sign of Ramsey.

The rest of that night was a blur. Twice he called Chandler House, and neither time was the phone even answered. He raged up and down the town, drove madly through the country, yearned for a fight, a chance to smash someone. He did not drink, or, though once or

twice he could have had his fight, vent his frustratio
that way. He would not give Chandler the least excus
to have him rousted out of town or locked up tight. H
held himself in check, slowly cooled, and set himself wit
stubbornness to wait it out, looking for some new angle c
attack. If he could only talk to Ramsey—

Which was impossible. The Old Man had sealed he
up in that big house like a princess in a tower. Eve
when the phone was answered, the butler made it plai
that she was out. He haunted the river house, but sh
never came. Twice he went back to Chandler House it
self, seeking her; the butler blocked his entrance, an
Andrew, fighting down the impulse to smash that smu;
dark face, turned away. This went on for three days. O
the fourth he got a note that she had somehow mailec
*For God's sake, don't leave. DON'T LEAVE. We won
give up. I love you.*

There was no danger of his leaving. Now, in fact, h
would not even quit his room longer than necessary fc
meals for fear she'd try to reach him there and fail. Tw
more days on the borderline of insanity in that dingy li
tle cubicle, with its scabby wallpaper and battered furn
iture . . . then the landlady plodded upstairs, knocked o
his door. Her face was full of wonder and curiosity :
she handed him an envelope bearing the trademark an
return address of Chandler Mills, just delivered by
chauffeur in a Cadillac. Andrew ripped it open wit
shaking hands, extracted a sheet bearing the mill lette
head. *It would be a favor to us if you came to Chandle
House at eight tonight.* Ducally, the broad-nibbed ma
culine scrawl was signed merely *Chandler.*

That was at four; the intervening hours were agon
an eternity of depression and elation, hope and fea
Then, precisely at eight, Andrew confronted Heat
Chandler again in that same living room, while Ramse
and Claudia looked on.

He was in exactly the same position as before, leanin
against the mantel. When Andrew approached, hea
thudding, body geared for anything, he did not com
forward to shake hands. He only took a cigarette fro

his mouth and said, "Hello, Andrew," in a tone neither stiff nor friendly. Ford looked at the women for some clue. They sat tensely on the sofa's edge, the mother's face apprehensive, Ramsey's a study in fear, bafflement; it was obvious that she did not know what was about to happen.

"You sent for me." Andrew's voice was a foolish croak.

"Yes." Then, wordlessly, Chandler ran his eyes over Andrew, tilting his head this way, that, frowning slightly, as if it was very necessary that he know every aspect of the younger man's appearance. He could have been a trader inspecting a horse he had thought of buying. Then, when Andrew could bear it no longer, opened his mouth to speak, Chandler abruptly turned away. He braced his elbows on the mantel, put his head between his hands, as if engaged in concentration so profound it racked him. A full minute passed while he stood like that, oblivious to Andrew and the others, who looked at him blankly. Then, suddenly, he whirled around. His eyes met Andrew's; all at once the face broke into a slow, warm smile. And, as Andrew gaped stupidly, he said briskly, "All right, Andrew Ford. You win. When and how do you two want the wedding?"

Part Three

1 THE LIGHT SHONE eerily through the blue
windows—many of them already smashed by rocks—into
the deserted mill. The silence in here was profound; and
it seemed strange to see all the ranks of machines motionless, inert, freed from the endless cat's cradles of roving
and yarn, the ancient looms of the weave room bereft of
cloth. Andrew could remember when this place had
seethed and hammered with merciless activity, lint flying
like snow, and, sometimes, steam from the boiling water
poured on the floor to maintain humidity making it a
kind of hell.

Lyle Butler, vice-president of Butler Mills and son of
St. John Butler, said, "How soon can you give us an
answer, Andrew? Like Daddy said, Chandler Mills has
got first call on anything you can use, then we'll let the
others in. After that, what's left goes up for auction or to
the junkyard."

"It's all pretty old and rickety, Lyle."

Butler was almost a duplicate of his father, tall, very
lean, handsome. Andrew wondered what he would say
if he knew how many times he had been the envy of a
hungry, desperate boy sweeping in the spinning room
because his father was rich and he lived in a big house
in Macedonia. And, for that matter, what he would say if
he knew that boy walked beside him now on equal terms
as Heath Chandler's son-in-law and representative.

"Yes, sure," Butler agreed. "That's why this plant was

418

expendable. Still, we hope you'll find there's something here you can use."

Andrew folded the inventory sheet, stuck it in his overcoat pocket. Somehow the February chill was worse in here than outside. Suddenly he wanted to be out of this place. "I'll let you know within three days, Lyle. But I don't think there'll be much."

"Well, bargain prices, Andrew. Bargain prices. It's worth it to teach the union a lesson. It was barely breaking even, and this will throw the fear of God into all our other hands. And into yours too." He laughed slightly. "That ought to be worth something to you."

"Yeah," Andrew said. They went downstairs and out into the steep, narrow yard of what had been Butler Plant Number One at Brackettville. Butler carefully locked the main door and then the plant gate behind them. He paid no attention to the four or five chilled-looking pickets marching up and down with scrawled signs. "Thanks for coming, Andrew," he said, shook hands, and got into his Cadillac. Andrew watched him drive away, then went to his own.

He stood there beside it for a moment, looking at the scabby mill village perched on the hillside above the river. It seemed to him that he could feel eyes from up there, watching him. He shivered, got in the car, started the engine, and turned on the heater. The plant was dead, the town was dead; and those people up there in the houses were dead, too, so far as ever finding another job in textiles was concerned. At one stroke St. John Butler had wiped them out, all of them. Brackettville had always been the end of the line, the last resort of those too old or incompetent to hold better jobs elsewhere. Now even it was gone. And every mill hand up there in that village who had joined the union was on a blacklist; his name was known; he would never work in a Carolina mill again.

The big car pulled easily up out of the river valley, across the bridge. There was, Andrew thought, really no reason for him to feel such a sickness. A place like Brackettville should be eliminated anyhow. He had been on the management side of the business long enough now to understand Butler's motivations. Paying the lowest wages in the industry, with the worst working conditions, the mill had been an easy target for the Textile Workers Union of America. They had organized it, and, on the day they had won their plant election, without even waiting for the certification of the election or any negotiations, St. John Butler had closed the plant forever and put the equipment up for sale. Thus at one stroke he had erased a town from the map—and, since it was his mill, his town, he had the right to do that.

As Lyle had said, it was a masterstroke; the hands at all the other Butler mills had had their warning; they would think a long time before they listened to union overtures. Maybe, indeed, the whole industry owed a debt to Butler.

And maybe, Andrew thought, I have been a mill hand too long to share Heath Chandler's sympathy for this move.

At the far end of the bridge he stopped a moment, looked out across the valley. Little threads of smoke climbed up from mill-village chimneys against a slate-gray sky. But not many of them; the greater part of the population of Brackettville had already left or been evicted. The few somehow remaining must feel like survivors of a shipwreck, adrift on a vast, hostile ocean, hoping against hope for miraculous rescue.

Well, he could offer them none; Heath Chandler had been firm about that. The blacklist held for Chandler Mills as well; and by this time he knew the Old Man too well to think of arguing.

He started the car again, drove swiftly through a winter-bitten countryside, wanting to get away from Brackettville as fast as possible. After all, it was no longer part of his life. His life now was the big house in the pecan grove and his office in the Chandler Tower and his vice-presidency of Chandler Mills and his wife and son and father- and mother-in-law, and his forty thousand dollars a year. He had come a long way since Brackettville, and even if it were not entirely the one he had meant to travel, he had no cause for complaint. The restlessness and sadness he felt now would vanish when he got home and had a drink.

But as the big car purred along he had nothing to do but think, and his mind returned again to that pivotal night in 1946, nearly ten years ago, hearing once again Ramsey's delighted cry breaking the stunned silence, seeing Chandler grinning as he himself stood numb and foolish with surprise, relief; and then Claudia moving swiftly to embrace him, eyes shining, lips touching his cheek. "Andrew, I'm so happy. Welcome to the family."

Welcome to the family . . . In that moment, with those words, he had become a Chandler with full credentials—not suspecting what a complicated thing that was. Ramsey kissed him wildly, delightedly, then whirled to her father with the same exuberance. She and Claudia created a shrill pandemonium, and as it swirled around them, Chandler took his arm. His voice was different now, immediately establishing intimacy. "Okay, Andrew. Looks like they were way ahead of me. Three rings, clowns, trained bears on bicycles, seals tooting tin horns, all-day preaching, and dinner on the grounds. Gonna be some wedding. Let's get out of the line of fire and have another drink. I believe we'll need it."

In the booklined room Chandler sat behind the desk, and Andrew faced him tensely, glass in hand. But again the Old Man's voice and manner reassured him.

"Well, the first thing's to get you out of that roach ranch you've been inhabiting. Tomorrow you bring your gear and move in with us until the fatal day."

Doing that, he had entered a new world—and he wondered if they knew what a momentous thing it was for him suddenly to be an accepted, valued member of a family. In Brackettville he had been the poor relation, tolerated, but never cherished. Here it was as if there had been a vacancy that they could not thank him enough for filling.

It was, of course, a world beyond his experience, one of wealth, grace, sensibility, and power, its customs and its artifacts wholly strange to him. But, gently, diplomatically, efficiently and with love, they taught him what he needed to know to move reasonably well through all this strangeness; and he had absorbed their teachings gratefully, without sense of inferiority, and, he prided himself, swiftly enough to win their admiration.

But it had not been easy; he knew so little and there was so much to learn. He had become Claudia's almost helpless captive at once, for she was his chief mentor; and, in a different way, had fallen as hopelessly in love with her as with Ramsey.

His relations with Heath Chandler were more complex. Once the barriers were down between them, they found themselves linked by a bond that had nothing to do with the impending marriage; they liked each other immensely as men, with much in common despite the differences in age and background.

To begin with, they were both survivors, though of different wars, and this had bred in both a kind of fatalistic realism, a contempt for hypocrisy and self-deception. Both, too, were sensualists in a masculine way, with a liking for good liquor, tobacco, women, speed and action, challenge; both were imbued with the gambling instinct, and, as it turned out, both were good, canny poker players. Each had a sense of humor and a bawdy wit; and it was soon evident that, under any circumstances, given a chance, they would have become friends, comrades. But for Andrew there was more than that. Here was a man whose superiority of knowledge and personality was so undeniable that there was no sense of sacrificing independence or pride in submitting to him, learning what he had to teach. Here, Andrew acknowledged to himself, was the kind of man he himself would like to be someday: that was a goal it would be less than simple to achieve. His admiration for Chandler made it easy, satisfying, to settle into a relationship not only of friendship but of son to father.

Only on one matter did they not see eye to eye. "School," the Old Man said a few nights after Andrew moved into Chandler House. "We talked about that once,

but we ought to again. Of course, this wedding's going
to be such a protracted business, it appears, that there's
no hope of your entering before the spring semester."

"I know," Andrew said apprehensively.

Chandler looked at him speculatively from across the
desk. "Have you by any chance reconsidered your plans
for the future? I mean the far future, after graduation."

Andrew flushed. "It's a little early—"

"You mean *no*," Chandler said wryly. "You're still not
panting with desire for the textile business. That it?"

Andrew hesitated miserably, unable to frame an answer
that would seem neither ungrateful nor arrogant.

"All right." Chandler smiled. "Ease off. I'm not going
to pressure you. You've earned the right to make your
own decision on that. I won't deny I'm hoping you'll come
into the company eventually, but I won't make a big
issue out of it. I'd rather not have you at all than to have
you sullen and resentful because you weren't doing what
you wanted to. Anyhow, I'm good for a long while yet,
and there's time." He put his feet up on the desk. "So
we'll forget textile school, and you go ahead at the university. In the long run I'd rather see you get a good
liberal-arts education anyhow. I can hire textile engineers
in profusion, but men with background and flexibility are
harder to come by. Now," he continued briskly, "you've
earned your G.I. money, and I want you to use it. All the
same, Ramsey's used to living in a certain way, one I
don't think the framers of the G.I. Bill envisioned. Besides, you've got a lot of lost ground to make up, considering the quality of your education up to now, and
you're going to need all the elbow room you can get to
do it. You'll do a lot better job in school if you don't have
to sweat every nickel you spend. So I hope you won't take
't amiss if I provide enough financing so you and Ramsey
can both get degrees without having to struggle just to
stay alive."

"Both?" Andrew stared at him.

"Well, she doesn't have one. Never quite ready for the
discipline before, or the being on her own. But maybe
now— She and Claudia have talked about it, and it makes

sense to me. Besides, she can't just twiddle her thumbs while you study." He grinned. "So we'll provide the wherewithal for the two of you to make it—only don't count on footmen, a polo string, or mink-lined toilet seats."

So that was settled. And then, at last, the wedding.

His memory of that, Andrew thought, was still one great colorful blur. The First Baptist, biggest church in Chandlerville, overflowing with a crowd of the powerful and legendary—Chandler's friends, myths made flesh, legends filing down the line at the reception afterward in Chandler House, famous pilots, actors and actresses, soldiers, politicians, bankers and businessmen, and of course the great families of the textile country: Springs, Cannon, Cone, Haines, a host of others. Ramsey was pale and glorious in white satin, Andrew stiff and awkward in cutaway, Olin Clutterbuck calm and reassuring as best man, and Chandler dignified yet at ease, dominating all the rest with his presence. Andrew remembered, too, the handsome, slender, graying man who had shaken his hand, kissed Ramsey on the cheek, smiled cordially and moved on; not until he was farther down the receiving line did Andrew realize this was St. John Butler.

One of their wedding presents from the Chandlers was an ornately wrapped shoebox containing thirty one-hundred-dollar bills. The first week of the wedding trip was spent in New York, the next two in Bermuda. And, as miraculous as everything had seemed to Andrew, Ramsey was still the greatest miracle. He was still in a kind of daze when they returned to Chandlerville, whence, a week later, they left for the university.

Chandler's allowance was generous; they found a small apartment, plunged together into studies. Ramsey, for no particular reason, decided to major in sociology. Andrew, with Willie Morgan's memory and example fresh in his mind, chose journalism. There was within him a desire to make things happen, to exert pressure, force, on the world, to have a lever with which to turn over the rocks under which creatures dwelled like the major who had put the two automatics in his gear and sent him to the stockade. The country, the world, he had decided, was full of such people; he would take up where Willie had left off, making them writhe in the searing light of public exposure, of uncompromising truth.

Now he smiled faintly at his own naïveté. Still, he thought, no life should be bereft of that period of youthful idealism and intensity, dedication. Better to break your heart against the world in giving up your dreams than never to have realized that you had a heart at all.

At first, in school, he was swamped, terrified. As Chandler had warned, he had vast deficits to make up. Soon, though, he discovered in himself a capacity for effort and concentration that Ramsey wholly lacked; she was too happy, too self-realized, to need more accomplishment. Then, as his mind flexed, limbered, some spark of latent intellect burst into flame; miraculously, almost overnight, he could grasp what before he could only grope at, and his mind leaped forward, exulting in its own strength and range.

Chandler was delighted with his grades, and Andrew drank his praise and still craved more. Now he had justified their faith in him, and Willie Morgan's too. More important, his own faith in himself grew. Now he could admit how afraid of failure he had been, of having to slink back under Chandler's wing, with no choices left except some sinecure in Chandler Mills. But he was safe; he was free; the future was one vast tempting feast at which he could sample any dish he chose.

Then he got Ramsey pregnant.

That should have made no difference, caused no abridgment of his independence. Indeed, by siring Lloyd he had given Heath and Claudia the one thing they had most desired, had thus repaid them for all their kindnesses and cleared the balance sheet.

Even now, Andrew thought, he could not sort it all out, make clear sense of what had happened. But suddenly he had lost control over everything without even realizing what was taking place. There was no reason why the pregnancy should have been so difficult; Ramsey was strong, healthy, had followed the doctor's orders. Yet the

child within her seemed a kind of poison; she sickened
and dropped out of school.

That was in their senior year, and for a while their
marriage had been tainted by the poisons in her body.
Andrew, striving to finish college in a burst of glory, was
distracted by her sickness as well as frightened. She
needed attention, reassurance that he could not provide.
When the Chandlers suggested that she come to live at
Chandler House he felt both deserted and relieved. She
seized the invitation with eagerness, and, as it turned out,
it was well she did. Lloyd Andrew Ford was six weeks
premature, and there were postpartum complications.
Ramsey lay ill for some time, drained and listless, with
Claudia relieving her of responsibility for the baby and
Heath Chandler standing in its father's stead.

Still, it might have worked out if Lloyd had not been
such a sickly child. Partly that was due to prematurity,
partly to some inexplicable quirk of heritage, for which
Andrew assumed bitterly he must take the blame, since
he was the one without pedigree or knowledge of his fore-
bears. Anyhow, the baby was never quite well; one ail-
ment after another, so that Ramsey was never quite free
to rejoin Andrew at Chapel Hill. And when he graduated
neither she nor Lloyd was in shape to travel anywhere.

Oh, he thought now, driving, it had all been so subtle.

At least you could listen to him, Ramsey said.

*What good would that do? Damn it, why do you think
I've worked so hard? I know what I want to do. I love
your father, but I don't love his God damned mills!*

*I don't mean forever, darling. But just until we're well
enough, Lloyd's in shape, to go with you. A few months
anyhow—*

And then Chandler, open, frank, and businesslike.

"Andrew, you know we'll be happy to see to Lloyd and
Ramsey if you want to take that New York job. And
frankly, if I were you, I wouldn't turn it down. Damned
few greenhorn graduates get a crack at the big time right
away—mostly, as I understand it, they serve apprentice-
ships on small-town mullet wrappers. You can go ahead
and rest easy that they'll be in good hands."

"I don't know what to do," Andrew said miserably.
"God damn it, Captain, we've been apart so much already . . ."

"I know," Chandler said. "Sometimes it seems as if life is nothing but choosing between the lesser of two evils over and over again. Still, Andrew, there is one alternative I can offer. But only if the terms are clearly understood."

"What do you mean?"

"I mean that I am about to present you with a proposition. This is not a seduction, and it is not a sop I throw to you out of the goodness of my heart because you're my son-in-law and such a dear, sweet fellow." He grinned sardonically, then sobered. "It's something I'm going to do, something that'll take a man with certain qualities to handle, and a challenge that will strain to the breaking point the nerve and guts and ingenuity of anybody who takes it. If you don't accept it, I'll find somebody else. If you do, you'll be expected to perform; and there won't be any easy out for you if you flub it. In short, it's strictly business, stand or fall on your own two feet. With that understood, do you want to hear about it?"

Andrew looked at him warily, but with aroused curiosity. "Captain, let me make one thing clear. I am not the least damned bit interested in this business. I don't want to get entangled in it. I know what I want to do."

Chandler shrugged. "Then at least give me your response to the idea. I value your judgment, and that's all I ask."

"I'll go along with that. Shoot."

The Old Man leaned back, tapping his somewhat irregular and jagged teeth with a pencil. His office in the tower was silent for a moment. Then he said, "Andrew, we've never advertised. Neither have our competitors. We sit down here in obscurity, grinding out our cloth, sell it to the cutting trades; they advertise the garments they make out of it, or the sheets or pillowcases or what have you, and nobody gives a damn who provides the fabric. When Mrs. Joe Doakes goes out to buy a shirt for her spouse or a bra for herself she knows the trade name

Arrow or Maidenform or whatever, and makes her deci
sion accordingly. No prestige attaches to the fact that the
cloth was made by Chandler Mills."

He paused. "It has occurred to me that this is stupid
Even though we don't sell to the final consumer, there
could be vast advantage in making sure that he or, more
often, she knows about us, in establishing an image of
Chandler Mills and Chandler products in her mind. Then
when she goes into a store to buy she will be concerned
not only with the manufacturer's name but with who fur
nished the materials out of which the product is made. In
short, if we can con the consumer into *specifying* prod
ucts made from our constructions, we force the manu
facturer to favor us over our competition. Then it's to
his advantage to feature us in *his* advertising, and the
whole thing pyramids. It gives him an edge and us an
edge; and in this business that's all-important—the edge
The edge is what I've survived on. See what I mean?"

"I think so."

"Now, the time to get such a campaign started is be
fore somebody else gets the idea and gets the jump on
us." He flung out an arm. "Today nobody outside the in
dustry knows or gives a damn about Chandler Mills. Si
months from now I want the first question a consume
asks before she buys to be 'Did Chandler make the cloth?
If we can do that, it could mean one hell of a lot o
money in the till, and, God knows, with the expansion
program I've projected, we could use it. Begin to com
prehend?"

He leaned forward. "I'm not talking about peanuts, and
that's why it's too serious a matter to hinge on nepotism
The trick is to find the right handle, to make Chandle
Mills a well-known name, like Sanforizing, overnight. I
we can do that I'm prepared to shell out some importan
dough. I want to set up a full-fledged advertising depart
ment, establish contact with the New York agencies, find
the right program and approach, and retain full contro
over it from here, and get this thing rolling in the mini
mum of time with maximum impact. To do that I'm go
ing to need somebody wildly creative and with the con

stitution and endurance of a locomotive. When I find that somebody I'll give him a free hand, almost, retaining final approval of course, but with nobody else but him and me having any say. All he has to do is produce, make Chandler a name that everybody knows and asks for, and do it in six months or a year from a standing start. Simple, eh? Maybe you could do it. Or if you can't, maybe you know somebody who could."

He tapped the pencil on the desk. "Because it's going to take a very special sort of man, Andrew. You don't get into the good graces of the family purchasing agent, the great American female, God bless her ample fanny, without all sorts of complicated wooing. She's as practical as a Hungarian pawnbroker and yet as susceptible as a virgin full of Spanish fly. I've already read all sorts of surveys on her purchasing habits and motivations, and they're enough to make strong men weep. Making her fall in love with us is a challenge for any man, and Christ only knows how it can be done. But what I want is this: something that'll rivet everybody's attention instanter. No time wasted. We can't afford the slow approach, four-color pictures of a loom or two slack-jawed females whining over whether a Chandler shirt or pillowcase stays whiter longer. What we have to do is avoid the banal like dogshit on the sidewalk, reach out and grab old Madam Consumer right where she's most ticklish. The man I want will find a way to do that, and his success will show up loud and clear on the balance sheets. If he fails I'll can his ass quicker than Campbell does a soup. Given those terms, are you interested?"

Andrew was silent for a moment. He felt a reluctance, a kind of warning bell ringing in his head. And yet . . . damn it, it was a challenge, a creative one. And he could take it without leaving Ramsey and Lloyd. It was an answer to his problem, tailor-made, God-sent—and yet he knew Chandler well enough to understand that the man meant every word he said. It was business, and he would stand or fall on his performance.

"Well?" Heath asked.

Andrew sucked in a breath. "I'm interested. But one

thing. Whether I succeed or fail, this: I can leave when I want to, and no questions asked, no hard feelings."

Heath smiled. "I would expect it that way. I only hope by then you'll have things rolling so a successor can take over. But even if you don't, when Ramsey and Lloyd are ready to go and you want to move on—" He shrugged. "I won't raise a hand to stop you."

"Then I'll do it," Andrew said.

The Old Man's face lit up. "Fine!" He shoved forward a voluminous file folder. "Here are all the surveys, data, I've accumulated, and a projected budget. Now, climb on your horse and ride off in all directions, and don't come back until you've got something to show me."

"Madam Consumer," Andrew said, lying in darkness with Ramsey beside him. This trip to Manhattan had done wonders for her; she seemed to have regained her strength and to have lost the edginess that had made their marriage tense for the past few weeks. It was good to have her by him like this again, relaxed, beautiful, vital, and very loving. The only thing depressing had been the endless conferences over the past few days with advertising agencies, and the lack of imagination they'd revealed. Experts, more experts, and none able to come up with anything that had not been done a hundred times before. Like sheep, playing it safe, following the leader.

"Madam Consumer," he repeated. "The Old Man says to grab her where she's ticklish. Dammit, where is she ticklish?"

"You know where I'm ticklish." Ramsey moved suggestively.

"Yeah," he grinned. "But if I grab the average housewife there she'll scream rape and call the cops."

"Oh, would she? Maybe not."

"Huh?"

"Most women like to be grabbed there—isn't that what it's for? The thing is, to use a little finesse. Anyhow, I always thought the whole theory of advertising was, when all else fails, use sex."

"It's pretty damned hard to make gray goods sexy. We've tried, and it always comes off either silly or smarmy—nothing the Captain would stand still for."

"I know, I've seen the presentations." She laughed. "How dismal and prissy can you get? Have you ever thought of trying to make it funny?"

"The agencies have done a lot of research. Women don't think sex is funny."

Ramsey voiced an indelicate word. "That's how much they know."

"You think it's funny?"

"Oh, no," she said owlishly. "I think it's divine and sacred."

"You go to hell," he snorted.

"Well, put yourself in a woman's place. Not mine, of course, darling." She stroked his stomach. "But the average housewife's. After a few hundred unimaginative lunges, or a thousand. By then she's either got a sense of humor or she's up the wall."

"I'm not sure I appreciate that statement a God damned bit."

She giggled. "I wasn't lumping you in with the common herd. But you do insist on making something complicated out of what's basically so simple."

"I always thought it was the other way around."

"That's because it's a man's world. Men aren't happy unless things are complicated. They insist that everything must mean *something*. Anyhow, if you appeal to a woman's sense of the ridiculous . . ."

"They just don't have one. I've surveyed women's magazines until I want to vomit. Ketchup, yes. Two thousand ways to cook hamburger. Girdle advertisements that look like illustrations from a Nancy Drew book—"

"But those magazines and advertisements both are made by men—the same pompous bastards you're dealing with right now. They can't get it through their heads that women appreciate a little honest bawdiness. Oh, with cleverness, insouciance—not blatant smut, the way men like it. Sure, they'd howl, but only for appearance's sake, to keep their men happy. Deep inside they'd be flattered that somebody gave them credit for being able to appreciate something besides two thousand ways to cook hamburger. And even if you do outrage 'em, they'll never forget you."

"Hmmm," said Andrew. "And how would I go about this?"

"That's your problem." She threw her thigh across him. "But if it will help any, you're welcome to the use of my ticklish spot."

"Hell's fire," Chandler said, shuffling through the proofs. "These are pretty God damned moldy, Andrew."

"Yes, sir."

"Chandler fabrics cover a multitude of sins—especially between the sheets!" He slammed the desk. "And this picture! What's he doing under there, taking her temperature with a rectal thermometer? And you want me to stake the image of my company on *this?*" But the corners of his mouth twitched as he picked up another layout. "Oh, Jesus, Andrew, come off of it. *Booby Trap.* You want to get every brassiere manufacturer we sell boycotted? And *this* picture! Where'd you get it, from a postcard salesman outside the Louvre?"

"An old cover of *Film Fun.* Cheaper than commissioning an original painting."

"Film Fun? I thought that went out with *Captain Billy's Whizbang!* Good Lord, like two gallon jugs filled with whipped cream. Let's see what else you've got. . . . *No lady ever lost by gambling on a Chandler sheet.* Andrew, are you serious?"

"You wanted something to get us talked about."

"Yeah, but not tarred and feathered. What does the agency think of this?"

"Well, I had to try three different ones before I found one who'd rough it up and try to place it if you okayed it."

"And the magazines?"

"Luce publications, *Look,* they'll take it. So will the fashion magazines. The rest almost threw us out bodily. But we'll get good coverage."

Chandler rubbed his face. "I don't know. This ain't quite what I bargained on. No other company ever used a campaign like this."

"Ramsey thinks it's the right approach."

"Ramsey isn't running Chandler Mills." He raked the proofs together. "Okay. I'll show these to Miss Claudia. She's the only one in the outfit who can lay claim to impeccable taste. If she doesn't upchuck, then I'll consider it."

The next morning he seemed stunned. "Women confuse me sometimes. Claudia can smell vulgarity a mile away, and these things are saturated with it. But"—Heath looked at Andrew blankly—"she thought they were funny. Said it was time somebody recognized women's sense of irony." He rubbed his face. "In my experience women understand irony the way a pig does Beethoven, but you seem to have struck a chord. She's all for 'em. So, okay. We gamble. Finish the damned things, publish them, tighten your sphincter, and get ready to duck."

And after that, no question of leaving Chandler Mills. The campaign's audacity stirred up a minor tempest, provoking articles in magazines, newspapers, a flood of letters ranging from the amused to the outraged—most of the latter, interestingly enough, from men. Andrew could from then on have had his pick of jobs in advertising, but proud and gleeful, savoring his first success, he was eager to follow up, as, overnight, Chandler Mills became literally a household word, and orders poured in from manufacturers eager to capitalize on the publicity.

And that, he thought now, is when he should have heard the jaws of the trap closing—but how could he when they were lined with velvet?

It was, he told himself, absurd. He pressed down on the accelerator, and the car whipped forward. What was there to regret? He had made the choice himself, had been old enough to know what he was doing. He had all the things he had ever dreamed of, and more. In the past five years Chandler had carefully edged him up and out of his initial function into every other aspect of the business: sales, engineering, financial, manufacturing, and the management of the town. And he had mastered all of it, proved himself in every way, and now he was third man in the company, after Heath and Olin. He had reconciled himself long ago to what lay ahead of him: someday he would inherit all of it, the Chandler empire. Since the war it had expanded steadily, plant after plant, and Chandlerville itself, still wholly owned by Heath, sprawled like an octopus. A fortune, millions—so many millions that perhaps not even Heath himself knew their true total, and certainly no outsider did. But wealth that would rank high on any national scale. He thought of the bleak little town he had just left. The distance between there and Chandlerville was far enough for one man to travel in a lifetime; and at thirty-five he was wise enough and old enough to master any disappointment that he had not traveled farther. He shivered again despite the warmth of the heater. The visit to Brackettville had been an ordeal. It, of course, was what accounted for the emptiness in him and the feeling that it had been a long time indeed since he'd been truly happy.

2   THE HOUSE—big, rambling, of antique brick—sat at the foot of the knoll on which Chandler House was built, in a position where it, too, could be viewed from above; and it had cost thirty-five thousand dollars four years before and had been a present from the Chandlers. When Andrew stopped the car in the drive he saw the Royces were already here.

Entering a large foyer dominated by a portrait of Ramsey as a child, painted by Olin Clutterbuck, he went directly to a big room off the living room. On the architect's plans it had been called a drawing room, but with built-in bar, television set, and casual furniture, it was something else now and the center of the Ford family's activities. As Andrew had expected, Ramsey and Vic and Mildred were at the bar.

As always, at his first sight of Ramsey after a day away from her, he felt a pang of love and admiration. A decade had changed her not a bit, except for the addition of a few pounds, which became her. Stunning in beaded white, a Dior Claudia had bought for her in Paris, she came to him, her blonde hair piled on her head emphasizing the sharp cheekbones, great green eyes. He kissed her soundly and felt better at once, that sensation of emptiness fading.

"Hello, darling," she murmured. "Oh, your face is cold."

"A martini will warm it up. Mix me one, huh?" He kissed her again, then turned to Mildred Royce. She came to him and kissed him as soundly as Ramsey had, though more chastely. A small, intense woman in a black sheath, she looked a decade older than his wife, although they were almost the same age. Bearing three children had spread her hips; raising them had overlaid her black hair with silver. Still, she bubbled all the time.

"Ramsey's right," she said. "It's like kissing a healthy dog."

Vic Royce moved in behind her, an enormous man, well over six feet, weighing more than two hundred and fifty, with massive, hairy wrists and legs like oak trunks. His head was almost completely bald, his blue eyes, behind thick-lensed glasses, keen, good-humored. He neither drank nor smoked, but his passion was for sweets, especially ice cream, and his clothes, though expensive, always seemed a bit too small, just outgrown. "Andrew," he rumbled, putting out a great, thick-fingered hand.

Vic Royce had appeared unexpectedly late on a summer's evening four years before while Andrew and Ramsey had been prowling the skeleton of this house after the workmen had left. Just as they turned to go, an old Chevrolet pulled up in the service road, a bulky figure got out, frowned, then grinned strangely. "Hey, Andrew!" it called. Andrew stared, then, struck with incredulous recognition, whooped and ran to meet him.

By then, more than a decade had passed since he and Vic and Paul McCloskey had left houses on the same street in the Brackettville mill village to fight a war. But time made no difference; that childhood bond had been so strong that he and Vic had picked up their friendship exactly where it had left off, for, although both had changed in diverse ways, their lives had run curiously parallel. Vic had served with the artillery in Europe; and that had opened up new vistas. Government money had put him through the first four years of college, and Mildred, whom he had married in his junior year, had worked to get him through law school. He had practiced in Chicago, but after the birth of their third son had decided that a big city was no place to raise a family. Casting about, he had made connection with Bass & Norwood in Macedonia, corporation lawyers representing most of the Macedonia textile manufacturers.

Vic's junior partnership could not, of course, command an income that matched Andrew's, but, nevertheless, the Fords and Royces ran together, almost inseparably, for Ramsey and Mildred had struck it off at once. Andrew managed to ease some of Vic's financial strain by giving him management of the Fords' personal legal affairs. There were weeks at the beach together, shopping trips for the women to New York, Richmond and Atlanta—and a relief from loneliness for all of them, an alternative in an arid environment to the Chandlers or the banal gaiety of the Macedonia Country Club.

"Have a Coke," Andrew said. "Let me go get squared away and look in on Lloyd." He took the martini Ramsey gave him and walked down the hall. There he halted before a door, grimacing. Even out here he could smell the vaporizer. He wondered again how a child sired of such stock could be so sickly. It had to be his fault. Look at Chandler, Claudia, Ramsey—even Fox Ramsey, who had been tough as hickory up until the day, three years ago, when, nearing eighty, he had simply fallen dead in the country store that he had resolutely tended all these years. Thinking of Fox, Andrew felt a pang. He had liked the wizened little man, the outlaw strain of independence in him, the hard clarity of his thinking right up to the end, and his total lack of awe for Heath Chandler. So Lloyd's weakness must have come from him, through his unknown father or some other scrubby ancestor, poor-white farmer or mountain man, whose own sire must have been cast out from God knew where. Whatever Lloyd's deficiencies, they had changed his life drastically, but he must not put that blame on his son; he must take responsibility for that himself.

Then, as he entered the boy's room, compassion and love promptly replaced a certain faint resentment. Lloyd looked around. "Daddy?" He lay propped high in bed, his enormous head dwarfing a seven-year-old body hardly more than a wisp. At Andrew's entrance his blue eyes lit with pleasure in a thin face touched with curious sweetness. There were times when Lloyd seemed older than his age, as if born that way or matured by the constant trial of recurring sickness, but now his delight was vast and wholly childish. Andrew sat down on the bed, kissed his cheek.

"What's this?" The bed was covered with red paper, crayons, scissors. "Been making Valentines?"

"Yes, sir. Wanta see the one I made for Grandma? You can't see the one I made for you, it's a secret." Lloyd held up a huge heart of scarlet construction paper trimmed with lace from fancy paper napkins. Embellished with drawings of birds and flowers, which Andrew thought showed real talent, it bore in the center the scrawled legend, *I love Grandma. Love, Lloyd.*

"That's real nice," Andrew said, but the smell of menthol and eucalyptus in the humid room almost gagged him. "Look, we've got company now, I'll see you later. Okay?"

"Okay." Lloyd picked up the scissors and a piece of paper. Andrew kissed him again, turned his cheek for the boy's kiss in return. Then he went out, and in the hall he sucked in grateful draughts of fresh air.

He went into the bathroom, washed his face, combed his hair, brushed his teeth. The countenance that looked back at him from the mirror was only a little fleshier than it had been in his twenties, and his body was fairly free of fat. He kept himself in shape. A little gray at the temples, that was all. He drained the rest of the martini, and then, because he wanted another one right away, hurried back to the bar. The two women, drinks in hand, had moved to chairs before the fire, were perched on the edges of their seats, chatting. Vic nursed a glass of Coca-Cola at the bar. As Andrew made a fresh drink he said, "I understand you went to Brackettville today."

"That I did."

"How was it?"

Andrew paused. "You haven't been there?"

"No. Since Mama died I try to stay away from there. It's not one of my favorite places."

Andrew saw again those few threads of smoke against a bleak sky, felt the chill of the empty, silent mill. "It was like a God damned tomb," he said. "That's how it was."

Vic nodded. "Will you buy any of the machinery?"

"Probably not. Some of it's the stuff that was there when we were. St. John will sell it at auction; maybe it'll go for scrap."

Vic rolled his glass between his hands. "See anybody we know?"

"I didn't look for anybody. They might have asked me for a job."

"Which you can't give them, naturally."

"Naturally."

"Chandler's supporting St. John Butler?"

"Everybody's supporting St. John Butler. Everybody always supports everybody else when it comes to something like that—the union. Even if you hate his guts, like Chandler does, you support him. It's one for all and all for one against the union."

"And they can't sell the people at auction," Vic said. "Not even the scrap dealers buy people."

"No," said Andrew.

"I'll tell you something in confidence," Vic said. "The union's gonna challenge this before the National Labor Relations Board and in the courts. Butler's right to shut down and sell off his plant. To kill his town."

"I'll tell you this," Andrew said. "Butler can do anything he wants to do. So can anybody else in this busi-

ess. With plants, towns, and people. I don't know
whether the court will uphold it, but it can't change a
act of life." He gestured. "Brackettville's gone. Nothing
-court or anyone—will bring it back."

"Maybe. Anyhow, Butler's approached our firm about
andling the case. There's talk that it may fall to me.
ndrew, if I could take this and win it, it would set the
rm in solid with Butler, and me in solid with my part-
ers. Do you think I ought to take it?"

Andrew looked at him in surprise. Then he laughed
oftly. "Our trouble, Vic, is that we have a tendency to
ive in the past, you and me. Here we are, we've worked
ike hell, or lucked up like hell, to get out of that mill
illage over yonder, we hated it like poison while we were
here . . . And yet we can't stop identifying. Look, we're
ut of that world now and in another one, and neither
ne of us has left anything behind—and if we don't re-
nember that, we'll both be schizophrenics."

He drank, waved his hand in a gesture. "Listen, I do
what Butler did every day on a smaller scale. About three
nonths ago the Old Man assigned me total responsibility
or the town, for Chandlerville. I hold a meeting once a
veek and lay down policy; I receive reports from spies
nd informers; I settle and arbitrate disputes, and always
n favor of the mills. That's part of my job, part of the
rice I pay for . . . for all this. And sometimes I have to
ust . . . wipe out people . . . banish them from the king-
lom, take away their livings, their homes . . . I had a case
ike that the other day. The newspaper hired a young
eporter, just out of journalism school, all full of beans.
Ie never did get it through his head the way things
vork here, he kept trying to *expose* us. In our *own* news-
aper. I had to tell Ed Fisher, the editor, to fire him."

"Wait a minute," Vic said. "I didn't mean to open a
ucket of worms."

"Well, you have to talk to somebody, and so do I. Any-
low, I'm citing an illustration. The facts of life are that
n a company town the company calls the turn, and you
lon't get crossways of it if you know what's healthy for
ou. And that holds true for Chandlerville just as much

as for Brackettville. I'm not equating the Chandlers wit
the Butlers—Christ forbid. But there are certain impera
tives, the imperatives of the mills, and either you g
along with them or you get out; it's as simple as tha
If you've got a big chunk of your life invested, like yo
and me, for better or for worse, you don't get out. I kno
how you feel—there was a while this afternoon when
wanted to gag. But then, suppose the union had brough
it off? It's just another competitor." He tapped the ba
"All it's interested in nowadays is dues, money—an
power. The only question being who uses the Bracket
ville people for pawns, the union or Butler? Hell, yes, tal
the case, and fight it, win it, make a name for yourself

Breaking off, he could feel Vic staring at him. "I nev
heard you talk like this before," Vic said.

"It's the hangover from Brackettville. That and a
proaching male menopause." Andrew laughed short
Then, as the telephone rang, he said, "Excuse me." H
picked it up. "Hello? Andrew Ford."

"Andrew." The voice at the other end was rich, viri
though Heath Chandler was sixty now. "Good evenin
son."

"Evening, Captain."

"You've been to Brackettville?"

"Yes, sir. Captain, there's nothing over there we war
Just a mess of junk."

"I figured that, but we had to do St. John the courtes
I wish you would see me in the office tomorrow, thoug
and give me a complete rundown. Meanwhile I've g
another little chore for you, considering the fact that (a
it's cold outside and (b) you're the official town wh
now."

"Yes, sir."

"I originally committed myself tonight to crown
queen. Seems Bolivar Junior High's electing a Queen
Hearts tonight at its Valentine's party, and they want
high mogul from the company to bestow the crown.
wonder if you'd run over there about nine and do th
honors for the pubescent princess? I stepped out the fro

oor and that wind went through my old bones like a
arrage of razor blades, but I do think somebody ought
be present to show the company flag, and your circula-
on's a hell of a lot better than mine. Would you be dis-
ombobulated terribly?"

"Not at all."

"Good for you. I would vastly appreciate it. And, look—
y ten tomorrow? I've got several important things I
ant to talk over with you."

"Yes, sir."

"Smooch Ramsey for me. Not to mention Lloyd. Much
bliged, son. Good night."

"Good night," Andrew said, and hung up. He looked at
ic wryly. "My master's voice. We've got to go out in a
ttle while. But meantime I can snatch another drink and
e can have some dinner."

With Ramsey beside him in the front, the Royces in the
ack, Andrew drove across the town.

It was not a short trip to the other side of Chandlerville,
here Bolivar Junior High, built by the county, was lo-
ated on land donated by Heath Chandler. Their journey
ook them past mill villages, through an ever-enlarging
usiness district, almost deserted at this time of night, but
s shop windows lit and fairly opulent, and then through
new development of small brick ranch houses, into
hich some of the hands had moved after careful screen-
g by Chandler Mills. A few enclaves like this, in which
eliable employees could own their own homes, with fi-
ancing from Chandler banks, had been set up in prefer-
nce to building more mill housing, although it almost
terally hurt Heath, Andrew could tell, to relinquish title
a square foot of his domain, vitiate his control by even
hat much. But since he held the mortgages, there was
ot much dilution of Chandler authority.

Thirty thousand people now; and Andrew could not
elp a certain awe at the realization that he himself, as
rown prince of this state within a state, could dispose of
hem and their affairs as he saw fit. Only Kannapolis, the
olding of Cannon Mills on the other side of Charlotte,

equaled Chandlerville in size; together they comprised
the two largest unincorporated towns in the United
States. There were still plenty of small company towns
scattered across the country, but only Chandler and the
Cannons owned full-sized cities outright, and ran them to
suit themselves.

And every day it grew larger, Chandlerville. Partly that
was the result of Heath's expansion mania, partly the result of external forces. Farming, more mechanized every
year, and with small crop allotments, required less labor,
and people from the country swarmed to town. Even the
Negroes—though no one hated blacks more than the people who had fled to the mills to escape their competition.
There were few jobs for them in the company. But as
other businesses sprang up to cater to the expanding
population, most of them somehow found work, and for
the first time Chandlerville was developing a black
quarter.

Andrew, after all his time in Chandlerville, did not discount the errand he was on tonight. It was just another
way of forestalling challenge to Chandler rule. The carrot
of paternalism, Andrew thought, the Chandlers always
working hard to maintain the ancient fiction of clan and
chieftain, binding loyalties to the family in more ways
than one. And the whip of economic interest; Chandler
Mills was the heart from which the money pumped
through all the veins and arteries of this place, and no one
dared to take the risk of being cut off from that vital circulation. Nor was there any interference from state government. Textiles owned it; and Chandler was a name to
reckon with in textiles.

Yes, Andrew thought, he had learned a lot about power
in the past ten years. Heath Chandler had taught him
that in many ways.

Then, ahead, he saw the yellow oblongs of the lighted
windows of the junior high school gymnasium. He eased
into the crowded parking lot behind the big new building,
stopped the car, got out. As the Royces followed suit, he
went around to open the door for Ramsey.

He took her arm, and they went into the gym, the oyces following.

Inside, the vast room was festooned with swags and bbons of crepe paper, decorated with paper hearts displaying in their construction more enthusiasm than artistic enius. Music whanged from the jukebox paid for by Chandler Mills, to blend with the raucous, unstable voices f a swarm of adolescents. And, despite its temporary and omantic new incarnation, the whole place smelled irreeemably of musky, athletic sweat. The sexes had coascsced into opposing clots on either side, boys gawky and esperate in coats and ties; girls like slim-stalked flowers n their party dresses on the left, a few of them, exasperted, dancing with one another in the center. The genders iingled only at tubs of iced soft drinks along the walls nd tables laden with potato chips and grocery-store upcakes, while harried teachers ranged the place with uspicious eyes, and a cluster of adults hovered around dais made of wooden crates covered with red paper, opped by a decorated office chair set up as a throne. The 'ords, of course, were recognized. And as they entered, ripple of excitement went through the crowd, a flashulb popped as a photographer for the *Free Press,* owned otally by Chandler Mills, took their picture. The princial, a bulky, crew-cut man of thirty, who looked like an rmy major even in a blue serge suit too heavy for the eat all these bodies had generated, registered relief as e came to welcome Andrew.

"Captain Chandler couldn't come," said Andrew, shakng the man's hand. "I hope I'll do."

"Fine, fine." The major—no, Andrew thought, principal -mopped his forehead with a handkerchief. "You folks ave a Coca-Cola?"

"No, thanks. Actually, if it fits in with your schedule, ve'd like to get right down to the coronation."

"We'll make it fit. Now—you know the way this works?"

"Not really. I never crowned a Valentine's Day queen efore."

"Well, first I'll make a little speech, you know. Read out he names of the runners-up, maids of honor. They come

forward, and you don't have to do anything then. And
then I name the queen, and— Miss Harnett, you got that
crown there?" He took it from her, made of heavy cardboard taped all around with gold paper. "Here. You put
this on her head. You know—'I crown thee Queen of
Hearts of Bolivar Junior High, long may you reign,' or
something. Then you give her this Valentine box of candy
from the PTA."

Andrew was careful not to meet Ramsey's eyes or those
of the Royces. "Sure," he said seriously. "It doesn't sound
too complicated."

"Oh, no. Everything's bound to go all right." Suddenly
Andrew felt compassion for this harried, sweating man
so tense in royalty's presence—not that of the putative
queen, but of Heath Chandler's kin. "Miss Harnett, if
you'll unplug that piccolo . . ."

"Who is your winner?" Ramsey asked.

"Oh, we knew she'd win all along. The most popular
girl in school. And the brightest too. Her name's Linda
Vereen."

"Does she have any connection with the mills?"

"Oh, yes, her father's worked there for ten years. Her
mother's dead." The principal grabbed Andrew's arm,
bent close. "Mr. Ford, this is a remarkable ninth-grader.
She's got a straight-A average, she's president of the senior
class—the only girl in the history of Bolivar Junior High
to hold that office."

Andrew nodded, forbearing to mention that the school
had been open only three years.

"Anyhow," the man went on, "she's earned it. Especially
when you consider that her mother died years ago. I
don't see how she does it—all our important clubs, the
Girl Scouts, First Baptist Church, one-hundred-percent
attendance at Sunday school, you know." He let go of
the arm, backed off a step. Now he was serious and even
impressive. "I respect this girl, Mr. Ford, and I'm glad
she won. She's overcome a lot of handicaps, being mother-
less and all." In that moment, beneath the layers of bureaucracy, Andrew discerned a man who had found a
vocation, and his own face lost what surely must have

een a smirk. "We don't get many like her. I want you to
ake a good look at her. Remember her. Because I don't
hink she'll ever make college on her own, but if she does
s well in high school as she has here . . ."

"We'll keep an eye on her," Ramsey said. "Our policy
s to make sure nobody worthwhile is wasted. What did
ou say her name is?"

"Linda Vereen. She's fourteen now. . . . Look, will you
xcuse me, since you're in a hurry?"

"Go ahead," said Andrew.

"Thanks." He mounted the dais. His voice rang out
bove the crowd, already silenced by the abrupt cessation
f the music. "Ladies and gentlemen—"

"I like that," Ramsey whispered. "He didn't call them
oys and girls."

"Hush," said Andrew.

". . . moment we've all been waiting for, the crowning
f Miss Bolivar Junior High 1956 Valentine's Day Miss
Queen of Hearts. We're greatly honored tonight to have
vith us Mr. Andrew Ford, vice-president of Chandler
Mills, Mrs. Ford, and their distinguished guests. Mr. Ford
vill bestow the crown on the lucky winner. Now, of
ourse we can't all be winners in a contest like this, but
ve can all learn something from the process of voting for
ur favorites—democracy in action . . ."

Andrew waited for the three interminable minutes of
nspiration that followed. They were all so *young!* he
hought. Those smooth, unlined faces upturned suspense-
ully, awaiting revelation. What would become of them?
Thinking that his own life had turned out to be so much
etter and so much worse than he had ever dreamed, he
elt a huge compassion for them.

". . . and in the best tradition of America, we congratu-
ate the winner and say '*Well done*' to those who tried!
Remember, the majority rules, and it's the will of the
najority that has made this country great. Now, heh-heh,
've talked long enough. Let's get to the important busi-
ess." He surveyed the massed children with deliberate,
antalizing silence. "Maids of Honor. First Maid of Honor
—Miss Earleen Jones!" He clapped high-held hands loud-

ly, and there was vast applause as a willowy, breastless
girl in a dress matching the furious pink of her complexion came forward. Taking her hand, the principal led her
to the left of the throne.

"Next, *First* Maid of Honor—Miss Mary Jo Tewl!" The
applause was louder as a really striking brunette with
breasts that were more than intimations mounted the dais
and took regal station to the throne's right.

Now the gym was hushed. The principal cleared his
throat. "And last but certainly not least, Bolivar Junior
High's Miss Queen of Hearts, 1956"—he paused, flung up
both hands—"*Miss Linda Vereen!*"

The roar was deafening, punctuated with screams and
whistles. The principal bent down to Andrew. "Mr. Ford,
if you will—"

Andrew stood blankly. Ramsey nudged him. "Give her
your *arm*, dolt! Escort her to the throne!"

"Who?" Andrew stared at the crowd. Then he saw her.
When she materialized at its edge, the garish light
caught the color of long hair more delicate than Ramsey's
spun gold, arranged around a plump, oval face, ivory
white, with huge, long-lashed gray-blue eyes. She was
not tall, and she was a few pounds overweight, and must
have designed her white dress, which was demure with
ruffles, to hide this fact, but it could not mask either
breasts or hips far too large and voluptuous for a girl so
young. The moment Andrew's eyes came to rest on her he
knew she was the one; there could be no other. Meeting
his gaze, she smiled shyly. The uproar continued, swelled
as Ramsey pushed him and he went forward to get her.
He presented his arm with all the suavity he could muster
and she took it with a matter-of-fact ease that would
have done credit to a Plantagenet or Windsor.

Up close he could see that her complexion was flawless,
her features kittenish, childishly rubicund, yet concealing
the promise of great beauty. She smiled at him as he
looked down at her, and her lips, bereft of makeup, were
pink enough and soft and ripe, revealing white, perfect
teeth. Her fingers dug down through his sleeve, and it
was she who gave the signal to start, straining forward

a little, and he led her up to the dais. Not once did she display awkwardness mounting that orange-crate eminence. And when the principal took her hand she turned, very gracefully and smoothly, and manipulating the full skirt with her free hand, sat down slowly, adjusting the fullness and flounce of the intricate dress unconsciously, smiling out at the crowd exactly as if she were saying "cheese." That hit Andrew as he climbed the dais: How many times, in her imagination, had she done this? Bette Davis in *Elizabeth and Essex*? Or Deborah Kerr, or who? One of the maids of honor, the least beautiful, leaned over and kissed her impulsively on the cheek, as if even female envy could not stand against her radiance; and a flashbulb went off.

Then the principal handed Andrew the crown. "Like I said—Miss Bolivar Junior High Queen of Hearts, 1956."

"Yes," answered Andrew. Crown in hand, he moved to confront the girl. She looked up at him with those great gray-blue eyes. Sparkling at first, suddenly they fastened on the crown, and then they were astonishingly sober. As Andrew lowered it she raised both hands in an instinctive, greedy gesture. "No," he whispered, but she had already caught herself and dropped them. He put the gilt-wrapped cardboard on her head. When it touched her hair she let out an involuntary and completely juvenile nervous giggle. Andrew grinned. "I crown thee," he bellowed, "Miss Bolivar Junior High Queen of Hearts, 1956! Long may you reign!"

He wheeled aside, raised his hands and clapped them. Pandemonium erupted in the gym. The other maid of honor curtsied and presented the queen with a scepter—a length of gilded broomstick wrapped in ribbon. Then Andrew took a four-pound heart-shaped box of candy from the principal and laid it in her lap. She stared down at it, then raised her face. "Thank you," the pink, full lips said soundlessly. Tears glistened on white, rounded cheeks. "Thank you."

"All right," Andrew whispered. He turned away. Somehow he felt shaken, affected, by this encounter.

Later, after he had made his speech, they left the gym. The night air was crisp and biting. "Wow," Vic Royce said. "Wish I was fourteen again."

"Mentally you are," said Mildred brassily.

"A fine speech, Andrew, a real fine speech. The future of Chandlerville is its youth. Not cannon fodder; loom fodder."

"Go to hell," said Andrew quietly. He was thinking about the girl.

Ramsey slipped her arm through his, and her hip brushed him. At the same time she laid her angular face against his shoulder. "I know," she said with perception. "She was quite something, wasn't she?"

"Yeah," Andrew said.

"And coming from that background—" They walked around the car, and he opened a door for her as Vic did the same for Mildred. "And only her father—" Gracefully she slipped in. "Yes," she said before he shut the door. "Yes, I'll have to tell Mother about her."

Andrew and Vic got in from the other side. "Look," Mildred was saying. "Of course she made that dress herself. But think of her incentive. She knew she'd be picked."

"Certainly," Ramsey said. "She knows there's too much of her to waste on some ignorant linthead."

"Don't worry." That brassiness was still in Mildred's voice. "She won't waste it. What you saw back there is the material your movie stars are made of, and your great courtesans."

"Maybe." Ramsey paused. "Still . . . she was just a child. So vulnerable."

"Child, shit," said Mildred. "That one will make it, don't worry. It's written all over her."

"All the same, I'm going to speak to Mother about her."

Andrew started the car. "Yeah," he said, "I think Claudia would be interested in her."

"I'm interested in another drink," said Mildred. "That's what I'm interested in."

"Andrew," said Vic, "do you have any ice cream at home?"

"As a matter of fact, we do," Andrew said. "We knew ou were coming. But I'm sorry. It's only a quart."

When the Royces had gone Andrew and Ramsey went to their bedroom. He watched her undress after she had taken off makeup and the barbaric earrings she had worn. Her body was still lithe and youthful, and she moved before him naked without shame, even with enticement. He could read desire in her muted exhibitionism. And she was, he thought, so damned lovely, and—

And yet, oddly, for the moment he felt no response. That was for him unusual. He looked at her, padding to the closet, staring at the line and curve of body, so long familiar, yet so well loved, and suddenly he felt something he had never felt before. It was a surge of bitterness, almost hatred, that welled up in him, and it was directed at her mindlessly, without reason. It startled, even frightened him, and then it ebbed as quickly as it had come, a strange mindless jealousy and fury at being wronged. But she had not wronged him, in no way had she wronged him. Why, in that instant, had he seen in her an enemy?

Then he was all right again, feeling contrition at his own momentary aberration, and the contrition turning into love, and love turning into desire, and when she came to bed he was ready for her. They made love, and not until it was over did Andrew feel anything but exhilaration.

Afterward, though, while she slept he lay awake, staring at the ceiling with a growing oppression, a sense of grief and loss, a longing to possess again something he had never owned. It nagged him until at last he drifted into fitful sleep.

3 AT THIS TIME of morning, long before dawn, the big house was hushed and seemed itself to be sleeping. What an enormous container for two small humans, Heath thought, careful not to disturb Claudia as he got out of bed. Objectively, it was ridiculous for only two people to lay claim to so much space, to surround themselves with so many artifacts and to require so much service, not for themselves, but for their trappings. It was neither a comfortable nor a gratifying place in which to live, and yet there was no question of their leaving it, ever. Whether he liked it or not, it was necessary to him and as inescapable as a turtle's shell; to rule, it was necessary to be set apart in a castle. Besides . . . sometimes here he could encounter Bolivar again and feel his presence. Along with the town and with the mills, it was all the father he had left.

In pajamas he padded to the window, pulled back the curtains, and looked down on sleeping Chandlerville, a vast blur in darkness, but with its streets outlined in a jeweled, crisscrossed pattern of lamps, punctuated with the night-lights of business and, here and there, a lighted house window, symbol of trouble, strain, sleeplessness, sickness, perhaps tragedy. He felt an outleaping of empathy and compassion for the people behind those yellow squares: families of fathers, mothers, daughters, sons, engaged in combat with the fleshly, psychological, spiritual ills that human flesh was heir to. In his time, he thought, he had known them all; and that was what it took to feel compassion—experience. From the moment men were born, he thought, they were all in combat, and only a veteran of the war could know how dire those battles and skirmishes were and what scars they left. In that moment, if he could, he would have reached out to them. He was himself feeling very much the loneliness and pressure of his own humanity, his own mortality.

He turned away, went to the bathroom, and, knowing that there would be no more sleep—as he got older he waked earlier and earlier, needing no alarm—surveyed himself in the mirror. His carcass *looked* all right for a man of sixty, he thought. The outside was fine, the muscles, nerves, and bones perfectly serviceable, like the casing of a well-made clock. It was only a spring or two inside that, from too much use and constant overwinding,

ad worn out. It seemed a dirty shame, a waste, that all
hat perfectly good apparatus must soon be cast aside be-
ause of the deterioration of a few insignificant key parts.
'he human body, he thought wryly, was an uneconomic
nd overelaborate machine; God should have subcon-
racted its design to a German engineer.

Then he sobered. Well, God had not. And he had to
ace the facts. Two specialists, both agreeing. Oh, what
ey had said must have sounded perfectly reasonable to
oth; it must have seemed to them that the hope they
ffered was adequate. *If you will revise your style of
ving, slow down, take it easy, then you may very well
ve for years. But if you continue at your present pace . . .*
'hey thought they had given him an out, a reprieve, but
e knew better; if their diagnosis was right, they had
olled a bell for him. *Slow down?* How could he slow
own? Especially now, when things were closing in on
im, events running him down like wolves with slavering
ws pursuing a droshky, and the horse beginning to tire.
'hat was the way it was; the more perceptibly the horse
altered, the more predators joined the chase.

He went back to the bedroom, looked down at Claudia,
leeping soundly. Then, as he began to dress, he thought
bout the conference last week with Ryall.

"Captain Chandler," Ryall had said. "Good of you to
ome." He was tall, muscular, about Andrew's age, and
is clothes, Chandler guessed, had come from Savile Row.
[Ii]s hand was soft but strong, the dark eyes beneath his
rew cut keen, intelligent, not quite as warm as his smile.
[L]ike, Chandler thought, something modeled almost, but
ot quite, out of plastic. Ryall was just a little too per-
ect—a businessman certainly, but with an insecurity
omewhere deep inside that required him to bolster his
onfidence by dressing the role and surrounding himself
ith the proper stage scenery to enable him to play it to
[th]e hilt. "It really wasn't necessary, though," Ryall con-
nued. "I'd have been happy to go back to North Caro-
na. I've been looking for an excuse to visit home, any-
ow."

"Well, I had business in New York, so it wasn't any trouble." Heath followed Ryall through various offices into a vast space that could have been the living room of a mansion save for the uncluttered desk. He contrasted it mentally and sardonically with his own cluttered tower office. The roar of Fifth Avenue traffic was inaudible at this height, behind sealed windows. "Anyhow," Chandler went on as Ryall closed the door, "I'd rather talk here. You know how small towns are. Break wind at one end, everybody at the other knows what you had for dinner."

Ryall laughed delightedly. "God, it's good to hear home folks talk again! Sit down, Captain. You're alone? No attorneys or advisors?"

"I know my business fairly well," Chandler said.

Ryall laughed again. "In that case—" He went to a door, opened it, thrust his head through. Chandler saw a conference room beyond, with half a dozen men at a table. "Gentlemen," Ryall said, "I don't think I'll need you after all. Captain Chandler and I will talk in privacy. Thank you for coming." He turned, grinning, closed the door. "I know mine too. Still, for some people you've got to put on a show." He sat down on a sofa. "I'm flattered. I really was afraid you wouldn't meet with me."

"Oh, I'm like an old whore; I'll listen to any proposition."

Ryall laughed once more, then sobered. "In that case shall I get straight to the point or shall we shilly-shally?"

"Shilly-shallying's not my long suit. Let's get to business, Stewart."

"Right. Well, you'll already have guessed. Captain, I don't want to sound arrogant, but . . . I'd like to take you under my wing."

"Maybe I'm a little big to fit there."

"I think Ryall Cloth and Fibers is big enough to cover you. Can you stand a chart or two?"

"Roll 'em," Heath said.

Ryall went to an easel, placed it in the center of the room, turned around a poster board, taking a pointer from a tray. "Well, here's the parent company, former

around the mills my father left me. These are the subsidiaries I've built."

Heath's eyes ran down the complex chart. "You've
parlayed your old man's mills into a bundle."

"You, of all people, realize that wasn't easy. There was
only one way to do it—break with tradition. A family-
held corporation simply doesn't have the capital to become a national industry. The answer was to go public,
and, in my case, to synthetics. So . . . The parent company. Then these others, wholly or partially owned by
Ryall Cloth and Fibers. Ryall Synthetics; Ryotex Print-
ing and Dyeing; Mulhauser Mills; Morno Fabrics; Global
Tire Cord. And then the carpet companies."

"Imposing."

"Here's a new one—Ryall—Arizona. Long-staple-cotton
farming, totally industrialized. We've acquired lands and
irrigation facilities in the Southwest, the whole idea being to beat the two-price cotton subsidy, whereby foreign
mills can buy American cotton on the export market
cheaper than we can at home. Not to mention certain
gravy in price-support payments from the Agriculture
Department. Anyhow, Captain, this is where Chandler
Mills comes in. Morno Fabrics sews cottons, shirts and
sheeting. The tire-cord company, the carpet mills . . . We
need another chain of cotton mills to complete and balance out our operation. Hopefully, Chandler Mills."

"They're not for sale," Heath said promptly.

Stewart Ryall looked at him keenly for a moment. Then
he said quietly, "Captain, are you sure?"

Something in his voice riveted Heath's attention. "What
made you think they might be?"

Ryall chewed his lip. "May I be frank?"

"You'd better be."

"All right." He perched on the edge of his desk. "Two
reasons. First, I happen to know that St. John Butler just
made you an offer, and that you've been talking with
him."

"Only long enough to turn him down out of hand, the
way I just did you."

Ryall nodded. "Perhaps. Second . . . All right, Captain.

You had a physical two weeks ago. High blood pressure, incipient hardening of the arteries—the prognosis is not too good. You have been advised by your doctors to retire from active management of Chandler Mills."

Heath jumped up. "How the hell did you find that out?"

"It's true, isn't it?"

"I'll make no statement in that respect!"

"Of course not. You refused even to let the specialist inform your wife. Captain, I'm not trying to spy on your personal affairs. But before making any offer one has to get the facts, all of them. And with a family-held company like yours, which doesn't have to publish one iota of information, it's not an easy thing to do. Sometimes one has to use certain tactics. Anyhow, don't take the doctor to task. The nurse has already been fired, I understand—"

"With a nice stash of cash from you." Heath grinned sourly. "Stewart, you're a tough cookie."

"Have to be in this business—you know that. It would have been much simpler if you'd been a public corporation. I could have moved in on you, and there would have been matters of record. But— Well, I know how it is. My father was the same way. He didn't want *anybody* knowing what he was worth or what his margin of profit was. His philosophy was the same as yours: the minute anybody knows how much you've got, you become a sitting duck, a target for everyone—the unions, the reformers, the government. And it's awfully hard to be one of the boys with your own hands when they have their noses rubbed in how rich you are." He shrugged. "That's all well and good up to a certain point. Beyond that, if you're really going to grow you've got to make certain concessions. And, truthfully, Captain, I've had it both ways, and this is easier on a man. You don't know how much of a relief it is when you can make decisions impersonally."

"I've managed all right my own way."

"True." Ryall nodded. "In fact, while a lot of people may hate your guts, you're the only universally acknowledged genius in this business. Nevertheless, Captain, the fact remains: we all grow old, and nobody lives forever. And—after you, what? I'm sure you must have asked yourself that question."

"And answered it. Stewart, if I died tomorrow, nothing would change at Chandler Mills."

Ryall arose, began to pace the room. "Captain, I think a great deal would change. Oh, I know there's Olin Clutterbuck, but after all, he's your age, and—" He halted. "And then, of course, there is Andrew Ford."

"Yes," Heath said. "There's Andrew."

"But is he the man?" Ryall stared at Chandler. "Ask yourself, Captain. *Is he the man?*"

Heath stared back at him. "What do you mean by that?"

"I mean nothing that's derogatory to Andrew. I've met him, I like him, and I've been impressed by him. The question is, is Andrew Ford another Heath Chandler? Because that's what it's going to take to continue Chandler Mills in its present form. Another genius, and not only that, but a man of certain dedication. A man of vast incentive, and energy, and knowledge; a man who lives, breathes, exists for Chandler Mills, as you do." He paused. Almost matter-of-factly, he said: "It's quite possible Andrew is that man. But I would have more confidence that he was if he were your own flesh and blood, if he had grown up in a family tradition, the way you did, I did. I'm not saying he isn't competent. But to replace Heath Chandler, competence isn't enough."

He stopped, took a cigarette from a box on the desk, lit it. "I've got a hundred men of great competence working for me. They're good, and they're interchangeable; I can shuffle them from slot to slot and they always fit. But, as yet, in all that number, Captain, I see no replacement for myself. That's because none of them's a Ryall. But if I died tomorrow, the structure of my company's arranged so that Ryall Cloth and Fibers would survive undamaged. That's not true of yours."

"Andrew Ford," Chandler rasped, "will be ready when the time comes. I'll see to that."

"For your sake I suppose I hope so. Still . . . I know he didn't come into the company of his own volition. I know he was educated for a different career—one, according to his classmates, that he had every intention of pursuing. And I know, too, some of the maneuvering that went into sidetracking him. You did it cleverly, Captain, caught him like a spider traps a fly. I wonder, though—if even I can see it, can't Andrew? And if he does, I wonder whether or not he might resent just a little what has happened to him. Maybe I've just got a Byzantine mind, maybe it didn't happen that way at all. For your sake, I trust that Andrew has no inkling—"

Chandler stared at him coldly. "Stewart, you're getting out of line."

"Yes, you're right. I'm sorry. I'm sure I've read more into my files than was actually there. Still, two thoroughly dedicated geniuses in a row, not even related by blood? What a phenomenon that would be, Captain. And one of them only five years out of school, with less experience than that in actual management . . . You've got all your eggs in one basket, Captain. I hope it's big enough to hold them."

"It will be," Chandler said. "You can fold your wings and quit hovering over my carcass, Stewart."

"Captain, I didn't intend—"

"Oh, yes, you did. But you're not the only one; there'll be others. I suppose it shows that I'm slowing down a little. Butler's already tried, the others will soon, I suppose—Burlington and Stevens and Celanese and the like. And they'll get the same answer you did."

"Captain, I did not mean to offend you."

"No, I'm not offended. In fact, I appreciate your objective comments. I think they've helped clarify my thinking. I'll be honest, Stewart, I've known you all your life and I respect you and what you've done. If I sold to anybody, it would be to you. But I have no intention of selling. I have Andrew and I have a grandson; I have my succession. Thank you just the same."

Ryall hesitated. "Is that final?"

"Yes."

"I'll accept it, but only for the moment. In case you should change your mind, my offer will remain open until further notice. We haven't talked money, but it'll be a price you couldn't resist." He thrust out his hand. "And, whatever you do, take care of yourself, follow doctor's orders. This industry can't afford to lose you. You're the gadfly who keeps all of us on our toes."

Heath went downstairs through the sleeping house. The cook was not yet in the kitchen, and in the utter emptiness of the lower floor he would not have been surprised to encounter Bolivar or even the ghost, the shadow, of his own youth, now equally as dead. The fluorescent lights of the great kitchen did nothing to dissipate the sensation, imparting a corpselike pallor to the hands with which he prepared a dish of cold cereal.

And yet, he thought, mortality did not frighten him. What did was leaving behind so much unfinished business. The thought of what would happen to the mills if he should drop dead today was terrifying. For them, for the Chandler empire, the next few months were crucial.

First, there was the expansion program, conceived in his own style, to be implemented in a way that only he understood. And if it were not, then everything he had put into it would go to waste, enormous resources already committed. Worse, the mills would lose their ability to compete; modernization to offset foreign competition was essential.

More than that, though ... He shoved the plate aside, his appetite gone. They would be coming after him again. What had happened at Brackettville was just a harbinger; the union was coming south once more. Not this time as a shouting rabble, to be quelled by bayonets, but as a big business, with a fat treasury, sharp lawyers, and half the United States government in its pocket. No underdog now, but a competitor, seeking to wrest from Chandler workers a fortune in dues, seeking to wrest from Heath Chandler himself his control over those same workers, to put itself in his place. He felt, suddenly, menaced by memory: that other winter morning, the great red flame, the screams . . . And suddenly he was trembling and there was a taste in his mouth like brass. Soon, yes; and when they came they must be beaten. And beaten this time so it would be another twenty years before they dared menace him again. This time they must be repaid. That was what he could not bear—the thought of dying before he paid them what he owed them; and he was the only one who could do it.

And yet he had no assurance. He might, as he arose from this table, even full of the pills they had given him, fall over. And if he did that now, at this point in time, it was all a mockery, everything he had ever done, paid, was wasted, would come to nothing. That above all was what must not happen. And so there was no time now to lose; he must move, and quickly. It would be rough on Andrew; it would be brutal.

He made the decision. Then he arose, went into the study. Bolivar's portrait looked down coolly at him as he sat in Bolivar's chair at Bolivar's desk, found pen and paper and began to write. This, he thought, was all he could give Andrew in compensation for what had been demanded of him so far and for what would be demanded of him in the future. He finished, blotted, folded the paper, sealed it in an envelope, wrote a single word on its outside and shoved it deep into the drawer.

Then he arose. He stood there for a moment looking at Bolivar. Then he went out, put on his overcoat and left the house.

Outside the eastern sky was just paling. The cold, clean air felt good. As he walked to the car the wake-up whistle blew, its crass, familiar scream blaring across the valley.

4   WITH NO ONE in the car, Ramsey could indulge herself. She still loved speed, and now, bound home from Macedonia, she mashed the accelerator of the Thunderbird and felt a guilty thrill when it leaped for-

ward as if suddenly unleashed. Curves and turns slammed toward her, narrow bridges, but, tires squealing protest, she slowed for nothing, exulting in her rapport with the car, the skill she had not lost.

Andrew would never let her drive like this, and she did not dare with either Claudia or Lloyd in the car. But when Heath Chandler rode with her he took her style for granted, seemed not even to notice, much less protest it. He and Andrew were very much alike, and she loved them both madly, she thought, whipping around a slow-moving truck, but still, they were very different too. And she was a lucky woman. Whatever one could not supply that she needed, she got from the other; not even Claudia was that fortunate, though maybe she had been before Grandpa Ramsey had died.

Then, sliding deftly back into the lane before the truck, she slowed. This was not, after all, fair to Andrew or her son; and she had no real need for risk. It was not like that nightmare interval that had ended ten years ago, when she had not cared what might happen to her, had, indeed, hoped something would.

She put that thought out of her mind, eased the accelerator a little more. Now she drove almost sedately through the winter-barren landscape. No, all of that was finished. Andrew had saved, rescued her. It was easy not to think about it now. It was something that had happened to someone else. She could feel pity for the girl, but no kinship with her. The speed was merely for its own sake, it had no other purpose; she neither ran from nor to anything now, and she could forgo it. Suddenly she was impatient, very impatient, to be home. It was late, and Andrew would already be there waiting, and dinner would be ready, and they could have a drink together and talk, and . . . that was all she needed. That and later in the bed. He would be glad, she thought, to hear about Vic. She hoped Vic hadn't phoned him with the news to spoil her surprise. But Mildred had been overjoyed at Butler giving his firm the Brackettville case and his partners assigning it to Vic.

No wonder. Ramsey knew how hard-pressed the Royces

were sometimes, and certainly Mildred had earned a break. This would change their lives; and Ramsey had been careful not to spoil her excitement by any slighting reference to the Butlers, although for as long as she could remember they had been the object of her father's contempt.

Her mind busied itself with plans for the party they must have to celebrate. Something private, just the four of them. She groped for the cigarette pack on the seat, found it empty, remembered she had smoked the last one just before leaving Mildred's house. Damn! And not a place along the road for miles to buy a pack.

Then, as if her craving had conjured it, the place appeared. She passed it before she saw that it had been reopened, then skidded to a screaming halt, glanced in the rearview mirror. The truck was far behind. She backed up swiftly, deftly, turned into its drive.

Two years ago Heath Chandler had seen to it that this roadhouse closed. Even he could not tolerate the bootleg whiskey that it sold—literally poisonous—or the card games in the back, run by professionals, that had cleaned too many Chandler people out of a full week's pay in an evening. Since then the long, low, wooden building had sat untenanted, gas pumps wrenched off their islands, windows smashed by vandals.

Now, though, it had been rehabilitated. Freshly painted, new glass in all the frames, over the door a sign, *Harry's Place. Pepsi-Cola*. A pickup truck was the only vehicle in the drive.

Instinctively Ramsey freshened her makeup, pulled off her head scarf, gave her hair several strokes with a comb. Then she slid out, smoothing the dress beneath the coat of Persian lamb. As she opened the door of the place she thought fleetingly of Billie Ray's. It had been years since she had entered such a place unescorted.

She was in a big, deserted room that smelled of fresh paint and new lumber. Booths, a dance floor, a jukebox and a bar, but no sign of anyone to wait on her. She turned to go, deciding that it really wasn't open yet. Then she heard the footsteps. She supposed it was Harry who appeared in tee shirt and khaki pants. "Yes, ma'am," he grunted; and then he really saw her and his expression changed.

Apparently he'd been sleeping; his eyes were bleary, his thick, black, oil-smeared hair tousled, although he tried to smooth it down. He was big, well above six feet, his shoulders wide and sloping, his chest banded with muscle. The last of sleep went from his eyes as he raked them over her, appraising her not as a customer but as a woman.

Ramsey looked back at him. His brows were heavy, the eyes beneath them like molten tar, swirling, glistening. His nose was small and straight, a small black mustache, neatly trimmed, spread across a full, red upper lip. His cheeks were pocked with scars of old acne, his chin big and cleft. On the inside of one thick, muscular forearm was a tattoo.

She found her voice. "A pack of Pall Malls, please."

He did not move at once, just stood there looking her up and down with an insolence undisguised. He was, she guessed, a few years younger than she was, but he seemed older, and there was something about him that made her realize acutely how alone the two of them were. Suddenly she felt naked and unprotected, almost threatened.

He turned, bent to get a pack from behind the bar. His hips were as narrow as his chest was wide. He was, she thought, a stallion of a man and knew it; and when he confronted her again she resented the confident knowledge on his face of the impression he had made. He laid the cigarettes on the counter. "Anything else?" His voice was surprisingly high for such a man, but not shrill.

"No," she said. "No, thank you." Fumbling in her bag, she found a quarter, gave it to him. He simply covered it with his hand and went on looking at her. She felt blood mounting in her cheeks. She took the cigarettes, turned away swiftly.

"Come back," he said as she closed the door behind her. Something in his voice infuriated her. She got into the car, careful not to show any leg, ripped open the pack, lit a cigarette. He was standing at the door, looking at her through the glass. She blew smoke, then started the car, whirled it around, ripped out of the drive with an especially spectacular maneuver that threw gravel against the truck, a kind of vehicular flounce. Then she roared off down the highway.

"Well, sir," she thought, "you picked the wrong mare this time. I can assure you, sir, that your credentials will be thoroughly examined." Then she laughed aloud, amused at her bourgeois, matronly concern; but all the same it somehow reassured her. By the time she got home to Chandlerville and saw her father's car in the drive as well as Andrew's he was forgotten. She parked, entered the house, found them all clustered around the bar—Andrew, Heath and Claudia. And the moment she caught sight of Andrew's face she knew at once that something was wrong.

As she entered he twisted on the stool, a lock of hair falling down across his forehead. His face was pale, his mouth smiling, but there was something wrong with his eyes; they looked curiously stunned, and she thought she saw in them a kind of pain.

But before either he or she could speak Heath Chandler stepped forward, grinning broadly, and put one hand on Andrew's shoulder. "Good afternoon, Mrs. Ford," he said, and she saw that he had been drinking heavily. "May I perform an introduction? Mr. Ford, meet Mrs. Ford. Mrs. Ford, meet the new president of Chandler Mills."

Ramsey stared from Andrew to her father and back again. Of course it had had to come—but so soon? All at once she was very pleased; then she felt a surge of real pride. Not only for Andrew but for what it meant to be a Chandler. "Wonderful!" she cried, and then she ran to Andrew and kissed him. He returned the kiss nicely enough, but Chandler said, "Hell, boy, you can do better than that." And obediently he did, making a thoroughly theatrical production out of it. Then he stepped back. " guess you'd like a drink."

"I certainly would!" She looked from one to the other of them. "How . . . how did this all come about?"

"I'll be damned if I know," Andrew said, pouring from a pitcher. His eyes were better now. "I walked into his office this morning, and he called Olin in, and we both sat down. Then he looked at Olin. 'Would you like to be president of Chandler Mills?' he asked, and Olin said, 'Hell, no'—like that. So he turned to me and said, 'Well, I guess that does it. It's up to you, Andrew.' And that's as much as I still know. You want to know more, you'll have to ask *him*."

"Pluck and luck," Heath grinned. "Do and dare. Risk and rise. Work and win. In short, sheer talent. Also, he's the only son-in-law I've got." Then he was serious. "I did it because it was time to do it and because Andrew's earned it. And if he hadn't, he would never have got it, even if I'd had to call in outside help."

But now questions crowded into Ramsey's mind as she took the drink Andrew passed to her. "Does this mean you're *retiring?*"

"In phases, yes. Immediately, no. You don't think I'd dump Andrew into a job like that and then run out and leave him holding the bag? No, I'm staying on as chairman of the board, for a while at least. That means I'll lay down broad policies and let Andrew work them out. I'll be available to offer advice, assistance, encouragement, and an occasional I-told-you-so. But by and large he's the whip from now on; in the regular management of the company he reigns supreme. And, insofar as possible, I'll keep my clammy hands off and get some well-earned rest!"

"That's a promise Andrew and I will hold you to," Claudia cut in, her voice edged enough to make Ramsey look at her.

"And one I intend to keep. Of course I'll have to work closely with him for a while until he's caught up on all the details, but then—" He grinned at Ramsey. "I figure about three months, anyway, until he's in the groove. And in case you're wondering what's eating on your mama, I promised her that after that, everything being in order, she and I are gonna elope to Europe together for a while, just the two of us—and she's so afraid I'll renege she's about to strip her gears." He put his arm around her. "Don't worry, madam. If the creek don't rise or the blight hit the rhubarb crop, we'll make the Grand Tour together." He was, Ramsey saw, on a very high horse indeed. Then his voice and face both softened. "You've earned it, and more."

Claudia closed her eyes, then opened them again, and Ramsey saw moisture in them. "I'm not thinking of myself," she said. "I'm thinking of you—and Andrew. You need the rest. And Andrew is entitled to be rid of you and have a chance to do things his own way."

"He's already told me he's going to. That's the condition on which he took the job. He made no bones about it, he wants his authority. Hell, I wouldn't be surprised to come back from Europe and find the sign on the watertower changed to FORDVILLE." He clapped Andrew on the shoulder.

"I think we'd better go now," Claudia said. She looked at Ramsey and Andrew half smiling. "It's going to take me hours to get him calmed down enough to eat his dinner. Andrew, I'm very happy and proud. Please . . . may we take Lloyd up to Chandler House with us to spend the night? He'll be a calming influence on his grandfather."

"He'd love that," Ramsey said. "I'll get him."

When they were gone she took Andrew's hand. "I'm like Mother. I'm awfully proud and happy."

He nodded, then pulled his hand away and went back to the bar. "Big Deal," he said. "Very big deal." He poured another martini, drank half of it at a swallow.

Startled by something in his voice, she looked at him. "What's the matter?"

"Nothing. Not a damned thing." He drank again. "What the hell. I guess I never believed in free will, anyhow."

"Free will? What's got into you? I don't understand." Like all men, he could at times be maddeningly contrary, but today of all days . . .

"Nothing's got into me, there's nothing to understand.

Let's just say that I'm somewhat . . . overwhelmed." But his voice was dry, even bitter.

"Well, of course you are. But you can do it. Besides, you always knew—"

"Of course I knew!" He set down his glass so hard the dregs spilled over. The lock of hair had fallen across his forehead. "So why whoop and holler and fire off rockets? The only thing I ever did to earn it was to have the guts to face him about marrying you; after that it was all cut and dried. Like a Good Conduct Medal in the Army, if you can go for a whole year without fucking up. But it's not something you go around bragging about having gotten."

She was strangely angry, hurt. "Andrew, you're behaving like a child."

"Well, that's what I am—a nice, sweet, obedient child, who does his duty by the paterfamilias without complaint. And I guess that's what I'll keep on being—" He broke off. "Oh, hell, I'm sorry. Viewed objectively, it's quite a thing. One of the finest votes of confidence I ever had. It would have been nice, though, maybe it would mean a little more, if I'd had some competition for the job. Or even if I could be sure that he really meant for me to run the company."

"He said—"

"I know what he said. I'll believe it when it actually happens." Suddenly he turned to her, voice changing. Now it was low, earnest, and thoughtful, as if he were sorting out his emotions for himself as well as for her. "I suppose I ought to feel as if it was the beginning of something, but I don't. I . . . feel more like it's an ending."

"An ending? Of what?"

"I don't know. Of Andrew Ford, maybe. Or at least of his having even the least control, the least power, over his own future. Maybe I always felt, deep inside of me, that there was some . . . kind of chance, anyhow, an alternative— But today when he told me I knew this was it. I just felt . . . swallowed up, as if something were closing over my head. Or as if somebody had finally shut a great big door behind me, once for all."

He was not making sense, at least to her. She was distressed, perturbed, and a little angry herself, or at least impatient with this irrationality. With all he had, with all that had been done for him— Somehow, too, she felt threatened. Still, she made a great effort not only to understand but to console and encourage him. "Has it occurred to you that there's another way to look at it?"

"Like what?"

She sat down on a bar stool, reached for the martini pitcher, all at once badly needing a second drink. "That this is your opportunity. That he's given you so much to work with. Whatever it is that you wanted to do, you can do it now your own way—and look at all the resources you have. He was right in a way. You can't change the sign on the water tower, but you can certainly make sure that people know who's in charge. I don't see why you should feel swallowed up. I'd think you'd feel liberated, free, glad to have all that power and authority finally to make things happen the way you want them to happen. Not to have to answer to anybody—"

"But him."

"He said—"

"I know what he said."

"Andrew, you're—"

"Behaving like a horse's ass. Okay, I'll go along with that. Let's just call it my last fling. It won't happen again." Then his voice hardened. "You're right, Ramsey, I've thought of that. In fact, it's the only hope I've got left. I had sense enough to make that clear to him, anyhow, and he'd better believe I meant what I said. If Andrew Ford is president of Chandler Mills, then Andrew Ford runs Chandler Mills, and does it in his own way, win, lose, draw. If he wants to fire me, he can; otherwise he'd better keep his hands off me. I am not"— and suddenly his eyes glittered—"going to completely submerge and lose myself for ever and ever in this family."

She slid off the stool. "I don't think anybody's ever asked you to."

"No," he said harshly. "Nobody's ever *asked* me anything."

She looked at him a moment silently, fighting back her own angry, cutting words. Then she said, control regained, "I'll go see to dinner."

"No hurry. I'm not very hungry."

"Then I'll tell Frieda to slow it down."

She went out. When she came back from conferring with the cook he was still at the bar, a fresh drink before him, his wallet by it. He held something over an ashtray, a folded piece of paper. Carefully, slowly, he thumbed back the cap of his cigarette lighter and snapped it into flame. He held the flame to the end of the clipping, and the ancient, worn piece of newsprint caught immediately. Andrew dropped it in the ashtray and watched it burn. When it was reduced to ashes he ground it to powder with the bottom of his glass. Then he raised his head, saw Ramsey standing there. "So much for that," he said, and drank.

She was baffled, disturbed, and made a little angry by the discomfort of the rest of the evening. They ate together in careful, overpolite silence, what little talk they made skirting the subject. She told him of Vic's good luck; he only nodded. There was a tension in the room like that of an impending quarrel, and carefully afterwards they separated; he watched television while she sat at her desk and answered letters that were long overdue. But finally they had to come together in the bedroom and in the bed.

She sought desperately to break the tension, restore perspective. Stripping off her stockings, and doing it as seductively as possible, she laughed. "This ought to be some night. I've never slept with the president of Chandler Mills before."

He turned, unbuttoning his shirt, and gave her a curious, opaque glance. "I guess that's true," he said quietly.

They lay in bed together. She kept her body carefully against him, her arm around him, waited. Strangely, she did not really want him tonight; the tension had pinched off desire. But she wanted him to want her. She would have made the first move, but somehow she sensed that in his present mood she must not. Once she thought he was about to; he rolled over, put his arm across her waist. But almost immediately he took it away, rolled over again. Baffled, she said with almost curt finality, "Good night."

"Good night," he said.

But it was a long time before she slept.

5   AFTER A FULL DAY at her desk Claudia still had work to do.

An east-wing room at Chandler House served as her office, a secretary coming in from the plant three times a week to take dictation. The affairs for which she was responsible were complicated, and often appalling or heartbreaking. Her concern and province were the problems of the women of the Chandler empire.

The duty was hers by default, but too important to neglect. Heath's power and influence spread like spilled ink across the Piedmont as the mills went on expanding, moving into one moribund little town after another in search of an untapped supply of cheap, abundant labor; and each time he located a new plant the burden on her increased. Andrew and Olin dealt with hard, practical matters, prodding the city fathers into giving the company tax concessions, forcing them to build new power, sewer, water systems to serve the mill, acquiring, for all practical purposes, political control through the power of the purse, the payroll. They handled the men, but left the women to be dealt with by her.

And, as Chandler Mills stirred such places to new life, there was plenty for her to deal with. For the first time the women there had a link with the outside world, a higher power outside the church to whom to turn, someone with money and authority enough to assume the roles of Lady Bountiful and Lady from Philadelphia simultaneously. Letters, requests, petitions flowed across her desk in an unending stream. She ate one dreary luncheon dish after another and made her succession of dreary talks at their meetings, showing the Chandler flag, doing what she could to inspire in all those ample breasts admiration for and loyalty to Chandler Mills, to get the women on the team. It was a vital duty, but one that bored her and that she detested; soon it would fall to Ramsey.

What did not bore her, what appalled, sometimes terrified her, were the real problems, the dreadful human problems of life and death and grief and heartbreak that came to her in a flood of poignant, frequently almost indecipherable letters, and that, in the final analysis, she could do little to solve. She could not, after all, restore pregnant teen-agers to virginity, reform drunkards, stay the hands of wife-beaters, bring deserters back to abandoned families, make adulterers faithful, or untangle brains and nervous systems hopelessly knotted by poverty and frustration.

Now, at four in the afternoon, arising from her desk, freshening what little makeup she wore, and preparing to go out, she tried to assess what she had accomplished in years of dealing with those problems.

Not much, really; they had affected her more than she had them. She had never really comprehended how much misery, squalor, and sheer bestiality had pooled itself at the bottom of society until she had come back to Chandlerville and assumed this responsibility. Now, though, she knew what human beings could do to one another, of what they were capable, and it chilled and sickened her. It took all the resources she could muster to retain some faith in people after reading all those letters. In a sense those little towns were mills themselves of a different kind, grinding their population with stones of ignorance and conformity and boredom and poverty. And she understood all too well why, caught inextricably in such places, young men drank themselves mindless, girls threw the defiance of pregnancy in their elders' teeth, older men despaired and vanished. There was not much she could do about it—the limits set on her authority were iron-clad; though sometimes she yearned to take such places, turn them upside down and shake them.

But she could not, she thought, as she went downstairs. The mills would not allow the status quo to be disturbed. The imperative was the labor pool, and, beyond certain limits, nothing could be done to injure that. Ignorance could be fought exactly to the point where knowledge made a man a better worker, and not beyond. Too much education made hands unfitted for the monotonous work of tending machines and performing the same operations over and over for the rest of their lives. Excessive ambition must be discouraged; it meant new wage demands or emigration or, worse, receptivity to unions. The shackles of local custom and conformity must not be struck off; these held people where they were, provided a ready means to control them. And so, usually, her hands were tied. She could treat symptoms, but not the disease itself —which, she thought, she had suffered from herself. On the veranda she glanced toward the water tower, still dominating the town: CHANDLERVILLE.

Some things, though, she had accomplished, she told herself as she got into the Oldsmobile which had been brought around for her. Two things she had struck at ruthlessly and with all the power at her disposal: the two ghastly crimes that seemed endemic to such places—child abuse and incest.

They were the curse of poverty, she thought, starting the car. She had never known before how sickeningly common they were, the vices of frustration and over-crowding. Among people who bred like rabbits, children were devalued, no blessing, only curses, added burdens, and all too often helpless objects of senseless hatred, an outlet for all pent-up grudges directed against the environment, even against life itself. Wherever it came to her attention she moved ruthlessly to stop it.

And incest—that had become a joke in every mill town. "A virgin is a six-year-old mill-hill girl who can run faster than her brother or her daddy." They laughed at that at the country club; but for her, more than once, it had become grim reality. Again it all came back to poverty and overcrowding. Swarming families jammed into three rooms, four, privacy unknown . . . Oh, she knew all about it, what caused it, how routine it was in the rock-bottom stratum of society in those little towns. But not something for which the mill economy was solely responsible; it was almost a tradition among the poorest of the whites, one brought into town with them from little sharecropper shanties or isolated mountain coves. Anyhow, she hated it. She hated it, and she fought it, and, thank God, it was diminishing as people moved out of the mill villages, prospering enough now to buy houses more spacious in the developments, financed by Chandler banks, which were beginning to offer them an alternative.

Still, the mill villages remained. The one to which she drove was the oldest in Chandlerville, not far from Chandler House, high on the valley wall above the river. Here the little houses ranked dusty streets in identical rows, their dooryards minuscule, their wooden flanks painted a uniform off-white. There were better villages spotted around the town; this was a sort of living museum, preserved across the decades by undue expenditure on maintenance. Still, it had a purpose, the Chandler equivalent of low-cost public housing. Unincorporated, the town was not eligible for state or federal grants, but here, on Hill Number One, the rock-bottom element, the transient, the unlucky and unthrifty, could still find minimal shelter for minimal payroll deduction. And places like this were the source of her greatest satisfaction. When she could find in such a place someone worthy of rescue, lend a helping hand, transform a life, then she felt that much was justified that she had endured.

It was warm today, and the women were on their porches, hair rolled up in curlers; grubby children with snot-smeared March faces played in the dusty yards; a few lank men, off shift, tinkered with cars or gathered around the little grocery. While the car bounced along a washboard street she watched the house numbers, finally found the one she sought, parked, got out, drawing her camel's hair coat about her under the gaze of idly curious eyes on the adjoining porches. The house was like all the rest, except that its front yard had been fenced with chicken wire to protect the rudimentary flower beds in its front yard; and she was pleased to see that, unlike the other dwellings, junk and scrap lumber had not been stuffed underneath the house.

Ancient steps sagged even under her meager weight as she climbed them, and the boards of the porch bent under her feet. Then she smiled wryly; compared to Fox's cabin, this place was well built and luxurious. Gittin above your raisin, she thought, amused at her own fastidiousness. Then she knocked on the door.

A moment passed; she knocked again, heard footsteps inside. The door opened, and the girl was there.

"Hello, Linda," Claudia said, smiling. "I'm Mrs. Chandler."

There was nothing of the familiar vacuousness in the child's huge blue eyes, and her smile was neither shy nor forward. Fourteen? thought Claudia, suddenly feeling as if she were confronting almost a contemporary. She had a quick impression of preternatural knowledge and age. Then it dissolved as the girl spoke, and Linda Vereen came back in focus, neither more nor less than what she was—a lovely and fairly poised young girl about whom, except for her looks, there would have been nothing exceptional any place but here.

"Oh, Mrs. Chandler. Ah, come in."

She pulled the door wide, standing back, looking a little abashed now as Claudia entered a front room scrupulously clean but, despite all the effort that had been put into decoration, remorselessly shabby. Linda had been able to make curtains for the windows and a slipcover of cheap cloth for the sofa, but evidently reupholstering the sag-bottomed easy chair had been beyond her powers; its arms were worn through to the stuffing, its back greasy where heads had rested. And she could not, of course, have done anything about the cracked, scabby linoleum that covered the floor or the ugly eminence of the coal space heater with a pipe bent back into a chimney, standing before a fireplace that had been blanked off with a sheet of poorly painted tin.

"I, ah, please, ma'am, won't you sit down?" Linda's chubby hands twisted together; her rounded cheeks were pink; Claudia knew that she was seeing these surroundings through Claudia's eyes. Immediately she sought to put the girl at ease.

"Thank you. Oh, I love these curtains. Did you make them yourself?"

"Yes, ma'am. Daddy brought the cloth home from the mill and I dyed it and hemmed it."

"I know, but where did you get that color?"

Linda smiled. "I just mixed dyes all together until I got something that looked right."

"Well, they are certainly nice." Claudia sat at one end of the sofa, feeling every tired spring in it through her buttocks. "And that skirt, did you make that yourself?"

"Yes, ma'am. And the blouse." Linda wore a plain white blouse and a navy skirt, both of them quite professional in workmanship. "Ah, would you like a cup of coffee or somethin?"

"No, thank you." Claudia smiled. "You know, before I was married I lived in a house much smaller than this and not half so nice. Just a little cabin out in the woods, just my father and myself. I didn't have anything like your talent for fixing things up."

"I like things nice," Linda said, still standing.

"Of course you do. I did too, but I didn't know how to make them that way. Oh, I had to study and study before I learned how to do the simplest things. Please sit down." Claudia gestured. She was genuinely impressed by what she had seen so far, and her comments were sincere. There *was* talent here. "Of course you got my note," she said as Linda dropped into the rump-sprung chair.

"Oh, yes, ma'am. I was so excited"—the chubby hands kept on twisting—"I just didn't know what to do."

"Well, there's no reason to get excited." Claudia took out cigarettes. "My daughter was very much impressed by you and about what Mr. Morton said about you, and we always try to, well, pinpoint people who have something special to offer . . . not just to Chandler Mills but the, well"—her cheeks burned, it sounded so banal—"the world," she finished. "Please, may I have an ashtray?"

Linda looked around, flustered. "I, ah— Just a minute. I don't smoke, you know, and my daddy, he don't believe in tobacco. Doesn't, I mean. Excuse me." She jumped up, ran out.

Again Claudia looked around the room. On a table a fat family Bible lay like a stranded walrus by a lamp. But there were other books, not many, in a case nearby. Mostly Nancy Drew, but two books on sewing and a couple of ancient novels by Bertha M. Clay and a number of religious tracts. Then she smiled. In addition to the movie magazines on the bottom shelf there were several copies of *Vogue*, *Harper's Bazaar*, and *Seventeen* and a thick *McCall's* pattern catalogue. Feeling that she knew Linda much better now, she waited to light the cigarette until the girl returned with a saucer that had once been part of a set of excellent china.

"Maybe this will do," she said shyly.

"That's Haviland," Claudia said. "Where did that come from?" She picked it up, held it to the light. "Bone."

"It was Mama's."

"Let me use this," Claudia said. She lit the cigarette, put her lighter back in her handbag, and indicated she would use the cheap clay dish on the end table in which sat a lard can wrapped in aluminum foil and containing a potted geranium. "You must be careful with this." She put the saucer beside her. "It's the best."

"Mama liked—"

"Nice things. Yes, I'm sure she did." On the wall there was a framed photograph of a pretty girl with the long hair and violently made-up mouth of the 1940s. "That your mother?"

"Yes, ma'am." Linda hesitated, then asked shyly, "Don't you think she looks like Ann Sheridan?"

"Very much," said Claudia. "Very much indeed. You're just like her except for the color of your hair."

"I get that and my eyes from Daddy," she said proudly.

"How long has your mother been . . . dead?"

"She died when I was eleven." Linda's eyes stayed fastened on the portrait. "Polio. She got real sick all of a sudden and I—"

"I'm sorry," Claudia said. "It's a blessing, though, that you didn't get it. Did she teach you sewing?"

"Yes, ma'am—some. Some I learned myself out of books. Then this year I had a year of Home Ec at Bolivar Junior High." Linda brightened. "I made an A."

"I'm sure you did. Well, Linda . . ." Claudia hesitated. "You know we at Chandler Mills" (Oh, God, what a tinny phrase, and mandatory) "always have an interest in bright young people—and I must say, Mr. Morton and your pastor both are most enthusiastic about your potential. That's why I sent you the note and that's why I came to see you." She put ashes in the dish under the geranium. "Tell me, do you have any plans for the future?"

Linda blushed. Apparently she blushed easily. When she did, Claudia thought, she was totally charming. "Well, I—"

"No, I mean, what would you really like to do? If you could be educated to do anything you wanted to."

Linda stared at her a moment, assessing how deeply, Claudia guessed, she could take an older woman into her confidence. "Well, I want to be a fashion designer. I want to make pretty clothes that nobody else has thought of. I just— I been around cloth all my life, you know, and—" She broke off, suddenly inarticulate.

Claudia kept her face carefully serious and business-like. "What do you know about designing fashions?"

"Well, not much except what I got out of *Vogue* and all those magazines. And they cost so much. But I designed this skirt and blouse, and look"—her enthusiasm was rising now, overriding her shyness—"something else, let me show you." She sprang up, ran out, came back with three dresses on hangers. "These, I worked up the design and made 'em myself."

Claudia arose and took each dress and examined it, and she was impressed. In some respects the work was crude, childish and unfinished, but she recognized here something burgeoning, as a gardener might identify a plant by its seed or sprout. Her voice was full of honesty as she laid the dresses on the sofa. "Linda, they are marvelous, all things considered."

Again that pinkness flushed the rounded cheeks. "Thank you." Her eyes glowed, as if she had received the ultimate compliment.

Before all that gratitude Claudia turned her head. She sat down again. For a moment she saw herself in Fox's cabin, barefooted, dirty, ignorant and full of longing. And if, with so little talent, she had come this far, what might not this girl be? In that instant some arc of mutual knowingness flashed between herself and Linda. Suddenly they became involved with each other; and Claudia knew she had taken on a new responsibility. She was committed.

She motioned Linda to sit down. "Well," she said, "I will promise you this. If you maintain your grades in school and work hard at studying design on the side, I'll see you get the best possible training afterward. Chandler Mills will provide a scholarship to Richmond Professional Institute or some other good school of design. And I think when you graduate you can be sure of a job if you're really serious and do good work."

"Oh," Linda said. "Oh."

"It will all depend on you," said Claudia. That sounded too austere and dogmatic and banal. "No, it won't either. I mean, the company has a considerable library on this subject, and so do I. I go to all the showings, you know, in Paris, and I know all the designers there." She leaned forward, caught up in resolve. "You could come up to Chandler House and use my books and magazines. And if you get something out of them—who knows? Maybe when you're older and I go to Paris—"

"Oh," Linda said. "Oh, oh." Then she said, "Thank you." Her eyes had turned moist. "I never thought—I mean—" Claudia looked at the geranium. "I'm always home on Friday afternoons. If you want to come up to Chandler

House then . . . Or any time you want to use my books, I'll leave instructions."

"Mrs. Chandler," Linda said, voice tremulous.

"It's all right," said Claudia thickly. "You're always welcome. As long as you make good use of the material I give you." She looked at her watch, then arose. "Why don't you come by next Friday?"

"Oh, I'd love to! I'd—"

"I'll expect you after school is out. Say four-thirty?"

"Yes, I—" Then Linda hesitated, looked crestfallen.

"What's wrong?"

"Daddy," she said. "He gets off at four. When he comes home he wants his supper."

"Can't he cook for himself?"

"No, ma'am." Linda was staring at the space heater, in which a fire flickered behind the isinglass window panel. "He don't—doesn't know how to cook much. I do all the cooking—"

"What does your father do?"

"He's a doffer in the spinning room." Again her cheeks turned pink. It was a lowly position for a man with a fourteen-year-old daughter, a man who had worked in the mills for years. Something cold touched Claudia's heart. Then she smiled; there were some advantages to wielding power. "Well, somebody will talk to him and explain the situation. I'm sure he'll understand if Mr. Ford speaks to him in person."

Their eyes met. Something wholly female sparked in that contact, and then Linda laughed; and when she did, it was as an intimate of Claudia Chandler. "Yeah," she said. "Yeah, I'll bet he will."

Again Claudia had that curious sense of being in the presence of a contemporary. Whatever else this girl knew, she understood the uses of authority. Or power. But, then, anybody who lived on this mill hill had to.

"Well, I must run. I'll see you Friday, then."

"Yes, ma'am," said Linda with certainty in her voice. "You'll see me Friday, sure."

"I'll look forward to it," Claudia said, and realized she meant it. "Goodbye, my dear."

"Goodbye." Linda arose and followed her to the door. Then, as Claudia was about to leave, she burst out, "Mrs. Chandler."

"Yes?"

"There ain't . . . I mean, there isn't any way somebody my age can get a scholarship any sooner, is there? I mean, go off to school somewhere and study what I really want to study?"

A kind of desperation and intensity in her voice caught Claudia off base. She realized then how much eagerness and yearning she had kindled, what force, power, and drive there were in Linda. "No, my dear," she said, "I'm afraid there isn't. You'll just have to be patient and do your best here. If you do your part, don't worry. I promise you, Chandler Mills will do its part too."

Linda looked a bit crestfallen. "Yes, ma'am. I was . . . only wonderin. I didn't know."

"Don't worry, child. You won't be forgotten." Claudia opened the door.

"Mrs. Chandler!" The voice halted her again. Linda ran to her, embraced her, kissed her cheek. Then she drew back, appalled. "Oh, Lord. I hope I didn't do the wrong thing."

Claudia looked at her, something stirring. "No, Linda," she said softly. "That wasn't the wrong thing. That was exactly right. I'll see you Friday." Then she went out, strangely shaken, and yet with a kind of warmth, even exaltation, glowing within her, a renewal of faith.

Driving back to Chandler House, her own words echoed in her mind. *You'll just have to be patient and do your best here. If you do your part . . .*

Well, she, too, had done that. For thirty years, almost. She and Linda both had rewards awaiting them. Both had liberation to look forward to.

She smiled faintly. Thank God for Andrew Ford; thank God for the miracle of his coming, which had saved them all. To this day she did not understand Heath's abrupt reversal of his attitude over that week's span, after the boy had first confronted them; the only reason he had

iven her was his admiration for the young man's guts
a daring to do it at all. Considering who Andrew was and
vhere he had come from, it had taken courage enough to
vin even his admiration; and courage was something he
ut the highest value on. Still, she had almost for a while
espaired; she had pleaded Ramsey's cause with all her
rength, to no visible effect; even that night in the sitting
oom when he had given his consent, she'd had no idea
hat his final verdict was.

But, she thought, he had that talent. Unlikely people.
he remembered herself on the porch of Fox's cabin
iat dreadful, wonderful morning; and later in the car:
ake me with you! He could see things in people, things
iey themselves were ignorant of possessing. More than
iat, he dared. He dared to take responsibility for chang-
ig their lives. She wondered if he knew how, after all
iese years, she still stood in a certain awe of him, won-
ering at the mysteries in his brain beyond her compre-
ension. Sometimes, she knew, even beyond his.

Anyhow, Andrew was here, and he had liberated both
f them. He was taking hold, moving decisively as presi-
ent, even beyond Heath's expectations. Savagely, almost
efiantly, he gathered authority to himself, exerted bold-
ess. And now Heath no longer had any excuse. Now,
fter all these years, she could reclaim him, take him for
er own again. That promise he had made, that they
ould go to Europe this summer, the two of them, pick
p the threads of life that Bolivar's sickness, death, and
tter had chopped—Andrew had made that possible.
nd she would hold Heath to it inexorably. Strangely,
ie thought that it would not take too much pressure.
[e was tired lately; seemed willing to disengage. That
orried her, and yet it pleased her.

Anyhow, she thought, they had served their time. Now
iey were free at last.

6   BEYOND MACEDONIA Olin turned the ca
off the highway up a dusty drive stretching for a quarte
of a mile between twin ranks of giant old cedars. Ahead
on the hilltop, Ellen's small house was strangely off-cente
in the grove of oaks and maples. Once the Quentins ha
owned one of the few genuine plantations this part of th
country had boasted; but most of the land had long sinc
been sold or taken in foreclosure, and the main hous
had burned in 1916. Since then the family had lived i
what had been the guest house. Now Ellen lived ther
alone, the last one left.

Around the cottage the lawn was green, and flower bed
made crazy quilts of vivid color, riotous with June. Oli
parked the car, got out, entered the house without knocl
ing.

The rooms were small, exquisite, containing not on
family heirlooms but all the pieces Ellen, with impeccabl
taste and a pawnbroker's eye, had accumulated; a fe
were presents from Clutterbuck himself. He went directl
to her studio at the back, a long room with a norther
exposure, constructed of the same materials as the hous
itself. This wing was only fifteen years old, but she ha
searched determinedly for pine and oak to match the ori
inal, had built it bit by bit, doing much of the carpent
herself. In it, she sat on a straight-backed chair befo
an easel, her black hair, now faintly overlaid with silve
bound with a cloth against her absentminded habit
running paint-smeared fingers through it, a man's shi
serving as a smock above blue jeans, on which she h
wiped hands and brushes until they were the colors of
rainbow. Leaning forward, gray eyes squinted in conce
tration, she stared at the portrait on the easel, the eve
present cigarette dangling from her lips. Her lanky, sma
breasted body, narrow-hipped, long-legged, almost ma
nish, was intent, every muscle taut. Smiling, Olin watch
her for a moment without her knowledge as she look

om the half-finished picture to the photographs on the
ble.

She had been his mistress for nearly twenty years. Back
Chandlerville, after that interval in Vienna, he had
one through some bad weeks. Then Claudia, maneuver-
g deftly, had arranged for him to meet Ellen Quentin,
d after that things were better. She had studied in
ome and Paris; her father had just lost his money and
cceeded in drinking himself to death; she had been
rced to come home to care for a mother never really
ell since; and her need of Olin at that moment had been
great as his need for her. Drawn together by that, and
t, painting, they had become lovers. Meanwhile, turn-
g all that expensive training to doing portraits of the
milies of moneyed people as far away as Charlotte, she
ad managed somehow not only to support her mother
ut to save this remnant of the Quentin land. Now, with
e older woman dead the past eight years, she limited
erself to two portraits a month, at three hundred dollars
ich, enough to live on and indulge her passions for an-
ques, flowers, and horses. By now the question of mar-
age had been disposed of; each had worked out a pat-
rn of life and independence that, they both understood,
arriage could only complicate and spoil; with Olin sixty
d she forty or a few years past, their ways were set.

"Damn," she muttered now, riffling through the snap-
ots.

"Forget it," Olin said. "It's quitting time."

She turned. "Hi." Her face, long, narrow, a little horsey,
ghted. She took off her glasses, laid them aside, padded
bare feet across the room, and kissed him. "You're
eaky. I didn't hear you come in."

"Too wrapped up in that juvenile delinquent's fea-
res."

"That juvenile delinquent happens to be a very nice
y of twelve and the heir to the Tillman peanut fortune."
e turned. "I am having a little trouble, though. In every
cture he seems to smirk, and I'm trying to de-smirk him
the portrait. But I can't figure out whether he smirks
ith his mouth or eyes."

Olin followed her to the easel, thumbed through the photographs, squinted at the painting. Then he picked up a brush, cleaned it, mixed colors, made a few strokes. "You took all these snapshots with the same lighting. It's that shadow."

Considering, she nodded suddenly. "I hate you," she said. "I absolutely hate you. Why didn't you come sooner?"

"I'm a professional de-smirker. If you hate me, put poison in my drink."

"Poison it yourself. I'm going to have a wash. Make me one too."

The kitchen was like her life—not spacious, but uncluttered, very clean. She was a contradiction, possessed of a man's direct mode of thought acquired over years of being responsible for another, weaker woman, yet with no sacrifice of the feminine love of color, nicety and order. He knew where everything was, and everything was always where it belonged. By the time the drinks were ready she reappeared, her thick shag of hair unbound and combed, her hands clean, smelling of turpentine and soap. He kissed her again, gave her a glass, and they were out on a rambling porch that crossed the rear of the house. Here they sat in old wicker-bottomed rocking chairs, while in the pasture below, two bay geldings cropped grass, their muscles, like compressed fluid, rippling beneath well-kept hides in slanting light.

"Tell me all the news," she said, putting bare feet on the railing.

"No news. Heath and Claudia are in London. Andrew taking full advantage. And me, slowly but surely, I'm becoming obsolete. My function when Heath left was to lend Andrew aid and comfort. If he needs either one, he hasn't asked for it."

"I had no idea he was such a powerhouse."

"I haven't seen such a sight since Heath moved in, took over. The boy's good, very good. Almost fanatical. If Heath doesn't look out, Andrew will out-Chandler him."

"That's what Heath wants, isn't it?"

"I presume so. Although it may crush his ego a little bit. He's not used to being out-Chandlered."

"Well, let him worry about that." Ellen was silent for a moment. Then she said, "Olin, why don't you seize this opportunity to get out?"

He whipped around. "What?"

"Heath's disengaged. Andrew doesn't need you, doesn't want you, you just said. Olin, now's the time to get out, while you can. Go back to painting. You still have things to say, and now you can say them."

There was something in her voice that brought Olin's head around. "Ellen—"

"It's true! We could go somewhere and—"

"We?"

She stood up. "Yes. If you'd like it that way."

Olin arose from his own chair. "Now, wait a minute. You always said you had everything arranged. Everything you wanted. And now you're talking about . . . giving it up?" He swept out his arm to encompass house and land.

"I wouldn't have to give it up. But leave it, yes."

"You mean, getting married?"

She shrugged. "If you'd like. Any way you want it." She raised her head. "I would have agreed long ago, done anything you'd wanted, if I'd thought I had any chance against Heath Chandler. I knew there was no hope of your ever leaving him, nobody does—not as long as he needs or can use them and decides to keep them. But now he's bowing out, and Andrew is perfectly capable. And you're not bound to Andrew. And I think you've still got too much left in you to waste any more of it."

He opened his mouth, but she went on. "I know, your age. What difference does that make? Picasso, Casals—people still create when they're old, they have mastery then. They know who they are. And if you moved out from under Heath's shadow you would too."

She came to him, put her hands on his shoulders. "I don't know how much money you have—"

"Roughly eight million dollars," he said wryly.

"That doesn't mean anything—I can't even comprehend that much money."

"Neither can I."

"Except it means this. You have no worries about being free. You don't need Heath, or anybody. You can do anything you please."

"Yes," he said. "I could."

She stepped back. "What are you afraid of?"

"I might fail," he said. "I did once."

"What difference does it make?"

"A lot. I'm too old to risk anything now. I've put it all away. I don't want to bring it back out again. It might . . . hurt."

"You've gotten soft. But you're old enough to stand the pain. So am I. You have given Heath Chandler most of your life. Why not take the rest for yourself?"

Olin did not answer, only looked around, at the pasture, the last truncated remnant of ancestral land; the geldings; the house crammed with the artifacts of her whole life; the oaks and maples and flower beds, the unfinished portrait in the studio . . . And she would give it up for him. And she deserved— There was so much he had wanted for so long to give her that she would not take, and now she was offering to accept and— He had intended to leave her the money anyway. . . .

Then he thought of Heath, Claudia. All at once he was terrified, as he had been before, so many years ago, that morning at breakfast in Chandler House. They were his whole life. To tear away from them, uproot—

Then the fear vanished and a different sensation took its place. He looked down at her. "I couldn't just walk out tomorrow."

She smiled, and what he saw in the gray eyes made him feel foolishly unburdened by his years. "I didn't expect you to. But if you would just promise—"

"Oh, hell, yes! We can be married tomorrow, for that matter."

"No. Not tomorrow. Not until I'm sure you're free, so I won't be caught up too."

"All right," Olin said. "I'll stay until Heath comes back, keep an eye on Andrew until then. And after that—" He hesitated. "I'll leave." It felt strange, to say out loud that he would leave the Chandlers. "I'll leave," he repeated; and now he knew he could, and would.

Then they looked at each other; they had been lovers for so long and neither was a child, but still he reached for her, and she came to him.

At last Ellen stepped back, face glowing. "I'll be so damned glad not to have to paint any more peanut people! I'll be so glad to see you painting again! Where, Olin? Paris—Rome—I've always wanted to see Copenhagen! I—" Then, as if it was unseemly for a woman her age to show so much joy, she said casually: "We can plan it later; that's the most delicious part. Now come talk to me while I fix dinner."

7 As USUAL these days, Andrew worked late in the silent tower. The past four months had been a blur, the most taxing, strenuous period of his life. For three of them he and Heath had worked side by side, day after day, as Andrew reached out and grasped the details that, until now, the Old Man had carried in his head. It had been a hammering, relentless education, but the fact that Heath had finally allowed himself to be dragged to Europe meant that he had come through with flying colors.

Well, he thought grimly now, staring at his heaped desk, he had meant to. He would not give the Old Man a single excuse to cling to the active management of the company. Because now that was all he had left, his one chance to prove to himself that he still existed as a person, not as a shadow of another man. He was not Heath Chandler, and he would not run these mills Heath Chandler's way; and when the time came, he thought, he might just change the name on the water tower after all. His mouth curled wryly. He would like to do that anyhow, just before the Old Man came home, let it be the first thing he saw when he returned to Chandlerville, even if it had to be repainted the next day.

Then his mouth straightened, thinned again. Suddenly the weight he bore crushed down on him. He had a long way to go before he could afford insolence like that. Despite determination, resolve, he had, since Heath had left, felt like Sisyphus, laboring under a tremendous burden of work toward a distant goal, only to achieve it and then have to start all over again. But it was the price he had to pay, and he would pay it.

Slowly, stiffly, he arose, left the office, took the private elevator. It carried him to the roof; in the garden built there crickets chirped in earth high above earth. He went to the parapet, leaned against it, lighting a cigarette. Below him the mill thundered and rumbled, the high, impregnable fence around its enormous sprawl brightly lighted with post lamps, like the perimeter of a prison camp. A few windows gleamed yellow in the darkness; the great blue ones had long since been walled in, as air conditioning and climate control spread to every area of the plant.

Beyond it, up and down the valley, were the spangled lights of Chandlerville. His eyes turned toward the knoll; even with Chandler House closed, the mansion still dominated the town, lighted not from within but by floodlights all around it, illuminating it as if it were a monument. White, enormous in its setting of trees, it shone in the night.

Then his eyes dropped. That cluster yonder at the foot of the knoll—his own home; Ramsey was there. He made a sound in his throat, ground out the cigarette. What was wrong? God damn it, what was wrong?

To one person only had he talked about it—Vic. There was no one else to talk to. "It's not physical," he said. "I can't explain it. It's as if . . . as if some connection was broken. Between here"—he touched his head—"and here" —he touched his loins. "Two months—more—now. We go to bed, and . . . and I can *feel* her waiting, wanting, and I want her too, only I can't— At first I tried, but it wasn't any good. It was bad, bad as hell, worse than not trying at all. But I don't know *why*. I can't understand *why*."

"Too much work," Vic said. "You're too tired."

"Maybe that's part of it. Not all, though. There's something else. It's almost as if I'm waiting for something. In suspension. As if, until then, until it happens, whatever it is, I don't want to. Not with her."

"With anybody?" Vic looked at him narrowly.

"Once," Andrew said. "Once I had to go to Charleston, and . . . I met her in the bar of the Francis Marion, a schoolteacher from some little town down south, on a binge. It was all right, I was all right. Then, with her, a stranger. It didn't mean anything, you see, but I had to prove to myself that I could. That it wasn't that I couldn't, that it was something else. It's almost as if I'm taking some sort of revenge against her—and I don't want that."

Vic rubbed his face. "Maybe you'd better see a psychiatrist." He grinned. "There's no answer for that in my law library."

"I don't have time for a psychiatrist or any other crap like that."

"Then take a long vacation, the two of you together, work it out, huh?"

"A long vacation!" Andrew laughed harshly. "For the next year I'll be lucky to have time enough to go to the water house to pee." Then he was sober. "My God, Vic. Two months, and it's already bad. When I go home at night the tension is thick enough to cut. A year? What if it lasts a year?"

Vic was silent for a moment. Then he said, "I guess it comes and goes. My own performance has shrunk drastically since I took this Butler case. You talk about being in suspense; that's true. You're gambling for high stakes, and you don't know who or what you are until you win or lose, and nothing else seems important but that, you're in a kind of limbo."

"But sooner or later you'll either win or lose. Me—there's no clear-cut way to tell."

"I guess not. But maybe it'll wear off. When the Old Man comes home you can let him run things long enough for you to go off with Ramsey and—"

"He is not getting his hands on things again," Andrew

said harshly. "That's the one thing he's not going to do. If he does, I'll never pry him loose. No, not that."

Now he kept on staring at the lights of his own house. He could almost see Ramsey down there. Maybe she was undressing, going to bed early. He could, in his mind, watch her strip away her clothes, revealing breasts and belly and golden pubic thatch and long slim legs—and in that moment of imagining, of fantasy, he wanted her, felt a physical stirring. It was often like that, wanting her from a distance, abstractly. It was only when he actually approached her, came near her, that something died, the circuit was broken. Then, full of confusion and bitter self-hatred at his own, involuntary, perverse inadequacy, there would be times when he hated her too, transferring his own failure to her, seeking reason to blame her. And that frightened him. Because he did not hate her, he loved her, never wanted to hate her, always wanted to love her. And what he really hated was what was damaging him, so that he was damaging their marriage. Whatever it was, that was what he had to find, strike out at.

He grunted a curse, tried to put it out of his mind. Another hour, anyhow. By then she'd be in bed, asleep. It would be easier to go home then. For now— He turned from the wall, went back to the elevator.

The tower was hushed, except for a faint purr of air-conditioning machinery. The office felt cold and clammy, and, sealed, it was tainted with cigarette smoke. He went to a window, opened it, let the warm, sweet air of June pour in. Then the telephone, connected by a direct night line to the switchboard, buzzed. Ramsey, he thought, wanting to know how much longer he would be. Maybe hoping that tonight, anyhow—

He picked it up. "Chandler Mills, Andrew Ford."

"Andrew."

"Hello, Vic."

"Look, Andrew." There was a strange urgency in Royce's tone. "I hate to bother you this time of night, but would it be at all possible for you to run over to Macedonia? To my office, not my home."

"*Now?*"

"Now. Right away."

"What the hell's wrong?"

"Nothing wrong, exactly. I can't tell you on the phone. But it's important."

"Well, Vic—"

"Look, can you come or not?"

Andrew hesitated. "Sure. If it's that urgent."

"It is. The watchman will let you in. Come straight on up. I'll be waiting for you. The door will be locked, but just knock."

"I'll see you in about three-quarters of an hour."

"Good," Vic said. Then he hung up.

Andrew stood there, wondering. Vic handled no company business, but of course dealt with his personal affairs. He had better tell Ramsey how late he would be, although she was used to his being late now, no longer commented on it.

When she came to the phone her voice was cool. "Andrew?"

"Yep." He told her what Vic had said. "I don't have any idea what this is all about, but I'll be late, don't wait up."

"I won't wait up. But, Andrew—"

"Yeah?"

She hesitated. Then she merely said, "Be careful driving home."

The Law Building, nine stories high, was the closest thing to a skyscraper Macedonia boasted. Across the street from the ancient, white-columned brick courthouse, its dark granite flanks were punctuated by only a few lighted rectangles. The watchman had been expecting Andrew, who took the self-service elevator to the fifth floor. In a deserted corridor he passed three doors bearing the name of Vic's firm before he reached the entrance to the suite. It was indeed locked, but when he rapped on the frosted glass a bulky shadow moved behind it. "Come in," Vic said as it swung open; and, when Andrew did so, closed and locked the door again.

"Listen, what's all this cloak-and-dagger—"

"Wait a minute. This way." Vic led him through the spacious and expensively furnished reception room to his own office. Its door swung inward on a room furnished with a nice balance between prosperity and functional austerity. Vic shut it behind them. "Now," he said.

"Hello, Andrew," said the man slouched in the chair across the room.

Andrew looked at him blankly: round, sunburned face with gray eyes beneath sandy brows, a bulbous nose, small, nearly feminine mouth. White shirt, tieless, open several buttons down to reveal a hairy chest and hugging the bulk of what could only be a beer belly; the trousers of a cheap suit, and unshined shoes. There was a glass in the big, freckled hand, and a rumpled jacket and discarded necktie lay across the back of the chair.

"I told you, Vic," the man said, grinning. "Once they reach the top they forget all their old friends."

And then it clicked in Andrew's mind. "Paul!" he blurted. "Well, hell's bells! Paul McCloskey!" Suddenly he laughed, then they flung themselves at each other cursing, half embracing, shaking hands. Vic stood beaming, like the godfather at a christening. "You see?" he crowed. "You see? Stuck his head in the door while I was working late, didn't even knock. First thing I knew, here's this idiot telling me an ambulance just went by. I'd better hurry if I aimed to catch it!"

"Well, damn!" Andrew backed off, looking McCloskey up and down. Brackettville: memories surged back. Paul thick and blocky even then, sandy-haired and freckled. And luckier than most, for his father was a weave-room foreman. The three of them, on the same street in the mill village, had been inseparable, from shooting marbles to working in the mill. How long? Andrew wondered. Sixteen years, and Paul fat and balding . . .

Andrew turned to Vic. "You bastard, with your cloak-and-dagger stuff. I thought the IRS was on me, or something."

"There was a reason for the cloak-and-dagger stuff." Vic gestured to a bottle, glasses, ice and water on his

desk. "Have one if you want, I'll go get another Coke."
He went out.

Andrew and Paul McCloskey stood grinning at each
other. "I can't believe it. I just can't believe it," Andrew
said. "Where'd you get that pot?"

"Worked for it, damn it. It's about the only thing I got
to show for my whole career. Andrew, you look good.
Haven't changed a bit, except a little dark under the
eyes. Like you could use a good night's sleep."

"Hell, I'm president of Chandler Mills, I'm not supposed
to sleep." Andrew turned, reaching for the bottle.

"Andrew," Paul said.

Something in his voice halted Andrew. "Huh?" He
faced Paul again.

McCloskey now was strangely serious, almost uneasy.
"Before the festivities start, there's something I ought
to tell you."

"Like what?" Andrew frowned.

Paul licked his lips. "Well . . ." He grinned faintly,
almost bashfully, then was very sober. "The fact of the
matter is, Andrew, you might want to turn around and
walk out of here right now. Because, you see, I . . .
am an organizer now for the Textile Workers Union of
America. And the reason I'm down here is to organize
Chandler Mills."

There was a moment when Andrew's brain seemed
turned to flint, unable to absorb those words. "Paul, you're
joking."

"I'm afraid not. I am that dread and fearful creature,
the union man. And if you want to get the hell out right
now, before some of the goofer dust blows off me and
contaminates you, I won't blame you. But I hope you
won't. Because I'd like to talk to you, and this may be our
only chance."

Now Andrew had grasped it. "You really mean it, then.
You are an organizer?"

"Have been, for the past ten years almost." Paul went
to the bottle, poured a small splash of whiskey into his
glass, added water from a pitcher. "And . . . this might

be a bad move for me. I mean, popping in on Vic like this, and then asking him to call you. But . . ." He grinned, and that lighted his face with warmth. "Whatever the outcome, I wanted to see you and Vic—personally—while I had a chance. It's been so damned long."

Vic returned then, Coke in hand. "Did you tell him, Paul?"

"Don't you see how unhappy he looks?"

Royce perched on the edge of his desk. "Now you know why the secrecy. If my partners or my clients got wind that *he* was here, that I not only entertained a union organizer, but with the firm's booze—"

"The kiss of death." Paul nodded, and his grin faded. I'm sorry. Maybe it wasn't a smart idea. If you'd rather, I can just walk out of here."

"You will like hell," Andrew said. His shock had dissipated now. "If you think I came all the way over here to let you make a couple of cryptic statements and run, you're crazy."

"Oh, that sounds like Andrew now." Paul smiled, lowering himself once more into the chair. "Only, I can see it in your eyes. Before anything else, you want to know what happened to good old Paul. How did a nice guy like him get into a business like this? Of course I really should be more surprised to find you two where you are. Anyhow, it's a long story. Want to hear it?"

He had joined the Navy, made a number of hazardous convoy runs across the North Atlantic as an armed guard crewman on merchant ships. "When I got out I figured on doing what you two did—get a college education under the G.I. Bill. Only it didn't work out that way. When I went back to Fall River, where Daddy had moved during the war . . . Well, he was in bad shape." Paul stared at his glass. "What we used to call the Monday Morning Chest. Now it's beginning to be called Brown Lung, like the Black Lung coal miners get, only slower and takes a while longer to kill you." He drank. "But it does, just as sure and twice as hard. Twenty or thirty years of dragging lint and bale trash dust into your lungs—"

"That's not what does it," Andrew said reflexively.

"Oh, come off it, Andrew—save that stuff for public pronouncement from on high. You and Vic and I, we've all three seen it, the old-timers with their wind shot. I know, the mills claim there isn't any such disease, because if there was, it would throw you open to paying workmen's compensation for it. But I saw my father die of it. By inches, gasping for every breath. Pneumonia finally put him out of his misery, thank God. When your lungs are that far gone, not even penicillin can save you—which in his case was a blessing."

The room was silent for a moment. Andrew and Vic were both remembering Ralph McCloskey, stocky, vital, open-hearted, with the Irish-Yankee accent that had set him apart in the Brackettville village. The deep laugh, the impartial kindness, the scarce food shared because they were his son's best friends and because they were hungry children . . . Andrew felt a deep and genuine sense of loss, of grief. "I'm sorry," he said quietly.

"Thanks." Paul's voice was also soft. "Anyhow, that left me with Mama and two sisters to support and doctor bills to pay, so instead of school, I had to go back in the mills. Which was all I knew, there not being much market for training in how to serve a three-inch gun. Anyhow, the union came in up there and organized the mill—after a long, mean strike. Well, I was hot on it. Then I was made shop steward of the local. And one thing led to another and— Well, the TWUA needed organizers, men who knew the mills and spoke the language, so to speak, to come into the field down here. And here I am. Eight years now I've been playing boogerman all through the South. And when the time came to move against Chandler, I was the logical choice."

He broke off, drained his glass, and set it aside. "First, let me congratulate you, Andrew. I thought I had come a long way, but you hold the record. And Vic says you've earned it, every bit. I'm proud of you, boy."

"Thanks," Andrew said wryly. He and Paul looked at each other and laughed. Then Andrew said, "Let's back up. What's all this crap about you trying to organize Chandler Mills?"

"I thought we might shoot the breeze a while before we came to that."

"We can shoot the breeze later. Right now I want to know whether you're serious or joking, and what all this is about. And especially, damn it, why us? Why not go after somebody like St. John Butler?"

"We already did, at Brackettville." Paul's face was serious. "And, frankly, we sort of got a bloody nose. And I'll admit that was my fault."

"Yours?"

"Right. I recommended that little caper." All at once his face was grim. "I had a score to settle with St. John Butler, you know? My daddy. It ended in Fall River, but that's where it began. And we were planning to come back down here on a large scale. They asked me for recommendations, I looked around, suggested Butler, with Brackettville as a start. Morale lower than a snake's belly, working conditions terrible, pay down on the bottom—it seemed a cinch. Matter of fact, it was. What I didn't count on was how cold-blooded Butler was. I never figured on him just wiping out a whole mill, a whole town, in one stroke, just because of us. That was pretty brutal even for him."

He paused. "But of course it served his purpose. He threw such a scare into all the other people at all his other plants that it will be a long time before they give us the time of day. And then he tied us up in court and—" He looked at Vic, smiled faintly. "Until that's settled we'll have to stand clear of him."

"Yes," Vic said tersely.

"So that leaves Chandler Mills, Andrew. You're the lucky winner. If we can crack you we can crack anybody."

Wholly relaxed now, Andrew leaned back in the chair. "Paul," he said, "I'm glad you called me over. We can save both of us a lot of time and trouble. You didn't by any chance time this, did you, by waiting until Heath Chandler went to Europe and I was in charge?"

McCloskey laughed. "It seemed a good time to get things under way. Seriously, Andrew, yes. I knew there'd be no talking to Chandler. But I figured at least I could talk to you. Maybe anyhow you would listen to what I have to say."

He leaned forward. "We are going to come back down here, and no ifs, ands, and buts about it. And we're going to organize this industry. Southern textiles is the lowest-paying industry in the country and the last big one left unorganized, and I think those two facts speak for themselves. I'm under no illusions; you people have a license to steal so far as your labor is concerned. You own the state government, and you've got your right-to-work laws, and so you pay the very lowest wages, the least fringe benefits, usually none at all. I'm not talking about Chandler, I mean the industry as a whole." His face hardened. "I saw what happened to my father; I worked myself to supply what company insurance and workmen's compensation should have. And I've seen it happen to too many others. I've seen people who've worked for a company thirty years thrown out on their asses to starve when they got too old to serve its purpose, treated the way you wouldn't treat a horse. I've seen them locked out without warning, and I've seen Brackettville and what happened there. I've seen them abused in every which way, and so confused by the way you people play Big Daddy to 'em and seal 'em off from the outside world and tell 'em lies that they didn't even know what was being done to them. You have too, Andrew, and you, Vic, so don't deny any of that." His eyes gleamed. "It'll be a long, hard fight, but we're going to make it, and someday we'll win it."

"Maybe. Anyhow, you do a lot of research before you hit a company, don't you?"

"Tons of it."

"Then," Andrew said, "you ought to know that most of what you just said doesn't hold good for Chandler Mills. We're the one company that's never locked our doors, regardless of how bad times got. We pay an employee bonus, and I'll invite you to examine our program of

fringe benefits. We've built a club for the employees
complete with golf course and swimming pool. We offe
scholarships to their kids, we've set up a hospital plan. It'
true that we don't pay union scale. We can't, not and mee
competition. But at Chandler the people have alway
come first. And they know it, and so do you."

"Exactly. Chandler's policies have been almost reason
able. That's one reason we picked you. Especially nov
that you are president. At least, you'll listen to my offer—

"Offer?"

"Right. This is gonna be a rough battle, like I said. Bu
it would be a lot easier if we could gain a foothold righ
away, without a lot of fighting. If somebody would giv
us that . . . Well, if we have to fight, when we win we'
take everything we can get, hold the company's feet t
the fire. But if we didn't have to fight, if we could b
certified and accepted without resistance, real resis
ance . . . Why, we would be prepared to moderate ou
terms considerably. And the company that lets us in lik
that will be in a very favorable position in relation to i
competition when the competition gets organized."

"A bribe," Andrew said, almost with amusemen
"You're offering me a sweetheart contract to let you i
and give you a start?"

"I'm saying that we'll organize Chandler Mills one wa
or the other. If you're reasonable it will cost you a lot le:
in the long run."

"I see." Revolving his glass between his hands, Andre
stared at it. "And with all this research of yours, did yc
overlook one thing?"

Paul was silent for a moment. Then he said, "You mea
Chandler's boy?"

"Yes. Hamp."

"We know about him. Everybody does."

"Then you know Heath Chandler would die before h
would deal with you. And kill me before he'd let me c
it."

"Listen, Andrew, the union didn't kill that boy. Esp
cially, not ours. We weren't even chartered until 193
Hamp Chandler was killed in 1934."

"Tell that to Chandler. A man named Freeman—"

"Freeman didn't do it. I've been in this business a long time. I've heard the old hands talk, all the inside scoop, drunk and sober. If anybody in any union had killed that kid I'd know it. Andrew, it must have been the Klan. Heath Chandler had just stomped down on them, hard; run them out of all his towns—"

"He turned the Klan inside out. And found nothing."

"It only takes one man. Anyhow, Freeman didn't do it. And Freeman's dead. He went off to Spain with the Abraham Lincoln Brigade and never came back. If Chandler wanted Freeman's ass, he can relax. Franco and the Nazis got it first."

He arose, went to the bottle, again poured a small drink. "Andrew, why can't you and I deal? Hell, we've had it, all of us, had our noses rubbed in it. Don't you remember?"

"Of course I do."

"Then, why? Why can't we—"

"Because," Andrew said. He also got up to make another drink. "I could give you a number of reasons, Paul, all the conventional ones. I could tell you that our conscience is clear—which, mainly, at least by comparison, it is. I could tell you that it would put us at a competitive disadvantage, and that if we let you in we'd be damned by all the rest of the industry as traitors and . . . well, there are ways in which that could damage, even ruin us. I could tell you that the hands don't want a union, that they hate unions themselves—"

"Sure, the way they've been brainwashed."

"I could go on and on." Andrew poured from the bottle. "But it all comes down to this. I am president of Chandler Mills. For certain reasons, which may not be the ones you'd think, it's important to me to be president of Chandler Mills, to have not just the title, but the power, the authority, the—"

"Money," Paul said wryly.

"No. That's the least of it. Anyhow, if you come after us and if I didn't fight you, if I didn't throw everything we had at you to stop you and send you home with your tail between your legs, just like Butler did, I'd be through. The least softness toward you, and Heath Chandler would be back here and jerk the reins out of my hands so fast it would make your head swim. I don't intend to have that happen. So I've got to fight you, don't you see? Maybe harder even than he would."

"I see," Paul said, his faint smile frozen on his face.

"But I'll make you a counteroffer. You go pick on somebody else. Raise the wage scale, get fringe benefits, whatever you can. And if it's the hands that you're really concerned about, Chandler will meet everything you can gouge out of someone else without your having to lift a finger. There won't be any union, you won't get your checkoff, but our people will benefit by everything you do."

Paul looked at him a moment, then the smile came to life again. "Sorry. Impossible."

"Why?"

"Because the decision's made. It's irrevocable. And . . . because you're the logical place to start. You're big, prestigious, and . . . you're vulnerable."

Andrew turned away, went back to his chair. "I'd call that a miscalculation. We're the least vulnerable outfit in the business. That's because Heath Chandler has worked for nearly thirty years preparing for this day. He's way ahead of you, Paul. We're not vulnerable. We're impregnable."

"I beg to differ, Andrew, old boy."

Andrew faced him again. "All right. How?"

"In several very important ways. Which, since it looks like push is rapidly approaching shove, I won't mention for tactical reasons." Then he grinned. "Final word, Andrew?"

"Final word."

"Well, at least that clears the air. Glad of one thing. If somebody's going to fight me, at least it'll be you. Maybe between the two of us we can keep it reasonably clean. At least no violence."

"Not unless you start it. I'll guarantee that. Those days are past, anyway."

"Are they?" Paul asked sardonically. "You know, Andrew, sometimes it works two ways. You talk about Hamp Chandler . . . I've got a wife and two daughters up in Baltimore. The way I work, I'm lucky if I see 'em once a month. I'd love to bring 'em down here, but I don't dare. You know why?"

He sat down. "A case in point. Two years ago, in a little town in Georgia, I tried to start my car and it wouldn't crank. So I opened up the hood, and there they were—three sticks of dynamite cuddled up against the block. And if the son of a bitch who put them there hadn't fucked up on his wiring . . . So the case of Chandler's boy is not exactly unique."

He drank. "Anyhow, I leave them up there, where they're safe from reprisal, and take my own chances. Because there are other things, you see? Ever been arrested for something like double parking, Andrew, and then hauled off to jail because the cop swears you cursed him? And while they're booking you, you 'fall down and hurt yourself'—you see? Or 'struggle, and they have to use force.' That's what they tell the judge. It accounts for all the cuts and bruises."

"Paul, we wouldn't—"

"Oh, come off it, Andrew. Don't tell me what you will and won't do. Chandlerville's a dictatorship, and you know it. The minute I enter it I am outside the protection of the laws of the United States and the State of North Carolina, and at your mercy. So if I've got to be at somebody's mercy, I'd rather it be yours."

His eyes glinted with amusement as he looked at Andrew. "I see disbelief. I don't believe you know the drill, not the way I do. But, I have no doubt, you'll learn it."

"You don't have anything to be afraid of, physically, in Chandlerville. I told you I'd guarantee—"

"We'll see," Paul said. Then his voice changed. "Well, that takes care of that. Thank God, the business is out of the way." He looked from Vic to Andrew, then grinned lewdly. "Say, you two remember that Turlington girl, I think her name was Sarah, the one with those enormous knockers? I've always wondered what became of her—"

8   ON THE BORDERLINE of drunkenness from both whiskey and fatigue, Andrew drove back to Chandlerville. It was nearly two, and the road was empty save for an occasional 'possum prowling for carrion killed earlier in the day by cars. Once he almost hit one, but swerved the car in time as it waddled stupidly away, eyes like emeralds in the headlights.

It had been better, he thought, after the talk had turned to sex and war: neutral ground. Paul drank sparingly, Andrew a little too much, and Vic sipped Coke. They traded pictures of their wives and children: Marion McCloskey was a handsome Irishwoman, a little raw-boned, and Paul's two daughters, fourteen and twelve, were in his image, with appealing, intelligent faces. Strain eased, they laughed and joked and needled one another, and for a while almost forgot why Paul had come. Then, reluctantly, he had arisen. "Damn, this has been good. But I've got to drive on to Charlotte."

"Oh, hell, stay and have another drink," Andrew urged.

"Nope, I've had my quota." He touched his stomach. "Matter of fact, I like the stuff too much. Have to watch myself. Especially in this territory." He grinned at Andrew. "Last thing I want is a driving-under-the-influence charge. You won't call the cops when I leave, will you, Andrew?"

"You go take a flying leap—"

"Sorry, that was a low blow."

"Paul," Vic said, "there's no need for you to drive that far tonight. You can stay at my house."

McCloskey looked at him and grinned. "Nope. Sure as fate, this would be the night St. John Butler decided to come over and crawl into bed with you." He picked up his coat. "That would really cook your goose." He turned to Andrew. "Well, lad, I'll see you soon, I guess."

"How soon?"

Paul grinned slyly. "You'd like to know, wouldn't you? But soon, believe me."

"Don't hurry, unless you'd like to change jobs. I'm looking for good men, trying to expand my staff—"

"Afraid not. Besides, I'm infected. I'd contaminate all around you." He thrust out his hand; then he was serious. "Andrew, I reckon it'll be a knock-down and drag-out; I'll lay on, and you will too, and may the best man win. But no hard feelings, eh? You know what I mean."

"No hard feelings. Anyhow, when you've thought it over, you'll change your mind in the cold, gray light of dawn."

"Not a chance. When it's all over, though, we'll have another drink, either way. Vic—?"

After Royce had showed McCloskey out, he came back into the office. "Well," he said quietly. "Well, Andrew, it looks like it has hit the fan. What are you going to do?"

"Just what I said." Andrew's voice reflected the confidence he felt. "Not give Paul even a toehold."

"You've never handled anything like this."

"No. But I've been briefed."

"Vulnerable. You think you are?"

"No. Not unless he was counting on my friendship."

Vic began to clear away the bottle and the glasses. "I don't know. Unless Paul's changed, you don't want to sell him short. He's a natural leader—you know how he used to make you and me jump through hoops. And stubborn as a mule—" He turned, his face grave. "Will you handle it all yourself, or will the Old Man come into it?"

Andrew drew in a deep breath. "I'm going to do my best to keep him out."

"Good. I know you'll play by the rules. With him there . . . I'm not implying that he'd resort to rough stuff, but I know how he feels, he might lean on Paul a little. And I'd hate to see old McCloskey get hurt. Beaten fair and square, that's one thing. Hurt's another."

"As long as he plays by the rules I can handle him. And

as long as I can handle him I can tell Chandler to keep out of it." Andrew hesitated. "It's Ramsey worries me."

"You think this might—?"

"I don't know." Suddenly it burst out of Andrew. "God damn it, Vic, you don't know how they are, the two of them! Like a religion, and them the only communicants. But not the flesh and blood of Christ, the flesh and blood of Hamp!" He drew in a long breath. "At the very least, it'll scare the hell out of her."

"I'm sorry," Vic said. He was silent for a moment. "Well, darn. Who would ever have thought—?" He rubbed his face. "Well, beat him, Andrew. I have to root for your side, my bread and butter depends on it. So go ahead," he added a little ruefully, "and I'll hold your coat."

"You sound like you'd rather be holding his."

"No. No, given a choice between the union and you and Chandler, I'd side with you anyhow. I'm no union partisan, I'm not that much of a hypocrite. Maybe it's just . . . dealing with St. John Butler. I guess my gorge has risen a little."

"He has a way of making it do that. Vic, I'm bushed. I'll head home now."

"Yeah, me too. I hope the kids haven't eaten up all the ice cream. I'm keyed up, it's gonna be a while before I sleep."

When Andrew reached home and got out of the car he was almost lurching with fatigue, and his brain felt as if it had been scrambled like an egg. Tomorrow, he thought. I'll sort all this out tomorrow, and then, after I talk to Clutt, decide what I'm going to do. He let himself into the house, then halted. A glow of light came from the bedroom in the rear. Oh, God, he thought. Please don't let her be awake right now. I don't want to have to answer questions.

But Ramsey was awake, sitting up in bed with a magazine propped against her knees. "Andrew? Darling?"

"It's me."

At the sight of him her eyes widened. "Good heavens. You look exhausted."

He sat down on the bed, began to unlace his shoes.
There was a hesitant silence between them. Then she
asked, almost timidly, "What in the *world* did Vic *want?*"

"Just a matter of business."

"Until two in the morning?"

"Yes," he said, voice edged, "business. Until two." Then
he turned on her. "Why? You think I was out with someone else, or something? Call him if you want to."

Ramsey's face went taut. "I didn't think anything.
Except to wonder where you were, to worry about you."

"I'm sorry," he said, and meant it. "I know." He rubbed
his face, passed his thumbs across his eyes. Then suddenly
he realized that he had to tell her. I must not, he thought
vaguely. I must not start thinking of her as my enemy.
And that, he suddenly realized, was what he had felt as
he questioned him. "All right," he said. "Listen. Do you
remember Vic and me talking about Paul McCloskey?"

She relaxed a little, even smiled. "Constantly."

"Well, he was in Vic's office tonight. He's an organizer
with the Textile Workers Union, and they're coming after
us, going to try to get into Chandler Mills."

"*What?*" She sat bolt upright, and in the glow of the
red lamp her face was pale as bone.

"Now, don't get all upset." And he told her.

She listened wordlessly, but when he was through she
laughed, a harsh, metallic sound. "So that's what it
meant."

"What what meant?"

"Last night. For the first time in years I dreamed of
. . Hamp again."

"God damn it, Ramsey, don't be absurd."

"I'm not being absurd." She shivered, looked toward
Lloyd's room. "There's nothing absurd about it after
what—"

"It's not even the same union. And Paul's my *friend*.
He's no"—wearily he groped for the name—"no Freeman."

"How do you know?" Her eyes were wide, frightened
in the lamplight. "After all these years, how do you know
what he is?" Then she said, "Well, you'd better call Father
right away. I've got their address and number in London."

"I'll call the Old Man when I'm ready to."

"Andrew, *now!* He's got to know."

"Of course he's got to know. But I'm not going to call him in panic and have him come flying home, barging in, taking over. I'll call him when I'm ready, when I know when Paul's coming, when I've got my own ducks in a row. This is my affair, not his, Ramsey. I don't even need his advice—there are no decisions he has to make. I know what he wants done, and I'll do it. Myself. And if I can't handle things, that will be time enough to yell for help."

"But he'll be furious." She was not making a statement, she was warning, threatening him.

"I don't care what he is." He got to his feet. "God damn it, either I'm president of this company or I'm nobody. It's all there is left of me, and I'm not going to have that taken away too, do you understand? I'm not—"

She looked at him strangely. "Andrew." Then she said, "You're so tired you can hardly stand. Darling, come to bed."

"That's what I'm going to do. Tomorrow will be time enough."

"All right," she said. "Just come to bed now."

Five minutes later he had done that. He lay there tensely. She lay beside him, body not quite touching his. Fireworks of weariness seemed to pop and flare behind his eyelids. He went to sleep almost at once.

But on one occasion he awakened in the night. She was not by him any more. Rolling over, he realized vaguely that a light burned elsewhere in the house; he heard the pad of footsteps. He half raised himself to call out to her, but then lay down and slept again.

9

His CHIEF PLEASURE in the past four weeks had been the pleasure they had given Claudia. For himself the return to Europe had not been without pain. Some of it he had anticipated; some had come as a surprise. But he had left too much of his youth overseas; all these years it had seemed to him that it waited there, untouched, for him to reclaim it. Foolish, of course; childish and naïve. But it accounted for the fact that save for two brief fortnight's trips in the past four years, he had avoided going back. His excuse had been the dreary and unappealing state of England and the Continent in the war's wake; actually, it was as if something valuable to him had been locked up for years in a sealed chamber, and he could not bear to open the door again and see what time had done to it. So long as he did not actually confront it again, it remained for him intact in his own imagination.

Not so any more. The stored treasure had been transmuted by the years, its gold turned to dross, its velvet threadbare; all of it smelled like dust and rot. The Second World War had wiped out his war, as a second wave changes the contour of the strand imposed on it by the first. His own no longer counted, was irrelevant. He still had friends and old war comrades everywhere, but their numbers had been diminished by the latest war or years, and those left reflected painfully his own aging and decline. Moreover, after all those momentous events in which they had taken part and he had not, he sensed in them a kind of pity for him, that he had not been with them on their St. Crispin's Day. Even the sensual pleasures he had so much enjoyed were forbidden now: the doctor had made clear to him how lethal the wine and food could be; long walks in the hills were beyond his strength; the single fox hunt in which he had ridden had left him drained and weak and shaken; everywhere he turned he was reminded that, like a clock, he was running down. It was maddening to walk among temptations everywhere, to be surrounded by things he loved and could not touch, to flame inside with youth and be imprisoned in that hulk of body reduced to a sort of childish impotence. Thus for him the trip had in some measure become an ordeal, and he could redeem it only by seeing that for Claudia it was as nearly perfect as he could make it. But with only a fraction of their time used up, he was growing nervous, jumpy, and irascible.

Then Ramsey's call brought him out of bed at six one morning, heart pounding with quick, involuntary fear. But as he listened to her that ebbed. He reassured Claudia with an aside as she sat up in bed, staring. Then, when Ramsey had finished, he said: "Don't worry. Don't worry about anything. Listen, as soon as Andrew's up and has had his coffee, tell him to call me. I'll be right here, waiting."

Three thousand miles away, she hesitated. "You're not supposed to know."

"The hell I'm not."

"He says he'll take care of it. But all the same, I thought I had better— He'll be furious at me if he knows I called you."

"I'll straighten that out with him. You tell him to phone."

"Yes, sir," she said. But she still sounded dubious.

"You did the right thing. This is something I had to know. Now, don't get all in a swivet. You tell Andrew to call, and give Lloyd a squeeze for your mama and me. Goodbye, honey." His voice was soft, loving, persuasive.

"Goodbye," she said, and she hung up.

Heath put down the phone and turned to Claudia. "Nothing drastic. Nobody sick or anything. Only a little cloud on the horizon." Then he told her what Ramsey had said.

She listened in silence, sitting there in bed. "Anyhow, when Andrew calls, I'll get the straight of it. It can't amount to much."

"Ramsey was afraid," she said.

"A little shaken up, yeah. More by the fact that Andrew didn't want me to know than anything else. However—" He took one of her cigarettes and lit it; he never carried any of his own nowadays. He tried hard to make his voice casual, reluctant. "I'm glad she did. I expect I'd better start checking airline schedules. I just might have to dash home to Chandlerville for a while." Then he could control himself no longer, began to pace, feeling

ood, younger, stronger, than he had in months. "Maybe
ought to call Andrew now, even if it means getting him
at of bed."

"No," said Claudia.

"But, damn it, it's only a little after two there. It may
e six, seven hours before he calls back."

"You can wait," Claudia said quietly.

Heath stared at her. "I don't know. It just might be
aat every minute counts."

"They're not there yet, are they?"

"They might be, for all I know."

"Well, if they are, they can't do much between now and
ae time you talk to Andrew."

He ground out the cigarette, reached for another. "You
on't seem to understand."

"I understand," she said tautly. "Let's get dressed and
ave some breakfast. I see no point in even thinking
oout it until you've talked to Andrew and got things
raight. I hope—" There was a hardness in her voice. "I
ope when you do, it won't be necessary for you to go
ack there at all."

He opened his mouth to challenge that, but her face,
ale, set, changed his mind. "Maybe you're right. Okay,
e'll forget it until then and go on with our regular
genda. But let's be sure to be back here in time for
ndrew's call."

Nevertheless for him the morning passed with leaden
owness. By one they were back in the suite, and he had
anch sent up. Then the phone buzzed. Heath set down
s coffee cup so hard it clattered, reached for the instru-
ent. "Heath Chandler here."

"Captain." It was a good connection. "I understand
amsey called you last night, this morning."

"That's right." He glanced at Claudia; she arose and
ent to the bedroom phone. He heard her say, "Andrew,
arling, I'm on the other line. How are you? Is everyone
l right?"

"Everyone's fine," Andrew said thinly. "There's nothing
 get upset about, absolutely nothing. I'm sorry Ramsey
othered you."

"Don't come down on her about that," Heath said. "She did the right thing. Besides, she was scared. You know—"

"I know," Andrew said. "No. I haven't fussed at her."

"Good. Don't. Now, I would like to have all the details From beginning to end. Everything you know about this joker and everything he said."

"All right," said Andrew, but Heath heard the reluctance in his voice. Then he began to talk. His narration was succinct, lucid, organized. Heath only rarely interrupted with a question.

"I see," he said when Andrew had finished. "Let me have that again—he said we were vulnerable?"

"Yes, sir."

"And this McCloskey. What's your assessment of him as a man—ordinary, smart, brilliant? How's he fixed for imagination? Is he a leader? And how tough is he?"

"He's smart," Andrew said. "Maybe not brilliant." He paused. "He's got imagination, and he's a leader, and he's tough. Of the three of us—him, me, Vic—he was the one who always called the tune. Got us into trouble, got us back out again. But I can handle him. I know him."

"I'm sure. All the same . . . The bastards. The damned bastards. I waited and waited for them to drop the other shoe, see who they were going to hit next after Butler. But they outwaited me. . . . Well, Andrew, the first step is to see that they don't even get a foothold, a lodgement. No motel, hotel, boardinghouse. An operation this size, they'll need a headquarters, a command post. We're not going to give them one in Chandlerville or any other place that we can freeze them out. I want you to see to that, that they get no aid and comfort from anybody. I'll have the hide of anybody that rents them a room or house or even toilet privileges."

"I'd already planned on that. It's my first move this morning."

"Good, son. You're on the ball. I'll be in touch with you later on, and I want a report by phone from you every day as to what's happening and what you're doing. Frankly, I think I ought to come home for a while."

There was silence at the other end of the line. Heath

sensed the suppressed displeasure in Andrew's voice when he finally spoke. "I don't see any reason for that. I know your policy. It's up to me to carry it out. If I need you I can holler for you."

"If it's not too late by then."

"Captain," Andrew said in a tone Heath had not heard him use since the first night he had seen him, "I don't need you here. I will handle this."

"I am sure you will, Andrew," Claudia cut in. "We have every confidence in you. Don't we, Heath?"

"Yeah, sure, of course. Only . . ." Heath hesitated. "Yes," he said. "But stay in touch, Andrew."

"I'll do that," Andrew said.

Chandler hardly heard the rest of the conversation as Claudia asked for news of Ramsey and Lloyd. Since Andrew was calling from the office they could not be put on the phone. Vaguely he heard Andrew tell her, "Yes, of course. She's a little upset. But there's nothing to worry about, absolutely nothing. I know Paul McCloskey, and whatever he does, it won't be anything . . . like the other time."

"I'm sure. I'll call her myself and talk to her later on. We love you, Andrew."

"The feeling's mutual"—and for the first time Andrew's voice really came to life.

"And you let me know the minute there's any indication when that son of a bitch will show," Heath ordered.

"Yes, sir, I'll do that. I will keep you *fully* informed." Again Andrew's tone had bite. "Goodbye, Captain. Goodbye, Claudia." And he broke the connection.

Heath turned away from the phone, began to pace. He felt as if shrouds and wrappings had been whipped away from his mind; it was free, no longer muffled, dulled. His imagination leaped ahead. Painstakingly he had studied the tactics of labor and the unions. They varied from industry to industry, shifted with the political climate, mutated with every new ruling by the government bureaucracy and the courts, every discovery in the psychology of public relations and the art of manipulating people. He kept abreast of all that, and had lately begun to make Andrew do so too. Vulnerable. That word rang in his head. McCloskey thought he was vulnerable. Or was it that he thought Andrew Ford might be?

"No," Claudia said from behind him.

He turned, to see her standing in the doorway.

"No, what?"

"We are not going back—unless Andrew asks you to come."

Heath halted. "I think that's a decision it's up to me to make."

She crossed the room, took a cigarette from a pack on a table, lit it, snapped shut the lighter, blew a plume of smoke. "It's Andrew's decision, not yours."

"This happens still to be my company. I'm the board chairman, with ultimate responsibility."

Claudia looked at him with eyes suddenly devoid of warmth, angry, almost contemptuous. The day was cloudy; in oyster-colored light penetrating the suite, mingling with the dim incandescence, every line and wrinkle was visible in a face still magnificently constructed but beginning to be ravaged. Her mouth was set, thin, and the sharpness of her features seemed accentuated to the point of bleakness.

"Your ultimate responsibility is to Andrew." Her voice rose a little. "You've asked everything of him he had to give, and he gave it to you because he loved you, Ramsey, maybe even me. Now it's time to pay him back."

She sat down on a chair arm, shook her head. "Why can't you see? Didn't you hear his voice on the phone? Didn't you see the way he looked that day when you made him president? You must have looked the same way when Bolivar put you to work in the mills—like a prisoner being condemned. Andrew's so much like you, a strong man, his own man. You've tied him to the mills the way you were tied, but at least when you came back you had a chance to be Heath Chandler. Aren't you ever going to give him one to be Andrew Ford?"

"He'll have plenty of chance when I'm dead and gone."

"Ten years from now, twenty, when he's an old man himself?"

Heath hesitated, searching her face. He had not told her anything of what the doctors had said, and, he realized now, she had not guessed. She had no idea of how short time was, how desperately short it might be, and what he must do before it ran out. And yet he could not tell her.

"Andrew will have his chance," he said, "and in due time. Meanwhile . . ." Heath took another tack. "Didn't you hear Ramsey? She's frightened. If I'm there she'll feel a whole lot better."

"It's not your responsibility to look after Ramsey. That's her husband's job."

Heath was silent for a moment. "Listen," he said quietly, "this time I'm not going to take any chances. Not any—do you understand?"

"Then stay away!" Claudia almost yelled. She jumped to her feet. "That's why you've got to stay away!" She made a quick, savage gesture. "Don't you think I'm afraid for them too—Andrew, Ramsey, Lloyd? Don't you think I can remember? That's why you've got to stay here in Europe!"

"You're not making sense."

"The hell I'm not! Andrew and McCloskey know each other, they're friends. They will not harm each other. Whatever happens, it can happen on some . . . some civilized level. But not if you go back!"

Her eyes glittered like polished stones. "I know what you want to do, I know what's in your head! *Oh, boy, they've come back at last, now I can get my hands on 'em, now I can pay 'em back for everything!* And if you go home you'll jerk everything out of Andrew's hands and try to roll over them like a . . . juggernaut, just crush them! And then they *will* have to fight back, and when that happens, who knows what else may happen? You won't even give them a chance to talk, negotiate, you'll go straight for their throats—"

"That's the only way to win!" he snapped.

"You won last time too, didn't you? With machine guns on the roof, and bayonets!" Her voice was brutal, cutting. "Oh, you won, all right, you won big, and look what it cost us!" Suddenly he saw tears glistening on her cheeks. "Do you think I want to pay a price for winning like that again?" Her voice rose. "What difference does it make if they unionize your God damned mills, so long as nobody gets hurt? Will the sky fall? Will the . . . the dead rise out of their graves? Other companies work with unions. You've overcome bigger handicaps than that, so can Andrew. What difference does it make?"

"A lot! A hell of a lot!"

She turned away, ground out her cigarette. "Only," she said hoarsely, "to one man, and he's been dead for nearly thirty years."

He looked at her back, bent as she rubbed the cigarette into the ashtray, saw the sharp points of shoulder blades against the fabric of her dress, realized the thinness and frailty of her body; and he went to her and put his arm around her and held her against him, his chin resting on the top of her hair. "Now, listen," he said quietly. "I understand exactly how you feel. I think, maybe, you're even right. I mean about Andrew having a free hand, what I might do if I mixed in. All the same, I think I should be there. Having no part in it, but just staying on the sidelines. In the long run it will be easier for Andrew."

"No," she said hoarsely.

"Yes. Now, look. I have one thing going for me, a kind of power that Andrew, no matter how he tries, can't muster. Don't you see? I'm the Old Man. To them, to the hands. Their loyalty isn't to the company, it's not to the main office and the tower, and not even to the paycheck. It's to me, because I have earned it, the hard way, and they know how hard, and so did my father before me. My God, don't you think I know the mistakes I made before, and what they cost me? How many nights do you think I've lain awake, wanting to just seize time with my hands and rip it, peel it backward so I could undo it all. And so I planned. I planned never to let it happen again. I planned to seal them to me so tightly that it could never happen, I would never need machine guns on the roof again. This is no mob from another plant to be defied, now. These are my own people, and we know what we owe each other. When any family—"

Claudia stiffened beneath his grasp. "They're not your family."

"They think they are. I have led them to believe that. And when any family is in trouble, when strangers try to divide them and turn them against one another, they are entitled to have someone to turn to to tell them what to do, what's right. And that's what I owe it to them to do. If I'm not there to show them that I care for them, that what they do matters to me—"

"They can turn to Andrew."

"Not yet. He hasn't been the Old Man long enough. Ten years from now, twenty, yes. But, no, not now." His arm tightened. "Damn it, honey, don't you see? This loyalty is our armor. I've worked since 1934 to make it strong enough to withstand any assault, so that all by itself it'll be enough. So there won't be any need to use other weapons."

"You'll use them."

"No. I promise you. But without me, there isn't any armor. If I'm not there, Andrew is . . . yes, he's vulnerable. Everything they throw at him will hit him. And you talk about his self-respect, his identity. Suppose he fails? In his first trial, suppose he loses, flops? What will that do to his identity and self-respect? If I'm there, if I can bring that loyalty into play, there's a brick wall between Andrew and McCloskey, one the union will see soon enough there's no profit in trying to knock down. If I'm not, Andrew's fighting in the open, unprotected, with both hands tied behind his back. And that way he can't win."

He felt Claudia shudder beneath his grasp. "No. No, I can't believe that. I know you too well. If you go home—"

"If I go home it will be only as a flag for the Chandler people to rally 'round. To make sure Andrew has their support. Beyond that it's all in his hands. I won't mix in. I promise you that."

She did not answer.

"Look at it from my standpoint. If I'm there and we

lose, I'll accept that. But if I stay and we lose, and Andrew has to swallow the bitterness of failure when I could have kept that from him, just by my presence, nothing else . . . That will do things to everybody nobody can predict."

"God damn you," Claudia said thickly.

"If it pleases you and Him."

"No. God damn you, because you make so much sense and I know you won't—"

Heath let go of her. "I will. We go home. I'm there, and if my being there is not enough, I can't help it. But I will not, beyond being there, infringe on Andrew." He turned away. "You don't send a kid to the store without money. Well, twenty-five years of being the Old Man is all the money I've got to give Andrew when he goes to buy whatever it is he wants."

Claudia did not answer, only stood by the table looking out the window. Then suddenly, without even glancing at him, she walked swiftly to the bedroom.

"Where are you going?" Heath flung at her.

In the doorway she turned, her face a mask. "Where do you think?" she rasped. "I'm going to pack our things. Call the airlines, call Andrew, tell him you're coming home. But I'll warn you now, you've made a promise. And I'll hold you to it. And if you—" She broke off. "We can be ready to leave tomorrow morning," she said, and slammed the door behind her.

10   THE HOUSE was in Village Number Two, across the river from the Chandler mansion, which McCloskey, as he stopped the car, could see, white, massive, brooding, on its knoll. As he got out of the three-year-old Chevrolet he felt a curious sense of nakedness, exposure, as if that house could see him, had already fastened on him its hostile gaze. Despite the heat of the bright June morning he shivered slightly, then laughed soundlessly at his own misgivings. Then he turned, looking up and down the street.

As an expert on mill villages, he had to give Chandler credit. Though a good forty years old, the four-room houses were sound and well maintained, and any that needed paint, he knew, were not owned by Chandler. They were the ones recently sold to their inhabitants under the new Chandler program of giving certain selected, loyal, and worthy employees the right to buy their dwellings. The rest, mill property, gleamed with fresh white paint, and though they were all identical, the lots on which they sat were larger than in Village Number One, across the river, and better kept, with trees, patches of lawn, even flower beds. And there were people on the porches, looking at him curiously as he dug in his pocket for the key the man in Charlotte had given him. "Morning," he said politely to an old woman on the porch of the house next door, who had stopped sweeping to stare at him, and he smiled and nodded.

"Morning," she answered. She kept on watching as he went up the steps, opened the front door, entered.

Inside he grinned. They would know soon enough who he was and what he was about. Then his smile vanished. So would Andrew. For a moment he wondered again if it had been a mistake, that midnight session with Andrew and Vic. Then he shrugged. It had been a good reunion, and what the hell. Two days advance warning to the Chandler management would make no difference one way or the other. He quit thinking about that and explored the empty house.

It had a large front room with an oil space heater; behind that a hall with bedrooms on either side, a kitchen in the rear, a somewhat primitive bathroom built as an afterthought, floored with scabby linoleum. Well, it would do; he'd used worse. He tried the water; the faucet hissed with air. Obviously it had been turned off, and so had the electricity. His grin was rueful. It was not likely they would be turned on either, but that was something he had already made allowance for.

Leaving the front door open, he went back to the car,

got his suitcases and the broom. The woman was still on the porch; he nodded and smiled again. Then he set his luggage in the corner and began to sweep, clearing out the dust before Brinton, Onslow, and the truck came. He hoped they would hurry up. Now that they were in the open, he did not want to be alone in Chandlerville any longer than he could help. It had been different on his other trips. No one then had known his identity.

Sweat poured down his round face as he swept vigorously and swiftly. Too damned fat, he thought, getting soft, must do something about this potbelly. Well, likely he would lose some of it here. He would be busy this time, not sitting around restaurants and beer joints and such places, as he had done on the other visits.

Over the past sixty days he had been here often, two and three days at a time, staying at a different motel each trip, familiarizing himself with the city and the people in it. He ate where the workers ate, drank beer with them in their taverns when they came off shift, hung around the little groceries, which, like country stores, were social centers for the people of the various villages and developments. He bought things, too, that he did not need in the downtown stores, striking up conversations with clerks and managers. He made himself agreeable, affable, to anyone who would talk, and spoke little himself, but listened carefully. During that interval he had subscribed to the daily *Free Press*, the town's one paper, wholly owned by Chandler, and read it carefully, down to the last engagement announcement and obituary, so that when the time came, he would already know something about the personal lives of the people whom he must approach. He had even read Heath Chandler's published plays, seeking some insight into the man and the way his mind worked, trying to capture the person beneath the legend.

And of course had digested the vast mass of information compiled by the union's research facilities, every scrap of data about the structure of the company, its operations, its finances, and the personal affairs of every member of the Chandler family and their chief executives. Despite everything, however, there was a curious paucity of such information.

Which he had expected. Such southern mill dynasties were all alike in this respect: they abhorred publicity. Carefully holding their stock within the family, they were secretive as so many Byzantine princes. Partly this was merely their nature. Dour Scotch-Irish with a rigid Fundamentalist tradition, like the other southerners of the region, they lived comparatively modest and unspectacular lives, as clannish and inward-turning as the mill hands themselves. Unlike the big tobacco families, they frowned on conspicuous and flamboyant marital scandals; Heath Chandler was the closest thing to a playboy they had ever produced. Mostly, though, their secrecy and virtual invisibility were defensive strategy. The size of their fortunes, if made public, would have shocked laborers working for the lowest wages in the country, caused them to wonder, given the union a weapon to use against them.

It was absolutely necessary, if the iron grip on their subjects' loyalties was to be maintained, that they never violate the fiction that they were no better than the most ignorant spinner or doffer, only luckier, beneficiaries of the American system of free enterprise, rewarded by a stern, just, all-seeing Jehovah for shouldering the vast burdens and responsibilities they carried. The revelation of their wealth, or flagrant violation of the rigid moral code of their employees, would have undercut their positions as chieftains of the clan, benevolent patriarchs and defenders of the faith, protecting the less fortunate from the evils of communism, racial equality, Yankee money-grubbing and soullessness, and all the other threats to the cherished southern way of life.

So they let nothing leak out that they could help, gave no interviews save to trade magazines, and usually made no spectacular gifts or endowments to such hoity-toity things as universities (except textile schools), art museums, or orchestras. In a sense, Paul thought, putting aside the broom, they were prisoners too, locked behind the cold, gray walls of what their workers deemed acceptable, reduced to the lowest common denominator by their

need to maintain their rule. Like, he thought, the plantation owners before the Civil War, the prisoners of slavery.

Well, those people had fought to keep their slaves,
maintain their own imprisonment. So would these.

When he went out on the porch again the woman was
gone, but two young girls, out of school and not old
enough for work in the mill, stood in the yard opposite,
staring and whispering. He smiled, said hello, and waved;
they giggled, then fled.

Paul looked up and down the street. Television aerials
glinted on every chimney or rooftop. Below, in the valley,
the city sprawled, huge now, still growing. In some places
it had overlapped the limits of Chandler land, fingers of
private ownership stretching out into farming country.
Cars by the hundreds crawled, like ants along a base-
board, up and down the streets and highways.

McCloskey smiled. Vulnerability. Wherever he looked
he saw it. It would not be easy, no. But it would not be
impossible either, as it would have been ten years ago,
or five. Nevertheless he felt a thrill of fear mingled with
expectancy. For now he was in hostile territory, surrounded by his enemies. He wished that his two assistants
would hurry with the truckload of office equipment, furniture, and literature. He did not like being alone; besides, it was bad policy. Then as he lit a cigarette he saw
the Cadillac swing around the corner, come toward him
along the street, moving slowly, and he straightened up.
He tossed aside one burned match, waited as the car
stopped before the house, and when Andrew got out he
smiled.

Ford came up the walk dressed in sports shirt and
slacks. There was a wry grin on his face as he mounted
the steps. Paul saw that his eyes were darkly circled, as
if he had not had much sleep since the other night. He
thrust out a hand. "Morning, Andrew."

"You didn't waste much time," Andrew said, shaking it.

"Neither did you. News gets around fast."

"Yes. We have our sources."

"Spies, you mean." With amusement on his face,

IcCloskey looked around the village, thinking of all
1ose watching eyes.

"Maybe." Andrew sat on the porch railing. "You can't
.ay here, you know."

Paul took from his hip pocket a folded paper. "This
ase says I can."

Andrew frowned. "Mind if I see it?"

"Hell, no. Look it over." While Andrew unfolded it
nd read, Paul went on. "All signed and in order. Closed
1e deal day before yesterday. That's why I had to go to
:harlotte." He grinned. "Don't feel bad, Andrew. A bu-
eaucracy big as yours can't catch everything."

Andrew folded the paper, handed it back. "Our real-
state department was supposed to have bought back this
ouse. I'll have somebody's ass because they didn't. How
id you get onto it?"

"Through a little skulking, keeping my ears open. You
old the house to a man named Bradshaw, a twenty-year
mployee. When he died his son in Charlotte became
xecutor of the estate. Young Bradshaw has no particular
ive for or obligation toward Chandler Mills. Your depart-
1ent did approach him, but it haggled over price, the
eal got hung up in your one-man system somewhere
long the line. So when I asked Bradshaw for a six-month
ease, he gave it to me. Simple as that."

"Yeah, very simple." Andrew looked at him a moment
/ith a mixture of rueful affection and exasperation. "So
ou've already outfoxed me."

"My two associates and our gear will be coming in any
ime. Where should I go to have the lights and water
ut on?"

"You know perfectly well where to go," Andrew said,
rinning coolly. "But it may take a little time—you under-
tand? Like you say, our bureaucracy moves awfully
low. It might even take six months."

Paul laughed softly. "Well, it won't be the first time I've
sed a chamber pot and worked by lantern light."

"You'll want to be real careful about sanitary regula-
ions," Andrew said. "That's one thing we're very strict
bout."

"Oh, I'm sure. I'll watch it. I'd hate to see this house condemned for anything. Of course, so would Bradshaw in Charlotte. He's a lawyer, by the way. We discussed that. If you condemn his property and interfere with its production of revenue he'll get an injunction."

"We've got lawyers too." Andrew took out cigarettes, lit one. "But for the time being we won't get mixed up in that. We'll let you go ahead and see what you're up against. It shouldn't take long to make a Christian out of you."

"Or somebody," Paul said.

Andrew's face was serious. "Paul, you're not fool enough to think you can really do it."

"I won't brag in advance. But there's a good chance, Andrew. Yes. A good one."

"Just you and a few others, with all we can throw against you? Hell, you can't even pass out pamphlets at the gate. That's Chandler property. You can be arrested for trespassing."

Paul laughed. "Not so. Go back and take another look, Andrew. The streets on two sides of the plant were taken into the state highway system for maintenance ten years ago. That saved Chandler some money. But it also means that state right-of-way runs up to his very fence. You can't arrest me when I'm on state right-of-way."

"Well, I'll be a son of a bitch," said Andrew. "I'll check that."

"It wasn't really Chandler's choice. But the state had to have some assurance that people could get back and forth and up and down the valley, so they made him give them special easements. You'll have to put all your gates on the other side if you want to block me off."

Andrew laughed too. "Well, I'm glad it happened before my time. The Old Man will chew me out about the house, but he can't chew me about that." Then he was almost grim. "He's coming back, you know."

"No, I didn't. But I expected it. I didn't figure he'd hold himself haughtily aloof."

"Well, I had hoped he would."

Something in Andrew's voice made Paul look keenly at him. "What's wrong?"

"What's wrong, for God's sake?" Andrew laughed bitterly. "You, among other things. God damn it, why couldn't you wait a year, two years, to come? When I had everything in hand—"

"Would you have dealt with me if I had?"

"Probably not. But it would have been easier for me to call my own shots. There are other reasons too, but none of your business." Andrew rubbed his face as if suddenly weary. "Paul, I don't know whether we'll be talking any more after this. But . . . I am going to try to keep control, you understand? I'm going to do everything I can to see that you don't get off the ground, I'm going to use every legitimate means at my disposal, and I'm going to make it as hard for you as I can. It's important for me to chase you out of here. For me to be the one, you understand? And not just to make points with Chandler either. So don't expect any . . . mercy. The quicker I can break you, the better off we'll all be."

"We?"

"You too."

"What you're trying to say is, if you don't beat me, then Chandler takes over. And Chandler plays rough."

"I'm not saying it'll be that way, I'm saying it's a possibility. With him there's no predicting." Andrew stared down the valley for a moment silently. "With me it's just a matter of business. With him it's"—he gestured—"something deeper."

"And just for the sake of supposing—if I start to win?"

"You can't. That's what I'm trying to tell you. How could you?"

"The same way you shake an apple off a tree. Ripe fruit falls."

Andrew grunted an obscenity.

"I mean it, Andrew. If my calculations are correct, you and Chandler might as well come to terms and save us all a lot of trouble. I need signatures of thirty percent of your employees to call an election; if we win, are certified, then we negotiate for a contract. I'm pretty sure I can get those thirty percent. In fact, there's no way you can stop me." He paused. "The Old Man may own Chandlerville, Andrew, but he doesn't control it anymore. It's grown too big, too diverse for one man to keep his thumb on."

"You don't know how total his power is."

"I know. I know exactly. Too total. More power than any one man should wield over other people in the United States of America in the mid-twentieth century. That's the trick, Andrew. The bigger they are, the harder they fall. Remember what happened to the dinosaurs." He broke off. "Chandlerville's a dinosaur, Andrew, something that shouldn't even exist any longer. You'll see what I mean soon." Then he tapped Andrew on the arm. "Okay, boy, give me hell. I'll hand it right back to you. But hold the beatings and the workings-over to a minimum, huh? I got a tender skin and I bruise real easy."

Andrew stared at him. "Don't talk like an idiot." Then he arose. "Well, I'll be going. Lots to do—Chandler will be in this afternoon."

"Would it do any good to come around and see him?"

Andrew laughed harshly. "You couldn't get near him. And you're better off if you don't. So long, Paul." He turned away, went down the steps. McCloskey watched him go, walking slowly, head down, and for a moment he felt a pang of compassion for Andrew, sensing unhappiness, something even more serious, in him. But he could not imagine what might cause it; Andrew had everything anyone could want.

At the car Andrew paused, turned, lifted his hand briefly, then slid behind the wheel. Paul waited until the Cadillac had rolled away, then he went back in the house and picked up the broom again.

Ramsey sat in the big car and kept the engine running so the newly installed air conditioner could function. Heat waves arose, shimmering, from the asphalt of the landing strip and the corrugated iron of the hangar as she yearningly searched the glaring sky for the black speck against the sun dazzle that would be the plane.

he had never expected to need them, to need *him*, again
s much as she did now.

In Claudia's absence she had taken over, probably for
ood, the function of liaison with the women of the
handler towns. Now she was the one to whom they
urned for help. But, she thought, she was as frightened
nd in need of help herself as any of those supplicants.

She thought of Andrew across the breakfast table two
mornings ago, face pale, eyes, circled with fatigue, angry
nd accusing. And there had been no way she could make
im understand. He was not the one who had begun to
ream about it again.

"So the first thing you did was run to Daddy." His
oice was harsh.

"I'm sorry. I couldn't sleep and—" She broke off. She
ould not tell him what she had felt lately that had made
er so vulnerable to the panic. How could she say, "He's
one, and you seem to have turned against me for some
eason I cannot understand, and now I feel I'm adrift."?
here was no way she could explain to him the chaos
rithin her. But she had learned this: at least one of them
ras necessary for her survival. "I didn't know you wanted
) keep it from him."

"Would it have made any difference if you had?"

She stared at him, astonished by the bitterness in his
oice. Then he went on, less harshly. "Never mind. I
ouldn't have kept it from him anyway. I just wanted to
ave things all in hand before he found out, came charg-
ng back." He folded his napkin, got up to leave. "I'll
hone him from the office." He came to her, touched her
heek in a ritual kiss, went out.

When he had gone, she remembered, she had wan-
ered the house aimlessly for a long time, though there
vere things she had to do. But she could not organize
erself or focus on them. All she could think about was
he truth that in these past thirty days she had learned
bout herself.

It was that she was not well. Ten years of marriage,
lacid, pleasurable, almost that many of being a mother,
nd yet she had been deceived. She had not changed at

all. She was still unreal—the swirling smoke in the bottle formless, shapeless—without either Andrew or her fathe. to give her form and being. It was as if she had some sort of disease for which their love was medicament abating but not curing it. They stabilized her, held her together. The hard, cold fact of the matter, she told her self, was that she was still an eleven-year-old child, need ing Hamp. Andrew fulfilled that need; so did Heath Chandler. Without either one she was still sitting on the pavement in the cold, screaming.

And now Heath had gone away, and Andrew—

It had been a long time since she had drunk anything in the morning. But, almost absentmindedly, she went to the bar that morning after he had left, made a martini took it to her room and locked the door. Sitting on the bed, she sipped it slowly, but the alcohol only added to the curious illusion that nothing around her had reality and it failed to moderate the anxiety, the fear, and sense of alienation within her. What did they call it? "Anomie —she had heard the word; the psychiatrists had used it Detachment. Detachment from reality.

It had not come to her swiftly, but had grown slowly insidiously, then hit her with full impact after her father left and she was alone. She slept with Andrew every night, saw him every day, but she was still alone, and she could not understand it. He was withdrawing from her, leaving her stranded, and the panic came, the same nameless panic that she had felt so long before, a kind of agony she did not think she could endure again.

At first she had attributed it to overwork. She knew what a burden his new job had laid upon him, not only of actual labor but of anxiety, the necessity to succeed It was his excuse too, and she had been willing to accept it at first. That would explain his inability to make love and that, the physical act, she could somehow do without. But she could not do without the rest of it, the other kind of love. And now it seemed plain to her that his body only reflected what he felt in his heart. He seemed to feel some nameless antipathy, even hatred for her now; he no longer touched her or held her, there was a missing spark. It was as if she had offended or hurt him deeply and he took revenge, but she did not know where or how she had transgressed. She did not know what he had against her, and she was afraid to ask. For if he told her, that might end it, there and then. I might, she had thought, cradling the glass that morning, just fly apart.

He was unhappy; that much she knew. And he held his unhappiness against her, deemed her somehow the cause. He was waiting for her to say something, do something, but she had said and done everything she knew of, and what he wanted was beyond her ability to imagine.

She had finished the martini, found no answer. It had only left her feeling rotten all day long. And that night had been a bad one; her father had phoned again; he was coming home. And she of course was responsible for that too. Yet he did not flare at her, berate her; that would have been all right—any reaction would have been all right. It was the way he withdrew into himself; and they were, truly, even in bed together and lying side by side, strangers that night. He was a man she had never met or know before. Again, then, she had dreamed of Hamp. Again the whole thing had happened once more, and she had jerked awake with mouth open in a silent scream and had lain sleepless for hours afterward.

Yesterday, she thought, still staring at the sky beyond the runway, had been a kind of blur. She had taken Lloyd to play with Mildred's children, then driven back along the Macedonia road. Still possessed by that curious, sourceless anxiety and fear, hours of it yawning ahead of her. Then she thought of the river house. It had been a long time since she had felt this way and gone out there alone to swim and drowse in sun on the dock, and drink— not much, but just enough to keep the fear and hagriding anxiety at bay. She had stopped at the roadhouse, bought four cans of beer from the man with the black mustache, enduring his bold eyes, like fingers pressing on her flesh. Something about him frightened her, and she had almost fled from the place. Then she had driven to the river house and managed to lose the afternoon in drowsing on the dock, in the flood of sunlight that was like a blanket of comfort on her body.

Presently, though, she came back to reality. She got Lloyd, took him home. He and Andrew built a model together that night, carefully excluding her from their intimacy of maleness. She lingered restlessly on the fringe of that closed circle, then went to bed. When Andrew came, got in beside her, she was suddenly possessed by physical desire so strong that it was almost uncontrollable, something she had not known in years. She did everything she could then to arouse him, to make him give her satisfaction; she was both as subtle and as wanton as she could be, in every way she knew he liked. But it did not work. And when she gave up, things were worse than they had been before; she felt in him not only withdrawal but humiliation; she herself still itched with desire, and yet her heart seemed at the same time turned to ice. For a moment she even hated him too. And she dreaded to give herself to sleep, knowing what dream would surely come.

Strangely, it had not. She had dreamed another dream. It lingered long after she had awakened to find Andrew already gone. Then she threw it off. Because she remembered: today was the day they were coming in. Her whole mood changed to one of eagerness, expectancy; when he arrived she would be all right again, and then she could think, figure out what was wrong.

Now she leaned against the window, feeling cool glass on her flesh. Soon, now, any minute, the plane Andrew had sent to the Charlotte airport to pick them up should be here. Hurry, she thought, now hurry. . . .

Then she saw it, a dark sliver against the glare, coming from the east. She flung open the car door, stepped out into heat that shocked the breath from her. The sliver grew larger, larger still, resolved itself into wings and wheels and fuselage, and slanted downward. Then it touched, rolled along the runway, came to a halt before the hangar. The propellers stopped. Presently a door opened, steps came down. The pilot descended, put up a hand, helped Claudia out. After her, moving slowly and carefully, came Heath. As he descended to the pavement he saw Ramsey, grinned and waved.

Her heart leaped within her; she waved back and ran across the runway to embrace her father.

11 BY THE END of August the drought had lasted for sixty days. In the searing heat streams and ponds recoiled from their banks, revealing secret shames of scabrous mud flats and snaggled, slime-coated rocks. Tree leaves dangled limply from their stems like tiny victims at the ends of gallows ropes. The heat bred violence: the sudden snapping of rubbed nerves, the quick grab for knife or pistol; the screech of tires and the engine thunder of cars roaring out of roadhouses in the dead of night. Swimmers and fishermen went out too far to seek embracing coolness, vanished, to surface later as strange, ugly, bobbing jetsam. Heath Chandler suffered from the heat, and like everyone else, slowed down to conserve strength and sweat. Only Paul McCloskey, he thought, with mingled admiration and bitterness as he sat in his tower office, was functioning at full speed.

He arose from his desk, went to the window, pulled back the drapes, looked out. The water tower, silver, hog-shaped, glittered in the sun, and in its glare the letters on it seemed invisible.

It was not that he had misjudged McCloskey, he thought, but he had misjudged a lot of other things. Perhaps, as much as that hurt, he had even misjudged Andrew.

No, he thought. No, that was wrong, unfair. It was not Andrew's fault. If he had misjudged anyone, it had been himself.

He remembered that first evening at Chandler House after their return. Ramsey had recalled the furloughed servants, arranged the dinner; she had been gay, sparking, obviously delighted by his return. It had, in fact, taken some doing to get away from her, seclude himself in the study with Andrew and Olin.

"Of course," he said, "I'm kind of taken aback by his getting the house. That was a damned stupid, inexcusable failure on the part of the real-estate department. But, then, this man struck so fast . . . Well, he knows, then, he's not going to get any lights and water. That was a good move."

"Thanks," Andrew said, with something in his voice that made Heath look at him. Of course, Heath thought. I would have felt the same way if Bolivar had still been alive and had interfered with me just as I was digging in my wheels.

"I want to make one thing clear," he went on. "This is your show, Andrew. Mostly I am going to stay home and putter one way or another. I've got a novel I started back in 1930 that I never finished, and that's going to engage most of my time and energy. But . . . let's run over the ground first, eh?—see where we stand."

He leaned back, made a tent of his fingers. "Well, he's got his command post, and right smack in the middle of the people he wants to influence. His next step will be to demand a list of our employees, and under present regulations, the government says we've got to furnish it. In a pig's eye we will! Stall. Stall, obfuscate, litigate if necessary—but no rosters! Let the son of a bitch dig for everything he gets."

He leaned back. "Thirty percent of the employees to call an election. That's over a thousand signatures he'll have to leg it to get. Likely he won't even try to have an election held until he's got more than that, enough to make sure he'll win. Anyhow, the only way he's going to get 'em is to pass out his propaganda at the gates, go house to house, he and his understrappers, like salesmen, soliciting—"

"He's not going to pass out anything at the gates, right-of-way or no," Andrew said. "I've already talked to the state highway patrol captain in this district. We've settled it with him, the sheriff, and our own police. There'll be no question of jurisdiction. He'll be obstructing traffic and subject to arrest."

"Good boy," Chandler said, brightening.

"I've also given strict orders," Andrew went on, "that if he's arrested I'll have the hide of anybody who lays a finger on him or on his men. I don't want this company exposed to any charges of strong-arm stuff."

"Of course not," Chandler said. "Besides, there's no reason to use it."

"There's no besides to it," Andrew said quietly.

"Probably," Heath said, "that was ill-phrased. I think you know me better than that, Andrew."

"I hope I do. I only want to get one thing straight. We fight McCloskey with everything we have, yes. But there are some things I won't stand for."

Heath was silent for a moment. "Suppose he starts playing it rough himself? This thing can be predicted, Andrew, traced through logically." He leaned forward then intently. "I have no doubt we'll block McCloskey before he ever gets to the point of calling an election. But let's consider the worst. Suppose he does, and suppose he wins. Then, as the certified collective bargaining agent for our employees, he will attempt to negotiate a contract. You realize, of course, that under no circumstances will we even discuss one with him. Then his next move would be to call a strike. In which case our next move would be to replace the strikers with nonunion labor. Under the right-to-work law in this state we can do that. They'd have to cross a picket line. When that time comes you may not find your friend McCloskey such a petunia blossom. When he gets his back to the wall, then we had all better watch him. Because I am not going to have my plant closed down. Under no circumstances. If we have to go to Nova Scotia or Patagonia to get workers, by God, we'll do it, and we'll get them through the picket line and to their machines. Then there will be some rough stuff—there always is."

"We'll worry about that when the time comes. If Paul starts something, that's a different matter."

"Certainly." Heath relaxed. "I'm just trying to point out that the best way to avoid violence is never to let it reach that point. Move hard and fast—and short of it, never fear—to stop him early in the game. All right. He can't block our gates, that's established. Now, what about the house-to-house part of it?"

"There's nothing we can do about that."

Heath smiled, glanced at Olin, then back at Andrew. "There ain't? Let me suggest this, son. Suppose we assign a uniformed policeman to each one of those jokers day and night. Not to sneak and hide but to follow them everywhere they go. Never to intimidate or threaten, they're to be under orders not even to speak. But suppose each one of them carries a clipboard and a pencil, and the minute one of these organizers knocks on a door, whoever answers sees a cop standing there taking down his name, making a record of what he does? Nothing else, just standing there writing, and being highly, highly visible."

"I hadn't thought of that," Andrew said. He frowned, shifting uncomfortably in his chair. "Christ, that sounds like the Gestapo."

"Cold water, that's all it is, throwing cold water on everybody who gets carried away and tries to deal with 'em. Sometimes cold water brings a man to his senses pretty damn fast. That's my suggestion—but whether you want to do that, of course, is your decision."

Andrew lit a cigarette with short, jerky motions. "All right. We'll do it."

"I think you'll find it gets the message through. Oh, he'll still get some, the soreheads, the nuts, the chronic malcontents. I don't begrudge him those; I hope he does. They'll scare off the levelheaded folks. Once they see what kind of goony birds are signing up with McCloskey, they won't want to be involved with such trash." He pointed a finger. "It's important, though, that if he holds a meeting, anywhere, to make his pitch, we have a full list of names of everybody who attends. We ought to plant enough of our people in his bunch so we know day to day who's coming over to his side."

"Yes," Andrew said, looking down at his cigarette.
"I guess that's necessary." He hesitated. "You're talking
'bout reprisals, though."

"If it comes to that. If a man attends as many as two
meetings. We ought to let anybody have the first one
free, allowing for curiosity. But two means he's getting
interested. Then more cold water's called for, some strong
hinting. Maybe a little tampering with his lights or water,
or if he's behind on a payment at the bank . . . Or his
supervisor can lean on him a little . . ."

Andrew nodded, but his face was pale.

Heath saw that and said softly, "Sticks in your gorge,
doesn't it?"

"Yes, it does. We've got a case to make. I don't see why
we don't make it first, while he's making his, instead of
resorting to—" He broke off. "Never mind. I know, you're
right. This is the way to handle it. I just didn't . . . expect
it to go against the grain quite so much. Maybe that's because McCloskey's my friend—but, hell, that's my problem, not the company's."

"I'll be truthful," Heath said, "and admit I don't like the
means any more than you do. They make me feel . . . But-
lerish. But consider the ends that justify them. Our whole
competitive position's at stake. The first company to unionize is the one behind the eight ball. The others will
take advantage of that to eat us alive. Which means, instead of helping the hands, McCloskey puts their jobs in
jeopardy."

He reached for the brandy bottle on the table, poured
a splash. "But there's more to it than that. Chain reaction.
The politics of this whole state is geared up to keep unions out. More than just our own profits are at stake; the
whole economy of the state is based on nonunion labor.
It's the pitch they use to bring in industry from the North,
and we're talking about fortunes, not only in textiles but
land, banking . . . We're going to have every industry,
the whole structure of the Democratic party, especially
since the Republicans are making headway, looking down
our throats, expecting us to stand fast. If we don't, then

we're in trouble politically. And that could cost us Chandlerville."

He set down his glass after sipping.

"There could be a lot of money for a lot of people in seeing Chandlerville incorporate. A lot of power too. Oh, we could still exert control, but . . . The wolves have been howling around it for a long time, drooling and licking their chops. The real estate, the taxes we'd have to pay, a chance to set up a new political base for somebody . . . You don't keep a place like this in your own possession without challengers. Our political clout has held them off. Let the union in here, be the company responsible for breaking the . . . the united front, I guess you'd call it, and we're at a disadvantage politically. We don't dare do less than our very best to fight this thing. If we don't, it'll be taken out of our hands. The state government will be under pressure to fight it for us, and maybe in a lot uglier ways. Because, like I said, this isn't a matter that just affects us; in the long run it'll affect everybody in this state. And I don't intend to be the scapegoat or let the wolves come in and take away my town, our town."

Then he grinned. "Besides which, McCloskey expects it. Hell, he might even be disappointed if he didn't get it. This is how he earns his living and makes his reputation. He makes his move, we make ours, it's all ritual, like the mating dance of the sandhill cranes. And believe me, when we beat him—and we will—he'd rather be able to have the overwhelming force we used against him to point to and save his face . . ."

He paused. "In the long run we'll save trouble, maybe even violence, if we move decisively now. It's up to you, you give the orders." He broke off, and now his face was serious, even grim. "But you know my policies. I will not have a union in my mills. I will not shut down one of my plants for a single day. And I will not lose Chandlerville. No matter what happens. Be guided accordingly."

"Yeah," said Andrew, arising. "I will."

"Where're you going?"

"Back to the office," Andrew said. "There's a lot I have to do. Tomorrow I'll have everything in motion."

Now, in the tower, Heath let the drapes fall shut.

No, he could not fault Andrew. The boy had done everything he could, even when, obviously, part of it had nearly gagged him. But McCloskey— He was like mercury; there was no way to put your finger on him and hold him down. Heath grinned sardonically. If he'd been in McCloskey's shoes he would have fought back the same way.

The electricity and water had never been turned on; the union organizers had bought Coleman lanterns, hauled in water in jerry cans, and made good use of service-station rest rooms. He could of course have had the house condemned, but that would have accomplished nothing; the owner would have fought it, and probably McCloskey and his men would have had to be evicted forcibly. Which in turn would have created more complications . . . especially with Andrew, if there was fighting.

Well, he had kept them away from the gates; they had understood and had taken the warning when the state troopers had made them move on. He had made sure they got no roster of employees, and he had mounted a massive propaganda campaign against them through the newspaper and through the churches. The churches were a chief focus of social life, and the word of ministers carried weight; and the ministers of Chandlerville knew which side their bread was buttered on, and they could give the message, the warning, to even those hands who could not read. Still, that was a minor list of triumphs compared to those McCloskey had scored.

He was smart, and a professional. A lesser man would have begun recruiting in the Old Village, among the drifters and the irresponsibles and ignorant, the lowest in the pecking order and the easiest to influence. Heath had hoped he would; a cadre of such people would have frightened away or disgusted those hands of real importance and influence. But McCloskey had sought bigger game, concentrating on the better villages, the housing developments and expanding suburbs, seeking the most highly skilled and prestigious of Chandler workers.

The police had followed him of course, taking names. But that had backfired; McCloskey had neatly turned their presence to his own benefit and against the mills. Cops could intimidate the smaller fry, but these were key workers who knew their own value, and, it turned out, were more resentful than afraid. They took the name-taking as a slur on their loyalty, a surprising symbol of distrust in those in whom the company should have had the most confidence, and it rankled; there were those among them who would not accept it meekly. In a show of defiance they made opportunity for McCloskey to talk, and listened to what he said. And, damn it, Heath thought, the man must be a spellbinder. He got them—not many, but enough to form an influential, articulate framework on which to build—and they drew others to them. Too late Andrew and Heath had realized that the surveillance was doing more harm than good, and had had it reduced, if not dropped completely; but by then McCloskey had rung a dozen effective propaganda changes on their threatening presence.

It was uncanny, the mill's spies reported. That potbellied, grinning little man combined sheer magnetism, Irish blarney, and a bedrock understanding of the psychology of the mill hand into a potent mixture. This was no raging, foaming, bitter Freeman, spouting ideology and waving the bloody shirt; this was a clever, subtle, soft-sell salesman, who patiently won the friendship of the hands, then their trust, and then showed them ways to rationalize joining for their own profit what they had always been taught was a malign and foreign enemy of their freedom.

And so, six weeks later, he had a band of powerful and influential people on his side, who had taken their loyalty from Chandler and given it to Paul. He had infected them with his own dedication, determination, briefed them on their rights, promised them protection—and then had led them down fatal ways for his own purposes, as cold-bloodedly as a butcher using a Judas goat to lead sheep to slaughter. He had encouraged them to recruit on the job, in the plant.

And, Heath thought, they were like a cancer in the body of Chandler Mills. And cancers had to be cut out. He had waited for Andrew to move. And when Andrew had not, there was nothing else to do but force him.

"Just these three," he had told Andrew an hour before in the adjoining office. "We'll start with them, and maybe the rest will get the message."

Andrew bit his lip, looking at the list of names. After a full half-minute of silence he asked, without raising his head, "On what grounds?"

"Inefficiency. The only possible grounds. Anything else, we'll have the law on us. You can't fire people for union activity."

"Excuse me a minute." Andrew arose, went out. Heath sat there before his desk, finally stole a cigarette from a box on the great console. He lit it, then turned his head to return the stare of Bolivar on the wall. "Well," he said harshly to the picture, "damn it, *you* know I can't help it."

Then Andrew returned. He sat down behind his desk again, breathing heavily, as if what he had done had strained him. He looked at Heath directly. "I just checked the personnel files. You know of course that among them these three have better than fifty years of service?"

"I've known them for longer than you have," Heath snapped. "Hell, two of them I've hunted and fished with. But there's no choice—they left me none. They've turned against us, and I've got to make examples of 'em. I hope that'll be enough to bring the others to their senses." He paused. "They've got to be big ones, because when they fall I want them to jar the ground. Little ones wouldn't mean anything."

"All the same . . ."

Suddenly Heath jerked the cigarette from his mouth, ground it in the ashtray. "Damn it, don't give me any crap! Don't look at me like that! You want to gawp reproachfully at somebody, gawp at your buddy Paul McCloskey! This is his doing, not mine! Do you think I want to do this?" He broke off. "But I want them fired," he finished quietly, "and off the property by shift's end."

Andrew said, "That's not an order you can give."

Heath jerked erect. "It's not an order I can—?"

"No. Such matters are in my hands, my decision to make. I follow your policy, but how I do it is up to me, and that includes whom to hire and whom to fire." His eyes met Heath's. "But of course if you're dissatisfied you can always let *me* go."

Heath sat absolutely motionless for half a minute, trying to read Andrew's face. There was nothing on it to read; the younger man leaned forward slightly, massive head thrust toward Heath in the first real defiance he had displayed in years. A kind of warning rang in Heath but it was mingled with a pleasure that was real and deep. What he saw across the desk from himself was a man worthy of the succession—a man of strength and will, integrity and courage, fitting of the chair he occupied. A kind of rich, warm satisfaction grew in him. Yes, it had been worth it, the chance, the gamble. In that moment he loved Andrew in a way he could not express.

And yet it was necessary. It was absolutely necessary. "Maybe I should call a board meeting," he said. "Get Olin, Claudia, Ramsey, John Otis from the bank . . . If you want it handled by the board, we'll take that onus off you. I can understand your feelings. We can work it a different way." He paused. "Or, if you just want me to do it, take the blame . . ."

"No," Andrew said. "You stay out of it. I'll decide."

Again, another silence. Then Heath nodded. "All right. Then consider it only a suggestion. The decision's yours." He arose, went to the connecting door that led to what had once been Andrew's office and that now he used for his own. "It's up to you."

Since then he had been alone in here with his own thoughts. There was nothing else he could do today in the tower. He could walk downtown, follow his usual weekly ritual of strolling around Chandlerville, get a haircut, spend a half hour or more in the barbershop, that center of society where, while in the chair, he could make casual pronouncements that would be all over town in less time than they could have been spread by a sound truck, and with more weight. It was a vital part of his

nction, as he had made Claudia see. Their loyalty was
> him, to his *persona,* to the down-to-earth, sympathetic,
pproachable Chandler, the Old Man, who could speak
heir language, make their kind of joke, listen to their
roubles. They were flattered and appeased by personal
ontact, and reassured that he still cared for them as
eople. In turn he, too, got something from such sessions;
nd more than just a feel for the current of their opinion.
[e was, in a way, part mill hand himself, born and bred
f the same stock, and to be among them brought things
nto focus for him, gave him a sense of his own identity.
t was a way of maintaining his roots in their rightful
oil.

And yet he hesitated, feeling not so much reluctance as
ack of energy. Lately it had become an ordeal, partly
ecause of the diminishing of his own vitality, as much
ecause he was expected to know every name, every
amily history. Once he had, but there were too many
f them now, too many new ones, too many strangers.
'oo many faces with which he could not connect any-
hing; and, for that matter, too many indifferent to him,
eeing him not as friend and leader but only as the boss,
ource of threatening authority and money. Mercenaries.
. lot of mercenaries had moved in lately.

All the more reason why he must make the effort. They
ad to be bound to him as well. He must capture them
efore McCloskey did. Yes, tired as he was, hot as it was
utside, it was his duty to go down there for a while. He
ghed and turned toward the door. Then the door from
ndrew's office opened.

Andrew stood there, coatless, tie pulled down, a lock
f hair tumbling across his forehead. His face was set, yet
ithout expression. "I've considered it," he said. "I guess
's the only thing to do. They're to be off the property
ithin an hour." He looked at Heath a moment and then
urned away and closed the door.

12 THE MAN'S NAME was Baucom. The secretary had tried to keep him out, but, raging, he had pushed past her, flung open Andrew's door. *"Mr. Ford!"* he bellowed.

Andrew looked up, startled. Vaguely, he connected the contorted face, long and gaunt and lined, inset with blazing blue eyes beneath a few thin strands of blond hair, with a name. He laid down his fountain pen. Then, straightening, he said quietly, "You weren't announced, Mr. Baucom. But what can I do for you?"

"Do for me?" Baucom stood there incredulously. There were fluffs of lint still in hair and eyebrows; the arms beneath the short sleeves of his sport shirt were long and ropy with veins; his big fists were clenched. "You know damned well what you can do for me. They come to me ten minutes ago and told me that I was fard. Jest pulled me right away from my looms and put another man in there and gimme this!" He snatched something from his pocket, threw it down before Andrew. It was a pay envelope. "Well, lemme tell you somethin! I ain't about to take that money until I git some straight answers as to what this is all about. I've done worked here twenty years, I've done near about ever' job in this mill and done it right, and now they say I got to be off the property in a hour! What the hell's goin on here?"

Andrew picked up the packet; it was fat, containing in cash, current wages and two weeks' severance; Chandler Mills never paid by check. He let it drop, forcing himself to meet Baucom's eyes. "What did your boss tell you?"

"Told me"—Baucom nearly strangled on the words—"told me I was fard for inefficiency! Not gittin out production, hangin around the waterhouse too much, talkin too much. Inefficiency, my foot! I git my work done, always have! I ain't laid out or missed a day on the job in four years! I go to the waterhouse when I got to d

ny business, and that's all! And anybody that tries to say
I ain't efficient, I'll tell that man right to his face he's
a G.D. liar!"

Andrew searched for words. His own voice sounded
unctuous and repulsive to him when he found them.
'You'll have to talk to your foreman about that. His
recommendation was we ought to let you go."

"Talk to him? He said I'd hafta talk to you. What is
this, the old Army game?" Baucom's head swiveled.
'Where's the Cap'n! By damn, I wanta talk to the Cap'n!
He knows me, he won't let nobody get away with this
kind of thing!"

"The Captain isn't here," Andrew said evenly. "If you
want to see him, go to Chandler House. But it won't do
you any good. You were fired for cause, and"—he picked
up the envelope—"here's your pay."

Baucom stared down at it. Then something glittered in
his eyes. "Oh," he said, in a different voice. "Wait a
minute. Yeah, now I know. Me, Cofer, and Tinjen. Well,
you wait a minute, Mr. Ford. You can't do that. You can't
fire a man because he signed the union papers."

"Nobody," Andrew said evenly, "is firing you because
you signed anything. We expect you to do your job, get
the work out. You didn't. That's it."

"Don't lie to me," Baucom said.

"All right," said Andrew. "If you think you've got a
grievance, go hire a lawyer."

"With this?" Baucom turned the envelope in his hand.
"With three weeks' pay?"

"That's your problem. You should have been more
conscientious about your work."

Baucom stood there, rubbing the envelope. His face
twisted strangely; what Andrew was seeing, he suddenly
realized, was the breaking of a man's nerve, his pride, in
desperation. Then Baucom drew in a long breath. "Maybe
I should have," he said in a different voice. "But, look
here, Mr. Ford, after all the time I done put in— I've
worked here for twenty years, I'm past forty now, nobody
wants to hire somebody as old as me. And this thing

about inefficiency . . . You far me for that, I can't even draw unemployment."

"Maybe that's something you should have thought of . . . earlier." Andrew looked down at the papers on his desk. "It's nothing that can be helped now. I'm sorry, Mr. Baucom, but I'm very busy." He snapped the words. "I suggest you be on your way. We want you off the premises now. You've got two weeks in which to vacate your company house. I'm sure you can find some place else to stay by then."

"No!" Baucom snapped. "No, I ain't gonna be treated like this! Fard, thrown outa my house—!"

"I'm sorry," Andrew said. "These things happen." He could feel his stomach knotting; his hands were sweating. He laid them flat on the table so they would not shake.

"I won't move!"

Anger suddenly kindled in Andrew Ford. It was rage against himself, against Heath Chandler, against Paul McCloskey even— but the only target for it was Baucom. "You'll move or get thrown out!"

Baucom took a step backward. Andrew looked at the face, pale, bloodless, the frightened, angry eyes. He saw the hands clench on the envelope—the last anchor, the one barrier to disaster, oblivion. He felt hot bile in the back of his own throat, raw and sickening. Now the blacklist would go out. The man before him was, whether he knew it or not, destroyed.

Baucom knew it. There was a terrible moment when Andrew thought the man before him would either break into tears or launch himself across the desk. But he did neither. He let out a long, shuddering sigh, and his shoulders slumped. He had accepted it: the finality, the futility of fighting against anything as big as Chandler Mills. It was over; he would leave now and go home and somehow tell his wife and children.

Then, wordlessly, the man turned, shambled out.

He had more work to do, but he went home early that afternoon. When he had parked the car in the drive beside the house, got out, Lloyd ran to meet him, slamming his big head into Andrew's torso, dangerously near the crotch. "Daddy!"

Automatically Andrew picked him up, swung him high, kissed him, set him down. His hand caressed the flaxen hair. "Where's your mama?"

"She's out somewhere, said she might go to Charlotte, buy me a surprise."

"All right." They went in the house together.

"Look, Daddy, I got a new model today, a P-38, I already started work, you want to see it?"

"Later," Andrew said. "You get it finished, show it to me then. Do a good job."

Lloyd recognized dismissal; he had endured it often enough before. He turned to go.

"Wait," Andrew said.

The boy whirled around, brightening. "Yes, sir?"

"Bring it out to the bar. We'll have a look at it there."

They sat there, Andrew and Lloyd, the man with a martini, the boy with a Coca-Cola, examining the plastic airplane. Andrew thought of Luzon; he had seen those twin-tailed fighters go over often enough. "That's very good," he said. "But you ought to paint it before you put the rest of it together."

"Yes, sir, I'll do that."

"Then run on, get it done. I want to see a good job. Just like on the box. And I'm a hard judge, because . . . there was a time when I used to see them every day." He jerked his hand. "Now, go on, get to work."

"Yes, sir!" Inspired, Lloyd scuttled away.

There was a time . . . Andrew sat there, turning his glass around. Curiously, it was hard to remember now. So much else had happened, intervened. Even Willie Morgan . . . even the memory of him was fading. "It's a necessary war, of course," Willie had said. Andrew groped for the rest of the words. "But it's not the Japs we're fighting really, or the Germans. We're fighting something in ourselves too. I only hope we beat it."

And then two .45 Colt automatics thrown down hard on his bed, and the major's smirking face, his unctuous voice: "Soldier, you're in trouble . . ."

Andrew drank again. Now all he could see was Baucom's eyes. He must have looked like that, too, when the planted guns fell on the cot.

And now, he thought, I am the major.

He made another drink, hoping Ramsey would come in soon. He had things to say to her.

He was on the third one when she entered, wearing a red sheath, her hair piled high on top of her head. She looked surprised to see him home so early. "Hello," she said.

"Where are your packages?"

"What? Oh, I didn't see anything I wanted. I was just killing time, really." She came to him, kissed his cheek. "What are you doing here this early? It's not often we have the pleasure any more."

He gestured. "Sit down. I'll make you a drink. I want to talk to you."

Her eyes widened. "What about?"

"Something that happened today at the office."

"Oh," she said. Then she took a stool. "All right. What?"

Carefully, choosing his words, he told her, trying to make her see what it had been like. When he was through she said, "It sounds ugly, dreadful."

"It was."

She sipped her martini. "Still, I suppose it had to be done."

"Yes. It had to be done. And what will I have to do next time? What else will I become an accomplice in?"

Ramsey set down her glass. Andrew looked at her, trying to detach himself, look at her as a stranger would have, as he had seen her that first day. She was still beautiful, no other word for it, and the very sight of her sent a pang through him, and he did love her, he truly did, only . . .

Then he said, "I've been thinking about something."

"What?"

He shoved his glass around across the top of the bar. "I've been thinking about leaving here. Resigning from Chandler Mills."

There was an interval of silence during which he did

not look at her. Then she said, "Could you do that?"

"Why couldn't I?" He raised his head finally and met her eyes.

"But . . . why should you?"

"I don't know. Maybe so my soul could come home to my body again. Maybe so I could repair a connection. Do you know something? I would like to be able to look at you without averting my eyes. I would like not to have to be . . . strangers with you any more."

She sucked in her lower lip and bit it. "Andrew—"

"Don't give me any song and dance. We don't live in this house, we haunt it. I'm getting tired of being a kind of ghost."

"What do you mean, a kind of ghost?"

"You know God damn well what I mean." He swallowed his drink at a gulp. "I remember when we took Manila. The Chinese cemetery out north of town, all the big, fancy tombs. We fought through them, but people were living in them too. Only that's not the point. The point is that in each one of those tombs there was an altar, and on each altar there were wicker baskets, and each basket was full of bones—ancestor's bones, there to be worshipped. Sacred. Well, I'm getting tired of it, Ramsey, this living in a tomb. I'm mixed up. I don't know whether I'm supposed to worship the bones or be the bones."

Her eyes flickered to the martini pitcher. "Darling—"

"No. You know what I mean." He paused. "I'm caught up in something I didn't count on. And something I have no control over. I made some mistakes, and you did, too, to get in such a mess, but it's not too late. I'm not like Baucom, I'm not too old, and I won't be blacklisted, and even if I was, I wouldn't give a damn so long as I was free. Ramsey, I want to leave, I want to quit, I want to get out of here. While I've still got a chance, anyhow. Before I turn into something—" He saw them again, the two cold pistols, irrefutable, on the Army blanket. And the major's gloating eyes. "Before I'm something I never intended to be."

Ramsey sat there, very rigid, for seconds. Her fingers

laced and unlaced on the bar, like pale snakes writhing. Then she said, "You know I'll do whatever you want to. If it is what you want. I want to do what you want to do."

"I wish I could be sure of that."

"Andrew—"

"Do you? Then why did you play his game when I got out of college? Why did you let him use you?"

"Use me?"

"God damn it, you know what I mean. There was a time when—"

"So I'm responsible. Totally responsible." She sucked in a breath that made her breasts move.

"No, I didn't say that. But partly, yes." Suddenly he spread his hands. "It doesn't make any difference now. It's beside the point now. You weren't the only one seduced, I can see that. I'll take my blame. But if only— The thing is, now. If we could leave, go away. You, me, Lloyd. We wouldn't have to take anything with us. I wouldn't want to. Not except our savings, the part that isn't in Chandler stock, that I feel I've earned. But—"

He broke off, looking at her. She was staring back. "All right," she said. "I told you, whatever you want. But . . . what will he do?"

"I don't care what he does. What would he have done if I'd never existed?"

"I don't know. What would I have done if you hadn't?" She drank. "Only, Andrew, he's old, and he's not well. And Uncle Olin is leaving when this is settled, the union thing. You know, he and Ellen Quentin . . . So if you go, what has he got left?"

"That's his problem, not mine," Andrew said thinly. "The point is—"

He was interrupted by the doorbell. Before either could arise to answer it he appeared, the Old Man, in sport shirt and slacks.

"Hello, children," he said. "Can a man who's been down in the town showing the flag and talking dialect get a drink here?" He halted. "Or am I interrupting some important dialogue?"

Andrew did not look at him; he looked at Ramsey. She

urned, and her face lighted. "Of course you can," she
aid. She arose, went to him. "You look tired. Come and
t down," and she kissed him on the cheek.

Chandler put his arm through hers. "I am tired, and
rateful for your concern and ministration. You'd be
urprised what an ordeal it is to get a haircut in this town
ght now." Then he looked at Andrew. Their eyes met.
But I wouldn't want to intrude. Send me on my way if
m intruding." He squeezed Ramsey's hand.

Andrew looked at him and her, and then he knew it
as impossible, and all the steam built up in him oozed
ut, leaving only a kind of sludge of bitterness behind
im. "No," he said. "You're not intruding. Sit down and
ave a drink."

He turned, and in doing so knocked a glass off the bar;
shattered in a thousand pieces, but that made no dif-
rence. The cook could sweep it up.

13 IN EARLY SEPTEMBER the dry weather
roke; and then it rained for four days straight, and the
emperature plummeted. But the change did not break
e tension; by now it was too strong for that. You could
lmost smell, taste it, Heath Chandler thought, driving
rough the downpour; it was in the streets like smoke.
hirty thousand people, and by now half, it seemed,
rned against the other half, with a bitterness running
eep and strong. Rain could not wash it away, could
ot erase the breathless expectancy of something about
) happen, of imminent explosion, coming decision.

Heath ran the car's heater despite the heavy sweater
nd the raincoat he wore. It seemed to him that nowadays
e was always cold.

Turning the car into the streets of Village Number
wo, he admitted to a sense of guilt; but nowadays, it
emed, he had to sneak to run his own business. Still,
e situation was slipping rapidly out of Andrew's control,
nd he was entitled to take a hand. Maybe he had waited

too long already; but maybe, too, this was worth trying
It was of course a long shot, but one he had convinced
himself was well worth taking. If he won, the payoff was
enormous; if he lost, the most he had to face was
Andrew's wrath, and he could cope with that. Somehow
He had this going for him anyhow, with Andrew: love
He had worked hard over the past ten years to wir
Andrew's love, and thought he had it. And if it was no
enough, there was always Ramsey. If he could not reacl
Andrew himself, he could always reach him through her

He slowed the car to a crawl. What he had to do now
was get his thoughts in order and ducks in a row. The
man he would confront was sly, clever, even brilliant
maybe as brilliant as himself. Look at the way he had
whiplashed those firings.

He had known from the beginning that it had been
gamble. Either the three men fired were skeletons on
gallows hill to serve as warnings or they were martyrs
As it had turned out, McCloskey had made them martyrs
Christ! Heath thought, but the man was a superb rabble
rouser!

No man who worked for Chandler Mills was safe
McCloskey had trumpeted through the town, no matte
how well or faithfully he did his job. Here was wha
Chandler Mills could do, and the only shelter from i
power was in the union. He made the fired men a rallyin
point, their names war cries, and in this he'd had hel
from a few of the larger newspapers in the state, whic
had recently come under liberal ownership. And th
upshot of it was that though the firings had frightene
many hands away, they had scared others into Mc
Closkey's embrace. Too many others.

The trouble was, it was hard to frighten people now
adays, especially the younger ones. They had too man
alternatives; lean on them and they'd jump in their cars
they all owned cars—and go. Heavy industry was comin
into Charlotte, with government contracts and federa
pay scales four times what the textile mills could offe
Skilled labor could go there, defy him, desert him, leav
him only with the dregs.

Another thing he had not realized was the strength of the force in Chandlerville for incorporation. That would mean self-government, and though, as the biggest landholder and employer in the town, he could cope with that, it would vitiate his rule. That was not the point, though. The point was that Bolivar had left him Chanlerville in trust. And if he lost it, he had betrayed his trust. He was a lesser man than his father if he broke up his father's holdings, and he would not be that. But McCloskey had courted and mobilized that faction too.

Then the Cadillac crested a rise. He knew which house it was, knew it well; he had visited Clyde Bradshaw here. He and Clyde had worked together in those long-gone days before he had rebelled. It seemed ironic. Clyde had been not only easygoing but dead loyal, his fealty to Chandler Mills complete. That was why he had been allowed to buy the house in the first place. But of course Clyde's son was a different breed of cat.

Heath parked the car, got out, ran hunched through the rain to the shelter of the porch, then hammered on the front door.

The squat, potbellied, sandy-haired man looked at him through the glass pane. He squinted, then incredulous recognition overspread his genial face. He opened the door. "I don't believe this," he said "You're Captain Chandler."

"What's left of him. You're McCloskey?"

"In the too, too solid flesh." It was the kind of answer Heath liked. He and McCloskey looked at each other, and something flashed between them, a kind of rapport, a quick understanding. In one thing at least they were alike: professionals. They knew their business and where their interests lay. "Come in," McCloskey went on. "It's cold out there and wet."

"Thanks." Chandler followed him into a room crowded with equipment: hand-cranked mimeo, file cabinets, desk, a couple of old swivel chairs. Then McCloskey thrust out his hand. "Captain Chandler, how do you do?"

"All right." Chandler looked into eyes both impressed

and amused, and he would have known immediately, even if McCloskey had not already proved it, that here was a man as close to his equal in every way as he would ever meet.

"Sit down," McCloskey said. Then he perched himself on the desk's corner. "It's good to meet you, Captain. I've . . . heard so much about you."

"Yeah," Heath said, grinning. "Likewise, Mr. McClos—"

"You might want to call me Paul. It's shorter."

"Paul. Okay. Well, Paul, I'll have to admit you've been doing very well, all things considered."

"Oh, I'm satisfied with my progress."

"Don't be. The worst is still to come."

McCloskey laughed, almost soundlessly. "For which one of us?" Then he sobered. "You, I hope. We—we're almost over the hump."

"The hump?"

"Sure. I figure another couple of weeks. Then we'll have enough names to go before the NLRB and have an election authorized."

Heath shook his head. "Never happen. You might get enough to hold one, not enough to win one."

"Did you come here to tell me that?"

"Maybe partly." Heath sat up straight. "You can't possibly have enough votes—you know that."

"Remains to be seen. The election will tell the tale."

Heath laughed. "I'll challenge it."

"Sure. When it gets to Federal Court we'll win."

"You're pretty damned sure of yourself."

"Dealing with Heath Chandler, I need to be."

Heath laughed. "You're damned right. Even if you got every hand in my mill on your side, I wouldn't sign a contract with you."

McCloskey said quietly, "You know, that would mean a strike."

"Yeah," Chandler said. "What did you expect?" When McCloskey did not answer he leaned forward. "Don't think you could close Plant Number One with one either. I'm on to you, McCloskey. I know now why you said was vulnerable. One reason was that you knew I wouldn't sell out, like Butler. Or even shut my doors for a day. You think that gives you leverage. Well, it doesn't."

"Let's put it another way," McCloskey said. "You and I, or Andrew and I . . . we could work out things. I made him an offer."

"A sweetheart contract?"

"I wouldn't call it that. But an inducement."

"To sell out my own company and the rest of the industry. No. If you want a strike, we'll have one." He took out cigarettes, which, under pressure, he had begun to carry again. "You see, Paul, I'm worth a lot of money. And I'll spend every nickel I have, if necessary, to keep you out. I'll hire as many strikebreakers as I need for as long as necessary and have the state troopers take them across your picket lines. You can't beat me. All you can do is cost your treasury a wad and make everybody see what a phony you are when it comes down to bedrock. You can discredit your union for a quarter of a century."

"Then that might happen," McCloskey said tersely.

"But it doesn't need to."

Outside, across the street, somebody was changing a tire in the rain. Iron clanged against iron as he beat the bead off the rim. Presently McCloskey said, "Explain that."

"Uh-huh. You've got a wife and two kids, right?"

McCloskey half rose. "Chandler, if you're threatening—"

"Sit down. I'm not. You're protected by your friendship with my son-in-law, if nothing else, and you know it. But it gets pretty lonesome away from them all the time, eh?"

"I don't see where—"

"And I imagine fairly expensive, what with them up here and you down here, even on the expense account. What do you make a year—seven thousand?"

Something in McCloskey's eyes told him he'd hit close. He smiled. "Not much for the risks you take. Not much to raise a family on either."

"Captain," McCloskey said, face red, "if you're offering me—"

"A bribe? No. Not trying to suborn you either. But I might be offering you a damned good job."

McCloskey's breath went out in a long gust. "Go to hell," he said.

"Eventually that's likely. But I'm not ready yet. Paul, I'm retiring when this is settled. My associate, Olin Clutterbuck, is too. That leaves Andrew as the whip. And he'll need good men, men who know cotton and who can handle people. And aren't afraid of responsibility. People like that are hard to find—the world is full of ribbon clerks. And a man who knew his business, and who could work with Andrew—well, he could make twenty-five thousand, maybe more, with Chandler Mills without working up a heavy sweat. And that's only just to start."

Whoever it was went on clanging the tire iron against the rim. The rain drummed on the roof. Heath watched McCloskey's eyes, saw the kindling in them.

"Without sacrificing his self-respect," Chandler went on. "You offered us a sweetheart contract. It would be less sacrifice than that."

Still McCloskey did not answer.

"You wouldn't even have any responsibility for labor relations. You could be put in another area entirely. I wouldn't want you to think that I would set a thief—"

"To catch one." Again that gusty sigh. "Captain—"

"Twenty-five thousand. Plus stock options."

McCloskey's thick-fingered hands were on the desk before him. He looked down at them hard. Then he said, "All right, Captain Chandler, I'll take it."

Something leaped in Heath; he fought down the exultation of triumph. Then McCloskey raised his head. "After this is settled one way or another," he went on, eyes meeting Chandler's. "When I've fought as hard as I could and either won or lost. Then, if you want me, I'll take the job."

Heath tried to control the falling-down sensation of disappointment. "What I'm offering you is for acceptance or rejection now."

"Then I can't take it," McCloskey said. He laughed softly, a little hoarsely. "And if I did, what kind of future would I have? A man sells out once, he'll sell out again. Neither you nor Andrew would trust me around the

orner if I came to you like that, nor would anybody
se."

He leaned back, folded his arms. "I'd love to be rich.
od knows, all my life I've wanted to be. I fell into the
bor movement by accident, because my father was
ying. What I really wanted to do was go to school and
et an education and learn something useful that people
ould pay me a whole lot of money to practice."

"You have."

"Maybe. If so, too late, too much the hard way." He
rose. "Captain, it won't work. It's funny, you and I are
o much alike. You don't want the union in here because
ou think it killed your son. I *know* the mills killed my
ather. I don't think the union will kill another son of
ours—I hope of anyone. But unless something's done,
ontrol passes, the mills will kill a lot more fathers. Choke
em to death, the way mine died. Well . . . you're
etermined not to sell your son out no matter how much
costs you. Should I sell out my father?"

He broke off, and there was only the sound of rain
ouring from the eaves. McCloskey raised his hand in a
erpentine gesture.

"That's what it's all about, isn't it? If the sons betray
eir fathers—or the fathers betray their sons—what else
left? Let's put it this way, Captain. If you want me, you
ight get me later on. But not until afterward—you
nderstand?"

"Then we can't deal."

"Not on those terms."

"There are no others. Paul, you haven't even seen what
can do—"

"I've got an idea of what you can do." McCloskey's
oice was quiet. "But this time it's not enough." He
aused. "I'll let you in on a trade secret, Captain. I told
ndrew you were vulnerable, and that's proved true. And
o you know why? Because you have absolute power; and
bsolute power has become obsolete. Like every other
ictatorship, yours bears within it the seeds of its own
estruction."

"You're talking—"

"Foolishness? The proof of that is in how far I've gone so fast." McCloskey smiled thinly. "Think about it, Captain. What it's like to be one man wholly in another's hands. To depend on him for everything you have, your job, your home, your very existence—and to know that no matter how benevolent he might be, he holds the power to squash you like a bug. To give complete control of your own destiny to someone else, Captain, is a frightening thing to have to do. And people do it only when there's no alternative."

He paused. "That's why we came here first, Captain, why it was the logical place to come, because this was where the power was most absolute. This was where the alternative was most needed. And they can see, understand for the first time, that if they have courage and band together, there is a counterforce, that if we win there is a shield between you and them, so that even by carelessness you can't squash them the way an elephant might squash an ant without even knowing it."

Chandler opened his mouth, but Paul went on.

"Oh, I know. There was a time when it served its purpose. There was a time when it was their salvation and I admire you and respect you for all you've done and so do they. But time's run out, Captain; you're dealing with a new breed now. They know now that you need them as much as they need you. They know now what you should have seen long ago and didn't—and if you had, I would never have got to first base—that the time is past when people can own other people. We've fought too many wars to prove that, and they fought in them like the rest." He smiled quite warmly and without animosity. "You're too big and too strong, and that's your weakness, and that's why you can thresh around all you want to, like a dying dinosaur, but you're finished."

Chandler also smiled. "You think I'm finished?"

"Yes. I'm afraid the age of giants is over. Andrew knows it too, though he wouldn't say it. But he understands— Maybe that's because he's no giant, no Chandler."

"Andrew is a Chandler," Heath said. "He will prove that to you."

"And maybe I know him better than you do, despite all ou've done to make him one. The fact remains—"

Heath stood up. "All right, McCloskey. I guess we nderstand each other."

"Yes," Paul said. "I guess we do." He put out his and. "Captain, thanks for coming by."

"You're welcome," Chandler said. Slowly, reluctantly, e took the hand. He shook it once, then let it go. "Good ay, McCloskey." He turned, went to the door, halted here.

"One piece of advice from a dinosaur," he said tersely. Don't get overconfident. Or else you might still get quashed." Then he went out.

14 THE TOWN, PENROSE, lay thirty miles outh of Chandlerville. With a population of six thou- and, it had two years ago been dying, as cotton farming lied around it. Then Heath Chandler had selected it as he site of a gigantic new combed-yarn mill, to be rought into production in phases. The city fathers were lesperate and met immediately the hard terms he laid lown, passing an ordinance that created in the middle of he town an area totally exempt from property taxes, training the faltering credit of the town to supply the ewer and water service the Chandler plant in that free one would need. But it had been worth it. The payroll f the first-phase employees had revived the town as lood revives a wounded man, and now, on Saturday ight at eight o'clock, there was still life in it. Looking hrough the window of the restaurant in which he ate /ith Bill Mullinax, the new plant's manager, Andrew /atched the hands who had drawn their week's pay at ne o'clock this afternoon swarm along the sidewalk. Now /as the moment for which the merchants of Penrose, as /ell as the bootleggers, held their breath all week long, nd for which the mill hands lived—the next thirty-six

hours their weekly allotment of freedom in which to lead
their own lives, taste their pleasures, rediscover their humanity, before the whistle blew again on Monday morning. Andrew felt a touch of envy. That was not much time
in which to enjoy freedom and irresponsibility, but for
him it had been a long while since he had known even
so brief an interval of liberation. Wherever he went, he
thought, whatever he did, he seemed to drag Chandler
Mills behind him or wear the company like an albatross
around his neck.

"I think we can wind up everything in the morning,"
Mullinax said. "It's going to have me humping, but when
the machinery gets here we'll be ready for it. Are you
driving home tonight and coming back, or will you stay
over until we're finished?"

"I'll stay over."

"Good. Then you'll spend the night with us."

"No. The motel will be all right. It would be an impo
sition on your wife."

Mullinax went on protesting, but Andrew hardly heard
him. The motel was what he needed; to be alone, to
think, to get things straight and ordered. He had to do i
somehow, and soon; because he and Ramsey could not go
on this way. Maybe a night away from Chandlerville
even in a place like this, would enable him to do that
Especially a place like this; it would close down tigh
in another hour, and then there would be no distractions
He was glad to get away from Mullinax, glad to seal him
self in the room with its plastic furniture and smell o
unchanged air and human habitation. He kicked off hi
shoes and stretched out on the bed.

He had not wanted to spend his weekend in Penrose
Heath Chandler had insisted. Yesterday, just before noon
he had come into Andrew's office, and though they saw
each other every day, Chandler seemed to Andrew t
have changed, aged suddenly. For the first time Andrew
perceived how slowly Heath moved nowadays, and how
that face, worthy of adorning a coin or medallion, ha
shrunk over its bony structure. Chandler looked old
tired, and grim.

"Well," he said flatly, "there's no point in putting it off any longer. We've got to make some plans. I've just done something you may not like, but something I deemed necessary." And then he told Andrew about the meeting with McCloskey.

"So you tried to bribe him," Andrew said, "and failed. I could have told you that you would." Curiously, he felt no exasperation at Chandler moving behind his back. It seemed to make no difference.

"Well, I had to make the offer." Heath straightened up a little painfully, as if his joints hurt. "Anyhow, he seems sure he's got the votes. And after meeting him, getting the cut of his jib, damned if I don't think he's telling the truth." He paused, and Andrew saw that he was suffering, not physically but from the impact of the knowledge that he might even lose, that all the effort of nearly thirty years was wasted. He looked bitter, disillusioned, yet unbelieving, like a cuckold betrayed by a trusted wife. Coming to grips with this was what had aged him, and Andrew felt a surge of compassion for the Old Man— who was now truly old—and love; for this was the only real father he had ever known. But, coldly, he fought that back, for he was coming to understand that it was something he could no longer afford.

Then Chandler was brisk, as if the fact that there was action to take had revived him. "Anyhow, a showdown's not far off. We'd better start getting ready. I want to plan for an immediate shift of production from Number One to other plants."

Andrew was incredulous. "You're not going to shut down Number One?"

"Hell, no. That's where he's had us by the balls all long, knowing I wouldn't shut down or pull a Butler on him. But—" Heath broke off. Then some of the animation went out of him. "But the bastard just might have the strength to shut us down. If he calls an election, wins, and we won't negotiate, and he sets up a strike—" His fingers plucked nervously at his sweater, he looked away from Andrew as if he was just coming to terms with that knowledge too. Andrew saw his mouth thin.

"Anyhow," Chandler went on, "there's a possibility of a slowdown at the very least. I'm not through fighting by a long shot, but we might as well get organized, plan for the worst, so we can deal from strength. With the backlog of orders and the shipping dates we've got, we could be in trouble with any sort of interruption here. Let's not have that happen; I wouldn't give him the satisfaction."

They spent the rest of the afternoon in conference and on the telephone. When they were finished, Chandler looked even more haggard, but there was satisfaction in his voice. "That locks it up, except for Penrose. God damn it—the timing. If we could get Phase Two under way now, move it up by two weeks, a month . . ."

"Impossible." Olin Clutterbuck shook his head.

"God damn it, nothing's impossible. I'll guarantee the manufacturers overtime to get that machinery shipped, and I'll pay overtime to get the plant in shape to take it. Andrew, tomorrow morning you go down there, talk to Mullinax. Tell him all hell's about to break loose around his head. And see that he gets on the stick."

"I can't go tomorrow. I'm up to my ass in things already. I'd planned to work all this weekend to—"

"You've got nothing more important than this. I want you in Penrose tomorrow morning, and that's an order."

Andrew looked at him, feeling a surge of rebellion. "I'll send Ross Manning. It's an engineering problem anyhow."

"I'll be damned if it is; it's a morale problem—to get Mullinax and everybody down there in high gear. I want you personally breathing down his neck and knocking down any excuses he comes up with. Time's running out on us. Either you go or I go."

Andrew hesitated. "If I get mixed up in it, it'll take me all day Saturday and part of Sunday. Be reasonable, Captain—"

"I'm tired of being reasonable." Chandler's voice rose "I've had being reasonable up to the top of my craw What I want now is to jerk a knot in your friend McClos key. And Penrose is part of doing that, and one of us i going to be down there until we're sure that part's ready. Hell, I'll go myself"—and he stood up.

Andrew looked at him. And then he knew he had no choice; Chandler meant it, and it would overtax him. So it had to be himself. Still, it was senseless, there were other ways it could be handled without his having to be out of town when he already had so much work.

"Very well," he said thinly. "I'll go."

It was well after seven when he went home that evening; and Ramsey, in a tight white dress, was sitting at the bar; and he knew immediately that the martini before her was not her first. But they had both been drinking more lately; and he could not begrudge or condemn her. The guilt, the deficiency, was his. He loved and wanted her and wanted everything to be right with her, and he had tried, God knows he had tried; and it did not work; that connection was still cut. Each time, with every failure, it got worse for them. It was not that sex had been the sole connection between them, but always it had been the symbol and summary of their relationship. And now something in him was rejecting her, and she was hurt and frightened by that rejection, and the lack of their ability to intermesh that way had been the measure of their inability to come together in any way, not the source of the disease but its symptom. But it was the symptoms that made diseases dreadful.

"Hello," she said thickly. "Lloyd and I have already eaten; he's spending the night with Mother and Father. Have you eaten?"

"No."

"I'll have Frieda fix something."

"Later. Now I'll have a drink. What have you been doing?"

"The good works department of Chandler Mills has been running full blast all day long. The letters I've answered—" Her mouth twisted; she looked down into her glass. "Everybody," she said. Everybody, it seems, is screwed up and unhappy nowadays." She laughed slightly. "Everybody wants me to bail them out. Imagine."

"Claudia isn't helping you?"

"Not any more. She's glad to be rid of it. One last protégée left, she sees her all the time, that's it." She brushed at her hair as he made a drink. "Andrew," she said, "I have an idea. A dreadful, terrible, scandalous idea."

He tensed. "What's that?"

"Let's leave Lloyd at Chandler House. Let's you and me go out to the river house and spend the weekend there, and let's both get roaring, stinking drunk, and . . . you know? For two whole days. Nobody but the two of us."

He looked at her, and suddenly he knew what she was driving at, and he came around the bar. "Yes," he said. Then he hesitated. "No. I mean, I can't. I've got to go out of town tomorrow."

She raised her head, looked at him with smoky green eyes that were full of anguish in a taut face. "Andrew, please don't!"

"I can't help it. The Old Man's orders."

"Oh," she said. "Oh."

"Well, don't look at me like that. It's not my idea." He explained to her what was happening, and saw that she comprehended. Then he said, "But, you know what? I *can* stay. He can raise hell, but there's no reason why I can't stay." He broke off, waiting for her answer. He held his breath. Suddenly it seemed to him that something precious, crucial, teetered in the balance in that moment. Just that much defiance—no more than that—from her. He could have made the choice himself; but this was one he wanted her to make.

Then she said, "It would make him angry, though."

Andrew felt as if something swollen in him had collapsed. "Yes," he said tonelessly. "It would make him mad as hell."

She was silent for a long while, and so was he, a kind of rage rising in him. Then she said, "But we still have tonight."

"Don't we though?" His voice was edged.

She looked at him, ignoring that. "I think we ought to

send Frieda home and get nice and drunk tonight and—"

"What good would that do?" he said harshly.

"Oh," she said again. Then she said desperately, "It might do a lot of good. You don't know, you can't tell. Andrew, please—" But then she read the expression on his face. "Pour me another drink," she said, shoving forward her glass. He did; she sipped it. Suddenly she burst out, "All right. I wish I knew what to do. I wish I knew how—"

She shook her head wildly, yellow hair flying. "What is it? What is it you want? What can I give you that I haven't? We can't go on living like this, we just can't, Andrew." Suddenly her eyes were wet. "I don't know what you want or what to give you anymore; it's all too complicated. It's like I see you through . . . through glass. I keep trying to reach out for you, and my hand just hits something it can't go through. And sometimes I feel you reaching out for me, and . . . it's the same. Can't we break the glass, Andrew? We've got to. I'm . . . scared of what will happen if we don't."

She halted, trembling, and he came around the bar, suddenly full of love, resolve. "Yes," he said. "God damn it, we'll break it. We'll—" He put his arm around her, held her, *I must*, he thought. He lifted her up, embraced her. Buried his face in the soft, perfumed flesh beneath her ear. "We'll break it," he rasped. "Come on."

She was tense beneath his grasp. She whispered something he did not catch, leaned against him as they went to the bedroom. There he closed the door, put his arm around her, and she clung to him, and he kissed her and she kissed him, carnally, with pent-up hunger, tongue avid, while she took his hand, thrust it against her breasts. Her body moved against him, and now, indeed, he felt the stirring of desire and hope, and she sensed that and pushed against him harder. They hurried to the bed, and her hand worked at his belt, and then, as he fumbled with his clothes, she pulled off the dress, threw away the bra and peeled off the thin underpants and was naked on the bed, thighs open wide, and he was, too, then, and she reached up and took his hand and pulled him down beside her and groped for his mouth with her own again. Coming to her, he thought, I love her. I love her, and I've got to prove that, and if I can, everything else will work.

"Christ," he said minutes later in an agony of disappointment and shame.

"No, don't give up." Her tongue played around his face. Her hand was desperate, yet gentle. "I love you. Oh, darling, I love you, I want you to— Wait, wait, don't pull away, wait— Now, please, let me— Lie back. Just lie back. Oh . . ."

Suddenly he sprang from the bed. "Damn it," he croaked, "it's not going to work! Can't you see it won't work?"

She lay there, staring at him, sprawled in a posture of desire almost ludicrous, obscene. Then she closed her thighs. "Andrew—"

He turned away; he could not bear to look at her. Not even to stand naked before her. He groped for his clothes. "It's no use," he said. "Not now. Not here."

"Then where and how? Andrew, I need you. I'm just— I'm afraid that I will—"

He sat down on the bed. "I know," he said more calmly. He touched her arm. "It's not your problem, it's mine. I've got to solve it, I'm the one who has to . . . find what it is." He rubbed his face with his hands. "Maybe it's just as well I'm going out of town. It will give me a chance to think." He shook his head. "Yes. Something must be done."

Now, lying on the motel bed, he remembered how, after that, they had been like strangers. Wanting to reach through that barrier, touch each other, unable to. And how she had fled, gone up to Chandler House, and had waited carefully until he was asleep to come home again.

And on that night some sort of dividing line had been reached; either they had come to an end or a beginning. He did not know which. All he knew was that, in a chaos of love and fractured intentions, their faith in one another had broken down. He was as afraid as she. He was beginning to distrust love. He was beginning to hate it.

Once he did that, there was no repairing what was wrong.

He could bear the empty room no longer; he got up and drove back downtown. He walked the streets of Penrose, needing the physical action to unwind and tire him. He watched young couples, hand in hand, with Chandler money in their pockets, inventory all the marvels in the store windows. He saw the laughing young people waiting in line for the second show at the town's one theater, which had been reopened since the Chandler payroll had come to town. In the car again, he went out the highway to a drive-in restaurant. Its parking lot was jammed with cars, and in the dark privacy of their seats, young hands and mouths made connection, young bodies squirmed, while neon flashed on and off and music from a loudspeaker pounded with sullen, rolling, erotic beat. He drank a beer, watching the affirmations all around him. Then, very tired, his brain seemingly frozen, he went back to the motel. This time he undressed completely, showered, donned pajamas, got into bed. He cut off the light; presently he slept.

The telephone awakened him. He came out of sleep groggily, picked it up, looked at the luminescent dial of his watch. It was after two o'clock. "Hello?" he mumbled.

Vic Royce's voice said, "Andrew? Don't be afraid, nothing's happened to your family. It's Paul."

"Paul?" Andrew repeated blankly.

"That's right," Vic said tonelessly. "Do you remember a girl named Linda Vereen? Last February you crowned her Queen of Hearts. She's not but fourteen. Well, the cops have picked up Paul, Andrew, and he's been taken to the Macedonia jail for safekeeping. She says he raped her."

15 "Hello, Mildred," Andrew said.

"Come in." She stepped aside to let him through the door of the Royce's pleasant house in a suburb of Macedonia. Somewhere in the distance a church bell rang. There was no levity or banter in Mildred's voice now; Andrew could see that she was afraid. "Vic's waiting for you in his den."

"Okay." Andrew went down the cluttered hall; children chattered and argued in adjoining rooms, pleased to be free unexpectedly of Sunday school. Two radios were playing, mingling the sound of pipe organ and choir with rock and roll.

Vic's room contained a desk with typewriter, a file cabinet, many books, a couple of chairs. He met Andrew in the doorway, unshaven and in his shirt sleeves, the thick hair of his chest a crawling vee above his open collar. He looked tired and probably was, for he must have been up all night.

"Hi, Andrew. Have you been to Chandlerville?"

"No. I came straight here."

"The Old Man didn't call you?"

"No. Vic, let me have this all again. And . . . I want to see Paul. This morning."

"I think I can arrange that. Sit down, let's have some coffee." He stuck his head through the door, yelled to Mildred to bring them some. Then he dropped heavily behind his desk. "I haven't been over there today. But I'm going in a little while. No reason you can't come along. If he'll see you, that is. I don't know. He was pretty damned bitter last night."

"Yeah, I guess. The girl. Have you talked to her?"

Vic grinned without any humor at all. "Are you dreaming? She's in Tom Capps Memorial over in Chandlerville for observation, and Chandler's got her incommunicado. Right now nobody sees her but him and his lawyers."

He spread his big hands on his desk. "Here are the

562

rough outlines of the story. Her side, which I got in fragments from the cops and Paul's. Hers first. Well. She had been uptown to the movie; when the nine-o'clock show was over, she walked home, alone. On the way it began to sprinkle, and she was afraid it would ruin her hair. So when Paul—she—says stopped and offered her a ride she took it. She knew him of course, everybody does by now. Anyhow, she says, instead of taking her home, he drove out in the country, so fast she was afraid to try to jump out. He parked somewhere down by the river on the Macedonia Road, took a bottle of whiskey from the glove compartment, rammed it in her mouth and made her drink until she was drunk and woozy. Then he raped her. After that he took her home, dumped her out in front of her house, raced off. She was groggy, drunk, hysterical, didn't know what to do, her father was out somewhere— her mother's dead, you know. But then her daddy came in and found her, and she told him and he called the cops. They came and took her to the hospital, and another detail went to Paul's house. According to their story, they found him in bed asleep, nobody else there. And they say he reeked of booze, was drunk when they awakened him. They took him into custody and called Heath Chandler; he told them right away to bring him to Macedonia for safekeeping. He said when word got around there might be trouble. That girl was apparently damned popular all over Chandlerville."

"Yeah," said Andrew. He had a quick vision of a kitten's face, blue eyes flaring as she made a greedy, involuntary reach for the crown. "Well . . . go on."

"Paul called me from the Macedonia jail—the one call they allowed him. The union has lawyers in Raleigh and Charlotte, but he knew he had to have someone on his side fast, he said, someone to make sure the cops didn't work him over. Otherwise they'd have had all night to play with him before his attorneys got there."

He broke off as his wife came with coffee. After, wordlessly, she had set it down and left, Andrew looked at him incredulously. "And you were fool enough to go?"

"Somebody had to. The chief from Chandlerville and

his lieutenant delivered him here in person, and they were mad as hornets. Both of them had known that girl since she was a baby, and they were just itching for an excuse to open up on Paul and clobber him. He would have been pulped if I, somebody, hadn't been on hand to intervene."

"No wonder Mildred looked so scared. Damn it, Vic, don't you understand what answering that call could do to you? When St. John Butler finds out—"

"You don't have to tell me," Vic said shortly. "I've already advised my partners and had a thorough chewing out."

"Then why go back today? Won't the lawyers from Raleigh and Charlotte be in by now?"

"Soon, anyhow. Meantime . . . He has to be checked on, Andrew."

"I'll check on him."

Vic looked at him with strange coolness. "By his attorney." Then he relaxed. "When the people from Raleigh and Charlotte get here I'll fill them in. Then I'm out of it, I hope."

"What do you mean, you hope?"

"Never mind that. You want to hear Paul's side?"

"Hell, yes. Has he got an alibi?"

Vic Royce leaned back in his chair, tapped his teeth with a pencil and fastened his eyes on Andrew. "Of course," he said. "He claims Heath Chandler framed him."

Andrew sat there, feeling no shock, no surprise, only a kind of sick, gnawing doubt that had been in him since Vic's phone call had awakened him. "Yeah," he said. "Sure. He would say that."

Vic did not answer him directly. "Here it is, his version. Neither he nor his assistants have had any time off in weeks. He gave them this weekend to go home and see their families while he kept watch; besides, it was too far to Baltimore. So he was alone, and, as he pointed out, a house without lights and water isn't exactly a pleasure dome to hang around in by yourself. So he drove out to the Steak House on the Macedonia Road, took a bottle with him, had a few drinks and supper, called

his wife collect from the pay phone. Then he said—"
Vic's eyes narrowed. "It seems the Old Man tried to bribe
him the other day."

Andrew let out a long breath. "Yes."

"It . . . bothered Paul. Was haunting him. He was afraid
he might even consider it. And, according to him, he
drove around out in the country for a long time, thinking
about it. He's not sure how long—maybe ten minutes,
maybe an hour. He had a drink or two more, then went
back to Chandlerville around eleven, maybe a little later.
Went straight to bed. Next thing he knew, well after midnight, somebody was shaking him awake. Cops; they'd
entered without knocking. The rest of his bottle had been
poured over him, and he and his blanket reeked of whiskey. Then they took him in. He was careful not to fight.
Not until they reached the station did they even tell him
why. After that they hustled him to the county jail, put
him under special guard."

Andrew looked down at his coffee cup, trying to fight
off sickness. He had not felt like this, he thought, since
he had got word of Willie Morgan's death. He felt as
if there was some slow poison in his blood stream, spreading through the arteries and veins and capillaries of every
part of his body. He had felt it from the moment he had
laid down the phone after Vic's call, and now it grew.
He tasted the coffee, set it aside.

"You don't have to answer, of course," said Vic, "but—"

Andrew raised his head. "How do I know?" he said
hoarsely.

"I'm not accusing you. But Chandler—"

Andrew said more quietly, "I just got through telling
you. I don't know. But I can tell you this, Vic. I'll find
out. Believe me, I'll find out." Then he stood up, unable
to sit any longer. "For Christ's sake," he said, "let's go see
Paul."

The courthouse and jail drowsed in its grove of oaks
on the square. As they reached its front steps Andrew
halted, assaulted by the sight of two khaki-clad men with
badges and western straw hats at the entrance, shotguns

cradled in their arms. The blued steel of the weapons, the equally metallic eyes of the sunburned men, were like a blow across the face: reality's hard fist. The guards knew Vic and looked at him with resentment as he and Andrew passed between them; by their lights he was a traitor to his own region, heritage, his own manhood.

The jailer's plump buttocks swayed ahead of them as he led the way up the steep stairs. Andrew shuddered, almost overcome with a kind of suffocation. The stockade, the Army prison . . . It had been so long, but the smells were the same—reek of humanity, disinfectant, and despair—and it all came back. Entering such a place was like going to the moon, passing beyond the decent rules and laws and mercies of society. Law here was master, not servant, and that made everything different, and frightening. They walked down a hall, and the jailer paused before a cell. "Here," he said, and Andrew looked through the grid of steel at the gray figure sprawled on the chain-hung cot. "Paul," he said.

McCloskey sat up, startled from a doze, looking at them in involuntary panic. In the detention uniform he seemed older, puffier and shapeless. Then he came back to reality, and the fright faded, erased by recognition; a ghost of a familiar smile moved his mouth.

"Gentlemen," he said, arose and came forward as the jailer unlocked the door. He looked at Andrew with neutral eyes and did not put out his hand. "What brings you here?"

"I thought maybe there was something I could do."

"For whom?" Paul's mouth warped. "Tell me, Andrew, has she got it yet?"

"Who? Got what?"

"The pubescent perjuress. Has her red convertible been delivered? Or is that deferred until she's old enough to drive? Or maybe it's a college scholarship, a year's supply of hair curlers, and a pair of red silk panties for every day in the week, with coy mottoes on the crotch—"

"Stop that, Paul!" Vic snapped.

"Excuse me," he said politely. "This place has a tendency to get on one's nerves. Well, Andrew, where were you when it hit the fan last night?"

"Out of town, in Penrose. I—"

"That figures. So he faked you out, eh, before he made his move? What's the matter, afraid you'd venture objections?"

Andrew did not answer. Paul spent a moment staring into his face, probing with his eyes as if they could peel away any mask he wore, strip off artifice, see through deceit to truth. Then he sighed. "Okay, Andrew. Sorry. I never thought it was you. But it wasn't me either. What would you like me to swear on? Old friendship? The Bible? My father's grave? Because I didn't do it. I was framed. And you know by whom."

Still Andrew did not speak.

"Has Vic told you my story?"

"I came to hear it from you."

"Yes. Well, I should have known better. I've been around long enough." He walked back to the cot, sat down, hands clasped between his thighs. "When they try to bribe you and that fails, then the next move has to be something drastic. You let down your guard one time, they get you."

He raised his head. "But it wears on you, you know? You batter away at 'em, convincing the unconvinced and making the disbelievers believe, and it's like bein a priest who has to preach a sermon every hour, seven days a week. And they cut off your lights and water, make even the simplest things of living hard, and the cops follow you, and you know you're in unfriendly territory always, like an English explorer I read about one time who went to Mecca in disguise among the Arabs; and if you make one mistake, you get hung up by the thumbs.

"So it got to them, those two kids, and I took the chance, sent both home at once. Which was wrong; one of the first rules is always to keep a witness with you. So last night— Well, the drinks and callin Marion just made it worse. I got to feelin sorry for myself, wonderin why I should inflict that kind of life on myself and wife and kids when it would be so easy to take the Old Man's offer. . . .

"So I just drove around, here, there, anywhere. And made some sort of peace with myself, went back to that Taj Mahal we call headquarters, tried to read by lantern light, gave up, had another drink, and went to bed. Next thing five cops with drawn guns around me, and my bed drenched with liquor—"

Suddenly his control broke, voice crackling with naked outrage. "Oh, he planned it beautifully, give him that! His spies knew my men were gone, he knew I was out that night! The master stroke, though, was pickin the one girl who could make it plausible, the perfect combination of sexpot and Shirley Temple! Hell, yes, I've seen her and drooled and had some nasty thoughts; you tell me one man that hasn't, she gives off a kind of radiation— Oh, she'll be impressive on the witness stand, won't she, the little bitch!" He stared at Andrew fiercely. "I really had him scared, didn't I? To hit me with something carrying the death penalty!"

"You know you won't—" Andrew began.

"Won't I? Wish I had your confidence in justice in these precincts. Oh—" Paul relaxed a little. "I know he's not really plannin to murder me, just ruin my reputation and the union's and take me outa circulation. But slip-ups happen, you know, even with the best of intentions, things might get out of control."

Andrew put a hand on his shoulder. "Listen, Paul, calm down. I haven't seen Chandler yet, but I'm going home now and talk to him—"

"Oh, you are?" Paul stood up, and beneath the fat and puffy face one leaner, harder, seemed to take shape with intensity. "Well, when you do that, tell him something for me, will you, Andrew? You tell him that this is a hell of a thing for my two daughters to see me stand accused of. You tell him that any father who would do this to another father is a lousy son of a bitch, beneath contempt! You tell him I said that!"

Andrew stepped back, shaken by his fury. "Word for word," Paul grated, and sat down, breathing heavily.

There was silence in the cell, except for the panting sound he made. Then Andrew said, "Paul. Listen. I'm president of Chandler Mills. And whatever the truth of this is, I'll find it out."

McCloskey did not look at him. "You'll find out what he wants you to know."

"I'll find out the truth!"

Paul stood up then, and when he looked at Andrew this time, what was in his eyes was almost pity. "The truth," he said, "is whatever Heath Chandler and St. John Butler and all the rest decide it is. You'll get a choice, that's all—of whom to believe, him or me." Then his voice softened. "Andrew, thanks—"

"Time's up, gentlemen," the jailer said behind them.

"I'll be back. Tomorrow, maybe," Andrew said. "Soon."

"Any time," Paul said. "I'll be around."

They went out, down the stairs, between the shotgun guards. Outside, Andrew sucked in great breaths of clean, fresh air. "Christ," he said. Then to Vic, "What do you think they'll ask for?"

"That's up to Chandler. It depends on what count they try him on. They've got a smorgasbord to choose from. Five, ten, twenty years . . . Unless, of course, it can be proved he's innocent. If the girl can be tripped up in court." He paused. "Conceivably it could be the gas chamber."

"No," Andrew said.

"No, of course not. But what difference does it make when a man's convicted on a charge like this? Even one year—it doesn't matter. He's ruined. For life." They got into Vic's car; he started it, turned it homeward, so Andrew could pick up his. "I wish—" he began after a moment, then broke off.

"You wish what?"

"That I could have a hand in his defense."

"You know what that would do to you, for God's sake. Besides, the union will furnish plenty of lawyers."

"I know. But I know the local court, the psychology of the kind of jurors there'll be, that would count for a lot. He needs somebody local." Then he laughed bitterly.

"Well, it's impossible, but—" He turned to Andrew, and
there was almost a look of pain on his face. "But, damn
it, why should a man have to eat a half-gallon of ice
cream every night to convince himself he's had some
satisfaction out of life?" He was breathing hard. "If it
weren't for Mildred, the kids—"

"Forget it," Andrew said. "You've got too much at
stake."

"Yeah, of course."

They were silent until they reached Vic's house. Mildred met them at the door. Andrew recognized the shock
of catastrophe on her face at once. She ignored him,
turned to her husband, and her voice was a whisper when
she spoke. "St. John Butler called you," she said, "and
wants you to call him back right away."

16 IT WAS ALMOST TEN that Sunday morning
when Claudia awakened after having been up most of
the night. From the moment she opened her eyes she
was assailed by foreboding, a sense of disaster, as if
in the aftermath of nightmare. Then full consciousness
returned, and she remembered that it had been no dream.
And what had happened, she thought, was bound to
affect them all—no good could come of it for anybody.
Except, of course, she told herself, sitting up, for *him.*

It seemed to her that he was a presence in the bedroom, as he had always been a presence in this house.
Brushing back her hair, she looked around. She herself
had bought every stick of furniture, chosen paper, carpet,
curtains, paintings. And yet it did not belong to her or
even to Heath. It was still his, as the rest of the house
was, as everything in Chandlerville still was. She remembered from weeks ago, on their return from Europe,
the house, as they approached it: white, massive, glittering with windows, and hostile. She had felt no sense
of homecoming; it had offered her no welcome. Nor ever
would . . .

Heath was already up, would be downstairs. She
rung out of bed and, a little shakily, went through the
utine of the morning, but with last night's events
owding back into her mind. The ringing phone past
idnight jerking her out of sleep, then Heath's crisp
ice and reassuring gesture as he noticed her awake.
ie tried to ask a question, but he waved her to silence,
s face clear of sleep. "Yeah, go on." Then: "All right.
et me know as soon as you've picked him up. Mean-
hile I want the girl examined by a doctor—no, two
octors. Get the best gynecologist in Macedonia and
ing him over here. I don't want any question about the
sults because Theron Winters is on my payroll. And I
on't want McCloskey in our jail either; I want him at
e county jail in Macedonia, under guard; we're not
ing to take responsibility for him. All right—if I'm not
re I'll be at the hospital. Stay in touch." He put down
e phone.

"Heath, what—?"

He arose stiffly, got a cigarette from her pack. His silver
air was tousled in curly points around his temples. "I
ave some good news and some bad news," he said.
'm sorry, but . . . Your little protégée, Linda whats-
rname."

"Vereen?" Claudia felt sudden fear; her hand went to
r throat.

"Yes." He paused. "She's been raped."

"Oh, no."

He nodded. "By Paul McCloskey." Briefly he told her
hat had happened. "When her father found her he
lled the police."

"Good Lord," Claudia whispered sickly.

Heath began to take off his pajamas. And now his
ice was changing, growing exultant. "But, my God,
hat a break for us! Fantastic!" His face was like some-
ing hammered out of metal in the lamplight; suddenly
e laughed, then hit his thigh with clenched fist. "A
iracle at the last minute! Don't you see? This winds it
, ends it! The stupid son of a bitch! He almost had me!

He almost had me, and then he threw it all away becaus
he had to dip his wick!"

"Heath!" Looking at him, listening to him, her stomac
roiled; for a moment she thought she would vomit. "Don
talk like that!"

He paused, looked at her, then relaxed a little. "I'r
sorry. But it's still a miracle."

"I don't call the raping of a little girl miraculous," sh
said hoarsely. She thought sickly of Linda, so young an
vulnerable and yearning, and for a moment he was no
her husband; he was a repellent old man taking lewd jo
in tragedy.

"I don't mean it that way. But if it's true, all the same—
And her. That's the thing about it, *her!* Not some promis
cuous little slut that might have picked him up and egge
him on and blown the whistle on him when he wouldn
pay, or— But a decent girl, a sweet girl—"

"Heath, for God's sake!"

"I know, I'm sorry for her, but don't worry, don't worr
about her, we'll see that she gets the best of care. We'
make this up to her, I promise you. But her misfortune
still my gain! Oh, that stupid, horny McCloskey!" H
turned away, perhaps so she could not see his face.

Claudia swung out of bed.

"Where are you going?"

"Down to the hospital. I want to be there and see ho
for myself. She has no mother. She'll . . . need somebody

"Her daddy's there with her."

"All the same—" She began to dress, hands tremblin
An anger, a rage, not so much at McCloskey but at li
itself racked her, what life could do to people. Its hunge
for victims was never satisfied.

Almost, she was sorry that she had gone. Linda had n
needed her; by the time they got there she was und
sedatives. Claudia looked down at the swollen, puf
face with its cut lips and chipped tooth and bruise
turned back the cover. She raised the neckline of th
hospital gown; Linda's breathing was slow, husky, heav
and she did not stir. Again Claudia felt that rage as sh

oked at the bruises on the round, white breasts and e unmistakable marks of teeth. She dropped the cloth, ulled up the sheet, and went out to join Heath, the girl's ather, and the chief of police in the hall.

"Whoever did this," she said, "deserves anything he ets."

"I shouldn'ta let her go to the picture show alone," the an on the chair in the alcove said. He sat, head down, ands twisting between his knees, small, wiry, in a white hirt without a tie and blue jeans. The back of his neck as brown and webbed with wrinkles, his close-cropped air was thinning. "I ought to of knowed better. But I ever thought . . ."

"It wasn't your fault, Vereen," Heath said.

"No, I should've run up there and got her. Only she's lone it a hunderd times and nothin ever happened— nd then, when I come in and found her layin there, all nessed up . . . I shouldn'ta called the cops. I shoulda aken my shotgun and took care of him myself."

"It's a good thing you didn't; it would only have made t worse for her. Don't worry. The man who did it'll get vhat's coming to him—I'll see to that." He broke off as he room door opened and closed and the two doctors ame out. "Theron, Dr. Webb. What's the report?"

"Maybe it would be better if we talked in my office," Theron Winters said. Chief of staff of Tom Capps Memo-ial Hospital, he was tall and gaunt and hard-faced. The loctor from Macedonia was smaller, plump and sleek. Vinters glanced at Vereen, who had not raised his head, till sat as if in shock. "It'll be better if I wait to talk to im," he whispered. They went into the office, and Vereen seemed not even to notice as they left.

Winters' office was spacious. Bolivar had founded this ospital, but Heath had enlarged it and spared no ex-ense to make it modern and efficient. Winters sat on he corner of his desk, and they ranged around him: Heath, Claudia, Chief Lawrence, and Webb, the gy-ecologist.

"Well," Winters said, "there was definitely sexual intercourse within the past few hours, with fresh, viable sperm in the vagina."

Claudia cut in with instinctive feminine anxiety "You've—"

"Yes. Spermicidal douches; the chances of pregnancy are minimal. But if anything occurs, we'll . . . take other steps." He went on coolly. "It's obvious the act was forcible. Bruises on the face and upper body, the mark of teeth on breasts and abdomen. She said the bottle was forced in her mouth; the chipped front tooth bears that out."

"We'll want that capped," said Claudia. "She has perfect teeth."

"After the trial," Heath said. "Go on, Theron."

"The percentage of alcohol in her blood was low comparatively speaking, but in view of her youth and lack of conditioning to it, probably enough to render her helpless. We've taken all the matter from beneath her fingernails; the State Bureau of Investigation will have to analyze it, but, curiously, there doesn't seem to be any skin, blood or tissue."

"That was the whiskey; she couldn't fight," Heath said. "You've left out the most important thing."

"Yes. Well, until tonight she was virginal. No doubt of that."

Claudia heard Heath's expelled breath of relief and gratification.

"Then there ought to be blood in his car," Lawrence said. "We've got it impounded. We'll check. As I understand it, she was forced into the back seat. The son—the subject picked her up, told her he'd take her home, then went out the other way so fast she was afraid to try to jump, parked somewhere off the road down by the river she's got no idea where, poured the booze in her and—"

"Yes," Dr. Webb from Macedonia said. "A brutal affair."

"When can I question her?"

"Tomorrow, maybe, late," said Winters.

"All right. In the meantime I want a guard on that door. I don't want anybody allowed in that room," Heath said, "except her father, law-enforcement officers, and myself—you understand?" He arose. "Well, I guess there's nothing else we can do here. Thanks, Theron, Dr. Webb."

They went out in the hall. In the waiting alcove Vereen was pacing now, smoking a cigarette with jerky puffs. He was not a tall man, hardly larger than Claudia herself, and, curiously, his daughter bore no resemblance to him at all. She was, it seemed, wholly her mother's child in nature and appearance. Yet she was devoted to him, and as Claudia had learned, he in his own awkward way to her; certainly he had worked hard to make up for Linda's lack of a mother. Claudia had never liked him very much, but now she felt compassion for him. She went to him, took his hand. "Mr. Vereen, I'm so sorry."

He raised his head, looked at her with dazed, haunted eyes, and she caught a breath of stale beer; he had, he'd said, been at a tavern while she was at the show. "She's going to be all right," Claudia said. "Don't worry; she's getting the best of care."

"Yeah," Heath put in, laying a hand on the man's shoulder. Vereen jumped nervously and drew his own hand from Claudia's. "Look," Heath continued, "you're in shock yourself. You'd better spend the night here; they'll give you a room and something to make you sleep. Don't worry about work tomorrow, take as much time off as you need. And of course the company will stand for all the bills."

Vereen dragged a hand across a weary, twitching face. "Cap'n, I appreciate it," he mumbled.

"We look after our own," Heath said.

On the way home they drove in silence. It seemed to Claudia that there was a great weight in her chest, resting on her heart. As Heath turned the car up the hill to Chandler House he said at last, "The son of a bitch. Well. Now I can throw the book at him with a clear conscience."

Claudia did not answer. Right now she wished that Fox were still alive; for some reason she had a desperate, instinctive need to talk with him.

Now, this morning, as she came down the stairs she heard Heath's voice through the half-open door of his study. "Am I to take that as a compliment, St. John?" he asked sardonically. "Well, you're wrong. I'm afraid I deserve no credit." Then, angrily, "Damn it, I mean it, and I don't want that kind of talk going around, you understand?" he paused. "Very well. Apology accepted. Don't worry. There won't be any bail, and no slip-up in the prosecution. No! No, thanks. This is my affair, and I'll handle it! If a special prosecutor's necessary, I'll pay him myself, but that's a decision I'll make. Yes. Well, thanks, I appreciate your confidence in me. Your support. Yes, if I need you, I'll call on you. Come to see us, St. John." He hung up, then came through the door, face haggard, dressed in sports shirt, sweater, slacks. "Oh, good morning," he grunted when he saw her, went to her and kissed her.

"You look tired. What time did you get up?" They walked through the house to the breakfast room together.

"About six. I couldn't sleep. Besides, the phone's been jumping off the hook. The news has already got around: Butler, the governor, the newspapers, everybody—" He made a sound in his throat. "You know what they all think, of course. Congratulations pouring in, the old Machiavelli has done it again, by God! This'll teach 'em not to mess around with Heath Chandler." They sat down at the table, and he accepted a cup of coffee from the cook. "I wish to hell Andrew would come on home. I'm going to need his help. This thing is starting to get out of hand, too many people grabbing for a piece of it. Everybody from the governor on down wants his finger in the pie to make easy points."

"I don't think you ought to take any more calls—you ought to rest."

"I'll rest when Andrew gets here." Heath drummed his fingers on the table nervously. "Mullinax said he checked out of the motel down yonder early this morning; I don't know where the hell he's got to."

"Yes, you do. He must have heard. He'll have gone to Macedonia to see McCloskey."

Heath's lips thinned. "I suppose so. Well, it would have
een a nice gesture for him to call me or come here first.
only hope he's not infected with the virus everybody
lse has—the isn't-Heath-Chandler-a-clever-bastard-to-
ave-taken-care-of-McCloskey-so-neatly virus. I suppose
'll have some explaining to do to him, but maybe a look
t that girl . . ."

"Yes," Claudia said. "That ought to—" She broke off as
omething going past the window caught her eye. "What's
hat?"

Heath hesitated. Then he said, "A cop. A guard."

Claudia's heart seemed to jump, then bind up within
er breast. "A guard?"

"Some more blowback. McCloskey had this town split
own the middle. Naturally his partisans think the same
hing everybody else does. When the news got around,
here were some carryings-on downtown. Well," he said
s if he begrudged her the knowledge, "a bunch of 'em
ried to march up here. The cops stopped 'em. And I
hought it might be smart to post a guard here, and at
ndrew's house. Olin's downtown now with the chief,
eeping an eye on the situation. If we need state troopers
e'll call 'em in."

"Oh," Claudia said. "Oh, good Lord!" Her hands
lenched. "So here we are again. Another flying squad-
on—"

"No, nothing like that. It's all under control—"

"Is it?" She stared at him, and the fear, the terror, rose
n her like a sickness. Trembling, she sprang to her feet.

Heath's eyes widened. "Where the hell you going?"

"To get Ramsey and Lloyd and bring them here!" she
ried. "Until Andrew comes! Then I want them all to
o away!"

"Go away?"

"Do you think I'll live through that again? Wondering,
orrying, never knowing—?"

"Andrew can't go away! I need him! I'll protect—"

"Protect." She looked down at him, and her mouth
wisted bitterly, and her words were hoarse, cutting. "Yes,
rotect. Like you protected—?" She made a wild gesture,

as if she could not say the name. "No. No, there won't be that again. Not as long as I'm alive. They're coming here, and then they're leaving, for somewhere out of reach—" She turned, everything in her knotted with a fear she could not control. There were extra car keys on a board in the butler's pantry. She ran to them, seized a pair. As she came out into the kitchen Heath caught her shoulder. "Wait! I'll send police."

"I'll go myself." She jerked away, ran through a door. Outside, nearly a half-dozen uniformed men, guns on hips, made a loose circle around the house. One of them whirled at the slam of the door.

Heath was behind her. "Brewster! Get Mrs. Chandler's Olds from the garage and ride with her."

"Yes, sir."

Claudia bit off the words almost savagely. "Be sure to check under the hood before you start it!"

"Damn it, Claudia," Heath began. "There's no chance—"

She whirled on him. Their eyes met, and whatever was in hers made him step back, almost as if from a blow. She sought for words and none came. Then she said quietly, "You stay here and see to the interests of your company. I will take responsibility for the children."

There was the slam of metal, the grind of an engine; she tensed instinctively, but then it purred to life and the car was there. She got in, and as she did so, looked at Heath again. He was standing wordlessly on the steps.

"Grandmama!" Lloyd ran into her arms, and she knelt in the living room of the Ford house and hugged him, something unclenching with relief at the sight of him. "Look, we got policemen out there! One let me touch his pistol."

"I know," said Claudia stiffly, getting to her feet. "Where's your mother?"

"She's gone off."

Claudia went cold. "Gone off? This morning? Where?"

"I don't know. Maybe Frieda does."

"Yes. Well, get your things together. Toys, books, what

ver you want. You're coming up to Chandler House for while."

"Oh, boy! Sure!" He ran off. By then the servant was here. "Frieda, pack some clothes for Lloyd. Enough for two or three days, anyhow. Where's Mrs. Ford?"

"Miz Ford go off this mornin about nine, say she may not be back till late afternoon. That jest before them policemen come. She didn't say where."

"At the Royces', maybe?"

"She not dressed like that. I think mo' likely the river house. She go out there right often nowadays."

"The river house," Claudia said. She shook her head; it was hard to think. That made no sense, but nothing did this morning. Panic still clogged her brain. She went outside, summoned the policeman who had ridden with her. "You take the boy up to Chandler House in that." She pointed to a squad car parked nearby. "See him into the house yourself."

"But I'm supposed to stay with you," he protested.

"I don't need you. I"—it was instinct now, sheer instinct, combined with a different kind of fear—"have somewhere to go that I must go alone."

He hesitated, then, under her eyes, nodded. "Yes, ma'am."

In the house again, she told Lloyd: "You're going to ride in a police car. Don't ask him to blow the siren, it'll only upset people. I'll see you in a little while when I've found your mother. Frieda, when Mr. Ford comes in, you tell him everybody's at Chandler House, and we want him there too. And . . . you don't have to be afraid of anything. The police will stay here."

"Yes, ma'am. But—"

She did not wait for explanations, only kissed Lloyd again, and got into her car. Very swiftly she drove away. Her route took her through the town. There was no sign of trouble, only the usual Sunday-morning somnolence. Church bells were just beginning to ring, and there were cars around the churches, and people in their Sunday best. She felt their eyes on her as she drove past. The business district was almost deserted, save for policemen with the Chandler patch on their sleeves. Everything looked so ordinary, peaceful, and yet—

She knew the violence beneath the surface. They had not come far enough from that day when a mob had shouted and cursed outside the house while men within stood guard with rifles. Nor from that Christmas season when the roar of dynamite had ripped more apart than the bodies of an old man and a child. She speeded up, now she was on the highway. Miles slid by, and she passed without looking at it a side road, well graded, lightly graveled, that led into a patch of woods. It had been a long time since she had been able to bear going down it to the ruins of Fox's house. Presently she turned onto a smaller paved road, and after a few minutes cut her speed. Ahead and to the right was the entrance to the river house.

Claudia stopped the car. The chain that blocked the drive was up and locked in place, and then she realized that she had no handbag and no key. She bit her lip, then pulled the car over on the shoulder, parked, got out. It was a long way down the slope, a longer one back up, but she could ride back with Ramsey if the girl was there.

Undergrowth clawed at her as she bypassed the chain, then she followed the winding drive downhill. Curiously, out here she was not afraid for either Ramsey or herself, the danger lay in Chandlerville. She went carefully; at her age a fall could be serious. Ahead, presently, she saw the glitter of sunlight on the windows and white paint of the river house. Then she saw it gleam, too, from the chrome of a car and let out a breath of relief; Ramsey was here. She walked on more slowly; now the house and the turnaround behind it were in full view.

But when she saw the old pickup truck parked beside Ramsey's Thunderbird, Claudia stopped.

For a long while she was paralyzed with panic and had no idea what to do. Then, heart pounding like a drum within her chest, mouth dry, stomach clenched, she left the road and circled downhill through the pines. Her shoes slipped dangerously on the glassy carpet of needles

ie kicked them off and went on, barefoot. She followed
wide arc that brought her back toward the flank of the
ouse under cover of the trees. Then a flicker of motion
aught her eye. She halted, frozen, behind a big pine's
unk, staring; and for a moment it seemed impossible to
reathe.

They were on the porch, their bodies visible from the
aist up through the glass, and they were naked. As
:laudia watched, Ramsey drank directly from a bottle,
aade a face, then laughed. Claudia heard the sound
aintly, harsh and brassy. Then the man reached for her,
ulled her to him, crushing her breasts against a thick,
auscular chest. He bent his head to kiss her; his hair was
aick and black and glinting with grease; she caught a
limpse of a little black mustache before Ramsey's head
locked his face from view. Claudia fought back vomit
a her throat as they clung together. Then she turned
way and, still barefoot, padded wearily uphill through
ae woods. When she reached the road she put on her
aoes, got into the car, exhausted. She sat panting behind
ae wheel, then fumbled désperately in the glove com-
artment, found a pack of cigarettes. Her hand shook so
aat she could hardly use the car lighter. Then she started
ae engine and drove away. But the shaking got worse
astead of better, and by the time she reached the other
raveled side road through the trees she could hardly
rive. She had turned off the highway onto it before she
ealized it. Somehow she got the car down through the
roods and halted it before the vine-clad mound of rub-
le, old wood and scattered stones that filled the center
f the clearing. She opened the door and swung around
a the seat and sat there in the silence of the forest for a
ang time, staring at the cabin's ruins.

17 WAITING FOR ANDREW in his study, Heath
eard Lloyd thumping around upstairs, and despite the
atigue and apprehension in himself, he smiled. The boy's

presence had helped, his ceaseless chatter mitigating the
silence and emptiness of Chandler House, until he had at
last talked himself out and gone upstairs to play. Now
Heath Chandler was alone again, and as the morning
stretched out interminably he wondered, *When will
Andrew come?*

As hour after hour had passed and there had been no
word from him Heath had grown more and more uneasy,
and had felt a kind of fear he was unable to suppress.
Andrew should have called, he should have come straight
back home, he should have— What did this silence mean?

Heath leaned back in his chair, looked at the big
photographic portrait of the Old Man on the wall near
the door. It had been made in the late twenties, through
a soft-focus lens, and heavily retouched; Bolivar looked
almost aristocratic with his silver hair and in his best
black suit. But no lens or brush could soften something
in the eyes, the mouth; there, Heath thought, was a man
steeled to meet his responsibilities no matter how heavy
or how crushing. Those eyes seemed to challenge Heath,
and under them some of the apprehension ebbed. He
opened the drawer of Bolivar's desk, reached into its
depths, and touched the envelope there. Then he got up,
went to a file cabinet across the room, took a key from
his pocket, unlocked its top drawer. He took from its very
rear a manila folder, its edges sealed all around with tape,
stood there balancing it in his hands. Then he put it back.
He felt better now. It would be all right, he told himself
as he locked the drawer again. Andrew would come in
here outraged, convinced like all the rest of them that
what had happened was only another of Heath Chandler's ruthless master strokes. But there was a difference
between Andrew and the rest. For he and Andrew loved
each other, and the boy was obligated to understand
and trust him. The love, that was the important part. If
he had built it strongly enough, it would withstand
anything.

He sat down again, lit a cigarette impatiently. And
Claudia had not returned and . . . Damn it, where *was*
Andrew? Why was he alone? Even Clutt was— Then he

traightened up, as a car stopped outside. Its door
lammed, hard. Heath did not move; no need to meet
ndrew; the boy would find him. But his heart leaped.

He heard the front door close, the sound of footsteps
n the hall. Then Andrew was there, all right, in the door-
vay, coatless, tieless, sleeves rolled up, a lock of damp
air falling across his forehead. "Captain," he said
narshly, "I want to talk to you."

Heath swiveled the chair around. "I figured you would.
Come in, son, and sit down."

Andrew entered, but he did not seat himself, only
tood before Heath's desk, his eyes opaque. "I've been to
Macedonia. I saw Paul McCloskey in the jail there. He
swears he's innocent, that he never touched that girl."

"What else would you expect him to swear?"

"Wait a minute," Andrew said. "I want to hear some-
hing from you too. I want you to answer me one
question."

Heath leaned back in Bolivar's chair and nodded. "I'll
answer it for you, yes. I may be sunk in sin and depravity
and considered by the general public capable of anything. But I hope you know me better than to think I
would use a fourteen-year-old girl to satisfy any quarrel
or grudge I might have against a man, when, if it came
down to that, I can still walk on two feet and hold and
aim a pistol."

Andrew and he looked at one another for a very long
moment, their eyes locked, and then Andrew let out a
gusty breath and sat down. "You did not frame him or
have a hand in that."

"No."

"It looked— You sent me out of town. Then, while I
was gone . . ."

"I know how it looked. I've sat here all morning imagining how it must have looked to you and waiting for you
so I could tell you."

"Christ," Andrew said as if a great burden had been
lifted from him. He dropped his head and rubbed his
face, and Heath felt himself unknot inside; for now he
knew Andrew believed him.

"I went . . ." Andrew said, "I went to the jail with Vic. He protected Paul from the cops last night, served as his lawyer, his friend's lawyer, for one day, a lousy day. When we got back from the jail St. John Butler had called up and fired him from that other case."

"We can see that Royce doesn't starve."

"No. No, he's decided now to associate himself with Paul's defense. After that he'll probably move away. He's through with the mills and people like St. John Butler and . . ."

"And us?" Heath asked.

Andrew did not answer that directly. Instead, he sat up straight. "All right," he said. "Paul didn't do it. You didn't frame him." He paused, looked straight at Heath. "Obviously the matter needs further intensive investigation. I'm going to order Lawrence to see that it gets it, and I'll contact the FBI to see if this qualifies as a kidnapping over which they might have jurisdiction, and, if necessary hire private detectives."

Heath sighed wearily. "No," he said.

Andrew kept his eyes on Chandler's face. "What do you mean no? Someone raped the girl, it seems. Either she's lying about who it was or she's mistaken. Either way the matter's our responsibility, she's one of our people. And I believe that's the theory behind Chandler Mills—that we take care of our own. Anyhow, I'm going to do it. As president of the company, it's not only my obligation but my right."

Heath was silent for a moment, then he leaned forward across the desk. "Your obligation," he said, "is to Chandler Mills. You say that Paul McCloskey didn't do it. I say that a girl of spotless reputation has accused him of it. If she changes her story, that's another matter, but after what she's been through, I will not have her harassed."

He paused. "Given a choice between her word and McCloskey's, we take hers. McCloskey—what do you know about him anyway? It's been fifteen years and more since you two ran together. People change in time; I've changed, you have— A man away from home, alone, without a woman and with a bottle to suck on, how do you know what goes on in his mind, what he might do just on drunken impulse? Good God, boy, the most virtuous of us thinks, imagines things every day that would get us lynched or burned alive or stuck in an insane asylum if we carried them out. Of course McCloskey afterward would swear—"

"But—" Andrew began.

"Wait." Heath leaned back. "If he's innocent, he'll have his day in court. All his high-priced lawyers and your friend Royce as well will try to tear that little girl apart; if she's lying, can she stand against them? Don't bleed for him, he, too, has money and power behind him."

"That's not the point," Andrew said, voice crackling. "If he's innocent, I want it proved, and now. He's got a wife, Captain, and two daughters. And if that girl's lying, they're entitled to know it right away." He stood up. "Paul sent you a message, Captain. *Any father who would do this to another father is a sonofabitch beneath contempt.* He said to tell you that. Maybe you'll understand. I do. I'm a father myself."

Heath sat there motionless, carefully gathering strength, force. "I am too," he said at last, "and a son as well, and I have my own faiths to keep, and so do you. And the only way they can be kept is for this thing to take its course." He also arose, went to the window, looked out, staring at the water tower with its legend, high above the town. "If McCloskey's innocent, he'll be acquitted. But there has got to be time for the threat he has presented us with to collapse, time for the union effort to break. As long as he's under suspicion they're finished here, and that is what we've got to be sure of, that they're finished."

He turned, faced Andrew. "Don't you understand? Where we had no chance at all to break the union, now we can do it, it's been done for us. And we don't have any choice but to take it. If we don't, do you know what will happen to this company? The whole industry and the whole political structure of the state will come smashing down on us. You don't know the calls I've had, how much people have already staked on this. We're in too deep now to get out. If McCloskey's innocent, let him be acquitted in due course. But with what's at stake—"

"And if he is innocent, who really raped the girl doesn't matter? All that matters is the company?" Andrew's voice was harsh. "No, Captain. It's not your responsibility any more to decide things like that; it's mine. I'm going to turn everything upside down until I find out—"

"No," Heath said. "You are not. That's final."

They looked at each other for a moment. Andrew stood spraddle-legged, big head thrust out, mouth thin and hard. *Christ*, Heath thought . . .

Then Andrew took a folded piece of paper from his shirt pocket and laid it on the desk. "All right," he said. "There's a present for you."

"What?" Heath stared at it.

"My resignation as president of Chandler Mills." Andrew smiled coolly. "It's a little rough; I wrote it using the railing of the bridge at Brackettville for a desk."

Heath shook his head, disbelieving. "Brackettville?"

Andrew nodded. "Yes. When I left Macedonia I went there. I don't know why. To think, maybe. Maybe to try to remind myself who I really was and where I came from. Anyhow, I found myself standing on the bridge, looking at that big old bull-bitch of a mill, remembering what it was like, looking at that town, empty, now, killed, destroyed. Like Paul, like Vic, like my marriage—"

"What?" Heath blurted.

"My marriage," Andrew said tonelessly. "It's a victim too. You can only use a thing so much and then you wear it out, and I figured that out, too, on the bridge, Captain. I haven't even been able to make love to my wife for nearly four months. She's been used too much, and I've been used too much, and what we had between us has been used too much. So I decided, Captain. I didn't start out to be a mill hand, and I'm not going to be a mill hand any more. I gave you your chance, to let me be something more, but I never thought that you would take it. So I wrote that."

"Don't be absurd," Heath said.

"There's nothing absurd about it. I'm through. I'm going."

"You can't." Heath's hands were sweating and yet he shivered. "There isn't anybody else but you."

"Oh, yes, there is," Andrew said. "There's your daddy and there's Hamp. All the ones who really count." Then his voice softened. "I don't want to have to go, but . . . it's costing me more than I can pay. I love you and Claudia and Ramsey and Lloyd, and my love keeps getting used so much that I . . . have got to leave before I don't believe in love any more. I—"

"Andrew," Claudia said from the doorway.

Heath whipped around. Neither he nor Andrew had heard her come up or knew how long she had been standing there.

Before Heath could speak Andrew said, "Claudia. I was telling the Captain that I was leaving. I'm through. I'm taking Ramsey—I don't know whether she will go or not. Maybe he can keep her here. He knows exactly how to be Hamp when he needs to, and I don't, all I can be is myself. But—"

"I heard it," Claudia said. "Yes, Andrew, that's the thing to do."

"Claudia, wait—" Heath said it frantically, then looked at Andrew. "Both of you, there are things— Wait."

"Hush," Claudia said, moving forward. "Be quiet. Andrew, Ramsey's not home, but she'll be there after a while. When she comes, just take her and Lloyd away, you understand? There's nothing else you have to do that's more important. Don't worry about McCloskey or the girl or anybody—I'll see to them." Her voice rose, trembling. "Just get her out of here. She'll go. If she won't, take her anyway!"

Andrew's eyes went to her, to Heath, then back to Claudia. The breath he drew in made his chest swell. "Yeah," he said. "That's what I intend to do." Then he stepped past her and through the door.

"Wait! Son!" Heath started after him.

Claudia blocked the doorway. She looked at him in a way he had never seen before, with so much ferocity in

her face that he drew back, astonished. "Don't you try to
stop him," she said. "Don't you ever try to stop him again
do you understand?"

"I have to—"

"No." The single word. Then, outside, Andrew's car
roaring into life, wheels on driveway.

Heath shook his head. It had not ended, it had not, he
would not let it. All at once he relaxed, summoned
strength and confidence. "All right. He can go for now
But he's not leaving. I won't let him. I won't let Ramsey
go with him, and he won't leave without her."

"You'll let her go with him," Claudia said. "You'll turn
her loose. Hamp's dead. Dead, dead, dead. So is Bolivar."
Then she wheeled around. "I'm going to make a phone
call."

"What?" He strode after her into the hall.

"Don't try to stop me." It was a vixen's face, snarling
Wide cheekbones, pointed muzzle, lambent eyes of yel
low-green. "I just came from the hospital. I didn't realiz
I, too, was sealed off from her. But I didn't let that stop
me; despite your orders, they let me in to see her." He
lips peeled back from sharp, white, vixen's teeth. "And
after all, I'm the only one she trusts. And I used her trust
very subtly, drew it all out of her."

"What are you talking about?"

Claudia's eyes flared. "You know damned well what I'm
talking about. You knew last night, and so did I, at leas
subconsciously, but I didn't want to believe it, ever
though I've dealt with the same thing a dozen times, a
hundred, in the past ten years. And because I understood
what drove her. Once I, too, wanted to escape that badly.

"You're not making sense. I didn't—"

"No. You didn't do anything except make sure that hi
story wasn't questioned, because you couldn't afford fo
it to be. I kept waiting, wondering, when you were going
to have them put him through the wringer too, but yo
never did. And I didn't speak up. I don't know why. May
be because I knew how much it meant to you, and I loved
you enough to . . . Maybe, too, because I even felt sorr
for him. He tried to be good to her. Maybe he was drunk

Maybe he couldn't stand the sight of all that woman when he was so weaselly and little and couldn't get one of his own. Maybe they had just lived together too long, too closely, for it even to have seemed wrong to him . . ."

Claudia's voice was harsher. "Maybe she even teased him unconsciously, drew him on; I don't know. I've seen stranger things happen between daughter and father."

"Listen," Heath said.

"Be still. She admitted it—when I told her all the good things we were going to do for her, how we would help her escape. She was terrified that she would be stranded here, lost, doomed to spend the rest of her life on a mill hill when there were so many great things inside of her. She didn't plan it, no; he came home drunk and . . . but she must not have fought him, not very hard. But when it was over, both of them were terrified. And it was her idea, you see? Oh, she's brilliant, it came to her like that, because she'd seen McCloskey driving past, out of town. And she knew that he was the one man everybody would want to be guilty—and, I tell you, she's a genius. That's what's so terrible, so horrifying. She could have stood up in court, it's just that she couldn't believe that I would betray her if she told me. Besides—" Claudia turned away. "She felt sorry for her father, she pitied him, she was trying to save him, because when it was over, he wanted to kill himself or turn himself in— She had to do it to save him." She picked up the telephone. "But I'll swear out a warrant against him. I have to do it. Maybe I can salvage her somehow later, but I doubt it, maybe she's too far gone, maybe the mills have already—"

Heath knocked her hand away from the phone, clamped it on its cradle. "Wait. You can't. This thing's gone too far. I can handle Andrew and Ramsey. You don't know. Let me tell you. But for now McCloskey's got to be kept out of action, in jail. He'll use this against me, and then the union will surely come in—"

"Let it," Claudia said.

"It'll destroy—"

"Fuck what it'll destroy," she said. "This morning I saw our daughter at the river house. There's been enough destroyed already. Now move, I want to—" She broke off. There was a smash of breaking glass in the sitting room opposite, and then, outside, a sharp, prompt spatter of gunfire.

Heath whirled away from the phone. The smell of gasoline was rank in his nostrils, and from across the hall there came a low roaring, crackling sound. He ran into the sitting room, then recoiled. Beneath the shattered window flames swirled across the heart-pine floor and licked the dry wool of the Oriental carpet, and the draperies were blazing.

"A fire bomb!" he yelled. Reacting instinctively, he ran to the fireplace across the room, seized the hearth shovel, began to beat at knee-high flames rising from the carpet. Then a hand clamped his wrist, pulled him around with savage strength.

He stared into Claudia's contorted face, huge green eyes gleaming with a kind of madness. "Let it burn!" she shrieked. "Let it all burn!" Suddenly she released him, turned, ran out. Then she reappeared with the portrait of Bolivar in her hands. She threw it into the leaping flames, and Heath's catching gesture was futile. It landed face down and caught immediately. He scraped for it with the shovel, but it dissolved into tatters of fire that flew up, drifted around the room, and ignited whatever they landed on.

"I said, let it burn!" his wife screamed. "It never was my house anyhow. Never anybody's but his! Never anybody's life but his! I'm tired of animals that eat their own young! God damn you, let it burn!"

Eyes almost blinded, nostrils clogged, Heath backed away from the wall of fire, seized her arm. "You're crazy!" he yelled.

"Maybe," she yelled back. "Maybe it's my turn! You and Ramsey had yours!" Smoke swirled between them. Then Claudia stiffened, and suddenly her face went sane. "Heath, My God! Lloyd. Where's Lloyd?"

And then he remembered too, and threw the shovel aside. "Upstairs!" He charged past her. "Get the servants out!" He dodged into the hall, faced the stairway's base.

It sucked up smoke like a flue. He drew in what breath he could, then scrambled up the stairs, hauling himself along with a hand on the banister rail. His lungs hurt, heart pounded, but he made the second floor, and there it was a little better. He could breathe again. "Lloyd!" he screamed, but there was no answer. Somewhere he heard people yelling—the police, he thought, getting out the cook and maid. He turned toward Lloyd's room, halfway down the corridor. When he shoved open the door, smoke surged in around him. Lloyd lay sleeping placidly on the bed, one leg dangling to the floor, an arm thrown across his breast.

Panting, Heath shook him hard, and the boy sat up groggily. Fire engines were howling in the town; the guards must have used their radios. "Come on, little chum," Heath said with careful, reassuring calm. "We're having a little excitement downstairs. Seems the house is on fire. Let's get out. Now. Now, don't be afraid. I'll see to you."

Lloyd blinked, rubbed his face. Heath wrapped him in a blanket from the bed, picked him up. Light as he knew the boy to be, the body seemed very heavy. Lloyd, drowsy still, put his head against Heath's chest unquestioningly. Perhaps he thought he still dreamed. Heath lurched back into the corridor with Lloyd in his arms. The smoke was terrible, devouring oxygen as it surged up the stairwell. At the head of the stairs he halted. Flame roiled below, spilling out of the sitting room, dancing across the foyer.

He felt his mouth twist in a ghastly grin. Well, he had faced fire before. Every day when he had gone up in France. He made sure that the blanket was well wrapped round his grandson. Then he went quickly and unsteadily down the stairs. The flames reared themselves into an orange wall before him, and he heard their gusty, greedy roar. His lungs were bursting, but he dared not breathe; there was nothing to do but go through, and he closed his eyes, tightened the blanket around Lloyd's head, and ran.

The fire licked around his shins, his thighs. Then he was

through it, and ahead, the front door fortunately was wide open, and he lurched out onto the veranda, sucking in gulps of air. His face hurt, and his clothes were smoldering, but he had been through worse. Then a hand reached for Lloyd, lifted the weight from his arms. Heath opened his eyes, realized his trousers were on fire, and began to beat at them. Claudia was there then. "My darling, darling— Are you all right?"

"I'm fine." He coughed. "Just a little singed." He put his arm around her; it felt good to lean on her. They steadied each other as they went out on the lawn. There Lloyd, unswathed, was jumping with excitement.

Behind him something was being covered with the blanket he had discarded. Heath twisted his head. The guard looked up at him before he covered Baucom's face. "He come in behind me when I warn't lookin, thowed it, run. But I got him, all right; you bet I got him."

"Yes," Heath said as the man dropped the blanket. Two weeks, he thought automatically, and rentals ran from Saturday to Saturday, and yesterday Baucom would have been evicted. Heavily he turned away. Flame and smoke billowed from almost every window of Chandler House now. The fire trucks were squalling up the long, winding drive, but it was obvious that they were too late.

Claudia leaned against him, and he and she held each other tightly. "Heath—" she said thickly.

"Hush," he said. "It's all right. I love you. Maybe it wasn't ever my house either. Let it burn."

"But—"

"It doesn't matter."

Curiously, it did not seem to. He had lived in it for most of his life, but it was not even a symbol to him now, meant nothing at all. The mills were still there, and his children were still safe. He searched his mind for some suitable epitaph for the place, but he was very tired, too tired to think right now. Then a hand grasped his arm, and he turned his head to look into the face of Clutterbuck.

"Heath," Olin said. "You—?"

"Hello, Clutt," he said. He looked back at the burning house and laughed unsteadily. "You wouldn't happen

have a package of marshmallows on you, would you?"
Then it hit him, suddenly, terribly, without warning,
squarely beneath the breastbone, exactly like the impact
of a large-caliber bullet. "Jesus Christ, Pearl," he heard
himself say, and dropped, feeling himself go away. Vaguely he heard her scream.

18   FOR A WHILE the pain had been worse
than any he had ever known before. He was in darkness
and very lonely, even with all those hands touching and
busy on him. Then the pain was better. After that the
darkness deepened and he was unconscious. When at last
he opened his eyes he looked up into a nurse's face. "Lie
still," she cautioned. "Don't move at all. Don't talk. It's
very important that you lie absolutely still."

He did not disobey; indeed, lacked the strength to. His
curiosity, however, had not deserted him. His eyes were
blurred with drugs, but he could see the glitter of the
enveloping oxygen tent, and beyond, the bottles—glucose,
he supposed—on racks, and tubes running to arm and
ankle. He was not quite sure how he discovered the tube
in his penis, the catheter, but he became aware of that
too. He was surprised; he had not known you were so
trussed and harnessed for a coronary.

The nurse stayed there and Theron Winter came and
went; or maybe he did himself. Because when he awakened again, someone or something else was there too.
He could not see or smell or feel or hear it, but it was
here; and then he began to be afraid. Because there was
till too much for him to do.

*A boy as big as you, said Bolivar. Doing that in your
pants. Shame.*

But the God damned Camels always went into a right-
hand spin.

Thanks, Olin. You saved my bacon. I owe you a drink.

Oohh, sweetness, she said. Keep on doing that. Just
keep on doing that.

You don't understand, Mr. Chandler. What you are asking is impossible.

Because Buckingham is more effective. It sets them on fire. Always a sure kill.

A scream. A red scream in cold morning darkness.

"I love you," Claudia said. "Oh, I love you so much."

Get down on your knees. Do you hear me, sir? Get down on your knees!

Seven hundred thousand spindles.

Worth Street Rules. With respect to osnaburgs, 40 inches and narrower, the constant 6,000 divided by, the width in inches multiplied by the yards per pound . . .

Everything stuck in her but the ax handle . . .

Herewith our report on subject, Andrew Ford . . .

I love you, Ramsey said.

If we change the machining on the cylinder head . . .

Phil Montague: Now, what the public wants—

Daddy. A red scream.

"Lie still," said Theron Winters. "You mustn't move or talk."

"Fuck you. I've got things to do."

"Be quiet. You'll never do them if you insist on—"

"I'll never do them if I lie here like a lump of horseshit on the highway. I want to see my family."

"All in good time."

"I don't have any good time left."

"Captain Chandler—"

"All of them. And Clutterbuck."

"Your wife has been here. You're not ready for more visitors."

"Hell, I've already got one."

"Sir?"

"Damn it, if you don't let me see my family, I'll up and die on you. That's a threat."

"Very well. If you insist. But I can't take responsibilit for the consequences."

"Fuck the consequences. I've been taking responsibilit for the consequences all my life."

"Captain Chandler, you're impossible."

"No, only highly improbable."

That exhausted him. He lay there in limbo, thinking. Because. The mills. They had not burned. They were still there. And Andrew. Andrew must.

And now he had to tell him. Until now there was no justifying it.

But it was a pool, wasn't it? And a man's life was a pebble, cast in, making rings, and those rings spreading, ever widening. So that a soldier dead at Gettysburg and another marching home insane and a slut moaning in the darkness of the riverbank and a hard, righteous old man and a brilliant, innocent, murdered child and a barefooted girl with something burning inside her slender, breastless body, and himself . . . It was magnificent. The intricacy, the sheer subtlety and control and over-all design was breathtaking. Not a pool, a fabric. Woven, interwoven, embroidered, but with the design always firm in the weaver's mind. He wanted Andrew. He wanted to make him see what a magnificent fabric had been woven and was still to weave.

The file. It was burnt. The letter in the desk. That was burnt, too. But he could still tell Andrew, and the boy could not disbelieve him now. Yes, he thought, it fits, it fits the fabric, the design. The way he and Ramsey loved each other right away, what they saw in each other at first sight . . . And even after his refusal to let them marry, how he had been haunted by something ineffable, intangible, in that spraddled stance, head thrust forward. The name, Ford, and the hasty investigation by the detectives in Charlotte. The same woman, no doubt of that, and the timing matched. A hundred others, maybe twice that, but he was sure; his seed. But he must believe and disbelieve, because if he believed too strongly, it would have been forbidden, and it could not be forbidden, because Hamp was dead, and then another Hamp had come when he and Ramsey had needed another Hamp the most. And now he must tell Andrew. Andrew would understand, and he could not disbelieve, not now. And he would know what he must do. He might leave Chandler Mills, but a son could not leave or betray his father.

That he had learned himself, through too much hard experience.

Drifting, drowsing, he waited. By now he had recognized who waited with him. They'd had business together often enough. "Stay away," he whispered. "Just a little while. Until I settle my affairs."

And then they came. For fear that any conversation would be too much, Winters had let them come all at once, and that was something he had not counted on. He mustered all his strength, using sheer will to keep the other, unbidden visitor far away. He looked at them through drug-swimming eyes. "Andrew," he said. "I want Andrew."

And then his son was standing over him, looking down at him with grief. And, Heath saw with surprise, Andrew already knew. Or if he did not know, it made no difference; there could have been no more love on his face, or grief, even if he had read the file or letter. He knew how closely they were linked, and he had accepted, loved enough to accept. He only waited for the words to bind him, with love and with fear of what he knew was going to happen to him, and with a sort of yearning.

Heath licked dry lips. All he had to do was speak, and he was quits with Bolivar and would have paid his debt.

But no words came. Andrew waited; and while he waited touched Heath's hand with his own.

And then Heath knew. He had no debts to pay, not to the dead. He was too close to them to owe them anything; like himself, they were beyond need and beyond desire and beyond—as he would soon be, perhaps—even love. But Andrew was not, nor Ramsey nor Lloyd. And then he understood that love was for the living, and he wished he had known that before, because now there was so much he could not make up to Claudia or to Ramsey or Andrew. He had wasted so damned much on the dead.

He held Andrew's hand a moment, then took his away. "Clutt."

"I'm here."

"Ryall."

"What?"

"Ryall."

Then he saw by Olin's expression that he understood. "That's what you want?" Olin asked thickly.

"Yes."

"I'll see to it," Olin said.

"Thanks." He and Heath looked at each other for a moment, and then words came to Heath out of the past, words spoken ritually on cold dawns while engines thundered. "Good hunting," Heath heard himself say.

"The same," Olin said calmly, unawed, accepting.

It was a scene, he thought, in a damned bad play. But when your strength was gone, there was no other way. So few words had to mean so much. "Ramsey," he said. "Is she here?"

Then she was above him, face pale, eyes enormous.

"Look," he said. "You can make it all right without me."

"Oh," she said thickly. "Oh."

"The living don't need the dead," he said. "That's what you've got to understand. And . . . the dead don't need the living. So it doesn't matter, you see, except for Andrew and Lloyd."

"Oh," she said again, and he thought that she was very beautiful and that he had created her too; and pride strengthened him. They had let Lloyd in, which he was sure he approved of, but it was good to hold the boy with the one hose-fed arm thrust from beneath the tent, good to feel the tenderness and vitality of his youth. The slender form throbbed with life.

Then Heath was impatient. "All right," he said. "I love you, but go on. Everybody. All but my wife."

She was there then, by him. "I want—" he said.

"Don't talk."

"I want. To say." Then he ran down.

"I know." She held his hand against her face. "I love you."

"Yes. I love you. Stay with me."

"Yes," she said. "Oh, yes."

"Tell them, please." He would have sworn he heard engines roaring, and there was a cold wind in his face, morning wind. She was there, and he knew it—could feel, touch her—but he was alone all the same. Even with her hand on his, he was wholly alone. But then, at such a time everybody was.

Then he was not alone any more. Claudia seemed gone, but he was not alone. His dearest friend and most bitter enemy came forward finally. He tried to rise, but, gently, it pressed him back. He found the strength to say or think he said, "All right you son of a bitch. I guess you're over-due to win." And, tired of fighting, yielded.